# THE O'BRIENS AND
# THE O'FLAHERTYS

**Lady Morgan** was born Sydney Owenson in about 1776. There is some debate about her birthplace, the favoured version being (symbolically) on the Irish Sea halfway between England and Ireland, when her father was returning to his native Ireland with her English mother. She began governessing to help pay her father's debts, acquired a title on her wedding day and won a large and eager readership for her novels, like the spectacularly successful *The Wild Irish Girl* (1806), which is also reprinted by Pandora. Lady Morgan was the first woman writer to be granted a pension – £300 per annum – for her service to the 'world of letters'. A brilliant conversationalist and hostess, Lady Morgan had definite feminist sympathies, one of her (unfinished) works being entitled *Woman and her Master: A History of the Female Sex from the Earliest Period*. She was also a patriot, a brave and resilient woman whose 'national tales', like *The O'Briens and The O'Flahertys* (1827) – 'tissues of woven air' as she called them – were serious enough to influence politics and policies, and to contribute to the ideas upon which modern Ireland was founded. Lady Morgan died in 1859.

**Mary Campbell** spent her early life working in the documentary film industry where she was one of the few women involved in writing, directing and editing films for the Central Office of Information and other official bodies. Marriage and children put an end to the life of going on location, but she continued to work as a freelancer in film, television and radio. A stint in advertising was made bearable by the discovery that she could write for the printed word and, for the last few years, she has written for the Arts and Studies pages of *The Irish Times* as well as many other publications. Her biography of Lady Morgan, *Lady Morgan: The Life and Times of Sydney Owenson* (1987) is published by Pandora.

PANDORA PRESS REPRINT

MOTHERS OF THE NOVEL

# MOTHERS OF THE NOVEL
*Reprint Fiction from Pandora Press*

Pandora is reprinting eighteenth and nineteenth century novels written by women. Each novel is being reset in modern typography and introduced to readers today by contemporary women writers. The following titles in this series are currently available:

The companion to this series is *Mothers of the Novel: 100 Good Women Writers Before Jane Austen* by Dale Spender, a wonderfully readable survey that reclaims the many women writers who contributed to the literary tradition. She describes the interconnections among the writers, their approach and the public response to their work.

# THE O'BRIENS AND THE O'FLAHERTYS

## A NATIONAL TALE

LADY MORGAN

Introduced by Mary Campbell

**PANDORA**

London, Sydney, Wellington

*First published
in paperback by Pandora Press,
an imprint of the trade division of
Unwin Hyman Limited, in 1988*

*Introduction Copyright © Mary Campbell 1988*

*Unwin Hyman Limited
15–17 Broadwick Street
London W1V 1FP*

*Allen & Unwin Australia Pty Ltd
8 Napier Street, North Sydney, NSW 2060, Australia*

*Allen & Unwin New Zealand Pty Ltd with the Port Nicholson Press
60 Cambridge Terrace, Wellington, New Zealand*

*ISBN 0–86358–289–3*

*British Library Cataloguing in Publication Data
Morgan, Lady
The O'Briens and the O'Flahertys : a
national tale. — (Mothers of the novel).
I. Title  II. Series
823'.7 [F]    PR5059.M3*

*Printed and bound by
The Guernsey Press Co. Ltd., Guernsey, Channel Islands.*

# CONTENTS

# INTRODUCTION

When Sydney Morgan published *The O'Briens and the O'Flahertys*, she, more than any other novelist writing at the time, had created a reading public eager for her type of 'national' table. For more than twenty years she had been processing Ireland's history from the old Gaelic past to the political struggles of her own times into the material of her novels, and she used and even manipulated that history boldly in order to plead Ireland's cause. She always claimed that her sole purpose in life was to serve that cause. Although a Protestant, she claimed that her novels were 'undertaken with an humble but zealous view to the promotion of a great national cause, the emancipation of the Catholics of Ireland'. When the 'great "O" novel', as it was called, came out in 1827, Daniel O'Connell, the leader of the Catholic masses, had put the Irish question so urgently before Parliament and the English public that it was obviously only a matter of time before the centuries old discrimination against Catholics came off the Statute book. The timely appearance of *The O'Briens and the O'Flahertys*, just when the English were anxious to know what the Irish were really up to, sent it through three editions in the first year. Sydney had written her first 'national tale' *The Wild Irish Girl* in 1806, and between its sensational appearance and the publication of *The O'Briens and the O'Flahertys* she had grown up, become internationally famous, acquired a title, and was now a political hostess in Dublin, influencing not only the Viceroy and his court, but noticed by the powers in London: 'I was as of late I have constantly been', she wrote in her diary, 'the centre of a circle'. That 'circle' of statesmen and politicians eventually brought Catholic emancipation into being in 1829, and after all the tumult and the shouting and the years of agitation, it was to all intents and purposes finalised in her drawing room, to the tinkle of teacups. Such was the power of her personality and her pen.

It was not, however, her social skills, great as they were, that allowed her to be an effective political force, but the influence that she had won over English public opinion with her four 'national tales'. When she began her mission to make the English reading public aware of Irish history, and sympathetic to the social, economic and political problems that had come out of that history, she was treading on very dangerous ground; when she started to write, English readers knew less of Ireland than they did of most other European countries, and what they did know came to them through selective and often prejudiced sources. For centuries they had been fed on the tales of soldiers returning from the wars of conquest and colonisation; grim and bloody stories of wolves, deadly ambushes, and wild savage people with strange clothes, stranger haircuts, and an incomprehensible language. Elizabethan London had seen the outlandish Irish chieftain Shane O'Neill swagger through its streets, flanked by his saffron kilted 'rug headed kernes'; he came to offer false allegiance to the Queen, which like many other Irishmen before and after him, he had no intention of keeping. The Irish were seditious then, and continued to be so. The historians said so; Shakespeare said so; so did Edmund Spenser, Marvell and Milton and all the writers of any consequence up to Sydney's own time. The Irish geographically so close, were totally alien in language, culture and religion. Particularly in religion. For some perverse reasons the Irish had rejected the glorious Reformation and, consequently, had made conspiratorial pacts with England's traditional enemies, the rest of Catholic Europe. They had sought aid from Spain and, later, in Sydney's own lifetime, from France: 'This peasant nation with no leaders but the priests, and no sympathisers but the enemies of England', as G.M. Trevelyan, an eminent historian of our own times, wrote in his *History of England*.

As a young girl Sydney had read all this history, and pondered over it; but she had also heard the stories from the other side; in the West of Ireland she had witnessed the total ruin of the Catholic Irish gentry brought to paupery through dispossession and discrimination; she identified passionately with the tragic flight of the Wild Geese who had to leave Ireland and find foreign service, and with those who stayed behind to become outlaws on the hills because, from her early childhood, she had heard her father sing the elegiac songs of these exiles and outlaws, and as she grew up she not only absorbed this history, she lived through it. As a girl, she had seen the Volunteers, in their bright uniforms and sashes, in a brief flush of aristocratic patriotism, swear allegiance to the Irish Nation; her father had managed a theatre in the West of Ireland where the young Wolfe Tone, leader of the '98 Rebellion, had acted in a light comedy; she herself had been in Sligo when the French were in the Bay, and where disaster overtook Wolfe Tone, and she, with the rest of nationalist Ireland had mourned for Lord Edward Fitzgerald, brother of the Duke of Leinster, but dedicated United Irishman when he died of wounds in a house close to her father's theatre in Dublin. Now, thirty years later, with the passing of the Act of Catholic Emancipation which would change the whole structure of Irish life she had herself helped to make history. Out of all this material through which she had lived closely and passionately she would make her national tale *The O'Briens and the O'Flahertys*. By the time *The O'Briens and the O'Flahertys* came out, the education of the English public with regard to Ireland was well under way. Her contemporary Maria Edgeworth had also been labouring for many years in the same field. But Maria was no nationalist. Although she was critical of many aspects of the relationship between landlord and tenant, one of the most controversial issues of the day, and she knew the foibles, humours and weaknesses of the Irish people on both sides through her status as administrator of her landowning father's estate her aspirations for Ireland looked to a conservative status quo, an eighteenth-century ideal of reason and rational behaviour. All would be well if the landlords would only behave with sense and good husbandry, and if the peasants were hardworking and loyal. She wrote with irony and humour, to great critical acclaim, and was very much admired by other writers, like Walter Scott, and even Turgeniev in Russia. But it was Sydney Morgan's romantic extravagance, style and exotic Irishness that caught the imagination of readers both in Ireland and England.

The 'national tale' had become a very popular form of fiction by the time Sydney's fourth novel of the genre had appeared. Walter Scott was now master of the historical novel but when he wrote his first novel *Waverley* in 1814 he followed the Irish writers and said that he wanted to introduce the natives of Scotland to English readers 'in a more favourable light than they had been placed hitherto, and so tend to procure sympathy for their virtues and indulgence for their foibles'. He thought he was emulating Maria Edgeworth and acknowledged his debt to her, but the plot of *Waverley*, where a young Englishman is introduced to the heroic life of the old Highland clans owes more than a little to the adventures of Lady Morgan's *Mortimer* hero of *The Wild Irish Girl*, published in 1806. Scott's intentions for Scotland were entirely in keeping with Sydney's own desire that England should recognize Ireland's worth, but whereas Scott wrote his historical novels long after the actual events had taken place, when the wounds had healed and the lost causes had become respectably romantic, her material was immediate, hot from the battle front as it were, with the struggle for nationality and cultural identity still raging. This is particularly so in *The O'Briens and the O'Flahertys* where the time scale covers her own life-span. Her fascination with the history of old Ireland, that half forgotten and heroic age symbolised by the ruins of the past that were scattered all over the countryside, and reinterpreted by her in *The Wild Irish Girl* by golden bodkins, cloaks and harps, had now turned into a study of the history of her own time – the terrible history of what was then modern Ireland. In her lifetime her native land had already come through such turning points as the Constitution of 1782, granted to Grattan's Parliament, the Rebellion of 1798, The Act of Union in 1800 when Ireland's Parliament was dissolved, and the rise of Daniel O'Connell, and the campaign for Catholic Emancipation.

The Chinese have a saying 'May you live in interesting times', which really means 'may you be cursed with too much history.' The Irish are notoriously addicted to history which with them has often been a curse and is very seldom impartial. Lady Morgan was haunted by history and she always wrote as a patriot. *The Wild Irish Girl* was the product of her youthful worship of a half mythical past. Twenty years later the 'great "O" novel' marked her progress through romantic nationalism into a kind of political reality. Passionate partisan that she was, she was now caught paradoxically between the two nations – the Protestant Ascendancy, and the Catholic peasantry. Neither completely native Irish, nor English by birth, but the child of a mixed marriage, it was the same with religion. She subscribed to no bigotry and ultimately could not come down on either side in the new Ireland that had taken the place of her longed for Republic of Reconciliation. Her nationalism was emotionally radical, but her romantic commitment to her idea of the aristocracy and her faith in their ultimate willingness to serve Ireland were politically naive. Her generous liberalism had made her support the cause of Catholic Emancipation in the name of natural justice, but the price to pay for the triumph of her cause was beginning to reveal itself and make her think again about the nature of patriotic fervour. The demagogy of Daniel O'Connell, who had roused the peasantry to a dangerous fury against the landlords, had nothing to do with the old Gaelic world of

Chieftain and faithful retainers that she had dreamed up for the Prince of Inishmore.

Her imagination was already working on the political implications of this new Ireland and in *The O'Briens and the O'Flahertys* she tries to steer a path through the inconsistencies and dangers of the situation. She brings her passionate interest in Irish history, the political complications and social consequences of the time and all her own life experiences together in this story of two families, and the different ways the history of their native land has treated them. Both the families are of old Catholic Irish stock dispossessed and uprooted by the Penal Laws. The O'Flahertys have survived by going abroad and taking service in foreign armies and the Church, where they have prospered. Murrough O'Brien, the young scion of the other family is the focal point for all the social tensions that bedevilled the Catholic gentry remaining in Ireland. Murrough, for a while a student at the pro Ascendancy University of Dublin, had nevertheless been educated secretly as a child by the Jesuits. He and his father – who is a powerful official in Dublin Castle – are now nominally Protestants, in order to survive in Irish society. But he is an independently minded young man, who has lived on the Continent and is aware of the revolutionary philosophies current in France. All of which make him sympathetic to the aims of the United Irishmen, who are now recruiting strongly and even making converts in Trinity College. Murrough, who of course is extremely handsome, is also involved with the ultra fashionable ladies of vice-regal society, very emancipated in their high camp talk and in their behaviour. Sydney Morgan knew this set intimately. She had been both their pet and their victim and in the set pieces of fashionable life there are very lively portraits of ladies and gentlemen she had known well enough to pay back a few scores. Murrough moves through all this complication of plot, with numerous O'Briens and O'Flahertys in subsidiary roles. Because of his support for the Volunteers, he is expelled from Trinity College, which leads him straight to the United Irishmen, and the revelation that 'Ireland is my vocation . . . here, in this unhappy land, stands the altar of my first and warmest vows'. Speaking from her own heart, Lady Morgan has expressed here the central idea in Irish nationalism which has not yet disappeared. But the failure of that feverish patriotism to achieve any other object except death or exile for its activists brought her to a deep pessimism, expressed later by Beavoin O'Flaherty, heroine of the book, who although starting her part in the story as an Abbess in a Connemara convent, ends up in Paris, married to Murrogh O'Brien, now a general in Napoleon's army. With Lady Morgan all things are possible. Beavoin is made to say 'To be born an Irishman is a dark destiny at the best. . . . Here virtue is made to turn traitor to itself, and the same passions that rouse the patriot to any sacrifice, urge him into the snares of the profligate. . . . here, genius is the object of suspicion to dull rulers, and of insult to petty underlings, and all that bends not – falls.'

The 'great "O" novel', did not have the resounding triumph of *The Wild Irish Girl*, but it is Sydney Morgan's strongest and best work. It is also her bravest, with the usual appeals to patriotism supported by full-blooded attacks on government and the 'oligarchs' of Dublin Castle; but now there is an attempt to understand the other side and show the burden that Ireland's unhappy history has placed upon the Protestants themselves – their uncertainty and uneasiness of tenure in a country that is always ready to reject them. She herself knew the penalties of her commitment to Ireland while writing for an audience that would be largely English. In her Preface to what would be her last 'national tale', she said 'In again presenting an Irish novel to the public I hope I am not doing a foolish thing, and yet I feel, as far as my own interests are concerned I am not doing a wise one. To live in Ireland and write for it, is to live and write "poignard sur la gorge", for there is no country where it is less possible to be useful with impunity, or where the penalty of patriotism is levied with a more tyrannous exaction.' History served up as fiction runs the danger of being romanticised and made trivial. It might end up, in the wrong hands, as a lurid 'bodice ripper', but again it could come out as *War and Peace*. Lady Morgan was no Tolstoy, but her intentions were honourable. The purpose for which she wrote – to help the English to understand the Irish better, and perhaps learn to love them – has probably not yet been achieved, but more than any other writer of her time, she presented Ireland and its people as worthy of study. All the facts of nineteenth century Irish history, social, economic and religious, can be read, of course, in modern academic studies, but the real flavour of life as it was then lies in the contemporary novel. Highly coloured, sometimes completely stretching credulity and extravagant of plot, yet the *The O'Briens and the O'Flahertys* takes us much further than the dry facts of history. We are involved with the men and women, real and imaginary, but all authentically recognizable as those who could make history happen; by an act of our own imagination we can share in all that 'delirium of the brave'. Sydney Morgan wrote about a world that was breaking up even as she was writing, but such was her understanding of its complexities, and so passionate was her sympathy with all human aspirations for liberty and justice, that there is nothing dated or dusty about it. That is why her book illuminates many of the problems of Ireland today.

# PREFACE

IN again presenting an Irish novel to the public, I hope I am not doing a foolish thing: and yet I feel, that as far as my own interests are concerned, I am not doing a wise one. To live in Ireland and to write for it, is to live and write *poignard sur la gorge;* for there is no country where it is less possible to be useful with impunity, or where the penalty on patriotism is levied with a more tyrannous exaction. Called, however, to the ground by the sarcasms of enemies, and by the counsels of friends, I venture forth once more, with something less perhaps of intrepidity, than when I 'fleshed my maiden sword' under the banners of 'The Wild Irish Girl;' but in the full force of that true female quality, over which time holds no jurisdiction – perseverance.

I anticipate upon this, as upon similar occasions, that I shall be accused of unfeminine presumption in 'meddling with politics;' but while so many of my countrywomen 'meddle' with subjects of much higher importance; – while missionary misses and proselytising peeresses affect to 'stand instead of God, amongst the children of men,' may not I be permitted, under the influence of merely human sympathies, to interest myself for human wrongs; to preach in my way on the 'evil that hath come upon my people,' and to 'fight with gentle words, till time brings friends,' in that cause, which made Esther eloquent, and Judith brave? For love of country is of no sex. It was by female patriotism that the Jews attacked their tyrants, and 'broke down their stateliness by the hands of a woman;' and who (said their enemies) 'would despise a nation, which had amongst them such women?'

The epoch I have chosen for illustration has, in the present state of exhausted combinations, one great recommendation to the novelist – it is untouched. It has also a deep interest in a national point of view – it embraces events which prepared the Rebellion, and accomplished the Union. An epoch of transition between the ancient despotism of brute force, and the dawning reign of public opinion, it was characterized by the supremacy of an oligarchy, in whose members the sense of irresponsible power engendered a contempt for private morals, as fatal as their political corruption.

The portraiture of such an epoch is curious from its evanescence, and consolatory by comparison with the present times, – times the most fatal to faction, and favourable to the establishment of equal rights, which Ireland has yet witnessed. It may also serve as a warning to a large and influential portion of the public, which has yet to learn, that to advocate arbitrary government, is to nourish moral disorder. In the ranks of intolerance, are to be found many, who make the largest pretensions to purity of principle, and to propriety of conduct. Should any such deign to trace, in the following pages, a picture of manners, far below the prevalent tone of refinement now assumed as the standard of good company, it may diminish their confidence in their favourite political maxims, to remark, that all which has been thus gained for society, has been obtained by a progressive abandonment of the system they advocate.

The personages introduced on the scene, are those which belong to the times described. They are alike necessary to the *vraisemblance* of the story, and to the fidelity of the portrait: and 'I beseech, very heartily, at my desires, my requests, and my petitions,' the zealots of party spirit, and the purveyors of private scandal, to refrain from the application of my characters to their own purposes; and from the fabrication of false 'keys,' by which their petty larceny has heretofore attempted to rob me of the little merit of that 'fearlessness' with which I have held the mirror up to nature, without subterfuge and without evasion. May I be permitted here to observe, that with the exception of those public characters, whose delineation was almost a plagiarism, and whose peculiarities arose out of the political state of Ireland, and were necessary to the display of its story, I have drawn none but such as represent a class, or identify a genus. Even my Ladies Llanberis and Dunore were illustrations, not individuals. They were intended to represent the spoiled children of high society in all ages, from the charming Duchesse du Maine, with her inimitable *il n'y a que moi qui ai toujours raison*, to the modern mistresses of supreme *bon ton*, – all alike the creatures of circumstances the most unfavourable to moral consistency. However I may have fallen *á main basse* on popes and potentates, – taken the field against Austria, to 'hang a calf's skin on those recreant limbs,' and put forth my protocol against the Holy Alliance, I have held private life sacred, and have religiously abstained from bringing forward a single anecdote or circumstance incidental to the life of any private individual. The only 'key,' therefore, that I acknowledge, is that which is to be found in the great repository of human nature.

*Au reste*, I grieve that, in self-defence, I must wound the self-love of those walking 'ladies and gentlemen,' who affect to tremble lest 'Lady Morgan should put them into her book,' – by dropping into their 'unwilling ears' the secret that *tout bois n'est pas bon à faire Mercure*. Like Macbeth, 'I cannot strike at wretched kernes;' and not even for the benefit of a puffing 'key' would I transfer to 'my book' the obscure insignificance and flippant pretension that bore and worry me in society. I also take this opportunity of averting the wrath of half the fair *bureaucratie* of Ireland, roused by my palpable hit at a certain red velvet gown, in Florence Macarthy (for of the genuine aristocracy either of rank or wit, I have no cause to complain), by informing those whom it may concern, that the said red velvet gown belonged to a person, with whom I had every right to take every liberty – even to the libellous extent of 'putting her into my book,' when, where, and how I pleased, – that is, to myself.

Sydney Morgan
Kildare-street, Dublin
Oct. 1st, 1827

# The O'Briens and the O'Flahertys

## VOLUME ONE

# CHAPTER I

●

## *Correspondence*

Look into the chronicles. We came in with Richard Conqueror. Therefore paucas pallabris. Let the world slide: *Sessa!*

*Taming of the Shrew*

Avocat, ah! passons au déluge.

*Les Plaideurs.*

### LETTER I

*To General Count Sir Malachi O'Flaherty, of the Hy-Flaherty, Tanist, or Chief of the Hy-Tartagh, or West Country, or Jar Connaught, in the province of Connaught, Lord, or Prince of Moycullen, hereditary standard-bearer of the Bally-boe of Conmacnamara (vulgò Connemara), Knight of the order of Curaidhe na Croibbe Ruadh, or Knights of the Red Branch, Chevalier de St Louis, Gentilhomme de la Chambre de S. M. le Roi de France, and Colonel of the 2nd Regiment of the Irish Brigade:*

à son Hôtel,
Rue de l'Università, F. St Germain,
à Paris.

Per favour of Major O'Gara,
of said regiment.

St Grellan, Barony of Jar Connaught,
Co. Galway, April 1st, 177– –

SIR MALACHI O'FLAHERTY,

I take leave to address you by your unalienable title of hereditary knighthood, since neither the law of the land, nor the degendered customs of present times, will bear you out in taking the title or captainship of your tribe or sept; – the same having been renounced, disclaimed, and surrendered for ever, with all the Irish customs to the same name incident, by your ancestor, Murrogh ne Doe O'Flaherty (to the moan and shame – then and long after – of him and his), by his writing, signed with his signet, bearing date the 30th Eliz. 1609; at which time, it is notable here to mark that the said Murrogh ne Doe 'coming in,' as the phrase is (or was), did surrender, give, grant, or confirm to the said queen, in her chancery of Ireland, his principality of Hy-Tartagh in Connemara, belonging to the sept, family, or sirname of the O'Flahertys, together with all manner of manors, castles, demesnes, messuages, lands, tenements, rents, reversions, services, mills, meadows, feedings, pastures, forests, woods, underwoods, houses, edifices, granges, dovecotes, fisheries, warrens, watercourses, ponds, loughs, lakes and turlochs, patronage of abbeys, churches, chapels, chauntries, presentations, advowsons, oblations, obsentions, tithes, pinsions, portions, courts-leet, views of frank pledge, together with all perquisites and profits of the same, and all other rights, possessions, commodities, uses, liberties, and hereditaments, as well spiritual as temporal, with all and singular their members, rights, and appurtenances universal in your principality of the Hy-Tartagh, viz. in Moycullen,[1] Both-Cowna, Bally Cowark, Ballynonaghe, Cornevecaghe, Bog Moy, Ballyslattery, etc. etc. etc. etc. with the ancient township, burgh, or bishoprick of St Grellan, the chief town or burgh of the barony of Moycullen, in Connemara, county of Galway, province of Connaught; which was a manor exempted from all taxes, enjoying privilege of market or fair, Seneschal's court to determine litigations, etc. etc.

The said Sir Murrogh ne Doe, having so come in, and surrendered with the intent (and no small blame to him) to receive back the same, by letters patent, from the said queen, under the great seal and signet of the kingdom of Ireland, she did give or grant to him, the said Murrogh ne Doe, Knt., his heirs and assigns for ever, the said demesnes, castles, lands, tithes, signories, reversions, etc. etc. etc. etc. with all and singular their appurtenances; – he receiving the same (though his unalienable right from the year of the world 2000, – as may be seen in the annals or green book of St Grellan, now in my possession) of the queen's special grace, certain

[1] At Park, in the Barony of Moycullen, was born the celebrated author of 'Ogygia,' Rod. O'Flaherty, An. Dom. 1630.

knowledge, and mere motion. 'But to be holden' (saith the patent) 'of us, our heirs and successors, by part of a knight's fee, etc. etc.: provided always, that these our letters patent, or any thing contained in the same, shall not exonerate or change any rents, customs, duties, and services, to be performed to us, our heirs and successors, etc. etc.: provided always, that this our grant do in no wise extend to the damage, hurt, or prejudice to the rights of any one or more of our subjects, except such pretended rights and titles as any of them shall or may claim, by the name of O'Flaherty, the head, captain, or thane of that name; which name *we here extinguish for ever*, by this grant: provided, lastly, notwithstanding, that if, hereafter, it shall sufficiently appear that we, our heirs or successors, are entitled, or have, or ought to have, any right on the said premises, or any parcel thereof, or any of the rights, profits, or services issuing out of the same, that this our present grant, and these our letters patent for such of the premises as we, our heirs and successors, are entitled, or have right unto, shall be void and of no effect against us, our heirs and successors; any matter above expressed to the contrary notwithstanding.'

Now, Sir Malachi, you will little marvel if this patent turned out Talagh-hill talk,[1] as we say in Ireland; for little cause was wanting to show that her majesty, her heirs and successors, were entitled to have rights and estates of or on the premises; so that eantred after eantred, liberties and hereditaments, spirituals and temporals, went one after the other; the queen and her successors paying off services done them with the lands of the 'popish O'Flahertys,' granting, at one slap, the barony of Bog Moy and the lordship of Ballyslattery to the Mac Taafs of the Fassagh, who had come in and reformed, of which them slapper-sallaghs,[2] my sister-in-law (devil squince[3] the relationship), the Miss Mac Taafs are seized at this day.

Then came the Cromwellians; then prisals, and reprisals, and forfeitures, and reclamations; and then the act of settlement, which unsettled everything; and then your grandfather, Sir Bryan Ruagh O'Flaherty, having little left but the estates of Moycullen and Bally-nonaghe in Barony Ross, County Mayo, and some chief rents, went

---

[1] An Irish phrase for words that mean nothing. Talagh Hill, near Dublin, is the site of the Archbishop's palace.
[2] Draggletails.
[3] Query, Devil quench.

to Chichester House, to make good his rights before the court of claims, giving himself out for an innocent papist. But a particular time having been given to examine these claims, and the numbers being so great, that when the commission was closed, seven thousand gentlemen were still unheard, of whom one was Sir Bryan, an act of explication was passed, forbidding all who were unheard ever to prefer their claims again.[1] So Sir Bryan returned to his property in Jar Connaught, living, and holding his patrimonial hereditaments, as it were, by stealth; placing part in trust with a protestant neighbour, and holding the rest *sub rosa*. Then came the penals; and a bill of discovery completed the ruin of the family of the Hy-Tartaghs; and then it was that your father abandoned the fine old abbey, that had been fitted up as a mansion-house, and retired to a small castle, hard by convenient, the first stone castle raised in Connemara. But them that were to flourish by his ruin, missed their mark. For few tenants were there to till the land, or take it; and rack rents, and cottiering and short leases ruined all; and great emigrating – the poor to America, the gentry to foreign parts. So rents fell rapidly: and lands were pilled and polled, and the protestant discoverers themselves began to quake, and the hereditaments of the O'Flahertys, which had brought thousands to the original proprietors, brought not hundreds to the usurpers. Meantime the beautiful barony of Moycullen became as it were a desart, the land wasted, the turloughs[2] spreading, the rivers overflowing their banks: mills, mansions, and castles crumbling to the earth, and the roads, mams,[3] passes and bridle ways, filling up by the falling in of rocks, rubbish and earth. But for all that, there are

---

[1] 'Mais la prorogation ayant été refusée par Clarendon, la cour établie pour l'examen des prétentions des innocens fut obligé de cesser ses fonctions et de se séparer. Clarendon créa alors un nouveau tribunal, composé des gens dont la plupart avaient userpé les terres dont les légitimes propriétaires sollicitaient la restitution. Les premiers, ainsi devenus juges et parties, quelle espérance restait-il aux derniers? Pour leur rendre à jamais la justice inaccessible, le parlement fit un nouvel *acte d'explication*, qui leur interdisait toute démarche ultérieure à cet égard.' *Histoire d'Irlande, par l'abbé Geoghegan.* 'Voilá,' says the author, 'les leçons de morale que ces réformateurs donnaient aux Irlandais:' and such has ever been the morality which has presided over the proconsular government of that people, down to a secretary's last unblushing assertion, that the treaty of Limerick was only available to those who were within its walls at the time; as baseless a subterfuge as 'the equivocating fiend' of intolerance ever rested upon.

[2] Marshy grounds.

[3] Mam – defiles in the mountains – nearly synonymous with 'pass.'

those in the present day who are willing to purchase the abbey lands of Moycullen at any price. Nor need I tell you that this abbey was founded by Beavoin O'Flaherty, daughter of Earva, King of West Connaught, Anno 944, lineal descendant from Duaeh Tèan gumha, or the *silver-tongued*, fifth christian king of Connaught. This Beavoin was mother of Brian, great monarch of all Ireland, called Brian Corru; and in her native mountains did Beavoin O'Flaherty ny Brian, queen of Ireland, retire after the death of her royal husband, and found this same abbey, for nuns of the order of St Bridget, and under the blessed invocation of Mary, John, and Joseph; and with her of blessed memory began the alliance of kith, kin, and kindred of the O'Flahertys and the O'Briens; and, from that hour to this, they have ever been engaged in love, or in war, and ever will to the end of time, until the prophecy be fulfilled.

And be it known to you, that the person who now addresses you, is your near kinsman and first cousin, once removed, the son of your first cousin, Onor ny Flaherty, of the Flahertys of Ballinsorbeagha, county Mayo, and Rory Oge O'Brien, the descendant and representative of the O'Briens, Clan Tiegs, princes of the isles of Arran, and lineal descendant of Brian Borru: which royal race of the O'Briens of Arran were by the O'Flahertys, in the reign of Queen Elizabeth, expelled from. . . . ; but of these more hereafter. To take up the thread of my narration, I say, there are them, who would purchase the abbey lands of Moycullen at any price, from their present supposed proprietor, Archdeacon Hunks of St Grellan, son of the discoverer; which lands, though let below their value, and at a short lease, to a Midhain,[1] who again parcels them off at rack rents to poor scullogs[2] and beggarly tenants, who ruin all, the archdeacon refuses to dispose of – assigning no reason but that he fears them would take them at so great a price, came not well by their means; and would fain turn the fine old ruins of the abbey, tower, chauntry, and castle, to some popish and superstitious uses; some saying that the talk was, and is, of the nuns of St Bridget, now lodged over Paddy Blake's shop in the Claddagh of St Grellan, that they were to be restored to their ancient premises; and others, having it that the old church or chapel, which stands in good preservation in the abbey, is to be fitted up for popish service (the wooden

[1] Middle-man.
[2] The lowest description of Irish farmers.

chapel serving for eight parishes having been burnt), and what not; and surely it would be well worth restoring that ancient, old, and beautiful abbey, if it was only for the honour and glory of the country. For though founded for the nuns of St Bridget, yet it being no place for faimales, in regard of the troubles, the septs of Connemara fighting through other after the old fashion, the chiefs of the Hy-Tartagh took it into their own hands; and from the twelfth century to the reformation, the abbot was ever an O'Flaherty. In 1542 Abbot Hugh surrendered by indenture, covenanting to furnish the king with sixty horse, sixty kerns, and a band of gallow-glasses, whenever the Lord Deputy came into the province. On this condition the abbey was insured to him for life; and after his death, his nephew, Malachi O'Flaherty, continued seized of its temporalities, in despite of the king and deputy, being upheld by his sept: and when Malachi died, it was granted, as heretofore mentioned, by Elizabeth to your immediate ancestor Murrogh ne Doe, for ever, in free soccage.

Now this Abbot Malachi, after whom you were named, was a mitred abbot, and a peer of parliament under Queen Mary; and preyed more cattle, and kept up more hospitality than all the Tannists in Connaught; and governed his monastery with sovereign controul; and had his choral monks from Italy, and his church organ from Amsterdam; and his wines from France and Spain; and kept his almoner, and his pittancer, his chamberlain, and his cellarer (and troth that was no sinecure), and lived as well as the protestant bishop of St Grellan at this day, as by law established, every taste.

Be that as it may, there are them do suspect the truth to be that the archdeacon cannot make a title to the property; and there are them who will engage to restore General Count Sir Malachi to his rights and hereditaments in the barony of Moycullen, commonly called the abbey lands of the monastery of St Bridget, provided always that the Count agrees thereunto, and backs by his presence, influence, and interest (the thing being to be brought before the House of Lords) his law-agent, champion, and advocate, who, without fee or reward, or any consideration of lucre or gain, but being as it were employed by the Count in the said causes, and acting under his, and counsel's instruction, hereby undertakes to pursue the claim, and signs himself the Count's

Humble servant, friend, cousin, and kinsman,

TERENTIUS BARON O'BRIEN,

of the Clan Tiegs of Arran.

P.S. – It will be needful to obtain from the Miss Mac Taafs leave to look through some papers in the old box of the Brigadier Mac Taaf, called the brigadier's coffre: – a word through the Abbé O'Flaherty, P.P., who arrived here lately from France, will suffice. The inclosed case will more fully explain your situation. It shall be submitted to counsel for approval, on the receipt of your order to that effect.

### Case

The father of the defendant Hunks was decreed, as a protestant discoverer, to the benefit of a statute staple taken by a papist. It can be proved that this discoverer was of papist parents of the old English stock; and that, though becoming a protestant, he had never filed any certificate of his conformity: and therefore that his claims as a discoverer are void and null. It can be proved that the said father of the defendant, having been till the age of discretion a papist, had never received the sacrament, nor subscribed the declaration, nor taken the abjuration oath, nor filed a certificate thereof in a court of justice; and it is submitted that according to the – -th statute Anne, § 14, he cannot be deemed a protestant, within the intent of the act, notwithstanding that the person so professing himself a protestant shall have procured a certificate from the bishop. And it is submitted that the claims of Count Malachi O'Flaherty, the lineal descendant and heir of Sir Bryan O'Flaherty, on whom the discovery had been made, are available against said defendant, Hunks.

### LETTER II

#### (INCLOSING THE FOREGOING.)

*To the Abbé O'Flaherty, Post Office, St Grellan, Galway, Ireland.*

Paris, rue de l'Université, 177 –

MON RÉV. DIRECTEUR ET CHER COUSIN,

What do you think of the inclosed? and what do you know of the writer? Is he of your communion? Is he *compos mentis?* and, for his sins or for yours, is his conscience in your keeping?

Car il m'envoye un parchemin escrit,
Où n'y avoit seul mot de Jésu Christ;
Mais où il ne parloit que de plaidoirie,
De conseillers, et d'imprimerie.

It appears from the *plaidoirie* of this Connaught Mons.
Chicaneau, that you are arrived at your *living* in the wilds of Connemara, to which, by divine indignation, and the favour of your uncle,
the titular Archbishop of Tuam, you have been appointed; where
a catholic priest is a felon by law, and a martyr by choice; and
where you are destined to the full enjoyment of all the pains and
penalties annexed in Ireland to that perilous calling. *Cela m'échauffe
la bile.* – That a man of your force of intellect, your condition, your
philosophy (all priest as you are), with your Port Royal morality,
your Jansenism, and above all, your tastes and habits – but I have
not time now to fight the ground over again. I have been *sous les
armes* all the morning. For Abbé Hussey and O'Leary breakfasted
(fasted) with me on a *pâté d'anguilles d'Amiens*, and a flask of *mousseux
d'Ai;* and their fanaticism about Ireland, is at least equal to your
own. Like you, they pant

D'aller à Domfront, juste ville de malheur,
Où l'on est accusé à midi, et pendu à une heure.

I write *le pied sur l'étrier*, Mons. le Duc de Lauzun waiting to
accompany me to Marli, where we are going for a particular
purpose, *en polisson* (not being '*du voyage.*)' Here is more English
than I have put together on paper these twenty years; and you will
discover, that like Arlequin, 'je ne suis pas fort sur l'orthographe.'
I dare not trust myself on the subject of the inclosed papers, till I
hear from you; lest I should give myself a *ridicule ineffaçable.* 'Princi-
palities and advowsons! spirituals and temporals,' *de par tous les
diables!!!cela fait venir l'eau à la bouche.* What think you of Abbot
Malachi the second? music from Italy, and wines from France,
*figurez-vous!!* The lance and the crozier have ever quartered well
together. St Ignatius and a hundred other saints were '*des braves
militaires,*' and fought their way to Paradise sword in hand. Hugues
Caput, le Grand Capitaine, was called Hugues l'Abbé, The council
of Henry the Third of France proposed to erect all the abbeys in
France into secular commanderies, and to bestow them on the
officers of his court and army. Are there not at this moment *des
pauvres pères spirituels* in Germany, who command a regiment of

guards? and am I not already a military lay-monk as knight of the holy order du Saint Esprit? – 'Persuade me not, Sir Hugh;' my probation is already made! Was it not the abbot of Cluni that was called '*l'abbé des abbés?*' but what was he, or all the abbés of the earth, compared to the abbot of Moycullen, with a noviciate made in camp and court, and transported from Marli and Versailles, to the mountains of Connemara? What new lights I shall bring with me, in addition to the efficient graces of the abbots Malachi and Hugh! *En attendant*, I shall not take my vow till I have further heard from you on the subject, nor resign my colonelcy and my charge *de gentilhomme de la chambre*, with all privileges and immunities of that Alhambra of courtiers' wishes, '*les petits appartemens*,' until assured by you that my spiritual vocation has a chance of being backed by a competent portion of the good things of this world.

Write to me immediately *en large et longuement*. Egoist as I am by habit and by necesssity, there is one green spot in my heart, over which the world's blast has not passed, nor the chill of exile (which withers all) withered. It is sacred to the impression of early ties and of passed association; for I too have my lay vocation to the land of my birth, if I had the folly to indulge it. But I keep down the brute instinct, and still believe, or endeavour to believe, that '*le pays où l'on doit vivre est celui où l'on vit le mieux*,' and in this heresy I subscribe myself, your penitent in the confessional; *et partout ailleurs*,

Your affectionate friend and kinsman,

THE COUNT O'FLAHERTY.

P.S. If you do not approve of the inclosed letter for my cousin the baron, who is, I take it for granted, some black letter barrister of the Chichester House[1] school, write what you like better in my name. Also, if the whole be not a day-dream of the baron's, wait on the ladies of Mac Taaf, the *slapper-sallaghs!* (*Della Cruscans! et vous, les quarante!* find me in your dictionaries a word comparable to that in sound or sense), and see what is to be done about the brigadier's coffer. I direct to you at hazard, not quite certain whether

---

[1] Chichester House, so called after the Chichester family, who erected it, was, in 1641, the residence of the famous Lord Justice Borlase. Parliaments were afterwards assembled there; and the court of claims being opened in it, it became the constant resort of the old Irish families, who, ruined by forfeitures, had always claims to make. That magnificent and beautiful fabric the Parliament House, now the Bank of Ireland, occupies the site of Chichester House.

your nearest post town is in Nova Scotia, or 'our own good city' of St Grellan. I send this under Lord Stair's diplomatic cover, with the English dispatches; so I reckon on its arriving safely. Write, write, write; and direct always to the F. St Germ. If it is not felony for a priest to ride, pray mount your horse, and pay a visit to my dominions, temporal and spiritual, of Moycullen, that you may report on their condition. Once more, *sans adieu*,

Yours, M. O'F.

LETTER III

*A Mons. le Général Comte O'Flaherty, à son Hôtel, rue de l'Université,
F. S. G., à Paris.*

MON CHER Général et beau COUSIN,

I thought to have dated my first Irish letter from 'wretched Dublin, in miserable Ireland,' to use a phrase of Swift's, as applicable now as when it was first employed. Many causes, however, have urged my immediate departure from the capital. My poor brethren of the Augustinian Friary, in St John's-street (consisting only of the old prior and two regulars), where I intended to lodge, *en chemin faisant*, had been obliged to fly from the new persecution against all the regulars in Ireland. My friends and travelling companions, also, the Lord and Lady Clandillon, who, after their long exile, were returning to purchase estates and settle in the land of their fathers, have stopped short in London; where letters met them with an account of the prevalent intolerance both of the laws and system of government, and of the disturbances in the south. So they mean to return once more to the Continent, and with sad hearts to resume their foreign habits, and breathe their last in a distant clime. Thus it is that Ireland is deprived of its capitalists. Many families who have acquired large fortunes on the Continent, and in India, and who were disposed to bring back to their native country their wealth, their enlarged views, and industrious habits, are driven back from its shores, by those barriers to all national prosperity and moral improvement, the penal laws, and the state of society arising out of them. My brother, too, my excellent brother, to whom my untravelled heart returned with such hopes of a permanent intercourse, he is gone. I had only time to embrace him, after a separation of twelve years. He has closed his partnership with the house of Mahony and O'Connor, resolved to place the little he has saved by twenty years' labour beyond the reach of those penalties and forfeitures, to which his unfortunate castle daily exposes him.

At the present moment, all commercial interests are suffering deeply under the common affliction of the country – the monopoly enjoyed by the merchants of the established church. The laws which favour them with superior influence, credit, and early information, expose their less orthodox brethren to injury and depression, and greatly prejudice the trading community at large. It is in vain that we strive to extricate ourselves from these toils; on every side, new suspicions are to be allayed, new mortifications are to be endured; and, distrustful of the present, as hopeless of the future, we are reduced to the choice of acts alike abhorrent to out natures, apostacy or treason. What then is left but flight? And yet this is a sad alternative! The horrible system pursued for a century, to degrade and pillage the catholic population, has worked its end. The peasantry appear morally and physically to be reduced to a state, to which, that of the beasts of the field is preferable. The spirit of the few gentry, now to be met with in the capital, is as broken, as their whole condition is fallen. Nothing like a political sensation exists among them, for though O'Connor of Ballinagar and others, whose smuggled education has given them a moral existence, have endeavoured to get up a committee; yet the catholics are still satisfied with being permitted to carry a slavish address to each successive viceroy, which is treated with all the contempt it deserves.

The frightful shock, the utter dislocation of society, given by the Revolution, is still felt in faint and remote vibration, though at the end of a century. The displaced classes are not yet shaken down into their permanent positions. Many of the gentry have melted into peasants, many of the lowest persons have risen into sudden wealth; while consideration is confined to power and office, and all distinctions are ill defined, save those conferred by legislative influence, or church supremacy. A third insurrection since 1759, has recently broken out. With names as wild[1] as their vengeance, the wretched

---

[1] In 1759, the white boys directed their vengeance chiefly against tithe proctors, but the church and the chapel, the priest and the parson, were usually attacked on the same night, with unsparing impartiality. In 1763 the hearts-of-oak boys, and in 1770, the hearts-of-steel boys were abroad. A commission appointed by government to inquire

peasantry, maddened into violence by want and injustice, have beset their petty local rulers, with such arms as nature ever lends the oppressed. They overrun the park, and trample down the meadow; they assail the glebe, and lay waste the farm. Clustered in numerous array, under the shelter of darkness, for the purposes of midnight depredation, they spring up in by-ways and lone places, and avenge their wrongs with a cruelty, proportioned to the barbarous policy by which they are oppressed.

You will not wonder then, that I hastened my departure from Dublin (which is still[1] the same, ill-built, filthy, and badly-policed city, I left it twelve years back), and that even the wilds of Connaught appear preferable to the moral desolation of that disgusting capital. I accompanied my venerable maternal uncle, the titular Archbishop of Tuam, as far as his residence: and then proceeded, by Galway, to my parish in Jar-Connaught; a parish, in point of extent, equal to an English bishoprick. Its duties extend by land and sea, bog and mountain, over a surface of some thousand Irish acres; as it partly lies in the great isle of Arran (*Ara na noaimhi*, or Arran of the saints) and partly among the southern mountains of Connemara; that is to say, in your ancient fief of Moycullen, of which Arran-more is the half barony.

I have just returned from my ocean parish, after a delightful sail of three hours; and *peu s'en faut* that I do not make it my domicile, and send my coadjutor (who at present officiates there, in a ruined monastery, founded by St Ængus) to Moycullen. Are you aware that the Isles of Arran were royally governed by the clan Tieg O'Briens, up to the time of Elizabeth; when, as the old records of Galway attest (for the Clan Tiegs, and the town of Galway were always in mutual alliance, offensive and defensive), Murrogh Mac Turlogh O'Brien, chief of his sept, lord of the isle, and in full possession of his lawful inheritance, 'was by the usurping power of the O'Flahertys thence expelled?' But upon information being received by the queen's government, the O'Flahertys of Jar-Connaught were in their turn expelled, and the queen issued a commission, declaring 'that the islands belonged to her majesty in

---

into the disturbances, reported that the authors of these riots were of different persuasions, and that no marks of disaffection to his majesty's government appeared in any of the people.

[1] Anno 177– –

right of the crown.' This was ever the old way of settling disputes between quarrelsome neighbours, in Ireland. Since that time, these more romantic islands, the foyer of druidism, of christianity, and of all antiquarian research, have passed through various hands. In 1641 the Clan Tiegs, who to this day claim them as their inheritance, surrounded and attacked them on all sides (so numerous and powerful was this sept); and they were only frustrated in their designs by the Marquis of Clanrickarde, at the head of an English army. Even at the actual moment, a new claimant to this property has arisen, in the person of one Baron O'Brien (one of our barons by courtesy, I take it)[1] a profound Seanachy antiquarian, and Irish philologist; who, to fulfil a prophecy 'that the sept of the Clan Tiegs will never regain their dominions in the islands, till one of the direct line be born in the ruins of Dun Ængus' (a most curious remainder of Irish military architecture), 'has twice carried the baroness from her snug brick-house in St Grellan, to give an heir to the head of the "quinque familiæ"[2] in their ancient fortress. Unluckily, a *fausse couche* has twice proved that the star of the Mac Tiegs does not hold its ascendant. But the Irish have great faith in odd numbers; and the third voyage of this future mother of the Irish Gracchi has been just undertaken. I passed the royal barge, 'big with the fate of Cato and of Rome,' on my voyage home. Thus all here tends to the past;

E di memoria nudrirsi, più che di speme.

I have obtained this *Shanaos*, partly in Irish, partly in bog Latin, and partly in Connaught English, from Shane na Brien, the son of a weird woman, or *Benied* of the Isle of Arran-more, one of the

---

[1] 'Of the title of barons (not lords) there are several families that yet remain in this kingdom. Many are extinct, and some are advanced to higher degrees of honour. Of old, we had in this country (Westmeath) the baron of Moynshell (Tuitt). The family remains in good reputation and port, although the title be almost obsolete. The baron of Rathconrah (Owen), the family now reduced to one poor brogue-maker, the chief of a few mean cottiers. In the county of Meath, the baron of Navan (Nangle), the baron of Galtrim (Hussey); in the county of Kilkenny, the baron of Burnchurch (Fitzgerald); in Munster, the baron of Loughmoe (Purcell), and several other families in this kingdom. This honour is hereditary in the several families, though the style (I know not by what neglect) be almost worn out everywhere.' – *Survey*.

[2] The 'five families of free gentlemen,' descended from Milesians, were the O'Briens, O'Connors, O'Neales, O'Donnels, and O'Kevanaghs.

sept, and who moreover 'wears a girelle,'[1] Mor-ny-Brien[2] is to be the Juno Lucina ('according to the prophecy,' says Shane) and the fosterer of the young prince of the isles. Shane himself, the son by a former marriage of this Sybil of the Isles, is a fine specimen of the mere Irish animal, in its highest physical perfection. A young giant in structure, he possesses all the qualifications of that race, whom the English army of Henry Fitzempress 'hunted through the woods, but found it impossible to take, while the leaves were on the trees.' With senses as keen as a beast of prey, he sees and hears, when neither sound or object meet more civilised organs; yet is he obtuse and dull, to all subjects that do not reach him through his local interests or his hereditary attachments. He is one of the last representatives of the true 'green born rapparee' of the early part of the century. His immediate ancestors, gentlemen of high descent, had been among the victims of revolutionary rage; and being reduced to the alternative of 'Hell or Connaught,' chose the latter, as a *mezzo termine*, and gradually degenerated among the savage regions of that remote province, from loyal gentlemen (martyrs on a good principle, to a bad cause) to desperate outlaws. They were in one generation, the fierce bog-hunted tory; in another, the predatory rapparee; and in the next, were broken down to the mere wood kern. Shane leads a genuine greenwood life, fishing, fowling, climbing, diving, and paddling his canoe round the isles. His powerful memory, and more powerful imagination (the one stored by his mother, a celebrated *Scealuidhe*, or story-teller of Arran, and the other fed by the fantastic superstition of the Arranites), are proofs of his true Irish organization; which bad laws and institutions may have degraded, but have not destroyed. I should like to educate and lure him into the lines of civilization: at present he follows the perilous and picturesque profession of a clifter, or puffin hunter; and I doubt not he will be the Chiron of the future Achilles of the west.

What a contrast between the scenes and associations of this island, and my entresol in the *rue du Bac, entre cour et jardin;* or

---

[1] For an account of the consecrated Irish girdle, and its miraculous powers, see Walker's History of the ancient Irish dress.

[2] Ny, 'the daughter;' the female prefix, answering to the 'O', or titular distinctive of the males. 'O" properly applies only to the chief family; 'Mac,' signifies the son of; and 'Na,' the genitive case of the article, is appropriated to the humbler followers of the clan.

even between its romantic solitudes and the 'priest's house' on the main land, surrounded on all sides by objects of squalid misery, and physical and moral disgust. By a strange anomaly, the deeper you go in Ireland, within the boundaries of civilization, the more you are struck with the degradation of society.

This moment, 'Paddy the post,' a red-shanked runner between the town of St Grellan and the mountains of Connemara, has brought me your welcome letter, and its curious enclosure. Its *odeur musquee*, transported me at once to the *boudoir au pavillon, rue de l'Université*, and the sight of your writing, gave me the first thrill of pleasure I have experienced since my arrival in this land of suffering and sadness. What a curious coincidence between your inquiries and my historical notices of the Clan Tiegs. I shall dispatch your letter to the Baron by an Arran sunfish boat this evening, and immediately pay my respects to the Miss Mac Taaffs of Bogmoy. The expression of your friendship touched me sensibly. Never were feelings and habits more at variance than yours. '*C'est un bien mauvais sujet*,' said *la Duchesse de Coigny*, speaking of you the night before I left Paris, and I have often thought that you illustrated the dogma of Porphyry, that the souls of men were angels, who, in the great conflict between good and bad spirits, were doomed to corrupt bodies, to try their sincerity; and never was angelic soul more tried by the appetites and passions of a worthless body, than your own. I leave however to time, that great reformer of life, and director of conscience, to effect that for you which I have failed to do; not for want of zeal, but means: and in the interim, must love you for the virtues you have, in expectation of those that as yet 'you know not of.'

Your vocation to the monastic life is quite *en règle*, for you have long since qualified for giving more joy in heaven by your repentance, than the ninety and nine just persons who have never erred. I have seen many such as you, *désabusés sur tout*, digging their own graves at La Trappe, or treading the snow at St Bernard,

> Car helas! les plus aimables
> Sont souvent les plus coupables.

Among the lingering recollections of your boyhood, can you not recall an old dreary building, which stood on the edge of the Fassagh, on the road from Moycullen to St Grellan, between shore and mountain; and which, with the name of Bogmoy House, presented in its composite order of tower and gable, bawn and barn, thatch and shingle, 'fair limestone house, and wicker-work edifice,' a monument of the progressive history and vicissitudes of the country? In our times, it was the domestic fortress of a certain brigadier Flavius Mac Taaf, who volunteered, with many other Irish gentlemen, to follow George the Second to his German wars, – who as gallantly defended himself against a host of besieging creditors at home, as he had defended his king against his enemies abroad; – and who, having fought and tippled away his limbs, health, and temper, continued to the last to swear like a trooper, drink like a fish, to run his own claret into the smuggling caves of his own Fassagh, to distil his own poteen in the security of his own bawn, and to claim half the titles and all the estates of the province, on the testimony of his own Connaught Shanaos.

This Shanaos, with his bogs, barrels, still-pots, and lawsuits, he bequeathed to the Miss Mac Taafs, his three nieces and co-heiresses, the sole representatives of their acute, wary, and pugnacious sept. As they are of an old protestant family, accustomed to look down on the new converts, and in alliance with all the catholic families in Connaught, they have all the toleration towards our unhappy caste, which is wanting in the more modern sectarians. The parish priest has always a duplicate key of their gardevin, and a cover at their Sunday dinner table; and he is a never failing adjunct to their party, at 'five and forty' and cribbage. Although I have not yet availed myself of these privileges, which my predecessor (I hear) did not permit to lie idle, I have left my card at their door, and have received an invitation to dine with them next Sunday, written on the back of a dirty knave of clubs, which I suppose, in the words of their favourite game, has been, 'thrown out for the rob.'

You shall hear from me as soon as I have made the necessary inquiries touching Terentius and his claims: meantime

and ever, I remain,

Your's, etc. etc. etc.
ABBÉ O'FLAHERTY.

LETTER IV

*To Gen. Count O'Flaherty, etc. etc. etc.*

MY DEAR COUNT,

I have delayed writing, that I might write to some purpose; and finding that it was possible to combine my temporal agency with my spiritual mission, I have rendered each subservient to the other. In penetrating into the remote wilds of my diocese, and making the personal acquaintance with the poorest, as well as the wealthiest of my flock, I have obtained the requisite information respecting both your interests and my own. All this I have done under the guidance, and with the full benefit of the advice, information, and superior knowledge of our kinsman and legal champion, the Baron O'Brien; with whom I have visited your castle, abbey, and feudatory domains, under circumstances that have put me perfectly *au fait* to his character, views, and springs of action, both with respect to himself and to you: – for you are not to suppose that all his exertions are '*pour l'amour de vos beaux yeux.*' No, there is an outstanding prophecy to be fulfilled. The sacrilegious crimes of Murrogh O'Brien, Lord Inchiquin, Cromwell's apostate general, are to be redeemed through his descendants. But above all, there is a long account of vengeance to be paid off to the Archdeacon Hunks: 'a true Irishman (says the baron) never forgives an injury nor forgets a kindness.'

Now, who do you think this Terentius Baron O'Brien turns out to be – this head of the 'quinque familiæ,' this living representative of the ancient Brehons and Seanachies of the land, whose professional success has enabled him to purchase estates in the dominions of his ancestors, and to drive a carriage emblazoned with the royal arms and supporters of the O'Briens? '*Devinez, s'il vous plait. Je vous le donne en quatre, je vous le donne en cent; jetez votre langue aux chiens:*' you will never guess; what do you think of little *Terneen na garlach,*[1] the *noistroir*[2] of the mass cave in the old abbey of Moycullen, the supposed illegitimate offspring of your cousin Onor ny Flaherty, who, as the '*Calleen dhas dhu*'[3] of Turlogh Carolan's amatory muse, and as the possessor of the Abbess Beavoin's

---

[1] *Terneen na garlach*. Little Terence the base-born.
[2] Sacristan.
[3] *Calleen dhas dhu* – The pretty dark girl.

cross, obtained a sort of poetical and pious celebrity, which has not yet passed away in her native district? But I forget that your early expatriation, and the world through which you have passed, and which effaces everything, must have obliterated these early recollections; which my frequent visits to Ireland, peculiar situation, and professional habits, have preserved in all their original freshness. Well, then, to suit my narrative to your *jucunda oblivia* of Irish life (for what is there of Irish misfortune which it is not pleasant to forget!), you are to know that Onor ny Flaherty was the only and posthumous daughter of one of those gallant officers, who, after the capitulation of Limerick, assembled amidst the ruins of the abbey of Quin, to make their election between remaining in Ireland, or going into exile. Of this deliberation, a voluntary expatriation was the result; and the English government saw with dismay and mortification the flower of the Irish nobility and army, headed by Sarsfield, Lord Lucan, march to the coast, from which they embarked, to the number of four thousand, to give to Europe her most gallant soldiers, and most skilful leaders.

The death of Col. O'Flaherty, who fell at the battle of Veletri, left Onor a houseless orphan, and enlisted her of necessity into that legion of poor cousins, who then billeted themselves on the few of their own caste, who had rescued any portion of their property from the general proscription. Poor Onor, condemned by her insolvent, but proud gentility, to lead an idle and wandering life, continued (in the phrase of the day) 'to walk up and down the country among her fosterers and kindred,' with no earthly means of support, but 'the run of their houses,' and the little revenue derived from the Abbess Beavoin's cross, an hereditary relic, like the Cathach of the O'Donnels:[1] the country people coming far and near, in all their petty litigations, to swear upon it at a tester the oath. Onor was wont upon these occasions to throw in a prayer *gratis;* for Onor was a great voteen, a sort of unprofessed nun (when none other was permitted by law), who had moreover vowed herself to the Virgin,

[1] The lower Irish in general esteem no oath as binding, which is not made on a crucifix, or something in a shape of a cross. The crosier of St Monalagh (Dr Warner observes) is still preserved with great care. It is called the boughal, or stick, and is of curious workmanship. It is held in such veneration, that oaths are taken on it with great solemnity, and a shilling is paid for its use, to a poor woman who gives it out to the applicant, and it travels safely from cabin to cabin. – See *Statistical View of the County of Clare.*

and was of the confraternity of the blessed rosary. Onor, too, had the voice of an angel, and whoever once heard her sing Carolan's '*Gloria in excelsis*,' or the '*Miserere*,' with Irish words, will never forget those heartbreaking tones; tones which are so peculiar to the plaintive and melodius organs of her countrywomen.

It happened, however, that while Onor was enjoying the odour of sanctity, ere her vow to the Virgin was yet dry in the records of heaven's chancery, there arrived in St Grellan, to the peril of all vestal vows, one of those 'idle young gentlemen of this kingdom,' who (in the words of the statute) 'having nothing to live on of their own, will not apply themselves to labour, but doe live idly, and inordinately, coshering upon the country, and cessing themselves, their followers, horses, and greyhounds upon the poor people and gentry.' Yet, in spite of all acts and statutes, when this 'idle young gentleman' came galloping down the main street of St Grellan, with his followers trotting after, and his greyhound running beside him, every hat was touched and every eye smiled; for all knew it was Rory Oge O'Brien, of the Clan Tieg O'Briens of Tromra, once lords of the Iles of Arran; whose name was a passport to the reverence, respect, and good will of the whole province. His father, Colonel Daniel O'Brien, to avoid the act of *præmunire* then held *in terrorem* over such papists as either taught their children at home, or sent them abroad for education, having fled with his youngest son while yet a child, to the Continent, fought in the service of the King of Spain and the two Sicilies, and in the Commandery of Calabria, and fell at the battle of Cremona. His young son was thus left a pupil in the Jesuit College of Naples (and is the now celebrated ex-jesuit Abbé Ignatius O'Brien). Meantime, Rory Oge, the heir and Tanist of the sept, remained in Ireland, and preserved the old influence of clanship, and the old habits of gentlemanly idleness; literally 'coshering upon the country, and cessing himself, horse and greyhound,' upon friends, relations and neighbours. But as there was no penal statute for maiming, or otherwise defacing the person of a handsome papist, nocent or innocent, Rory Oge contrived to prey the country, as his ancestors had done before him: not indeed, carrying away herds, but hearts: and breaking more vows to the Virgin, than the Iconoclasts ever broke images.

Now, it happened that Onor ny Flaherty stood telling her beads and looking at the kissing and quarrelling of the market people in the main street, from the Spanish bay window of a kinsman's house, when Rory Oge rode into the town of St Grellan. Rory was an experienced watcher of windows on a market day; and he saluted the lady with a flourish of his Ramilies hat, as, riding up to the porch, he claimed his coshering with '*Eanaght* and *Edraugh*,'[1] after the old prescriptive fashion. There he not only cessed himself, horse, follower, and greyhound, for one calendar month upon Onor's hospitable Connaught cousin, but lodged himself for life in that sanctuary which the Virgin, till then, had exclusively occupied – poor Onor's tender heart.

O'Brien, who, like Madelon, was of opinion that '*ne faire l'amour qu'en faisant le contrat de mariage,*' was '*prendre le roman par la queue,*' had as yet no inclination '*de venir de but en blanc à l'union du mariage;*' but Onor was a gentlewoman born and bred, and though Rory Oge was as ardent as all the Rory Oges ever have been and ever will be to the end of time, yet Onor was as pure, though not as frail, as her own vow to the Virgin. The result, as might be expected, was a compromise between love and conscience. One fine morning Onor mounted *en croupe* behind Rory Oge, accompanied only by his horse-boy and greyhound, took the road to the mountains of Moycullen, by the then desolate and unfrequented pass of Glen-murrogh, and presented themselves at the cell of the titular Bishop of St Grellan (a persecuted prelate, who, under your father's protection, and at a great risk, took shelter among the ruins of the Abbey of St Bridget, whence he addressed his letter to his exiled friends abroad, '*ex nostro ultimo refugio*).'[2]

The jealousy of the statute book against holy wedlock then ran so high, and the premiums on catholic concubinage were so much above par, that it was perilous for a catholic priest to celebrate the forms of marriage between any parties whatever; and notwithstanding the two ancient catholic names that now presented themselves to be indissolubly united, the bishop hesitated. There was, however, something in the air of Rory Oge (to say nothing of the ides of May, and the solitary pass of Glen-murrogh), that induced

---

[1] See Statute of Charles II., against coshering.

[2] About this time a proclamation was issued by the privy council of Ireland, for the detection of catholic prieests, by which, in addition tto ttthe rewards offered by acts of Parliament, the informers were promised, on the conviction of an archbishop, bishop, or vicar-general, the sum of 150*l.*; for every priest or other person exercising ecclesiastical jurisdiction, 50*l.*; for every person, having property to a certain amount, and entertaining, concealing, or relieving a priest, 200*l.*

him, for Onor's sake, to risk a compliance. But when the sacrament of marriage was over, and the bishop proposed the celebration of a still more solemn ceremony, O'Brien started, hesitated, and at last confessed that he was by accident, and without his own knowledge or consent, a member of the church as by law established, having been converted by a process of persuasion then very prevalent, which saved the soul and the property of the proselyte by the only means deemed security for either. To recover a very small estate, Rory, who was no bigot, had undergone a temporary conformity; with the mental reservation of relapsing as soon as he should have sold his few acres so recovered, and placed his money in safety in some foreign security.[1] For this act, he boasted at the time that he had *good grounds;* and he declared that he would rather trust his soul with Providence for a few months, than leave an acre of his land for one day at the mercy of the statute book.

On this avowal, which struck poor Onor to the heart, the bishop made no observation; but coolly taking down a book, read aloud as follows: – 'If a catholic clergyman happens, *though inadvertently*, to celebrate marriage between a catholic and a protestant, not previously married by a protestant minister, he is liable by law to suffer death.' Onor, already feeling the penalty of her breach of one vow, by the fatality of another, swore at the feet of the crucifix, before which she had just pledged her faith to O'Brien, never to reveal her marriage during the life of her revered pastor; while Rory swore 'by all the books that ever were opened or shut,' not to betray a secret which, under any circumstances, it had never been his intention to disclose.

Shortly after Rory left the country, never to return; and poor abandoned and betrayed Onor remained to stand the brunt of his desertion and of her own disgrace. She soon lost not only her fine spirits, but, what was worse, her fine form. No longer the welcome guest of even Connaught cousins, she was looked coldly upon by all. A superannuated court lady, then sheltering her titled head in Castle O'Flaherty, who had in her fair youth wooed the smile of the Duchess of Portsmouth, or courted a nod from Sedley's profligate daughter, now turned her eyes askance when poor Onor came in

---

[1] 'Necessity, that makes a man ten times forsworn,' rendered this a very common practice in Ireland at the epoch alluded to, when every species of demoralization was forwarded and protected by the law of the land.

her way; and when, deserted by all, she gave birth to Terence O'Brien, in the cabin of a poor cotter in the mountains of Moycullen, she had the mortification of hearing the sobriquet of '*Terneen na garlagh*'[1] bestowed upon the legitimate descendant of Brien Borru. In a short time afterwards Onor and her infant son disappeared from the neighbourhood of St Grellan, and nothing was known of her for some years, except that she was living in the isles of Arran, and had been occasionally met by wayfaring people, wandering lonely in lone places, in the mountains of the Hy-Tartagh, with her son in one hand, a pilgrim's staff in the other, and her hereditary cross in her bosom. There she was revered as a saint, by the title of '*Onor na Croise*,'[2] and indeed was regarded as a martyr also; for, while making a pilgrimage to St Patrick's purgatory, she was caught in the act of praying at the holy well, and thus incurred the penalty of a fine; which as she had not the means of paying, she suffered the punishment of a whipping, denounced against every person 'who shall attend or be present at any pilgrimage, or meeting at any holy well, or reputed holy well.' To this punishment, some say she submitted, as a voluntary penance; but this is not probable.

The death of the persecuted bishop, for whose sake she had undergone so much ignominy and suffering, released her from her vow of silence.

The castle of your father, limited as were his means, was at that time the rendezvous and asylum of a number of unfortunate catholic ladies and gentlemen, reduced from rank and opulence to houseless poverty, by the proscription which followed the revolution. There was in those dark times, an affectionate party attachment, the relic of the old feudal clanship, which new associations of mercantile and metaphysical ideas, together with distrust of all, felt by all, have now abolished. It happened, that on the Christmas eve, which followed the death of the titular bishop, the party of the castle had assembled for midnight mass, in the cave under the chauntry in the abbey, which still bears the name of 'the mass cave, or *priest's chamber*.' MacCabe[3] had just played on the harp, the fine 'Gloria'

---

[1] The illegitimate.

[2] Honor of the Cross.

[3] One of the last of the composers and harpists of the old school, who played in the halls of the nobility and gentry of Ireland.

of Carolan, and had struck up the Miserere, when a voice of the most heart-breaking pathos, that drew tears from all eyes, issued from a remote part of the cave. The voice of poor Onor was never to be forgotten; and when the service was over, the vision of her former self was recognised, advancing to the altar, her child in one hand, and a paper in the other, which she presented to the officiating priest. She was wrapt in the old Irish mantle, and her long hair, no longer the raven locks of the *Calleen dhas dhu,* but white as snow, hung round her fine tall figure, and with her upraised eye, recalled the Magdalen of Guido. The priest read the paper she presented aloud, from the altar. It was the bishop's certificate of her marriage. All knew his seal and signature affixed to the instrument, that restored her to her fair fame; and all were willing to make the *amende,* for all were sensible of poor Onor's pious sacrifice. But Onor, with the double vindictiveness of female, and of Irish pride, wounded beyond all solace, did not forget, and could not forgive. She had vowed, never to sleep beneath 'the shed of a shingle roof;' and she would accept of no hospitality, but from that humble class which had never deserted her. She continued, however, for a short time, on Sundays and holidays, to frequent the mass cave, where she sung the Miserere in Irish, while her little boy, pranked out in a tattered stole and cincture (for she had devoted him to the church), served as Noistroir or Sacristan. I was then a boy; but I see him now, as I saw him at the time, walking barefooted and barelegged, after the officiating priest, with his bell and book in either hand, bowing to the right and to the left according to the forms; snuffing with his fingers the tallow candles, that lighted up the rude rock altar, chaunting out the responses, and tingling his little bell, with a low and muffled vibration, as if he feared its prohibited sound should be borne on the blasts, that rushed through the secret mass cave, to the ears of the bishop, 'by law established.' Oh, my dear O'Flaherty, these are the scenes, and these the recollections, which render the catholics of Ireland, *the most catholic* of any in Christendom; which array the heart and fancy, on the side of a persecuted religion, and bind both of them to forms and creeds, which I much fear are losing their influence over every other part of Europe.

It was just before I was sent to Douai, that Onor, returning to her hovel in the Isle of Arran, was found on a spring morning dead among the ruins of Dun Engus, 'with wandering spent and woe;'

and poor Terry, the little descendant of the heroes who raised that great military fortress, having wept himself asleep on his mother's body, on the night of her internment in the family vault, set out the next day on his travels in the quality of a poor scholar. With 'the world before,' and a satchel of books behind him, and with the Abbess Beavoin's cross for his sole inheritance, he continued to lead much the same wandering and precarious life he had led from his cradle (alas! there were many of the sons of the proscribed Irish gentry who had then neither so certain nor so honest a means of subsistence). It happened that Terence, no longer *Terneen na Garlach*, but Terence *na Librach*[1], was pursuing his vocation on Sunday in the cemetery of St Grellan's cathedral, and was reading out the '*Seven wise maisers*,' for a circle of less learned auditors, at a halfpenny a head, when he was suddenly seized by Prebend Audley Hunks, under the statute which 'impowers a protestant minister to pick up any stray child receiving charity in the parish, and to bind the said child to a substantial protestant as a menial servant till his twenty-first year.'

Now one of the most substantial protestants in St Grellan town was Geoffry Hunks, an old black letter conveyancer, who, at his brother's, the Prebend Hunk's suggestion, willingly availed himself of the letter of the law: for little Terence had become accidentally known to the reverend prebend as the expounder of many old Irish and Latin inscriptions on the tombs and monuments of the cathedral of St Grellan. You are aware that at this period, while the natural resources of the soil were abandoned to neglect and waste, the bogs were gradually overspreading rich vallies, and fertile tracks, the intellectual and moral resources of the nation were alike doomed to sterility and uncultured wildness.

One of the ends pursued in the early part of this century, with little regard to the means, was the impolitic measure of compelling catholics to educate their children in protestant schools, and to force on the cause of proselytism by the very modes which have always tended to retard it. The result was the degradation of the lower classes (till nothing was left but their powerful instincts and vehement passions), and the driving away the youthful catholic gentry to foreign countries (as in the instance of yourself), from whence they seldom returned; or if they remained, only to flourish

[1] Terence of the books.

like the wild shrub of the desert, sending forth their vigorous shoots of intellect in luxurious disorder, and frequently in mischievous strength. A few gloomy and concealed convents still indeed existed (and still exist) in the provinces of Connaught and Munster, where a sort of smuggled education was perpetrated (in defiance of the law, because unknown to it), by some simple, ignorant, and bigoted friars, who taught their bare-footed scholars to translate the poetry of Homer and the eloquence of Cicero into bad Irish, and worse English. There, too, some dreaming old annalists or antiquarians (such as initiated Geoffry Keating in those fables to which he has given the name of history), still taught the 'hard Irish,' and affected to translate the branch Ogham into versions which none could dispute, since none could understand them.

In such seminaries, led by his wandering mother, had little Terence acquired that sort of learning which rendered him as precious an assistant to the old black letter conveyancer of St Grellan, as the young heavenborn statesman, Jonathan Swift, was to Sir William Temple. Hunk's business lay exclusively among those litigious Connaught gentry, who, dissatisfied with the judgments of successive suits, spent their last doubloons in asserting claims involved in all the obscurity of parchment and of pedigrees, which, both for their Irish and Latin, might have puzzled even Geoffry Keating himself.

Even still these 'bondsmen of the law,' backed by counsel's opinion, as given by Counsellor Hyacinth Daly of Galway, or Counsellor O'Sullivan Bere of Kerry, continue to urge and to boast of claims merged in the successive forfeitures of ages, with all the pertinacity of ignorance worked upon by pride – the refuge, vice, or virtue of the oppressed and degraded of all countries.

The success of Terence in deciphering these hieroglyphics, and above all, his version of an old inscription in Runic Ogham (as he called it), found on a stone in the abbey (said to be the very stone on which the annals of the Ballyboe were first began), induced old Hunks to change his indentures of menial servitude into a patent of professional gentility, and to create Terence a gentleman by law, as he was by blood, alliance, and descent. For this, however, a preliminary act of regeneration was necessary; for, saith the statute, 'whereas, by experience, in this kingdom, it hath always been found that papist solicitors and agents have been the common disturbers of the peace and tranquillity of his Majesty's subjects, his most excellent Majesty, for the remedy thereof, by the advice and consent of the lords spiritual and temporal, has decreed that none can practise as attorneys or solictors who do not declare against all interpretation of the Gospel, but such as the existing hierarchy of the land promulgateth.'

Terence, from the hour of his birth the predestined victim of statutes, who, under their influence had one parent exiled and the other dishonoured, – who had seen his mother flagellated, himself bastardized, the rites of his religion celebrated in midnight mystery, – and who moreover trembled at the name of Hunks, could not be supposed to possess that sort of moral courage which gives the church its martyrs. As his ideas of the 'hierarchy of the land' were Friar Pat and Father John, and as the Gospel was imaged to him by the little leather bag (so named), tied round his neck by his mother, to keep off the chincough, he had little hesitation to agreeing to any interpretation of it proposed to him; and when called on to avow if he believed the thirty-nine articles, he himself replied, 'Ay, troth, and more if your honor plases.' Thus docile to the existing influence of the time, the descendant of Brien Baroihme, the sacristan of the mass cave, became an indented attorney, and a member of the law church; while solicitor Hunks was eulogized to the skies for having rescued a soul from that 'damnable heresy' which turned even the professed conservators of the law into 'common disturbers of the peace and tranquillity of his Majesty's subjects.'

The age and indolence of the unlettered Hunks, the diligence, learning, and activity of his apprentice, soon gave the younger and more vigorous limb of the law the *dessus*. Old Hunks finally admitted him to a share of that business of which, in fact, he had long done the whole; and Miss Deborah Hunks, his only child and mature daughter, who for thirty years had flirted through the entire chapter of St Grellan, cracked the voices of more vicars choral, and disappointed the hopes of more aspiring young choristers than any Connaught heiress of the day, at last disposed of her heart as her father had done of his affairs; and when Terence had completed one indenture, he entered unresistingly into another; doubtful whether there was not some penal statute by which the comely young apprentice of an old solicitor was obliged to marry the plain, elderly daughter of his master by 'the advice of his Majesty's council, spiritual and temporal.'

The death of old Hunks, in the fifth year of Terence's marriage, left him in full possession of a good country business; and there was not a more pains-taking and protestant attorney in the province of Connaught, when the sudden appearance of Terence's uncle (the expatriated younger brother of Rory Oge), superior of the Jesuit convent of '*Il Gesù*,' at Rome, gave a new colour to the story and circumstances of his nephew.

The Abbate Don Ignatius O'Brien, whose restless and zealous character has since come out with such force, in his public struggles to prevent the suppression of his order, and secretly to perpetuate its influence; and whose active life has proved that '*Cucullus non facit monachum*,' had come over to Ireland ostensibly to find out his nephew, and to establish his legitimacy according to the statute book, as it was already proved according to the law of God. Rory Oge, who had died an officer of the Pope's guard, and a brother of the '*Penitenti*' to boot, had, it appears, left a certificate of his having returned to the catholic church before his marriage with Onor; and confessing the *supercherie* of having concealed the fact, bequeathed a sum of money to his long abandoned son, with all his nominal rights, privileges, and immunities in the isle of Arran. The ambitious marriage of Rory with the indigent widow of an insolvent Roman *principe*, a representative of the S.P.Q.R. of ancient Rome, during the lifetime of his first wife, had rendered illegitimate the birth of his only child by this marriage; and at the early age of sixteen, the daughter of the Italian princess and the Irish prince, took the veil in an Irish convent at Rome, supposed to be under the special protection of the Jesuits.

Such was the ostensible motive for the Abbate O'Brien's visit to his native country. The authorities of St Grellan, however, looked upon his mission as governed by other views. An ex-Jesuit, superior to the richest house of that powerful order in Rome, who travelled in his own carriage, who had removed the remnant of the order of St Bridget from their retreat in a garret over the shop of a grocer in the market-place to the old monastery of Mary, John, and Joseph, in another part of the town, who expended considerable sums in charity, and who in his progress through the wilds of Connemara and the isles of Arran was followed like another St Patrick, could not fail to excite suspicions in times when nothing was talked of but 'popish banditti spirited up by agitating friars, and Roman missionaries sent over to sow seduction, and spread heresy and

rebellion among the people.' The charities of the abbate soon
furnished an excuse for his persecution, in a land where charity
was made the pretext for open and forceful robbery.[1] In a little time
he found himself the object of an infinity of petty intrigues, the
victim of the most absurd calumnies, the subject of a protracted
*correspondence with the castle;* and on the point of being arrested by
a secretary of state's warrant – I know not under what ridiculous
charge – was at length compelled in self-protection to retire from
a scene and country in which, though his existence was not recognized by the law, his life was embittered by its odious and persecuting enactments. Thus a man, whose bigoted ambition, haughty
character, and temporal views for the supremacy of ultramontane
principles, and above all for the maintenance of his own pernicious
and enterprising order, was the least calculated to succeed with the
Irish catholics (whose national notions resembled in independence
those entertained by the Gallican church), was elevated to the
glory of sanctity and martyrdom; and his sudden departure from St
Grellan will be long commemorated as their Hegira by the natives
of Connemara and the isles of Arran. You will see in these animadversions what you call the *dernier rejeton de Port-Royal* and the leaven
of Jansenism – but let that pass.

The persecution of his uncle rendered Terence more protestant

---

[1] It is laid down, not only by the statute concerning superstitious uses, and other
English statutes, but also generally, that the King, as head of the church, and as
entrusted by the common law to see that nothing is done in maintenance or propagation
of a false religion, is entitled to all grants and gifts made for such purposes, so as to
appropriate them to other uses that are held lawful. This principle of general policy,
which may be pushed to any extent that to a chancellor may appear necessary, applies
equally in the law of Ireland and England. The commissioners of charitable bequests
form a board expressly appointed to hunt out catholic charities, and divert them to
protestant uses; and their zeal and activity in the discharge of their ungracious functions,
completely frustrated every attempt to provide a permanent maintenance for the catholic
ministers of worship, their places of education, and other pious and charitable foun-
dations. It may, by the by, be remarked, that this same dictum of the common law,
appointing the king to the supervisorship of religion, is another of those gratuitous
inventions by which the judges manufacture laws for whatever suits their convenience.
The common law of England arose in the woods of Germany, when the religion of
Woden was 'by law established;' and it grew up to maturity under the catholic kings
of England. The *ne quid detrimenti* authority must therefore be two steps removed from
protestantism; and the seizure of property to protestant uses, a direct infraction, instead
of a fulfilment of common law: at least, so common sense would say. But what has law
to do with common sense?

and loyal than ever. He even carried his subserviency to the length of subscribing to the 'black petition' against the catholic claims;[1] for, the more unmeasured the oppression, the deeper is the dissimulation it demands. But though all cried out that 'O'Brien was a pretty name to open a pew[2] door with,' all were pleased to see the legitimized son of Mr O'Flaherty drive to the cathedral porch with the arms and supporters of his family in his – one-horse chaise, and his 'boy' in the crimson livery of the O'Briens. The death of his elderly wife, and an open breach with her dictatorial and intolerant kinsman, the proselyting prebend of St Grellan, released O'Brien from the tyranny of a family, which, in making his fortune, had, in his estimation, risked his salvation; and which, in forcing him under the protection of the statute book, could not place him beyond the persecutions of his own conscience.

'And now, Abbé O'Flaherty,' said the Baron O'Brien, in touching upon this part of his story – for I am giving you a brief abstract of his own biography, as we wound through the almost impassable pass of Glen Murrogh, on the way to Moycullen, – 'and now, being no longer a slave, nor an indented apprentice, but feeling myself one of the five free gentlemen of Ireland, and at liberty to dispose of my heart and person, without the fear of act or statute; and it having pleased Divine wisdom to take the first Baroness O'Brien, alias Miss Hunks, to itself; I begun to look about me for the ould blood flowing in good protestant veins, that the mother of the future representative of the tribe of Dalgais (founders of the Irish monarchy under CAS, son of CONAL of the swift horses), should not throw a *flan deargh*[3] on the scutcheon of the family; and so I consulted my late ould clients, Brigadier Flavius Mac Taaf, of Bogmoy, and he offered me his oldest niece and co-heiress, Miss Mable Mac Taaf, and said if he had an oulder he would give her to me. But, Abbé O'Flaherty, I resolved to be a Hussian,[4] and fight for pay no longer; and though Miss Mac Mable Taaf is a comely fine woman, and in her prime, as I may say, – likewise Miss Monica – yet, do ye see, I had a vocation towards the cadette, Miss Bridget,

[1] See Harding's *Galway*.

[2] Pews are peculiar to protestant churches.

[3] A term in Irish, signifying in heraldry a standard or colour; used also as a disgrace or blot in an escutcheon.

[4] An Hessian.

who was the Cinderella of the family, and who was often sent to slip down to our office in St Grellan with a bond to be signed, or a deed to be executed. So, having slipped in, one fine day, she forgot, the cratur, to slip out, till she was Baroness O'Brien, and then she wrote to her uncle for pardon, a letter that would mollify a stone; in which I enclosed the grey mare to Miss Mable, to soften her heart: but all would not do. Well, *Foghal Foh!* wait a while, but to this blessed hour Miss Mac Taaf hates the ground I walk on.'

So much for the history of your cousin, law agent, and hereditary foeman. With respect to his character, it is a study; and is combined in a singular degree with the temperament of his sept, and the qualities of his social (or rather anti-social) position. It is evident that Terence, physically brave as the fiercest of his family, is morally timid, as the most degraded of his caste. Always ready to risk his life on a point of personal or of national honour (and I am told that he fought a duel with an English officer who had observed that the legs of the Connaught ladies and the Connaught heifers were formed on the same model); yet he shrinks from legal infliction, however remotely threatened, and is ready to prostrate his opinion to any constituted authority, from a king to a constable. Courting the notice of the great, even in the party he hates, he enjoys himself only in the intimate familiarity of the lowly and oppressed. Secretly attached to the popular party, without one popular feeling, or one constitutional idea, he is ready to restore, but unwilling to reform. With thoughts ever retrospective to the glories of 'ancient ould Ireland,' with its green banners, and harps, and collars of gold, – and with that religious tendency to passive obedience with which we catholics are accused, he is a rebel and a royalist on the same principle. These conflicting opinions he veils under an exterior of the most unlimited submission to the powers that be; giving no further vent to his fears and his hopes than may be safely expressed in his favourite adage of *Foghal Foh*, or 'wait awhile.' Distrusting all, and not confiding even in himself, he lives in perpetual fear of becoming, without his own consent, that thing 'hated of gods and men!' a *relapsed papist*, – as he became at the direction of the others, a protestant proselyte. In a word, he is not only a 'brief abstract' of a large class of his countrymen, such as six centuries of degradation have made them; but is, in his own person, with all his contraries and inconsistencies, a part and parcel of the law of the land, a leaf torn out of the Irish statute book, a comment on that code written in human blood, which stands accountable for the perversion of a national character, as gallant and as good as was ever checked in its progress to improvement, and driven back disgracefully and disgraciously to the starting-post of civilization, by a system that renders legalisation a bye word, and government a crime.

With respect to O'Brien's professional character, he is, that *rara avis in terris*, an honest attorney. His high calling in the profession, forced on him by circumstances, has given him a sort of historical dignity in the suits he undertakes. He brings up evidences, as Hecate called up spirits, and marshals a dozen of Irish kings in sad array, to scare the wits of Scotch adventurers, and extinguish the claims of protestant discoverers; giving to his causes a sort of bardic interest, and making his suits the very poetry of litigation.

I pause for a moment at this recollection, struck with the different destinies of two men, each representing the story of their country in different ways. The chief of the O'Flahertys driven into exile, to fight on foreign grounds for foreign interests; but by so acting, recovering his 'simple state of man,' and shining out in all the original brightness of hereditary endowment, – elevated by rank, distinguished by titles, loaded with honours obtained through qualities which ever find their own level, where no partial institutes impede their progress, and convert all talent to misery or to abuse. The descendant of the supreme monarchs of Ireland was on the contrary chained by a concatenation of evils, to the stake of disqualifying persecution; dragging his historical name through the mire of sordid poverty and debasing dependence, and predestined before his birth to inevitable degradation. With a spirit doubtless as brave, energies as active, and feelings as vehement, as the most high-minded of his forefathers, yet with the sources of all these ennobling gifts poisoned at their spring, he is beaten down by statutes, into a disgraceful subserviency, which settles, after sone ineffectual struggles between nature and fate, into a suppressed indignation and profound duplicity, and leaves the individual victim, who represents so large a portion of his fellow countrymen, a heterogeneous particle of a heterogeneous mass. Secretly devoted to one religion (for Terence, live as he may, will die '*ferme catholique*') but affecting to uphold another, – a patriot, loving Ireland 'not wisely but too well,' he is more calculated to injure than benefit its cause, and that by the very means he would resort to for its redemption. *Au reste*, he is the finest possible specimen of his caste and class; speaking, like all the old catholics, and protestants too, in Ireland, the English of Queen Anne's days, with the accent of Queen Elizabeth; and, evidently dressed by the statute book, no reformed chief of Henry the Eighth's time, who had saved his head by cropping it, and presented himself to the lord deputy unmantled and unbendelled, glibs closely cut, and Crommeale closely shaven, was ever more loyally and guardedly habited.[1] Still he looks the very personification of a recusant or nocent papist; and though tall and comely like all the O'Briens, effaces the original nobility of nature, by an air cowering and servile, which marks the moral degradation of his position.

O'Brien has met my advances on your behalf with the most enthusiastic ardour: and the opinions of two eminent lawyers are so clearly in favour of the case, that I have no hesitation in urging you to proceed.

I conclude abruptly, though (for your patience), not briefly; having just found means to dispatch this, *via* Bordeaux, through the Frenches and Blakes, whose argosie now rides at anchor within view of my window. I shall write again to-morrow, for I willingly take refuge in your affairs from the sad impressions of pauperism by which I am surrounded, and from the daily mortifications here inflicted upon all, who, for worshipping their God, in the form once practised throughout Europe, are the prostrate victims of an intolerant and impolitic code, that renders them aliens in their native land.

Adieu! I commend your spiritual welfare to the Husseys and the O'Learys, and for the rest, *Cura ut valeas.*

Yours, etc. etc.

THE ABBÉ O'FLAHERTY

[1] The jealousy of Irish manufacture was as keen in the middle of the last century, as in its commencement, when Dean Swift, having published 'a proposal for the universal use of Irish manufactures,' it was by the men in office construed to be 'a seditious and factious pamphlet.' The printer stood his trial for its publication; and the jury persisting in finding him not guilty, the chief justice sent them nine times back, until, tired out, they left it to the mercy of the judge by a special verdict! The chief justice, laying his hand on his heart, solemnly declared that a proposal to encourage the manufactures of Ireland was a design to bring in the Pretender.

LETTER V.

*To Count Malachi O'Flaherty, etc. etc.*

MON BEAU COUSIN,

*Vos affaires vont leur train.* The inclosed will convince you that
your cause, already bruited about (for our Baron is *très-démonstratif*)
is popular, and that the old feeling to the old family anticipates its
success. The Hunkses (the delegated authorities of the Proudforts,
the reigning toparchs of the country), are, for their insolence of
office, detested by all sides and parties. *D'ailleurs*, a change is ever
a sensation; and a lawsuit in Connaught is always a *ben trovato*.

I have had audience of the Misses Mac Taaf; audiences, alas!
where, for two mortal hours, I was 'sole auditor.' *Des memoires contre
le genre humain*, with six centuries of wrongs at their fingers' ends,
and the 'abductor of that simple *omadaun*, the cadette, that turncoat papist, Terry O'Brien,' for the refrain of all. All this too, in a
sustained drone, the fluent monotony of which, if you have never
listened to Connaught Shanaos, you cannot conceive; though the
drone of the Scotch pipes has some resemblance to it. Meantime
the Brigadier's *coffre* is ours; and a sort of *trève de Dieu* has been
patched up between O'Brien and the heiresses of Bog Moy, who
have even consented to see the mother of the young chief of the
isles, on her return from her accouchement. 'And let the Count
know, Abbé O'Flaherty,' said Miss Mable, 'that I have done for
him what I would not do for the thirteen tribes of Galway.' The
fact is, O'Brien thinks that, both as evidence and as authority, they
can be of infinite use; 'and will, I'll engage,' says O'Brien, 'and
have their own raisons for that same, Abbé dear; and what was the
heart and person of Baron O'Brien, in comparison to Count Sir
Malachi O'Flaherty? and Miss Mac Taaf is a comely fine woman
to the fore, and has fine acres, townland and turloghs, stretching
up to the Pass of Moycullen, if they were well worked. And it's
herself would not throw a good offer over her shoulder, as the
saying is of the priest and the poteen.' Indeed, from certain hints
of both ladies, I rather suspect O'Brien's surmises are well founded,
and that you would find no difficulty in quartering the arms of the
O'Flahertys with those of the Barons of Bally Slattery and the spurs
of the Green Knight.

On my visit to Bog Moy (where I found every thing *in statu quo*, as in the Brigadier's time, – even to the ruined roof, which fell in during the great storm of 42, leaving one-half of the fabric uncovered), Miss Mac Taaf observed, 'You see here is a fine place, Abbé O'Flaherty, if there was one to keep things together, and make the most of it; and hopes, before the Count arrives in the country, to see it another thing; for myself and Monica have it *in contemplation* (a favourite word with her uncle for thirty years before his death) to raise that roof this spring, plaze God, which covers the great dining-room, and to *flure* (floor) the new parlour built by my grandfather Sir Columbus; and whenever the suit is terminated with Martin of Dangan, and gets lave to work the quarry claimed by the Darcys and Blakes, and to which we have every right in life – which Terence O'Brien, the poltroon knows, if he would spake out like a man – manes to build up with Connemara marble the great gate pillars of the bawn, and has had it long and late in contemplation to drain the turlogh and plant the demesne (an unreclaimed bog), but would be glad to have the binefit of the count's advice.' Thus you see 'if the dial speak not, yet it makes shrewd signs.'

As for O'Brien's own views in urging on the promotion of your interests, it seems to me that your suit once gained, he wishes to become the purchaser of the abbey lands, ruins and all (which are magnificently picturesque, and in wonderful preservation), either for himself, or in trust for others. I think I can detect the intriguing jesuitical spirit of the Abbate O'Brien under all. Since the suppression of his order (which never has been suppressed), the Pope has given him several missions, and participates more than ever in his views. With all the imperturbability of a narrow but zealous mind, he is acting upon principles, which however operative in the days of the La Chaises, and the Telliers, and of their credulous dupe and victim, Louis *le Grand*, are as inapplicable to the spirit of this age, as they have in all ages been injurious to the interests of society.

As a proof, he has sent over his Italian niece, Rory Oge's daughter by the *Principessa*, and O'Brien's half sister, to preside over and to reform the order of St Bridget, now represented by the poor sisters of Mary, John, and Joseph at St Grellan (for female orders in Ireland have held their ground, when the abbeys and monasteries have lost theirs). It was in vain that in religious vicissitudes of three centuries, the sisterhood had been frequently driven from their altars, by the reforming halberds of Elizabeth, and the pious pikes of Cromwell; that their holy houses were laid bare, and that deeds were perpetrated within their consecrated walls, which made 'the shrines all tremble, and the saints grow pale.' The nuns fled for shelter to their orders in Spain and France, or lay hid in the castles and fastnesses of their friends at home. It was in vain that the government sent orders to the mayor of St Grellan, 'to keep a strict eye' upon the nuns of Mary, John, and Joseph (four old ladies, the wreck of the order, which had suffered persecution from Cromwell to William). Though twenty times exiled, they had twenty times returned; and when in the year 1740, the last inquisition was taken of their house, and when the mayor reported that he had searched it and only found ten beds, in which it was 'apprehended that the reformed nuns lay before their dispersion,' the old ladies still held their ground *perdues* under the beds, where the mayor had forgotten to look for them.

From that period, government gave up the unequal contest, tired out and convinced that the double pertinacity of the church and the women was too much even for the penal laws; and that the different fate of the brotherhood and the sisterhood of St Dominic, St Bridget, and St Augustin, proved that '*ce que femme veut, Dieu veut.*' In spite, therefore, of the law of the land, which makes monastic vows felony, the venerable sisters have preserved theirs; and have still received the vows of others, at the altar of Mary, John, and Joseph, as if no such law existed. The life they lead is as pious and useless, as prayers and idleness can make it. The house they occupy is as comfortless, dirty, and unwholesome, as time, poverty, neglect, and the want of all ventilation, has left it. Still the poor nuns, though maintained by charity, are objects of veneration and respect, and the little well in their narrow garden, dedicated to the blessed Virgin, and to St John the Baptist, is still visited with faith and unction, and still performs as many miracles, as the celebrated virgin of the Rosary, in the Abbey of Moycullen, mentioned by John Heyne.

To reform or rather to revive this order, the abbate has translated his niece from her *couvent à coton* on the Corso (one of the *mignon* establishments at Rome, under the special government of the Jesuits), to the convent of St Bridget in the Cladagh of St Grellan. Imagine this Italian nun (who, by the by, is *Italia-nissima*), with the true temperament and organization of her country, brought up amidst the splendid ceremonies of her church, fed upon soft sounds, and brilliant lights, not speaking a word of English nor of Irish, and suddenly dropped among the *bonnes grosses mères* (of St Bridget's), who speak nothing else. Of course, as others have done in the same situation, she will return in disgust, by the first opportunity, to her own country. Meantime she is drawing crowds to her chapel, even protestants, by the singular beauty of her voice and person; and so far, the Abbate has not hit upon a bad expedient for bringing papacy into fashion. For, says O'Brien, who worships his new found sister as a thing inskied, 'with woman and music, Abbé dear, you might proselytize all Ireland, far better than by all the peynals, and all the persecutions that ever were invented:' and wonders but the government never hit upon it.

On the first of the month we move to Dublin, to take the field, under the standard of Messrs Ponsonby and Egan. As soon as you are wanted, we shall write for you.

*En attendant*, do the honours by the Baron, and the Miss Mac Taafs. I enclose Miss Mac Taaf's envelope to me, with her letters for you: it is as characteristic as its enclosure. – *Vale*.

Yours, etc.

Abbé O'Flaherty.

ENVELOPE.

### To the Rev. Abbé O'Flaherty.

The Miss Mac Taafs (Mable and Monica), of Bog Moy, present regards to the Abbé O'Flaherty. Take leave to enclose him a letter for his cousin, General Count O'Flaherty, not knowing the Count's present abode in Paris. The Miss Mac Taafs (Mable and Monica) forgot to remind the Abbé, that they had the pleasure of making his acquaintance, when they were slips of girls, at the Mayor of Galway's, Patrick Lynch; more betoken it was a drum (dry), not all as one, as in the old times, as I hear tell, by my uncle the Brigadier, when chocolate, rosolia, and usquebagh, were served round, more plenty than *cathbhruidh*[1] may be had in Galway town now. And for all that, as my sister Monica pleasantly says, there was as much pride as poverty there; the Bells, Blakes, and Bodkins, and the rest

---

[1] A sort of curds and whey.

of the thirteen tribes, being as high in the instep, as if they had ever an acre of land in the province, barring what they got by trade; not all as one as the ould residenters and ancient proprietors of the place, since the flood and before.

P.S. It gives the Miss Mac Taafs the greatest of pleasure to learn the probable success of the O'Flaherty cause; and wonders but the Abbé would employ Counsellor Costello, who does the Miss Mac Taafs' business to their entire satisfaction, and would, with the Miss Mac Taafs' assistance, make a far better hand of it than that Terence O'Brien, who got what proofs he has out of the Brigadier's bureau. For it is yourself, Terry O'Brien, that had the plunder of it and us, when you had the run of Bog Moy house, as the chartered school apprentice of old Hunks. And a poor creature you were, with scarce a skeed to your back, though you ride in your own chay now; and were glad to truck the Brigadier's old black camblet coat for ten masses for your mother's soul, to poor Father Blake, for all your going to church on Sundays, like any kiln-dried protestant in St Grellan. And it is a pretty return you made us, abducting and perverting that unfortunate cratur, that was but a child in the eye of the law. To say nothing of her being seduced and disgraced to ally herself to one every way below her, an attorney; for which, if God forgive you, Terence O'Brien, the Miss Mac Taafs never will, and

I am,

Abbé O'Flaherty's<br>Humble servants,<br>MABLE AND MONICA MAC TAAF.

LETTER VI.

*To Gen. Count O'Flaherty, etc. etc.*

The Count OFlaherty will surely be plased, without being surprised, that the Miss Mac Taafs (Mable and Monica), nieces and coheiresses of the late Brigadier Flavius Mac Taaf, of Bog Moy (which is but a mole hill to their estates on both sides the Shannon, to which the Miss Mac Taafs are entitled, setting aside the male tail, if every one had their due), should take up the pen to wish the Count every joy in life, on the probable success of his cause against the Hunkses; the Miss Mac Taafs having themselves, from documents purloined out of their uncle the Brigadier's coffer, by his attorney, Terence O'Brien (now Baron, as he has proved on the evidence of an old tombstone[1]), contributed thereto; and moreover, as being near relations of the Count; no two families in the province being more nearly related by kin and kindred, gossipry and alliance, than the Mac Taafs and the O'Flahertys, the Count and the Miss Mac Taafs (Mable and Monica), having one common ancestress, Mabilia, sole daughter and heiress of Mac Oge Illivan O'Mailly. By the said Mabilia's second marriage with a Geraldine, the Count and the Mac Taafs claim kindred with the Fitzgeralds of Maynooth, or Leinster family, the Talbots of Malahide, the Barnwells of Turvey, and most of the great Pale families, – to say nothing of the celebrated Granuaile,[2] or Grace O'Mailly (remarkable for having had six husbands), daughter and sole heiress of Duondarragh, son of Cormac, the son of Owen Omailly, chief of his name. Her daughter Margaret became the wife of Sir Murrogh na Doe O'Flaherty, of Aghnanewer; and the Count is surely apprised that the Earl of Carlingford, dying in 1730 without male issue (my cousin, Rodolphus, Chancellor of the German Empire, Lord of Ballymote, having only succeeded to the Ballymote title, a barony), the Carlingford branch is represented by Miss Mac Taaf, who would bring the earldom, together with the Barony of Bally Slattery, into any family she might chance to marry into; also the Green Knight, which she is in the female line: for that title (which my uncle the Brigadier often proved was more ancient than the three Knights of Desmond, viz. the White Knight, Knight of Glin, and Knight of Kerry), would in right belong to the heiress of Bog Moy's husband, if he pleased to make claims thereto. So that whenever the eldest Miss Mac Taaf plases to change her situation

---

[1] The Roscommon Peerage, now before the House of Lords, is claimed on a similar testimony.

[2] This celebrated lady, when wife of Mac William Oughter, was so determined and persevering in her hostility to the English, and committed so many acts of depredation, that it was found necessary (1579), to send troops from Galway, under the command of Captain William Martin, to besiege her romantic castle of Carrick na Uile, in the county of Mayo. The expedition sailed from Galway on the 8th of March; but so spirited was the defence, that the English troops were obliged to retreat on the 26th, having very narrowly escaped being made prisoners, a circumstance which would have been followed by the instant death of the entire party. The names of the men sent are entered on an old MS, formerly belonging to Sir Ed. Fitton.

(as my sister Monica says), she will bring as her dowry, undisputed claims upon the earldom of Carlingford, the Barony of Bally Slattery, and the most ancient knighthood in the country, which she can herself prove in any court in Christendom: and should Count O'Flaherty be inclined to make a visit to Ireland, she would point out to him a way of recovering the greatest part, if not all of the O'Flaherty country under which the Mac Taafs held vast tracts of land, by Fearon Allod[1] (for far be it from me to dispute that we were only *Righ begs* or petty kings[2] under the O'Flahertys); and the aforesaid lands were re-granted to *us* under the great seal on *coming in*, with other grants, in lieu of services done; and a *non obstante* for life to the Brigadier's great grandfather, Sir Daniel Mac Taaf, as in the grant of Sir Thomas Cusack: all of which we should be reprized in (the same being forfeited), should Count O'Flaherty recover his property of the Hy-Tartagh, particularly a moiety of the Suck and the parish of Kilfarboy, anciently given by your ancestors to found the abbey of St Bridget, to which you have every claim and right, and might distrain for tithes to-morrow if you plased. It is well known that the adventurers in Charles the Second's time did willingly deliver false certificates to the Court of Claims at Chichester House, which I can prove from the Brigadier's papers, and which, if proven, saith the act, 'such adventurer of his assignee doe forfeit the rents, profits, etc. etc. thereoff.' But all now standeth at stay, in regard of the Count's absence, who could, if present, rejust all (the Miss Mac Taafs aiding and abetting thereunto). For it is an old Irish saying, that 'the elm tree is not to be cleft but by a wedge of its own timber;' and the presence of General Count O'Flaherty would surely set all to rights, and show the Hunkses and Proudforts who was who in the province: and have the honour to be the Count's humble servants and kinswomen,

Signed for self and sister,

MABLE AND MONICA MAC TAFF.

P.S. There were three of us, as the Count well knows, and will marvel to hear no mention of the cadette, which is a great heart-break; having disgraced herself by marriage with one reputed to be

---

[1] Military tenure.

[2] The chief of each noble family in Ireland was styled king, the only title in use among the Irish to distinguish the nobility from the inferior gentry, until the arrival of the English, who introduced the title of earl. – See Keating's *History*.

a base-born of a cousin of the Count's, and worse than that, an attorney, now employed in the O'Flaherty cause: and hopes the Count will have no raison to repent, Counsellor Costello being the man.

P.S. Miss Monica Mac Taaf takes lave to notify to Count O'Flaherty (of which she reminded her sister last night, as forgotten by her), that in case the Count recovers Bally na Um hal (the owl's country), he will find by papers in Miss Mac Taaf's possession, that same is encumbered with certain tributes to the Mac Taafs, in lieu of services done by them for the O'Flahertys during their feuds with the Mac Tieg O'Briens of the Isles – yearly, ten cows, fifty hoggs, two barrels of corn burnt in the straw, fifty oaten bannocks, and ten bandals of ratteen dyed in the wool; and often heard tell by my uncle, the brigadier, that it was an old custom, that with the tribute came in the making of two clever mantles a-piece for the ladies of the family of Bogmoy, a great courtesy on the part of the gentlemen of the O'Flaherty family, one of which, but little the worse of the wear, hangs up in the ould tower to this day, only faded by lying bye; it is of two colours, after the Spanish fashion, and my sister thinks it was a Spanish mantle of Sir Gioll O'Flaherty, Knight of the military order of St Jago, for services done to the King of Spain, and has it in contemplation to get same scoured this spring, plase God, as a great relic.

P.S. – Takes lave to inclose a latter from Turlogh O'Flaherty, a follower of the families, and an honest poor cratur as breathes the breath of life, now a scullog[1] on the Ballyslattery estate.

(Letter inclosed in the Miss Mac Taaf's.)

### To General Count O'Flaherty.

Plaze your honour, Sir, I'm the boy who has the soward, with which your honour's grand-father, Sir Bryan, fought for Shamus at the battle of the Boyne; the curse of the crows on him day and night, I pray Jasus, for it's himself sould the Pass. And plaze your honour, Sir, the soward was found in the black bog, near your own place in Moycullen; and if it had a blade would be a good soward, being the same ancient ould trusty that the great O'Flaherty More,

---

[1] *Scullog* – a small farmer.

would flourish when he declared war agin the toun of Galway.[1] And would go to your honour every step of the way, and fetch it to you in France myself, if your honour's glory, long life to yez, would order Baron O'Brien Torney of St Grellan to give me eighteen thirteens to pay my journey over say and land; and would make it on my bare knees, truth I would, for your sake and the family's, and think little of it. Your honour, it's well known, and Father Festus, of the Dominicans, will prove the same, that I am of your honour's oun kin and blood, though never tould it to any sowl living or dead, out of respect to your honour and the family; and never will, barring Father Festus and the Miss Mac Taafs: and hopes your honour will spake a good word for me to Mr O'Brien, in respect of a bit of grazing ground in a luib of the mountains, when ye get back your own – which was my father's before me, time out of mind; and wont sell it over my head, being of the family; and would be sorry to see Darby Lynch, a notorious sae Pirate, put above me, which is what I will never be reduced to submit to, cost me my life or his. So no more at prisint, only the greatest of joys at your honour's success; for the heart of me wass too big for my bosom on that day, I heard tell that the downfall of the Boddah Hunkses was coming – and long may yez reign, which is the last prayer of now and ever more amen,

Your loving friend and kin,

his

TURLOCH X O'FLAHERTY.<br>mark

LETTER VII.

*To the Miss Mac Taafs, St Grellan.*

Per favour of the Abbé O'Flaherty.

Count O'Flaherty begs to offer the expression of his homage to the Miss Mac Taafs. He is quite sensible (it is impossible to be more so) of the honor conferred upon him by their gracious and amiable letter; and he assures them that among the many very interesting details it contains, nothing touched the Count more

---

[1] A tradition of the family.

profoundly, than the privilege granted him of claiming kindred with ladies so amiable and accomplished. The invitation held out to the Count to visit his unhappy, but always loved country, is a reason the more for doing that which he had long desired and intended. He looks forward at no very distant period to offering to the Miss Mac Taafs the expression of his gratitude for the kindness they have shown in his favour, and the still greater kindness they may yet confer on him. Touching his claims on the Abbey of St Bridget, he has every possible desire to establish them, and trusts he will find no very obstinate resistance on the part of the ladies of that venerable order, which he understands now flourishes under the control of the reverend Mother Abbess O'Brien. With respect to the tribute offered by the cavaliers of the Hy-Tartagh family to the fair ladies of Bog Moy, it is a token of fealty which the Count will be charmed to renew with other marks of his homage. In the mean time he begs their acceptance of a piece of Lyons silk (*cuisse de la reine*), and a Flanders *coiffure à la Du Barry*, which are at present making the rage at Paris – they will be sent *via* Bordeaux by the Count's wine-merchant to the care of French and Blake, Galway. The Count has no doubt that these foreign commodities, like Spanish wines, will improve by the voyage, and acquire new graces from the amiable wearers, to whom they are destined with sentiments of the profoundest respect and devotion.

Paris, Rue de Bac, 177– – .


### LETTER VIII.

### *To the Abbé O'Flaherty, St Grellan.*

CHER ABBÉ

*Place aux dames!* Inclosed is a note for the heiresses of Bog Moy. I have rubbed up my old Irish, or rather, done my French gallantry into English to answer them. They are *impayables*. The importance attached to the dignity of our respective dynasties, by these well-preserved specimens of other times, is delicious. It reminds one of Mademoiselle Montpensier's remarks on the *liaison* of Mademoiselle Rohan and the Chevalier De—— (when such things made up the soul of French government and society) – '*Cette affaire entretient toute la terre durant l'hiver.*' What is most ridiculous in all this, is, that I am myself infected by the very absurdity I laugh at, and have been actually seeking over an old map of O'Flahertys country, for some of those atrocious names of town-lands and Bally-boes, which have the same charms for me that Versailles and Fontainebleau have for the *privilégiés* of the French court. The memory of early impressions is that which survives all others; it is the memory of the heart. All that I have since seen, struggled through, suffered, or enjoyed, has passed like shadows over the surface; while all I saw, and heard, and shared in, before I left the rude mountain fastnesses of my forefathers, is graven in deep and graphic images on my mind. I see even now that *grosse masse de batimens*, the stern and gloomy hold of the chiefs of my sept; and the beautiful ruins of the adjacent abbey, reflected on its own still lake, as distinctly as when I saw them for the last time, the morning we sailed for France. How strongly the parting scene of that eventful day rushes to my recollection! Even now the tearful faces and grosteque figures that filled up the fine old archway of the court gate, as we issued forth after parting with my mother in the black oak room, old M'Cabe seated on the stirrup-stone, with his harp on his knee, playing tremulously, 'You take the summer along with you,' – a poetical farewell to two Irish youths, heirs to six hundred years of misery and oppression, driven by national adversity into a foreign land. My father too (I never saw him or my mother after!) with fixed eye, compressed lips, and clenched hands, keeping down the emotions of parental sensibility by a sort of muscular resistance. The venerated titular bishop of St Grellan, with his mild and martyr looks, had come forth from his hiding-place in the abbey, to give his parting benediction to the son of his protector. You too, my dear Abbé, with your pale, thoughtful, but boyish countenance, already mounted on your little Connemara pony, giving a hand to one and a smile or a sigh, as it happened, to another: even my grandfather's old greyhound, and the great chained wolf-dog (the last of the breed I believe), are prominent figures in the picture.

There is one heart-rending circumstance connected with my departure from Ireland which I did not then know. The difficulty of giving a suitable education in Ireland to the representatives of an ancient and noble family, the barbarous English then spoken, and the bog Latin then learned by the young gentry of Connaught, were the pleas urged by my father for sending me to a foreign seminary, and permitting me to a foreign service. But his most cogent reason was, as I have since learnt, that atrocious and inhuman law, called the gavel act, which tempted the sons of the catholic gentry in Ireland to betray their own fathers, and which, by the law of the land, gave to the child a power over his parents, in defiance of the law of God. My father used to call this clause a law against the fourth[1] commandment.

By what a variety of ways did the penal code of Ireland attack those morals which are founded in the affections! I shall never dispute that the English might not have acted wisely in exterminating the Irish at the time of the revolution, and thus getting rid of a race which they looked upon as armed in the cause of despotism and bigotry (for we, '*of the Irish nation*,' who have seen these things *de près*, have other notions on these subjects, than those entertained by our brethren, who have staid at home to brood over their misfortunes, under the lash of actual inflictions, and to mix up their wrongs with their opinions).

Having, however, permitted the Irish to live, they should not have deprived them of all the rights which give life its moral dignity, and alone raise the human above the brute animal. What madness too, on the part of the Irish catholics, to refuse the offer of the Prince of Orange.[2] But when have we acted with consistency, with unity, or under other influence than that of vehement affections and impetuous passions, and (I must say it) personal, or if you will, national vanity. How often do the agreeable *singes-tigres*, among whom I live, recall you Irish to my mind! Still, however, driven back as you have been to the infancy of society, and kept there, your governors (like those of other children), and not yourselves, are accountable for your follies and your faults.

Do you know that your last letter quite unfitted me for Versailles, where I was just going to risk a few louis on the cards of the pretty

---

[1] The fifth in the protestant decalogue.

[2] 'The Prince of Orange was touched with the fate of a gallant nation, the victim of French promises, and who had run headlong to ruin, for the only purpose of advancing the French conquests in the Netherlands. He (Orange) longed to find himself at the head of a confederate army, with so strong a reinforcement. In this anxiety he offered the Irish catholics the free exercise of their religion, half the churches in the kingdom, half the employments, civil and military, and even the moiety of their ancient properties. These proposals, though they were to have had an English act of parliament for their sanction, were refused with contempt. They had no confidence in the promises of a country, which had already broken her public faith with respect to the articles of Limerick.' – *Sir Charles Wogan's Letter to Swift.*

duchesses, when your *gros parquet* arrived. Onor na Croise, however, takes the *pas* of the *superbe de Grammont*, and Rory Oge, and Terence O'Brien are objects of more importance to me than even that troop of '*Marquis charmans, poudrès et embaumés*,' who from the height of their seven quarterings and red heels, look down upon the rest of the human species, as the *canaille* of the creation. I write by this post to O'Brien, acknowledging the relationship, in a manner that will flatter his genealogical pride; and with respect to his poetry of litigation, *je le laisse faire*, and have given him *carte blanche* to act as he pleases.

Pleasantry apart: – I have just now a strong vocation towards Ireland; and should I be reinstated in some of my *droits de seigneur*, as Tanist of Moycullen, I am not quite sure that I shall not re-edify the old abbey, and quit the world before it quits me; like other '*pieux fainéans*,' who have nothing to do but to

> Chanter les oremus, faire les processions,
> Et répandre à grands flots les bénédictions.

But of that hereafter.

For a man, *blasé sur tout*, Ireland is the place. But if we fail, and I am forced to yield before the Hunkses, then I will abduct you *vi et armis*, and carry you back to France. I prophecy that, with your talents and moral courage, you will inevitably expose yourself to that jealous irritability of power which bears no resistance, and you will incur that personal proscription which has banished all the talent of the land. Here, at least, we have blue skies, and we have not an Irish penal code. The remorseless zealots, whose sanguinary policy preferred extermination, to the prolonged agonies of legalized torture, have in France for ever set at rest the question of religious differences. You shall still have your old *gîte* in the *Rue du Bac*, and your *taudis* in the pavilion of my garden of Bretigny; and as we grow old together, we will gather with our own hands the grape, whose juice '*fait danser les chèvres*.' There, instead of making dreary pilgrimages to Patrick's purgatory, or incurring a flagellation by hanging a rag at a holy well, we will light a taper to Rabelais at his *presbytère* of Meudon, or commemorate the classic fêtes of Jodelle and Ronsard among the vineyards of Arcueil: and when at last we shall suddenly find ourselves '*un de ces vieillards qu'on appelle heureux, dont le bonheur consiste à ne pouvoir jouir d'aucun plaisir de la vie*,' we will die as we have lived, – you, as a saint; and I, as one who, long the sport of uncontrollable events, desire only, with Rabelais, '*qu'on tire le rideau, la farce ètant jouée.*'

I shall certainly go to Ireland, as soon as I can obtain a *semestre* from Duc de Fitzjames; for which, however, I must wait the return of Colonel Eugene Macarthy, of Spring-house. Commend me to the prayers of the abbess of Mary, John, and Joseph. *Dio buono!* what a reformer. Oh! ye Calvins and Luthers! Women and music! Those Jesuits are like Madame la Duchesse de Ferté; – '*Il n'y a qu'eux qui ont toujours raison.*' Adieu! write frequently. Nothing but letters from Connemara can amuse *les peu amusables, tels que*

*Votre très-affectionne,*

THE COUNT O'FLAHERTY.

P.S. Pray give a guinea on my account to my cousin O'Flaherty, of the sword; but do not give him 'the eighteen thirteens' for travelling charges; lest he should put his threat into practice, and visit me at Versailles.

# CHAPTER II

———•———

## *St Grellan*

'Cela mérite bien qu'en oyez un motelet, avant que venir a mon principal discours.'

*Satire Ménippée.*

AMONG the variety of evils which distracted Ireland at the period of the revolution, and for nearly a century afterwards, one of the most perplexing and least remediable, was 'the confusion worse confounded,' in which a large portion of the landed property was involved. Five hundred years of successive forfeitures, – possessions held for ages by prescription, won by the sword and reconquered by the sword, – tenures obtained by force or usurped by fraud, – partitions of the soil carelessly made over to successive 'adventurers, soldiers, patentees, and polatines,' in grants, regrants, debentures, patents, commutations, and reprisals, gifts of 'mitre land,' consecrated by his holiness the Pope, and now conferred, by our soveriegn lord the King, – with trusts perpetually violated, and discoveries nefariously made, – had rendered the laws a chaos, producing a series of contradictory decisions and ludicrous statutes; which (to borrow the language of the legislature itself), had long puzzled both executors and regulators.'

Down to the middle of the last century, a feeling of insecurity in all classes prevailed through this anomalous condition of things; which, while it kept capital out of the country, paralyzed industry, and, misdirecting the restless energy of the people, awoke a spirit of litigation, that has long been a ridicule and a reproach to the national character. The small but ascendant party of protestants, scarcely less harassed than the victims of their own oppression, suffered through their fears

of the disabilities they had themselves imposed; and largely participated in the insecurity of property, which they had inflicted on their
catholic opponents. An agitating though suppressed emotion pervaded
the whole population; and whatever brought the question of property
into debate, was sure to throw the community into fermentation:
insomuch, that at one epoch, the government had ordered the Irish
bar not to defend the revived claims of an Irish noble of the old caste.[1]

While, however, scarcely one of every hundred claims was justified
by law or equity, and the fabric of many a litigious vision fell before
the inquiry it courted, the issue of a cause between a protestant
ecclesiastic (supported by the Proudforts, one of the most powerful
families in the kingdom), and a catholic gentleman in the service of
the King of France, excited, when known to be in favour of the latter,
a considerable anxiety and alarm. The coffee-houses of the capital,
then the centres of all the political, literary, and legal gossip of the
day, rang with the intelligence: Lucas's (once Cork-house[2]) was then
exclusively the resort of the protestant and official gentry of Dublin;
– the catholics rarely appearing in public, and (when they did come
forth *in churchtime on Sundays*,) herding at 'The Globe', in Essex
Street.

It was in the long room at Lucas's, where the Boyles, the Burling-
tons, and the Orrerys had held their statesmen-circles, and literary
coteries, that the triumph of Count O'Flaherty was announced by one
of the *habitués*, who read aloud the decision of the court, from the
columns of Faulkner's Journal. The news was heard by the descendant
of many a protestant discoverer with fear and trembling; and not a
few doubted, what it was so painful to believe: for the measure of
men's faith generally lies in their interests; and Bramah and Mahomet,
at least, owe as much to rice fields and green turbans, as to pure
conviction and disinterested assent.

'I will venture to swear,' said a rival editor of old George Faulkner,
who was present, 'that this turns out one of George's blunders; like
his own house in Parliament Street, which he has built without a
staircase; or his yesterday's erratum – for *her* grace the Duke, read
*his* grace the Duchess.'

The reperusal of the paragraph was called for, but it afforded
no refuge for interested incredulity. 'So, here is a pretty precedent

[1] Lord Clancarty.
[2] Built by the celebrated Earl of Cork and Orrery.

established,' burst forth a little gentleman, whose clerical hat and cassock detected his calling (the learned professions then still retaining their distinctive liveries in Ireland). But though evidently of the church, there was a certain pendulous movement of the shoulders, an approximation of the knees, a squaring of the elbows, and a poking of the head, which indicated another vocation, and pointed him out as one better qualified to run for the cup, than to start for the mitre. He was a noted character of the day: by some deemed mad, by none deemed wise; he was cherished and upheld by the party who committed their interests to his absurdities; while his folly and his ambition went so well together, that all who listened to his ravings and knew their true object, might have exclaimed –

Ma foi! c'est être sage, que d'être fou comme lai.

'We shall have the papists,' he continued, 'rummaging out old claims, and proving their rights to all the landed property of the country; and his Majesty's protestant subjects of Ireland will have nothing to expect but poverty and persecution, the overthrow of the church, the murders of forty-one, the massacre of St Bartholomew, the dragonades of France, the inquisition, the popish plot, Guy Faux, and Bloody Queen Mary! We shall have the scarlet old woman of Babylon holding levees at the Castle, papist archbishops celebrating high mass at St Patrick's, and all our church lands, tithes, glebes, and parsonage-houses, fox-hounds, hunters, and old Bordeaux, passing into the hands of monks, abbots, and friars.'

This prophetic threat, including all the bugbears of terrorism, and all the images of ruin then conjured up in Ireland with unfailing effect, was heard with approving nods and affirmative exclamations. The laying down of newspapers and coffee-cups, the resting of chins upon gold-headed canes, the turning of all eyes to the place where the speaker sat, indicated a wish that he should proceed with the subject; when a person, from a distant box at the remote end of the room, observed, that 'he hoped the government was too wise to listen, and too politic to give heed, to such unfounded insinuations as had been then broached. Whatever a few interested persons might think, or rather circulate, to the contrary, the catholics of Ireland, whose property had, every acre, been twenty times confiscated, and changed its owners alternately in favour of catholics and protestants, were neither so ignorant nor so mad, as, by the revival of obsolete claims and the questioning of established settlements, to involve such of their own estates as by the connivance of the law they were yet permitted to hold; most of which had been purchased on the faith of forfeitures. The interests of men are ever the strongest security for their peaceable demeanour; and the reverend gentleman may depend upon it, that no danger can reasonably be apprehended either to church or state, from the claims of the few representatives of Milesian proprietors still unsettled. The case in question,' he continued, 'is one of a singular and, indeed, unequalled description; and any other decision than that given, would have rendered the laws a jest, and the statute book as idle, if not as amusing as Joe Miller, or Jonathan Wild: for it would have proved that for catholics there was no justice.'

'Catholics, forsooth!' exclaimed the little advocate of ascendancy, 'Where are they? Who are they? Where do they burrow? Where do they roost? Where do they earth? Show me their marks, and prints? Trot me out here an Irish papist, and I'll take the odds, I show you sport for a week! An Irish catholic! who ventures to acknowledge that such a thing exists? – not the laws of the land: the chancellor has settled that point. He has given it from the woolsack, that a papist only breathes by the connivance of the government.'

'And yet,' said the mild but emphatic speaker from the remote box, 'it does happen, that by a dictum, superior even to that of the Lord Chancellor, a connivance paramount to that of the government, four millions of Irish catholics are at this moment breathing as healthfully and as vigorously, as though no acts of parliament, to deprive them of their being, were on the statute book.'

'A connivance paramount! a dictum superior!' re-echoed, somewhat incoherently, the man of lungs. 'Where is it, I beseech you, my voice from the Vatican? Is it ould infallibility the fisherman's? or the Council of Trent's, or the Lady's of Loretto? or – '

'No,' interrupted the party appealed to, in a tone of deep and firm emphasis, 'it is the connivance of a power above all prelates, princes, and potentates: a power, reverend Sir, of which you, I take it, are the minister on earth; a power, that has upheld the persecuted for conscience's sake, in all ages, and in all climes – the power of a just and beneficent providence!'

Silenced for a moment, by the appeal made to his holy calling, the champion of ascendancy soon recovered breath and spirit; and, flattered by the circle that had gathered thickly around him, set to for another round, exclaiming, 'Now, my hearties, you all know that I am no Jesuit, in or out of disguise; I thank God for it; I have none of St

Peter's logic at my fingers' ends; and I can neither dogmatize, nor prevaricate, nor double, nor turn, nor break cover, as it suits the purpose. Nor shall I stop to strip off the foliage of Italian drapery from any defender of the faith, who may please to start up. But this I will say, and let me see who will deny it, that his present Majesty, like his predecessors, is imposed upon;[1] and if the government of this country, that is, the ignorant cabal of his Majesty's council, and the weak men at the head of it, do not change their tune, and listen to wiser heads than their own (the chancellor and archbishop of Dublin, always excepted), there is an end to church and state; and Luther and King William may go and hunt hares together. Mind my words, my worthies, if this new conciliation system, as it is absurdly called, goes on, the ouldest amongst us will live to see the repeal of the whole penal code – we shall see papists riding blood horses, and the first protestant gentlemen in the land, not daring to seize a hair in their tail – we shall have papists purchasing land, and bequeathing it by will – teaching publicly in schools, and speaking publicly in places where a few years back they dared no more show their faces, than in the castle-yard – we shall have papists called to the bar, admitted to the king's inns, allowed to marry protestant wives, and educate their own children in the catholic faith – we shall have Jack priests stalking about, as if they were not felons by the law of the land, – and emissaries of Rome and Spain, prowling in our very coffee-houses. In a word, Gentlemen, we shall have papist barristers, papist attornies, papist constables, papist watchmen, papist ladies'-lieutenant holding drawing-rooms in the castle; and to climax all, we shall have papists enjoying the elective franchises, and in due time we shall send papist members to a papist parliament, and live to see our protestant House of Commons perverted into a conclave of cardinals.'

The lighted torch thrown by the Pope among the congregation at St Peter's on Maunday Thursday (after the *Cœna Domini*), and

---

[1] The two first Georges, like the gallant William of Nassau, were friends to religious toleration, but were obliged to truckle to the all-powerful oligarchy, who, though then sharing the prejudices of the English people, were as independent of them, and as much the main spring and moving souls of the government, as they are in the present day, in which the minister can neither give liberty to an Irishman nor bread to a Briton, but according to their good will and pleasure. The first sovereigns of the House of Hanover relaxed, as far as they dared, the penalties annexed to the catholic worship; and George the Third began his reign by following in their footsteps, till 'Hanoverian toleration' had passed into a by-word among the ascendancy party. – *See O'Connor's Life.*

imagining the thunder of his own anathemas, never gave more alarm to the conscience of the timid sinner, than the denunciations of the little protestant pope of Lucas's, now excited among his prejudiced, ignorant, and self-interested auditory; when the '*imperturbable*' of the remote box, whose fine and characteristic head only was visible above the high oak screen-work, behind which he was deliberately taking his chocolate and dried toast, coolly observed, that 'all that the reverend gentleman had predicted, with the exception of a papist parliament and conclave senate, would eventually come to pass; and that too, at no distant day. It is in the order of things,' he added, 'that, as the intemperate times which occasioned the infliction of penal statutes pass away, the impolitic laws should pass with them; together with the petty and personal vexations, which grow out of them, to the destruction of those social pleasures, which the Irish, beyond all other people, are calculated to enjoy.[1] To inflict civil punishment, where no civil crime is committed, to make men's private creed the measure of their public principles, to vindicate the Deity by fires, and mulct faith by forfeitures, are expedients that belong only to an age in which the nature and end of legislation are either totally unknown, or are forgotten or set at nought, amidst the conflict of contending factions.'

The advocate of toleration then arose, threw down the amount of his bill, and courteously bowing to the company, withdrew from a contest, forcibly illustrative of the jargon of the times. He was a person of distinguished appearance, with a countenance full of intelligence, softened down by an expression of melancholy. He was scarcely middle aged; and his dress and *tournure* recalled, to those who had travelled, the French ecclesiastic of rank, so frequently found in the highest circles of Parisian society. His accent was, however, perfectly Irish, though with something of a foreign rhythm. As he passed through the hall of Lucas's Coffee-house to his chair, the crowd of link-boys, coachmen, and chairmen, who then usually thronged in such places, took off their hats, and cheered him with 'Long life to your Reverence Abbé O'Flaherty! – Connemara for ever! – the O'Flaherty cause, and long may they reign! – Hurrah for ould Ireland!'

[1] So far back as the year 1725, Swift alludes in one of his letters of Sheridan, to the 'glorious and immortal memory,' being a party signal, occasioning many quarrels. The Bishop of Cork, Dr Peter Browne, wrote a pamphlet called, 'A treatise against drinking to the Memory of the Dead.' Cumberland also gives an account of the fatal effects of unnecessary insults heaped on an oppressed and persecuted people, by the ascendancy party.

The information communicated by this vociferation of the populace excited a general sensation. Some wondered at the courage of the Abbé, others swelled with indignation against him, as one whose existence was denied by the statutes, and who thus, like the Genoese *galérien*, bore the word *libertas* upon the chains which galled him. All considered this unwonted boldness in a papist, a priest, and a regular, as a bad omen; and many prophesied the result of that temporizing system, which, though they themselves might not live to see the evil consequences, would, they said, throw their children upon 'evil men and evil times.'

The striking of the castle clock now sounded the tocsin for the evening's occupations and amusements. Some adjourned from the coffee-room below to the private apartments above; where oards and hazard assembled the legitimate predecessors of the future members of *Daly's* and *Kildare-street*. Others ordered their chairs to the Parliament House, or to the theatre in Smock-alley. The *habitués* of Lady Brandon's private box, at the new theatre in Crow-street, hastened, in obedience to her ladyship's morning commands, to support her 'dear Mr Mossop;' and all who were of the musical faction (the *'coin de la reine'*), the Leinsters, Conollys, Belmonts, and Westmeaths, proceeded to the Italian Opera in Capel-street; where the bewitching Sestini, in *'La buona Figliuola,'* and Pinetti, in the *'Isola d'Alcina,'* elicited a rapturous, but judicious applause, even from the gallery, which it would now be vain to look for from the most refined audience that Dublin can supply.

But if the issue of the O'Flaherty cause had excited some sensation in the capital, there was a spot where it was deemed of no less magnitude than the acquisition of Silesia had been to Prussia, the dismemberment of Poland to Russia, or the results of the war of the succession to the House of Bourbon. This spot was the remote, romantic, and venerable district and town of St Grellan; the former a long and winding tract, between sea and mountain, indented with picturesque harbours and beautiful bays, lying in all the still repose of sheltering rocks; – the latter, like all old Irish towns, consisting chiefly of a long, narrow, rutted main street, intersected by the market cross, and terminating in a ruinous, over-peopled suburb, called the *cladagh;*[1] which, with a few diverging lanes, passages, and courts,

[1] Cladagh, literally – the dirty place.

leading 'up to the mountains, or down to the sea,' made up the whole of its straggling circumference.

With all its defects, however, St Grellan, when viewed from a distance, had still a venerable and imposing air. Its picturesque ruins of monasteries and towers, and, above all, its Spanish-built castles, or castellated mansions, raised round narrow courts, and opening to the main street by ponderous archways, recalled, on a diminished scale, the Stradas of Seville and Badajos. Upon these models they had been evidently built, by the burghers of the town, who, in times of turbulence, had found such fortifications necessary for the preservation of their wine cellars and counters against the inroads of the toparchs of the Milesian race; when, on pretence of claiming 'connowe and meales, due to them by the testimonial of many auncient, ould and credible persons,' the native chiefs were wont to come down upon the town, from their raths and forts in the mountains, in utter contempt of the impotent by-laws of the good mayor and corporation, which decreed, that 'Ne Mac, nor O, should strut, ne swagger, in the streets; nor ne Irishman brag ne boast upon the town.'

But in process of time, when the chiefs of the old race dropped into the lines of civilization, it became their pride to rear their mansions also within the town wall, and to sculpture over their massy portals their ancient armorial bearings, and expressive mottoes, which distinguished them from the plebeian residences of the '*gailobh*,' or tribe of merchants. Many of these patrician edifices still remained, though fast falling to ruin; and were no less revered by the natives of St Grellan, than the palaces of the Massimi, with their imperial arms and cardinal hats, are by the modern Romans. Few of them, however, were in the possession of the descendants of the ancient proprietors, whose name they still bore. Almost all were in litigation; and some were claimed as the estates of two or three different families: the first story being held in fee by an O, the second by a Mac, and the *rez-de-chaussée* being possessed and inhabited by some pains-taking tradesman of the Cromwellian stock, who proved his right in the premises by 'a debenture of Colonel Stubbers,' or a grant of some other of Cromwell's Connaught governors. A stone staircase, and two dark closets, were claimed in Mac Taaf's Court (an old house in the Cladagh), by the Miss Mac Taafs, who were still carrying on the suit, begun in the year forty-five by their uncle the brigadier.

All beyond the coast and plain of St Grellan, called the Fassagh, and the lower range of hills, which formed its land boundary, had become *terra incognita* to its indolent and unenterprising inhabitants; and the river Pactolus, Golconda, or the ruins of some ancient Irish Palmyra, might have existed in the interior of the mountains of Connemara without awakening their curiosity, or stimulating their research.

The military passes, made through these romantic mountains by the Lord Deputy Clanrickard, and his rebellious kinsmen, the *Clan Earla*,[1] were long blocked up by the caprice of torrents, which yearly changed their course, or by the fall of rocks, which yielded to the fierce storms engendered in the surrounding ocean. The bridle tracks still cut through in the gorges of these stupendous hills were but little known or frequented, except by smugglers, passing from the coast to the interior of Mayo and Galway, or by other lawless persons, the successors of the Rapparees of Queen Ann's and George the First's day.

At the distance of five Irish miles from the town of St Grellan arose the castellated domes of Beauregard, like a fairy structure in a desert, backed by inaccessible mountains and dreary wastes. The object of its noble owner in choosing this site, was to oppose and conquer the country physically, as he had already succeeded in doing in the moral sense. But the riches, the magnificence, and the extent of this almost royal palace, were in vain opposed to the deep-rooted prejudices of the people in favour of their ancient chieftains. The power, the influence, the measureless expanse of estate were all on the side of the Proudforts; but the chiefs of the Hy-Tartagh, the forfeited and abdicated O'Briens and O'Flahertys, with their '*gestes et faits*' in th' ould times, held their supremacy in the public imagination. It was in vain that on the head-stone of a ruined arch of one of the town gates of St Grellan, might still be read the timid invocation, 'From the ferocious O'Flahertys deliver us, O Lord!' It was in vain that the marks of a ring were still pointed out in the fragment of an embrasure of the town walls, as the place where a chain had been drawn across the western suburbs, to prevent the O'Flahertys from rushing down from the mountains and galloping through the town, to plunder the honest burghers, the descendants of a company of English merchants; – it was in vain even that the O'Flaherty of the day was branded with absenteeism; and that for thirty years he had given no other proof of his recollection of such a spot, than his annual demand of the few chief rents which still remained to him: in spite of all these 'damning

---

[1] The Earl's sons.

proofs,' there was yet a magic in the name; and while the gallantry and misfortunes of the brave sept were still sung in many a merry planxty, or chanted in many a doleful cronan, the faults and ferocity of its turbulent chiefs, with their cuttings, and cosherings, and black rents, and other barbarous exactions of their feudal power, were all forgotten. All the recollections of these Alpine districts were associated with the names, fortunes, and fate of that fallen but revered dynasty; the recent triumphs of whose representative now conveyed such general satisfaction to the mere Irishry of the Bally-boe.

General Count Malachi O'Flaherty, the hero of the day, was of the highest order of Irish exiles, whom the misrule of their own country has driven to become the ornaments and defenders of another. With considerable talent, courage, and great personal beauty, he was less indebted for his rapid, but late, promotion in the French service, and his favour at the French court, to these superior natural endowments, than to the degrading accident of his relationship, being claimed (not proved) by the profligate Count Du Barry, and to the condescension with which he permitted the king's mistress to call him cousin in the circle, where cringing peers and crouching priests received their appointments, and canvassed their promotions from the smiles of the royal concubine. Previous to this mortifying distinction, he had only won unprofitable honours, in a service which afforded to the Irish exile no prospect, but that of growing more unhappy as he grew old in it; but from this epoch his military promotion was rapid; his illustrious Irish descent was acknowledged in his patent of French nobility, and he had his '*charge à la cour*,' and the '*entrée des petits appartemens.*' If in the first era of his favour, his high martial spirit, his sense of family honour and hereditary glory, had to struggle against privileges and distinctions, so degraded by the source from whence they flowed; yet long absence from his native land, his habitual intercourse with a nation of slaves, in a country where there was no public opinion, no private morals, had gradually blunted, though it had never extinguished these feelings. An indignant remorse in the midst of his good fortune, would frequently rise to embitter the present, and lead him to regret the dignified adversity of the past. This mood of mind was not peculiar to Count O'Flaherty. The unfortunate and exiled catholic gentlemen of Ireland, dependents abroad, as slaves at home, carried about with them a dark repining temper, which rendered them not less suspicious of favours conferred, than they were jealous of distinctions withheld.

In politics, Count O'Flaherty, as a feudal aristocrat, was a stern upholder of the divine right of kings; but though upon principle a jacobite, he was, by sentiment, a contemner of the despicable family in whose cause his own had suffered ruin, almost to extinction. In religion, he was a Roman catholic, upon point of honour; but while he regularly (in the Irish catholic phrase) 'attended his duty,' and assisted *à la messe du roi*, at Versailles, he was, at Paris, in the '*coterie d'Holbach*,' and of the prevailing faith of all the *esprits forts*, and fashionable philosophers of the day; who admitted no infallibility but in the wit of the patriarch of Ferney, who borrowed their texts from Rabelais, and who took their epigraphs from the Lutrin of Boileau. A man of pleasure, in the truest sense of the word, but '*en homme comme il faut*,' always in love, rarely out of debt, addicted to play, and spoiled alike by his mistress and his creditors, he was scarcely accountable for a character, to which he had been predestined by the history of his country; nor answerable for irregularities, into which he was hurried by a vivacity of constitution, the temperament of his nation. Unrestrained by those wholesome ties, which men placed under the control of public opinion in their own country acknowledge and obey, still handsome, and still, '*en bonne fortune*,' the Count had yet attained the age, when the tide of life is on its ebb – when the vain are vainest, and men of gallantry most gallant. Touchy and jealous of the triumphs which once sought him, but which he was now obliged to seek, he was the more dangerous, as he was less passionate. The penalties of time were paid off from the treasury of experience; and the ambition of supporting a reputation, which had placed him in the ranks of the Lauzuns and the Lauragais, left him ready for any adventure which circumstance and situation might throw in his way.

Such was the man, whose recovery of a small part of his patrimony excited so strong a sensation in St Grellan. The event was exaggerated, as all such events are in Ireland. It was considered as 'the happy prologue of a swelling theme,' in which the Irish pentarchy was to be restored, according to the imaginings of those whose forefathers had been all kings.

The Count O'Flaherty only arrived in Dublin in time to witness the completion of his hopes, and to go through the forms which the law required. He then set off on his royal progress to St Grellan, with a suite of two carriages, and accompanied by his champion and kinsman, the Baron O'Brien, by the Abbé O'Flaherty, and by two young French noblemen of his own school and caste, who had visited Ireland in a frolic.

The eyes of the protestant ascendancy of the town, as they glared from the balcony of the episcopal palace, beheld with amazement the multitudes who followed the chariot of the victorious client of Baron O'Brien. At the Cladagh, the horses were taken from the Count's carriage, and he was carried to the Proudfort Arms on the necks of his sept. The Baron too was chaired through the town, to his own house, by a party of 'Isle of Arran boys,' led on by Shane, whose mother, Mor-ny-Brien, in her Arranite costume, stood in a window, with the young chief of the Mac Tiegs, the Baron's only son, in her arms; and the Miss Mac Taafs in their *coiffures à la du Barri*, from the bay window at which Onor O'Flaherty had formerly saluted Rory Oge, on his visit to St Grellan, waved their white kerchiefs to the Count as he passed; whose gracious smile, and graceful bow, gave them full assurance that '*le coup fut parti*,' and that he had already made up his mind to the Green Knighthood, and Barony of Ballyslatterie, as Miss Mac Taaf, the elder, had made up hers to be Countess O'Flaherty, of Moycullen.

As the evening advanced, preparations were made for the old Irish demonstration of all sorts of joy, and triumph – a bonfire. The whole town and Ballyboe were in movement. Children came bounding down the mountains, with their tributary *brasneens*;[1] the old folk were busied in collecting turf, mould, bones, and sea-weeds, to heap up in particular stations; and the fishermen of the Cladagh marched up the main street, in a sort of confused procession, carrying bundles of reeds on poles (as on the eve of St John), to contribute to the general conflagration. Young females, carrying small brooms of dock stems, touched the passengers with their rustic *fasces*, with the simpering request of 'honour the bonfire,' 'honour the bonfire of the O'Flahertys and the O'Briens;' and those who refused to comply with this demand by moving the hat or bending the knee, did not withhold their homage with impunity. It was to little purpose that the Honourable and Right Reverend the Lord Bishop of St Grellan fulminated a bull from his ecclesiastical residence, against bonfires and riotous assemblies; that the mandate was proclaimed by the beadle with bell and staff, and with three '*Uaishts*;'[2] that it was repeated by the verger *in pontificalibus*;

---

[1] Bundles of underwood and brambles, picked up in the hedges, etc.

[2] '*Uaisht*,' listen: the '*Oyez*,' or rather 'O yes,' of the Connaught town criers.

echoed by two squeaking choristers, and intonated by a bass vicar choral – the brasneens still came in, and the fires blazed out. It was to as little purpose that the state came in aid of the church; that old justice Hunks, brother of the archdeacon of St Grellan, rummaged all the statute books, from William to George, to find some act 'for the better putting down of seditious and popish bonfires:' the evil had escaped the attention of the legislature, the law had provided no penalty; and had not the great oligarch of the town and county, the Lord Viscount Proudfort (brother to the bishop, uncle to the dean, and cousin, or kinsman, to half the rich rectors and prebendaries in the diocese), in his quality of governor of the town, ordered out a military party to suppress the incendiary symptoms of insurrection (which, under the simple names of *bonfires*, were in fact the *boute-feux* of incipient rebellion), there is every reason to suppose, that the bonfires would eventually – have gone out of themselves.

As it was, a riot ensued! a life or two were lost, some half dozen, half-naked, turf-cutters and bog-trotters, were incarcerated in the cells of the town-jail – some few limbs were fractured, some few heads were broken, and some few brave English soldiers (worthy of a better cause), were wounded by that unfailing missile, a well-directed stone, thrown by a well-practised hand. Thus, before midnight, the social order of St Grellan was restored; but, lo! as the grey dawn broke upon the silent town, the bonfires were found blazing higher than ever, from cliff to cliff, from rock to rock, along every high point on the coast; as if the sun, as he rose from behind O'Flaherty's mountains, had kindled them with his own celestial rays. It was thus in ancient times he was wont to light up the fires of the god Samhuin, at the same high places, and at the same season; while druid priests sang his praise, and sold his dispensations.

There were many in St Grellan who, when they heard of this phenomenon of the quenchless fires, crossed themselves. Some there were indeed who could account for the fact upon very simple principles; but the majority preferred the belief, that the whole was a miraculous interposition of Heaven itself, in testimony of its special protection of a family and of a church, which, in spite of these occasional proofs of celestial favour, were still prostrate before human power, and subjugated by human events.

# CHAPTER III.

———————•———————

## *The Review (i)*

Beauty, and such a stock of impudence,
As to the playhouse well might recommend her.

ETHERIDGE

The warrior, Liberty, with bending sails
Helm'd his bold course to fair Hibernia's vales;-
Firm as he steps along the shouting lands,
Lo! Truth and Virtue range their radiant bands;
Sad Superstition wails her empire torn,
Art plies his oar, and Commerce pours her horn.

*Botanic Garden, Canto II.*

TIME went on; and in less than a quarter of a century, 'nay not so much,' from the epoch of the O'Flaherty cause, the force of circumstance, bearing down, as it ever does, the systems of human policy, effected changes in Ireland, which the legislatures of centuries had deemed impracticable, and which the bigotry of interested ignorance had shunned, as ruinous. Within this 'brief and petty space,' the shock of opinion (first felt in American) had vibrated to the remotest regions of civilization; and wherever the deep and awful convulsion had passed, the long-during edifice of despotism had crumbled under its influence. Even Ireland, the *cul-de-sac* of politics and of society – inert and stagnant as she had long lain, under the pressure of the penal code – participated in the movement. The Irish – or, to give the people of Ireland a more definite designation – the Irish catholics, though excluded from all privileges, were reluctantly acknowledged to exist as citizens; and were allowed to pray, as conscience dictated, without incurring the penalties of felony. They were permitted to hold their own estates in their own hands, without fear of the treachery of their children; they could ride blood horses, worth fifty pounds, without the risk of being obliged to part with them for five; they might fill the state offices of watchmen, and constables, and enter into the liberal professions of attorneys and notaries, without being considered as disturbers of the peace and tranquillity of his Majesty's subjects; they could raise their timid voices in coffee-houses, and show their proscribed faces in the castle yard. Yet with all these long-dreaded innovations – these bugbears to loyalty and ascendancy – the isle was not 'frighten'd from her propriety.' No civil war of 1641 was rekindled, no massacre of St Bartholomew ensued! Every wise concession had served but to strengthen national confidence, and to develop the national resources. The fearful alternations which had agitated the community for more than a century, the vague and wasteful exertions of delirious strength, the troubled sleep of exhausted violence, were gradually subsiding in the enjoyments of rights obtained, and the consciousness and foretaste of rights to be conceded.

America had revolted; and England, in her hour of peril, fearing Ireland, as the oppressor in times of danger always fears the oppressed, reluctantly abandoned a part of that all-pervading and comprehensive system of tyranny, which had hitherto paralyzed the energies of the nation; and by this *'premier pas'* rendered the ultimate emancipation of the people, morally, and almost physically, inevitable. It was not, however, until a French fleet rode triumphantly in the Irish seas,[1] that

---

[1] To what purpose, it may be asked, are these bitter recollections revived? Certainly neither to irritate nor insult the English nation, from whose justice and good sense Ireland has so much to expect. The fact, however, being as it is, it is neither unfair nor unwise to remind the party in England, who are perpetually vociferating, both in and out of parliament, 'we won't be bullied,' and who endeavour, by alarming the timid, and by arousing the passions of the people, to seduce them into no-popery fanaticism, that the Tory faction (calling itself the State) *has been bullied* and *may be bullied;* and that, as it never has granted any thing to justice or generosity, the turbulence of the catholic agitators is not quite as groundless, or devoid of policy, as their opponents affect to imagine. It should not be forgotten, that though a brave and high-spirited people can never be threatened into a tame submission to wrong, nothing is more common than for the most powerful to be forced into a concession of rights. There is an inevitable efficiency in moral propriety, from the mere constancy of its action: accident, at some time or other, must conspire with it; and small circumstances are enough to render it irresistible. The outcry against being threatened into toleration is, therefore, mere empty declamation. A reasonable apprehension of the natural

the attempt was made to bribe Ireland into tranquillity, by relaxing her chains. Then indeed the experiment was made; and England found that the people she had so long oppressed, were not quite debased. Permitted to arm in their own defence, the Irish stood forth with all their ancient valour, and with more than their ancient unity, to protect their native land from foreign aggression; and to realize that splendid dream of political philosophy – a national army – self-associated, self-organized, self-paid; each and all having an interest and a property in the land they had risen to defend.

Such were the Irish volunteers, whose brilliant, but short-lived story, forms the only illuminated page in Ireland's dismal annals! Such was that gallant band of patriots, who, during the short epoch of their existence, rescued their country from bondage, and redeemed it from disgrace. Attracting the attention of other countries, and winning the veneration of their own, the Irish volunteers made daily acquisitions of strength by an alliance with all classes. Nobles sought the distinction of becoming their officers; men of boundless wealth were proud of being enrolled in their ranks; all sects and all religions united under their banners; and the moral dignity attached to the service created prepossessions, which its imposing exterior was not calculated to diminish. A race, which had ever been deemed comely, became improved by military discipline. The use of arms, while it rubbed off the uncouth awkwardness of the lower orders, gave energy to the languid movements of the highest. Volunteering became a vogue, as well as a principle. The women (and Ireland was then deemed the Corinth of Europe) took them under their special protection, presented their banners and dictated their devices. Gallantry and patriotism were never in a more strict alliance; and national vanity, occasionally supplying the place of national feeling, enlisted many in the volunteer corps, whose natural vocation, by birth and caste, lay all another way.

To defend the land from foreign invasion had been the original motive which armed the volunteers of Ireland; but this was only a temporary remedy, applied to a temporary evil. The result, the important result, was an effort to emancipate the nation from six centuries of unmitigated suffering, and to re-open those sources of

---

consequences of moral wrong is prudence, not fear; even though the argument be advanced in the spirit of hostility. But, after all, what has the conduct of the agitators to do with the policy of the main question?

national prosperity which had so long been dried up, or turned aside. The impulse gave a new spring to the spirit of this military body; and an armed association of thirty thousand citizens, assembling by their representatives, struck terror into minds inaccessible to the suggestions of sound policy, or of fair dealing. The eloquence of men with arms in their hands was not to be resisted. A free trade, the rejected prayer of ages, was conceded; Ireland's legislative independence, the long, but hopeless aspiration of millions, was acknowledged, and the government consented to abandon pretensions which it was no longer in a condition to assert.

When, however, America triumphed, and peace was proclaimed, England – punished but not taught – returned to her old policy; and having no further occasion for that flame she had permitted to kindle, she resolved to quench it. But the Irish spirit, like a long compressed spring set free, though somewhat too rapid and irregular in its movements, was still too forcible and vigorous to be readily reduced to its former subjection. The volunteers still continued to debate in their convention, and the highest in rank and talent presided in their assemblies, and took a frank and approving part in their deliberations. They continued to hold their military reviews in all parts of the kingdom, and their graceful movements, performed under the rewarding eye of beauty, were executed to the exhilarating sounds of their national music. Such meetings were considered as historical epochs by the people, and such reviews were regarded as national festivals.

A military institution, so singular in its nature as to include the several gradations of nobles and commons, merchants, yeomen, and mechanics, always prompt to combat the views of an unfriendly government, and make head against the corrupt influence of a banditti of dictators,[1] soon became to the state, which had eulogized its first organization, an object of amazement, and a source of vexation. In their infancy, the volunteers might have been suppressed – in their present state, to resist them was difficult; to control them, vain; to disband them, impossible! But to disunite, to undermine, to sap, to slander, and to vilify, were always practicable in Ireland. Corruption, the old medium, was again resorted to. Religion, the old state engine of Engish policy, was again brought into play. Ridicule, under many

---

[1] 'Three of four grandees had such an influence in the Irish House of Commons, that their coalition commanded a majority upon any question.'

forms, launched by the witty and the profligate, the hireling satirist and the pensioned buffoon, was set to work to raise 'that dread laugh,' against which even virtue is not always proof. The volunteers themselves, like all sanguine reformers, and like all Irishmen, over-shooting or deviating from their mark, occasionally furnished their enemies with arms against themselves; and divisions, industriously sown between the leaders and their corps, were rapidly breaking up their unity, when the French Revolution broke forth – a brand from the altar of American independence – an event that terminated the struggle between kings, and began the contest between governments and nations.

The French Revolution, at its dawn so splendid and so temperate, produced in Ireland an effect the most powerful and electric. Reorgan-izing in their legislative assembly a new empire from an old despotism, breaking the fetters of ages, and calling forth a national army to replace their liveried and foreign forces, the French had obtained the suffrages of the wise and good of all parties; but in Ireland their proceedings awakened more than admiration – they aroused a powerful sympathy, and a deep and self-reflecting interest. They gave an example of which Ireland had but too much reason to avail herself; and the Irish volunteers boldly, though not prudently, commemorated the great event of the revolution by the most public demonstration of opinion. It was then that the government, taking new alarm, resolved upon the destruction of a force, which, if it had no other demerit, must have been at once odious and suspicious, because it was – national. Yet, ere the hand of power fell with an annihilating weight upon the devoted bands, while public opinion yet suspended the coming blow, the volunteers continued to exhibit to their partial fellow-citizens that admirable discipline to which they had so long and so cheerfully submitted; and their reviews continued to embrace all classes, either as actors or spectators, from the viceroy to the lowest populace.

It happened that while the army of Ulster were celebrating, in their province, the anniversary of the French Revolution, the army of Leinster, with less ostensible motives for reunion, were summoned to a grand review in the Phoenix Park. The reviewing general, upon this, as upon every other occasion, was the great Earl of Charlemont, the general of the volunteer army of Ulster, the father of the volunteer army of Ireland; one of those men who hallow a whole people, and lift up all who live in their time. Presiding over a great army for years without reward, he had assisted to establish a revolution[1] without blood. The Earl of Charlemont was then advanced in years, and suffered under their consequent infirmities; yet still at his post, he gave to his country what age in its usual egotism requires for itself – his health, his time, his tastes, his repose, and, it is melancholy to add, his peace.

On the evening previous to this review (one of the last and the most splendid), the several corps were seen marching into the capital from various directions. They were met by the cordial inhabitants, who accepted their billets with cheerfulness, receiving them with boundless hospitality, and entertaining them with emulous profusion. In the morning (and it was a bright May morning), Dublin was all bustle and movement. Military music was heard in every direction. The carriages of the nobility and gentry, colonels and commandants of the various provincial corps, came rolling into town from the seats and villas of their distinguished owners. The different corps assembled to beat of drum, or sound of trumpet; forming themselves into brigades in the most spacious streets, or along the noble quays of the Liffey: and by eleven o'clock the army of Leinster, led on by the Dublin Volunteers, headed by the Duke of Leinster, were all marching to the scene of action. A multitude preceded, followed, and surrounded them; and all who did not, or could not, accompany them to the field, hailed and cheered them as they passed, from the windows, balconies, and roofs of the houses.

The Phœnix Park – the old manor of *Fionne uisge*,[2] gallantly translated by Lord Chesterfield into '*Phœnix*,' – once the domain of the powerful priors of Kilmainham, now the '*bel respiro*' of the Anglo-Irish officials, from the viceroy to the chamberlain, from the secretary of state to the clerk of the kitchen – the Phœnix Park is, perhaps, one of the most beautiful suburban pleasure grounds that any city in Europe can boast. Since the Union it has been deserted by the dispirited citizens of Dublin, and wholly abandoned to the temporary residence of the English members of the Irish government. At the epoch here alluded to, it was not only the site of many villas belonging to the nobility, but the Hyde Park and Kensington of the Irish metropolis. It was the daily resort of the rank, beauty, and fashion of the capital, where the *corso* was performed with all the punctuality of an

---

[1] In 1782, well denominated 'Ireland's life-time.'
[2] Fair Water.

Italian town. It was the weekly promenade of the lower and middle ranks, who assembled there, not only for health and amusement, but to witness that emulous display of splendid equipages and numerous cavalry, which it was then the vanity, and sometimes the ruin of the Irish gentry to indulge in; and above all, it had been the site of all military exercises, from the '*joustes et fêtes*' of those belligerent monks, the knights templars of Kilmainham, to the reviews of the Irish volunteers.

Its diversified scenery, the vast variety of its surface, and the accident of a broad and uninterrupted plain, called the 'Fifteen Acres,' admirably calculate the Phœnix Park for military evolutions. Rising from the banks of the Liffey, in a succession of gentle eminences, it commands an exterior view of that embellished landscape, which swells on the opposite side of the river to the base of a ridge of mountains, whose bold and daring outline forms the back-ground of the whole. Within the park innumerable swellings of the surface and shaded glens, intersected by the gleaming waters of small natural lakes, diffuse an air of rural beauty, even over the pleasure grounds of a court; while groves of luxuriant hawthorn, of large and venerable growth, spread their shades over many 'an alley green, dingle, and bushy dell,' in whose recesses groups of deer repose undisturbed, and add a touch of wildness to a scene at once romantic and cultivated.

On the occasion of the volunteer review, now alluded to, the park was all green and gold, verdure and sunshine. The Liffey reflected skies blue as any that ever tinted the waters of the Arno; and the rich bloom of the hawthorn, pushed forth by a mild winter and an anticipated spring (so common and so delusive in Ireland), already clothed the trees with beauty, and loaded the air with perfume. The Dublin mountains, cutting darkly against purple the lights of their horizon, gave relief to the city, which exhibited, as it spread down to the port, many a spire and steeple, mingling with the flags of vessels, which then rode into the very heart of the metropolis. Tents, for the entertainment of the lowly, and pavilions of every colour and kind, for the repose of the great, were pitched among the glens and defiles, so as not to impede the movements of the troops. Some few, upon well selected eminences, attracted attention, by their peculiar elegance, by the guards that sentinelled their draped and curtained entrance, and by the banners that floated on their summit. One of these, with the royal flag over it, was the vice-regal banquet tent, reserved for his Excellency, the Lord Lieutenant, and his party. Another was a gallantry, on the part of the Dublin Volunteers, to their illustrious commander. Its scarlet banner, with the motto of *Crom aboo*, denoted that it was reserved for the Leinster family.

All the several gates of entrance to the park were thrown open to receive the multitude, which poured in from the capital and its environs. For the Irish, always prone to pleasure, or to what they deem pleasure, are the people in the world.

> De vivre heureux – s'ils avaient de quoi vivre.

Towards mid-day, the tide set in with great force. Parties of men, women, and children, escaped from the foul air of the 'Liberty,' or 'Patrick's Close,' already seated upon various hillocks, and covered with dust, were, in their own language, 'moistening their clay,' by a recurrence to that resource, which rarely fails the lower Irish, even in the worst of times – whiskey. Groups of bare-legged spalpeens, with their ragged jackets on their arms, their brogues on their shoulders, and their short sticks in their hands, came trooping over the green heights; their brawny breasts exposed to the sun, and their staring eyes, searching for 'a place to see the Review,' where they might admire the manœuvring of their own village or county corps, and be thus enabled, on their return, to relate the prowess of the heroes of Pucks Town, or Hazle Hatch, County Kildare, or County Cavan.

The pedestrian spectators, who 'took time by the forelock,' were followed by the humbler order of vehicles of all kinds; the old Irish *Tim whiskey*, the *Chaise marine*, that capacious Irish family vehicle, and predecessor of modern jingles; the *Noddy!* that humble, unpretending, public carriage, which placed the driver, his horse, and his companion, in such intimate, close, and social contact; the Dublin hackney coach, that short process to dislocation; the *pochay*, from Castle Knock, or Castle Dermott, from the 'Black Bull,' or the 'Man of War;' with the one-horse chair of the Dublin cockney, or the new-invented '*Duchess's gig*,' the unpopular novelty, sported by an unpopular corporator, who, as the pasquinade of the day had it –

> ——Set up his gig
> With the money he got for sticking a pig,[1]

all jumbled, jostled, shambled, and shattered along, with emulous

---

[1] The *vaudevilles* of Dublin were then as much a vehicle for giving vent to public discontent, as those of Paris in the time of Cardinal Richelieu.

rapidity. The 'Judys' and 'Juggys,' from Bally-bough, or Bally-tore, from Glassneven, or Glassmanogue, mounted *en croupe* upon the stout lean garrons[1] of their husbands, displayed 'their broad beaver hats, and red cloaks all so fine,' to the envious eyes and invidious sarcasms of their less opulent pedestrian neighbours.

Last, and late, and long after the plebeian spectators were assembled, came the splendid and numerous equipages of the aristocracy; the greater number drawn by four, and some by six horses; with liveries that sparkled in the sun, like cloths of gold, and outriders mounted on steeds, that looked like chargers. Driving up the most perilous sites, and 'seeking glory, even in the cannon's mouth,' came rolling on, the female charioteers, supreme above all in splendour and attractions; some of whom, mounted in lofty phaetons, and guiding their fiery coursers with more spirit than discretion, seemed like the spoiled child of the sun, only to have 'obtained the chariot of the day, to set the world on fire.' These splendid personages, were, however, as few as they were conspicuous; for high phaetons and female charioteership were then alike novelties in Ireland; and were exclusively confined to those great female oligarchs who governed society, as their husbands governed the state, and ruled in the coteries of the capital, as their consorts ruled the country, in all the insolence of exclusive privilege, and all the lawlessness of unlimited power.

Conspicuous amongst the most conspicuous of these stars of the ascendant, was a lady, who took the field with an *éclat*, a brilliancy, and bustle, which for a time fixed the attention of all upon herself. Although a fine woman, in the strictest sense of the term, and still handsome, though not still very young, she was even more distinguished by her air of high supremacy, than by her beauty. She sat loftily in a lofty phaeton, which was emblazoned with arms, and covered with coronets; and she played with her long whip, as ladies of old managed their fans, with grace and coquetry. She was dressed in a rich habit, whose facings and epaulettes spoke her the lady of the noble colonel of some provincial corps of volunteers. A high military cap, surmounted with a plume of black feathers, well became her bright, bold, black eyes, and her brow, that looked as if accustomed 'to threaten and command.' The air had deepened her colour through her rouge, as it had blown from her dark dishevelled tresses the mareschal powder, then still worn in Ireland – (the last lingering

[1] Garron, a lean horse.

barbarism of the British toilet, which France had already abandoned, with other barbarous modes, and exchanged for the *coiffure d'Agrippine* and the *tête à la Brutus*). Her *pose*, her glance, her nod, her smile, all conscious and careless as they were, proclaimed a privileged autocrat of the Irish *bon ton*, a '*dasher*,' as it was termed, of the first order: – for that species of effrontery called *dashing* was then in full vogue, as consonant to a state of society, where all in a certain class went by assumption.

The lady had arrived rather early in the field, for one whose habits were necessarily on the wrong side of time and of punctuality. She came bowling along, keeping up her fiery steeds to a sort of curveting gallop, like one deep in the science of the *manège* – now deranging the order of march of the troops, by breaking through the ranks, in spite of the impertinent remonstrances of the out-posts and videttes, at which she laughed, at once to show her teeth and her power; – and now scattering the humble crowd, 'like chaff before the wind,' as, giving her horses the rein, she permitted them to plunge headlong on, while skifully flourishing her long whip, she made on every side a preliminary clearance. Many among the multitude announced her as the famous Kitty Cut-dash; and nodded knowingly as she passed them; but the greater number detected in the beautiful charioteer, the equally famous Albina Countess Knocklofty, the female chief of that great oligarchical family, the Proudforts – a family on which the church rained mitres, the state coronets, and the people – curses.

Beside her sat, or rather lounged, another dame of quality; bearing the stamp of her class and caste as obviously, yet less deeply marked, than her companion. More feminine in her air, more foreign in her dress and entire bearing, her faultless form, and almost faultless face, had all the advantages of the new democratic toilet of Paris (adopted by its court, when more important innovations were still fatally resisted); and she appeared in the Phœnix Park, dressed much in the same costume as Maria Antoinette and her female favourites are described to have worn in the gardens of Trianon, or in the bowers of St Cloud, – to the horror of all old *dames d'atours*, and all the partisans of the ancient regime of whalebone and buckram! The chemise of transparent muslin, or *robe à la Polignac, chapeau de paille à la bergère*, tied down with a lilac ribbon, with

Scarf loosely flowing, hair as free,

gave an air of sylph-like simplicity to one, whose features, though beautiful, were marked by an expression foreign to simplicity, evincing that taste, not sentiment, presided over her toilet, and that '*chez elle, un beau désordre fut l'effet de l'art.*'

This triumphal car was followed, or surrounded, by a host of beaux; some in military uniform, and with true English faces and figures; but the greater number in the civil, though uncivilized, dress of the day, and with forms and physiognomies as Irish as ever were exhibited in Pale or Palatinate, to the dread of English settlers and Scotch undertakers. Ponderous powdered clubs, hanging from heads of dishevelled hair, – shoulders raised or stuffed to an Atlas height and breadth, – the stoop of paviers, and the lounge of chairmen, – broad beavers, tight buckskins, the striped vest of a groom, and the loose coat of a coachman, gave something ruffianly to the air of even the finest figures; which assorted but too well with the daring, dashing manner, that just then had succeeded, among a *particular set*, to the courtly polish for which the travelled nobility of Ireland were once so distinguished. Such, in exterior, were many of the members of the famous *Cherokee Club*, and such the future legislators of that great national indignity, which had procured them a contemptible pre-eminence in the black book of public opinion, by the style and title of 'the *Union Lords.*' As they now crowded round the cynosures of the day, there was something too ardent and unrestrained in their homage, something too emphatic in their expressions and gestures, for true breeding; while in their handsome, but 'light, revelling, and protesting faces,' traces of the night's orgies were still visible, which gave their fine features a licentious cast, and deprived their open and very manly countenances of every mark of intellectual expression.

The volunteers had now nearly all marched into the park, and awaited only the arrival of the Lord Lieutenant (the Duke of Belvoir), and of the reviewing general and commander of the forces, before they commenced the usual operations. Meantime it was curious to observe the interest excited by these native legions among the spectators, as each corps, bearing some well-known standard, passed the groups and parties stationed in various positions. Each body was hailed with cheers and plaudits, according to its own popularity, or the popularity of its distinguished leader. Even the smallest company, from some little hamlet in the vicinity, had its partisans, and was named with pride by friends and townsmen. One of these, the spokesman on the occasion, was an old Fingalian, as great an amateur of volunteer reviews, as George Selwyn was of executions; and he continued to announce to his party each company and its 'great captain,' as it marched beneath the little hill on which he was seated. The appearance of the Duke of Leinster, at the head of his own corps, drew forth one continuous cheer of universal approbation; for at this epoch, the old prejudice in favour of the Geraldines was in full force, nurtured by the active patriotism, which was deemed the inalienable inheritance of the Fitzgerald family, and which some of the illustrious members too soon afterwards shed their blood to prove.

As his Grace passed beneath the hill alluded to, which was studded with joyous faces from base to summit, the cries of 'the Leinster lads for ever!' – 'Success to the Maynooths!' and '*Crom aboo* to the ind of time, and long after!' were heard on every side, from crowds led up by the Fingal oracle, Tim Doolin of Portran, who, in expectation of the arrival of the corps of his own townlands, liberally did the honours by every other.

'Now, boys,' cried Tim, 'up with your heads, and off with your hats! Here comes the Malahides and the Coolocks – Talbot's own fencibles for ever, with three cheers, boys, hurra! And now look to your lift, marching from Stony Batther gate to the tune of Langolee; thim's the Balruthries; and close on their *traheens*, in scarlet and blue, comes the Portrans,[1] my cuishla they are, and Captain Hampden at their *hid*. Now, boys, jewels, up with your hats, and off with your hids! Oh! by the powers, here's the raal things, any how! the "Dublin Indipindints!" Hould your *whuisht* now, every sowl of yez; the Volunteer's March, do ye hear that? There they go; three cheers for the great and grand Dublin Indipindints, and Counsellor Grattan for ever, huzza!'

This popular corps, one of the finest and first raised in the Leinster army, was this day headed for the last time by one of the greatest men that Ireland ever produced; and as the Irish Cicero rode on, amidst deafening acclamations of popular gratitude and enthusiasm, there was something in his eye and air that might well recall to the classic mind the liberator of Rome, the father of his country. Grattan had lately merited and obtained a similar title, and his eloquence was

---

[1] Portran, a beautiful peninsula, darting out into the Bay of Dublin, at that time the seat of Hampden Evans, now the residence of his son George Evans, Esq. a good landlord, a liberal politician, and one of the few who still hold by the country which gave them birth and subsistence, and reflect back upon it the high benefit of enlightened and well-directed patriotism.

daily raised to oppose the corruption of more than one Verres, and
to put down the conspiring audacity of more than one Catiline.

While the cheers of a grateful people were hailing the name of
their champion, other public characters succeeded to elicit popular
applause. The officer next in command to the immortal colonel of the
'Dublin Indipindents' was, like him, of the 'true antique mould.' With
the head of a Brutus, and the figure of a Hercules, yet with the air
of one practised in the graces of a court, Archibald Hamilton Rowan
received the cheers of admiration with all that peculiar suavity and
cordiality, which, springing from the heart, still survive, with principles
that never varied, and spirit that never quenched.

Other corps followed, each hoisting colours expressive of the tone
and feeling of public opinion. On one was inscribed, 'The five free
nations, America, France, Poland, Great Britain, and Ireland;' on
another, 'The nation, the law, and the king;' on a third, 'The asylum
of liberty;' and on a fourth, 'Unite and be free.' The leaders of all were
remarkable for their manly bearing and intellectual countenances; and
the 'long lives' wished to them by the populace (the Irish, as it was
the Jewish benediction), seemed rather a promise than a vow. Yet in
a few short years many of those young lives were offered up upon the
scaffold, a sacrifice to sincerity in that cause, which, wrong or right,
was by the victims deemed the cause *of their country*. These victims
were then all full of youth, life, love, and hope, surrounded by
admiring compatriots, and gazed on by eyes whose smiles were immortality – by eyes soon to be dimmed with tears which time has not even
yet dried up.

Several provincial corps succeeded, only less distinquished, because
less known to the people of Dublin and its vicinity, than their own
immediate companies; until *one* approached, which seemed to challenge a species of feeling beyond all vulgar admiration. On the silken
flag of emerald green which preceded it, was woven in gold letters,
'The Irish Brigade,' with the Irish harp, and the motto of 'I am new
strung.' On the reverse was inscribed, *'Fais ce que day, arrive que
pourra,'* an old epigraph, adopted by a peculiar branch of the O'Briens.
There was something bold, and it might seem perilous, in such
devices; but they were the fashion of the day, and as yet unreproved
(though not unnoticed) by government. The corps had been recently
raised. The *dernier rejeton* of the old stock of the Irish volunteers, its
last vigorous offset, not numerous, but select, – it was almost exclusively composed of the *élite* of the youth of the capital and the university.

A certain brilliant petulance of look and movement, with a gallant and military bearing, not always found in the best disciplined home-bred troops, distinguished this band of boy-citizen-soldiers; and the *éclat* of their appearance, well became their age and vocation. Martinets in dress and discipline, their elegant and highly ornamented green uniform, of a foreign cut and novel fashion, gave them the air of Polish hussars, enlisted under the free banners of some gallant Kosciusko; and a few novelties in their exercises, introduced by their young captain (who, it was understood, had seen foreign service), gave them advantages, personal and military, which had obtained for them the *sobriquet* of the 'Ladies' Own.' Preceded by a fine band, and headed by a youth whom nature in her partiality had called out of the common roll of men, they presented, as they marched into the park, in quick time, a splendid image of precocious patriotism, *gaillard* as the '*Jeunesse dorée*' of the French Revolution, and honoured as the '*gioventù armata*' of the best days of Florence.

'Why, then, who are they at all, Tim, dear?' demanded a Skerries fisherman, who had during the day consulted *Tim Doolan*, as his oracle.

'Why, then, I couldn't tell you thruly, barring I'd lade yez astray, Pat Doran,' replied Tim; 'for 'bove all the volunteer throops, in the Phanix, this day, thim's the boys I don't know nothing about at all, at all; but thinks to the best of my belief, they are Lords' sons, or the College boys.'

'Why, then, I wouldn't wonder,' said the Skerries man. The question, however, repeated to another bystander, was suddenly, and, it should appear, oraculously, answered, like the druidical oracles of old, from the top of a tall and magnificent oak, which, rooted at the base of the acclivity, overshadowed its summit with thick and lofty branches. 'O'Brien aboo,' shouted with an echoing yell the respondent: and the cry, long, loud, and shrill, was taken up by Tim Doolan, repeated by Pat Doran, and reiterated by the imitative multitude. While yet but half pronounced, it had caught the quick ear of the young leader of the Irish brigade. He started – threw his eyes up to the oak, whence the cry had issued; then cast them suddenly down, and reddened, and grew pale – and gave the word of quick march! to his company. But when the cry of 'O'Brien aboo,' found an echo from the popular voice, he seemed proudly to apply its meaning to himself, and saluted the multitude with his sword, and smiled with all the popular grace of a young Roman tribune.

'What does O'Brien aboo mane?' asked Pat Doran, hoarse with shouting it.

'Why it manes the same as *Crom aboo*,[1] to be sure, what else would it mane,' replied Tim Doolan; 'and often heard tell by my gossip in Fingal, that it was wid that same watch-word, that Brien Borru diffinded the great pass of Bally-bough bridge agin the Danes, at the battle of Clontarf.'

'Why, then, I wouldn't wondher if that comely young chap at their head there, was Mr Brien *Boreyou's* own son, Tim Doolan, for he looks like a lad would head a ruction, bravely, as the father that bore him.'

'Whooh, man! that's mortally unpossible,' replied the antiquarian of Fingal; 'sure that battle was fit in th' ould times, afore the battle of the Boyne, or Aughram, fifty years! ay, troth, a thousand (and more) out of the memory of man, Pat Doran, dear.'

'Why, then, sorrow ache, their hearts ache, that fought at that fit, any how, Tim.'

'Oh, thrue for you, Pat; sorrow ache, and never did, not all as one as now; for th'ould times was the fine times, and will be ever more, amen, plaze Christ.'

It was not, however, from the clients of the Portran oracle, that the Irish brigade alone attracted notice, and awakened inquiry. Many bright eyes followed, and many bland smiles shone upon the *élite* of 'the Ladies' own.' But none so bright or so bland, as those which emanated from the fair occupants of the splendid phaeton, already described; which had drawn up parallel to the halt made by the Irish brigade.

'O'Mealy,' exclaimed the fair and noble charioteer, with a prettily lisped, but technical, 'steady, now; steady, I tell you;' addressed to her horses – 'O'Mealy, what corps is that with the green standard and uniform?'

'What corps is it, Lady Knocklofty? why, then, give you my honour, I don't know a corps in the Volunteer army; 'pon my honour I don't! We, *reglars*, never know any thing of the train bands, and more

---

[1] 'O'Brien aboo,' the cause of the O'Briens. Aboo! the war-cry of the ancient Irish, was adopted by the Norman or English settlers, as – Butleirach-abû, the cause of the Butlers.

Crom-a-boo, the motto of the Geraldines, is literally the *cause of God*, 'Crom' being one of the many names of the Deity in the Irish language.

partickilarly, we cavalry make it a point; besides, there are some ugly customers among them, such as one's tailor, or shoemaker, upon my honour!'

This answer was made by a handsome, flashy looking person, in military uniform, with large features, scattered at random over a broad face, with a leering smile, good bold eyes, high colour, and a perfect chevaux-de-frize of powdered whiskers. He had long been sidling his horse up to the phaeton, and had obtained, with some difficulty, a position which he maintained with some effort.

'What a very fine young fellow that is,' continued Lady Knocklofty, not attending to the assertions of O'Mealy, and keeping her magnificent eyes steadily fired on the face of the young leader of the Irish Brigade; who, perhaps, not quite unconscious of the gaze, either in the confusion of vanity, or under the oppression of heat, removed his plumed cap: as he displaced and scattered the dark unpowdered locks (then a mark of singularity, if not of disloyalty) which clustered round his high and intellectual temples, he exhibited one of those heads which painters love to copy, and sculptors to model.

'What a handsome head, and what a singular one!' said Lady Knocklofty to the lady beside her.

'Yes, I have seen many such at Paris, this winter,' was the reply, 'it is called *tête à la victime.*'

'Do, like a good soul, O'Mealy' (cried Lady Knocklofty), 'find out who he is; I am sure it is some one I ought to bow to, for he seems to canvass a salute. Can it be one of the Carrick, or Mount Garret Butlers.'

'He is one of the *mount garrets*, I dare say,' replied Lady Honoria, laughing. 'Many of these volunteers heroes, I believe, descend from their altitudes to take the field; and exchange their leather aprons for their leather belts.'

'What eyes!' continued Lady Knocklofty, keeping her own fixed; 'those are what Hamilton, the painter, calls Irish eyes, large, dark, deep set, and put in, as it were, with dirty fingers; O'Mealy, do find out who that boy with the eyes is.'

'Is it the chap with the squint?' demanded the captain; 'that's my boot-maker, of the Golden Leg in Ormonde Quay. If your ladyship ever wears top-boots, I'd take the liberty of recommending him to your pathronage and protection.'

'I suppose, Captain,' said the other lady, 'you infer that her ladyship occasionally wears top-boots because she sometimes wears the – ;'

and the most beautiful lips in the world boldly pronounced a word that would now shock even ears which do not pique themselves on being ears polite, to listen to.

Captain O'Mealy raised a horse laugh, which showed his large white teeth from ear to ear. 'Bravo! Lady Honoria, I will make it a point to report that at mess to-day; give you my honour I will.'

'I am sure you know who he is, O'Mealy, if you chose to tell,' said Lady Knocklofty, pettishly; 'there, I mean that tall boy, with the eyes – '

'Tall boy' (repeated Lady Honoria), 'do you call him; he looks more like a console, I think.'[1]

'Oh, the young captain there, in green,' said O'Mealy, conceitedly; 'that's a young journeyman tailor, one of Roger Sweeney's men, who himself commands a corps here to-day.'

'A tailor!' said Lady Honoria, '*Où les beaux yeux vont-ils se nicher!*'

'A tailor! nonsense! impossible!' said Lady Knocklofty, haughtily.

'Give you my honour, Lady Knocklofty, if I'm not grately mistaken, and I take it for granted I am not, he is a tailor. If your ladyship wants a habit, I'll ingage that's your man.'

'A habit!' said Lady Honoria, 'a fancy, you mean.'

'Bravo! again, Lady Honoria; I'll report that at mess to-day, give you my honour I will; and what I shall report would have no credit, were not the proof so high, as the immortal Shakspeare says.'

'What is the meaning of that Irish motto on that green flag?' asked Lady Knocklofty, wholly preoccupied with her subject; 'at least it looks like Irish.'

'That, Lady Knocklofty? – never had one word of Irish in my existence.'

'Nor two of English' (muttered Lady Honoria). 'Now, upon your honour, Captain O'Mealy, of all tongues, living or dead, which is your favourite?'

'Why, then, upon my honour and conscience,' replied Captain O'Mealy, emphatically, throwing round his large eyes, and pulling up his black stock, anxious to observe if his intimacy with the two great ladies was noticed; 'and what's more, upon the honour of a soldier and a man, Lady Honoria, I have no choice.'

'But Hobson's,' said Lady Honoria, gravely, and both ladies burst into an immoderate fit of laughter, with very little consideration for

[1] Two fasionable pieces of furniture, the *armoire* and *tripod* of the day.

the feelings of the object of their mirth; who, to evince that he had none, joined in the laugh also, – too happy to keep his enviable station, at any expense.

'Lady Honoria takes horrible liberties with your parts of speech, O'Mealy,' said Lady Knocklofty.

'Her ladyship may take any liberties she plazes with me, Lady Knocklofty,' replied the Captain, with an impudent leer; 'and the freer the welcomer, 'pon my honour; so, I'll beseech you, let her will have a free way, as I said last night at the private thayathricals, in the Moor of Venice.'

'The Moor of *Ennis*,' said Lady Honoria, in allusion to the Captain's strong county of Clare accent; –'apropos, Captain O'Mealy, what did you mean by refusing the part of Captain O'Blunder, as Lady Ely cast it for you the other night at the Attic?'

'Lady Ely? why, I mane Lady Honoria, I never could lay my tongue about the Irish brogue, give you my honour; and besides, O'Blunder is intirely too low for me.'

'Do you really *mane* that,' asked Lady Honoria, broadly; and both ladies again laughed in his face, while he again joined them, though a little less heartily than before; adding, "Pon my honour, I am highly delighted to see your two ladyships in such charming fine spirits to-day, considering the bating the countess got at the brag-table last night, or rather this morning, after the private thayatricals at Lady Ely's.'

'O'Mealy,' said Lady Knocklofty, yawning, 'what have you done with Miss Macguire?'

'What have I done with her, Lady Knocklofty? why, as any young lady would like to be done by; as your ladyship will own, when I tell you that I have left her with the whole staff, riding along the line in the Fifteen Acres.'

'Well, now, do go like a good man, and stay by her, and see that she don't play tricks with my mare; Kitty Macguire would spoil any horse in Ireland. She has left Rowdelam not worth a shilling, and ruined the mouth and gait of Mrs. Slamikin beyond cure. Do go,' continued her ladyship, impatiently, as the Captain, flanking her to the left, impeded the view of everything but his own sprawling person.

'Certainly, Lady Knocklofty; born for your use, I live but to obee you;' and he was backing out, when again turning round, and pulling up his stock, he demanded, affectedly, 'I hope I am to have the honour of meeting your ladyships at the small, leetle, private paurty at the Castle to-night?'

'Oh, *you* are asked, are you,' said Lady Knocklofty, with a look of insolent surprise. 'I suppose you are on guard at the Castle, to-night.'

'Why, I should be on the Castle guard, I believe,' said the Captain; 'that is, I take it for granted, I will; but whether or no, Lady Knocklofty, I assure your ladyship, I would be asked; as it has long been her Excellency's polite intintion to have me at all her small, leetle, private paurties.'

'Oh, if you *would* be asked, there is not a word more to be said,' observed Lady Honoria gravely, 'so, *au revoir.*'

'Ay, *au revoir,*' said Lady Knocklofty, impatiently nodding him off; 'and mind you return to Kitty Macguire, and look to the mare.'

The captain again backed out and flourished off, making way for a heavy dragoon (who had long and patiently waited for the reversion of his place); and continuing to repeat to himself as he trotted on his mission, '*O rewoir, O rewoir;* that's not in the grammar as far as I've got, but to be sure I am not further than *Jay*, I have, *tu wah*, thou hast. *O rewoir*, well to be sure!' and the captain added, '*au revoir,*' or something that sounded like it, to a vocabulary he was industriously composing, from the crumbs which fell from the rich man's table.

Suddenly and unexpectedly introduced into high life by the very absurdities which should have kept him out of it, he felt that, as *la nature n'apprend pas l'orthographe*, some aid from art was necessary to supply her deficiencies; and believing that learning, like a 'wise-bearing carriage, is caught as men take diseases one from another,' he had put himself through a course of education, to which all his great friends unconsciously contributed, in conjunction with 'the immortal Shakspeare,' whose acquaintance he had recently made by acting in the singing characters, and filling up that useful range of parts included in 'mutes, guards, attendants, and others,' at the Countess of Ely's Attic theatre in Ely-place.

'How that vulgar fellow gets on,' said Lady Knocklofty, cutting dead the heavy dragoon by turning her back to him, and addressing her companion.

'Get on! to be sure he does,' said Lady Honoria; '*il est fait pour cela*. With his immaculate brogue, his pushing manners, and divine voice, how could he fail?'

'Oh! his brogue and manners are detestable; but what would he do, if he lost his voice?' said Lady Knocklofty.

'Do?' said Lady Honoria, 'why, do without his dinner very often; unless you appoint him to the *état* of dry nurse in perpetuity to Kitty Macguire.'

'I am tired of them both,' said Lady Knocklofty, yawning; and, for want of excitement, just then tired of every thing: 'I wish,' she continued, still cutting the dragoon, 'they were married to each other.'

'What! the Hon. Kitty Macguire, with her high blood and her (sometimes) high airs, married to Barney O'Mealy, the son of an innkeeper at Ennis! *Oh! la mésalliance!*'

'I wish then Lord Knocklofty would not bore me with his hangers on and poor cousins, if he has no means of providing for them.'

'He has provided for the Captain,' said Lady Honoria.

'He? not a bit. It was Captain Macheath that made a Captain of Barney O'Mealy. The Duke was so pleased with him at Lady Ely's.'

'Yes, but who introduced him there to please the Duke? But as for young Kitty, *soyez tranquille*. Kitty will provide for herself, some how or other. In the mean time, she is the most useful bit of furniture in Knocklofty House. She talks to the bores, flirts with the boys, takes a hand with the dowagers, fills the beau-pots with flowers from the country, and sings slang songs to amuse Lord Knocklofty, when he returns from the house, badgered into an ill temper by the patriots of the opposition, with their eternal *refrain* of places, pensions, penals, and all the old list of Irish grievances. By the by, where *is* your husband to-day, my dear? I don't see him upon the ground.'

The question was asked with a carelessness, too careless not to seem studied.

'Lord, child, I have enough to do to mind other people's husbands, without looking after my own,' replied Lady Knocklofty, laughing:– 'but I really thought he was with you this morning when I called to take you up in Stephen's Green; I thought, at least, I saw a frosted head between the Venetian blinds in your dressing-room.'

'Oh! that was *my* deary's head, *tête de mari au naturel, que cependant j'ai bien coiffé* before I left him, for we were going over the old ground – '

'What old ground?' asked Lady K., who had now fairly shouldered out the dragoon.

'Want of money; simply that, my dear,' said Lady Honoria.

'The only want I cannot complain of,' said Lady Knocklofty with a sigh; 'but by the by, I heard the Duchess ask Lord Knocklofty to join her 'awkward squad,' as she calls the household. You know the ministerials have sent her over a new consignment of younger sons to provide for. Oh! here she comes, the vice-regal Venus.'

'A Venus in brass (said Lady Honoria, spitefully), as old Lady Slipslop (*Hislop, par parenthèse*) names the 'Diana in bronze,' when she undertakes to show off her husband's museum. O dear, I forgot she was your aunt, child!'

'Oh! never mind that; spare my friends, and do as you please with my relations. But you should remember every one has not travelled like you,' said Lady Knocklofty, sharply. 'Yet you have your nickname, as well as my aunt, Hislop.'

'Oh, I have, have I? and what do they call me?'

'Madame de Polthogue (said Lady Knocklofty, with a pretty little malignant smile that always became her); from your constant use of French phrases, and, as they pretend, from your patriotic preservation of the Munster accent.'

'And what does polthogue mean?' asked Lady Honoria, biting her lips.

'In Irish, a thump, or blow, I believe.'

'Well, I do give them some hard knocks, now and then, that is certain. I hold them all (the set or *clique* excepted) in utter contempt. To my French phrases, I plead guilty: for the phraseology of the mere *bel air* of Dublin is so *baroque*, so anti-European, that of necessity I take refuge in the French. But I deny the Munster brogue; I deny the coach horses, Sir Peter. And now draw in, for Heaven's sake, or we shall be run down by your friend, the vice-queen.'

Lady Knocklofty tightened her reins, and the next moment the low and splendid phaeton of the Lady Lieutenant – small, light, and elegant as the biga of the Vatican, – came sweeping over the ground. It was drawn by four tiny steeds, which looked as though some such fairy godmother as Cinderella's had recently converted them from white mice into white ponies. They were whimsically driven by two little, jet-black postilions, turbaned and draped in eastern costume: and they strongly contrasted their moorish visages, and ebony countenances, with the pretty fair faces of two little boys, who sat *sur le devant*, and who might have passed for loves, if they had not been loaded with the military finery of vice-regal pages. Alone in her triumphal car, surpassing all, even these who '*surpassed the passing fair*,' sat the fairest representative of royalty that ever was delegated by foreign policy, to win over a refractory people, by means which might have succeeded, when weightier measures failed. But party spirit is not gallant; and politics and chivalry have ever stood aloof. It happened therefore that her Excellency, the idol of the court, formed to 'engage all hearts, and charm all eyes,' was not a favourite with the people; who confounded the gaiety of her drawing-room with the impolitic measures of her husband's cabinet. And though, whenever she came forth into public, a sudden burst of admiration, which nature sent from the hearts to the lips of all parties, hailed her approach, yet it was too frequently chilled by prejudice, or checked by misdirected indignation. She appeared at the review in a habit of Rutland blue, faced with scarlet, and embroidered in gold. Her faultless face was too much shaded by the broad leaf of a white beaver hat, surmounted by a *panache blanche*, which, like that worn by the best of the Bourbons, was the oriflamme of many a devoted heart. As she passed along, she bowed gracefully to all; and familiarly, and with a significant glance and smile, to the ladies in the phaeton. Her splendid appearance extorted involuntary homage from every eye – and voluntary sarcasms from many lips. 'There she goes,' said Lady Knocklofty, 'the "queen of hearts," with St Leger, and St George, and St John, and all her train of saints after her.'

'And sinners,' said Lady Honoria, significantly.

'I hope you don't count *my* lord in the number, poor man,' said Lady Knocklofty, 'for he is close upon her chariot wheels, you see.'

'Yes!' said Lady Honoria, with humour, 'she is at all in the ring.'

'If she is at him, it will be love's labour lost,' said Lady Knocklofty, 'or coquetry's; for if I know any thing of Lord Knocklofty, he is not to be taken, alive or dead.'

'Well!' said Lady Honoria, "*sur ce chapitre on peut se rapporter à vous*,' as Ninon says; and it is as well to be put upon one's guard at once.'

'I don't mean to say that Lord Knocklofty is not to be won,' said his wife, coolly; 'but it will not be by a woman, who, like the Duchess, is neither actuated by passion, nor by avarice; and who, spoilt by flattery herself, never thinks of offering it, where flattery alone will take. Lord Knocklofty must be wooed, and not unsought be won. He has no time to make love. A clever woman might do anything with him, who would take that trouble off his hands. As for the Duchess, she, you know, means nothing by her conquests but the pleasure of making them.'

'Humph!' ejaculated Lady Honoria; 'I am not quite so sure of that.'

Here the flourish of trumpets, the roll of drums, and the striking up of the English national anthem by the several bands, announced the arrival of the Lord Lieutenant, General and General Governor of Ireland. In the prime of life and manly beauty, gay, careless, and spirited, splendidly attired, and numerously attended by a brilliant *cortège* of young English military of rank and fashion, he came, not pompously, but dashingly on, smiling and bowing to the host of beautiful women, who hailed him as he passed; while, among the multitude, but few 'threw up their caps, and cried, "God save King Richard!" '

The reviewing general (the Earl of Charlemont), and his staff, immediately followed. Then the popular voice swelled into acclamation to the remotest confines of the multitude; hats were waved, and handkerchiefs flaunted, and the old national air of 'Patrick's Day' honoured the progress of the father of the Irish Volunteers. He rode on slowly, as if at once to spare and gratify the people, who crowded closely on him, and almost under his horse's feet; his venerable head uncovered, his white hair contrasting with his dark impending brows, and with a certain severity of look, softened down by a beneficent smile. As he passed the Knocklofty carriage, the ladies bowed coldly, but respectfully; while to the Lord Lieutenant, who seemed disposed to stop and speak to them, they nodded familiarly, and smiled sportively.

'How handsome he looks!' said Lady Honoria.

'Yes; but he wants expression,' said Lady Knocklofty, 'a certain sentimental ardour of look, without which there is no beauty for me.'

'Oh, pooh!' interrupted Lady Honoria, impatiently, 'I am half inclined to exclaim with Charles Surface, "curse your sentiment;' but how unpopular he is; – only observe.'

'I am sure, I don't know why,' said Lady Knocklofty; 'he does every thing to please them: he scarcely ever goes to bed sober, and he bespoke tabinet furniture the other day to an immense amount.'

'It is the '*patriots*,' as they call themselves, that are doing it. What do you think of that insolent fellow, Curran, talking something about 'a paltry viceroy' the other day in the House? However, we have all made a party to go to the gallery with the Duchess, to witness the putting down of this young patriot by dear Fitz; we are to have an exhibition by command.'

'It was at my house that it was arranged,' said Lady Knocklofty.

'One would think,' added Lady Honoria, 'that the Duke was the very *beau idéal* of an Irish Lord Lieutenant, made on purpose for them. But there is no knowing where to catch the dear Irish, and "I *will* be drowned, and nobody *shall* save me," as it is their own grammar, should be their motto.'

Here the subject of her animadversions, attended only by one aide-de-camp, rode up to the phaeton (having hastily acknowledged the military honours with which he was received). His Excellency was evidently *aux petits soins* with Lady Knocklofty; and Lady Honoria, like a true woman of the world, left them to their *chuchoteries*, and turned her whole attention to the carriage of the Lady Lieutenant, which was a little in advance. Humming the then popular French air of '*Je suis Lindor*,' she observed through her glass, with an involuntary sneer of pleasure, the cold, phlegmatic deportment, which Lord Knocklofty preserved, while among the crowd of servitors with whom he was confounded.

The observations of Lady Honoria Stratton (a woman of the world, in all the force of the term), with respect both to the chief governor, and the country he governed, or misgoverned, were not unfounded. If Ireland ever did possess the true '*beau idéal*' of a popular Lord Lieutenant (to use her Ladyship's phrase), it was in the person of him, who now seemed especially marked out by popular prejudice for aversion. Young, beautiful, generous, and gallant, – but too much addicted to social pleasures, and but too prone to convivial indulgence, – this sem-Hibernian chief governor epitomized himself the leading traits of temperament and habits, ascribed to the Irish character. In his early youth, he had been distinguished in the English house of peers, as the apologist for the popular disorders in Ireland, by judiciously and courageously ascribing them to their true causes; yet it belonged to the anomalies of the most unfortunate of all countries, to consider its early friend as a present enemy; to make him answerable, on his first arrival, for the errors of the administration he came to replace; and to hold him accountable for measures over which he as yet had no control. Impatient (as the long-suffering always are), occasionally unjust (as those to whom all justice has been denied frequently will be), the Irish acted upon the impulse of irritated and hasty feelings; and received with a whoop of insult, the man who had long sympathized with their sufferings. In the petulance of wounded self-love, and the hauteur of high rank, the offended chief governor suffered every prepossession in favour of Ireland to yield to unconquerable disgust. Love of ease, with the sense of unmerited indignities, combined to withdraw the votary of pleasure from the drudgery of business; and, hastily and imprudently yielding up the reins of the state to more interested and less safe hands – to hands long used to direct it, by the whip and curb – be abandoned the cabinet for the banquet hall, changed the council 'into merry meetings,' turned his sceptre to a thyrsus, and braiding

> His brows with rosy twine,
> Dropping odours, dropping wine,

he converted the strong-hold of an ascendant faction into the court of a Comus, and like Beuvron, the *fainéant* courtier of Louis the XIIIth, '*il fit très bien sa charge, quand il n'y avait rien à faire.*'

The troops to be employed in the sham fight, were now assembling near the fifteen acres. Piquets of cavalry, supported by infantry, were distributed in various directions; some concealed in the luxuriant bushes near the great ravine, and others in the knolls and clumps of the reservoir. A few videttes remained on the skirts of the back woods, their arms glittering through the foliage; and aides-de-camp and orderlies scouring across the intervening plains, gave to the scene the air of a field of battle on the eve of a great engagement.

The spot chosen for this display of calculated evolutions, was called the *Star Fort*, the attack and the defence of which formed the principal features in the manœuvres of the day. It appeared the ruin of a strong and ancient hold, covering a regular polygon, of considerable dimensions; but was, in reality, of modern construction. It was raised by the celebrated Earl of Wharton as a retreat for safety in the event of an insurrectionary movement in the capital – some symptoms of such an event having manifested themselves in an attack upon the statue of King William III, on his lordship's arrival in the country, to take the reins of its government. But the apprehensions it had awakened proved groundless; the Fort, ere it was quite finished, was permitted to fall into a picturesque and premature decay (presenting to the eye the image of a once impregnable place; and adding to the fine scene it dominated a feature of characteristic interest and great effect), and it continued to be long identified with the reign of him who erected it, by the name of 'Wharton's Folly.'

The defence of this place had been assigned to the Dublin volunteers, who occupied a position extending along 'the Nine Acres;' with their right resting on the Fort, which they had strongly garrisoned, and their left upon the first bridge, which, at a short distance from the approach to the vice-regal lodge, is thrown across the piece of water, which runs in a parallel direction to the road leading to it. The second bridge, equally well guarded, served as a key to the centre of their well taken position. The assault was reserved for the 'Irish brigade,' and the manner of conducting it was left (with the exception of the usual sketch of a 'project for a field-day') entirely to the skill and discretion of its youthful leader. There appeared to be two ways only of approaching the Fort, which he was appointed to attack, and both were equally disadvantageous. He must either carry the bridges upon which the enemy were posted, or enter upon the rear of their position, by making a long *détour* to the right, or to the left. The leader of the enemy was aware of his own strength, and was equally prepared for his antagonist's adopting either of these alternatives. The first, he knew, would be difficult to accomplish; and the second would occupy so much time that it could hardly be accomplished at all. There was, however, one advantage which the Irish brigade possessed: they had a full and complete view of the whole of their opponents' position, and could see distinctly any movements that they made; whilst their own motions were concealed from the observation of the enemy by the thickness of the foliage, with which their part of the park was so luxuriously shaded.

Shortly after, within view of many thousand spectators, and under the eye of many veteran officers, the Irish brigade commenced the action, by a spirited and simultaneous attack upon both the bridges. For these attacks, the enemy was well prepared, and the defence and assault were conducted with equal obstinacy and skill. But while the enemy's attention was exclusively directed to the defence of these important points, the leader of the Irish brigade, putting himself at the head of his light infantry, and taking advantage of the inequality of the ground near the Royal Military Hospital, proceeded in double quick time, made a *détour* to his left, and keeping close to the south wall of the park, succeeded (unobserved by the enemy) in establishing his columns among the thorn bushes, which lay scattered irregularly between the wall and the Star Fort. Here, with the eye of a lynx, and the patient vigilance of a young tiger ready to spring on its prey, he awaited the result of the operations of the other part of the brigade. The bridge on the enemy's left, after a persevering defence, fell at last before the skill and ardour of the assailants; who instantly passing their victorious columns over it, wheeled short round to the left, under cover of the ground which slopes down towards the water, and proceeded rapidly to attack the rear of the enemy, employed in defending the bridge in the centre. This bridge had held out long and obstinately, in consequence of the fire of a twelve-pounder having been directed to check the progress of the assailants. Meantime the leader of the besieged had perceived the last skilful movements of the besiegers; but not suspecting the presence of an enemy in the immediate vicinity of the Fort, he drew out of it a large body of his troops, and led them to the support of his centre. Upon this movement, the young chief of the Irish brigade had calculated; and allowing the enemy to advance beyond the possibility of a recall, he rushed forward, sword in hand, at the head of his light infantry, scaled the unprotected ramparts, and, forgetting for a moment the unreality in the ardour of the attack, forced the artillery men from their guns, and, amidst cheers and shouts of the excited and anxious spectators, he planted the colours of the Irish brigade in the centre of the Fort.

The Reviewing-General, who had watched with much interest the progress of the fight, and to whom this last movement was as unexpected as it was to the enemy – observed to his staff, that by all the rules of war the Irish brigade had conquered; and ordering the bugles to sound for a cessation of hostilities, he rode up with his staff to the youthful and spirited leader, smilingly congratulated him upon his victory, and seriously commended the skill which he had displayed in achieving it.

The young man received commendations thus flattering, from one whose praise was fame, with head uncovered, with eyes flashing beneath their downcast lids, and with a face glowing with a deeper flush than that which the activity of his recent feats had kindled. The veteran general, and the youthful soldier, as they stood in contact and in contrast, exhibited the splendid representation of the men of Ireland's best days.

The great body of the army of Leinster now proceeded to the Fifteen Acres; the vanquished party taking up its ground, in contiguous columns, on the spot where the Chief Secretary's lodge now stands: while the victors diverged to the left, and passing on the rear of the Hibernian military school, halted and piled their arms on the rising ground which overlooks the white houses and ivy-covered church of the village of Chapelizod.

# CHAPTER IV

---

## *The Review (ii)*

Sir, you have wrestled well, and overthrown more than your enemies.

*As You Like It.*

HEATED and animated, with the strong excitement of the combat still fluttering in every heart, and throbbing in every pulse, the Irish brigade and their leader stood at rest along the highest ridge of the acclivity – the gaze and admiration of the multitude, who were crowded along its base in vehicles of all sorts, public and private. It was to this spot, where the mock combat had terminated, that Lady Knocklofty urged her restless steeds, though the ascent was steep and the way encumbered. She had followed the progress of the sham fight with the eye, if not with the science, of a practised tactician. The conspicuous form of the young assailant had seldom eluded her observation, through all the evolutions of the corps: and she had perceived that while, with downcast looks and crimsoned cheek, he stood modestly receiving the eulogies of Lord Charlemont, his furtive glances had more than once been directed towards the spot she occupied. The sight of the lynx, and the scent of the hound, are dull instincts when compared with the rapid perception with which a vain woman detects the admiration she has awakened, and the interest she excites.

She now halted, and drew in half way up the hill, flanked to her right by the line of the Irish brigade, and to the left by a confused mass of gigs, noddies, cars, and private carriages, so as to have all approach cut off on that side where Lady Honoria Stratton was placed. Evidently out of spirits and out of temper, silent and sullen, that lady sat enveloped in a white satin cardinal, which she had drawn round her fine figure; her pouting pretty face just peeping above it, like that charming picture of Miss Farren, in a similar costume, which was once the ornament of every dressing room. The fact was, Lady Honoria had not during the day been fortunate – the Lady Lieutenant had kept many of her own particular men, and one in particular, in constant attendance on her vice-regal progress; and while several young military and some of the household contrived to squeeze their horses between the wheel of the phaeton, and the acclivity fringed by the Irish brigade, for the purpose of paying their homage to Lady Knocklofty, all Lady Honoria's prospects were bounded by an old shattered carriage, whose hind wheel had got fast locked in that of Lady Knocklofty's phaeton – a most ludicrous *mésalliance!*

'This is a capital position,' said Lady Knocklofty, throwing a *batterie d'enfilade* of smiling looks along the line of the Irish brigade, every one of which hit its man. 'This is a capital position, is it not, Honoria?'

'*C'est selon,*' said Lady Honoria, dryly; who as usual, preferred speaking the language she had acquired in the best circles of Paris, to the dialect she had learned in her native mountains.

'How *selon?*' demanded Lady Knocklofty.

'Why, according to the object you have in view.'

'Oh! my object,' replied Lady Knocklofty, laughing, 'is to see the manœuvres in the Fifteen Acres to the best possible advantage?'

'The best manœuvres are not those gone through in the Fifteen Acres,' said Lady Honoria, with a humour in her tone that did not escape her friend's penetration; who, looking in her face, demanded, in the drawling French accent, acquired in her paternal castle in Connaught, from her mother's Swiss maid, '*sur quelle fleur avez-vous marché, ma chère?*'

'*Sur une pensée,*' was the quick reply, with the true *grasseyant* tone of the Faubourg St Germain.

'Apparently,' said Lady Knocklofty, with that acrimony which dear friends in high life will sometimes feel towards each other, 'apparently your "*pensée*" is not "*heart's ease.*" '

'No,' said Lady Honoria, throwing up her meaning eyes to the Irish brigade; 'neither is my *pensée* (or, as the Irish call it, my *pansée*) a *Narcissus.*'

'You are a greater adept in the language of flowers, as in every other' (said Lady Knocklofty coldly), 'than I am; and I confess your meaning escapes my comprehension.'

'I wish I could escape from this atmosphere of bad smells,' said

Lady Honoria, looking round with disgust; 'pah! we have got into a pretty mess here!'

'What the devil, Albina, could have driven you to take up this position?' demanded an authoritative voice from behind the carriage. Both ladies started, and turned round. A gentleman, for whom the two outriders had backed to make way, had got his horse between the hind wheels of the phaeton. He was a tall, fair, slight, cold-looking person, with a phlegmatic countenance and haughty demeanour; but more distinguished by his splendid volunteer uniform, and his blue ribbon and star of St Patrick, than by any other mark of exterior supremacy. It was Lord Knocklofty. Lady Honoria stood up, and leaned over the back of the Phaeton, with a face, from which every trace of ill humour was banished, and was succeeded by radiant smiles. Lady Knocklofty carelessly turned round her head, and without noticing the conjugal inquiry, addressed her steeds with 'Steady now, dears, steady,' continuing to tip their ears with the whip, in a manner to produce a very contrary effect from that her words directed. Lord Knocklofty pressed significantly the fair hand presented to him by Lady Honoria, with the murmured observation of 'How beautiful you are looking to-day!' Then addressing his wife, he added, 'I say, Albina, do get out of this as soon as you can – what could induce you to drive up this hill?'

'To show my learning, as your lordship's coachman calls it,' said Lady Knocklofty, playing with her whip, and smiling archly at 'a case of coxcombs,' who were in waiting by the side of the phaeton.

'Your pedantry you mean,' said Lady Honoria pointedly.

'Exactly,' said Lord Knocklofty; 'you are a witty creature.'

'More witty than wise,' said Lady Honoria, laughing, 'or I should not trust myself with such a neck-or-nothing driver as her ladyship here.'

'Why did you let her scramble up this hill?' added Lord Knocklofty, while his lady was talking to one of her *cavalieri serventi*.

'Needs must' (said Lady Honoria, shrugging her shoulders), 'when the –' she paused and laughed.

'*Devil drives*, of course,' added Lady Knocklofty, sharply, and suddenly turning round. 'But observe, my dear, your coming with me to-day was your own proposition.'

Lady Honoria looked mortified, as if her proposition had been her alternative, between coming in Lady Knocklofty's phaeton, or not coming at all.

'Well, at all events, get out of this as soon as you can,' said Lord Knocklofty; 'and pray don't tease your horses so, Albina.'

'Why, I'm only tipping them the silk,' said Lady Knocklofty, 'just to keep them alive.'

'I'll be d——d but they'll throw you.'

'I'll be d——d if they do,' said Lady Knocklofty, not with Lady Townly's 'gulp,' but with such a look and such a smile, and such an accent that the coarseness of the imprecation was almost neutralized in its utterance, and its very profaneness almost turned into a grace by the dramatic simplicity and archness with which it was given. Such were the manners of the day in Ireland; not so bad, indeed, as in the days of Queen Elizabeth, when fine ladies were wont to *'jurer leur Grand Dieu,'* at every word; nor yet so coarse as when the prettiest lips uttered the broadest *double-entendres* in the days of the Mary Wortleys. Still they were bad enough; *en arrière* with the age, and even in Ireland peculiar to the domineering and ministerial oligarchy, whose lawless power was thus well illustrated by manners as licentious. All the men laughed vociferously at the playful *nonchalance* of Lady Knocklofty's imprecation, who added, in a coaxing tone, to her cold and sullen Lord (himself occupied in listening to some muttered witticisms of Lady Honoria),

'Well, don't be angry, Lord K——, and 'pon honour, and, as O'Mealy says in Macheath, "may my meer slip her shoulder," if I don't escape out of this, as soon as I can extricate myself from this file of carriages.'

'Why, then, long life to your honour, Marram, I hopes you soon will, plaze Jasus, with the help of God; and that your ladyship's honour will just let go my bit of a hind whill, Marram, which you have kotched here behind to the rare.'

This prayer, which produced a general laugh, was uttered by the postillion of an old-fashioned and cumbrous vehicle that seemed of foreign build, except that it was unemblazoned with arms; and as its blinds were drawn up, and the glasses were down, it was probably unoccupied. The ragged postillion, and the miserable cattle he drove, justified all that ever was said, written, or sketched in the broadest spirit of caricature of the genuine Irish posting of the eighteenth century. He was a short, thick-set, sunburnt person, with an old hat on one side of his shock head, and a broken pipe in one corner of his arch mouth. His eye was sly, his visage shrewd, and his attitude, as he sat lack-a-daisically, that of a person, in whom 'patience per force, with wilful choler meeting,' was very humorously obvious. He had preceded his appeal for the emancipation of his hind wheel, by many a supplicating look, first at the captive wheel, and then at the captivating lady, and by many a true Irish 'Och hone!' though he was evidently neither an unamused nor an unwilling auditor of the superior beings with whom he was thus accidentally brought into such close contact; and when he now audibly made his petition, with a look and gesture correspondent to the words, he heard the very general laugh with which it was received by the grandees with the same unaltered air of plaintive supplication which he had all along assumed.

'Famous, by Jove! capital,' exclaimed a pretty boy officer of the Prince's Own, on the watch for Irish fun, expecting a wit in every peasant, and a *bon mot* in every word uttered by the common people. 'Capital! come, we shall have some vastly good fun now. Do draw him out, Lady Knocklofty – now pray!'

'So, friend,' said Lady Knocklofty, 'I see I have got you into a predicament.'

'Perdicament! och! you have, plaze your ladyship; and am'nt the first, I'll engage,' looking archly round at the gentlemen.

'Capital!' said the Prince's Own; 'but I say, why don't you take your pipe out of your mouth, you rascal, when you address a lady?'

'Is it the *dhudeen*, plaze your honour,' taking out the black stump of a pipe, looking at it complacently and then placing it back, between his large white teeth; 'och! then, Sir, so I would, only sorrow puff in it, nor won't till I get back, for want of a spark; barring I might light it at her ladyship's eye.'

'Bravo!' exclaimed the officers, 'bravo! excellent!'

'Very well, indeed,' said Lady Knocklofty, with whom the coin of admiration was always current, pass through what hands it might. 'Come, that's a compliment worth paying for. Oh, Kitty Macguire has my purse. There she is, St Leger, with Captain O'Mealy,' pointing to a fair, fat, fashionable looking girl, in a faded green riding habit, and mounted on a magnificent horse. 'But, stop, who will lend me something? – Lord Knocklofty, Lady Honoria?'

'You know I never carry money,' replied Lord Knocklofty.

'You know I never have any to carry,' said Lady Honoria.

A hundred purses had now 'leaped from their' waistcoat pockets. Lady Knocklofty took Colonel St Leger's (one of the most distinguished members of the Irish court).

'Oh! there is nothing here but gold,' she said, looking into the purse as she drew the strings. 'Stay, here is a seven shilling piece,' and she flung it to the driver, adding, 'there, friend, that's to drink your mistress's health.'

'This is paying for flattery *à poids d'or*,' said Lady Honoria to Lord Knocklofty.

''Tis just like her,' he replied; and then whispering to Lady Honoria, took leave with a '*good bye till this evening;*' for an aide-de-camp had called him off to the Lord Lieutenant.

The driver looked at the bright coin thus carelessly thrown at him; and then in the bright eyes of his generous donor, as if he doubted his good luck. 'Sure I a'n't to keep it all, my lady,' he said, dropping his pipe from his mouth, and throwing an expression of gratitude and delight into his mobile countenance.

'Yes, yes,' said the lady, laughing, 'I don't expect any change.'

'Why then, may I never live to have a happy death, if ever I drive the Castle Knockgarrons again, oncet I get rid of my load.'

'Your load!' exclaimed the ladies and the beaux, fixing their eyes on the close blinded carriage. 'Why, have you any one shut up in that old chaise?'

'Is it in the chay?' (said the man, rubbing his head, with a slight contraction in the muscles of his face), 'sorrow, christian, how would I? Sure thim's returns' (pointing to the horses), 'fresh as they look and nat a hair turned, the animals – ' and he stroked down the necks of the blind and broken-winded beasts, which had scarcely a hair left to turn.

'What do you mean then by getting rid of your load?' said the Prince's Own.

'What do I mane is it, plaze your honour? Why then, what would I mane (scratching his head in evident perplexity), but my own self, Sir? There is many a man would be glad to get rid of himself; and what *bether* way could I do it than in drinking long life to her ladyship's honour there.'

'You mean then' (said Lady Honoria), 'you will get beside yourself as soon as you can.'

'That's just it, long life to your ladyship, mind, and body;' and looking back at his locked wheel with an expression of anxiety, and an evident desire to extricate himself and be off, he added, 'and hopes it's no offence, only just if your Ladyship would back a taste, sure I'd get off in a jiffey.'

'No, no, pray Lady Knocklofty, don't let him go,' exclaimed the

Prince's Own; 'he is worth any thing, he is by far the best fun we have seen since we arrived. I say, Paddy – '

'That's not the name that made a christian of me, plaze your honour.'

'Well then, come, do tell us what *is* your name, my worthy?'

'Barny Houghloghan is the name's upon me, Sir, off you plaze.'

'Well, Barny Orlegan, if you are so impatient to be off, what brought you here, may I ask?'

'What brought me here, is it, Sir! – the cattle did,' said Barny dryly, and smacking his whip.

'Capital!' said the young officer, chuckling; 'and so your horses came to see the review did they?'

'Och, plaze your honour, they are not such asses as that, any how, nor myself neider; we have someting else to be doing, nor to be looking after diversion at this hour of the day, Sir!'

'Then how did you get into the scrape, Bawney?'

'Och, I didn't get in at the scrape at all, but in at the Castle Knock gate shure; to cut across the Phanix, and to shirk that divil's own Knock-maroon hill on the low road; and just made down to the Fifteens, to see if I could not catch a taste of the Castle Knock infantry doing their revolutions, when one sentry driv me here, and another driv me there; and throth, if they'd been army soggers instead of our own volunteers, I wouldn't have been driven out of my own road by any of them: and so they kipt driving me here, and driving me there, till I was fairly driven in amongst the quality; and it's how I came by the great honor of being kotched fast by her ladyship; many a bether man's luck afore me, and will again, plaze God.'

A general laugh followed this allusion, which gained much, by the leer, the look, and the accent, in which it was uttered.

'Well,' said Lady Knocklofty, throwing round her eyes, and drawing out Barney, much less for the amusement of the English beaux, than for the crowd in general, and for the corps of young brigades in particular – 'Well, now I have kotched you, I shall keep you, you may depend on that.'

'Oh, very well, my lady, your honour will do as you plaze with me, and troth I'd ax nothing better, than to stay wid yez all day, only – ' and he looked back at his chaise, and then at his wheel, 'as one perplexed in the extreme;' when suddenly elevating his eye to the Fifteen Acres, and resting it on rather a rustic troop, who were going through their evolutions to the left, he cried out – 'Oh, by the piper that played before Moses, if thim an't the Castle-knocks, and Master Thady, the master's son, at the head of em, in his new regimintals; oh, thim's the boys! I'd back thim, afore any corps in the Phainix;' and seating himself, he continued to follow every movement of his native troops with intense admiration and scrutiny; uttering at intervals exclamations of delight, and shouldering his whip, and following the movements of his friends, with a precision, which evinced that even the postillion of Castle Knock was in heart an Irish volunteer. He was observed, and laughed at, as long as he amused; and then, sharing the fate of other tumblers, in other places, was dropped and forgotten.

Meantime, Lady Honoria was still excluded from the agreeable pastime of flirtation, by a blockade of carriages, and her old flanker the Castleknock; and Lady Knocklofty continued running through her 'tricks of singularity,' fixing every eye, and arresting every ear, within the sphere of her operations. She had missions and commissions for all her *patiti*, civil and military; who were all addressed by name, with a levelling familiarity, which showed no respect for titles and dignities, hereditary or professional. 'Edward Fitzgerald' was sent to his brother Leinster, to beg he would put off the private play at Carton; as she had got the Dean of—— to play Filch, who had to preach at St Patrick's on Sunday; so that his private vocation might not interfere with his public duties. Kilcolman, a young Tipperary Earl (and descendant of one of Charles the Second's playfellows and ministers), was sent on as embassy, such as his ancestor had occasionally undertaken, at Whitehall – with a single violet to the Lord Lieutenant. He hesitated. 'Go, go,' said Lady Knocklofty, significantly; 'he will understand it.' The Tipperary Earl rode off, with the nobility of six hundred years on his back. A handsome young page was dispatched to the Earl, his papa, to procure tickets for a concert at the Rotunda, at which the noble amateur was to take the lead. Colonel St Leger, the 'rose of fashion,' with 'Freddys,' 'Franks,' and 'Phils,' 'all honourable men,' were expedited on various missions; while Manser St George (one of the last and best of the Irish fine gentlemen in Ireland's most brilliant day), was sent to the Duchess, begging permission to bring Lord Charles Fitzcharles, of the Prince's Own, to her grace's *petit souper* and blind-man's buff that evening.

All flew to execute her 'infinite deal of nothings,' with a zeal and readiness which proved that the 'age of chivalry was not yet passed,' in Ireland. Neither was it. The Irish gallantry of that day had indeed the true smack of the chivalry of the old times. A mixed system of devotion and brutality; in which women, alternately treated as sultanas and as slaves, extorted all homage but that of respect; and excited all feelings, save those of tenderness. Adored today, *déaissées* to-morrow, fashion or passion ruled their momentary ascendant; and the old parts of the *roués* of the French court was played to the life by the *roués* of the Irish, who were all little Richelieus and De Grammonts in their way.

A long-drawn inspiration, as the last of her noble estafettes galloped off, indicated that their liege lady was not sorry to get rid of them. The two great ladies and dear friends, in evident *guignon* with each other, sat *dos à dos*. Lady Honoria, again, enveloped in her cardinal, was sulky, and self-concentrated. Lady Knocklofty, with looks and spirits all abroad, hummed an air from the Beggar's Opera; and playing her very pretty foot against the side of her phaeton, slipped it in and out of a little zebra shoe, which was the fashion of the day, and an exact type of a slipper from the seraglio of the Grand Signor.

This movement, conscious or unconscious on the part of the exhibitor, had attracted the eyes, and caused some confusion along the line of the Irish brigade. It more particularly attracted the young leader, who stood in advance of the corps, and who watched the twinkling of the little foot with such a glance as the hawk gives to the fluttering of a young bird nestled near his eiry. The slipper (as might be expected) at last fell to the ground! and the young volunteer, springing from his post, pounced on his pretty prey with a rapidity that distanced all other competitors for the honour of picking it up, and restoring it. With the slipper in one hand, and his cap in the other, he stood beside the phaeton, presenting it gracefully; his colour deepening, and his eyes raised with a look, not confident but intense, to the face of its distinguished owner. Finer eyes might be forgotten; but such eyes, – eyes that awaken emotion, by emitting it, once met, are remembered for ever!

Lady Knocklofty, instead of taking the shoe so respectfully and gracefully offered, looked round for a moment, then putting out her foot, seemed to say by the motion, and the smile more cordial than coquettish, which accompanied it, 'there! you may put it on for your pains!' The look was understood, as it was meant, and the slipper was put on; but with an air of such religious respect, as pilgrims give to the consecrated slipper of St Peter, when first permitted to kiss with 'holy palmer's kiss' the toe of infallibility.

The enviable office performed, the young volunteer bowed, was thanked with smiles, backed, and resumed his post: from that moment, orders ran along the line, and fuglemen figured in vain.

'*Ma belle*,' said Honoria, who had witnessed this silent intercourse of eyes (a drama, whose unities were included in an instant of time), '*Ma belle, avec un tel language on se passe de paroles!*' Lady Knocklofty (still pre-occupied) started, coloured through her rouge, and asked coldly, 'what do you mean, child?'

'Mean, child! why I mean that you seem to think those 'eyes right' there, which you have been endeavouring to set wrong all day, are "*d'assez beaux yeux, pour des yeux de province.*" '

'Yes,' said Lady Knocklofty, flirting her whip and smiling, 'they are terrible eyes, that's the truth of it, Honoria. He is altogether a very fine lad; much superior to the creatures he is hustled among. I wonder who he is?'

'Poh! what does it signify who he is? Of course, as O'Mealy said, he is some young tradesman. If he were *any body*, we could not fail to know him. But, be he who he may, gentle or simple, your permitting him to put on your shoe in this public place, was very foolish. We shall have it all in the "Freeman's journal" to-morrow, with an epigram from Curran, or Lysaght; or it will be sung as a ballad about the streets, with "the Duchess's gig;" and I am sure we are unpopular enough already with the swinish multitude.'

'Nonsense!' said Lady Knocklofty; 'it was all the thing of a moment, and nobody saw it.'

'Every body sees every thing; but my dear Albina,' said Lady Honoria, in an affectionate and admonitory tone, 'I must say you are the most indiscreet person in the world; for you not only take the oddest fancies, but' –

'Oh, come, this is too pleasant,' said Lady Knocklofty, piqued, 'as if you never had *your* fancies, as you call them.'

'Yes, to be sure, I have,' said Lady Honoria, laughing; 'but as Mrs Peachum says, "not with a highwayman, you hussey." Observe, it is as a matter of taste, and not of morals, that I consider these affairs; I am no straitlaced censor, *Dieu le sait;* for with me, as with the world, it is the rank of the parties, not the nature of the contract, that stamps it with indiscretion.'

'Why, yes,' said Lady Knocklofty, pointedly, 'you are tolerably aristocratic in *your fancies*, and none under nobility approaches Mrs Kitty.'

'To be sure,' said Lady Honoria, 'love has no better child's guide than the red book; and the Exchequer is your true Paphos, after all: see, who has governed France for the last fifty years.'

'Do you call that love? I call it calculation,' said Lady Knocklofty, significantly.

'Call it what you please,' said Lady Honoria, colouring slightly; 'but 'tis good taste, *pour le moins;* and that is precisely what you mere home-bred Irishwomen of fashion are perpetually sinning against.'

'We home-bred Irishwomen! And pray, what are you, my dear, pretty, Honoria O'Callaghan, with all your county Cork kindred –

> Pat O'Daisey,
> And Mistress Casey,
> All blood relations to Lord Donoughmore.'

'Why, my dear, to answer you (with a little variation in the text) from Paddy O'Carrol in the 'Register Office,' – It is true, that, as ill luck would have it, 'I comed over to Ireland to be born,' but I was never dipped in the Shannon for all that; and, thanks to my father, have lived too much abroad, not to be fully aware of the absurdities of my native home, since, by divine indignation, I have returned to it. It is a sure sign of barbarism when women make a parade of the vices they have not, and even exhibit more of the virtues they have, than is consistent with decency and *bienséance*. You Irishwomen are all, by temperament, cold and vain; you love display, and there is frequently in your flirting manners and unmeaning *allures*, an absence of taste and a want of keeping, which would in other countries put many a woman in keeping out of countenance. You look, and you sigh, and permit innocent liberties, – all meaning nothing at all, – and then, are rather startled some fine day, when a disappointed admirer turns, heigh presto, into an inveterate enemy; and you find you have lost your reputation, without gaining anything by the sacrifice. For instance, you have been playing off this foolish boy, merely for the pleasure of turning his head; as Mrs Colonel O'Gallagher got her husband broke for throwing his regiment into confusion, at a review in Kilkenny, through her coquetting with the fugleman.'

'Well, and how do you think I have succeeded?' asked Lady Knocklofty, sportively.

'Oh, I dare say you will send the boy back to his school or his shop, utterly unfit for book or business.'

'I believe,' said Lady Knocklofty, 'even if he is what you suppose, it would be difficult to make him now think

A shop with virtue is the height of bliss.'

'Oh, I grant you,' said Lady Honoria, 'that politics and patriotism, and the French revolution, are upsetting all, and playing 'the devil among the tailors.' But again, to quote from your prologue (which, by the by, Mrs O'Neil did not give last night with her usual spirits)-

> To check these heroes, and their laurels crop,
> And bring them back to reason and the shop,

would, for the present, be difficult, while such eloquent demagogues as Curran and Grattan are working on the folly and passions of the lower orders. Pray, however, do not you bring liberty and equality into fashion by your looks and smiles, lest you should, some day, have such a youth as that with the 'terrible eyes,' taking liberties which your quality would not stand; *car c'est le plus grand petit polisson,*' or I am much mistaken. Pray remember, Albina, that there is some one on the ground, and not far off (whose glass is now pointed at you), worth all the Irish volunteers that ever raised the flag of rebellion, or brogued vulgar nonsense in their factious convention – to the edification of their earl and their bishop;[1] and recollect, that for one of those *œillades* that you are throwing away upon that chit with the eyes there, you might command a place in the revenue for your butler, make a captain of the battle-axe of your groom of the chambers, or obtain a pension on the concordatum for that sprig of pauper nobility, your right honourable and ever devoted, but just now not very popular friend, the Lady Honoria Stratton.'

'Poh! my dear Honoria, you know you may have what you please; for if I command the viceroy, you may command one who 'is viceroy over him,' one over whom I have long ceased to have any influence,' and her ladyship sighed.

'I see what you allude to,' said Lady Honoria, 'but upon my honour you are wrong. I amuse Lord Knocklofty, and I aim at no more; and aim at that, only as it gives me the more opportunity of being with you, dear Albina.' The ladies looked in each other's eyes tenderly, and pressed each other's hands sentimentally.

'I love you very much,' said Lady Knocklofty, fondly; 'but you are so severe, so sarcastic with me; you would rather at any time sacrifice a friend, than lose your *bon mot.*'

---

[1] The Earl of Charlemont, and the celebrated Earl of Bristol, and Bishop of Derry, who took a leading part in these conventions.

'To act otherwise,' observed Lady Honoria, laughing, 'Lavater says, entitles one to canonization; and you know, dear, I am no saint. But seriously, you mistake me, dearest Albina; I am only vexed to see your romantic imagination perpetually getting the better of your judgment. Now, tell truth, haven't you conjured up that young volunteer into a regular hero of romance?'

'He has the air of one,' said Lady Knocklofty; 'surely you can't deny that?'

'What, because he is tall, has impudent eyes, and wears no powder! But you are always *dans les hautes aventures*. You know you once fancied your black footman was Prince Lee Boo, which produced that ridiculous scene at the castle, and committed you beyond – '

'I have, at least, never so committed myself as to forfeit my own esteem,' interrupted Lady Knocklofty, her temper rising, in spite of her friendship, at the allusion to Prince Lee Boo – a sore subject. 'And allow me to tell you frankly,' she continued, raising her voice with most unsentimental vehemence –

'Tell me what you please, and as frankly as you will,' said Lady Honoria, in a muttered and rapid tone, 'but don't tell it to me quite so loud, for I suspect we are overheard.'

'Heard, by whom – there is no one near,' said Lady Knocklofty.

'Don't be too sure of that,' said Lady Honoria; 'I much mistake if we have not some close auditors in that old chaise; for I have more than once caught something like a bright eye glancing through the fracture of the old blind.'

While Lady Honoria was still speaking, a sudden jerk was given to the chaise, which occasioned one of the blinds to drop down; and the chaise itself was immediately thrown into rapid motion by the wild gallop of the bare-boned, ill-trained steeds, excited by the smacking whip of Barny Houloghan, who dashing on through thick and thin, overturned a noddy, upset a tim whiskey, threw down an old barrow woman, extricating himself from all obstacles, as he continued his rolling, rattling, jolting, and serpentine course across the park, cleared his way to the gate, and then disappeared; but whether, according to the phrase of romance, 'in the haze of distance,' or in the first ditch that presented itself outside the Park wall, *reste à savoir!*

During the few minutes that the two ladies had been so closely and intimately engaged in their 'colloquy sublime,' Barny, crawling between the two carriages, had contrived to extricate his wheel; and taking advantage of an opening in the file of vehicles, made by the drawing off of the Lady Lieutenant's phaeton, 'which had stopped the way,' he seized the first moment of possible escape, and drove, as the drivers of Irish chaises still drive, in utter contempt of consequences, and a total forgetfulness of the frailty of all sublunary things – wheels, springs, traces, and bridles included.

He was almost out of sight before Lady Knocklofty, drawing breath, observed, in allusion to the discovery made by the dropping of the blind, 'How very extraordinary! Did you ever see such figures?'

'I suspected there was some one shut up in that old chaise from the beginning,' said Lady Honoria.

'There is something very mysterious in this,' said Lady Knocklofty, whose imagination was easily mounted. 'I wish Lord K. had seen them. You know there is 500*l*. offered for taking of Captain Right; and I should not wonder if he was one of those strangely disguised figures – for disguised they certainly were.'

'No, no,' said Lady Honoria, 'there was no Captain Right there; I saw distinctly the far off figure, who sat more prominent than the muffled one next to us. If not the ghost of St Dominick come down in his character of Grand Inquisitor, to reform his own order in Ireland, it is some intriguing monk from France or Spain, some Abbé Hussey, whom my father and I left digging his own grave in La Trappe, and who, the year after, was figuring away as an intriguing diplomatist, between half the courts in Europe. You perceived the old man was tonsured.'

'Yes; and what a countenance!' said Lady Knocklofty. 'It just met my idea of the monk in the Castle of Otranto; but the other creature looked like a female; though it was so veiled and muffled, it was difficult to make it out. Who, and what could they be?'

'Be they who they may,' said Lady Honoria, 'they have heard all we said, and the *frate* may turn our auricular confession to some account. These papists are on the watch for every thing, and would like to have the showing up of one of the Proudforts, their most powerful and inveterate enemies – to say nothing of a squib at a "privy counsellor's wife," or a hit at a "certain beautiful and witty member of the *beau monde*," as the Dublin journal calls me; for it has elected me as its "arch wag," and lays all its trash at my door.'

Here the *tête-à-tête* of the inseparables (as they were called) was interrupted by the accession of some new beaux of the second order, who not being of the official *coterie*, were tolerated, but not distinguished; and who, for want of something else to say, not being initiated, offered the usual common-places discussed upon such occasions: 'A fortunate day for the review – magnificent spectacle – all the evolutions well performed, in good time, and with life – men carried their arms well, marched, wheeled, and formed with exactness – the volunteers performed their manœuvres *but too well;* it was no joke, arming factious citizens,' etc. etc. Their observations, military and political, were cut short by the arrival of a young officer in the Prince's Own, for whom all made way, and who was received by both ladies with significant smiles, exclusively reserved for him, and such as him. It was Lord Charles Fitzcharles, the second son of an English Duke, whose eldest brother, the Marquis of B., was a lunatic, subject to fits, and likely to go off in one of his epileptic paroxysms. Lord Fitzcharles, with all the advantages of so distinguished a position, was ordinary in his person, and *brusque* in his address. He approached the ladies in a familiar and unceremonious manner, with,

'See what a pretty pickle I am in.'

He was covered with dust and spattered with mud.

'Did you ever see such a figure, Lady K.?'

'You look as if you had fallen into the hands of the non-importation confederates, and were tarred and feathered after their most approved fashion,' said Lady Honoria.

'I had a narrow escape indeed,' said Lord Charles; 'for just as I was turning short off by the Phœnix, to escape the four eternal Miss Roistrums, who came galloping down on me full charge, and flanked by four heavy dragoons, my horse took fright, and I was all but ditched and dished by an old ramshackled carriage with a mad driver and mad horses; I believe the devil was in the chaise.'

'Well, we have some reason to think he was,' said Lady Honoria, 'either the devil or a monk.'

'By the by, Lord Charles,' said Lady Knocklofty, 'I have engaged you to the Duchess for this evening; and pray get off your regimentals, and put on a romping frock;[1] we are going to play blind-man's buff at the Castle, in opposition to the Provost's kutch-a-kutch-choo parties, who is obliged to have innocent pastimes for the fellows and their left-handed wives. You must come.'

'I can't indeed; first we cannot go in plain clothes when in garrison,

---

[1] A simple coat of pepper and salt mixture, worn to conceal the impression of powder, by the members of the *haut ton* in Ireland about this period, when romping was the order of the day.

you know, and the chief there; besides, I am particularly engaged this evening.'

'Nonsense! I know there is nothing going on in town this evening. The Duchess expects you, and I command you.'

'Don't signify, I can't to-night, indeed, Lady Knocklofty. I'm in for a frolic, that's the truth of it, a regular set to; the whole party made this week back, expressly – '

'Where, what party? I hope not another drunken bout at Lord Kilcolman's, with those odious Cherokees, who broke all poor Lady Dunshaughlin's new furniture, the other night in Merrion-street.'

'No, I assure you; none of us English belong to that set.'

'Then where can you be engaged this evening? Are you going to play at Daly's? Has the Marquis got in his rents?'

'Don't know at all; but the fact is, we are going to. . . .' Here his lordship lowered his voice, and advanced his head; 'but you won't 'peach, either of you, now will you?'

'Honour bright and shining!' said Lady Honoria, laying her hand on her heart; 'but you must not tell us any thing naughty, mind; you must not do like the man in the gallery, the other night, at the theatre, who put the public into a particular confidence about our viceroy, which it was not good manners to allude to.'

'No, no,' said Seymour, 'it is only a frolic, which the lads of ours have entered into, *en esprit de garnison.* You know that one of us was knocked down by a tavern keeper, the other night; so we are going to take a dinner with him to-day, at the Strugglers, to see fair play, and pay off old scores.'

'The Struggles! what Struggles! where is that?'

'Why, the Strugglers in Wine Tavern-street; a sort of Hole-in-the-Wall, where the Duke and the Chancellor, and some of us, used to go last winter to eat beef-steaks, and drink whiskey punch.'

'Oh, yes! I remember,' said Lady Knocklofty, 'and where *some of you* got into a sad scrape; what was it all about, I forget now?'

'Why, our host of the Strugglers is one of your public spirited tapsters, a captain of volunteers; a legislator, with a musket on his shoulder and a sword by his side; a papist; a defender of the faith, and a leader of the tar and feathering bands! By the by, Lady Honoria, he was of the party by whose patriotic efforts your brother's London-built carriage was *si bien emplumé* last winter.'

'The wretch!' interrupted Lady Honoria, 'and who broke poor dear Madame Tournon's windows, in Dawson-street, and carried off her cargo of Lyons' silk and soufflet gauze, because it was not Irish poplin; well?'

'Well, but really I ought to get O'Mealy to tell you the story; we English always spoil your Irish stories, like the dull fellow in Joe Miller; and the long and the short, you know.'

'No, no, go on,' said both ladies, who loved gossipry, '*plus que vépres ou sermon.*'

'Well, it happened, that this host of the Strugglers abandoned the spigot and fosset for a review at Drogheda, was billeted upon some house where the guests were more numerous than the *couverts;* so that the captain, more hungry than ceremonious, after a long march, was caught helping himself, by such means as were resorted to before the invention of knives and forks.'

'Oh, the nasty beast!'

'But here comes the best of it. The supreme council of volunteer *bon ton* (for the volunteers are all gentlemen, by Jasus, and use knives and forks like other folk, while acting (that is ating), under the eye of all Europe, as the Belfast manifesto has it), after a court-martial, presided by the only officer who is a private gentleman in the corps, pronounced sentence of "ungentlemanlike conduct at table" on the primitive *gustateur;* and he was forbid to bear arms for ten months, for not having borne them at a dinner, taken *au bout du banc.* Meantime, as the captain's politics and politesse had nothing to do with his excellent beef-steaks, we had a scramble there a week or two ago; and the captain's wife, who always serves up the first dish, happening to be "as pretty a piece of flesh," as the man in the play says, as any – '

'In her own larder,' interrupted Lady Honoria, 'and quite as *mangeable* as her own beef-steaks, I suppose.'

'Exactly,' said Lord Seymour, laughing; 'and it did happen, that one of us stepping down to the bar for a glass of Tokay – for the fellow keeps choice wines – and being, I rather believe, something more gallant than this Brutus of the Strugglers thought right or proper——, I don't know how it was, but in the struggle, the Struggler knocked one of us down. A row ensued, in which the Struggler had the best of it; and when a complaint was made to the colonel commandant of his corps, not only no notice was taken of the insult, but the fellow was restored to his company, and permitted to figure away here to-day in the face of the lord-lieutenant, and the very noblemen and gentlemen he had so grossly insulted. Now it happens, my valet has bespoke a dinner at the Strugglers, to which a few friends are invited;

and, as I rather think there will be some fun, I suspect we shall not be in a plight for her Grace's party of blindman's buff, afterwards.'

'No,' said Lady Honoria, 'for I dare say many of you would have the advantage of us, by seeing double, instead of not seeing at all.'

'Take care, though,' said Lady Knocklofty; 'you will, I fear, get into a scrape; I hate those *frolics*, in which the common people are concerned.'

'Oh, my dear,' interrupted her friend, 'there is no interfering with public duties; and, truth to tell, a little summary justice after the manner of the "tarrers and featherers" themselves, is no bad thing. It is just as well to meet them sometimes on their own ground.'

'Exactly,' said Lord Charles; 'Lady Honoria is quite right. Lady Knocklofty, do your horses stand fire? We shall have the thirty-six rounds before these heroes have done. – Ay, there they go; now for it, *tenez ferme*.'

Her ladyship's answer was lost in the first volley which was fired; the horses stood it well, but with a little pricking of ears, and curvetting of hoofs. The firing now continued by companies, by grand divisions, by subdivisions, obliquely, advancing, and retreating, then by files and in squares, and finally concluded in one tremendous volley, which burst with a crash that resembled the explosion of a volcano. The too spirited steeds of the reckless Lady Knocklofty, overfed and under-worked, were startled by the shock, and plunged forward, breaking the traces. Loosely reined, wild, and unmanageable, they dashed down headlong among the troops, with a fearful velocity that scattered all before them, till they were lost in the dense smoke of the artillery, which left the fate of the two ladies in doubt. None of their *cavalieri serventi* had the presence of mind to go to their rescue, till their interference was too late; and when the smoke cleared off, the anxious spectators of this fearful accident were relieved by seeing the horses at rest in the plain below, panting and foaming, but quiet; their heads held by the leader of the Irish brigade, who was coolly directing the groom to adjust the traces. He had sprung down the acclivity, at the first plunge made by the unruly animals, had thrown himself before them in their wild career, and had all the success in his efforts to save the ladies, which such skill, courage, and presence of mind rarely fail to obtain.

The two ladies, though frightened into a misprision of hysterics, had not fainted. They had firmly and wisely held their seats; and as nerves were not the order of the day, and dashing was, they exhibited a fearless contempt of the danger they had escaped, which was ill borne out by their pale faces and quivering lips. The peril over, the phaeton (whose gaudy panels were either broken or disfigured) was surrounded by gentlemen. Among others, the Lord Lieutenant, and Lord Knocklofty were in anxious attendance, the latter on his wife's friend, and the former on his friend's wife. After a due application of Eau de Luce and Sal Volatile, provided from the sumptuary pocket of Miss Macguire (who with Captain O'Mealy and a party of horsemen and horsewomen had ridden up to the heroines of the catastrophe, with sympathetic look and smelling bottles), the two ladies were conveyed to a chariot in waiting belonging to her Excellency, who had driven up to make her inquiries in person. The carriage drove on, accompanied for a few paces by the Duke and Lord Knocklofty; each with a hand on the window near which they rode.

'Lady Honoria,' said Lord Knocklofty, 'you had better go to Knocklofty House with Albina. The sooner you get some hartshorn and water the better.'

'Had they not better go to the lodge?' said the Lord Lieutenant, with equal solicitude in his manner.

'No, no,' said Lady Knocklofty, 'pray let me go home. But first, I beseech you, Lord Knocklofty, go to that gallant young gentleman, who is still standing at the horses' heads, and thank him for the service he has rendered us; and pray get his address; for' (added her ladyship, who, like Maritornes, had occasionally some sketches and shadows of Christianity about her), 'under God, I do believe we owe the preservation of our lives to his timely and courageous interposition.'

'Yes, yes,' said Lord Knocklofty, without turning his head towards the spot where the gallant gentleman stood, 'Yes, yes, I'll see to that; but get home as soon as you can; you know we dine at the Castle. To Knocklofty House,' cried out his lordship, authoritatively, to the postillion.

'Farewell,' said the Duke, 'till this evening;' and the gentlemen rode off.

As Lady Knocklofty passed her dismantled phaeton, she pulled the check-string violently, and called out 'O'Mealy,' with a shrill and commanding voice, that was instantly obeyed by the Captain, who was following Lord Knocklofty.

'O'Mealy,' she said, 'go after that young gentleman in the green uniform, who is now walking towards the striped tent; don't fail to get his address, and tell him Lady Knocklofty is fully aware, that she owes her life to his gallant interposition, and that she hopes he will give her an immediate opportunity of expressing her gratitude *de vive voix.*'

'I *shawl*, Lady Knocklofty,' returned the Captain.

The carriage drove on.

'*De viv waw*,' repeated Captain O'Mealy, removing his large cocked hat from three hairs on the left side of his head, to three hairs on the right (a motion that always expressed the Captain's perplexity). – '*De viv waw*: well, the women of quality are the "very queens of the dictionary," as Sir Lucius says;' and looking round, he found to his infinite satisfaction that the 'young gentleman' had disappeared. Anxious to sidle into the suite of the Lord Lieutenant, by following in the wake of his patron, Lord Knocklofty, he galloped on to overtake the party, and insinuated himself between two young aide-de-camps. As he rode along the quays, wholly forgetful of his *protégée*, Miss Maguire, he pulled up his stock, shifted his hat, and threw a reconnoitring look, to discover if his brilliant position did not render him the observed of all observers. Occasionally, as he rode along, he repeated to himself, '*de viv waw* – I shall thank him *de viv waw* – I suppose that's Frinch for getting him a place or a pinsion, for saving her life. Well, to be sure, what luck I had, to be sent foostering and gostering after the honourable Kitty, when if I had been left alone to mind my business and stay where I was, I might have been thanked *de viv waw*, and sent down a brigade major to Ennis; or made collector of St Grellan at laste; who knows?'

# CHAPTER V

---

## *The Row*

Sa jeunesse fait tant de bruit qu'il n'entend pas.

MAD. DE SEVIGNE.

Now, Master Shallow, you'll complain of me to the king.

*Merry Wives.*

IN the year 1770, when the penal statutes were in all their fearful force, Dublin (some of its aristocratic palaces excepted) was a city of lanes and alleys, of cribs and dens; whose filthy avenues swarmed with a squalid and mendicant population; and whose trading streets exhibited but few images to cheer the eye, or to exhilarate the heart. From the year 1782, however, the city rose from its rubbish, and the hovel of mud became a palace of marble. It was from this period, that the partial amelioration of the terrific code, the influence of national independence, and the establishment of a free trade, awoke the spirit of the people. The ancient capital of 'one of the most beautiful countries under heaven,' as Spenser designates it, then began to acquire the aspect, and to exhibit the splendour of a metropolitan city. Then its dark lanes and narrow courts gave way to spacious streets and beautiful quays, where the air of heaven was permitted to circulate, and its blessed light to shine. Then edifices in the best taste, at once noble and simple, were erected for public use, or for individual enjoyment. The change was not operated by the despotic wisdom of some sagacious tyrant, but by the partial abolition of bad laws, and the limited introduction of enlightened principles.

While, however, the north and east shores of the beautiful river which winds through the Irish metropolis became crowned, as if by magic, with all the pomp of architecture, the west (or that part of old Dublin which once was enclosed by its fortified walls, including the castle, law courts, cathedrals, and the houses of the few gentry who anciently possessed mansions in the capital), remained but little changed. Here were yet to be found the wrecks and relics of the houses of the Geraldines, the Pettys, the Boyles, the O'Briens, and such of the chiefs of English and of Irish descent as had dropped into the lines of fealty. Even within view of the attic saloons of Moira House (then the Montague House of Dublin), might still be seen some of those ancient edifices of cage work and timber, covered with tiles and shingles, whose high pointed gables and pending balconies threatened destruction to the pedestrian passing beneath, – while they riveted the eyes of the antiquarian, and furnished the pages of the modern Stanihursts with some of their most interesting items.

One of these houses, a mansion of some extent, still stood upon that 'voyd piece of ground' then called Lord Galway's walk, and now denominated the military road. Old and dilapidated as it then was, a more delightful *rus in urbe* could scarcely be imagined, than it must have been in former times. It hung over the banks of the Liffey, commanded a long sweep of river scenery, with the rising and wooded grounds of the beautiful park on the opposite side. From its casements in the rear, it looked upon the mountains of Dublin, which gradually break down into the green and fertile plains that lie at their base.

If its rural beauties were many, its town advantages had not been few. It lay in the neighbourhood of the metropolitan cathedral and of the old law courts, – a spot which the litigiousness of the age rendered the focus of the vital interests of the land. It was at no great distance from the Tholsel or Toll-stall, the tribunal for petty delinquencies and small litigations, where all tolls on provincial commodities were paid. The edifice itself was not lofty, but lengthy; resembling the old black and white framework houses of old English towns. It was roofed with tiles, spotted with little casements, and was entered by an archway, disproportionately low and narrow. Along the breadth of the building was inserted a stout broad beam of Irish oak, on which was cut an inscription with armorial bearings perfectly legible, save where an upright piece of timber being mortised in the wall, had received the drippings of a projecting spout, fixed in the roof, and consequently was something rotted. The inscription was, 'VICTORIA MIHI,

CHRISTUS;' and an escutcheon of arms followed, with the date 16—-, and the united initials of M. M. O. B.

The house had been called, time immemorial O'Brien's Inn, nobody knew why; but every one supposed, that some one had kept an inn there 'in the ould times,' at the sign of the O'Brien Arms: for none but the learned knew (and they were then few), that *inn* (the translation of the French hotel) was the designation of all noble houses in former days, both in England and Ireland. O'Brien's inn had, in fact, been the residence of that branch of the O'Brien family, of which the celebrated Murrogh, Lord Inchiquin, a General in Cromwell's army, was the last lineal descendant. He was stigmatized by the name of *Murrogh an Tothaine*, or the incendiary, by the sect, family, and party he had deserted. Here Lord Inchiquin retired after the battle of Cashel, where he had earned his infamous *agnomen;* and the venerable mansion had been constantly inhabited by some one of the Brien family, until about a quarter of a century back, when it had fallen into litigation between two claimants. Since that epoch, the sturdy old fabric had, for the most part, remained uninhabited; save by an old crone, who occupied a dark room on the ground floor, and who (with the shelter of its roof for her hire) acted as housekeeper to the desolate building, and lived by the mendicity of her little grandchild.

While modern buildings rose on every side, O'Brien's inn stood, in its solitary and antiquated pride of gables and casements, like an old dowager in her hoop and *tête de mouton*, in the midst of a group of young beauties in adhesive draperies and braided tresses. In spite of the pious inscription, the premises had a bad name. There existed against it, and against the old woman who kept it, that natural prejudice, which is usually felt against all old women and old houses.

The old woman was asserted to be (on the authority of a Kilkenny carrier) no other than the famous Alice Ketyll, the traditionally celebrated witch of that ancient city, where

> Fire without smoke,
> Air without fog,
> Water without mud,
> And land without bog,

certainly do indicate the influence of some supernatural agency.

As, however, tradition does not trade in dates, no one knew the precise period when Alice had flourished; but every one knew that she had been cited and condemned by a Bishop of Ossory, for heresy and sorcery; that she had a certain attendant spirit called Robin Artyson; that she had killed 'in a certayne fourward way,' nine red cocks – had swept the streets of Kilkenny with besoms, 'between complin and curfew; ' and that two of her accomplices had worn the devil's girdle about their bodies, for which they were burnt, by order of the bishop and council; while Alice, mounted on her cowltre (an anointed stick), made her way without let or molestation.

From that time Alice Ketyll was never heard of, till more than a century or two afterwards, when she was *déterrée* by the Kilkenny carrier, who passed O'Brien's inn every Monday, on his way in and out of town; where he had seen her sweeping the pathway with a besom, after the old fashion, 'between complin and curfew.' The hue-and-cry, once raised against the old woman, had a deathless echo in the neighbourhood of Watling-street, and Lord Galway's walk; and persecution again raised its bloody arm, not indeed to light brands and erect stakes, but to throw rotten eggs at the old woman, and pelt stones at the casement of the old house. It was in vain that Alice's ex-groom of the chamber, Robin Artyson (a poor, half-starved, naked little boy), declared that his name was Dennis Mooney, and that Alice Ketyll was old Molly Mooney, his grandmother, for whom he had begged half-pence at the Tholsel steps every day. Whenever Alice put out her squalid head 'between complin and curfew,' eggs were pelted and stones were thrown: and if she was no longer cited before deans and condemned by bishops, to be burned alive, or driven as a last resource to the cowltre, it was because public opinion had taken another direction; and because the current of prejudice, which once had set so strong against heretics and witches, had turned into another channel, and was, with equal wisdom and policy directed against papists and popery. For the last ten years, however, Alice and her grandson Robin, had lived peaceably in the service of the lord and occupant of the old mansion, its triumphant claimant and present owner.

Lord Arranmore, an old nobleman, of the old Irish stock, was of recluse and singular habits. Much more celebrated than known, he had distinguished himself by the pertinacious pursuit of a title (long gone astray in his family, and recently revived in his person), and by some ingenious antiquarian papers he had contributed to the trans-actions of the Royal Irish Academy, of which he was the most learned and indefatigable member. For the rest, his lordship led much such a life as Seneachys and annalists of old – buried in the past, unconnected with the present – the world forgetting, and long since by the world forgot. His habits of seclusion were indeed so ascetic, as to be beyond even what a taste for studious solitude might inspire; and it was probable that this retreat from the world was superinduced by a recent mortification, publicly inflicted by order of the Herald at Arms. His armorial supporters were effaced from the old vehicle he sometimes exhibited in the streets of Dublin, though his claims to the peerage had been allowed by the House of Lords. As, however, he had been accused of being a relapsed papist, the insult was neither unprecedented nor extraordinary.

It was on the evening of the great review at the Phœnix Park, and some time after the corps had all been dismissed, and the crowd which this brilliant and national spectacle had collected for the last time had been dispersed, that the young leader of the Irish brigade, the victor of the Star Fort, presented himself at the door of the old edifice of Lord Galway's walk. It was slowly and cautiously opened by Robin Artyson in *propria persona*, who, but for his gorgeous crimson livery, oddly contrasted by his naked legs and feet, might have passed for the evil spirit whose name he still bore.

'Is my father returned,' was the question put to him, as the young volunteer, striding rapidly up the broad, low, creaking stairs, entered a dreary, comfortless chamber in the attic.

'My lard's not at home,' was the drawled out and mechanical answer.

The intelligence seemed not to displease the hearer. Making a somewhat hasty and partial ablution (a necessary refreshment after the heat and dust of the day), he drew the costly robe, appropriated by the university to its noble members (the *filii nobiles*), over his volunteer uniform; and exchanging his plumed helm for a square and tasselled cap, gave one glance into a ponderously set mirror, and was just issuing forth, when he suddenly turned back.

'Where is your mother, Robin?' he demanded.

'My moder! Is it my granny? Sure she's in bed.'

'She is not ill, I hope?' was the kind inquiry.

'Och, she is nat; only a weight at her heart.'

'Robin, you need not mention my having dressed here for the review this morning, except the question is directly put to you.'

'I will nat,' said Robin, shaking his head importantly.

'And should Mr Emmet inquire for me – You know Mr Emmet, Robin?'

'I do nat,' said Robin.

'Well, should any gentleman inquire for me this evening, say – but, stay;' and not daring to trust to the stupidity of one, whose intellect had been only awakened to extortion, and whom indigence had almost stultified to idiotism, he tore off the back of a letter and wrote – 'In my chamber till nine – at the historical society till ten;' and giving the paper to Robin, he desired him to give that to any young gentleman who might inquire for him.

'And mind, Robin,' he added, putting his finger upon his smiling lip, 'not a word of the review.'

'Nae, nae,' said Robin, with a grin, meant to be significant, but which was only ghastly: and eagerly pocketing the shilling slipped into his hand, he hastily slapped to the door.

With the rapidity of a shooting star, the student of the Dublin university, and captain of the Irish brigade, hurried back to his *Alma Mater*. He had already proceeded more than half way, when his sword, by impeding his movements, and nearly throwing him on the pavement, betrayed the hurry of thought, which had led him to commit so palpable an *étourderie*, as to retain it. He was returning with incredible velocity to deposit, in the attic of the old house, an implement so little suited to his academic exterior, when his steps were retarded, and his curiosity was attracted by a tumultuous assembly round the porch of an ancient and popular tavern, called the Strugglers.

The house stood on that old up-hill part of Dublin, which, opening to the Quays of the Liffey, still preserves its antiquated name of Wine Tavern-street. The host of the Strugglers, to whose private room the College boys sometimes stole to indulge in furtive potations, was a noted character, and had all those claims to popularity with one party, and to persecution from another, which then gave celebrity to individuals even of the humblest class. The moment also was one of great excitement. While the Irish senate was the scene of contention to the most stormy passions, the arena where the most powerful intellects were drawn out in the fiercest opposition, – while the walls of either house re-echoed to the eloquence of the most eloquent men that Ireland or any other country ever produced, – the people wanted no factious tribune to plead their lowly cause, or express their vulgar wisdom. Associated for the preservation of interests, then misunderstood by all classes, the manufacturing part of the community added to this general ignorance, a deep and irritating sense of suffering, which is apt to lead astray the best informed. Goaded by want, and

by the heart-rending conviction of the impossibility of finding employment for their skill and industry, they occasionally exercised a
summary vengeance on those whom they deemed the violators of the
national interest; and these violences rendered an association illegal,
which in its formation was intended for the most legitimate purposes
of self defence.[1] The melancholy feature in this case was, that the
government secretly fomented the very intemperance it affected, by
unconstitutional means, to restrain. If, at least, no preconcerted plan
of getting up a tumult can be brought home to the door of the
executive, it is notorious that the riots were aggravated by the imprud-
ence of what was significantly called the Castle party. Military force,
too often substituted for the civil power, irritated the popular resentment; and widened a breach which had for some time existed between
the English soldiery and the Irish populace; while it gave a sanguinary
character to disturbances, which of themselves would have been bloodless and unimportant.

The contests between the populace and the military, were now of
daily and fatal occurrence; and even the officers of some of the *crack
regiments*, quartered in the garrison of the capital, had been known to
mingle in the popular broils, and in more than one instance to have
found no unequal opponents in the students of the Dublin University,
– a body which for more than half a century had composed a very
formidable branch of the *social order* of those dislocated times.

[1] In the general depression of the manufacturing interests, the people then looked
(as many, not of the people, still look), for relief, to what is called the encouragement
of domestic manufactures; – that is, to the voluntary or compulsory preference of dear
or bad articles, of home manufacture, to better or cheaper goods brought from abroad.
The non-importers, in the pursuit of this mischievous chimera, destroyed the foreign-
made dresses, equipages, etc., which appeared in the streets of Dublin, – insulted and
outraged the persons who used them, – and attacked the houses of the great importing
merchants.

The causes of the depressed state of Irish manufactures are multifarious; of which,
the wicked and execrable destruction of the Irish woollen manufacture, a sacrifice to
English jealousy, if not the chief, is perhaps the original. In compensation for this act
of violence, various experiments have from time to time been made by Government
and by the upper classes, for introducing other manufactures, which wold spontaneously
have found their own way into existence, had the circumstances of the country been
adapted to their exercise. Such attempts, therefore, have at best had but a partial
success; by which numbers of starving struggling wretches have been called into being,
where there were no permanent and assured means of their support. Bad governments
are never so mischievous as when they turn sentimental, and interfere with the private
and pecuniary interests of the subject, under the notion of relieving distress.

The actual riot at the Strugglers was one of those outrageous frolics, in which the idle, the powerful, and the dissipated of the Irish capital were, at this period, wont too frequently to indulge.

Originating in the licentious gallantry of the noble cornet alluded to by Lord Fitzcharles, in the morning's conversation with Lady Knocklofty, it was not a little increased by the part which the host was well known to have taken in a recent broil between the military and a party of the non-importation confederates.

As yet the mob without (consisting chiefly of tradesmen and artisans returning home from their work) appeared much less interested than amused with what was passing in the house; and the spectacle of flying bottles and broken decanters, in a combat not very unequally carried on between the 'familiars' of the Strugglers and its military guests, excited less wrath than merriment. When, however, the handsome hostess, with dishevelled hair and clasped hands, appeared at an upper window, and with true feminine and Irish eloquence called for aid and protection, declaring to God and upon her honour, that that honour had been insulted by the impertinent gallantry of the English officers, who had incarcerated her husband in his own cellar, and were reducing his property to ruin, because he was a volunteer and a non-importation man – then a new impulse was given to popular feeling, a portentous movement was visible in the crowd, and the cry of 'Shame! shame!' resounded on every side.

'*Shame on those who stand by to witness such an outrage!*' exclaimed the young collegian, who had pushed his way to the very heart of the multitude, and who, rushing forward, sprung through a breach made in the bar window by one of the rioters within. His example had an electric influence. The mob wanted but an individual to lead them to the attack. The outworks were soon carried; and the assailed, who had thrown themselves in the entry to defend the keep (the cellar, where the host lay, confounded among his own broken bottles), were driven from their posts in various directions; the host was liberated by his young brother volunteer, and a skirmish took place between the combatants (at first more ludicrous than serious), as the 'rank-scented people' engaged hand to hand, and breast to breast, with the trim and perfumed heroes of the 'Prince's Own.' 'No military murderers!' 'No English importation men!' 'Trinity boys for ever!' and other party watch-words, inapplicable to the event, but not to the spirit of the affray, filled the air and enlisted new partisans. Still the efforts of the mob and of its young and gallant leader went no further than the most decided manual endeavours to clear the premises of the dashing Tarquins, whose deeds of violence the Lucretia of the Strugglers had scarcely exaggerated.

Dislocated chairs, shattered glasses, and smashed windows, broken-headed waiters, and screaming barmaids, denoted the feats of these military '*brise-maisons*,' who, ripe for a row, and primed with claret, gave, by their shouts of laughter and ill-timed pleasantries, the character of a frolic, to what was in fact becoming a very shameful outrage. At first, they had received the allies of the Strugglers upon the equal terms of animal strength; and clenched fists, and squared elbows, a well flung bottle, or a better directed blow, rendered the combat as yet both fair and equal; but when the brute force of the unwashed artisans began to prevail over the science of the patrician '*élèves*' of Mendoza, then it was that the temper of the higher powers wholly gave way. Taking close order and making a desperate rally, at the moment when they were nearly ousted, they imprudently and intemperately drew their swords on the unarmed populace; and a sanguinary and unequal conflict instantly began, which threatened the worst consequences.

The young collegian, who had hitherto stood 'a keen encounter' with many a well directed fist, and returned every attack with interest, now remembered the sword which had hung forgotten at his side; and throwing himself at the head of the mob, he stood in the gap of a door-way, and kept at bay more than one well armed assailant, until the populace effected their retreat into the street. Unfortunately, at that precise moment, when the enraged and bleeding people were preparing for a renewed attack, a non-importation confederate company, returning from a 'tar and feathering' expedition, fell in with the combatants. No preliminaries were necessary to the making a common cause – 'Rebellion lay in their way. and they found it;' and the new allies, reeking from their recent triumphs, were about to bestow the *beaux restes* of their unsated rage on the English party, when a military guard, accompanied by a strong civil power, who had been sent in search of 'the tar-and-featherers,' overtook them at this precise spot and moment. The soldiers saw at once the danger of their officers, and in a natural *esprit de corps*, though as yet unattacked themselves, fired without orders on the uproarious multitude. One of the populace fell dead; a few were wounded; some fled, hotly pursued by the military; others stood their ground, and in their turn were again forced to retreat. In amount twenty times the number of the military

– savage with rage and indignation, and 'all smarting with their wounds' – they tore up the pavement and pelted the soldiers with that favourite missile, with which the Irish have ever done so much execution. Again the soldiers fired, and the echo of their shots was answered by shouts of execrations, and by showers of stones. The civil power interposed in vain, and confusion and carnage reigned on every side.

One conspicuous figure, towering above the rest, still kept the *devant*, and by his savage shouts and Irish cries served as a rallying point, giving spirit and force to the popular party, which however he appeared to have only accidentally joined. In external appearance, he resembled none of those by whom he was surrounded, and was evidently a stranger from some remote district of Connaught or Munster. Wild, weird, gaunt, bloody, half-naked, and apparently half mad, he continued to move steadily on towards some given point. With wondrous strength and dexterity, he whirled a thick, long, twisted pole above his head, and occasionally let it fall with a fatal force on whatever opposed his way. He shouted in Irish as he moved along, '*Faere ghem! – Faere ghem!*' – '*O'Brien aboo!*' – '*Lamblaider aboo!*' – '*Faere, faere, mi cuishleen!*'[1] – and other incoherent exclamations, sometimes addressed to the mob, and sometimes to the young collegian, towards whom, with all his strength and agility, he was in vain endeavouring to make his way.

The collegian himself (the next prominent figure in the conflict) stood in the foreground of the fight, grappling hand to hand, and breast to breast with the officer who had been the primary cause of all this tumult, and who, having lost his own sword, was endeavouring to wrest that of his opponent from his firm and nervous grasp. Between these combatants there was no disparity, they were well and gallantly opposed. Each had insulted and struck at his adversary in the beginning of the affray; and as they now in their youthful strength and passionate vindictiveness wrestled for life or death, they appeared like two young vultures, intent on tearing out each other's hearts from the breasts in which they panted. Heads tossed back, teeth gnashed, eyes fixed, with fury in their glances, pain unfelt, danger despised, the instinct of carnage in full and fearful development, would have given the conflict a poetical character, on another site, and in another cause,

---

[1] 'Watch, watch, the cause of the O'Briens, the cause of the strong hand, etc., watch, my heart's vein.'

than those, on which such courage and such energies were now so uselessly and perniciously displayed.

This single combat in the midst of more vulgar conflicts, attracted the attention of all who were not deeply engaged in their own defence. Such tranquil spectators were chiefly composed of the occupants of windows, and of the old projecting balconies, suspended in front of the cage-work houses, then still standing in Wine Tavern-street.

Immediately next to the Strugglers (itself a very ancient edifice), stood a formless building, which but for its waving gables above, and its bricked-up arches below, might have passed for the high, dead wall of a state prison. One small grated casement alone diversified its gloomy surface, behind whose iron bars some restless object seemed agitated with a perpetual motion, like that of a wild animal in his cage. The figure was not only human, it was female; and as the dreary *masure* was the rear of a convent of Franciscan nuns, and the casement (the only one which looked on the 'busy haunts of man') belonged to the abbess's own apartment, she probably was the pious and restless spectatress of this sanguinary fray. Her curiosity was well repaid by the evidence it must have furnished of the wisdom of her retreat from the world, where human passions were still in such baneful and reckless activity.

Meanwhile, a hundred voices continued to cheer the collegian; and the champion of the military party had, by an effort of great dexterity, nearly wrested his sword from his grasp, when the protecting demon of the Irish cause reached the spot on which they contended. Whirling his long pole over his own head, he was about to let it fall on that of his destined victim, when the generous collegian, perceiving the treacherous attack as it was made, summed up all his strength, and throwing back the officer into the porch of the house, saved his life, and permitted the pole to fall innoxiously on the resounding pavement. Shouts of plaudits followed; and reiterated cries of 'The college boys for ever,' 'Long life to the Trinity, and the glorious Volunteers,' filled the air.

At length the civil force, which, with many of the chief authorities, had been involved in the pell-mell confusion of the first heat of the riot, began to prevail; owing to the courage and influence of one of the principal and most popular magistrates of the day. He had thrown himself between the military and the people, at the risk of his life; and by his eloquence, his promises, and his exertions, finally succeeded in checking the further progress of a tumult, which might otherwise have terminated in an insurrectionary movement. The soldiers, who had mingled in the affray, were marched back to their barracks; the young officers, whose frolic had began it, were put under an arrest; a general dispersion of the mob followed; and the ringleaders only, who had mingled in the row from the beginning, were pointed out by spies of the police, and taken up, to be reserved as examples of justice. At the head of these was the collegiate captain of the Irish Brigade, who had led on the mob, at the commencement of the combat. For him was reserved the distinction of being arrested by the sheriff in person, as he stood carelessly before the porch of the Strugglers, wiping the blood from his wounded forehead with one hand, while, panting and heated, he leaned on his sword with the other.

'That is the young collegian that was the first to enter the bar window, plaze your honour,' said a policeman, in the train of the sheriff. 'Sorrow stir the mob stirred, till he led the way, your worship.'

'You must give up your sword, young gentleman,' said the sheriff, addressing his prisoner.

'To you, Sir, certainly,' said the youth, coolly presenting it.

'I am sorry,' said the sheriff, 'to see the sword of an Irish volunteer so used, and the dress you wear, and the rank it bespeaks, so disgraced.'

'Disgraced!' reiterated the collegian, turning round indignantly.

'Constables, take your prisoner to the watch-house,' said the sheriff coolly, and walked on to a spot, to which he was summoned by the springing of a legion of rattles; where he found one of the guardians of the night struggling in the fearful grasp of a gaunt and gigantic figure. At the approach of the sheriff and his party, the savage let go his hold, and dashing down his prey upon the earth, fled with a velocity that distanced all pursuit.

While the young student was gathering his torn robe round him, and stepping forward to proceed with his guard, his military antagonist was led forth from the Strugglers, under an escort. Their eyes met.

'Lord Charles Fitzcharles, Prince's Own, Royal Barracks,' whispered the latter. 'Murrogh O'Brien, Trinity College,' was the reply of the former; and both passed on, the one over Queen's-bridge, to his quarters, the other along the quays, to that 'durance vile' of heroic spirits, a watch-house.

It was now a dark and foggy twilight; the sun, which sets with so fine and picturesque an effect behind the last bridge over the Liffey, had sunk portentously in black and lurid clouds. A premature obscurity had already involved the worst lighted city in the empire. The shops and houses in the neighbourhood of the riot, had been shut up at an early hour, and the mob and military, spreading consternation in their flight and pursuit, as a shout was raised, or as a musket went off, had so completely cleared the streets of pedestrians and carriages, that the capital at nine o'clock had the desolate and deserted aspect, which it was wont to assume in troubled times. In the previous morning the volunteer review had furnished an excuse for recreation to the most pleasure-loving citizens of any capital in the world. All had been bustle, light, and life: now all was gloom, silence, and apprehension. The great bell of the university, tolling out the ninth hour (that hour in the Irish university over which care holds no control[1]), swung its deep tones over the still and empty streets, as solemnly as if it were the vesper bell of a convent of the blessed Virgin, pealing through the silent cloister of the monastery of Hogges-green.[2]

The youthful prisoner (who had so acted, as inevitably to place himself under the ban of that rigid institution, whose discipline that bell announced) heard not its warning voice. He was now insensible to all external impressions. 'The tempest in his mind' solely occupied him. Agitated and preoccupied, his heart fluttering, his chafed blood all on fire, he paced on, in the centre of his guards, with a firm and rapid step. His arms were carelessly folded in tattered gown, and his square cap was worn over his left eye, as if in defiance; but in fact was so worn, to check the drops which oozed from a scar in his temple. There was nothing in his bearing that corresponded with an appearance so pitiable, and a position so perilous; and it might have been supposed, to judge by his air and motions, that a triumph, and not a prosecution, awaited him. A flashing eye – a distended nostril – an occasional haughty toss of the head – and a tone of voice, which, whether replying to, or demanding a question of the guard, who almost 'toiled after him in vain,' had something scoffing and disdainful in its accent, – spoke one worked on by powerful excitements, and intoxicated by that exaltation of the mind, which raises its subject above all sensible impressions, and leaves even physical pain unheeded, if not unfelt.

---

[1] This bell formerly summoned the students of the university to the October cellar, where a potation, equal to the far-famed Trinity audit ale of Cambridge, was distributed.

[2] Hogges Green, now called College Green, from being the site of the University, was, down to the commencement of the 17th century, strewed with religious houses.

The day, in truth, with all its uncalculated incidents and adventures, was a day big with consequences to him, on whose head it had risen (as spring days arise upon the young and hopeful), in light, in lustre, and in joy. He was one, whose generous enterprize and reckless daring bespoke a temperament, which leads men from the beaten track, through ways of danger, to fame and glory, – rarely to happiness. The circumstances of times so stirring and so consonant to the aspirations of the brave and the imaginative, had contributed to the early development of passions, which in the ordinary progress of nature, might still have slept; and the incidents of a day had thus probably decided the destinies of a life.

The peace officers who conducted the prisoner, had nearly reached one of those horrible dens, where folly and crime are so injudiciously incarcerated and confounded together, when to their surprise and consternation, a shrill and savage shout burst upon their ears; and a mob, led on by the same uncouth figure as had already attracted the attention, but evaded the vigilance of the police, came pouring forth in dusky groups, and in great number, from one of the many dark alleys which then opened on the quays. The contest that followed was so unequal, that an almost immediate rescue was effected, in spite of the spirited resistance of the police, and even of the remonstrances of the young prisoner himself. The populace (now masters of the field) raised the hero of the evening on the shoulders of the stoutest of their party; and at the peril of him they had sought at such risk to protect, ran with an extraordinary velocity along the banks of the Liffey; till their strange and uncouth leader halted before the antique and solitary edifice, from which his *protégé* had issued a short time before, unconscious of the portentous events in which he was soon to be involved. Three tremendous shouts announcing the arrival of the party, were echoed by the falls of a ponderous brass knocker; while the cries resounded of 'success to your lordship's honour. Here's your iligant fine son, Sir, brought safe home to you, plaze your honour, th' Honourable Murrogh, glory be to his name! Open the door if you plaze, my lord, afore the powlice comes down upon us and murders us intirely, plaze your honour.'

To this appeal, no answer was made. A window in the gable had, indeed, been opened, but it was as suddenly closed. The whole house seemed barricadoed, as if ready for a siege; and all was utter darkness, save when the moon, appearing for a moment through the massy clouds, fell with peculiar effect on the lofty figure and upturned head of the collegian. It was evident that, in the strong relief in which he stood, he must have been fully recognized by the person who had so immediately and timidly withdrawn. After a short pause, therefore, he addressed the mob to induce them to retire, and to secure their own safety, without indulging any fear for his.

He spoke not so much to the point, as to the passions of his hearers. Little practised in addressing a multitude, his eloquence arose out of the exigency of the moment; and coming fresh from the mint of a heated imagination, it abounded in those watch-words of Irish feeling, which are the clap-traps of natural vanity; they had their wonted efficacy.

The account of the rally and the rescue had been rapidly communicated by the fugitives of the discomfited party to one of the patrols, which paraded the city; who instantly bent their steps in the direction in which the rioters were supposed to have halted. They had reached the ascent of that very ancient bridge, whose sanguinary name[1] still attests the conflicts, of which its narrow pass was once the scene, when the mob, as they were still listening to the harangue of the young orator, caught the glitter of bayonets; and suddenly dropping the object of their triumph from their shoulders (contented with having left him at the paternal threshold), dispersed in various ways. One alone remained, moving like a strange phantom in the foggy distance; beckoning, by uncouth gestures, the object of his evident protection to join him; and waving his long pole through the misty air, with a faint exclamation of '*Faere ghem, Faere ghem.*'

The phantom, however, produced a far different effect on the object of its protection, from that which it appeared desirous to operate. It stunned, it stultified him. As often as he had caught a view of the huge, dark, and shadowy outline of that figure, he doubted the fidelity of his senses; and as he listened to those strange accents, deep and guttural as they were, he paused and shuddered. But as the military approached, the voice and figure faded away. The collegian alone remained to stand the brunt of the encounter. He had cast up his eyes to the window, where he thought he had seen his father. But no light or sound gave evidence that his fate excited further attention. The paternal door was evidently closed in wrath against him, – a

---

[1] Bloody Bridge, supposed to be so called from a battle fought upon it between the Irish and Danes; but more probably from the circumstance of several lives having been lost by the fall of a bridge on this site.

heart-chilling event in the life of the young and the cherished. Still the dark defiles of Watling-street, with its blind alleys, might have afforded him covert. To the right, and to the left, lay the open fields and burying ground of the Military Hospital, and all that swampy wilderness of desolation, of ruin and of wretchedness, which the trim military road now bounds along the Liffey's banks. The foot-fall of the approaching patrol fell quick upon his ear. Flight was still in his power. Flight! from what? from justice! Flight would have confounded him with the vulgar, timid, and capricious multitude. Far therefore, from retreating, he advanced boldly to meet the military. He had already been observed; and one of the soldiers sprung forth to seize him, when his carbine was knocked from his grasp to a considerable distance, by an unseen but powerful blow; and the man reeled back on his steps from the violence of the shock.

The student, stepping before him, presented himself to the commander of the party, touched his cap courteously, and said – 'To save all further trouble, I think it right to inform you, Sir, that *I* am the person in whose favour the rescue has been effected, and of whom I suppose you are in pursuit. I surrender myself voluntarily, and am ready to accompany you where you please.'

'Then march we to the castle guard-house,' replied the officer in a tone and manner but little suited to the occasion; while his party surrounded the prisoner.

'Soldier, have you recovered your piece?'

'No, plaze your honour, Captain O'Mealy, I have not: shure, it's the devil himself has ran off with it, I believe, captain.'

As he spoke, a shot was fired at the party, so well aimed, that it took off the feather in the officer's hat, as it whizzed by him. He instantly commanded a halt.

'Upon my honour, this is too agreeable,' he exclaimed, as he picked up his damaged plume. 'My bran new Captain Absolute's feather, that I'm to wear at Lady Ely's.'

'The shot was fired, Captain, from my own carbine, as sure as a gun,' said the soldier, who was still groping for his piece.

'Then the bloody-minded rebelly papist cannot be far off,' said the Captain.

A figure was, at that moment, dimly seen, in a creeping, crouching attitude, to pass along the walls of a ruined and dilapidated house.

'Fire!' said the Captain.

'Hold!' exclaimed the prisoner, earnestly and passionately; but his voice was lost in the noise of the volley, while a loud wild laugh, with the cry of '*Faere ghem, faere ghem,*' followed by a blast of a horn, was distinctly heard.

The next moment, a tremendous plunge in the Liffey disclosed the escape of the assassin, by means that seemed as perilous, as the fire from which he had so narrowly escaped.

'The villain,' said the officer, 'has escaped, after all; well, boys, leave him to his fate, which is not to be drowned, I'll ingage, any how.' And now, resuming his hat, he gave the word to march.

Surrounded by the military, the prisoner followed in the party, headed by the gallant Captain, and proceeded on his way to the castle.


END OF VOL. I

# The O'Briens and the O'Flahertys

## VOLUME TWO

# CHAPTER I

—•—

## *The Guard-House*

Turn melancholy forth to funerals;
The pale companion is not for our pomp.

MILTON.

Meanwhile welcome joy and feast,
Midnight shout and revelry,
Tipsy dance and jollity.
Rigour now is gone to bed,
And advice, with scrupulous head,
Strict age and sage severity,
With their grave laws, in slumber lie.

MILTON.

IT has always been the policy of the ruling party in Ireland, to exaggerate popular commotions into insurrectionary movements; and to assign to disturbances, merely local, a political origin.

The drunken riot at the Strugglers had scarcely commenced, when it was bruited about, by the secret service men of the government, as a tumult of the most deep-laid conspiracy – a *guerre à la mort*, between the people and the military, the volunteers and the garrison! the preliminary explosion of a long-concerted plot, which was to be followed up by the rising of the White Boys in the south, the Right Boys in the east, the Heart-of-Oak Boys in the west, and the Heart-of-Steel Boys in the north, with every other 'wild variety' of 'Boys,' which in Ireland, at all times (and particularly in the epoch alluded to), served as terms of terrorism, to scare the timid at home, and flatter the prejudices of the ignorant and credulous abroad.

The review in the Phœnix Park, distinguished by the most brilliant sham fight that had been exhibited on any similar occasion, evinced to the suspicious vigilance of government, that the old spirit of eighty-two had suddenly received a new impulse, and was again bursting forth with more than its original splendour.

Other scintillations of public spirit, it was asserted, were hourly exploding; which threw a light upon the state of public opinion. From the academic eloquence of the young and ardent members of the Historical Society (then the glory and pride of the university), to the less developed, but more formidable associations of the sober, civilized dissenters of Ulster, every thing intimated, to the heated imagination of the public authorities, some powerful impulsion; against which their vigilance was to be directed. The faintest breathing in favour of parliamentary reform, or Catholic emancipation, was deemed sedition; and the commonest street broil was considered an insurrectionary commotion.

On the first intimation, therefore, of the riot at the Strugglers, every demonstration of power and every show of fear were exhibited. Estafettes flew between the Royal Hospital and the Mayoralty; the castle sentinels were doubled, the castle gates were closed; and a captain's guard was thrown into, what was then called, the 'Old Guard Room' (situated in the lower court, near the ancient Chapel and Wardrobe Tower), a building long since swept away by modern improvement, and then only occupied in cases of emergency. Commands were issued to hold the troops in readiness to march upon the people; patrols were sent out; piquets established; the streets were cleared, the shops closed; and the awful silence of the capital was disturbed only by the trampling of steeds and the roll of carriages; whose flambeaux, flaring behind, reflected a murky glare from the arms of the military.

Power and pleasure, despotism and dissipation, were then inseparable images in Irish society: and while the city exhibited the appearance of a town besieged, the gay and the fair, the great and the dissipated, were reckless of public woe or weal; and hastened to their various rendezvous of amusement – to the innocent pastime of the *kutcha kutchoo* party at the provost's house, or the more select *media noche* of the castle, – which, like those of Versailles in the pious and profligate reign of Louis the Fourteenth, were at once puerile and licentious.

Composed of persons, congregated like monkeys, for the sole purposes of love and mischief – frequently beginning in a game of romps, and occasionally ending in a suit at Doctors' Commons – these private relaxations were independent of all control from the cares of public duty. Nor were any public disturbances permitted to intrude upon the elegant *délassemens* of the high officials and their particular *côteries;* except such as might be discussed to the amusement of the Lord Lieutenant after dinner; when fun and frolic gave a zest to business, when puns were manufactured with insurrections, heads and walnuts were cracked together, and rows and risings, – a drunken broil, or a White Boy irruption, – were treated with equal seriousness; that is, with equal levity.

The account of the tumult had reached the castle, just as the lovely vice-queen and her bevy of beauties had risen from table, amidst acclamations much too loud for the quietude of modern *bon ton*. These were called forth by the true Irish gallantry of a young and devoted admirer of her Excellency's, who observing the water in her finger-glass tinged with the dye of black gloves, which had sullied the rosy tips of her fingers, drank off the polluted beverage to her health; declaring, in all the ardour of Tipperary enthusiasm, 'that it was sweeter than nectar, and far superior to His Excellency's champagne,' though that was Ferns's best!!

It was reserved for the fortunate Captain O'Mealy to announce the event of the tumult at the Strugglers; for which purpose he called out the under secretary, a pretty boy diplomatist, the Honourable Freddy Fitzjohn, in the hopes of being called *in* himself (for the captain's social and civil manœuvres were infinitely more scientific than his military). The result answered to the intention. The captain was called in, and while the under secretary whispered the news to the chief, the chief passed it (with the bottle), to the chancellor; who gave it, with the toast 'of Kitty Cut-a-dash' to the commander of the forces; and the commander communicated it, without note or comment, to the Lord Lieutenant. Captain O'Mealy was then called on for a song; and he chaunted forth 'None can love like an Irishman,' an axiom denied by his Excellency, who was seconded by all the English officials present.

The board then proceeded to transact business; and the members of His Majesty's most honourable privy-council fitted their glasses, and gave their opinions. The contents of many wise heads, and many bright flasks were now poured forth together. More troops were ordered out, and more wine was ordered up. The state butler and the first aide-de-camp were kept in perpetual activity. The wine was declared prime, and the times perilous. The disbanding of the volunteers, and the knighting of Ferus, were orders carried in council, without a dissenting voice. The policy of elevating some to the peerage, and others to the gallows, was then started by Lord Knocklofty, whose family had progressively prospered by such measures; and it was agreed to by the Lord Chancellor, with a comment on the propriety of exterminating all the Catholics (one of his lordship's most favourite schemes); while the wisdom of multiplying jails and jobs, of raising barracks, for which there were no troops, and building fountains, for which there was no water,[1] was admitted *nem. con.*

The genial current of private feeling now flowed freely, with other genial currents. Particular interest mingled with general concerns; and, as confidence and claret circulated together, politics and pretty women were discussed with equal frankness and ardour. Then were brought upon the table, the services done to the state by the Ladies Knocklofty and Honoria Stratton, in a late contested election; when the Proudforts (the provincial bashaws of the country for half a century) were nearly worsted by a patriot, whose name was destined to make a part of the history of his country. In consideration of such services, Lord Knocklofty solicited a cornetcy of dragoons, for his fair friend Lady Honoria (nothing else being get-at-able at the time), which was instantly granted; and '*la belle soldat,*' was immediately toasted by Lord Kilcolman, in as good French and as honest a feeling as those in which one of his celebrated countrymen afterwards toasted '*la belle sexe,*' at a similarly 'highly contracting' party. Lady Knocklofty, too, was hinted at by his Excellency, as a proper person to fill the station of judge advocate, on the demise of the present incumbent; and the Chancellor, in complimenting the high judicial talents of his

---

[1] When the erection of fountains for the *accommodation of the poor* was decreed, the jobbers fixed upon Merrion-square as one of the sites. The inhabitants justly objected that there were no poor in the immediate vicinity, and that a fountain would be a public nuisance in the most elegant square of the capital. Sir Jno. De——, the advocate of the job, promised that the building should be ornamental; and that, upon his honour, *one drop of water should never be admitted into it.* He and his representatives have been true to the engagement; and the fountain, to this day, continues as dry as if it had been built for a powder magazine.

Over the edifice may yet be seen the following appropriate inscription, as if in mockery of the people, –

'His saltem accumulem donis, et *fungar inani Munere;*'

an unlucky allusion to the decease of the Lord Lieutenant at whose command the project was undertaken.

own widowed sister, declared that her sex only incapacitated her for the situation of attorney general, which he had recently vacated. In compensation for this *salique* disability, the affectionate brother said she would accept of a pension on the concordatum list, which was ordered to be enrolled *instanter*.

Amidst such national discussions, the council sat late and drank deep; occasionally receiving intelligence, and issuing orders; and they exhibited an unity and a mutual good understanding, for which the Irish cabinet has not always been remarkable. Even the Lord Lieutenant and his chief secretary agreed upon most points; his Excellency, for once, took the lead at the board; and his secretary, for once, did not affect to act 'as viceroy over him.'

While the Duke was thus giving up to a 'party, what was meant for mankind,' a little curly-headed page ran into the dining-room, and with an arch look, presented him a bit of twisted perfumed paper. It was opened and read with *empressement;* and the page was instantly followed into the adjoining and but half lighted throne room. The temporary absence of the governor, and general governor of Ireland, afforded infinite mirth and innuendo to the whole 'council assembled;' and when he returned, toasts were given, and puns were made, which left the representative of majesty in no doubt, as to the suspicions created by his sudden absence. The first to join in the jest, of which he was the subject, he observed that affairs of state must be attended to, ordered every man to fill a bumper, called on the chancellor for a toast, and desired 'Nosey Tisdall' (the court droll of the day) to sing a song, *à l'apropos*. The droll obeyed, and chaunted forth –

'Oons! neighbour, ne'er blush for a trifle like this;'

while all the 'members present' joined in the chorus of –

'No age, no profession, no station is free;
To sovereign beauty mankind bends the knee;'
etc. etc. etc. etc. etc.

Meantime the Duchess and her '*allegra brigata*' waited in mortified impatience for the breaking up of the *privy council*, to begin her games of magical music, blindman's buff, or puss in the corner; amusing themselves as they might, sometimes, like the ladies of the villa of Schiffanoza, with tales and stories, which had some points in common with those of the Decamerone; and sometimes by mystifying a drowsy page, or 'selling a bargain' to an unsuspecting aide-de-camp; both of whom they occasionally sent forth as scouts to bring in news of the row, and to make returns of 'the killed and wounded.' The arrival of some of their own elect, the clique of the castle, in their romping frocks, drove the privy council out of the heads of the fair states-women; who soon found they could 'better spare' those 'better men,' whose devotion to business and to the bottle outweighed the attraction of their own splendid charms.

The play of high spirits, the excitement of inordinate vanity (the one so often mistaken for wit, the other for passion), were now in full operation; and called forth whatever was brilliant and buoyant, in look or temperament of either sex. Warm blushes bloomed warmer, bright eyes shone brighter, as the plumage of tropical birds grows more vivid in the season of those transient loves, which in flutter and in brevity do not ill image the commerce so peculiar to British gallantry, called flirtation.

While each was thus engaged with each, and all with all, the patron-ized *protégée* of the evening, a foreign female harpist, was led in by the master of the ceremonies, in vain. The pedal harp was then such a novelty, that its very form was '*a lion;*' and yet the splendid performer, though anticipating the excellence of a Krumpholtz, had scarcely run over a few modulations, when she was called upon to symphonize the game of magical music, – a game as favourable to particular *tête-à-têtes*, as it is advantageous to forms, which in their doubtful search after the enigma of the mission, have the whole range of graceful action at their command. The paying and releasing of forfeits, however, constituted the point of the game; and Lady Honoria, as judge, contrived to turn every penalty into an epigram, showing little mercy to her enemies, and none to her friends.

It was now Lady Knocklofty's turn to be guided by the forte and piano of the harp. After sailing round the room with the theatrical grace of one to whom stage effect was not unknown, vainly warned, by the harmonious performer, of her remoteness from the object of her search, she became petulant, and got as much out of temper as she had before been pre-occupied; until, tearing off her diamond necklace, she flung it into the Duchess's lap, which held the forfeits, exclaiming 'there – give me a task and I'll perform it; but save me from the insipidity of hunting under cushions for hidden handkerchiefs, or the bore of taking Lady Mary O'Blarney's scarf and tying it round Lord Muckross's head.'

At that moment the Captain of the guard in sash and gorget, all powder and importance, joined the circle and soon became its centre. Called upon for news of the tumult, he drew up, took snuff, looked grave, and with the face of one who brought 'news of price,' narrated the important events of the evening, in which he had played himself the most important part. He talked of 'moving accidents,' of mob and military, of rescues and reprisals, of his rencontre with the son of a catholic peer in disguise (the real Captain Right he shrewdly suspected); and of his own feather cropped, and three hairs of his whisker singed (the parties were produced in court as corroborating testimonies). But when he discovered that Captain Right, who had acted so very wrong, was not only the son of a catholic peer in disguise, but the volunteer victor of the Star Fort, 'whose officiousness,' added Captain O'Mealy, looking at Lady Knocklofty, 'prevented every man on the ground from flying to her Ladyship's assistance,' then the last '*colpo di pennello*' was given to the picture; though some doubted, and some disbelieved, all were interested, because all were amused and excited.

At the Duchess's request, however, the unfinished game of magical music was again resumed. Lady Knocklofty was called upon to redeem her forfeit; and Lady Honoria, the judge of 'what was to be done to the owner of that superfine thing,' decreed that she should fulfil a task which appeared impracticable to all, and which was possible only to one too interested in its performance to hastily abandon the attempt.

While the collective wisdom of the nation had been thus occupied, in the dining-room of the castle, in providing for the exigencies of the times, and the ladies in the drawing-room in providing for their own amusement, the tumult had been quelled, by the wisdom, prudence, and activity, of a single magistrate; and the most conspicuous actor in the conflict, placed under the guard of Captain O'Mealy (who had been obliged to relinquish the distinction of his Excellency's society, to take command of a patrol), had been marched a prisoner to the castle guard-house. He had walked firmly and rapidly in the midst of his mounted guard; while Captain O'Mealy, riding on one side, and occasionally throwing his eyes over the person of his prisoner, somewhat shadowed by the group in which he was merged, sung out, for his own amusement, and the benefit of the public, his favourite air of

> 'We Irish boys, both high and low,
> Are clivir, brisk, and handy,

> And the ladies, every where we go
> All swear we are the dandy.
> To be sure we are, and indeed we are;
> With my hie! folathrum Leary.
> To be sure, etc.'

This jocund genuine Irish air he sometimes varied for the more placid melody of '*Maw chare amy*,' which he gave with a *cantabile* that had often excited the admiration, and drawn to the window many a '*chère amie*,' to whom his vocal powers were not unknown, in the neighbourhood between the barracks and the castle – his

> 'Daily haunts and ancient neighbourhood.'

Though Ennis born, the Captain was Dublin bred; and he had served his time to a button-maker in Wine Tavern-street, which had been the scene of the night's conflict. With 'a soul above buttons,' and a voice above par, – with the most dauntless impudence and the finest baritone – Barnaby O'Mealy had pushed and sung himself into the first company in the capital, and into the last company of 'Royal Irish,' one of those regiments '*de circonstance*,' something between a job and an expediency, which served the purposes of the government for the time being, and filled the pockets of the Colonel permitted to raise it.

When the patrol had reached Wine Tavern-street, the Captain commanded a halt on the scene of the recent action, which was still strewed with commemorating fragments of the battle. The old dilapidated taven of 'the Strugglers,' lay in deep shadow (the moon rising behind it), and was confounded with the formless mass of walls of its ill-assorted neighbour, the Franciscan nunnery; where a faint twinkle of light streamed from the solitary grated casement already noticed: haply some votive taper of a vestal shrine, which was suddenly extinguished, as the clanking of hoofs resounded on the pavement beneath, and scared the vigilance of the pious votarist 'by sounds unholy.' A sentinel kept guard at the shattered door of the tavern.

'Cintry,' cried out Captain O'Mealy, 'did this thing appear again to-night? as Hamlet in the immortal Shakspeare says; – that is, did any of thim rebelly, ruffianly, papist mob appear here upon the premises?'

An answer in the negative, with the assertion 'That all was right,' satisfied the Captain; who had only asked the question and made the halt, in his love of habitual display. But a man loitering near the place having volunteered some vague information, instantly engaged his attention; and much idle and unmeaning talk ensued, which produced the effect intended by the Captain, gradually gathering an auditory around him, and bringing heads to every window, and spectators to every door.

When a full half hour had thus been dawdled away, the word was again given to the guard, and they continued their route, followed by many of the mob; while the captain again raised his clear, mellow, but vulgarly modulated voice, to the reiterated *refrain* of –

> 'Maw chare amy – he-he,
> Maw chare amy,
> Maw chare amy – he-he-he,
> Maw chare amy.'

The party had now turned into High-street, which was more spacious and better lighted than the remoter avenues, giving to the Captain a more perfect view of the person of his prisoner, whose head was now in strong relief, though the rest of his figure was in shadow. Captain O'Mealy neared his horse, and taking the place of one of his men, accosted the prisoner with – 'I believe I have seen you somewhere before to-day; at laste, I take it for granted, if not much mistaken?'

''Tis probable, Sir,' was the cold reply.

'If I'm not greatly decaived, you are the young lad who led on the attack upon the Star Fort, – I think I recollect your prawfile?'

'I had that honour,' said the youth, with animation.

'It was a mighty nate thing, 'pon my honour, – that is, for the volunteers. The reglars (barring we cavalry) couldn't do it better; you must have had a good many rehearsals to get it up so well, as we say at Lady Ely's Attic; and it's a pity but so genteel a beginning should have so – so – '

'So what, Sir?' interrupted the prisoner, petulantly.

'So unlucky an inding, Sir, that's all,' said the Captain; 'for though a row is a good thing in itself, and what no gentleman need be ashamed of, yet it all depinds upon the style of getting it up. It's only a little while ago, that my friend, Lord Knocklofty, myself, Kilcolman, and the three Honourable O'Mullins's got into the devil's own row, returning a little disguised, as we say in Ireland, from the Lord Chancellor's, and were all clapped up in the watch-house – give you my honour we were – which reminded us of the prince and the chief justice, in the immortal Shakspeare; but there is every difference in life, in getting into a scrape with men of quality, and fighting with the commonalty, and taking their parts.'

'There is, indeed,' replied the prisoner, emphatically.

'And it's pity but a fine young fellow, like yourself, should get into a scrape, that may be the ruin of you; for if you are an indintured apprintice, as I suppose you are, – and, by the by, may I ask your trade?'

'My trade, Sir?'

'Oh, it's all in the way of kindness,' continued Captain O'Mealy, with a patronizing air; 'for I might be the making of you, in the way of getting you the pathronage of the greatest lady in Ireland; for I'm hand in glove with thim all, from the Lady-Lieutenant down – '

The young man tossed his head haughtily, and drawing up his college robe, which had fallen midway down his figure, so wrapped its folds over his arms, as to display, in full light, the gold tassels still pendant from its hanging sleeves. As they glittered in the moonlight, they caught the eye of Captain O'Mealy, who now first observed the University cap and robe of his prisoner. He remained silent for a moment, as if collecting himself for a new train of ideas; and then dismounting, he gave his horse to one of his men, and taking his place beside the prisoner, observed – 'I ask pardon if I've made a little mistake in taking you for a mechanic, Sir; but I believe I have the honour of addressing a young collegian, and a *non nobis domine.*'

'A what, Sir?' demanded the young man, smilingly.

'Why, a nobleman's son; at least I suppose so, from the gold tassels. Sir, I beg to introduce myself to the honour of your acquaintance; my name, Sir, is Captain Barnaby O'Mealy, of the Royal Irish.'

'And mine, sir,' said the prisoner, touching his cap, 'is Murrogh O'Brien.'

'The Honourable Murrogh, son of the Earl of Inchiquin, I presume?'

'No, sir; a son of Lord Arranmore.'

'Lord Arranmore! I have not the honour of knowing his lordship, which is extraordinary; as I may say the whole rid binch are my intimate frinds and particular acquaintances; a new crayation, I presume?'

'No, Sir, a very old title revived.'

'Humph! Mr O'Brien, you are a happy man, Sir.'

Mr O'Brien smiled, in the probable conception that his position was a singular one for a happy man; while Captain O'Mealy, passing his arm familiarly through that of his prisoner, continued – 'A very happy man, Sir; for I believe you are the very identical individual, now I look at you close, that saved the life of Lady Knocklofty, by stopping those devil's own skittish animals of hers, and – '

'Was that Lady Knocklofty?' interrupted the prisoner, with an obvious interest in the question.

'It was, Sir; the most intimate friend I have upon earth, and wonder but you should know her, Mr O'Brien; for, if I'm not intirely deceived and much mistaken, all people of quality know each other.'

'I have not been long in Ireland; and since my return to my native country, my time has been exclusively occupied by my collegiate pursuits. Had I gone into society, I could not fail to have distinguished a person so attractive as Lady Knocklofty.'

'Oh, that alters the case intirely,' said Captain O'Mealy; 'but thim that never went among the people of fashion, might know Lady Knocklofty: she drives on Sundays in the Phaynix, and on the Circular every day in the week, with her Excellency; and, as the ballad says –

> If you'd wish to see her Grece,
> The circular road it is the plece;
> For there ache day she drives her gig,
> With her hair tied up like a swadlere wig.'

'Is her ladyship a widow?' asked the young man, with interest and pre-occupation.

'A widow, is it she? Why, Mr O'Brien, you must be a stranger indeed, not to know that Albina, Countess Knocklofty, is the wife of the Right Honourable Claudius Antoninus Marcus Frederick Proudfort, Earl of Knocklofty, Baron St Grellan, Viscount Mount Raven – a Baronet and Lord Lieutenant of the county of Mayo; a member of his Majesty's most honourable Privy Council, Knight of the most noble Order of St Patrick, Colonel of the Royal Irish, Captain of the St Grellan Loyal Volunteers, Keeper of the Privy Sale, Chief Remembrancer of the Exchequer, First Commissioner of the Customs, Reversionary Secretary of State, Governor of the Lying-in and Foundling Hospitals, Master of the Revels, and Searcher, Packer, and Guager of the Port of St Grellan; Brother to one archbishop, and nephew to another; uncle to three bishops, four deans, and two archdeacons; and the head of the greatest, most powerfullest, and loyalest family of his Majesty's dominions of Ireland.'

The captain here paused for want of breath, and his prisoner observed – 'He is a happy man; Lady Knocklofty is a very attractive and beautiful person.'

'Oh, she's a lovely fine creature surely –

> The brightness of her cheek would shame those stars,
> As daylight does thim lamps,

as the immortal Shakspeare says; only she wears too much rouge, as I often tell her. Lady Knocklofty, dear, says I, I wish you would allow me to rouge you; for it's I have the notes for it, and paints all the faces at Lady Ely's for stage effect. By the by, Mr O'Brien, if you get out of this scrape, as I expect you will, being a lord's son, I'll inthroduce you at Knocklofty House, I will, 'pon my honour; and between ourselves (lowering his voice confidentially), you are not quite unknown to her Ladyship, for I pointed you out to her as she was driving off after the accident. Lady Knocklofty, says I, that's your *haro*, says I, – 'pon your honour! says she; 'pon my honour, says I: upon which, O'Mealy, says she, tell him, says she – in fact, she said as much, as that she meant to provide for you *de viv wau!*'

The prisoner was a moment silent; and then said, 'Any mark of Lady Knocklofty's notice, could not fail to be a distinction; and I would certainly rather receive it *de vive voix*, than by any intermediate means.'

The answer evidently puzzled Captain O'Mealy; but, resolved rather 'to burst in ignorance' than betray it, he continued to hum, 'If you would wish to see her Grece,' while debating in his mind what sort of an appointment *de viv wau* might be, which the son of a nobleman preferred to any other.

The party had now passed by the guarded gates of the upper Castle-yard (the residence of the viceroy), and descending Cork-hill, presented themselves at the lower court; when signs and countersigns were asked and given, pass-words whispered, and all the military mysteries of times of civil broil strictly observed. They were then permitted to enter.

The Castle of Dublin, a strong fortress, erected in the thirteenth century, for the defence of the capital, and of the English government, had once contained within its moated walls, the high court of Parliament, and courts of justice, with state prisons, state dungeons, state chapel, state gambling houses, and all the other appendages of state, belonging to an order of things founded on force and violence. Though few vestiges now remained of these features of a feudal despotism – though no draw-bridge or portcullis impeded the ingress, though no constable of the keep or gentleman porter was visible on the walls, though no body of warders or troop of archers, or pike-men bearded the ramparts, to scan such as, once entering them, 'left hope behind,' – still this ancient fort, and modern château, appeared to the imagination, and low-toned spirits of the prisoner, sufficiently awful. He had been in lands, where such strong-holds were more than monuments of the lawless power of darker and more distant times: he had lived under institutions, which made the will of one the law of all; and where a word or breath sufficed to incarcerate for life in such fearful edifices, the young and hopeful, the brave and bold. But recently returned to his native country, with a memory stored by reading, and early associations, with its ancient history, the towers of the Castle of the pale were still beheld with emotion, by one who considered himself by name and by descent the representative of the 'mere Irish.'

The lower castle-yard still indeed bore some resemblance to the description made of it in the preceding century, as a 'space or court, to the east of the castle, where stood the chapel for the service of the household, a lodging for the office of groom-porter, or gaming table, the Provost-Marshal's prison, the armoury and dwelling to the smiths and armourers, the wardrobe tower, the stable of the chief governor, and a range of fair buildings, the offices of war, ordnance, treasury, and for the regulating of the deeds and conveyances of the kingdom and the like.'[1] Most of these offices remained, and were now guarded by pacing sentinels; while the moon, as it shone from behind the wardrobe tower, and its ancient adjunct, the Castle chapel, threw a broad and picturesque shadow upon the pavement, with a singular effect.

' "I do not like the towers of any place," as th' immortal Shakspeare says,' observed Captain O'Mealy, pointing to the building.

'Nor I neither,' said the prisoner, with a sigh.

'Did Julius Caisar build that tower?' asked the Captain, still quoting from the only author with whom chance had made him acquainted.

'No,' said the prisoner, replying with *naïveté* to the question, and falling into the general error of mistaking the wardrobe tower for the Birmingham. 'It was erected, I have read, by the English deputy, John de Birmingham, Baron of Athenry, in 1342. From that tower the

[1] Ware's *Antiquities*.

gallant O'Donnel, of Tyrconnel, escaped from the tyranny of Elizabeth. From that tower, high as it is, escaped the brave Lord Delvin, one of the unfortunate few who, struggling for the independence of Ireland, sought to effect it at every risk.'

'Lord Delvin, do you tell me that? – why, he is one of our private thayathricals at Lady Ely's, and acts in "the gang" to my Macheath.'

'I mean the Lord Delvin of 1600, who was committed in ward here for joining in a conspiracy with the Earls of Tyrone and Tyrconnel, my own ancestors.'

'The Earl of Tyrone,' interrupted the Captain, confused by names so familiar. 'Is it the great Beresford, Earl of Tyrone, my partiklar acquaintance and intimate friend?'

'No,' said the youth, smiling, 'the great O'Neal, Earl of Tyrone, who, in league with the Lord Maguire. . . .'

'Oh! I know, – a relative of the honourable Kitty's?'

. . . . 'O'Cahan, and other chieftains of the sept of Ulster, intended to surprise the castle of Dublin, cut off the Lord Deputy and council, dissolve the state, and set up a government of their own.'

'O the rebelly papist thieves,' interrupted Captain O'Mealy, indignantly.

'On the contrary,' said the youth, with an earnestness singular in one in his position, 'it was a papist who betrayed this conspiracy; but though Lord Delvin was in charge of the constable, the stern Tristram Eccleston, he escaped. There are resources in the brave and the enterprising, which, like those of Heaven, are inscrutable.'

As the prisoner spoke with vehemence, Captain O'Mealy gazed on him in evident doubt and amazement, mentally observing, 'I wouldn't wonder if the Honourable Murrogh was Captain Right, devil a wonder;' a suspicion that brought with it a host of speculations, which afterwards formed the ground-work of his details in the Duchess's drawing-room.

The party had now drawn up to the guard-house, which formed a part of the mass of building adjoining to the old chapel, and had been one of those 'nameless towers'[1] which have since been taken down to make room for other necessary buildings. The prisoner was conducted in the usual form, and given up to the lieutenant of the guard, a pursy, ponderous, elderly gentleman, whom Captain O'Mealy introduced as Lieutenant Ellis, of the Royal Irish. In consideration of the prisoner's

---

[1] Ware.

rank, as Captain O'Mealy observed, he would be permitted to remain in the officer's room, to which he was at once conducted, till he should be given up to the civil power in the morning.

'And now, my dear O'Brien,' said the Captain familiarly, and drawing his dear O'Brien into a little den, which a camp-bed and dressing-table showed to be the sleeping-room of the officer on guard; 'I've just a word for your private ear, while I *tit-a-vate* myself a taste for her Excellency's little private paurty, and shake a dust of powder into my whiskers. I needn't tell you, you've a friend in court in your humble servant, and will spake to Lady Knocklofty to back you out of this bit of a scrape: I'm just stepping in to meet her at her Grace's private paurty, and – '

'To Lady Knocklofty! no, I entreat you,' interrupted his prisoner eagerly.

'Death alive, man! the women of quality will like you the better for a bit of a row. Why, what is there so much the go as Viscount Killkelly and Baron Killcoachy, as we call my friend Sir Terence Flynn, of county Galway, the chief of the Pinking Dindies, who nateley pinked his friend in a duel in the morning, and killed his coachman with a tinis ball in the afternoon; and an't them *Cherokees* too, an't they the life of the place; frightening all th' ould ladies in their sedan chairs, smashing the fine furniture of their particular friends, and playing H-H and Tommy through the town? But, at all events, hadn't I better go to my lord your father, for I suppose he knows nothing of your situation, and introduce myself to him as – '

'I am not quite sure that my father is in town; at least he was not this evening.'

'Well, any how, I'll go and thry to-morrow,' said Captain O'Mealy officiously; and secretly determined to add his lordship's name to his list of titled acquaintance – 'where does he keep, when he is in it?'

'At O'Brien House,' answered the prisoner with some hesitation.

'O'Brien House! humph! Well, sure I'll be there at cock-crow; some where about the new squares, or Stephens' Green, I suppose?'

'No, it's an ancient family mansion, and lies in what was once the principal quarter of Dublin.'

'And where is that?' O'Brien hesitated – then replied, 'Along the south bank of the river.'

'Oh, aye, I know, – near Moira House, where I'm to be introduced next week.'

'Further still, it occupies part of that ground, called Lord Galway's walk.'

'Why! it's like the house that Jack built, at the back of God's speed; but stay,' said Captain O'Mealy; taking up the almanack that lay on his table, and probably doubting the truth of O'Brien's information. 'Here's ould tell-truth; let us see Lord Arranmore! aye, here it is, the Right Honourable Terentius O'Brien, Baron of Arranmore – O'Brien House, Dublin – Castle of Dunn Engus, Isle of Arran – Grouse Lodge, Connemara. Well, Sir, if your father isn't well lodged, it isn't for want of houses; though, to be sure, they are something out of the line of fire, as we say in the Royal Irish. But now, mind, have a bit of a note ready by the time I come back from her Excellency's small, little, private paurty, and I'll find out his lordship, if he's above ground, and make your pace with him, to-morrow morning, 'pon my honour I will.'

'To save you all trouble,' said O'Brien, impatiently, 'my college-porter will deliver him a letter from me, if you will have the kindness to let your servant leave it at the Porter's Lodge of the University.'

'Well, my dear fellow, give you my honour I'm greatly intherested for you, and when you are out of this scrape, and enters bail, and that sort of thing, will get you to inthroduce me to my lord your father, and hopes you will both take a friendly dinner with me. So keep yourselves disengaged for some day next week; and I'll ask Knocklofty and the Chancellor, and a few others, to meet you: and now I lave you the reversion of my toylit, since you're a little flustered or so; and wash the blood spots off that comely fine face of yours, and I'll sind Serjeant Flanagan, who is a great bone-setter, to put a taste of gold-baither's lafe over the scratch on your timple, and a bit of black plaister over that, which will look for all the world like a beauty spot; and then Lieutenant Ellis will invite you to supper. So, fare you well till we meet, which will be soon, as I must return to my guard in an hour or two.'

O'Mealy then once more recommended his noble prisoner to the attention of his ancient Pistol, Lieutenant Ellis, and, titivated and powdered up to the highest bent of his personal ambition, the captain of the guard sallied forth to parade his vulgar absurdities to her Excellency's select *côterie*, where his reception has been already described.

The reversion of the toilette of the Irish military Adonis was an advantage of which O'Brien was happy to avail himself; and having benefited by the skill and black patch of Serjeant Flanagan, and pulled up his black stock, after the manner of Captain O'Mealy, ruffled his handsome head into a mass of curls, laid aside his customary robe of 'inky black,' and permitted the serjeant to brush the dust from his green uniform, he presented himself in the guard-room.

Lieutenant Ellis, a coarse, dashing, vulgar-looking person, alone occupied this apartment; and was seated at the fire, poring over the orderly book, and sipping brandy and water. He motioned to the prisoner to take a seat, and insisted on his swallowing a glass of the potation, with such importunity, that it was vain to resist. The refusal of a second glass, and a cold answer to his idle questions, soon gave him impressions of the prisoner's character and designs not very advantageous. Silence and sobriety were, in the estimation of Lieutenant Ellis, misprisions of treason: with him, the man who would not talk or drink, was 'fit for plots and stratagems;' and unwilling to keep company with one at once so dangerous and so dull, so sober and so seditious, he drained off his goblet, read out the last order to the serjeant of the guard, and retired to the little bedroom, where he soon gave audible intimation of *his* manner of keeping watch and ward.

The prisoner, meantime, had seated himself on an old-fashioned settle, beside the guard-room fire, and availing himself of some writing materials, which lay on the table, began a letter, dated from the castle guard-house. Having written 'my dear father,' he paused. To this dear father he had much to say; but the current of his ideas was dried up. The exhaustion of fatigue fell heavily both on body and mind; nature had gone to her uttermost; and the will and the intellect were alike in abeyance. The pen fell from his hand, his eyes closed; he sank gradually on the old settle, and life was soon to him as though it were not. As he lay with one arm pillowing his head, the other thrown listlessly over his breast, he imaged, in the grace of his attitude, and the youth and beauty of his person, the '*sommeil d'Endymion*,' such as the genius of painting, in various ages, has represented it.

The clock of the castle had struck, but he had taken no note of time! Ages or hours, a minute or a night, might have elapsed between the last sensation of slumbering drowsiness and the first of awakening consciousness, which was occasioned by a painful tingling that ran across his closed lids, and induced him instinctively to press them still closer. Though his eyes were deeply shaded by the long dark lashes, and by his upraised hand, the painful sensation became more and more intense; still starting up, in sudden and full wakefulness, he perceived that the uneasiness arose from a burst of light, held close to his face.

At his waking, the person who held it drew back abruptly into a remote corner; and he could just perceive that it was a stranger, muffled in a military cloak, and that they were alone. Before, however, he could make further observation or inquiry, Serjeant Flanagan came forth from Lieutenant Ellis's room, and giving the stranger a paper, said, 'Plaze your honour, it's all right – that's enough, Sir, if a man was condemned to five hundred – the prisoner is to attind you.'

The stranger now advanced a little, in the direction of a small, low arched door in the guard-room, which seemed to lead into the interior of the building. There he paused, and touching his hat with a slight *dégagé* military salute, observed, in an affected and effeminate voice, 'Serjeant, acquaint the gentleman with my order; or, stay – you had better show it to him.'

Flanagan presented the paper to the prisoner, who was now on his feet, and had taken up his cap, and drawn on his robe. It was an order, in the proper technical form, empowering the lieutenant of the guard to give up the prisoner, the Honourable Murrogh O'Brien, to the bearer. What was most extraordinary in the event was, that it was dignified by the signature of the Lord Lieutenant.

'May I ask, Sir,' demanded O'Brien, 'whither I am to be removed?'

'For the present,' replied the young officer, 'not I hope beyond the castle walls; for it is cursed cold' (and he folded his cloak more closely round him), 'and to-night's duty is no joke.'

'I suppose I'm about to be called up for examination then?' demanded the prisoner.

'Yes, for examination – there is no doubt of that.'

'Before a civil or a military tribunal?' asked O'Brien anxiously.

'Oh, *very civil*,' replied the officer, in an accent, that struck upon the just then irritable nerves of his prisoner to be jocular even to jeering. All the blood of the O'Briens rushed into his face; and resolving to ask no more questions, he followed his guide in sullen silence; who led the way through a low, arched postern – the serjeant lighting them with his guard-room light, which, as he held it on high, discovered an obscure stone passage.

'There,' said the young officer, 'take away our greasy light; the smell is suffocation. Can't government light guard-rooms, with something that an't grease? pah!'

The serjeant, offended by the haughty manner of this 'officer, who was no soldier,' but appeared to be some dandy youth of quality, recently initiated into the coarseness of military service, suddenly slapped the door, and left the guard and the guarded alike in utter darkness.

'By Jove,' exclaimed the young officer, 'this is a pleasant adventure! The lamp that hung here, too, is extinguished; but don't be afraid, Sir.'

''Tis not my habit, Sir,' replied the prisoner, abruptly.

'I know the way' (continued the young leader), ''tis a private one, between the lower and upper court; a short cut, though an ugly one. It saves exposure, however, to night air. Stay, Sir, here are three steps – give me your hand – one, two, three – and now on, and step boldly.'

The prisoner, with a feeling of extreme provocation, literally obeyed his finical guide, gave his hand, and 'stepped on boldly;' when suddenly, and with a movement not unobserved, he involuntarily removed his cap; for by some illusion of the senses, some dream of the fancy, he was struck by the odd conviction, that the ungloved hand that led him –

> – to whose soft seizure,
> The cygnet's down was harsh,

was – a woman's!

'You had better not uncover your head,' said the officer, looking over his shoulder, as a gleam of light, from the further extremity of the passage, discovered the act.

'I did so upon instinct,' said the prisoner, laughingly; 'I was scarcely conscious that I did it at all.'

'It must have been a strange instinct; to what conclusion did it lead you?'

'For an instant, that I was in a woman's presence.'

'Well, stand not upon the gallantry of your instinct, but resume your cap; for these passages are damp. Curse these boots; I wish the fellow that made them was wedged into one of them, up to his neck – they must have been made on the last of the Irish giant. I beg your pardon for a moment, pray hold my spur,' – and he paused to arrange the 'cursed boot,' which he had hitherto evidently dragged after him with difficulty. 'And so (he continued, in his lisping tone) you have had the romance to turn this no very pleasant event, of being brought up for midnight examination, into – a *bonne fortune?*'

'A *bonne fortune*,' repeated the prisoner angrily, and feeling his cheek tingle with a sudden blush at the coxcombical supposition.

'Ay, to be sure,' replied the officer, still fiddling with his boot, 'for if you could think that a lady led you along these mysterious passages, at this witching time of night, it follows of course,'. . . .

'No, Sir' (interrupted the prisoner petulantly), 'I thought nothing about the matter. The fact is, I am not yet half awake. I was taken by surprise out of a deep sleep; a soft voice and a soft hand did the rest, and led to the absurd idea.'

'Not so absurd neither' (said the officer). 'This castle is a frolicsome place; and women, who keep grown gentlemen at arm's-length, do sometimes interest themselves for us boys.'

'Because it is for us boys only, they can do so with impunity,' was the reply.

'Humph! not always, we flatter ourselves,' said the officer conceitedly, taking back his spur and moving on. 'It sometimes happens our spirits are too bold for our years.'

'Say rather,' said the prisoner laughing, 'that our years are too few for our spirits.'

'You may uncover your head now, if you will' (observed the officer, passing through a little grated door, through which the faint light had hitherto proceeded), 'for now you are on holy ground.'

The officer paused; and the prisoner perceived with surprise, that they stood in the centre of an ancient chapel, doubly, but dimly lighted by the waning moon, which streamed through its gothic casements of painted glass in many vivid lines, borrowed from the robe of St Patrick, or the girdle of St Bridget, – and by the flickering red light of a waxen taper, in a brazen chandelier, suspended above a little gallery, which had the air of a royal tribune in a Catholic church.

'Many a stout heart has quailed here,' said the young officer, with theatrical emphasis; 'for this chapel communicates with Birmingham Tower, the State Prison. Many an Irish rebel, many an O'Neil, an O'Donnel, and an O'Brien too, were shriven here, on their way to execution: "arch rebels all, time immemorial," they say.'

'Rebels, indeed!' exclaimed the prisoner with vehemence: 'there are still many, I believe, in Ireland, who sigh for the return of those terrible times, when love of country was a penal crime, and the life of a native Irishman had its price, like the head of the Irish wolf; but there are still, be it hoped, many who would die a thousand deaths, to prevent their recurrence.'

'Let such be silent here,' said the young officer, in an admonitory tone; and proceeding on, they passed through a lateral door, under the gallery, – but not before the prisoner thought he heard a rush of sounds above, like the flutter of birds disturbed into sudden flight. He was now much struck by the oddity of this manner of being 'brought up for examination.' A doubt, a confusion of ideas, or rather of sensations, left him without the power of reflection or inference; and all other functions were, for the time, 'smothered in surmise.'

'Does you spirit flag?' asked the officer, as they passed from a matted gallery into a stone and vaulted passage, in utter darkness, save from a distant flash which gleamed at its further extremity.

'Not a jot,' was the careless reply. 'Come what come may, I am prepared.'

'Give me a proof of your presence of mind,' said the officer, turning short round to his prisoner.

'What proof do you ask?' was the laughing reply.

'Quote me a line instantly from any author, in any language, no matter what; but be quick.'

> 'Di mia sciocchezza tosto fui pentito,
> Ma troppo mi trovai lungo dal lito,'

replied the now almost amused, and thoroughly awakened prisoner.

'Oh! you know Italian: where did you learn it?'

'In Italy.'

'In Italy? but you are an Irishman!'

'Soul and body.'

'Humph!' said the interrogator, significantly. '*Tant pis pour vous.* – You have, at least, the Irish qualities of wit and courage: but wit and courage without discretion, will not avail where you are about to appear.'

'I fear I should want both' (said the prisoner, in evident excitement, and again strangely puzzled by the oddity of the adventure), 'if that which is impossible should be true; like some dogmas in religion.'

'Oh! you are at your instincts again, are you?' asked the guide archly.

'May I beg to ask you a question?' was the eager reply.

'I can answer no questions now, Sir,' said the officer coldly, and quickening his creeping pace: 'I have already held too much parley with a prisoner, though all about nothing at all; and nothing can come of nothing. So now, follow, and be silent.'

As he spoke, they issued from the stone passage, into a spacious, handsome, and architectural vestibule. Its roof was supported by massive pillars; and its marble pavement was heavily paced by sentinels, who carried arms to the plumed helmet of the officer as he passed.

At the moment when they were about to ascend a broad and noble staircase, which branched into two flights at the first landing, the state-porter in the outer hall, cried pompously, 'The Lord Chief Justice's chair.'

'The Lord Chief Justice is coming down,' replied the footman, in the same vociferating tone, from the corridor above.

'The Commander of the Forces' carriage stops the way,' cried the porter, below.

'The Commander of the Forces is coming down,' was the answer from above.

At this solemn announcement of the approach of two great officers of state, the guide and guard of the prisoner suddenly turned back on his steps, beckoning to his charge to follow. Tripping lightly back, through the passage they had already cleared, he opened a door to the left of that matted gallery, through which they had issued from the chapel, and silently, but with a significant gesture, ascended a flight of narrow, ill-lighted, stone steps, terminating at another door. The door opened, and discovered an unexpected vista to the amazed prisoner. It was a long corridor, with a stuccoed and ornamented roof, containing many small cupolas; from each of which were pendant massy gilt chandeliers, filled with wax-lights. It opened on either side by a succession of doors, to different suites of apartments; while the intervals were filled with sofas of scarlet, on which lounged or slept, a numerous train of pages, grooms of the chamber, and footmen in gorgeous liveries. A door, flung open, at the further extremity, discovered an armoury, where a group of beef-eaters were gathered round the fire. To the right, a foreshortened view appeared of the broad stone stairs, with the pacing battle-axe; from which the officer had turned at the approach of the Chief Justice: (an incident which convinced the prisoner, that he was acting under some private and secret authority, unknown to the privy-counsellors.) Beyond all, and terminating the perspective, was visible the moon-lighted vastness of St Patrick's Hall.

At about the middle of the corridor, the officer paused. A groom of the chamber flew to open a door to the right, which as they entered was quickly closed after them; and the parties found themselves in a dimly lighted room. A solitary wax candle here and there just dispelled the utter darkness, and faintly designed the stately forms of a throne and canopy, with heavy draperies of dark velvet, and a few old pictures in cumbrous frames. All was silent and still, save a faint burst of merriment, which was scarcely caught through the double doors of an adjoining apartment; and which was soon overpowered by the full tones of a harp.

The air performed was not unknown to its spell-bound auditor; whose senses responded to the mellifluous sounds in most amazed sympathy. It was peculiar to that region, where he last had heard it; and was part of a celebrated litany, sung in the Santa Chiesa di Loretto at Rome, to which the modern auditory of Europe have since listened with undiminishing rapture.[1]

'Where is that music?' demanded O'Brien, eagerly.

'In the spheres,' was the reply.

Though too confused for conjecture, O'Brien was now half inclined not to advance further, till he had some explanation with his leader; who, with his hand upon the lock of a double door (within the deep and dark embrasure of which he already stood), beckoned him on.

'I cannot, Sir,' he said: 'I will not proceed further, till you tell me for what purpose I have been brought thus far.'

'A soldier, and afraid?' exclaimed the young officer, scoffingly. 'What danger do you suspect, Sir?'

'None; but I fear – '

'What? Out with it, man!'

'A ridicule,' returned the bewildered prisoner.

'A ridicule! a dainty fear truly for the ringleader of a riot, and a prisoner in the Castle of Dublin.'

'You talked of the castle being a frolicsome place,' said the prisoner, advancing to the door-way, and now full of the idea that he was the victim of some anti-chamber mystification – perhaps in the hands of a mischievous page, or possibly in those of the vulgar O'Mealy, who might be engaged to show him up for the amusement of his friends, 'the people of quality.'

'Why, yes,' said the young officer, lowering his voice, and beckoning to his charge to advance, 'so it is a frolicsome place; and I know it

[1] Well known, by Rossini's adoption of it, as the motive of *Di tanti palpiti*. I give the anecdote as I found it, without vouching for its accuracy.

was even proposed this night to Lady Knocklofty, whose life, by the by, you saved to-day. . . .'

'Lady Knocklofty,' said her champion, with emotion, entering the embrasure to catch the words.

'Stay,' said the officer, speaking in a whisper, 'close the door behind you, and I'll tell you all.'

The prisoner obeyed, and they were for an instant in utter darkness. The music ceased, and the officer, taking his hand, emphatically whispered, from the motto of his own colours – *'Fais ce qui doy, arrive que pourra,'* – then throwing open the second door, drew him quickly forward, into a blaze of light and beauty, – into the presence of the vice-queen, and her merry court. A shout of 'bravos,' received the officer and his charge; and while the latter 'stood a statue,' the former threw aside his helm and cloak, and knocking off the 'cursed boots,' from the silken slippered feet they had encumbered, discovered the imposing and splendid figure of Albina Countess Knocklofty.

# CHAPTER II

## *The Frolic*

Avea in ogni sua parte un laccio tesò,
O parli o rida, o canti o passo mova;
Nè maraviglia è se Ruggier n'è preso,
Poi che tanto benigna se la trova,
Quel che di lei già avea dal mirto inteso,
Com'è perfida e ria, poco gli giova;
Ch'inganno o tradimento non gli è avviso;
Che possa star con sì soave riso.

*Orl. Fur. Canto* vii, 16.

'THERE,' said Lady Knocklofty, throwing off her ponderous helmet, shaking out her ruffled drapery of soufflet gauze (which the cloak of Captain O'Mealy, borrowed for her disguise, had crushed), and resuming her turban *à la Roxalane* – 'There, good folks, give me your applause, for I have won it hard and well.'

'I fear we must give you more than that,' said Lady Honoria, peevishly, 'if you hold us to the letter of our foolish bets.'

'Hold you! to be sure I shall, my dear,' returned Lady Knocklofty, in the greatest possible excitement, and evidently concealing some flutter of feeling, under an affected eagerness about her bets. 'I have done *my* part; – now for yours. Duchess, my diamonds; Kilcolman, your cool hundred; Freddy Fitz-John, your ten to one; Lady Honoria, name your night for the sally-lun and raking pot of tea, after the play! A good let off, let me tell you, dear; so no grumbling.'

'I rise to explain,' said Lady Honoria, affecting humour, to cover up her real annoyance; for she had taken up some by-bets on the non-performance of Lady Knocklofty's frolic, which were not as easily paid off, as the sally-lun, and its raking accompaniment – 'I believe, Lady Knocklofty, that the bets stood thus – '

'My dear Honoria,' said Lady Knocklofty, laughing violently, and speaking vehemently, 'all your wit won't save your tea-pot. "Till thou can'st rail my seal from off my bond," ' she added, theatrically, ' "thou but offendest thy lungs to speak." '

'The betting-book will decide all,' said the Honourable Freddy Fitz-John (a pretty little sucking secretary), who, pert and priggish, passed the precocity of a smart school-boy, as the earnest of future talents he was destined never to exhibit; and who, as a considerable loser in the betting speculations of the evening, was mentally applying his 'Giles-Gingerbread' diplomacy to the raising supplies for the liqui-dation of his 'losses.'

'The betting-book, the betting-book,' called out the comptroller of the household (over which he held no control).

'The book, the book,' re-echoed the Honourable and Reverend the Dean of the Chapel (the first of his Excellency's thirty chaplains), who had just joined the party from the dining-room, full of the spirit, and without the grace to check an hiccup as he called for 'the book,' – which might have been the Talmux or the Alcoran, Joe Miller or Jonathan Wild, for all he knew to the contrary.

The '*compte rendu*' of the aide-de-camp's room was immediately produced; and one of the gentlemen in ordinary read out as follows from its pages: –

'The countess Knocklofty having, at the game of magical music, forfeited her diamond necklace, engages to redeem it by the perform-ance of the following feat, viz., she will release the prisoner brought this evening to the guard-house, in the lower castle-yard, by Captain O'Mealy, and produce him in the presence of her Excellency the Duchess of Belvoir, before the clock strikes twelve.

'N. B. It is understood, as stated by the Captain of the guard, that the prisoner in question must be a gentleman, namely, the Honourable Murrogh O'Brien, son of Lord Arranmore, and the same who distinguished himself as the leader of the volunteer corps of the Irish brigade this day, in the sham fight at the Phœnix Park; and therefore *presentable* in the society of her Grace the Duchess of Belvoir.'

A long list of bets followed, for and against the possible performance of this enterprize; made according to the confidence of the several bettors in the ways and means, headlong temper, and dauntless and romantic spirit of the chief actress in this frolicsome drama.

All eyes were now turned on him, who was recognized as the hero of the day; and whose captivity had thus so pleasantly been cut short. There he was, and consequently, the conditions being performed, there was no more to be said on the subject. Those who could pay their debts of honour on demand, paid them; and those who could not, pledged their honour to do so when they could.

'There!' said Lady Knocklofty, sweeping her winnings into her handkerchief, and still laying the agitation of her manner to the account of her cupidity. 'There! I flatter myself this is fairly won, and daringly earned; for what woman dare do, I have done.'

'Which is the short way for a woman to be undone,' said Lady Knocklofty's dear friend, Lady Honoria, to Lady Knocklofty's grateful *protégée*, the Honourable Catherine Macguire. Between these ladies there existed a confidence, if not a friendship, which had insensibly grown out of similar tastes and humours – a sense of the ridiculous – and that talent for ridicule which is so often found unallied with any other.

To the axiom of her ally, as applied to her protectress, Miss Macguire acceded, with one of those comical grimaces, which constituted a leading trait in her list of amusing abilities; and she added, 'You know, of course, how this was done?'

'Not by a *coup de baguette*,' replied Lady Honoria. 'She has had an audience, I take it; and the Eccellenza has yielded to "her most petitionary vehemence," and given her an order for the prisoner's release. Under the double influence of beauty and of Burgundy, the poor dear Duke would give away the whole kingdom, if there were any one fool enough to accept it.'

'Exactly,' said Miss Macguire; and pursing up her comical mouth, she hummed in her friend's ear, from the fashionable burletta of the 'Golden Pippin,'

> 'Jovey, my soul!
> What does it say?
> Fire the north-pole –
> Jove's your valet!'

'Exactly,' said Lady Honoria, laughing.

'But now,' said Miss Macguire, 'that she has got that handsome, stupified creature here, what will she do with him?'

'You do not know, then, that he is the *enjouement*, the Prince Lee Boo of the moment?'

'*Enjouement!* yes, perhaps; but here! and the Lord Lieutenant, the *cavaliere pagante* of the day!'

'Well; this handsome, stupified creature will be the *cavaliere pagato, comme de raison*,' replied Lady Honoria; and both the ladies laughed loudly, but prettily; as ladies of fashion only know how to laugh, when to laugh is notoriously becoming, and the object some particularly dear friend.

Meantime, the 'handsome, stupified creature,' the Astolfo of the adventure, had passed the short interval in a confusion of all the senses, which extended minutes to months, and gave to something less than half a quarter of an hour the importance of a century. Stunned, dazzled, abashed in the first instance; indignant, irritated, and perplexed in the next; gazed at by many, noticed by none (not even by O'Mealy, whose broad, vulgar face was notable over the shoulders of more elegant, though less lofty spectators), knowing not how to retreat, nor how to advance without making a scene, or giving *prise* to a ridicule, he still stood where his fair and false guide had left him. He leaned against the projecting wood-work of a window near the door by which he had entered; and was half involved in its crimson draperies, with an effect which rendered his person a picture. He still wore his black gown half drawn over his dark uniform; and his fine head, lighted by a chandelier, came out in strong relief, and harmonized with the rich hues of the well draped background.

The audible reading of the betting book had put him in full possession of the nature of the embroglio in which he was involved; and though there was clearly more of idle frolic than of premeditated insult in the part allotted him, still the conviction neither diminished his awkwardness, nor dissipated his perplexity. The dim, mysterious avenues he had passed; the soft hand that had guided him – that sudden burst of light and loveliness that had succeeded to darkness and solitude – the brilliancy of the drawing-room, and the persons by whom it was occupied, and by whom he was surrounded, all alike confounded and bewildered him. That he was then occupying a spot, in what he had deemed the den of political corruption; that he was surrounded by those who drew their very existence from the misery of his country (that country he would die to serve or save); that he stood confounded with those against whose system of aggression he had registered a protest, solemn and sincere as the patriot's last sigh on the scaffold of his martyrdom; that he was the laugh, perhaps the scorn of those he scorned, – were fancies or convictions, rendered insupportable by the morbid state of his feelings, and the previous depression of his spirits. They left him without the power, almost without the will to act; and wholly deprived him of that presence of mind, the want or possession of which mars or makes a fortune. What might have been turned to the account of personal advancement by those who knew how to make the most of it, was, by one 'so green and young in this old world,' only considered as a personal indignity, or a mark of disrespect.

In spirit and bearing, O'Brien was a '*petit Dunois.*' He had hitherto, during his short life, acted as if

> D'Orlando e di Rinaldo era cugino.

With a temperament all Irish, and a character made up of those elements, which in the poetry of life form its sublime, but in its prose tend a little to the ridiculous, – impetuous and spirited, as the genuine Hibernian always is, petulant and fierce as a foreign *militaire* usually affects to be, – his natural and national qualities had been sharpened rather than subdued by a life of early excitement and vicissitude. Too susceptible to impressions, as they flattered or mortified his passions and his pride, he now stood in a position the most painfully opposed to all that was strongest or weakest in his nature. He who had fought his way through half Europe sword in hand, had not now the courage to pass through a group of frivolous coxcombs of both sexes. He who had desperately led more than one forlorn hope, now in the midst of gaiety and pleasure, looked the picture of a forlorn hope himself. Infinitely more willing to be shot, than to be laughed at, he was devoutly wishing himself up to the neck in the trenches before Belgrade, where he had already distinguished himself, rather than in this enchanted palace of a '*possente Alcina,*' when the *possente Alcina* herself came forward,

> Con allegra faccia,
> Con modi graziosi e reverenti,

and changed in a moment the whole character of his sensations and course of his ideas.

The Irish Vice Queen, the beautiful Duchess of Belvoir, had hitherto stood in the centre of a group, the members of which, with the true effrontery of fashion – that affects no feeling, and knows no restraint – as coolly and deliberately were pointing their glasses and their glances at the victim of their supercilious notice, as philosophy directs its microscope at the insect it studies. But now, supported on either side by Lady Knocklofty and the old Earl of Muckross (the latter, *par parenthèse*, a dried specimen of a genus now almost extinct, the travelled Irish nobleman of the old school), she advanced in the direction where O'Brien stood, who retreated 'deeper and deeper still,' within the recess of the window. With her beautiful eyes fixed smilingly upon him, she said, in a good-natured and half audible whisper, 'Speak to him, Lady Knocklofty; the frolic, you know, was your own.'

'Mine, dearest duchess? It was every one's frolic. But, come, I have had the glory, and will perform the duties arising from it, – even that of asking Mr O'Brien's pardon for the liberty I have taken with him.'

O'Brien bowed, as men only bow who have learned to bow abroad; and blushed, as men only blush to whom the world is still new. His bow and his blush had their due effect; and were received at their full value.

'I am sure,' continued Lady Knocklofty, 'he will forgive the means, for the sake of the result, if your Grace will permit me to present him to you.'

'I desire particularly to make the acquaintance of Mr O'Brien,' said the Duchess, with her bland smile and tone; 'and to offer my apology at the same time. For though not a party concerned in the frolic, yet, as consenting thereunto, I believe I should come in for part of the blame.'

Lady Knocklofty then, with the manner of a master of the ceremonies, said, 'Duchess, in the absence of Sir Phelim O'Kelly, I will presume to do the honours, and present to your Grace the Honourable Murrogh O'Brien.'

O'Brien again bowed, and the old Lord Muckross, with an air between that of Lord Herbert of Cherbury, and Sir Lucius O'Trigger, requested his introduction also of the '*Camerara Mayor*,' as he termed Lady Knocklofty, and complimented the victor of the Star Fort on his military skill; adding, 'that he hoped his laurels, won in the morning, would not be tarnished by the adventures of the night; for that the saviour of Lady Knocklofty could not fail to be an object of interest to all who had the honour of knowing her ladyship.'

'It was a gallant rescue,' said the Duchess. 'I saw it all, and for a moment it struck me that your life was more in danger, than that of the object of your protection. How can you, my dear Lady K., drive such horses? I am not a timid whip; yet I would not trust myself to your greys, within sound of a cannon shot – no, "not for a wilderness of monkeys." '

'Except,' interrupted Lady Knocklofty, throwing down her eyes, with a peculiar expression, 'you had some *preux chevalier* near, to come to the rescue. *Alors le jeu vaut bien la chandelle.*'

'Aye,' said Lord Muckross, 'there it is. What is death to others, is sport to you tyrants. There is not on earth a more pitiless savage than a beautiful woman; and whether –

> Her hero perish, or her sparrow fall,

*c'est ègal*, provided she shows her power.'

'*Vous parlez avec connaissance de cause*,' said the Duchess, tapping him with her fan.

'I *have* seen service,' replied his lordship, taking snuff, conceitedly: 'they alone jest at scars, who never felt a wound.'

'Mr O'Brien, you do not seem to have escaped unhurt from the field, to judge by the mark on your brow. I hope it was not in my service?' said Lady Knocklofty, fixing her eyes on the black patch, which rather became than disfigured the wearer.

'I wish it had been, Madam,' replied O'Brien, confusedly. 'It is, however, so slight a scratch, that I am quite ignorant how or when I came by it.'

'I hear,' said the Duchess, 'that Lord Charles Fitzcharles has got into the same scrape that has brought you, Mr O'Brien, into the "durance vile" of our strong-hold; and to which, by the by, your deliverer, Lady Knocklofty, must soon yield you up. For you must not be found here by the big wigs,' she added, laughingly, 'who all dine with the Lord-Lieutenant to-day.'

'Oh, I'll send him back in due time, under the care of the Captain of the guard,' said Lady Knocklofty; 'but, dear Duchess, as one good turn deserves another, pray present *me* to Mr O'Brien, for he cannot, upon instinct, know who I am.' And she laid an emphasis on the word, that brought a rush of odd recollections to the mind of O'Brien which tingled in every fibre.

'Oh, my dear,' said Lady Honoria, who, with the rest of the exclusives, had now gathered round the party, 'we all take it for granted, that you and Mr O'Brien made your acquaintance in your journey through those long passages, which do not always "*lead to nothing.*" '

'No, upon my honour,' said Lady Knocklofty, vehemently, 'Mr O'Brien never discovered the disguise; and took me for an officer on duty, till I threw off O'Mealy's cloak and cap in this very room. I appeal to you, Mr O'Brien.'

'Appeal to him!' abruptly interrupted Lady Honoria, in the same jeering tone. 'Why, child, on such an occasion, his testimony would go for as little as O'Mealy's did, in the cause of Miss Juliana O'Gallagher, O'Mealy defindant.'

'Pray, let us have that,' said Lord Kilcolman. 'Now, Lady Honoria, in your best manner. O'Mealy, my boy, come into court – Miss O'Gallagher plaintiff.'

O'Mealy came forward, pulling up his stock, and roughing out his whiskers, with a look of affected bashfulness, that only added to the habitual expression of his invincible impudence. 'Give your lordship my honour, I have no notion of what Lady Honoria is going to tell: but I hope she will speer the leedy; that's all.'

'Now, Lady Honoria,' said Lord Kilcolman, rubbing his hands – for O'Mealy was his butt – 'now for it. Silence in Court.'

'Well,' said Lady Honoria, 'when Counsellor Cornelius O'Gallagher insisted on knowing the Captain's intintions, in consequence of a visit to the barracks of the Royal Irish, paid by Miss Juliana, and when he demanded that the Captain should pledge his honour that the lady was still as well qualified to preside as priestess in the Temple of Vesta, as before the aforesaid visit; the Captain then and there replied, "Upon my honour, Counsellor Cornelius, your sister is as innocent for me, this day, as the child unborn: and if she were not, Counsellor, I'd swear, upon my honour, to the fact, all the same." '

'I don't see the application of the anecdote, however well told,' said Lady Knocklofty, coldly and haughtily.

'Nor I,' said the Duchess, endeavouring to look grave; while all the rest of the party laughed loudly, on the pretext of Lady Honoria's admirable imitation of O'Mealy's mincing manner and indomitable brogue. Meantime O'Mealy, encouraged by being noticed at all, even for his absurdities, and now seeing that O'Brien had obtained a *grand succès*,' shook him by the hand, and with the whisper of 'I tould you I would do the needful for you,' turned to Lady Honoria, exclaiming familiarly, 'Upon my honour, your Ladyship is too sevaire upon me entirely. All that story of Juliana O'Gallagher had not a spark of foundation; for at that very time when people were talking of my seducing the young cratur's affections, and carrying her off to the barracks, I was in fact deeply and sariously attached to Miss O'Kelly, or at all events to Miss O'Tool.'

This confession, the result of garrulous vanity and inordinate folly, produced a general laugh, louder than the first; and all agreed that the price of O'Mealy was beyond that of rubies.

With all her wit and humour, Lady Honoria was sometimes *un peu trop forte* for the Duchess. Although her Grace had thrown off somewhat of the high manner of English *bon ton* since her arrival in Ireland, she had not familiarized herself with that breadth and freedom of speech which distinguished a particular class (and that the highest) in Irish society, among whom wit was seldom impeded by propriety; and who, whether they 'sold a bargain,' or told an anecdote, did both, with little reference to that *bienséance*, which, though coming under the head of minor morals, is rarely found separated from the great.

The Duchess did not therefore join in a laugh, so coarsely and indelicately raised at the expense even of a rival; and without appearing to notice the application, she coolly presented O'Brien to the Countess Knocklofty, as the lady whose life his gallantry had probably saved in the morning. With a graceful gravity that imposed on all, she then took Lady Knocklofty's arm; and seating herself on a sofa, motioned O'Brien to approach, and (by one of those acts of conscious power which dares do all, or of female caprice, which *does* do all), placed him between Lady Knocklofty and herself.

The effect of this conduct was instantaneous. Laughter was hushed into sneers; and sneers gradually were subdued into approving smiles. Hitherto, through all the apparent cordiality of the Duchess's manner to her accidental guest, there was a by-play, directed to the initiated, which spoke her subjection to the worthless and the worldly, by whom she was environed. A sly glance at Lady Honoria, or a significant nod to Lord Kilcolman, evinced the necessity of proving to the tribunal of Irish *ton* that her gracious reception was but a mockery, a civil mystification, played off on one whom 'nobody' knew, and who had been seen 'no where.' The few who composed the oligarchy of fashion and of faction in Ireland, were then deemed 'everybody;' and the whole of space not occupied by them, was termed 'no where.' '*Le même propos par le même jargon*,' has served the purposes of society under all its changes and modifications; and from the swearing, slanging, drinking Duchesses of Whitehall and the Cockpit, to the coarse, petulant Peeresses who presided at Kew, and who hunted down 'the pretty fellows' at Ranelagh; and from them to the cold, *brusques*, dull dames who reign amidst the more decent but less amusing coteries of modern fashion, all, in their passing supremacy, have condemned to utter insignificance the nobodies who were out of their clique, and have consigned to obscurity the places which were not consecrated by the exhibition of their follies, or the display of their power.

But the Duchess had now *pris son parti;* and whether her conduct was the result of good nature, or of female caprice, the object to whom it was devoted profited largely by its direction, and yielded gradually to its seduction. For man, however he may adhere to principles, cannot always command sensations; and if there is an age in which the influence of politics and of pretty women are at odds, O'Brien was yet far from having attained it. He was, indeed, a devoted patriot. His love of country partook of all that passion which leads men to things deemed great, or desperate, as circumstances direct. Life to him was of no value, when its sacrifice could promote the great cause of its adoption. But if such is the enthusiasm which in all causes makes martyrs, 'tis time only that makes saints; and the honest, but ardent novice, who now sat exposed to such temptations as St Anthony never dreamed of, sighed to think how much easier it is to suffer with a Mutius, than to resist with a Scipio. Convinced that the 'English interest' was, for once, committed to fair hands, he felt, in every fibre, that it was the female, and not the male oligarchy, which could most effectually 'do the king's business.'

The society of the vice-regal drawing-room was now broken up into groups, and formed into *petite pelotons.* Incipient flirtations were forming in the recesses of every window, and decided affairs were yawning out their *tête-à-têtes* in every corner. Some of the *Coryphœi* of the Curragh were betting upon their Eclipses and their Mrs. Slamakins; and some histrionics of the private theatricals were holding forth on the rival merits of Mrs O'Neil and Mrs Gardiner.[1] The intimates, or particular *cortège* of the vice-queen now drew near, and took their places, as ease and grace directed, round her, who, though many among the attendant graces were all divine –

> Yet still the fairest queen,
> Like Dian 'midst her circling nymphs, appear'd.

The group was picturesque, and with its accessories of light and

---

[1] Two beautiful and accomplished leaders of what was best and most intellectual in the Irish *bon ton* of the day. The poetical productions of Mrs O'Neil were as admirable as those of her friend Mrs Greville.

shade, of ponderous mirrors, and grotesque girandoles, would have painted well. From the variety of colour, form, and costume, it looked, indeed, like a carnival party designed by a Callot or a Canaletti, or like an antique masque got up by Ben Jonson, or described by Scott. The epoch alluded to was, indeed, a sort of saturnalia of the toilette; it was the only interregnum in the despotism of fashion on record, between the final breaking up of the old German costume, which came in with the English revolution, and the Greek, which came in at the French; – a brief pause, when beauty, for once emancipated from the tyranny of *ton*, pranked herself as she pleased, and never looked more beautiful.

The dress of the Duchess (her favourite dress), a hat and corsage of black velvet, with diamond loop and cross, and a petticoat of rose-coloured satin, full in folds and hue, recalled the heroine of the 'Merry Wives of Windsor;' while Lady Knocklofty (in the same turban and caftan, in which, a night or two before, she had played Roxalana) imaged one of those –

> Forms
> Which the bright sun of Persia warms.

Lady Honoria, always original and always simple, the glass of fashion, but not its reflector, might have passed for a Swiss peasant, the Claudine of Florian, or the *prima ballerina* of the Italian opera. Miss Macguire, plump and pretty, fat, fair, and twenty-five, wanted but the cornucopia, to exhibit as the goddess of plenty. The Ladies O'Blarney (the Duchess's inseparables), who had obtained the name of the Graces, whom they resembled in number and audity, were draped as if escaping from the bath, or ready to plunge into it. Others almost as fair, and quite as fantastic, – in large, full-feathered hats, and loosely flowing tresses, – their zones scarcely bound, and their drapery scarcely fastened (even by the precautionary pin of Sir Peter Lely), formed the outward line of this nucleus of beauties, who all

> In circles as they stood,
> More lovely seem'd than wood-nymphs or feign'd
> goddesses.

The presiding deity, the '*pulcherrima illa*' of Irish jobs, and Irish gallantry, beheld the arms and back of her sofa, surrounded by the manly, handsome representatives of the young oligarchy; while Lord Muckross, the last relic of the old, lay at her feet, in the attitude of

Hamlet's fantastic gallantry, playing with her fan, as fans were played with when such occupations had their use and influence; – when a course of flirtation was not a course of science; – and when love, not lecturing, was the end and object of the social system of the day.

Among the *dévoués* who were crowding round this queen of hearts, were two young looking persons, evidently in the first evening of their noviciate at the Irish court. They were both distinguished by the inalienable inheritance of the Geraldine race, golden fair, full blue eye, and a mild benignity of look and smile. As they now stood, in the prime of youthful beauty, there was a contrast between the elegant but manly softness of their thorough bred air and manner, and the style and bearing of the official hierarchy, the cold *hauteur* of the Proudfort party, or the broad dashing swagger of their political followers, and social disciples, the Kilcolmans, the Kilmallocks, the Kilmainhams, and 'others.'

The elder of these two youths was frequently addressed by the Duchess, by the title of Lord Walter Fitzwalter; and the latter by that of some inherited knighthood of romantic sound, and historic reminiscence, which bespoke him a descendant of that heroic branch of the Geraldine family, the Desmonds. They had both already taken their stand under the oriflamme of patriotism; the one destined to attest the sincerity of his vocation with his blood, the other by the sacrifice of almost all '*fors l'honneur*.' Such were the men whom the Machiavelian policy of the day endeavoured to lure into the snares of power, by baits which rarely fail, but which in the present instance did not succeed; for, if the heart sometimes yielded, the principle stood firm.

O'Brien thus encircled, enthralled in '*dolce prigione*,' was smiled upon by the three graces, interrogated on his adventures of the night by Lady Knocklofty (with that anxious maternity of manner, the more dangerous because the least suspicious), insidiously cross-questioned by Lady Honoria, drawn upon with a flattering familiarity by Miss Macguire (who had promised Lord Kilcolman to 'trot him out'), and plied by the Duchess with those courteous common-places which princes and their representatives so well know how to dispense. He replied to all with an impassioned bashfulness, and with an earnestness and *naïveté*, the natural expression of strong excitement. This was his first introduction to the society of British beauty; almost the first to the female society of any country. His young life had been divided between the ascetic solitude of the wildest part of Ireland, the monastic cells of a foreign college, and the rude haunts of a foreign camp. With his eyes now turned on the naturally impassioned countenance of Lady Knocklofty, and now fixed on the splendid orbs of the Duchess, who archly enjoyed his confusion, – he answered their multifarious questions 'neglectingly, he knew not what.' But whatever he did answer, pleased; and pleased perhaps for that very reason: for women ever prefer the confusion they excite to the wit they inspire.

'How well he speaks!' said Lady Knocklofty to Lady Honoria.

'So did Balaam's ass, when the angel addressed him,' said Lady Honoria; 'and you see the Duchess, the irresistible Duchess, has already inspired *your* Cymon.'

This intimation fell, as it was intended, on the heart of Lady Knocklofty; who suddenly interrupting one of her Grace's questions, rose and said: 'Come, Mr O'Brien, the Duchess must not make you forget that you are a prisoner on parole, that I am responsible for your surety, and that Captain O'Mealy must return to his guard, and will conduct you to your prison-house.'

'As long,' said the Duchess, laughing, 'as *you* keep guard on Mr O'Brien, you know, he is safe.'

'Mr O'Brien does not, perhaps, feel so,' said Lord Muckross.

'When chief meets chief, then comes the tug of war,' whispered Lady Honoria to Miss Macguire, delighted with the struggle for power between the rival beauties.

Lady Knocklofty replied coldly to the Duchess's observation, 'I believe my guard is relieved. But Mr O'Brien should know that the serjeant waits for him in the yeoman's hall; and he must not be found here, when the Lord-Lieutenant comes out of the dining-room.'

'That won't be ere rise of sun,' sang forth Miss Macguire, a stock witch in Macbeth: 'for I have observed, when once his Grace passes midnight at table, like other spirits, he never retires till cock-crow.'

'Then let us have supper,' said the Duchess; 'and place little Gore, as a vidette to warn us of the enemy's approach. When 'tis time to dismiss our Captain, I'll give him his *bouquet d'adieu.*'

'Give it him now then,' said Lady Knocklofty, whose temper brooked no control; 'for I must go; and I will not stir till Mr O'Brien is delivered back to the serjeant of the guard.'

'Well, do give it to him, Duchess, and relieve Lady Knocklofty from her responsibility,' said Lady Honoria significantly, and throwing her eyes, with a look, understood by the Duchess, on that beautiful bust where

> Nel bel sen le peregrine rose,
> Giunte ai nativi gigli.

The Duchess, with more of playfulness than of discretion, and more occupied with teasing an imperious rival, than in supporting her own dignity, actually drew from the *bouquet* that ornamented her bosom, a rose, and then looked and smiled; but still she paused! O'Brien's eyes followed the movement of her beautiful hand; and his unpractised gallantry, anticipating her intention, was almost ready to bend his knee to the ground, to receive the precious flower, half held out to him.

'Fairies use flowers for their charactery. You are a happy man, Mr O'Brien,' said Lord Muckross; and he cast a reproving look at the Duchess; who, at once recalled to herself by the remark, let the flower carelessly fall upon the carpet. O'Brien darted forward to seize it, but it was already under the foot of Lady Knocklofty.

'*Tour de comédie des plus plaisans,*' said Lady Honoria, clapping her hands; while the Duchess, piqued, and now 'every inch a woman,' and not an inch a queen, said,

'Well, Mr O'Brien, never mind, you shall have a fresher flower another day; and it *shall not be a bouquet d'adieu!*'

'Your Grace may console, but cannot compensate,' said the object of this flattering contest, almost inarticulate from emotion. 'The flower with which you intended to honour me, was' – 'consecrated,' he was about to say; but he paused. He felt he was saying too much, and saying it awkwardly; and yet he had said nothing, nothing that expressed his feelings.

'"Tis sport to you, but death to him,' whispered Lord Walter in the Duchess's ear, in strong sympathy, with feelings fresh and ardent as his own.

'Come,' said the Duchess, good humouredly, 'sit down, my dear Lady Knocklofty, and grant a few minutes longer furlough to your prisoner: he must take some refreshment before he goes. So, Arthur' (turning to the youngest aide-de-camp in waiting), 'order supper, and gather up those flowers, which Lord Kilcolman has thrown down with his Atlas shoulders.'

Arthur flew to execute his lady's commands, – to order supper, ere the fulness of time sent him to order armies; and to pick up prostrate flowers, ere his destinies sent him to restore fallen dynasties. The next moment a door was thrown open, *en suite* with that by which the Countess and her captive had entered, and discovered the little apartment leading to the round room in Birmingham Tower; which looked like 'Pomona's bower,' ornamented with spring foliage and aromatic shrubs, and filled with tables, which, though not piled with 'angel food,' groaned under more substantial fare, and were set off with

> fruits of delicious vines
> With freshest flowers crown'd.

The odour of *rôts* and ragouts, more gracious to the exhausted forces of rompers and rattlers, than that 'shed from love's dewy wings,' now caused a universal desertion from the drawing-room. A general rush took place; none standing 'on the order of their going' – but going 'at once,' with an indifference to forms and etiquettes enough to make the majestic portrait of the Duchess of Ormond (which hung over the reigning Duchess's head) start from its frame, and to *faire frémir d'horreur* the presiding chamberlains of castle ceremonies. A *buffet* was served in the drawing-room, in the centre of the Duchess's select circle, with fairy elegance and magical celerity. Iced champagne, and a high seasoned *Mayence*, were the principal items selected by her Excellency's *maître d'hôtel;* who, besides being lineally descended from that *preux* of the kitchen, Vatel, had served in the *petits appartemens* of Monceaux; where luxury still raised altars, of which Madame de Genlis doubtless never dreamed, amidst the convent cells of Belle Chasse.

At this period, supper was no less the favourite meal of the Irish, than it had been of the Romans and the French. Conviviality was then the predominant quality of their temperament; and the most excitable of all people were most excited by that light but stimulating meal, over which care in any country rarely holds an influence. The guests of her Grace's round table seemed to quaff wit with their wine; many a *bon mot* followed many a *bonne bouche;*

> Et l'esprit qui vient du corps'
> En bien mangeant remonte ses ressorts.

Tokay was recommended, Burgundy was sipped, the Champagne circulated rapidly; and looks as sparkling, though not as cold, gave it a zest worth all the *borraccio* in the world. The old Irish fashion of kissing the cup, to pass it to the rest, was quoted by the young knight of the Geraldines, and practised by the fair lady he pledged. The old earl repeated his usual *chanson à boire* –

Nous n'avons qu'un temps à vivre,
Amis, passons le gaiment,

and there was not a dissenting voice to the doctrine; while all, in the full enjoyment of the hour, seemed to feel that the present is the millennium of the wise, *'et que l'avenir est aux fous.'*

While the grosser senses were thus engaged, that which is most the slave of the imagination was fed with the magic of sweet sounds. A fine German military band played in an adjoining room, those delicious, languid measures (then a novelty in Ireland), which have since had such vogue; – an appropriate accompaniment to the smothered 'colloquies divine,' which say so little and mean so much. It was in that tone of voice, so indistinct to all but the ear to which alone it is addressed, that Lady Knocklofty continued to flatter to intoxication the auditor, to whom she addressed herself; who, inspired by the double philtre, poured from flasks and eyes, was yielding up the reserve of pride and the shyness of inexperience, to blandishments, powerful in proportion to their novelty. The canon law against grandmothers is not so absurd as some may imagine; and the siren of forty has always a chance against the sylph of fifteen, when the object is still of that age, when passion is not nice, and when the smile that solicits is, under all circumstances, worth the frown that repulses.

# CHAPTER III

———•———

## *The Frolic Continued*

Puis dit à l'âne: 'Or conte moi ta vie,
Et garde-toi bien d'omettre un seul fait;
Car si tu faux, je ne te faudrai pas.'
L'âne, craignant de recevoir puissance,
Répond ainsi.

WHILE *chacun avec sa chacune* uttered an infinite deal of nothings
that meant every thing, and said every thing that meant nothing, the
excitement of the scene passed with all, for the exuberance of sensibility, or the fervour of wit. Every man fancied himself in love, and
every woman believed it. All in their turn contributed to the general
festivity, and kindled at the reciprocal corruscations of gaiety, emitted
from eyes that sparkled, and lips that smiled. Even persons, by their
calling and *manière d'être*, the most displaced in such revels, partook
of the tone and spirit of the moment, and sanctioned by their presence
the follies which they did not personally promote; while their individual peculiarities and professional exterior of gravity served to
promote the fun, which such contrast ever heightens.

Among the latter class, was the Honourable and Reverend Lady
Mary Sullivan, more usually called the 'good Lady Mary,' sister of
Lord Knocklofty, and the wife of the bishop of St Grellan. *Her* place,
as she declared, being assigned by Providence 'among publicans and
sinners,' she yielded with submission to its dispensations; and was as
seldom absent from the public entertainments, or private parties of
the castle, as her husband, the bishop, was from its levees and audiences. Gifted, however, like the rest of her order, with a restless
abounding of sanctity, in season and out of season, her precepts and

her preachments yielded ample food for mystification, while they awakened an affected respect for her 'goodness:' and when she got credit for her intentions, she did not the less provoke infinite mirth by their displaced fervour and sincerity. She now sat at the Duchess's *petit souper*, eating her ice with an air of sober self-denial, such as that with which Madame de Maintenon fasted on a herring, while all around feasted on flesh at the merry banquets of the *Hôtel Scarron*.

Next to Lady Mary stood the very reverend the Archdeacon of St Grellan, soaking a Naples biscuit in a glass of Tokay; himself sufficiently soaked to render the advice of that dear friend and patroness nearly unavailable. To her urgent entreaties that he should follow the example of the Bishop, who had retired from the dining-table, without appearing in the Duchess's circle, he opposed the pertinacity of a fuddled man; and he continued to hold his ground, though he could scarcely keep his feet; and to stick to a theme which had enlisted some of the most acrimonious passions of his never very placable temperament in its discussion. This theme was the flushed, fluttered, and highly-excited youth, who, being placed between those to whom 'all bishops, priests, and deacons' then bowed, as 'the givers of all good things,' had become the accidental object of the Archdeacon's envy, as he habitually was the natural subject of his malice. For the Reverend Joshua Hunks was the son and successor, in the archdeaconry, of the Reverend James Hunks, whose title to the estates of Moycullen had been defeated by O'Brien's father, some three-and-twenty years before, in favour of the Count O'Flaherty.

Hovering near, without being invited to join the gay and fair party of the Duchess's *petit couvert*, he resembled, in his dusky canonicals, a croaking raven among a flock of birds of brilliant song and feather; and he fixed the victim of his mediated attack (as monkeys and maniacs select the objects of their mischievous antipathies), with an obstinacy which the prudent councils of the 'good Lady Mary,' for once, could not disturb. Primed with port and persecution, the flush of excess burning on his cheek, the power of protestant ascendancy beetling on his brow, the consecrated bacchant was a prophetic image of the more modern members of his caste, who, intolerant at the board as in the pulpit, and intemperate in both, make 'sweet religion a living fountain of gall,' and render society one protracted feast of the Lapithæ. Full of ire and envy, with every irascible passion mounted by wine, the Archdeacon had, with difficulty, restrained himself from a formal attack on the lion of the night, at the first moment when he had found him engaging the attentions of Lady Knocklofty; and when the Duchess, with the *étourderie* of a great lady, remembering nothing that did not directly concern herself, inquired of Mr O'Brien, 'if he was not of the illustrious house of Inchiquin,' the Archdeacon suddenly burst forth, and interrupting the answer of the person addressed, exclaimed –

'Lest the young gentleman should be too modest to answer for himself, Madam, I can answer for him that he is not of the Inchiquin family. He is, I think, the son of a townsman of mine, one Terence O'Brien, an attorney, who, having first brought himself into note by a litigious victory over my father, the late Archdeacon of St Grellan, in favour of a foreign papist, contrived afterwards to ruin himself by the pursuit of a dormant title; for the recovery of which he was indebted to the impatience of a committee of privilege, to which the king had referred him. Worried out with his pretensions, contained in volumes of fusty parchments, they, some time back, declared him a peer on his petition *in forma pauperis*. Upon which, by way of a grateful return, he must needs become a relapsed papist. I believe the young gentleman is also nephew to the two jacobite old ladies, the Misses Mac Taaf, who so vehemently opposed the Proudforts at the last election, and with a few paltry freeholders nearly turned the scale in favour of young Mr Daly.'

The brutality of this speech, which would not have been made in so gross a form, except under the influence of inebriety, had its natural effect; it produced disgust towards the reverend chronicler, in all not prejudiced against O'Brien; and these were principally the women. By putting Lady Knocklofty in the wrong, it put her in a rage, not the less violent for being necessarily suppressed; and by clouding the gaiety of the moment, it annoyed the Duchess, and almost tempted her to desire the page in waiting to order the archdeacon's carriage; since, like all the great, her Grace could suddenly draw up, and dash down obtrusive presumption, with the same hand that had capriciously caressed it into its perilous familiarity. But O'Brien instantly and exclusively fixed her attention on himself, by coolly observing to her inquiries (while the expression of his countenance spoke the struggle of indignant feeling, and the effort he made upon himself) –

'I am much flattered by your Grace's inquiries, and as I could "but little grace my tale in speaking of myself," as the archdeacon has observed, I am much obliged by his anticipating the little I could say.

I am, indeed, Madam, the son of the poorest peer in the realm, whose misfortunes are involved in those of his country; and who, in early life, persecuted into apostacy by that gentleman's family, has lately redeemed an involuntary error, by abjuring it. Of the anecdote he has related of my two female relations, I was ignorant; but I rejoice to learn that they have had the moral courage to oppose power in its strong hold, to assert the elective franchise, and permit their tenants to vote as conscience dictates. For the rest, Madam, I have no occasion to blush for a family, whose hereditary rank sanctions the condescension which places me in the enviable position I now occupy; and whose poverty is at least a proof of the uncompromising honesty which has accompanied a title that never was bought or sold.'

'Bravo! Mr O'Brien,' said the Duchess, who, with every woman in the room, was, for the moment, a partisan of the frank and spirited speaker – 'Bravo! I will take my iced sherbet to your Champagne. Will you, Lady Knocklofty, like a generous enemy, be *de la partie?*'

'With all my heart,' said Lady Knocklofty, gaily; and both ladies, laughing and nodding, touched their glasses with that of O'Brien; while the rest of the fair guests bowed, and sipped, and smiled at one, 'who, rich in title, if not in wealth,' had been endowed by nature with grace, spirit, eloquence, and beauty, – qualities which never fall unacknowledged upon female apprehensions.

From these, however, were to be excepted the Lady Honoria and Miss Macguire: the latter had views on Lord Kilcolman, which an obvious admiration of the hero of the evening might not promote; and the former, on the arrangements of the house of Proudfort, which the prepossession of Lady Knocklofty, if carried beyond a mere *goût passager*, would considerably discomfit. Meantime, the dean sat cowering and glouring by the side of Lady Mary's chair, like an ill-omen'd bird of prey, disappointed in his aim, and waiting for another pounce.

'I suspect, Mr O'Brien,' said Lord Muckross, who fancied he saw in the spirited youth *'un matador de sa jeunesse,'* 'that notwithstanding your very Irish name and birth, your education has been foreign, and – '

'Oh! that is obvious from his bow,' interrupted Lady Honoria, in her wonted tone of irony, 'which bow, by the by, I remarked at the review to-day. You mere Irish may smile as you will, but there *is* an air acquired by foreign education, which not all the dancing masters in Ireland, from dear Fontaine, "*avec ses graces,*" to Paddy Flanaghan, with his "dance up to the griddle, and down to the broom," can neither give nor take away. You have lived much in other and better worlds than this, our *ultima Thule*, Mr O'Brien,' added Lady Honoria, with a significant look at Lord Kilcolman, and a knot of kindred spirits of which he was the centre and the soul.

With the sensitive apprehension of a morbid pride, always on the *qui vive*, because always at odds with fortune, O'Brien had intercepted this look; and now suspecting himself the butt of the foolish and fashionable practice of hoaxing (the quizzing of that day), he took his position of defence, and, with lance in guard, was ready to meet the assault with at least as much force, if not with as much coolness as it was made. He replied therefore, drily,

'I have served abroad, Madam.'

'Mass,' whispered Miss Macguire to Lord Kilcolman, who answered in his Munster brogue –

'I'll ingage! I wonder what the devil Lady Knocklofty and the Duchess see in the fellow, to make such a fuss about him?'

'Oh! he is very handsome,' said Miss Macguire. 'Lady Knocklofty says he has quite a Roman head.'

'Roman catholic, I suppose she manes,' said Lord Kilcolman, laughing at his own wit, and unmindful of Miss Macguire's precautionary hint of 'Hush, for gracious sake, Lord K.; if you don't take care, we shall all be properly unpopular. You had better go with the stream.'

'If I do I'll be d——d!' said his Lordship. 'Upon my honour and soul, I never saw such a coxcomb in my life.'

'Do you mean,' said Lord Muckross to O'Brien, 'by having served abroad, that you have borne a commission in some foreign army?'

'I mean, my Lord,' said O'Brien, now suspicious of every question, and irritated by the look and laugh of Miss Maguire and Lord Kilcolman, 'I mean that I have served abroad as other mercenaries have served at home; and have been driven by necessity to turn that into a trade, which ought to be a profession – fighting for any cause, good or bad, that I was hired to defend. I have been for some years in the Austrian army – '

Lord Muckross drew up, and bridled like one of Richardson's 'charmers.' There was something revolutionary in this answer, something of the new democratic school, that touched his aristocracy to the quick, and diminished his prepossession in favour of the imprudent speaker.

'Your definition is a singular one, Sir,' said an old Colonel of the battle-axe, whose service had been confined to the castle yard; 'and allow me to say, as one who has borne His Majesty's commission for thirty years, that if it be a *trade* to serve one's king and country, hired or not, it is a glorious one.'

'It has not been my good fortune to be permitted to serve either, Sir,' said O'Brien. 'In the late war I should have fought against the interest and honour of both; and I rejoice that I was then too young to bear arms in a contest, which lost England the best of her colonies abroad, and exposed the weakness of the councils which too long had governed her at home.'

'*Ouf!* exclaimed Lady Honoria, 'and this within two steps of Birmingham Tower!'

Every one looked astonished at the utterance of a speech, to say the least of it, so impudent and misplaced; while the divine chuckled, rubbed his hands, and whispered something in the ear of the good Lady Mary, who in reply added – 'Ay, and atheistical too.' Even the good humoured Duchess looked displeased; and Lady Knocklofty, rousing a little page, who lay half asleep on a pile of cushions behind her, said,

'Go, my dear, into the supper-room, and tell Captain O'Mealy, that Mr O'Brien is ready to attend him to the guard-house whenever he pleases.'

The sleepy page toddled off, rubbing his eyes, and told O'Mealy that he might return to the guard-room whenever he pleased. Captain O'Mealy, however, did not please to return till he had finished a tumbler of punch royal, in which he was joined by his friend, Sir Phelim O'Flyn.

'If you have served in the Emperor of Austria's army,' continued Lord Muckross, 'which, for one so young, is a singular event, and for a student of Trinity College, I believe, an unprecedented circumstance, you probably have seen my old friend the Maréchal Lacy, and can give me some account of him; and of that Prince of wits and *preux*, the charming Prince de Ligne, the boon companion of some of my gayest days, ay, and nights too.'

'I carried the colours of the Prince's regiment under the walls of Oczakow,' said O'Brien eagerly, 'and had the honour of serving as his aide-de-camp in the last campaign. To the Maréchal Lacy I have the honour to be related, and the happiness of being obliged. I owed to his protection my rapid rise in a service, where all goes by privilege and influence. They were both well, when I left Germany; the one '*le Doyen des Heros du siècle*,' the other the model and inspiration of all the young military, for whom he has done so much, both by precept and example.'

'I am enchanted to hear it,' said the old Earl, warming to the reflection of his early reminiscences: for he had been the Adonis of Maria Theresa's Court; and the imperial prude had even given him the name of *le bel Irlandais*, with a snuff-box, which he now proudly produced, exhibiting her formal features and powdered *toupée*, ornamented with a sky-blue ribbon, and a rose on her expanded bosom, as full and faded as her cheek. He continued, in a tone of great exhilaration, '*Ah! c'étaient de beaux jours!*'

'What an old twaddle!' said Lady Ellen O'Blarney, passing the box to Miss Macguire.

'Twaddle! She was beautiful!' exclaimed Lord Muckross. 'Beautiful, as she was clever. Your Emperor, Mr O'Brien, was a great man, but not so great a man as his mother.'

A general laugh succeeded this observation. Lord Muckross pleaded his privilege.

'I should have said, not so great a sovereign as his mother.'

'There are many in the present day, my lord,' said O'Brien, 'of a different opinion.'

'Yes, the French democrats,' said his Lordship, with whom O'Brien again lost ground, 'who expect that the emperor will some day lay down his sceptre, like his great ancestor, and, joining their convention, exchange his iron crown for a *bonnet rouge*.'

'The emperor himself, my lord,' said O'Brien, 'has encouraged no such expectations; for though less foolish than many of his royal contemporaries, he has frankly declared, "*son mètier à lui est d'être roi.*" Opposed, as he is, to the dull race of Hapsburg, laugh as he may at the follies of his aulic council, and disposed as he has been to partial reforms in the barbarous institutions of his Gothic government, he is at best but a happy accident in a bad system, whose defects he may ameliorate, but will never remove.'

'The government of Austria,' said Lord Muckross, 'is at least as good as the wretched people for whom it exists deserve. But, I suspect, Mr O'Brien, that you have lived more in France than in Germany, from the colour of your opinions; for these are not the doctrines of the *salons* of Vienna.'

'I have only visited France, my lord, for a few months on my way home,' was the reply; 'and only remained there as the guest of a dear old friend and former preceptor, the now celebrated Bishop of——, one of the constitutional clergy of France.'

'You must have seen some hot work,' said the Earl, 'during your service in the Austrian army. Your emperor did not let the swords of his troops rest in their scabbards. He was, however, sometimes more prompt than prudent. The Turks beat you back *pas à pas*, in spite of the united arms of Potemkin and Saxe Cobourg, at one time.'

'I had not the mortification of witnessing the defeat you allude to – I was then with my regiment at Florence. But it was my good luck, shortly after, to join the grand army, under Marshal Loudhon, at Belgrade, and to see the power of the barbarous masters of the Greeks crumble before a force at least one degree less barbarous than themselves.'

'Are you a disciple of the Greek cause?' asked Lord Walter eagerly; who had listened with much attention and interest, to the imprudent but emphatic answers of one, whose ardour he shared, but whose misplaced frankness he regretted.

'I am fanatically so, my Lord,' answered O'Brien, smiling.

'I wonder you do not volunteer your service to the Great Catherine,' said Lord Muckross, archly; 'you are quite in her line.'

'I have no great confidence in her intentions,' said O'Brien. 'A Russian autocrat may plan the erection of a throne on the borders of the Euxine; but the partitioner of Poland can never advance the cause of freedom and justice, nor the mistress of a nation of slaves give liberty to other nations.'

'Liberty and equality for ever!' muttered Lord Kilcolman.

'French atheism and philosophy,' whispered the Archdeacon to Lady Mary.

'If you take the Greek cause out of the hands of Russia,' said Lord Walter, 'I fear you leave it hopeless.'

'I should hope not,' said O'Brien. 'There *is* a nation, which nature points out as the ally of the Greeks (resembling them in character and intellect), – a nation, which now struggling for its own liberty, may one day assist in giving back to Greece the rights that called into existence her Pericles and her Themistocles, her Solons and Lycurguses, – a nation, which having already annihilated the exclusive and pernicious privileges of its own worn-out institutions, may – '

'France, of course!' nodded Lord Muckross. O'Brien bowed assent.

'How eloquent!' whispered Lady Knocklofty to Lady Honoria.

'And how discreet,' replied her Ladyship. 'How "consults in all the genius of the place." '

'One may be goaded to say anything, anywhere,' rejoined Lady Knocklofty; 'but it is delightful to see any one think so freshly, and speak so frankly, and so unlike every thing and every body else.'

'I am sorry to perceive, Mr O'Brien,' said Lord Muckross, 'that, like many other young Irishmen of the present times, whose heads are as hot as their hearts, you are infected with doctrines of the new revolutionary school; and though it always shows blood, when a young steed resents the bit, and kicks at the curb at first starting, yet it is necessary to take care that such a spirit does not degenerate into vice.'

'In this country, my Lord, our spirit has been so thoroughly broken, that it is the spur, and not the curb, that is wanting. Those who have been for centuries under the yoke, and, like the racers of the Roman corso, are hemmed in on all sides, may be trusted without bit or rider. It requires but a little hooting and whooping to drive them to the desired goal.'

'Nothing can save him, my dear,' said Lady Honoria. '*Tête de victime, entendez-vous?*'

'I suppose, Sir,' said Lord Kilcolman, 'you have returned here, for the purpose of offering your services in reviving that deficient spirit, – that spirit which has already produced such admirable effects in France.'

'I would do so, Sir, with all my soul,' replied O'Brien, with uncontrollable petulance, 'if I thought such services as mine could become available.'

'Jockey of Norfolk be not too bold!' muttered Lady Honoria; while Lord Muckross, feeling for the perilous impetuosity of one so unguarded, whom he himself had drawn out, said, good naturedly,

'Come, Mr O'Brien, I will not take advantage of a fervour kindled, I suppose, in the Historical Society of the University, where you young orators, I hear, sometimes say very eloquent, but very foolish things. I will venture to assert now, that you are the Demosthenes of that, or of some other debating society, where young people overthrow old empires and imagine new.'

'The "Devil" in Temple Bar, or the "Black Boar" in the Strand,' said Lord Kilcolman, insolently and laughingly.

'My Lord, I have the honour of being an humble member of the society you mention,' said O'Brien, turning to Lord Muckross; 'a society which, so long as it is permitted to exist, with Locke for its legislator, and Grattan for its model, will, indeed, assist in reviving that national spirit, and awakening that national eloquence, without which, nations can have no political existence, nor any adequate champions of their rights. I have also recently been present at another assembly, not held at the "Devils," or the "Black Boar," but in the *Jeu de Paume*, at Versailles, consisting of the representatives of the greatest nation upon earth. I was present when they swore never to separate, till they give a constitution to their country, founded upon the overthrow of those oligarchical privileges in church and state, which had been alike fatal to the independence of the king and to the rights of the people. I was present, also, at the demolition of the Bastille, and I cannot help adding to this confession, the boast of having been one of those young men who gave the first *coup de hachet* to the chains of the portcullis, which led to all that followed.'

By the effervescence of his looks and words, O'Brien had now so well 'pointed his purpose to his hearers' hearts,' that, with a very few exceptions, all admired the speaker, even though they disapproved the speech. A short silence ensued, which was broken by Lord Kilcolman's observing, in a half whisper to Lady Honoria, 'He is come of a good school.'

'To try the bird, the spur must touch his blood,' said Lord Walter to Lady Knocklofty.

'Yes,' said Lady Knocklofty, 'and the bird turns out to be a young eagle.'

'A young goose!' whispered Lady Honoria; 'and a goose more likely to betray than to save the Capitol, I suspect.'

'Come,' said the Duchess, no longer amused by the conversation, and therefore now fully alive to its impropriety, 'no more politics, for patience sake. Miss Macguire, pray sing, "Arrah! will you marry me;" "*La Marmotte*," or any thing you please; only sing.'

'Dear Duchess, I've no more voice than a corncrake,' said Miss Macguire.

'Nonsense! sing when you are bid, Kitty Macguire,' said Lady Knocklofty, authoritatively, and rising to break the circle and to draw off others from the quarry which (in the language of hawking) she had ruffed, but not carried.

'I cannot sing without my guitar,' said Miss Macguire, to whom such imperious commands were familiar, as they were unresented.

'Do somebody get her a guitar,' cried Lady Knocklofty, who, in the conscious power of greatness, expected to find every thing she wanted, every where she wished.

'Do look for a guitar, Freddy Fitzjohn,' said the Duchess.

'Where shall I look for it?' drawled out the little secretary, with his mouth full of sugar-plums, as in all the dignity of office, he sat apart from the group.

'Look into the back-gammon box,' said Lady Honoria, gravely.

'Will this do,' said Lady Mary O'Blarney, drawing her fingers over the chords of a beautiful French harp, which, with its highly orna-mented *étui*, stood in a remote corner of the room.

Its deep soft tones, even when touched by unskilled hands, brought to the preoccupied mind of O'Brien, a recollection of the air he had heard in the throne room. It also recalled to the Duchess the performer who had so finely played it, unasked and unrewarded.

'By the by, what has become of the harpist, Sir James?' she inquired, languidly.

'She has just slipped off, I believe,' said the chamberlain; 'a few minutes back I got her a glass of wine and some macaroons; for she was very weary, and perhaps a little mortified at not being asked to perform again.'

'Poor thing! don't fail to send her something in the morning – five, or ten guineas, or whatever you think right. She sung that Italian air prettily, though she had a very husky voice.'

'Husky!' said Lord Muckross, a professed amateur, and president of the Irish Philharmonics. 'The very finest contra-alto! a quality of voice which has become extremely rare, even in Italy. But you all made such a noise, it was quite enough to confound her. Where did you pick her up, Duchess?'

'Don't remember at all,' said the Duchess; 'so many send petitions to exhibit before "her Excellency, at the castle," that somehow or other I mix them all up together. I thought we were to have had the musical glasses, Sir James, or the harmonica, or something.'

'Mr Cartwright, Madam, sent an apology to say he was ill; so I accepted this Italian lady's proposition, whose note I read to your Grace at your toilette, on your return from the review.'

'Oh, yes! I remember – that is, forget all about it.'

'It was simply to beg your Grace's patronage, and permission to play at your party this evening; desirous, of course, to be brought forward by your Grace's notice. It appears she is but just arrived in Dublin, and means to give concerts.'

'Well,' said the Duchess, 'we are all down, I suppose, for subscriptions; but send her something all the same.'

'I really, Madam, do not know where to send to her. There is no address to her note, and her messenger waited for his answer.'

'Don't be alarmed,' said Lady Honoria, 'she will not let you forget her. Besides, there is her harp in pledge, which will be redeemed with ten dozen of tickets, and a request for your Grace's name, patronage, and protection.'

'What an odd looking old trot it is,' said Lady Eleanor O'Blarney, 'coming here in a coal-box bonnet, and black mode cloak. These foreigners are always such odd, ugly creatures; don't you think so, Lord Walter?'

'Not always,' said Lord Walter, laughing. 'This person, though disfigured by her dress, and buried under the shadow of her horrible bonnet and balloon handkerchief, seemed neither old nor ugly. Her eyes, when they glanced through the short, black curtain which shaded them, were most enchantingly fine; but as I could not speak Italian, I could make nothing of her.'

At this moment a little page entering the room, cried out in a fluttered voice 'the Lord Lieutenant!' while the aide-de-camp on service, throwing open another door, the dinner party (those at least who, at an earlier hour, had not left the table, gone home, or *remained* under it) came forth. They entered the drawing-room with a burst of noise and laughter, which called from Lady Honoria the invocation of 'Mirth, admit me of your crew!' Taking the offered arm of Lord Knocklofty, she led him to a sofa, with a vigilant precaution, of which the president of the privy council seemed to stand in need. The Duke meantime hurried joyously, but not very steadily on, followed by his merry court; his eyes sparkling, his cheek flushed, and his hair disordered; and beauty and inebriety combining to give to his fine person the air of the youthful Bacchus, chiselled by a Buonaroti, or painted by an Albano. It was in vain that his privy council endeavoured to look as sober as their calling. The keeper of the seals could not keep his legs – the attorney-general was served with a *noli prosequi* – the speaker could not articulate a syllable – and the King's solicitor suffered judgment to go by default; while the chief baron (an old stager), rejected the admonition of his brother, who was also his register, with 'be aisy, you *omadaun*,'[1] and spouted out theatrically –

---

[1] An Irish phrase for foolish fellow.

'We are state drunkards –
Who shows a sober eye is traitor,
And I arrest him in the name of the Viceroy.'

On the first announce of the Lord Lieutenant, Lady Knocklofty
(who, under the pretence of examining the harp, had drawn O'Brien
to the corner of the room), feeling the necessity of his instant departure
(as his presence would have been a violation of the articles of her
treaty with the Duke, and of all the forms of *bienséance*), gently drew
him from the room into St Patrick's hall. The spacious amplitude was
lighted only by a single lamp, placed for the convenience of the
servants, and by the silver beams of a bright full moon. Through an
open door at the furthest extremity of the apartment, was visible the
long, illuminated vista of the corridor, by which they had first entered
the apartments, with the armoury intervening.

'There is your route,' she said: 'I will send O'Mealy to join you, if
he be not already gone; but,' she added, emphatically, 'if he be, I
think, Mr O'Brien, I may with safety trust to your honour.'

'In the present instance, Madam,' said O'Brien, laughing, 'the trust
is so trifling, that I think you may. But, in any instance, I hope you
will believe, that one whom you have distinguished by your notice,
will never prove unworthy of your confidence.'

'Yes,' she said, gaily; 'but you *very* young men have such odd
ideas of honour. Besides, you are so indiscreet – so impetuous. You
compromised yourself this evening, in a manner which, had you been
my son, I should indeed have gloried in, but not without trembling.'

'Your son! Oh, Lady Knocklofty, what an incongruous idea! – But
would you have your brother, or your friend, under such circumstances, speak otherwise, than as truth and feeling dictated? or truckle
to the insolence of arrogant rank, and deny the principles by which
he is ready to stand or fall?'

'All this is very noble and very fine, but very imprudent. I cannot,
however, stay to dispute against qualities I admire; were I to consult
my own feelings and sentiments, I should not perhaps have you think
or speak otherwise than you did. Strange as it may appear to you, Mr
O'Brien, though obliged by circumstances to live with those, whom I
– but (she added, with a deep sigh, for she had begun to *'enfiler la
grande route du sentiment,'*) 'I must bid you good night, or good
morning. Yet, ere I go, let me gratefully acknowledge a debt, the sum
of which is nothing less than life. I am aware it is not to be cancelled;

but this – give me your hand,' – (and she placed a ring on his finger) – 'this, when you look on it, may recall one, whose will to serve you you must never doubt, however feeble her power.'

'Good heavens! Madam, how can you talk thus of a common act of instinctive humanity!' said O'Brien, in confusion, and retaining the hand, while he gently rejected the ring it presented. 'I cannot,' he added, 'indeed, I cannot accept of any thing so valuable, or rather so valueless, when compared with words so precious as have now fallen from lips which – '

'Valueless, indeed,' interrupted Lady Knocklofty, scarcely struggling to withdraw her hand. 'Valueless, but for the sentiment it expresses; for, see,' and she held it to the lamp: 'it is but a single Lough Corrib pearl, set in Irish gold. 'Tis the family crest, with the family motto round the circle – *"Qui me cherche, me trouve."* You cannot refuse so Irish an offering – you cannot forget so *sincere an intimation;*' and she again passed the ring on a finger of the hand which lay trembling in her own. – 'And now,' she continued, 'never mind O'Mealy, but return to the guard-house, as soon as you see a clearance in the battle-axe hall. To-morrow must provide for itself! Meanwhile, remember, *qui me cherche, me trouve,*' and with the smile and air of the Roxalana she personated in dress, she suddenly disappeared, closing the door, with a violence that extinguished the light on the table, and left O'Brien in the vast, cold moonlighted hall.

The freshness of its air was balm, its silence was repose; after the heated atmosphere, and noisy and imposing circle he had quitted. In the distant vista light and bustle still prevailed. Battle-axes, footmen and pages, the uproar of announced carriages and chairs, – of servants called for, or lords and ladies *'coming down,'* afforded an obstacle to O'Brien's immediate, unobserved departure, of which he gladly availed himself, to remain, for a little while, where he was. In a confusion of ideas, more rapid in their succession, than 'the galloping of heaven's wings,' he was glad to pause, and to tranquillize, if it were possible, the emotions by which he was agitated. The little wine he had drunk (the more exciting to one who had hitherto lived 'in the darkness of sobriety') – the eyes he had gazed on, – the ring whose circlet pressed his finger, – the promise that accompanied it, breathing so sweetly on his ear, – the resulting exaltation of spirit and confusion of thought, all rendered the singular solitude in which he was placed, a resource and an enjoyment. Throwing himself, therefore, along one of those red benches,[1] (to obtain a place upon which, such sacrifices have been made of honour, principle, and patriotism), he gave free course to that illusory, but delicious, train of reverie, which lends to feeling its highest tone, and to thought its brightest scintillations. As he lay, with his right arm pillowing his head, and his eyes turned upward, he unconsciously fixed them upon the superb and richly painted ceiling; where the sycophancy of the times had depicted the regal state of Henry Fitz-empress, who is represented receiving the homage of the subdued Irish chieftains, as they stood, spiritless and crouching, before the Majesty of English power. The full and cloudless moon poured through the lofty windows the full tide of its beams; and the accidents of reflection gave a transient distinctness to the picture, that was strengthened by the deep shadows of the unillumined portions of the apartment.

For some moments O'Brien, pre-occupied by the world within, almost 'above the sense of sense,' saw nothing, heard nothing, and felt all that men feel under the double inebriety of the senses and the imagination. By degrees, as the moon shone more brightly on the frescoed story of Ireland's shame, he was struck by the subject, although but indistinctly seen. He sighed as he gazed. The image was opposed to his present condition, with a mortifying contrast, which awakened the compunctious visitings of conscience; so goading to those in whom principle and passion are at variance. His feelings, his views, with respect to Lady Knocklofty, were so vague, such mere phantoms of fancy and of vanity, of gratitude and admiration, that they had neither character nor consistency. But the wife of the leader of the Irish oligarchy, had she not hinted that she did not participate – . In recalling her words, his memory failed him; the exhaustion of his spirits, the distant hum, the immediate silence, contributed to his abstraction, and thoughts became dreams. His eyes still fixed on the picture of Henry the Second, his imagination still dwelling on his beautiful protectress, – his ideas by degrees faded, and he slept: if that could be called sleep, which, while it absorbed the corporeal faculties, and suspended the will, left the fancy wild and energetic beyond its waking powers; and bodied forth visions of such palpable

---

[1] The privileged seats of the peerage, on the birth-night and other court festivities, held in St Patrick's hall.

form and plausible combination, that mid-day consciousness could scarcely have given perceptions more acute.

From the chaos of incoherent images that attends the first slumbers of weariness, gradually arose a fairy fabrick, the Pomona bower, of which he had caught a view through the open door of the room in which he supped. It seemed all light and verdure; and canopied the fair, majestic, and voluptuous form of Lady Knocklofty, at whose feet he thought he lay, again receiving the pearl of Lough Corrib, and with it

> Such honied words and smiles
> As made the gift seem dearer.

Suddenly the flowers faded, the garlands fell, the lights grew dim, and the rude, dark walls of Birmingham tower appeared in all their original strength and dreariness. The bower of love assumed its ancient aspect of a state prison. No longer at the feet of the lady of his vision, he believed himself chained down to a stone bench, above which appeared, in dark and smoky letters, the names of 'O'Donnel,' 'O'Neil,' 'Delvin,' 'Lord Thomas Fitzgerald,' 'Lord Desmond,' and other illustrious patriots, both of the Irish and English stock, who, by resisting power, had been incarcerated in despotism's strongest hold. Preserving in idea the same uneasy attitude, in which he actually lay, his eyes were involuntarily fixed upon the same grim figure, as in the pictured roof represented Henry the Second. Gradually, however, that stern countenance resolved itself into the cold, phlegmatic features of Lord Knocklofty. His ancient armour was covered with the sash of St Patrick. One extended hand was armed with a dagger, which was gradually and slowly directed to O'Brien's thick-beating heart; while with the other he drew from the finger of his spell-bound victim's hand, his wife's most prized and treasured ring. O'Brien heaved and panted to resist or evade the murderous intent; and still half in dream and half awakened by his suffering, he caught the uplifted hand and griped it firm and fast. Its death-like coldness chilled him to the heart. The prickling of a thousand arrows tingled through his frame; yet still he continued to grasp the unearthly hand, no longer in a dream, but awake and conscious, though still motionless. He looked around him, and recognized every object. The light of the retiring moon faintly sketched the shadows of St Patrick's banners on the floor. The glittering throne was still visible; the hum in the battle-axe hall was heard; still, in spite of these tokens of returning sensation, he held the hand.

Making an effort to move, the motion, slight as it was, restored the blood to its circulation; and he perceived that the cold hand he clasped was – his own; – the hand of that arm on which his head had pressed. The clock at that moment struck three: the whole baseless fabric of his vision had vanished, still however leaving a wreck behind, in his excited imagination. He started on his feet, rubbed his hands, and walked about the obscure and spacious hall, under the disagreeable influence, which a terrible nightmare always leaves behind it. Then resolving to proceed without further delay to the guard-house, he passed the battle-axe hall unremarked, though not unseen; and was proceeding to the lower castle-yard, by the state porter's lodge (instead of the passage by which he had entered), when a chair passed him, preceded by a tall, gaunt figure, wrapped in a long, dark cloak.

The extraordinary height of this gigantic person, just sufficiently awakened O'Brien's curiosity to induce him to glance his eye under the stranger's broad flapped hat; when to his amazement and horror, he again saw, or fancied he saw, that wild and weird countenance which had so often, in the course of the day, congealed him by its apparition. The figure strode rapidly on, and O'Brien, unable to resist the impulse, was about to follow, when he was suddenly seized by the shoulder, with an exclamation of 'I arrest you in the King's name.' He turned and encountered Captain O'Mealy, who, though not tipsy, was just sufficiently elevated by his punch royal, to throw his natural humour and vulgarity off their guard.

'What a pretty fellow you are,' he continued, in an unminced brogue, passing his arm through O'Brien's, 'to lade me such a dance. Sure, I've had the devil's own search after you, Lady K. desiring me to take care of you; but sorrow ghost of you was to be seen nor heard either. So I thought you were carried off by the fairies. For, touch my honour, touch my life. I know you were not the man to give leg bail for your surety. Well, you had the devil's own luck, Sir; and owes it every taste to myself. I gave them th' whole history of you; and first I butthered them up about you, and then I slither'd them down, Sir; so that nothing would do, but you must be served up: so you see – '

'Have you any idea who was in that chair, that passed before us, just as you came up?' interrupted O'Brien, much preoccupied, and attending but slightly to O'Mealy's vulgar egotism.

'Is it any idea I have? Ay, have I, every idea in life. It was that poor cratur of a furreigner, that played so iligantly upon the harp; though nobody listened to her, only myself and a few conishures. When I came down, a little taste ago, there she was standing in a corner, behind the futmen and the flambeaux, waiting for her sedan. So I did the genteel thing by her, as if she was a lady of quality; and packed up her and her little instrument, myself, into the sedan.'

'Had she no servant with her?' asked O'Brien, with an affected carelessness, and fearful of drawing the attention of the captain of the guard to the mysterious person who appeared to have officiated in that capacity, when the chair passed.

'Sorrow, soul, or servant, or christian cratur.'

'And where was the chair ordered?' asked O'Brien.

'Why, have you a mind to be better acquainted with her too? You are a pretty lad – at all in the ring. Why then, I think you have enough to do; and if you mind your hits and take the ball at the hop, and keep the game in your own hands, devil a fear of you, but you'll prosper. Why, Sir, that handsome physognomy, and pale, penetrating eyebrows of yours, is as good as board wages. The little furreigner is a swarthy, poor cratur, and not worth picking out of the gutther, in comparison with them that. . . . Well, naboclish, "mum," says I, "budget," says you, that's the talk, as the great Shakspeare says.'

They were now at the guard-room door; and as soon as O'Brien had shaken off the obtrusive O'Mealy, who mounted his horse to visit the guard and go the rounds, he drew near the light which flickered in its socket on the guard-room table; and throwing round a vigilant glance, with the feeling of a miser visiting his hidden hoards, he raised the ring, the precious ring, to his eyes. At that moment the expiring lamp gave one bright flash, and discovered – not the pearl of Lough Corrib, with its pretty device – but a death's head on a dark onyx, with the well known device of the jesuits engraven in black characters on its circlet –

'Sub cruce latet.'

# CHAPTER IV

---

## *The Oligarchs*

And when we see the figure of the house,
Then must we rate the cost of the erection.

SHAKSPEARE.

PROUDFORT HOUSE was one of those magnificent mansions which, before the Union, were the town residences of the Irish aristocracy; and which, since that fatal period, have been converted into public offices. For such have been the anomalies of that country, 'where (Swift says) an honest man ought to be ashamed to live,' that its official splendour has increased, in proportion as its resources have dwindled, and its business diminished.

Proudfort House, at all times of the year, the shrine of place-hunters and pension-mongers, – of the needy and of the corrupt, was, – at that particular season, which is the carnival of life, as of society, the *rendezvous* of all the rank and fashion of the country. Ireland, during the last quarter of a century, has fallen far behind the rest of Europe; but it was at this period of its active demoralization, more liberal, than it now is in its stultified degradation. Society, though corrupt, was joyous. Party threw no cloud over pleasure. Fashion took no note of faction; and if many of the hereditary guardians of the country and counsellors of the crown – the first in rank as in talents – stood dignified and aloof from the Proudfort cabal and its chiefs; if they boldly entered their protest in the senate[1] against the scandalous measures originated by these political vampires, they did not suffer

---

[1] See the protest in the House of Peers, in 1790, signed by such names as Leinster, Charlemont, Moira, Portarlington, etc. etc.

their patriotic feelings to interfere with social festivity; nor, in that narrow and illiberal jealousy, which has since broken up society into cliques and coteries, refuse to mingle on public nights in the balls, masquerades, theatricals, and ridottoes of their political opponents. The members of all parties then filled up the ranks of amusement; and by encouraging trade, energizing industry, and stimulating the arts, they enabled the country to make a better stand against its oppressors; and, for a while, to uphold its struggling, but decaying manufactures.[1]

But if wit and beauty discountenanced the domestic display of party violence, they had not to encounter the resistance of that dark bigotry, which now lies like an incubus on the public pleasures. A feeble race of imbecile fanatics had not yet succeeded to a generation, whose vices, bold as their manners, did not permit them to veil their patricidal enormities under the sanctimonious garb of religious hypocrisy. Even the harpies who devoured the vitals of the land, showed more sense and more feeling for the people, than their heartless, brainless successors; and if they helped themselves largely and impudently from the public purse, they had not yet exhibited the scandal of purchasing heaven at the expense of their impoverished country, – of congregating to suffocation round the itinerant declaimer, to squander their super-fluities upon foreign missions, – nor of overlooking the thousands perishing in their streets and their highways, to administer with profusion to the fanciful wants of proselytes at the furthest extremities of the globe. As yet, the gayest capital of Europe was unclouded by the gloom of controversial theology; and the charities and the graces of life, still lingering where the sterner virtues had disappeared, were neither chilled by ignorant fanaticism, nor reproved by vulgar zeal.

The intimates, the *habitués* of Proudfort House, the daily guests of its lord, were, however, exclusively selected from the oligarchy, of which he was the leader. Strenuously occupied in the barter of power and principle, they exercised an unrestrained rule over the less privi-leged classes, engrossing all the offices of state, owning most of the property in the soil, and supplying from amongst their own cadets,

---

[1] These remarks apply only to the political and social intercourse between protestant and protestant. At all times catholics rarely and difficultly obtained admission into what is called *bon ton* society. Party feelings were perhaps too rancorous at first to render much intimacy desirable on either side; and eventually, those who were not seen in a particular circle, were deemed unfit for it.

the 'nursing fathers of the church,' (to use a phrase of archbishop King's), whose fosterage was more fatal to the interests and tranquillity of Ireland, than that of the olden times, against which so many acts were fulminated by early parliaments.

At the head of this caste, in power and in influence, stood the family of the Proudforts; whose numbers, like the '*race d'Agamemnon qui ne finit jamais*,' seemed to increase and multiply, with the resources they extorted from the revenues of the country. Arrogating to themselves an exclusive loyalty, as 'King's men,' they mistook the subjection of the crown to their will, for *their* devotion to its possessor: and if a minister, offended by their pride, or scandalized at their greediness, hesitated to uphold their political juggling, or questioned their right to a monopoly of place, they were as ready to turn against the sovereign, as against the people. More than once, a concerted *soulèvement* of the whole privy council, a *levée en masse*, against the viceroy, marked their determination to suffer no minister in Ireland, who was not of their own selection: and on one occasion 'seven of the eleven' constituting the Irish ministry, put the King into Coventry, and themselves *hors du combat*. Kings, however, like wits, have sometimes short memories; and his majesty forgetting to call in those who had so foolishly gone out, resigned them to the original obscurity for which nature had intended them.

The foundation of the Proudfort power was the Proudfort property: and this property was based on the church. The founder of the family had been the chaplain of King William's regiment; and a succession of prelates, *de père en fils*, had added to a small original grant of land (made by the military head of the church, to the chaplain of the church militant), a succession of estates, each purchased from the ample dower of the establishment. This vast landed property, spotted as it was with boroughs (close and rotten), was the *matériel* of family influence; and amply fulfilled the prophecy, 'that to him who has much, more shall be given.' For the rest, the Proudforts, without one quality which naturally places men above their fellows, were destitute of every means for attaining to eminence, save the pertinacity which usually accompanies the passion for family aggrandizement. They were indeed the happiest illustrations of what dogged dulness may effect, when unencumbered by genius to withdraw it from the beaten track of self-interest, or by sympathy with human suffering to distract it from the steady pursuit of personal ambition. Dull as the Dutchman from whom they were descended, tasteless, as they were talentless, they had yet given princes to the church, and commanders to the army; and stopping short only where distinction was to be exclusively acquired by merit, they had engrossed all places and all patronage, without giving to the Irish senate one orator, or to the Irish bar one advocate of eminence.

The Earl of Knocklofty, the head and representative of this prosperous dynasty, was more distinguished by the family organ of self-appropriation, than by any trait of individual idiosyncracy. Plodding, without a head for business; sensual, without a taste for pleasure; the gravity of his manner passed for wisdom, and the solemnity of his carriage for dignity. Always ready to scoff at public virtue as a phantom, he affected great respect for all the external forms of society; and he talked with plausibility of 'the great bonds which keep men together.' Regular in his attendance at church on Sundays, and at Daly's Club-house, on every other day of the week, he prayed and played with equal devotion. But though religious and loyal in the extreme, a pillar of the state and a corner stone of the church, he was, on certain points and morals, with which going to church has little to do, as relaxed as the members of his caste then usually were in Ireland. He had long survived the passion, which had led him into a second marriage with Lady Albina O'Blarney, whose portionless rank, and powerful beauty, had suited his ambition, and gratified his vanity. But his liberality of the wealth which she knew so well how to distribute, and which gratified his ostentatious habits, and the pride he took in his handsome children, obtained for him the reputation of an excellent private character; as if the selfishness which leads to public corruption, could be made compatible with private worth. Living with magnificence, his table exhibited all that luxury had then invented, in a department which has since become one of the fine arts; and his wines and his influence brought him a multitude of guests, who learned from his example, to enjoy, without remorse, those public emoluments which were purchased without restraint – by the ruin of the country. He had recently been elevated to the Earldom of Knocklofty; and the higher dignity of a Marquisate was said to be reserved for those future services, which the proprietor of many boroughs can always render to the party of his adoption.

The Countess Knocklofty was, by her social position, the great autocrat of Irish fashion; and she presided over the *bel air* of the Irish capital, as her husband ruled its political junta. Preserving all the beauty which does not exclusively depend on youth (a passionate expression, a graceful *tournure*), brilliant, though no longer blooming; her rank and influence gave her all the charms she had lost, and heightened all she had retained: for even beauty, in that little world called 'the great,' has no intrinsic value. It is the stamp of fashion that gives it currency; and with that stamp the basest metal is received without examination, while the sterling ore of loveliness, that bears not the mark of the mint, is rejected with disdain. Educated by a feeble and bigoted grandmother, with prejudices which passed for principles, and phrases which passed for ideas; and brought up in respect for forms, and in ignorance of realities, she threw off ties, on coming into the world, which, being founded not in influence but in authority, had no hold either on her judgment or her heart. Launched from the romantic solitudes of her father's castle in Connaught, upon the bustle and temptation of the world, she brought into society the unregulated romance of a retired education; with all the headlong propensities to pleasure of a wilful temperament. Vain, credulous, and impetuous, her vivacity was mistaken for passion, and her fancies for feelings. The reigning manners of the day, and the influence of her position, conspired to sanction the boundless indulgence of a disposition, as unregulated as her mind; and even the selfish pursuit of her own gratification passed for devotion to those who were flattered by being distinguished as its objects. With men of the world, there is a shorter road to the heart than even through their passions – their vanity; and none ever took it with more success than Lady Knocklofty.

It is a maxim of French gallantry (and axioms in love, like dogmas in faith, are always numerous in proportion as the religion is doubtful), that '*la femme, quand l'amour est passion, est constante; quand l'amour n'est que goût, elle est légère.*' According to this canon, Lady Knocklofty was the most passionless, as she was the most *enjouée* of women. Yet her predilections and her preferences, such as they were, were not the episodes, but the history of her life. Platonic or passionate, the fancy of a day, or the sentiment of a year, her flirtations or attachments were the business of her existence. '*Vertueuse, elle jouit de ses refus; faible, elle jouit de ses remords.*' Hitherto, borne out by that demoralization in the higher circles, which ever goes with despotic governments, and living on those terms of decency with her lord, which the world only requires (for nothing can save an imprudent wife, but the dupery of her husband, – or his depravity), Lady Knocklofty, though blamed by some, suspected by many, and talked of by all, still retained the reins of society in her own possession; and kept opinion in check, by having the whip hand, in the great career of rank, influence, and fortune.

To preserve her Ladyship in this enviable, but critical position, which enabled her to preside over the largest house, and command the highest circles in the Irish capital, was the vigilant, assiduous, and not very disinterested object of her friend, monitor, and constant companion, Lady Honoria Stratton. More gifted, more accomplished, more corrupt, and more experienced, than her noble *protégée*, Lady Honoria was one of the many illustrations of that golden maxim, 'that gallantry is the least fault of a woman of gallantry.' The *'vertu de moins'* of Lady Honoria was indeed the only point in her character that had the semblance of amiability. But the frailty which, in some, indicates a susceptibility to 'loving too well,' was in her the result of a necessitous poverty, which obliged her to love 'too wisely.' In risking her character, she calculated only on the profit and loss of a tender attachment; and with Werter in one hand, and Cocker in the other, she formed her estimates as much by the arithmetical conclusions of the one, as by the high-flown sentimentalities of the other. The world, however, always more apt to pardon the folly of vice, than its wisdom, had nearly thrown her beyond its pale, for the ruin she had brought on a young and popular Irishman of moderate fortune; when, luckily, her well directed coquetry at the cold phlegmatic vanity of Lord Knocklofty, and her knowledge of the world, as cleverly directed at the assumption of his wife, gave her an influence at Proudfort House; which opened the door of every other house in Dublin to her reception, and restored her to the caste which she had nearly lost by that which should have been deemed an additional cause for banishing her for ever from its ranks. Beautiful and witty, bold and adroit, the naturally fine dispositions and brilliant qualities of Lady Honoria had been perverted in her earliest youth by a neglected education at home, and a depraved one abroad. Living on the continent from her fifteenth year to her five-and-twentieth with a libertine father (a poor Irish peer), in the refined but profligate circles of the French court, she married at that epoch (in the expectation of a reversionary title and large fortune), the drivelling brother of an Irish nobleman, whose celibacy was deemed certain, till he wedded his cook; when the birth of an heir blasted the hope for which Lady Honoria had made such sacrifices.

Obliged by circumstances to live in Ireland – niched in a large empty house, in Stephen's Green, belonging to her brother-in-law, who resided habitually on his estate in Munster, – and conscious of her own superiority to those to whom her necessities obliged her to bend, she paid back the obligations her ruined fortunes compelled her to accept, by secret contempt, or by open sallies of wit and bitterness, which frequently purchased civilities that gratitude and complaisance might not have extorted. Admired by the men, and feared by the women, she used both as she wanted them; and called upon to '*désennuyer la sottise*,' she repaid the dinners she could not return, and the entertainments she could not rival, by a wit which was always amusing, though not always refined; and a humour which was reckoned somewhat too broad even for the Irish court.

A constant and welcome guest at Proudfort House, she gave a life to its festivities, and a style to its entertainments, which the taste and refinement of its owners were insufficient to confer. Flattering the dull vanity of the husband, and engrossing the confidence of the wife, she soon became a necessity to both; and was frequently a mediatrix in disputes, which her cleverness and subtlety prevented from exploding, to the total rupture of the matrimonial tie, that would have involved the overthrow of her own interests.

While Lady Honoria thus acted as *premier* in the diplomacy of the Knocklofty *ménage*, the Honourable Catherine Macguire was not without her utility in the domestic system of those, who by the very fortune which raises them, are disposed to depend so much more upon the resources of others, than on their own. The daughter of an aunt of Lord Knocklofty, who had run away with a landless papist lord, and had been ever afterwards thrown off by the family, the Honourable Catherine was received by her noble kinsman, as poor Irish cousins usually are – partly from pity, and partly from pride: and being destitute of that fine tone of feeling, which makes dependence misery, – and as highly endowed with that stout huckaback fibre, which stands the wear and tear of capricious favour and insolent pretension, she steadily kept the 'even tenor of her way.' False without feigning, insincere without hypocrisy, she frankly showed up to the world's laughter her present friends and her former creed; and quizzed the Proudforts, and ridiculed the papists, with equally unsparing candour. To the proselyting humour of 'the good Lady Mary' she was indebted for the new creed, which had been the passport to her cousin's protection; and she abandoned the faith of her fathers, with a conviction quite as clear as that with which she had originally received it. Pleasant as she was heartless, she had already passed through the world's hands; and had contracted from its contact that simple hardihood of manner, which often gives to the hackneyed the *naïveté* that is the charm of the recluse. Sure to please, as long as she amused the solemn mediocrity of her kinsman and host, she was well aware of her tenure at Proudfort House; and, resolved that it should be a lease renewable for ever, she silently inserted a clause of surrender, in case she should attain to the fee-simple of any other more advantageous possession.

'The good Lady Mary,' by whose agency Miss Macguire had been induced to accept the thirty-nine articles, and a seat at Lord Knock-lofty's luxurious table, – to swallow the precepts of the sister, with the *pâtés* of the brother, – was a happy precursor of all the *good* ladies of the present day, who have come forward in such numbers 'to justify the ways of God to man,' to complete what the Redeemer had left undone, and, in the fulness of time, accomplish and expound that revelation, which ordinary Christians imagine to have been perfected some eighteen hundred years ago. She was the first to bring into notice an inspired work, generally thought to have been long well known: and she was the original inventor of the protestant dray for carrying converted papists on their road to salvation. She was likewise the first among the great to send out invitations to tea and tracts; and to open religious shops for go-carts mounted upon protestant principles, toys against tolerance, and bible-only babies. It was in Lady Mary's cheap repository, that employment was given to idle ladies of fashion,[1] at the slight expense of those humble dependants on their own industry for their daily bread, who are persons of no fashion; and it was in her schools that education was first made subservient to the purposes of an insidious proselytism. Dull and mischievous, arrogant and interfering, she was among the first to contribute and collect for the conversion of Asiatic Jews; while the poor Irish peasant perished at the gates of the Episcopal Palace, unheeded, and the needy artisan fainted under the windows of the metropolitan mansion, unrelieved.

---

[1] She works religious petticoats: for flowers
She'll make church histories. Her needle doth
So sanctify my cushionets. – Besides,
My smock-sleeves have such holy embroidery,
And are so learned, that I fear in time
All my apparel will be quoted by
Some pure instructor.

                                        *Old Play.*

In her domestic capacity, too deeply occupied in saving the souls of her neighbour's children, she had no time to attend to the comforts of her own; and, while driving about from school to school, to teach tenets with tent-stitch, and encourage the growth of piety and plain work, she gradually saw the objects of her natural affections disappear beneath her unobserving neglect. One of her children had fallen into a pond, another had fallen out of a window. The eldest, Miss Sullivan, who was thrown from unwholesome confinement into a galloping consumption, *galloped off* with the apothecary; and the youngest, suffered to run wild from apprehension of her sister's fate, had been so much in the habit of trotting behind the coachman, that she trotted away with him one day to Gretna Green. Her three surviving sons, however, following in the Bishop's track (the 'milky way' of church promotion), bid fair for the Bishop's fortune. They already engrossed the three best livings in the Bishop's gift.

The bishop himself, who, as tutor to Lord Knocklofty, had won Lady Mary's heart, and as Dean of St Grellan had obtained her hand, was one of those '*personnages de position, qui viennent toujours au secours du vainqueur.*' He had wriggled himself into his proud eminence by siding successively with every party that prospered, and dedicating his various polemical volumes alternately to whig and tory. A Foxite to-day, a Pittite to-morrow – now a catholic advocate, and now the apostle of catholic extermination – his true religion was a mitre, his political principle a peerage; and knowing that the world, like the Baron in *La fausse Agnès*, '*est toujours dans l'admiration de ce qu'il n'entend pas,*' he took for the subject of a work, which was designed as the key-stone of his fortune, a theme, which, being beyond human comprehension, left no just measure of the intellect which he brought to bear upon its mystery. Having arrived at the object of his ambition, the pliant candidate for church promotion stood erect upon the pediment of church supremacy, with a look that might be translated, '*Sono Papa.*' A little Sextus Quintus in his way, his air became as papistical as his infallible pretensions: and whoever saw him mounted upon his ecclesiastical *haquenée*, ambling through the streets of St Grellan, saw the most faithful copy of an Italian Monsignore ever exhibited beyond the Roman corso: – all purple and pertness, pious priggery and foppish formality, with a beetling brow, and the best flapped hat that ever was perched upon three hairs of the erect head of a high, haughty, and overbearing churchman, – the genius of caricature could have added nothing to the picture.

Lord Chesterfield has said, that 'of all men who can read and write, a parson is, perhaps, the most ignorant.' This apothegm described the Archdeacon of St Grellan to a tittle. Ignorant of all but his own interests, his want of *savoir* was well supplied by his *savoir faire;* and the success of his well directed subserviency to the bishop, to Lady Mary, and to the whole Proudfort dynasty, proved that he had neither mistaken his means nor misunderstood his persons. The nephew of their law agent, Solicitor Hunks, – the son of their chaplain and *protégé*, the late Archdeacon, – he had in his favour the habit of the Proudforts to provide for his family; and he did not suffer that habit to wear out for want of frequent solicitation.

Pertinacious, as men of limited intellects usually are, irascible, as churchmen are accused of being, and envious, as mediocrity ever is, he had viewed the young and hardy 'engrosser of fame' and favour, the hero of the castle frolic, with a deeply founded aversion, sharpened by the sense of hereditary wrongs. O'Brien, as the son of him who had contrived to embezzle a part of the Archdeacon's family property, by embezzling the daughter of its richest member – of him whose legal knowledge had reduced the Archdeacon's inheritance almost to his hopes in the Proudfort interest, – had claims on his hatred, which he was determined should not lie idle; even at the risk of opposing the impetuous predilections of Lady Knocklofty.

Such was the party which, with the addition of Lord Kilcolman and Captain O'Mealy, assembled for dinner in the great saloon of Proudfort-house, at the then late hour of six o'clock – a quarter of an hour before the lady of the mansion made her appearance. Miss Macguire, however, received, amused, and talked with the guests; while Lord Knocklofty, always silent and abstracted before dinner, walked up and down, occasionally assenting, by a nod, to the bishop's emphatic philippics against the bad spirit of the times, as illustrated by the volunteer review of the preceding day, the tumult at the Strugglers, and other signs equally portentous of a state of things, which called on every loyal and religious man to put it down. To this all agreed in their different ways; from Captain O'Mealy's "'tis true for you, my lord, for as the immortal Shakspeare says, "the times themselves are out of sayson,"' to the pious ejaculations of Lady Mary, and the never-failing concordance of the Archdeacon with the sentiments of his superior.

'By the by, Albina,' said Lord Knocklofty, turning short upon his wife, as she entered and flung herself in an arm-chair, with a very slight inclination of the head to her guests – 'By the by, how have you disposed of your hero?'

'Disposed of *my* hero?' re-echoed Lady Knocklofty, evasively, and looking for resource to her friend, Lady Honoria.

'What! has she got a hero *de poche?*' asked Lady Honoria, laughing. 'Oh! I suppose you mean the volunteer, who, under heaven, saved our lives yesterday. I hope, Lady Knocklofty, you will assist me in paying the debt, by saying a word in his favour to the Provost; for, of course, he will be brought before the board, with the rest of the college boys concerned in the row last night.'

'I believe,' said the Archdeacon, 'that is past praying for. The Provost can do nothing; the whole affair being referred to the visitors. The Chancellor, as Vice-Chancellor of the University, has been long waiting to make an example of some of those young incendiaries, who are known agents of the jacobinical societies, now so numerous.'

'And this very O'Brien,' observed the Bishop, 'the leader in the riot, to whom your ladyship imagines yourself so much indebted, will, most probably, be rusticated, if not expelled: but as long as the historical society is permitted to exist in the College, and Locke on Government to form part of the College course, you will have a hotbed of sedition and a code of republicanism, whose influence is obvious.'

'Ay, and of atheism too, as the Archdeacon says,' observed Lady Mary.

'I think,' said the Archdeacon, 'that the denial of innate ideas leads irresistibly to such a conclusion.'

'I am quite of the Archdeacon's opinion,' said O'Mealy, pulling up his stock: 'I am, upon my honour; and so I believe is every loyal man in Dublin, in or out of College. For there is all the difference upon earth between a nate idaya, and an innate idaya.'

A general titter followed the assertion, and Lady Honoria demanded – 'Now, honour bright, O'Mealy, what is the precise difference between a *nate* and an *innate* idea?'

'Why, Lady Honoria?' said O'Mealy, calling fearlessly on a stock of impudence which he knew to be exhaustless, 'an innate idaya may be any man's idaya; but your ladyship's must always be a nate one, intirely, upon my honour.'

'*Pas mal,*' said Lady Honoria, nodding her head approvingly; while Lord Kilcolman cried out, 'Hear him, hear him!'

'You are aware, my Lord,' continued the Archdeacon, returning to the charge, 'that this Mr O'Brien, who affected to stop Lady Knocklofty's horses, when they had stopped of themselves, is – '

'That is not true,' interrupted Lady Knocklofty, vehemently and haughtily; 'it is utterly false: the horses were quite unmanageable, and both Lady Honoria and myself would have been dashed to pieces, but for the interference of *this Mister* O'Brien, who had the humanity to risk his life, and save ours. Is it not true, Lady Honoria?'

'I'll schwear to that,' said Lady Honoria, in the tone and accent of the Jew, in the School for Scandal.

'Well, then,' continued the pertinacious Archdeacon, 'this saviour of her ladyship's life is the youth, my lord, who, in the historical society, made a sort of killing-no-murder oration on the death of Cæsar; defending the regicide act of Brutus upon a great principle of popular right, applicable to all times; taking occasion, apropos to nothing at all, to introduce an invective against those whom he called the Dictators of Ireland, and sketching three illustrious characters high in the Irish government, as the triumvirate, who, with the same patricidal views as those of the Roman triumvirs, wanted only the courage and the talents to effect the same ends. The speech got into the opposition journal, which complimented the speaker with the title of the Irish Mirabeau, an imitation of whose eloquence, by the by, he gave us last night at the castle.'

'Indeed!' said Lord Knocklofty, pausing in his measured pace before his wife: 'and is this the person, Lady Knocklofty, whom you brought forward, as I hear you did, in so extraordinary a way, last night; availing yourself of the Duke's complaisance and good nature – is this the hero of your frolic?'

'Pooh, nonsense!' said Lady Knocklofty, carelessly, 'my frolic was everybody's frolic; and it was neither as improper as Lady Glenmore's frolic with the sweep, nor as fatal as your lordship's, when you and your friends personated highwaymen, in the Phœnix Park, to frighten the Ladies Butler; when you not only upset their carriage and broke Lady Anne's arm, but shot one of the postilions *by accident*, and scared to death old Lady Castletown, who never recovered the fright. Archdeacon, you are like old Croaker, in Goldsmith's 'Good-natured Man;' you have always some stock horror, some conspiracy or sedition on hand. I wish they would make you a bishop, and then you would be quiet. Kitty Macguire, do ring the bell for dinner; what are the people about?'

'Won't you wait for the Chancellor?' asked Miss Macguire, while the Countess's *sortie* produced a momentary silence in all; for even Lord Knocklofty's solemn haughtiness was at times borne down by his wife's vehemence.

'Does the Chancellor dine here?' asked Lady Knocklofty, with a look of annoyance.

'He proposed to do so an hour back, when I met him on the circular road,' said Lord Knocklofty.

'So he told me,' said the Bishop. 'I rode into town with him. He doesn't see the row of last night in the same point of view as the Lord Lieutenant, who considers it as a mere street brawl. He says that he has long had his eye upon this O'Brien, who hoisted the seditious flag in the park yesterday.'

'Who the devil is he?' demanded Lord Knocklofty.

Lady Mary and the Archdeacon both opened their mouths at once; and the latter exclaimed, 'He is the mischievous young scamp, who gave my father the nick-name of the arch dæmon; the son of Terence O'Brien, the present Lord Arranmore. Your Lordship may remember the fuss which was made about this seape-grace twelve years ago, when I discovered that, notwithstanding his name having been entered on the books of the diocesan school, he was for the greater part of the year actually under the tuition of a foreign priest in the isles of Arran: and this too in the face of the statute, which provided that the son of an attorney shall be bred in the established religion, and made it felony for any catholic priest to keep a school.'

'Well?' said Lord Knocklofty, impatiently.

'Well,' said the Archdeacon, 'a writ having been served, or rather sent by the proper officer to force this priest to appear before the constituted authorities of St Grellan, the people of the Islands, followers of these O'Briens, and bigoted papists, led on by one Shane, the son of the noted Mor ny Brien, and of one, the last of the Connaught rapparees, surrounded the priest's house for his protection: and this Shane, being pressed by one of the King's officers, murdered him on the spot; or rather caused his death, for the murdered man died within six months; and the fellow stood his trial, and was hanged at St Michael's Cross in Galway.'

'Well?' said Lord Knocklofty, still more impatiently.

'Well, my lord, the priest having escaped to the Continent, and the boy having shortly afterwards disappeared, and his mother dying (a sister, by the way, of those old catamaran jacobites, the Miss Mac Taafs), Terence O'Brien came to Dublin to pursue his claims to the title, where he spent his time and fortune in haunting the law courts, and searching the record and rolls offices. The boy had been sent to Douay to be made a priest of; but he suddenly reappeared at Trinity College, where he entered as a *filius nobilis*. As this happened just before I resigned my fellowship, I was struck with the name of Murrogh Mag Teig O'Brien on the books; and on further inquiry, I found that this youth had passed the last eight years of his life as a soldier of fortune, and has come from the Continent warmed with the precepts of his old tutor, the *ci-devant* parish priest of St Grellan. For the Abbé O'Flaherty, you must know, my lord,' he added, turning to the Bishop, 'has become a French bishop, and is one of those who are called the constitutional clergy; renegades to their king and their God, who have declared that the property of the church is national property; and who have consented to the abolition of tithes. In a pamphlet dedicated to his friend Talleyrand, Bishop of Autun, he has advanced, on the authority of scripture, that the clergy are the simple administrators of the church wealth; which was given for worship, and not to the priesthood. Such is the school, and such the precepts, to which the Irish university is indebted for its new honourable member.

'*Le pauvre homme*,' said Lady Honoria, looking dramatically at the Archdeacon; who was perspiring at every pore at the horrors he was relating.

'And who is this courageous Bishop,' said Lady Knocklofty, 'who dares to sacrifice his own interests to the general good? What is his name? Good heavens, how I should like to know him.'

'What nonsense you talk, Albina,' said Lord Knocklofty.

'When in Ireland,' said the Archdeacon, 'he was called the Abbé O'Flaherty, and passed for a cousin of that famous, or rather infamous Count O'Flaherty, who, you may remember, my lord, contrived to rob my father of a considerable part of his property, through the chicanery of Terence O'Brien; and who, received in Connaught as the champion of popery, ended by carrying off the foreign Abbess of St Bridget's, brought over from Italy by O'Brien's jesuit uncle, to reform the order in St Grellan.'

A general laugh followed this narrative.

'I was at Cambridge then,' said Lord Knocklofty, 'but I remember something of the matter.'

'Pray go on, Archdeacon,' said Lady Knocklofty, now interested and excited; 'carried off the Abbess?'

'Yes, Lady Knocklofty; or rather unfortunately, he did not carry her off, till he had scandalized the whole world, by taking her to the Abbey of Moycullen, where he had built apartments for the celebration of his orgies, which still attest, by their licentious pictures, the purposes for which they were fitted up.'

'What purposes?' asked Lady Honoria, demurely. 'What purposes, Archdeacon? pray tell us!'

'Lady Honoria,' said the Archdeacon, 'you will spare me the details.'

'Spare his blushes,' whispered Miss Macguire.

'Suffice it to say,' continued the Archdeacon solemnly, 'that all that was ever said of Cæsar, Borgia, and Heliogabalus, and all the profligate papists and pagans that ever lived, did not exceed the life led by the Count and his French friends; so at least I am told: for I was then a very young man, and such things were studiously kept from my knowledge by my father the late Archdeacon. . . .'

'*Le pauvre innocent!*' whispered Lady Honoria to Lady Knocklofty.

'I am told that he actually assumed the habit of an Abbot, dressed up his companions in monk's tunics, and established a sort of licentious club, called *The Monks of the Vine.*'

'Something like the Monks of the Screw here in Dublin, I suppose,' said Lady Honoria.

'Oh, worse, worse a great deal, Lady Honoria. They exceeded in profligacy all that was ever heard of.'

'Had they any six-bottle men among them, like our Cherokees?' demanded Lord Kilcolman.

'Lord Kilcolman, I know not what they had: the proceedings of Moycullen were fortunately hid from the world. I believe the Count admitted but few persons at the abbey; though, when he went out, he was well received; for he was a most insinuating and winning man in his manners.'

'He was indeed!' said Lady Mary. 'I was then almost a child; but I remember he always put me in mind of Richardson's Lovelace.'

'And you, *par hasard*, might have been his Clarissa,' said Lady Honoria, 'if the mammas and papas had admitted him to *Beauregard.*'

'I assure you,' said Lady Mary, evasively, 'he was received and pushed on by the Clanrickards, the De Burghs, and other catholic nobility; though my dear father refused to visit him for many reasons.'

'But from the time,' continued the Archdeacon, 'when he abducted, or rather was suspected of abducting the Abbess (for it was given out that she was drowned, her veil having been found floating on the rocks at St Grellan at the back of the convent, and masses were said for her soul in spite of the penal statutes), he was cut by all.'

'Well,' said Lady Knocklofty, 'and how did the romance end?'

'Oh! the catholic church has a way of hushing up all its scandalous romances, as your ladyship calls this event. The Abbess was never heard of more. The whole circumstance was denied by those, whose interests required that the truth should not be revealed. The Monks of the Vine dispersed. The Count returned to France, and was either killed in a duel, or assassinated in the Bois de Boulogne; and his property was bequeathed in trust to some foreign agent, for purposes which, if inquired into, would, I doubt not, be found illegal.'

Here the announcement of the Lord Chancellor, and the order for dinner, interrupted the conversation; and objects of more immediate importance at that season of the day, were discussed and digested, with a uniformity of opinion, unbroken by a single dissentient voice.

# CHAPTER V

────────────●────────────

## *O'Brien House*

Full of state and ancientry.

SHAKSPEARE

WHILE the party at Proudfort House were assembled round the sumptuous table of its ostentatious host, the object of this recent discussion
(released from his durance by means at which he himself blushed),
proceeded to that lonely and desolate house, where no sumptuous
table, nor brilliant guests awaited him.

At the epoch in question, when everything went by privilege and
favour, and life and liberty were in Ireland at the disposal of a ruling
caste; debts of a private nature were easily paid at the expense of
public justice or public wealth; and forms were daily violated, as the
spirit of the constitution was outraged, to answer some particular
purpose of a powerful individual, or to get rid of some obnoxious
opponent. O'Brien, at five o'clock of the day which followed his arrest,
found himself at liberty. No charge had been brought (or rather was
permitted to be brought) against him: and while the officious and
boasting O'Mealy acted as the immediate agent in the affair, it was
not doubtful to O'Brien, that the lovely and kind arbitress of his
destiny, was the all-powerful Lady Knocklofty.

O'Mealy having accompanied his *protégé* to the gate of the lower
castle yard, left him in the filthy defile of Ship-street; after having
disburthened himself of so much of the tediousness of his undisguised
vulgarity of mind and manner, as excited new wonder, that one so
below the mark of ordinary education, should have made himself the
associate of those whose rank was an assurance for their refinement.

O'Brien, as he still smiled at some of the Captain's absurdities, recalled a precept which he had often heard repeated by his Colonel, the charming Prince de Ligne, to the young men of his staff and regiment: '*Je veux que le militaire, qui a éte aussi aimable le soir que le grand Condé l'était chez Ninon, soit d'aussi bonne heure à sa troupe le matin, que fut toujours le brave Turenne.*' Such were the maxims upon which O'Brien's military education had been formed. But the grand Condé, Ninon, Turenne, and Captain O'Mealy of the Royal Irish!.... what a comparison!! He shrugged his shoulders, and sighed; for he felt that this first sacrifice to patriotism, on quitting the service of a foreign despot, was not the least, as he was beginning to feel, it would not be the last.

Released from the coarse and vulgar garrulity of his companion, he hurried home to O'Brien House by those obscure ways, bye streets, and dirty lanes and courts, which Stanihurst and Ware have rendered historical; but which are now the purlieus of a squalid indigence, that turns aside the eye of charity by the filth or vice which accompanies its wretchedness.

Threading the disgusting mazes of the liberties, where epidemic maladies are perpetuated by helpless, hopeless, irremediable poverty, his heart recoiled, and his senses sickened. Figures and faces presented themselves at every step, in which the impress of crime, or the traces of famine, left scarcely a human feature: and this too almost in sight of the architectural cupolas and gilded vanes of the seat of that government, which was answerable for every combination that had contributed to produce such an unparalleled order of things.

To these painful impressions succeeded reflections, rapid as his steps, on his own recent adventures, – the occurrences of the preceding day and night – his liberation – his liberatress. The ring so mysteriously exchanged for one not unknown, nor unconnected with his former life; the perpetual apparition of that wild, and to his apprehension, supernatural figure; the fate too that awaited him at the college, where he well knew that he was already watched; and above all, the annoyance which he must have occasioned to his father, who, after an absence of three months, had just returned in time to witness the part he had taken in the riot, all recurred to his imagination. He was almost certain that he had seen Lord Arranmore at the gable window of the attic on the preceding evening; and, that the paternal door had been closed against him in a moment of such exigency, was a proof how much and how deeply he had incurred the displeasure of one, who had but too many annoyances to contend against.

It was at this point of a reverie (which had more than once made him lose his way, and obliged him to apply for information as to the shortest cut to Watling-street), that he reached O'Brien House. It seemed to him to wear more than its usual air of sad and sombre dilapidation. The evening was bleak and gloomy. A drizzling rain was beginning to fall, and gusts of wind were blowing down the river, to which the solitary and isolated mansion stood singularly exposed. Almost all the window-shutters were closed; and some loose papers flaunting in the wind and hanging on the walls, intimated that an auction had taken place there since the previous night. With a sinking heart he tore down one of these advertisements, and could just make out from the fragment, the words 'sheriff's sale – inch of candle – valuable antiquities – materials of the house to be sold – fine old carved oak chimney-piece.' One of the old gossips of the neighbourhood, familiarly stopping and reading over O'Brien's shoulder, exclaimed,

'Why, then, they had better take it down while it stands; for sorrow long will it keep together. See there, Sir, there's a beam that's green and soaked with the wet, giving way already. I tould th' ould woman that, a week ago and more; and if you are a frind of the family, you'd be doing well to tell them the same.'

O'Brien thanked her for her information, and with a heavy heart knocked at the door. He had repeated his knock, before the window in the gable was slowly opened, and a head as suddenly drawn in as it was put out. After the delay of a few minutes, the door was opened by Robin.

'So, Robin,' said O'Brien, a little startled at the appearance of the porter, not only without his livery, but without shoes and stockings; 'is my father at home?'

'My lard's not at home,' was the mechanical reply.

'Not at home! why he arrived in town last night, did he not?'

'Ay, did he,' said Robin; 'but my lard's not at home now.'

'Pooh!' said Murrogh, passing impatiently by him; then suddenly stopping, as Robin closed the door behind him, he asked, 'Where is your mother? where is Alice?'

'There,' said Robin, pointing to a parlour on the left, which had never more than one window unshuttered, for nearly a century.

Murrogh turned in to speak with the scarcely more human, though more communicative Alice; but his blood chilled, and he stood fixed to the threshold, as he gazed round him. Dark and desolate, the spacious empty room was only lighted by a single tallow candle, placed at the head of the corpse of old Alice, which was stretched on a mattress, and shrouded in a sheet. The sight of death, under all its forms, is dreadful to the young, to whom life is an eternity. After a short pause, O'Brien demanded,

'When did she die?'

The graceless progeny of the old woman, as he stood coolly peeling and eating a turnip, answered, 'Last night, shure.'

'Of what did she die?'

'I don't know, shure.'

'She was alive yesterday?'

'Ay,' said Robin, filling his mouth with the last slice of his turnip, and shutting up his clasp-knife, his only property.

O'Brien, in equal disgust at the living and the dead, moved away, shuddering; and slowly and mechanically mounted the broad, old, creaking stairs. He was proceeding to the sitting-room on the first floor, when Robin, with more than wonted energy, sprung after him, and catching him by the coat, cried emphatically, 'Shure my lard's not at home – no, in troth.' O'Brien shook him off, though almost tempted to believe him from his earnestness. He threw back the door of the drawing-room, and found it empty. It was a long, low room, which ran nearly through the whole of the front of the house; save only where stood a dark closet, which lay at the further extremity, and led by a narrow passage to a flight of steep stairs that ascended to the attics.

O'Brien entered the room; the door of the closet was suddenly shut, as if by a blast of wind; but he heard, or fancied that he heard, a light retreating step. He flew to the door, but could not open it.

'There is certainly, Robin, some one in this closet.'

'My lard's not at home any how,' said Robin, with a dogged air; and O'Brien was again inclined to believe that he told truth, and to think that his own gloomy and heated imagination had deceived him. Not doubting, however, that Lord Arranmore would sleep (perhaps for the last time) in this miserable 'home;' and struck with the little or no anxiety he had expressed relative to his son's late peculiar situation, he resolved to await his arrival; and not to return to college, till the darkness of the night should shroud his own somewhat disorderly appearance. He had slept on the guard-house settle in his clothes (if that short feverish slumber he had taken for an hour after daylight could be called sleep); and the anxiety, fatigue, and dissipation of the previous night had impressed their traces on his countenance. Fortunately, a substantial luncheon, taken with O'Mealy in the guard-room, rendered him independent of that refreshment, which his father's house could not afford; for there 'pale fast, that with the gods doth diet,' seemed to have established his reign.

At no time, since the return of the heir of O'Brien House, had its appearance been suitable to the rank of its possessor. The greater number of its nests and closets, by courtesy called rooms, were utterly dilapidated and unfurnished; exhibiting upon their walls, and in their fixtures, curious relics of the style of fitting up houses in Ireland, in former times; when even the hangings were not permanent, when the walls were left bare and rude; and when, on the removal of the family into the country, the scantiness of the furniture obliged them to carry away the carpeting, cloth, or leather, that covered out the brick and mortar, and nothing but doors, windows, and chimney-pieces, remained stationary. Thus, however, it was, in the gorgeous reign of Louis the Fourteenth; when a princess of the blood, and the greatest heiress in the world,[1] travelled from her house in Paris, to her *châteaux* in the provinces, with her sumpter mules laden with the beds, on which herself and her court slept alike in town and country. Comfort and order are the privileges of a free people; and the French and the Irish, who had not then tasted of the blessings of constitutional liberty, were alike remote from all its necessary advantages: both were, even then, centuries behind England and Holland, in all the accommo-dations of domestic life.

The only room furnished in O'Brien House, was the great drawing-room, as it was pompously called by its lord; though its dimensions alone justified the description, by a comparison with the rest of the apartments. Even this state chamber was destitute of every modern comfort. No window closed, no door (and there were four opening into the room) hung firmly and freely on its hinges. All that an old, faded, and moth-eaten tapestry carpet did not cover of the black oak narrow-ribbed floor, was mouldered into rat-holes; and nothing of the original fixtures remained whole and complete, but a superb and curious chimney-piece, of the famous black oak of the once celebrated wood of Shilelah, the shelter of so many rebel heads, and the despair of so many English chieftains of the Pale. This chimney-piece rose from the surface on either side, and canopied, on high, the spacious,

[1] Madame de Montpensier

open, and ungrated hearth. It was curiously carved; and its delicate and laborious minutiæ were not unworthy of the chisel of Gibbons. It was crowned with the arms and supporters of the O'Brien family, surmounted by the royal Irish crown; under which was carved upon a label, and in old Irish characters, 'Thou who madest heaven and earth, bless this house, which Murrogh O'Brien and Onor his wife caused to be raised in the year. . . .' The date was worn out; but it was a tradition, that the house had been occupied by the O'Brien family, since the reign of Elizabeth, whose favourite (for the maiden queen had always a pet Irishman), the Lord Thomond, her privy counsellor and president of Munster, was the Murrogh O'Brien mentioned in the carving. This house was likewise the 'lodging,' whence the famous Lord Inchiquin (called the incendiary), the renegade General of Cromwell, had dated many of his letters; and lastly, it had been occupied by O'Brien, Lord Clare, of George the First's time, who died Marshal Thomond and Governor of Alsace.

The purchase of this mansion-house by the present Lord Arranmore, after it had been half a century in litigation, was among the items of uncalculated and ruinous expenditure, into which he had been betrayed *'par l'amour de l'antiquaille'* (to use a phrase of Rabelais); and the only furniture he had thrown into it was so adapted to the genius of the place, that the withdrawing-room of O'Brien House, would, in the present day, have made the glory of a genuine collector; and have rivalled the glass closet, blue room, and Holbein chamber of Strawberry Hill. There had stood the famous harp of Brian Borrû, now the choicest specimen in the Museum of the Irish University. There, too, was treasured the beautiful ebony crosier, tipped with gold, so powerfully wielded in the Abbey of Quin, by the celebrated O'Brien, Bishop of Killaloo, in Queen Elizabeth's day; a bishoprick which (said a label attached to the crosier), 'none could enjoy without the consent of the Mac-i-Brien,' the Tanist of the day. There, flaunted, 'all tattered and torn', over an old Indian screen, the 'rich footcloth of black velvet, trimmed up with gold and silver lace,' bequeathed in the will of the great Lady Thomond, 1672, together with her 'counterpane of tawny satin, quilted with silken twist.' There, likewise, stood much of the rich plunder of Malahide Castle, the cabinets and portraits of the Talbots; given by Corbett during the time that most beautiful of the castellated residences of the English lords of the Pale was in his possession, to his friend and brother officer Inchiquin; together with such tables and chairs, such stools and voydores, buhles and buffets, as had gone out of fashion with the battle of the Boyne; and have come in, as anti-revolutionary and loyal, during the late reaction of all that is old and useless, over all that is new and serviceable.

Such relics, however, with their historical recollections, will always have the fanciful and imaginative on their side; and the young student of the University, in the visits he had paid to his father's antiquated mansion, had examined them with intense curiosity and interest; more especially the fine old portraits, in their carved oak frames, of the bold, brave, and beautiful race from which he was descended.

Now, however, he was struck even to sorrowful amazement, on the life nerve of that family pride, so curiously mingled with his democratic opinions, – an amalgamation of incompatibles, which forms the weakness of almost all the liberal descendants of the great feudal families, both of the Scotch and Irish. A total change had been effected in the apartment, since he last had visited it. The portraits of the Bishop of Killaloo, of Marshal Thomond, and of the beautiful Lady Mary O'Brien of King Charles's court, were gone. So were the exquisite crosier of the Abbot of Quin, the screen, the foot-cloth, and the counterpane of the great Lady Thomond, – relics which O'Brien had often seen his father kiss with pious reverence. The cabinets and curious carved altar-piece of Malahide Castle still remained; but they were packed up carefully, and labelled, 'purchased by Colonel Talbot, of Malahide Castle, duty to be paid by the purchaser.' Nothing, of all the objects he had been accustomed to look upon with interest and pride, was there, save a corner cupboard (or, as it was called, buffet), so incorporated with the walls as to be immovable, two arm-chairs on either side of the fire-place, and an old table with twisted legs (called, from its hexapodal basis, a spider table). These were chalked 'unsold.' On the latter was a pile of very old books, with a label, 'sold for waste paper to Sheriff Vance, grocer, Capel-street.' O'Brien sighed deeply as he looked over them. They were, an odd volume of Dugdale's Baronage; Spelman, much torn and defaced; Selden and Bracton complete, but soiled; Howard's Popery Laws; a copy of the Penal Statutes, and a volume of Collins, which was marked by a strip of paper, and interlined with red ink.

The marked passage ran thus: – 'It is a rule that an honour, or barony, or a tenure by barony, does not enforce a conclusion that the possessor is a baron of parliament.' This conclusion was a point which Lord Arranmore had been toiling to overturn; for though he had recovered his barren title, he had not established his right to sit in parliament; the first Baron Arranmore never having complied with the writ, by coming in to take his seat. These had been the studies, and these the pursuits which had seduced Terence O'Brien from his industrious and prosperous calling, and had drawn him to sacrifice to pride of family (a natural, as it was a characteristic folly), that independence which is the sole base of the best and noblest pride. For if wealth has its vices, poverty has its weaknesses; and if the rich can often stoop to be mean, the poor are rarely enabled to be high-minded.

'What,' thought O'Brien, as he stood with folded arms, looking round him on the empty spaces left by the removal of his father's collection, 'what must it have cost him to part with these objects of his tastes, his research, and his pride! 'Tis so much easier to part with ordinary essentials, than with the superfluities, with which the passions have connected themselves.'

It was evident that a sheriff's sale had taken place during the morning; and O'Brien supposing that a newspaper which lay on the table might contain some account of it, he took it up; when to his surprise he found that it had concealed an open volume of illuminated vellum, with a small ivory pallet, and a hair pencil in a glass of water. The colours on the pallet were still wet; and in the open page of the volume was accurately and beautifully drawn the antiquated chimney-piece, with its crown, arms, and inscription. The drawing was not finished, but the first outline and tints were laid in with the hand of a master. He examined the book in astonishment. It looked like a splendid album of modern, modish, literary frippery; or, but for its freshness, it might have been mistaken for one of those magnificent missals, from which the ostentatious piety of past times loved to pray.

The room, it was evident, had very recently been occupied by the elegant artist. There was part of an old wainscoat burning on the great brazen dogs of the spacious hearth; and the ponderous leg of an old chair seemed to lie in store beside them, to replenish the embers which were now burning dimly. O'Brien looked into the buffet; and there stood a brazen candlestick, with a butt of one of those immense wax tapers used on church altars. It also contained that Irish *morceau* of *patisserie*, called a *Barneenbraec*, an old-fashioned cruet of water, and a small flask of that genuine Irish cordial (the *curaçoa* of the O'Donnel's, and the *parfait amour* of the O'Neils), Usquebagh, – or rather more classically, 'Uishge buy.'[1]

From all these evidences, O'Brien drew the conclusion, that his father was getting a drawing made of the family relic, which was now no longer his; and that both himself and the artist he employed, would return under cover of the evening, to finish a sketch so happily begun. Unwilling again to put the stultified fidelity of Robin to the test (who had evidently been bound over to secrecy, by some threat or reward, sufficient to preserve it), he was determined, more than ever, to wait the return of his unfortunate parent, in whose ruin his own was involved, but whose fate alone touched him; and he again turned to the table, to the examination of the volume, whose pure, rich, Roman binding of white vellum, ornamented with gold, with its silver clasps studded with Irish amethysts, so curiously contrasted with the dirty and ill-scented leather backs of Collins and Selden, and with the poverty of all around it. On looking at its frontispiece, which was beautifully illuminated with shamrocks and harps and rainbows, he read the following title-page:-

The Annals of the Isles of Arran and Moycullen,
or the
Green Book of St Grellan;
done into English by
The Abbot Malachi O'Flaherty,
called
Malachi an Leabhair, or, of the Book;
with Notes and Commentaries by
The Right Hon. T. O'Brien, Baron of Arranmore,
and illuminated by

\* \* \* \* \*

O'Brien had heard so much of this book in his childhood, of its superiority over the Psalter of Cashel, the Annals of Ulster, the Annals of the Seven Masters, the Leabhair Gabhala, or Black Book of Hoath, and the Blue Book of Ballytore; and even over that great national record (so much prized and praised by all Irish antiquaries, from O'Flaherty to Valancey), the Annals of Innisfallen, that his curiosity

---

[1]'Uishge buy,' the yellow water; from the saffron, which, being infused in it, imparts to that compound its fine golden colour.

had long been sharpened by the privation; and he was now much pleased to light upon it. When Sir George Carew and Sir Henry Sydney received orders to destroy all the Irish manuscripts they could find in the kingdom, this treasure of the bibliotheca Grellensis had been secretly conveyed out of the kingdom, and had been deposited in that great *répertoire* (beside things most valuable) of all the nonsense consecrated by antiquity, – the library of the Vatican. From this depository it had lately been taken by a powerful member of the Roman church; who, though an Irishman by birth, stood better at the court of the Quirinal, than many of the conclave; and who, though an exile from infancy, was now returning to the land of his nativity.

However different in temperament, opposed in opinion, or various in views the young may be, from those who give to their ductile minds their first impressions, many of those impressions will remain indelible. They will even survive respect for those, from whom they were drawn; and will cling to the mind with an habitual tenacity that sets reason at defiance, and loosens conviction from its strongest holds. The young O'Brien, an epitome of the regenerated age to which he belonged, going with its views, and animated by its spirit, a worshipper of La Fayette, a disciple of Mirabeau, partaking of all the 'glorious faults' which distinguished the youth of his times, as well as of their merits, was yet, with respect to Ireland, full of the 'vulgar errors of the wise.' On those national subjects, which have so long led the Irish from the better career of national improvement, and retrograded intellect, by directing its researches to the barbarous times, so falsely called heroic, – he was purely Irish. Knowing nothing of modern Ireland, but her sufferings and her wrongs; knowing little of ancient Ireland, but her fables and her dreams, his mind had been stored with popular and poetical fallacies relative to all that concerned her in the barbarous 'days of her glory;' and unconsciously partaking in his father's prejudices and sentiments, while he had stood opposed to him in his political and religious opinions, – he was, upon many points, as visionary and as fanciful as him, whose illusions he now so keenly deplored. Deeply read in O'Flaherty, and in Keating, in O'Connor, and all the celebrated genealogists and senaschies, ancient and modern, – and from his cradle the auditor of his Irish foster-mother, the famous weird woman of the Isles of Arran, Mor ny Brien, – his memory and imagination nourished these early associations; and recollections of family glory were the more fondly cherished, in proportion to the growing misfortunes and mortifications of his present struggling position: for, to the young and the aspiring, the struggles which arise between poverty and pride are the most painful contests to which the human will can be subjected.

Pleased, in a moment so suspenseful and anxious, to have lighted upon any subject, that could divert his attention from the melancholy point to which it was naturally bent, he drew one of the old chairs to the table, and began the examination of the sybil leaves of a record, which, besides being reputed the 'brief abstract' of the history of the nation, was deemed the best chronicle extant of the two rival families of the O'Briens and the O'Flahertys, whose destinies and stories seemed so mysteriously interwoven.

The first pages were vellum, covered with silver paper: they contained the armorial bearings of the O'Briens and the O'Flahertys, drawn with heraldic skill, and painted in the brightest tints; and in rapidly turning over the gilt leaves, O'Brien perceived that many of the adventures recorded of those families were illustrated with beautiful vignettes, admirably imitating the monastic portraits and illuminations of ancient missals, with an art still taught in Italian convents, as an appropriate acquirement for those whose talents are only cultivated for the service of the church. The text was in a fine Italian hand, such as is written by the professional scribes of Rome; who are equally expert in copying the legend of a saint, or in inditing a tender '*biglietto d'amore*.'[1] The notes and commentaries were written, in off-pages, in the well-known office hand of Lord Arranmore. The whole appeared to be an improved and beautiful copy of the very ancient original, which had probably been restored to its consecrated niche in the great counters of the Vatican collection.

While looking with a school-boy's eagerness over the glittering pictures, astonished by some, delighted by all, O'Brien found the grey light of a most sombre and rainy evening grow dim; and the wind, as it shook the windows, burst open the doors, and entered by every crevice, cranny, and broken sash in the room, rendered its desolate vastness so chill, that, trembling with cold, and desirous to read at his ease, he stirred up the embers, threw the old leg of the chair on the fire, lighted the bit of wax taper, and closed the rattling shutter of the window next the chimney. Then drawing his chair and table near the

---

[1] Mr Davis, an English artist of celebrity, has taken the *biglietto d'amore* for the subject of one of the prettiest compositions that English art has produced in the country of the Raphaels and Guidos.

suddenly blazing hearth, and with his legs stretched upon the dogs, he began a regular perusal of

# THE ANNALS OF ST GRELLAN.

# CHAPTER VI

## Annals of St Grellan

Instructed by the antiquary, Time.

SHAKSPEARE

The light of antiquity and wisdom of past ages.

*Letter of J.K.L.*

YEAR of the world 500. – Great pace and prosperitie of Innisfail, or Irelonde.[1] Under God's providence, the Ballyboe of St Grellan, aunciently called Croich-Fuineah, or the 'finall countrie,' being the last cantred of lande in the place, darting out into the great western sae, flourishes above the worlde; in salubritie far above Brittaine. Abounding in milke and honey; also not wanting in fish, foule, ne red deir. The people much given to learning and musick, great players upon the harpe, of lofty stature, and mighty comely. They multiply exceedingly!

A.M. 1525. – Arrivall of one Cesarea, a niece of one Noah,[2] who,

---

[1] 'To give a regular account of the first inhabitants of Ireland, I am obliged to begin at the creation of the world.' – *Dr Keating's History of Ireland.*

The doctor begins by quoting a celebrated antediluvian Irish poet, 'Cad aimsu an bleadha,' etc. etc. 'from the sixth day, when Adam first was formed.'

[2] 'Various are the opinions,' says Keating, 'concerning the first mortal, who set a foot upon the island. We are told by some, that three of the daughters of Cain arrived here several hundred years before the deluge; and the old poet gives us this account:

> Fri hingiona chaidhin Chain maraon ar
> Seth mac Adhamb,
> Ad chonairch an Banba ar nus ar mabhair
> Liom anionthus.

rigging out a navire, cometh to seek adventures, and falleth on the coaste of Connemara, together with fifty faymales, or gallads, or ladyes, having only three males, on boarde; one of whom was called Fintan, a great gramog,[1], or curinkey[2] of a fellow.

1595. – Whereas, in this yeare of the worlde, Noah began to admonishe the people of the general deluge to come, for their detestable sinnes, and more particularly the people of St Grellan, in regarde of the arrivaull of Cesarea and her fifty faymales, ladyes, or gallads; and Noah continued admonishions for one hundred and twenty yeares (while he builded himself an ark for him and his), which made the inhabitants of St Grellan say it was all Tallagh-hill talk, till a poure down of rayne, and the overflowing of the great river Suck,[3] caused an universall floode, and drowned them all; in which perplexities of minde and imminent daunger, Fintan transformed himself into a saumon and swoomed all the time of the deluge in the Suck, which, to this day, is famous for its saumon fysh, called by the people, in regard of the bushoppes dues, 'tithe fyshe.' And the saide Fintan recovering his former shape, after the sayde deluge, lived longer than Adam, and had greate *Shanaós*[4] of the ould times, which he toulde to his posteritie: so that of him, the common speech riseth to this blessed houre, 'if I had lived Fintan's yeares, I could tel as much and more.'[5]

---

> The three fair daughters of the cursed Cain,
> With Seth, the son of Adam, first beheld
> The isle of Banba.

Another poet, however, asserts that

> Ceasar inghion Bleatha bhuain dalta Sabhuill mac aionaill,
> An chead bhean chalma do chinn, an inis Banba-riandilion:

> Ceasarea, daughter of the good Beatha,
> Nursed by the careful hand of Sabhuill,
> Was the first woman, in the list of fame,
> That set a foot on Banba's rugged shore,
> Before the world was drowned.

[1] A buffoon.

[2] The Leader of the war dance.

[3] A river in Connaught. – A modern Irish epic begins – 'Ye sons of Suck,' etc. etc.

[4] Shanaós, genealogical gossipry, from 'Senachy,' an annalist.

[5] The learned and revered Keating expresses some doubt as to Fintan living two thousand years; because, he says, no authors of note have transmitted such an account to posterity. He, however, adds, 'I must own there is very good reason for me to believe,

1526. Ireland riseth out of the sae like a beautiful water-lily, or lump of Kerry-stone diamond.

1800. – Arrivall of three shippes in the port of St Grellan, and one barque, contayning three hundreth men, and one small boy or gassoon; being the familie and followers of one Japeth, led on by Bartholanus, a great sae captaine; greate skirmish and fierce battaille betweene the new comers and the ancient oulde Irish; the former claiming a righte to the place, in respect of theire kin, and Cousine Cesarea, who conquered the lande.

The Irish denying the same, a greate battaille ensueth, and the ancient oulde Irish are driven into the Fassaghs of Connact province.

1801. Greate pace and plentie in Irelande for six months and more.

1802. Where God hath his churche, the devil hath his chapell, for its seemeth that the countrie became uproarious, in regarde of the arrivaulle of the cursed seed of Shem, with their captaine, one Oceanus, who landed at the port of St Grellan, and gives his name to the sae thereabouts, which has ever since been called Ocean. Greate bickerings and skirmishes betweene the Giants and ancient oulde Irish, also the Bartholanian settlers: successe various betweene laweful governors and new usurpers – the giants are slayne, and throwne into the sae; greate pace and plentie throughout the yeare. The ancient Irish multiplie exceedingly.

1803. – More new comers or transplanters. Arrivaulle of the Belgians in a fleete, well rigged, led on by Slangey or Slang, prevaileth over the Bartholanians; but the Danans, a new colony, arriving, the Bartholanians forfeit their londes, and the Belgians are driven into the Fassaghs of Connact province, – only Slang, who accepteth a commission in the Irish militia:[1] his progeny flourish in the lande to this day. And now the Danans remayne masters of the sayde londe, 198 yeares, 6 months, and 2 dais.

Warres and uproares with the Belgians of the mountaynes, being frequent, in the neck of all mischief and hurli-burlies, in the yeare of the worlde 2828, there appeareth on the coast of St Grellan 120

---

that there was a very old man, in the time of St Patrick, who lived some hundred years before, and gave him a particular account of the History of Ireland.' But this man's name was Tuam, and not Fintan. – Note by the Baron O'Brien.

[1] For an account of the Fionne, Erin, or Irish militia, established before all recorded history, and of which the great Fingal was colonel or chief, see O'Halloran, Mac Pherson, O'Connor, etc. etc.

shippes, being the fleet of them boulde invaders, the Kirca-Scuits, or Scote, or Scots, or Scytoe, or Scythians, from Scythia, or Milesians from Milesius (as Trogus and Marianus Scotus, do write), whose sons, Heber and Heremon[1] did conquer the londe entirely, dividing of it betweene them, – Heber to South, and Heremon to North; but ambition, the mother of mischief, did not suffer them to remayne in pace, so they put on armes, and to battaille they goe, Heber he being slain by his own brother, and Heremon remayning cock of the roost.

1100. B.C. – Gathulus the Ardruith,[2] or Archdruid, planteth the true religion; the great idol of Croich Fuineah, or St Grellan, thrown into the sae, to the entire moane of the ancient oulde Irish. And Gathulus presideth metropolitically under the sovereign pontiff. And now, Heremon, his conscience being sore pinched for his brother's murther, he giveth great stretche of londe to the druids; and the greate wood of St Grellan, called Bally ny doire; and the reste of the londe is parcelled out among the chief captains. And Con Maol, of the Dalcascan race, founder of the O'Briens, son of Heber, son of Milesius, settleth along the coaste of Munster, to the Isle of Arran;[3] and the Hy Flahertys, or O'Flahertys, take to the mountains of Connamara, or the bays of the great sae, and found their kingdom of Iar Connaught, or the Hy-Tartagh, whereof Moycullen is the principal sate; and the Hy Taafs (now Mac Taafs) being ever a pitiful sept, stop in the Fassagh,[4] between hill and coast.

And now, as hath ever been in these kingdomes, greate change and alteration, by usurping and compounding among themselves, and by dividing of countrees, and skirmishes through other, and taking of preys of cattle, and forfeiting and reprizing.

And now the druids rule the londe, and prophecy the greate power of theire order, and write their mysteries in the boke in the old Ogham, and depositeth it in the greate college of Mur Ollivan at

[1] See O'Connor's Dissertations on Ireland.

[2] The Gauls had a sovereign pontiff, or head of the Druids. The druidical, or Celtic religion, was the same as that of the old patriarchs. They worshipped one Supreme Being; their temple was a consecrated grove; they believed in a future state of rewards and punishments; they offered victims to their god, and celebrated festivals in his honour. – See *Universal History*, vol. xviii, p. 351.

[3] For the rest of the pedigree of the O'Briens, up to Noah, see *General History of Ireland*, vol. i, p. 40. – Note by Lord Arranmore.

[4] Fassagh, a desolate place, or Moorland.

Feamor;[1] and the people, sett on by one Kinge Cormac O'Quinn, a great scholar and heretic, demanded sight of the sacred boke, at which the chief druid did fume and chafe, saying it was an impious abomination; and the sayd King Cormack O'Quinn, still conferring and confuting with the sayd druid, payeth dearly for the same!

Two hundred years before Christe, great uproares – druids taking the londe for their god Ball, and the people of Munster rising up against them. The wolves came down from the mountaines and devoured all the inhabitants of St Grellan, the rest being carried off with the plague. The druids declareth it a judgement for their pestiferous sinnes. And now the race of the O'Briens, the Dalcascan kings of Munster, of the race of whom cometh Brian Borrû, or Borreimh, king of all Ireland, flourish above the world, and begin the great Momonian war which is waged to this blessed day: so that the realm, as it were, submitted to the O'Briens intirely, and who but them, according to the Mulconeries.[2]

A.D. 390. – Christian religion beganne to roote in Irelande, as written in the Lyfe of Finn Lug, saint and bushopp; but not as some wilful men dreameth, by James the Apostel, neither by Patricius, Phaidrig, or Patrick,[3] but by the said Finn Lug,[4] who builded him a cell in the isle of the Black Lake of O'Flaherty's Mountain, which afterwards became a great Dominican friary, and is to this day, and will ever more, This friary became mother of the Abbey of St Grellan, and of others in France, Germanie, Suavia, and Italie.

---

[1] O'Connor calls this college 'the celebrated mother of all our philosophical schools.'

[2] See that great monument of Irish antiquities, the Codex Momonensis, or Munster Book, whereof I have an authentic copy. No regular chronology being observed in this work, which alone containeth the succession of the kings of Munster, of the Dalcascan race, I take leave to supply the defect in my genealogical account of the O'Briens, from the time of Logan More Moghnuagad,* in the 2d century, to 1541, when Murrogh O'Brien surrendered the title of King of Munster to Henry the Eighth. – Note by Lord Arranmore.

[3] Almost every province in Ireland claims the establishment of Christianity by its own patron and favourite saint. St Kiaran is said, by Mr O'Connor, to be the founder of Irish Christianity.

[4] This King is called, by a modern Irish historian, the greatest legislator of all our kings, as he was indisputably the greatest philosopher of our nation. It appears that he paid the penalty of his philosophy; for Mr O'Connor informs us, that by openly opposing the corruptions of the druids, and attacking the temporal power of their priests, they attacked him with a treasonable conspiracy, which cost that great monarch no less than his life.

Mr Walker, and most of the Irish antiquarians, call this king 'the Irish Lycurgus.'

The chief druid ordereth Finn Lug, sainte and bushoppe, to be burnt; but he, Lug, warned of same in a dreame, as by a miracle, escapeth, and travels to Rome, where he is made bushoppe, and has the Ballyboe erected into a see by Pope Celestinus. He hastens back to Ireland with Saint Patrick, apostle and patron. Saint Patrick converts Queen O'Brien, of Munster, and Finn Lug, the Queen O'Connor of Connaught, the kings following. Now the chief druids beganne to quake, no longer backed by kings or nobles, and falleth to railling; and Saint Finn Lug holdeth great converse with Duhbliach-Mac Logain, ardfileah or chief druid to the supreme king. He is converted, and composeth a hymn in honour of the christian religion. Druids, called magicians by Saint Patrick, are persecuted: they fly to the islands of Arran, and are protected by the clan Tieg O'Briens. Saint Patrick burns the bokes[1] in the college of Mur Ollivan, to the number of one hundred and eighty, as we are toulde by the learned Duald Mac Firbess: and now the whole island being converted, so that there were as many saintes as soules, they multiplie exceedingly; and the cell or monasterie of Finn Lug, in the isle of the Black Lake, alone containing three thousand monkes, being of the first of the three orders established by Saint Patrick, called the most holy order, which was composed of three hundred and fifty regular bushoppes, all of them saintes, who drank nothing but water, and fed on nothing but herbes.

200. – The O'Briens now lord it manfully; and Eagan More, King of Munster, the great Momonican hero, makes war upon Con Caedcathath, his cousin, who styles himself King of Ireland, and great murthur among the heroes of the O'Brien race, for divers usurpations in Munster and Connaught.[2]

(Here O'Brien, in disgust at the sanguinary absurdities, and

---

[1] It appears from the Life of St Patrick, written by the Monk of Furnes, that the apostle of Ireland brought with him that destroying zeal which has distinguished the saints of all ages. He destroyed King Leoguire's gold and silver images, asserting that the good king was a worshipper of devils; and he threw the poor man's two beautiful daughters, for the good of their souls, into a deep sleep, from which they never awakened. He had also the power of turning meat into poison in the mouths of his enemies; a power he frequently exercised, 'wherein (says the Rev. Jocelyn) we are sufficiently admonished not to offend the servants of God.'

[2] For an account of this war, see O'Flaherty's Ogygia: it ended in a perfect reconciliation between the rival kinsmen, til fresh disputes arising relative to certain duties of the port of Dublin, Eagan More O'Brien was surprized in his bed, and barbarously murthered in prison, by Con Caed Cathath. – Note by Lord Arranmore.

confused and barbarous details of the wars of his ancestors, was about to throw aside the volume, when a beautiful vignette of the head of the St Grellan, founder of his native town, induced him again to look into the text.)

664. – The saintes multiplie exceedingly, and the lande being overrun with them, many are sent into foreign countrees on the mission of the Propaganda; and Saint Grellan, a young novice, being ordered to Germanie by the abbot, is loth to lave the place. His heart being hardened, he refuseth to quit, and calleth the abbot, who was ould and deaf, a *Bodhaire*,[1] and is excommunicated by bell, boke, and candle light, for breaking the first rule of the churche – obedience – and is sent out of the island in a bottomless boat, and sees a greate star in the lake, and finds it was a toothe dropped by Saint Patrick two hundred years before; and takes it for an omen, and by light of same, walks the worlde long and lone, bare foot and bare headed, through bog and brake, fern and fassagh, and ford and plash; and reaching Croick Fuineah (now St Grellan), wake and weary, lyeth him down to die, sore suffering in sowl and sole. A deep sleep cometh on him, within reach of tide and floode, but the water retireth back on every side to the measure of four caracutes of lande, and left that place dry ever after, that is now the bawn or deer-cloose of the court of the abbey; and in memory of this marvellous miracle, Saint Grellan builded him a cell, of which that rock was the foundation, and stands to this day, nigh to the ould druid's cormach, by name of Carigny-Grellan-an-Sanctha – the holy rock of Saint Grellan. Out of this cell grew the great abbey, or *monasterium Crovense*, now the greatest in the lande, of which St Grellan was founder and first abbot, and builded a new city round it for the continual resort of Frinch, Alimandes, Saxons, or English, Picts, and Italians, and other barbarous nations, repairing there to be instructed in a strict course of lyfe; and was buried here; so that it may be called the store-house of learning and holiness for the christian worlde, and generall sanctuarie of saintes and apostels.

988. – And now the people of Connaught, headed by their kings and chiefs, and led on by the great O'Flaherty, King of Iar Connaught, invaded the territories of the O'Briens, from West Munster to the isles of Arran; and by way of bravados, cut down the famous tree of Maghadoire, under which the kings of the O'Brien race were crowned.

---

[1] A deaf or stupid person.

And it fell out, that Brien Borrû, now king of all Munster, stomached by this bouldnesse, saileth with a powerful army up the Shanon, and overrunning the western partes of Connaught, spoyled and laid waste the same, slaying O'Flaherty, and Murtoch son of Conor, king of Connaught, and other princes, without distinction; and returned home with the spoyle. The great Abbey of Moycullen, founded by O'Flaherty, chief of that name, and Prince of Moycullen, for the order of St Bridget, whereof his daughter, Bevoine O'Flaherty-ni-Brian was first Abbess; and this name of Bevoine became of great note and sanctity in the family ever after, till the mishap of Abbess Bevoine the Second, in the sixteenth century.

[O'Brien paused here in the perusal of the manuscript. The name of Bevoine O'Flaherty was familiar to his memory. Either it had found a place in some of the wild tales of his foster-mother, Mor-ny-Brien, in the isles of Arran, or he had lisped the name in his infancy. The sound, as he now audibly repeated it, came upon his ear as the echo of sounds known, and half forgotten – at once sweet and sad, the general character of old and broken recollections. He took up the manuscript and continued.]

1120. – And now descents and other trespasses by the O'Flahertys on the Clan Teig O'Briens of the isles of Arran, whom they bate back to the mountains. The Mac Taafs and the O'Flahertys fall to odds for a prey of cattle. Greate cosherings and cuttings on the people. Danish pirates spoil the lande, and put all to the sword, the rest carried off by the plague.

1260. – Murrogh O'Brien, chief of the Clan Teigs, prince, or lord of the isles, and near a-kin to the great king of Thumond, falls to odds with St Grellan – greate cutting and coshering; the Abbot excommunicates him, he refusing his Easter oblation; he, Murrogh, layeth stone and faggot to the Abbey walls, cleaves the Abbot's scull with a hatchet, and carryeth off greate spoyle to the isles. The O'Flahertys taking advantage of same, come down upon the town, and plunder the people with fire and sword, who cry woe! and ohone! (anglice, alack!) and the Mac Taafs waiteth for a pounce at the pass of Glen Murrogh, take a prey of cattle from the O'Flahertys; great skirmishes through other.

1150. – And now Murrogh of the isles, being stricken in years, became sore troubled of conscience, in respect of cleaving of the Abbot's scull with his hatchet, pays an eric for the Abbot's head of 3000 cows, and maketh over in gift and oblation every caricute of lande he had won or held in the Bally-boe of St Grellan to the Abbey, giving in lieu of the Abbot's head his best lands along the coast, also 500 herrings, and 5,000 oysters from every buss or barque, boat or picear, breaking bulk on his head land on the coast of St Grellan, called Knock-ni-huing, which are the best gifts in the bishoprick to this day, together with three holy crosses, brought from Rome, two embroidered vestments, for the Abbot, and a golden chalice. And so he took the cowl, and retired to a cell in the Abbey of Moycullen, in the habit of the order; where his tombe may still be seen to this blessed hour. He was callendered a saint by the Pope.

1161. – Strange shippes neare the harbour of St Grellan, thought to be English. The O'Flahertys goe to armes, and gather on the coaste; the strange shippes make off. The divill sett his foote after them.

1162. – King Henry Fitzempress of England, having caste in his mynde to conquer ould Ireland, seeing it commodious so to do, and being invited by the Irish princes fighting through other, gets a grant of the island from Pope Adrian (bad cess to him, Amen!) and entering by force of armes, breakes the bounds of Ireland, according to ould prophecy,

> At the creek of Bagganbun
> Ireland will be lost and won;

The invaders having no hope of the harbour of St Grellan, as I have shown.

1175. – Munster submitteth (to the greate moan of the lande). Rorie O'Connor, King of Connaught, calleth a gathering of the chiefs of the prowence, layeth before them the dangerous estate of the lande; for council and discretion are wont to stay hasty motion, and stop the course of rash device! So to armes they goe, horse and foote, kern and gallow glass, stockah and horse-boy, chief and tributary; the king at their head, the O'Flahertys bearing the banner of the province; which put the M'Dermotts in dudging, and the O'Briens of the Isles disputing the king's right, claymed of ancient privilege by the O'Flahertys of Iar Connaught: and so they cross the Shannon, and preyed the country to the walls of Dublin, where lyeth encamped Earl Strongbow, with his Norman gallants, who were fine in their apparel, nor could endure service in maresh and border, like the Irish, nor brooked open and remote places, prefering a warme chamber and furre gownes to woodes and bogges; standing upon the pantofles of their reputation, calling the Irish barbarians, polling, pilling, extorting, and what not.

And now the Irish chiefs, out of old grudges, fall to odds through others – the O'Briens against the O'Flahertys – and are surprised by the Strongbonians,[1] who show them small mercy; many are slayne, and many cross the Shannon, back with King Rorie, who maketh his peace with the English king, sweareth allegiance, and holdeth the kingdom of Connaught *ex sub eo;*[2] and so it was as ever more in the londe.

1179. – English first sette foote in Connaught province. O'Flaherty plasheth his woodes, and raiseth a castle of stone in St Grellan, at which the bards cry 'shame!' And Dermod More O'Brien, prince of the Isle of Arran, receives this yeare twelve tuns of wine for protecting the towns of St Grellan and Galway from all pirates and privateers. Now this Dermod More was immediate ancestor of Terence Baron O'Brien, now of St Grellan, but formerly of Moyvanie and Cluantes in Munster, and of Caoluisge in Connaught, with a Caput Baronicum castle, or battled house, raised not without king's licence in the liberties of Dublin, the capital of the realm, now called O'Brien's House.

King Henry III seizes on the province, bestows it on one Richard de Burgho or Burke, head of the Clanrickards, who marcheth on St Grellan, with English horse and foote, light armes, jacks and sculls, and bows and arrows, and two-edged swordes, to the marvel and terror of the people; but the English find ne dastards, ne cowards in the Ballyboe, but valiant men, stout hearts and handes, with horse and foote, and sling and sparth – the countrie faste with woode and bogge, and trenched and plashed. But of the towne and castle of St Grellan, the English make small worke; the castle they crumble to the dust; and the townsmen being net-fishers, small craftsmen, and retainers of the abbot and bishop, are put to flight; the church alone is spared. Then was seen Giolla Dubh[3] O'Flaherty More, issuing

---

[1] Speaking of this event, Harding, the admirable historian of Galway, observes, 'These unhappy dissensions were at all times the cause of their (the Irish) ruin.'

[2] This O'Connor was the last of the Irish monarchs; he died in the abbey of Cong.

[3] 'Gialla, or Giall, was a great name in the O'Flaherty family; but such is the sweetness, copiousness, and great antiquity of the Irish tongue, that I know of no name in English to answer truly thereunto. Gialla, or Giall, expressing manhood, or the state of man, in contradistinction to female, as one would say; for Gialla or Giall, means a male-hostage, or pledge, man-servant, boy, or lacquey; baggage-driver in the army,

betweene two dark woodes, descending from his mountains; his horse was fair, and ran as any stagge – he, tall of stature, well composed, and active, in countenance fierce; in his right hande he bore a darte, which he caste from him in token of defiance, then seized his sparth from one of his captaines, he flew forth at the head of his chiefs and gallow glasses, so as to break the English arraie! The Irish raise a shout! – but the wary English, clipping them in betweene hill and sae, get them on the champaign countrey. And now, being man to man, great strife ensueth – the English charging with their bows! – the Irish hurl their slings! The English, with their accustomed art, gette the Irish betweene them and the sae, falling on them with their two-edged swords. The Irish being in this strait, choose to die like men, rather than drown like bastes – no vantage ground is there now – it booteth not to fly on any side; they fight sore – no mercie, but dead blows; the Irish fall like leaves, within sight of their fathers' raths. The O'Flaherty More is left in the midst of his enemies; flourishing his sparthe or axe, swashing and lashing, like a lion among sheep, he backeth bravely towards the mountain. Some Irish, scattered among the bushes, raise the shout, and gathering together, come to the rescue; the English turn on them – the Irish make feint to rune away; the English following, are bogged in low moor-ground, and being environed with marishes, forsake their horses, and fighting valliantly back to back, doe free themselves from their bottoms, and make close retrait. The Irish eagerly pursue, and charge them with their slings. One De Courcey, with his company, turn their faces, and fight a cruell fight – the earth is strewn, the Suck runs blood! Each claimeth the victory, but who got the best, there is no boast now made.

The English gett off, under covert of night – the Irish that remayned, retraite to O'Flahertys' rath or fort in the mountaines of Moycullen, bearing the body of O'Flaherty More on their shoulders; his mantle well rent with English arrows, the ouldest blood in the nation gushing from his heart. The monkes of the abbey come forth to meet them with reed and rush, and raise the 'ullaloo.' The abbot did solemnize his exequies with great reverence; and to this day the

---

armour-bearer, poet, charioteer, waiter, butler, or lower coachman, postillion, footman, runner, cup-bearer, groom, ostler, page, train-bearer, porter, confidant, secretary, plough-boy, sweep, or solicitor, according to the word placed after it. Such is the copiousness of the Irish tongue.' See the *Sanasgaoihlgesags-bhearla*, or *Irish English Dictionary*, by O'Reilly, word Giall or Gialla. – Note by Lord Arranmore.

people talk of the battaille of the pass of Glen Murrogh, where O'Flaherty fell, defending his country: and no small blame was given to the Mac Taafs, who kept aloofe, playing fast and loose, laving their Fassagh without watch or ward, standing on the pounce, to take a prey of cattle from the O'Briens of the isles, who were then fighting valliantly the good cause, in Munster, under O'Brien, Prince of Thumond.

A.D. 1240. – The English, masters of all the champaign country, built towers, castles, and forts, and churches. The realm at this time in pace – the chief in his mountains – the priest in his church – the souldier in his garrison – and the plowman at his plow. English and Spanish merchants settle in St Grellan: charter of staple and murage granted, gate and town wall erected, and castle of stone and lyme builded. The town more English than Irish. The O'Flahertys come down and scour the place. The O'Briens of the isles make a landing, and carry off great spoyle. Great plague this yeare; also, upon the neck of it, comes over one Steffano, with the pope's apostolick mandate, requiring the tenth of all moveables, to mantayne his warres with Frederick, Emperor of Alemaine or Germanie. The lords and laity, as well English as Irish, sayeth, 'Nay, we will give the pope no tenths; neither subject our locall possessions to the church of Rome.' But the clergie, fearing the bulls of excommunication, with grudging yielded; the people sending after their money, bitter Irish curses; they being all driven to the worst, selling their goods to merciless merchants to pay their tenths; their cowes, hackneys, eadoes, cuppes, copes, altar cloths, chalices, and *aqua vitæ*. Father Thady Mac Taaf makes hard for the see of St Grellan, but misses the cushion. The Kyng endeavoures to lay greate taxes on the Irish, to help him in his warres against the Frinch. Great polling and pilling of the Irish, which they could not brooke; so to warre they goe with the English, – the O'Neils of Ulster, O'Briens of Munster, O'Connors of Connaught, and O'Flahertys of St Grellan.

1276. – Great slaughter of the Irish this yeare, and spilling of the ould blood – overthrow given to the English at Glendalory – Murtoch O'Flaherty, a notable rebel, taken and executed – Thomas, Earl of Clare, slays O'Brien Roe – The Irish draw such draught, they shut up the English in Slew-Bany, and oblige them to cry quarter – Friar Falburn, B. of Waterford, Lord Deputy at this tyme.

1280. – Rose cruell warres betweene the O'Flahertys and the O'Briens; great slaughter and bloode-shed; also, between the Mac

Dermotts and O'Connors. The Mac-en-earlies[1] overrun the country with fire and sworde. And now the English lordes and gentilmen begyning to incline to Irish rule and order, certain statutes are made for the preservation of English order, that no English subjects should make alliance by altarage, or fostering wyth any of Irish nacion; nor no Englishman to marry an Irishwoman, on pain of forfaiture of lands and tenements, with divers other statutes for benefit of that English nacion.

This yeare Monica Mac Taaf granted in Frankalmoigne to the cathedral of St Grellan, 3 void pieces of ground, her jointure lande and orchard, and her right to a mill on the river Suck, she retiring to a nunnery.

1331. – This yeare, greate rebellion in Connaught; ringleaders cut off every where. Great skirmishes betweene the O'Flahertys and the O'Briens. Great slaughter of the mere Irish (by the English of Leinster), in Connaught. A dearth ensueth, famine killeth where the sworde spareth.

1336. – On St Lawrence's day, the Irish of Connaught discomfitted by the English;[2] were slaine three thousand Irish. Great variance betweene Fitz-Ralph, Primate, and the four orders of begging friars. Great storme! wolves come downe from the mountaines and devoure the abbot's deer; he maketh offering to the three jewels of Ireland, St Patrick, St Bridget, and St Colomb; buildeth a stone fence, by an English mason of the towne; deer never devoured after – praise be to the jewels! – Greate garboils in the churche. Bushoppe of St Grellan claimes the tithe fishe and woode landes. Abbot of Moycullen proveth that the O'Briens gave ten acres of woode and stony grounde, in 1210, for ever in fee soccage, not in capite; also any black rent thereupon; also five hundred herrings, and five thousand oysters, from every buss or barque, boat or picar breaking bulk on his head-land on the coaste of St Grellan, called Knock ny Huay. Bushoppe showeth a grant of the Pope for the same – they fall to odds. The O'Flahertys back the abbot, the townsmen goe with the Bushoppe, who is backed by the Earl of Ulster, and English troopes from Galway. Bushoppe wins the day, and gets the oysters to this blessed houre.

1400. – Greate oblations come in to the Abbey, and tributary offers

---

[1] The earl's sons, the factious sons of the first Earl of Clanrickard.

[2] The defeat of the Irish, led on by Teahlim O'Connor, at the battle of Athenry, established the English power in Connaught.

from the great Irish families of the ould blood. Eel weir built. Holywell much resorted to.

1490. – Father Paddy Mac Taaf, a purveyor and a fine birder, brings down eighty curlieus and fifty rails in one day. Great goss hawk at the Abbey, called 'the Prior,' dies of a surfeit. Greate disorder among the monks. St Grellan's rule lost. Monks reformed by the friars of strict reformance of the Black Isle. Great glut of oysters this yeare; the Bushoppe translated to heaven after supper one night, which reminded the people of the goss hawk.

The Mac Taafs take English order, and goe in, doeing homage, and taking grant of their landes, before the Lorde Walter de Burgo, in the Castle of Portumna – also one of the O'Briens *facit fidelitatem et homagium.*

1530. – The O'Flahertys refuseth all parlance with the Lord President, denying English laws and statutes,[1] with great abusion of reproache for suche as take English rule, and order, and habite, and tongue, saying in the teeth of the sayd Lord President, 'that it be oone of the destructions of the Irish, their never being threwe to each other, but selling themselves ever, and their mother lande, for title, and place, and power; – as the oulde Earle of Tyrone, O'Briens, Earles of Inchiquin, Macarthys, Earls of Desmonde, O'Connor, and others; but as for him, he would stick, as his father had done, to the ould Brehon law, mantle, glibb, and crumhal;' and so he retired to his mountaines, and raised a fine pile of defence, a tower and rath (now called a bawn).

1534. – Lord President, at the head of his bandes, with the banner of the province, six score kernes, and their captaines, a score battailleaxe, and little guidons, and a hosting of the men of Galway, joined by the Mac Taafs, attack the O'Flahertys, and take the towne of St Grellan. O'Flaherty escapes to the mountaynes – three of his sones killed – the towne of St Grellan is bound in bond of recognizance, to observe the kyng's lawes, and pay obedience to the English governor; Lord President to receive fee-farme and cess of the porte (oysters and herrings secured to the bushoppe); no black rent to be

---

[1] 'So frequent were the breaches of public faith, and the insecurity of any pardon granted to the Irish, that they became hopeless, and maddened into resistance: for many, who were received into protection, without being guilty of any new crime, and without a legal trial, were afterwards condemned and executed, to the great dishonour of her Majesty, and discredit of her laws.' – Manuscript in Trinity College, Dublin.

paide to any Irishman; the President, for eight days, is to cut passes through the woodes adjacent to his majesty's subjects, and to cleare the mountaynes, so to rid the lande of the wilde Irish; and the President giveth regrantes of the Abbey landes to our lord, the abbot, also confirmeth the domayne of the bushoppe (both Englishmen); together with sock, sack, and toll, and judgement of fire, and water, and iron, and tryal by combat and jurisdiction of the gallows and pitt to one Kenelm Hunks, an Englishman, and scout-master of the province; to whom the low landes of the O'Flahertys, being 4437 acres, with rents of 512*l.* sterling, are also made over for his good services.

1536. – The O'Flaherty taken in armes by a hosting of the lord-president, and a quest being passed upon him, he was condemned to death, and the provost and officers led him to death. And he, dying stout-hearted, cursed his posterity, who should learne Englishe, sow corn, or build houses, to invite the English. He was succeeded, according to the law of tanistry, by Giolla O'Flaherty, his nephew: a powerful man he was, dark of aspect, and strong of arme, of great valour, and eminent piety; so that he re-edified and re-endowed the abbey, now fallen to decay: saying he would build for God, and not for man. He was a zealous and faithful childe of the catholick church.

1540. – Now heresy gaineth footinge in the londe: provost Hunks professeth it, and saying, 'the king is pope,' is excommunicated by the abbot. One Browne, an Augustinian friar, denyeth the pope's supremacy, and is made archbishoppe of Dublin; being the first of the clergy who embraceth the new heresy.

1545. – Dissolution of monasteries proclaimed by the lord-president; great hostilities and stirrings; Abbot escapeth to the Isle of Slattery; Bushoppe conformeth, and so keepeth his owne.

1557. – New heresy established by proclamation; the fine ould abbey church plundered of relics and images by English soldiers, and monks put to the sworde.[1] The abbey landes annexed to the see of St Grellan.

1551. – Mass restored by her most sacred majesty of blessed memory. Abbot and monks return to the abbey.

The abbot, an O'Flaherty, made bishoppe of St Grellan; an English garrison received by the queen's order; grant of immunity to the burghers thereof. Giolla O'Flaherty keepeth quiet in his castle; endoweth the nunnery of Mary, John, and Joseph, with foure cantreds

---

[1] See Theatre of Catholic and Protestant Religion; also 'Currey's Civil Wars.'

of mountaine lande, placing his daughter Beavoin O'Flaherty therein, as abbess, who receives a cross for the head of her crosier, from the Pope, containing therein a bit of the true cross, which, to this day, is sworne upon. She was a fine and lovely lady, a great alms-giver from her childhoode up, pre-eminent in learning and hospitality, and one who may be calendered for a saint, when her time cometh.

1560. – Abduction of the Abbess of Mary, John, and Joseph, by Murrogh O'Brien, chief of the Isles, who carryeth her off, she being on a pilgrimage to St Patrick's Purgatory. And now greate strife and hurly-burly between the O'Flahertys and the O'Briens; no tidings of the abbess for a year and more. Giolla O'Flaherty attacks the Isles, and after much strife and uproarious contintion, expels the Clan Teig O'Briens, man and baste, and carries back his daughter, the abbess; that is, her dead bodie, to Moycullen, where she lies in a faire tomb, in the new chauntrey of the abbey. And a great *chree* was raised over her by the women of the Ballyboe. The story runneth, that she being much beloved by the said Murrogh, her abductor, and loving him much, from early youth, was forced to her veil and vow by her father, who hated the O'Briens, after the ould grudge. And willingly went she with the said Murrogh to his Isles, where they were married by a Franciscan; for he, Murrogh, was of the ould descent, tall and dark-eyed and very comely, as the Dalgaiscan or Milesian race ever were, and a goodly gentleman, and of the sword, and heir to many subtracts of gentry, and had been sent more than once to bridle in the insolence of the O'Fflaherties, in ruffling times. He was, in his youth and prime, when first he beheld the most fair and lovely Beavoin, in the church of Mary, John, and Joseph, on an Easter day. And was called Murrogh na Spaniagh, from having been a sword and buckler man of the King of Spain, and fought valiantly against the Moors in Pagan lande. And the story went, that the Lady Beavoin was slain in his armes by her own father, who sought and found her within the walls of Dan Ængus, the rath or fort of the O'Briens of Arran and what not. – Be that as it may, the O'Briens of Arran never flourished after, as will be seen in history; the O'Flahertys holding possession of their islands of Arran, until the Queen, on pretext, backed by pike and gunne, did claim said isles, and get them: which showeth what doeth ever come of meddling with Godde's own.

And here it seemeth notable to mention the ould Irish prophecy in regard of the O'Briens and the O'Flahertys, that love and religion would ever be fatal to them; till the cross, first planted in the land by

St Grellan, should rise triumphant by Godde's grace, and by the strong arme of the O'Briens. For it is well known that Heaven did openly manifest its favour to the great Aongus O'Brien at the battle of Iveleathian, – a sword falling from a cloud at his feet when he was sore pressed; with which he won the victory, and killed with the same sword the usurper of his crowne and kingdom, Mog Muagad; and hence the crest of the O'Briens, a naked arm issuing from a cloud, brandishing a sword, all proper. Motto – '*Vigueur de dessus.*' And further goeth the prophecy of him shall restore his church and sept, an Irish distich, which done into fair Englishe, thus inditeth:-

> 'Midst Ængus forlorne
> Shall th' O'Brien be borne;
> And bear in his face
> The mole of his race.'

\* \* \* \* \*

Here O'Brien laid down the MS., which he had read with rapidity. He smiled to think how readily the accidents of his own birth and person might, in darker times, have been turned to the account of party, by the influence of superstition or craft, as in the instance of O'Donnel Baldearg. For the rest, the impressions made were very different from those which similar records, traditionally learned in childhood from the story-tellers of the isles of Arran, and confirmed by Keating and O'Flaherty, had awakened. In the fables of national vanity and poetical hyperbole, he had then seen only a race of saints and heroes, perfect as the types of the martyrology, and ideal as the chiefs of Ossian's poetic strains. He now saw them as they were, a barbarous[1] people, checked in their natural progress towards civiliz-ation by a foregin government, to the full as barbarous as themselves; their boasted learning, a tissue of monkish legends; their government, the rudest form of the worst of human institutions – feudality; their heroes, bold, brave, fierce, and false, as men acting under the worst political combinations, and the most vehement of human passions: constantly opposed in domestic quarrels, to the destruction of their common interests, and always oppressed, because always divided. Still he saw them valiant, proud, and spirited; highly endowed, full of that

---

[1] Barbarous as the rest of Europe, in the dark times which preceded the glorious middle ages of the south.

creative imagination which constitutes genius, and animated by those strong passions which anticipate time, and lead to social advancement, by prompt decision and uncalculated innovation.

In the story of Murrogh O'Brien and Beavoin O'Flaherty, there was something that touched and even affected him; rudely and simply as it was told. What a world of feeling! – what struggles of passion and piety! – of prejudice and predilection! – what incidents and adventures, in the church of St Bridget, in the wild fastnesses of Moycullen, on the turbulent Atlantic, and the rocky isles of Arran! The destiny also of the two families, thus engrafted on the history of a country, and interwoven with its wrongs! For the false combinations of a barbarous legislature nourished the provincial and municipal feuds, and cherished by persecution the institutions which so often quenched 'those best of passions,' love and patriotism.

It was curious to observe the same system still reproducing the same effects. His devout grandmother, Onor-ny-Flaherty, the origin of his own present adverse state, the victim of love and of a devotion equally ill-regulated. Rory Oge, the clan Tieg O'Brien of *his* day, – and again the mysterious rumours of the abduction of his aunt, the Abbess of St Bridget, by the accomplished but profligate Count O'Flaherty; which he had so often heard alluded to in his boyhood, but which his father, rather evasively than positively, denied. His granduncle, too, the Abbate O'Brien! the awful object of his boyish recollections! his father himself, writhing under some 'compunctious visitings of conscience,' connected with the religion he had abandoned, and to which he afterwards relapsed: – the perversion of his talents under the pressure of national prejudices, nurtured by national wrongs – his misfortune, his ruin, his long and mysterious absence – the inheritance of misery he had purchased for his son – a pauper nobility – the perpetual struggle between pride and indigence! – all these convictions crowded on his mind, and sunk him into the deepest despondency. He threw himself back in the old and creaking chair, and covering his eyes with his hands, yielded to impressions of wretchedness, which come with such fearful force when the spirits are previously prepared by malady or their own depression, to exaggerate circumstances in themselves baleful and disastrous. He sighed deeply and often – and once he thought he heard his sigh re-echoed – and so distinctly, that he started on his feet and listened; but all was silent.

save the pattering of the rain against the windows, or the beating of the wind against the old gables.

He again, therefore, took his seat, and was about to resume the old chronicle, when at that moment, either the rattling of wind in one of the apartments, which opened into the sitting-room, produced a singular noise, or somebody moved within. O'Brien arose, and advanced to a door exactly opposite the place where he sat; but it was fastened. Believing that the movement (if any other than that by which the increasing storm shook the old edifice, and more than once brought the old woman's warning to his memory) was occasioned by Robin, who kept his sad vigils below by the bier of his grandmother, he again stirred up the fire, trimmed his wax-light, and re-assumed the annals. In turning over the leaves, he perceived that two pages, enveloped with silver paper, had stuck together. He opened them with some difficulty, and discovered a superb vignette, the *chef-d'œuvre* of the book. It exhibited a faithful view of the Gothic archway of the Convent of Mary, John, and Joseph, at St Grellan, as he had last seen it in his boyhood. Within its deep shadow stood a woman in a religious habit, her head turned back, as if taking a last view of the altar (faintly sketched in the remote perspective) to which she had vainly vowed the sacrifice of all human passions. Without the arch, and leading her by the hand, with an apparently gentle violence, stood a young man in the Irish habit, as it was worn in Connaught in Elizabeth's time, in spite of laws and statutes forbidding truis and mantle, glib and coolun. O'Brien was struck by the bold outline of this figure, sketched as it was upon the sunny fore-ground, '*a colpo di pennello*,' after the manner of Salvator Rosa's strong, but careless figures. All but the head was a mere sketch; but that was a finished miniature. It was full of beauty, both in expression and colouring; and it seemed the high wrought copy of some original model, tinged with the idealism of the painter's fervid fancy. It was too much in nature, not to be a portrait, for there was even a dark mole upon the cheek, – but it was too beautiful, not to have received some of that 'purple light', with which genius knows how to embellish truth and nature. As he held the picture nearer to the light, he thought he had somewhere seen such a face. The mole, too, the O'Brien mole, like the cross of the O'Donnels;[1] such a mole as he himself had on his left cheek! He paused,

---

[1] A mark said to be common to the members of this family.

and looked again; and blushing deeply, though alone, he at last recognized his own flattered resemblance.

Amazement, the most profound, – amazement even to an emotion that quickened his breathing, and accelerated the pulses of his heart, took possession of every sense. Who was this charming artist, whose exquisite skill and delicate flattery had substituted his head for that of his celebrated ancestor, Murrogh-na-Spaniagh, one whose valour and heroism were on record, and who had died the victim of both, in the war of the Earl of Tyrone?

In assigning this introduction of his own resemblance to paternal vanity, he was still at a loss as to the ingenious painter who had taken so perfect a likeness, for which the original had never sat. Conjecture was vain; this little incident belonged to the mass of mysteries, in which his father had shrouded all his actions. Still such is the unconscious influence of self-love, that O'Brien took up the manuscript with a new and deeper interest; but in replacing the vignette, he again unconsciously examined it with increasing accuracy. Details came out in the scenery, with which he was well acquainted. Every thing was clear, but that which he most wished to behold; for the face of the erring abbess was shrouded in her veil. His excited imagination, however, lent to this victim of bigotry a charm, beyond that of mere mortal beauty, a charm which high wrought enthusiasm and deep seated passion ever give to the countenance and figure they animate and inspire.

Under the influence of particular impressions, accidentally given to a mind the most imaginative, O'Brien had formed an ideal model of female influence, arising out of a position which placed the object beyond the reach of man's pursuit, and therefore the more irresistibly attractive. Such a character, formed to lead, to overrule all within its sphere, he suspected, he believed did exist, hiding beneath the religious scapular and vestal's veil, energies and talents that are rarely found in women divested of strong passions and vehement affections. He believed this highly endowed and enlightened being, with powers misdirected and overwrought, was but an accident in a system, an agent in a cause, which blasted and perverted all that fell within its sphere. He imagined for a moment such a woman drawn off, and induced to abandon the great object for which she had been reared, and to which she had been devoted. He imagined in the invincible Abbess on whose veil he now gazed, such a woman – and the man!

– He sighed! What were a thousand Lady Knockloftys to such a being?

He again took up the manuscript and read; but read for a minute with distracted attention, until gradually falling in with the subject, it became again deep and concentrated.

\* \* \* \* \*

*(Annals resumed.)*

1560. – And now, Murrogh O'Brien gets a dispensation from the Pope, making his marriage lawfull with the Abbess of Moycullen; and his son, *Murrogh-an-Urlicaen* (Murrogh of the curly head), their issue legitimate. And of this issue of Prince Murrogh, of the isles, and Beavoin O'Flaherty, comes the family of the present Terence O'Brien, late of St Grellan, Esq., and claimant of the title of Arranmore.

1570. – Mass again put down. Litany ordered to be read in English, in the cathedral of St Grellan. Popish images and relics to be removed. Every catholic not going to church, to be fined. The cathedral walls painted white. Scripture texts wrote on the same 'in place' (sayeth the ordinance) 'of idolatrous images:' great and sore persecution of the pore catholics, townsmen, and burghers, English and Irish. Abbot flies to Arran isles. Monks driven into boggs and fassaghs by English souldiers. A large bible sent down to be placed in the midst of the choir of the cathedral church of St Grellan, to be read by the people, on penalty: (none reading English in that tyme, save the genteels, and few of them.) Castellated house built for the new prelatical bishoppe, called a palace, the ould castel, or mess, in the close, being much decayed. And now the Queen being *insensed* of the outrages of the O'Flahertys on the O'Brien's isles, a commission is issued showing that the sayd isles do belong neither to O'Brien nor to O'Flahertys, but to her majesty in right of her crown; so, by her letters patent, she bestoweth same isles upon an English captayne and his heirs, so that he would mantayne there twenty English soldiers. The county and towne of Galway and Bishop of St Grellan memorial the Queen in behalf of sayd O'Brien, Lord of the isles since the Milesians, but in vain; and the Mac Tiegs still claim these as their patrimony, and will evermore, to the ind of time and after.

1590. – And now the O'Flaherty being accused of declaring against
the Queen's supremacy, saying 'she was no pope;' and not obeying
the proclamation, and refusing to come in, at the rathmore of Mulloghmaston;[1] and also accused of saving and succouring the crew of a
Spanish bark, wrecked on his head lands; and he holding off with
delays and delusions to answer these charges, the Lord President
ordered the warre to be prosecuted gainst him, and a hosting to ride
forth into his mountains: and so his territory was plundered, his
tower taken, and he hunted into the woodes. And now the people of
Connaught are sore driven by their English Lord President, Sir
Richard Bingham: the sheriffs, and other officers following his
example, enter county and town, barony and Ballyboe, and burgh and
bishoprick of St Grellan, with large bodies of armed men, pillaging,
polling, violating, and murthering, where they list, and other
barbarities as 'were sufficient to drive the best and quietest state into
a sudden confusion.'[2] So that by famine, sword, and plague, the people
are brought to such wretchedness as any stony heart would rue the
same; out of every corner of the woodes and glynnes they came
creeping forth upon their hands – their legs no longer bear them, –
they like anatomies of death – they eat dead carrion, sparing not to
scrape dead carcases out of the graves. If they found a plot of shamrocks or cresses, they flocked unto it as to a feast; and the oulde chief
O'Flaherty flying into the woodes, was there in a cabin slaine, his
head cut off and sent to the Lord Deputy, having only a friar and
horse-boy with him.

And now the O'Flaherty (his son), is forced to come in. Though
at the head of a powerful body of kernes and gallow-glasses, he
submitteth, and surrendering all his possessions, received them back
by letters patent, that same yeare, reciting that, 'although the queen
and her predecessors were the true possessors of the premises, yet
that Rorie O'Flaherty and his ancestors possessed them unjustly
against the crown;' and he being truly sensible of same, the queen

---

[1] The English published a proclamation, inviting all the well-affected Irish to an
interview at the rathmore, at Mulloghmaston, engaging, at the same time, for their
security, and that no evil was intended. In consequence of this engagement, the well-
affected came to the rathmore aforesaid, and soon after they were assembled, they
found themselves surrounded by three or four lines of English and Irish horse and
foot, completely accoutred, by whom they were ungenerously attacked and cut to pieces,
and not a single man escaped. – See Currey's *Civil Wars*.

[2] The Lord Deputy Mountjoy's own words.

accordingly granted to Sir Roderic, chief of his name, by the service of a knight's fee, all his manors, lordships, and domaines, with a proviso of forfeiture, in case of confederacy against the crowne. He rendereth the queen a greate service; is made colonel in her army; is knighted, and builds a noble castel of tenure, adjoining his old tower, with flankers and donjons.

1603. – King James, of the ould stock (Milesian born), his access to the crowne; long life to him! Great rejoicings; fires on every rock and rack in the Ballyboe; light on the top of O'Flaherty's tower – seen six leagues off at sea. Irishry received into protection, which breeds much comfort and security in the hearts of men. Sir Roderick O'Flaherty elected a free man, he bearing scott and lott; sits in Parliament; disputes precedence with Colonel Teague O'Brien, which is adjudged to the former; they fight near Isod's Chapel,[1] in Isod's Park; both are wounded.

1617. – Proclamation, for banishing the popish regular clergy, made in St Grellan; great moan and marvel thereat. Sir Roger O'Flaherty censured in the Star-chamber of Dublin for speaking slightingly of the King's supremacy; retires to his castle in the mountaines.

1623. – Proclamation requiring popish clergie, regular and secular, to depart the kingdom, forbidding all converse with them; great moan through the Ballyboe; the Abbott of Moycullen holds his ground, backed by his sept.

1636. – Convent of Mary, John, and Joseph, of the order of St Bridget, and other religious houses, seized to the King's use.

1641. – Great Irish rebellion put down by the King's forces; in the heat of which, starts up one of the clan Tieg O'Briens to claim the Island of Arran.

1645. – Great rebellion in England; King murdered.

1649. – Parliament forces overrun the lande; great murther of the Irish; country burnt about Leinster – two thousand fires at once, seen from the steeples there; great plague and famine; meeting of chiefs, lords, burghers, and corporation of St Grellan, and Iar Connaught, and Galway – resolve to remain faithful to the King's majesty. Sir Murtoch Na Doe O'Flaherty raises a corps of two thousand men of

---

[1] Now chapel Izod.

his own people to join the royal forces; but he refusing to truckle to 'the excommunicator,'[1] and being a great catholic, got the name of 'the Marauder;' and lending his aid to the Lord Clanrickard in the King's behalf, kept his majesty's foes at bay, and often cleared the Ballyboe of the thieving Roundheads, but would join no foreigners.

Battle of Knock na Clashy – the last ever fought between loyal Irish and English rebel. The Parliamentarians win the day; old Sir Murtoch leaves three of his fine young sons dead in the field; the youngest Bryan, the Tanist, joins the King's standard in foreign parts. The town of St Grellan blockaded by Cromwell's troops under Coote and Stubbes; townsmen resolve to sell their lives dearly; famine rages; two vessels laded with corn getting into the harbour, are pursued and taken by the Parliamentarians. Proposals now sent to the besiegers; town surrenders to Colonel Stubbes; articles being signed, are all violated. Colonel Stubbes preaches a sermon on God's mercy at the upper four corners. Surrender of the town, followed by a great famine and plague.

1653. – The military governor (a great saint and preacher), under pretence of taking up idle persons, 'who knew not the Lord,' makes excursions nightly into the woodes, mountaines, and country; seizes a thousand persons and more, without respect of rank or birth, and transports them to the West Indies, where they are sold for slaves. Contributions raised, to the entire ruin of the town's-people; bible explained in the parish church, which is stripped of all ornaments; fifty catholic clergie, caught in the woodes, are shipped for the West Indies.

1654. – Petition from the English protestants of the towne to the council of state, that the mayor and chief magistrates should be English protestants, and the Irish or papists removed; ould corporation disfranchised; English souldiers made free men; orders issued, for all the popish or Irish inhabitants to leave the towne, to provide accommodation for English protestants. The St Grellaners, driven out of the towne in the midst of winter, – herd in ditches and poor cabins in O'Flaherty's mountains. The town now a great

---

[1] The Pope's nuncio, Cardinal Rinuncinni, so called. The catholic loyalists were divided into two bodies; the smaller, under the Pope's nuncio, were called the excommunicators; the others, adhering to the King, but resisting foreign influence, were named marauders.

barrack; houses fit to lodge kings fall to ruin. O'Flaherty's country portioned out to the Parliamentary souldiers. Mac Taaf's fassagh sould to adventurers. Prelatical church or cathedral converted into stables for dragoons; chalices used as drinking-cups; the lead of the ancient ould abbey of Moycullen made into cannon-balls; the choir turned into a brewery; and Abbess Beavoin's Cross, without the town, turned into a gallows. Bishop's verger hanged for decorating the cathedral church with holly and ivy on the nativity of our Lord. Parson Hunks fined and imprisoned for celebrating the mass done into English, on same blessed day; great meeting-house erected for 'the service of God,' defrayed by applotments on the papists; O'Flaherty's silver tankard, and great salt-cellar, with a coyer, seen on the English governor's table.

1655. – Court of inquiry held to try a young gentleman, one Donogh O'Brien, of the clan Tiegs, found hiding in the caves of Knock Na Huay, under the fort of Dun Ængus, in the great Isle of Arran, he being accused of murdering four protestants in the rebellion of forty-one. Proves he was not then born. Is condemned and executed same evening by torchlight, all the same, at Abbess Beavoin's Cross.

Now the story ranne that he was the O'Brien Mac Tieg, who was the direct descendant of Murrogh O'Brien and the Abbess Beavoin O'Flaherty, and that it was remarkable that he was hung upon the fine ould cross, erected by O'Flaherty Dhu for the peace of his daughter's soul (the Abbess of St Bridget), at the four ways; and upon St Grellan's Eve, above all nights in the yeare; and what was more remarkable still, that the said O'Brien was afterwards seen in the Isle of Arran, and swore many of the ould followers of the family upon the head of the Abbess's crozier to be true to the ould blood, and so sailed for Spayne.

1656. – Order issued that the governor of St Grellan do forthwith remove thereout all Irish papists, and that no Irish be permitted to inhabit therein, (unless disabled to remove through age or sickness), so that now no Irish are permitted to live in the town, or within six miles thereof.

1660. – Restoration of the King's majesty; great rejoicing – fires on every rock and rath in the Ballyboe. Many of the new settlers quit the place – old natives hold up their heads. King orders the Lords Justices to restore the old natives to their freedom and estates.[1] Great contintions of the new settlers and ould inhabitants. Lords Justices turn a deaf ear to the King's orders, who was said to have the two ways with him. Some of the ancient inhabitants flock to the town, but are expelled. Bishop and Abbot return together in a herring-buss – the one to his abbey in the mountains, the other to his palace in the town; they fall to odds about oysters and herrings. An inquisition taken, which finds that the abbey lands were vested in the crown in the reign of Henry VIII. The ould Abbot and four monks maintained in the ruins of the abbey by voluntary oblations. Old natives give security, backed by Lord Essex, Lord Lieutenant. Some permitted to return, but driven out again by the corporation. Colonel Sir Bryan O'Flaherty, the marauder, a great crony of the King's, and kinsman by alliance to the Lady Castlemain, his most sacred majesty's concubine (being one of 'those specially meriting favour,[2] and without further proof to be restored'), repossesses his estates; and the adventurers, or English settlers removed thence, were reprized in forfeitures upon the estates of the Hunkses, and others manifesting rebellious intentions against his late majesty; also on the estates of some of the O'Briens: they being 'Irish popish rebels of the confederate army, over whom his majesty hath obtained victorie by his English and protestant subjects.' Sir Dermot returns to Moycullen, to the great joy thereoff. Repairs the ould abbey, and fits up the place for his own residence. Clears the pass of Glen Murrogh, so that my Lord President's coach drives within one mile of the stone gate of the outward court, on the occasion of the young Tanist's birth. Great doings, and the ould hospitality. Silver tankard and great salt-cellar, with a cover, found in a bog and restored to the family. Colonel Sir Bryan O'Flaherty, in consideration of his allyance in bloode to the whole towne, he and his posterity shall hereafter be freemen of the corporation. Great discontent of the townspeople; they mortgaged most of the corporation lands, for several sums of money, which they handed over to the Lord Clanricarde for the King's service. After

---

[1] 'The catholics of Ireland, in the great Rebellion, lost their estates for fighting in defence of the king' (says Swift), 'and Charles the Second, to reward them, excluded them from the act of oblivion, and issued a proclamation, 1660, "That all adventurers, soldiers, and others, in possession of manors, castles, houses, or land, of any of the said Irish rebels, should not be disturbed in their possessions," ' etc. etc.

[2] ' "Who have, for reasons known unto us, in an especial manner, merited our grace and favour." Among these favoured persons were Lord Taaf, Sir Brien O'Flaherty, and a hundred others.' – See Irish Statutes, Charles II.

restoration, said loyal mortgagers were found to be forfeiting persons, the premises vested in the king under act of settlement, who granted the entire to a fair lady,[1] widow of one of the grooms of his chamber, and this was the entire ruin of the town.

1686. – His most sacred majesty James II proclaimed; all the ould natives and ancient inhabitants flock back to the town, without let or hindrance, and are restored to their properties and freedom. And now returns the O'Brien, chief of the clan Tiegs, from Spain, and recovers lands and fiefs, through the King's justices, and has good effects in Clare and elsewhere, and prepares his claims to bring before the Lords Commissioners of the High Court, established to that intent. The catholic clergy reclaim their respective places of worship. Abbey choir repaired, and windows sashed.

1690. – Great protestant rebellion, headed by the Prince of Orange. Protestant inhabitants of St Grellan supply stores and other materials for the fortification of the town. Colonel Sir Roderick O'Flaherty raises a regiment among his own people for the King's service. Great preparation in the town.

1691. July 12. – Battle of Aughrim – all lost. The town of St Grellan surrenders; English army burn the suburbs; the old natives and inhabitants quit the towne; papists disarmed. The prior of St Francis flies to Spain, leaving one of the community to preserve the order in the town. The ladies of Mary, John, and Joseph, sent upon the *Shaughraun*, flying to and fro, like doves in a dove-cote before a hawk.

1691. – A large frog found in the fossée of the old castle of St Grellan (now the jail), the first ever seen in the province since the time of Saint Patrick.

1691. – King William's army plunder and murder the poore Irish at pleasure, in spite of His Majesty's declaration;[2] and many protestants and officers of the King's army, who had more bowels and justice than the rest, did abhor to see what sport they made to hang up poore Irish people by dozens, without pains to examine them; they scarcely thinking them human kind: so that they now began to turn

---

[1] A Mrs. Hamilton.

[2] The wise and benevolent intentions of King William, with respect to Ireland, were frustrated at every step by a faction, and by the licentious and disorderly rabble of foreigners who formed the greater part of the army. – See Harris's *King William*, and Burnet's *History of his own Time*.

rapparees,[1] hiding themselves in the bog-grass of the Mac Taaf's fassagh, and in glens and crannies of O'Flaherty's mountaines. And others of the better sort of papists, being driven out of the towne to go upon their keepinge, turn rapparees, being forced to unquiet means. And before the woods were destroyed, or the mountains were cleared of their heath and underwood, nothing was commoner than to find many, who from too much melancholy, grief, fear of death, and constant danger, being turned in their brains, did run starke, or live in tatters, subsisting upon herbs, berries, wild fruit, and the like.[2]

[O'Brien paused, – he thought he heard the lock of the door turn. He listened; but all was silent, save the pattering of the rain against the windows, and the blowing of the wind in sudden gusts. He felt he was nervous, and again read on.]

.... subsisting upon herbs, berries, wild fruit, and the like; which gave occasion to the report of there being wild people in Connaught province, and more particularly in Connemara. And wild indeed were they, in these troubleous times, and down to the present; and when one of them was taken, which was very difficult to compass, by reason of their great nimbleness, exceeding even that of the common game, it would be with long and extraordinary care and management that they were brought to their senses, and sure were they ever to remain affected, or light.

---

[1] 'Those who were then called "rapparees," and executed as such, were, for the most part, poor harmless country people, that were daily killed in vast numbers, up and down the fields, or taken out of their beds and shot immediately.' Leslie's Answer to King's State of the Protestants, etc.

[2] Of rapparees killed by the army, or militia, one thousand nine hundred, and twenty-eight; of rapparees killed and HANGED by the soldiers, without ceremony, one hundred and twenty. – Dean Story.

# CHAPTER VII

———————●———————

## *The Rapparee*

By my troth, I will go with thee to the land's end. I am a kind of burr, I
shall stick.

*Ola Play.*

O'BRIEN had dropped the annals of St Grellan. There was a moisture
in his eyes that obscured their vision, and for a moment rendered the
perusal impracticable. The last passage, which he had twice read over,
as the timid recur involuntarily to the objects of their fears, had deeply
affected him, both by a general inference and by a particular instance.
There was something in its graphic delineation, which almost realized
the wretched outlawed Irish gentleman, and the hound-hunted Irish
peasant of Cromwell's time. It had touched a nerve in his heart, which
vibrated painfully to the impression. Twice he had passed his hand
across his humid eyes, and pshaw'd and pished away his womanish
sensibility; and, determined to read no more on a subject, which,
combined with the heavy storm without, and the dreary desolation
within, was unfitting him for the interview he awaited with his unfortunate father, he was about to amuse himself with the vignettes, when,
in the next page to the melancholy description that had so deeply
affected him, he found its illustration, in the full-length drawing of

A rapparee,
Or wild Irishman,
Of the 18th century.

It was evidently a portrait, being marked by all that truth, which a
close copy of nature alone preserves. It represented a man in rude,
vigorous senility. The figure was gaunt, powerful, and athletic; but

the countenance (the true physiognomy of the western or Spanish race of Irishmen), was worn, wan, and haggard, and full of that melancholy ferocity, and timid vigilance of look, which ever characterizes man, when hunted from civilized society; or when in his savage, unaccommodated state, ere he has been admitted to its protection. A dark, deep, and sunken eye, with the Irish glib, cumhal, and prohibited coolun, or long, black, matted lock, hanging down on each side, added to the wild and weird air of a figure, still not divested of manly comeliness. The dress, if a garb so tattered could be called a dress, was singular. It was that still worn at the time, by the natives of the isles of Arran: a frieze jerkin and truis, a conical cap of seal-skin, and the brog, or sandal, fastened by a latchet. From the shoulders fell a mantle, folded across the breast with a wooden bodkin; the whole giving a most perfect picture of a *wild Irishman*, as he was called, and exhibited on the stage in his traditional dress and deplorable humiliation, from the time of Charles the Second almost to the present day, – from Teague to Paddy O'Carrol.

Here again O'Brien, as he gazed sadly and intently, recognized the resemblance of one, once dearly loved, and still deeply lamented. Although apparently worn by time or suffering, the strongly marked countenance, the gigantic figure, the form and attitude, recalled his earliest friend and foster-brother – the Chiron of his infancy and childhood – the man who, in nature's own gymnasium, had taught him to climb, to run, to dive, to swim, to sling, to wrestle, and to hurl, – the man to whom he was indebted for that strength, agility, and adroitness, that robust and unalterable health, which had served him so materially in the arduous profession he had afterwards adopted.

As he now gazed, in wonder and in pity, on this fine representation of a fine and noble animal, degraded into savagery, he recollected, with deep and dire emotion, the last moment in which he had seen the person, who had given the model of this characteristic picture. It almost maddened him, even at such a distance of time, to remember the hour, the scene, the event. He had full in his memory the dauntless, bold bearing of a being so loved, when led from a mock trial to instant execution, 'unanointed, unanneal'd' – his cool and careless eye, the look of stoical indifference he had worn, until he saw pressing through the multitude his mother, leading by the hand a youth – a mere child. Then, indeed, his countenance had changed! O'Brien saw him turn his head, and hastily assist the executioner in the horrible preliminaries of his ignominious death: he saw the fatal cap, the rope

– but he saw no more! Even now, at the distance of eleven years, he sickened as he had sickened then; he felt the same fainting of the heart, as when he then fell senseless into the arms of the stern, tearless, and inflexible Mor-ny-Brien. The recollection suffocated him with emotion, he flung down the book, and rose to change the subject of his thoughts. But suddenly he paused, started back, shuddered. Doubting his senses, and as one spellbound, he stood fixed, gazed intensely, and breathed shortly, but spoke not – for before him, on the threshold of the door, stood the object of his melancholy reminiscence, the awful original of that fearful and affecting picture, which had curdled his blood even to look upon. It was indeed 'the rapparee,' not as he had seen him in the prime of manhood, but the same in form, in dress, in attitude, as the vignette represented him, and in that half-crouching position, the habitual posture of vigilance and fear.

'Shane!' exclaimed O'Brien, after a long pause, tremulously and doubtingly; 'can it be? – is it? – Gracious God!'

With a spring, like that of a wild beast restored to its ravaged young, Shane darted forward; and with a stifled burst of sound, which resembled the last whining howl of a dying wolf, – a sound such as those only emit who have learned to 'cry Irish,' fell at his feet.

Clasping the knees of O'Brien with his huge arms, he fixed his upturned eyes on his face with such intensity, such wild tenderness, as made its object shudder. O'Brien bent down, and embraced his foster brother and hereditary clansman, with all the earnestness of affection. It was a full minute before he could speak, or address him.

'Shane,' at last he cried, 'you live then? You are the person who has haunted me of late, who came to my rescue last night; you, whom I thought I had seen murdered! whose horrible fate first drove me forth a wanderer?'

'Ay, Musha! Shane I am; poor Shane *a vic!* Shane-na-Brien, who was hanged at Michael's cross, as was the fader afore him, for th' ould cause, praised be Jasus and his blessed moder, Amen! And the mark's left on me to this hour shure, like Moran's collar.'[1]

He bared his neck, as he spoke, and showed a black circle, discolouring its muscular surface like a collar. O'Brien still bending over him, his hands clasped in his iron grasp, smiled on him through his swimming eyes, but strove in vain to speak; while Shane, gazing

[1] See O'Halloran's *Antiquities of Ireland*.

on him with ineffable tenderness (for a visage so stern and wild), seemed wholly lost in the enjoyment of the meeting. At last, looking fearfully round, he dropped his deep guttural voice, and asked in a low mutter, 'Have you Irish?'

'Not enough to converse with you,' said Murrogh. 'I have almost lost my Irish, though I still understand it.'

'Ay then,' said Shane, still more wildly and vaguely, looking around him, with what seemed habitual caution; and then again fixing his eyes on the face of O'Brien, cowering timidly towards him, and muttering a phrase of Irish endearment, as if to disarm his apprehensions. He sighed deeply, exclaiming, 'Och! the great joy! and do I touch you again, my *Vourneen Urlicaen?*[1]

'You must rise,' said O'Brien: 'I cannot speak to you, while you keep this degrading and painful attitude. Pray rise, Shane; you must, you must indeed!'

'Huisht! huisht! a vic,' said Shane, evidently confused and wild, and with a mind as wandering as his affections were concentrated, 'Huisht! I wid not throuble you long. I'll only look on ye a vic for a taste, and just touch your little *crubeen*[2] once again, and then I'll be off to the mountains the night, and nivir throuble you more – no, troth and fait, only pray for ye on the knees of my heart.'

'Trouble me! Oh, Shane, how you mistake me! indeed I am rejoiced to see you – amazed, but still rejoiced. But after what passed last night, you are not safe here.'

'*Nil, nil,*'[3] said Shane, shaking his head.

'Much as I desire to know by what means that life has been preserved, I dread to endanger it, by detaining you here a minute. You are not safe, Shane, here – I must repeat it.'

'*Nilin,*'[4] sighed Shane; 'and am like the fox of Mam Turk, hunted from his lair, with the *arch-ghaid*[5] at his throath, and the pack at his traheens, ay indeed.'

'What could have brought you here, my dear Shane?' said O'Brien, gently forcing him to rise, and drawing forward one of the arm chairs, to induce him to sit down. But Shane, leaning against the old chimney-

---

[1] My darling, my curly head.
[2] Your hand.
[3] No, no.
[4] I am not.
[5] The hound which first scents the morning dew.

piece, as characteristic as one of its own supporters, rejected the offered seat, while O'Brien resumed his own.

'And what brought me here?' repeated Shane. 'Och! Musha, what but yourself, ma vourneen. Shure it's little Shane thinks of life, in regard o' that; and have kept watch and ward upon you, since I first seed you in the great scrimmage yesterday; and was in th' ould *daoire*,[1] and you took me for an *arrach*,[2] Musha, I'll engage ye did, and th' ould *chree* "*lambh laidre aboo*." '[3]

'The sound of your never-forgotten voice, the family war-cry, and your strange appearance, did indeed sorely amaze, confound, and agitate me. I knew not what to think of it.'

'Ay, Musha,' said Shane, with a half yell'd laugh, that gave to his visage an expression more grim than even was natural to it – 'and wouldn't show mysel for fear to shame yez.'

'And whence came you, my dear Shane, – from Connaught?'

'Ay,' said Shane.

'And how did you find your way?'

'Och! I followed the track of thim that led.'

'And who were they?'

Shane rubbed round his shoulders, and answered, evasively and smilingly, from an old Irish song –

> 'Che shin? Gudae shin
> Nogh wanneen shae gho.'[4]

'But how did you know I had returned?'

'Och! I dramed it,' replied Shane, 'ay, indeed.'

'When did you arrive in Dublin?' demanded O'Brien, perceiving it was in vain to ask what Shane chose not to tell.

'Och! Jasus be praised, yesterday, – and saw you afar off, a great *Gendreanaire*,[5] and knew ye by the knocking of my heart, and the mole on your cheek, and the eyes, and your mother's smile, agrah!'

'Then, you had just arrived by the Phœnix park, when I passed you under the tree at the head of my corps?'

'Arrah! Musha,[6] that's it intirely!' said Shane, gradually cheering

---

[1] Oak-tree.
[2] A fetch, or ghost.
[3] The strong hand for ever.
[4] 'What is it? What is it to any one, whom it doth not concern?'
[5] Officer, hero.
[6] Arra, or arrah: I pledge myself.

up: 'and never lost sight of you after (sorrow sight), till this blessed minute, Jasus be praised, and found you in the *Cean corrah*.'[1]

'You have learned to speak English fluently,' said O'Brien, 'since we last parted – but surely not in Connaught?'

'*Nihil*, but where it was well taught, shure.'

'And where was that, Shane?' asked O'Brien, almost amused.

'Och, in Rome!'

'In Rome?' repeated O'Brien, with incredulous astonishment.

'Shure enough, and larned it of the Irish Dominicans of our Lady of Peace.'

'And what could have brought you to Rome, Shane?'

'*Mea culpa, mea maxima culpa*,' exclaimed Shane, striking his breast with a terrific force; while a slight convulsion passed over his grim features; and he muttered with great rapidity and confusion some penitential prayers. Then suddenly assuming his wonted manner, he said, with a smile,

'A great place it is.'

'Then you went to Rome,' said O'Brien, with increasing amazement, 'on a pilgrimage of penance?'

'Ay, in troth: and the jubilee, and the *Santa Porta*, and the thrue cross!' And he drew from his bosom a string, to which one of those reliquaries was suspended, which are supposed by the faithful to contain a bit of the cross.

'And how did you get to Rome?' said O'Brien.

'Och! shure the grace of God and the blessed Virgin: and overtook in my corricle,[2] a Galway merchant bount for Leghorn; and begged and prayed my way to the holy city. And shure' (he added, rubbing his hands and turning their palms to the fire) – 'our own cousin is suparior, father Kelly: and might have my bit and my sup to this day at our lady's of pace, only for ould Ireland, and the great yearning, ay troth.'

'But how did you escape from – from St Michael's cross?'

'Och!' said Shane, cowering closer to O'Brien; 'Sure my moder wore the girdle dear, and see, here it is:' (and stripping back his ragged jacket, he displayed a small leathern belt, wrought over with

---

[1] Cean corrah: The Chief's House.

[2] These boats, made of wicker work, covered with hides, are the only kind that could live a moment in the violent surf that generally beats on this shore; and it is astonishing what a sea they will venture to encounter. – See Survey of Clare.

Irish characters)[1] 'and when they left me in great haste, the rain falling, and the storm blowing, and I like the branch of a withered tree, Mor-ny-Brien cut me down, wid her own two hands and the help of God: and she reigns in glory with Christ and his mother this day, she that bore and saved me, *in nomine patris et filii – Amen.* Shure no harm could come to me while she lived – the last of the *Binieds!*[2] And she it was cut me down wid her own hands; and in the caves of Cong, with fire and water, and the sign of the cross, gave back a pulse to the heart o' me, and breath and sight; and the first word I spoke was an *ave*, and the next was a curse on the inimies of me and mine, to the ind of time. May the screech of the morning be on them, soon and often! – May the evil eye open on them every day they sae light! – May they never know pace nor grace in this world or the next! – May they die in a lone land, without kith or kin to close their eyes! – May they – '

'Hush, dear Shane,' interrupted O'Brien, more shocked and alarmed by the expression of insanity, that was gradually distorting his haggard features, than even by his wild imprecations. 'Remember you have triumphed over your enemies, since you live and are here – changed, indeed, since we last met in the Isles of Arran, but – '

'Och, the sorrow much,' said Shane, brightening up; 'only in regard of the glib, and coolun, and cumhal;' and he stroked back his long matted locks from his visage, and roughed the stiff tufts which bristled upon his upper lip; 'and that's to hide me from th'inemy, since I comed here. For the heart o' me was in the place, and would rather be famished at home nor feasted far away; and be hanged in the midst of my people, nor have the stranger close poor Shane's eyes in a foreign land.'

'But where, and how do you subsist?' asked O'Brien, his interest increasing with his compassion, and his early associations returning in all their ancient influence.

'Where is it? and how? Och, Christ is good, and his holy mother, *Sancta Virgo Maria!* – But the paper[3] is still on the church door at St Grellan to this day, the blood-money for the informer! – But who

---

[1] Sir John Harrington observes, 'It is a great practice in Ireland, to charme girdles and the like; persuading men that while they weare them, they cannot be hurt by any weapone.'

[2] Wise women.

[3] The proclamation of a reward for his apprehension.

would inform against a Brien? Not the clan Tiegs of Arran, nor the
O'Flahertys of Moycullen; and so keeps by times in the isles, and by
times in the mountains, and sleeps where the fox has his hole, and
the eagle his nest; and never lays head under shingled roof, nor goes
near town or townland, nor where the Sassoni keep crock nor pan;
nor where the traitor leaves the track of his *traheens*.'

'But how do you subsist? – I mean, how do you live? I know there
is shelter in the hills and fastnesses of Connemara for the hunted and
the persecuted; but I remember when you fared well with our dear
and excellent Abbé in the isles, and when your mother's hearth gave
hospitality to all who needed it.'

'Ay,' said Shane, his countenance assuming great tenderness of
expression at the recollections of his insular home, 'Ay, and the cabin
down by the cromleck, and the cow in the bawn, and St Endeas'
Cross, and ating and the dhrinking, and the puffins, and the sunfish,
and the uishge, and the meed. And now the great-grandson of Con-
na-Brien Mac-na-Reagh, who built the first stone house in Arranmore, and killed six oxen at Holytide for all who came, to be a poor
wild *shular man*,[1] without cot or cabin, only for the christians that
throw him his bit and his rag. But what moan in that? God is good;
and the poorest has a soul to be saved! and there's berries on the
bramble, and cresses in the ditch, and wather in the ford; and is not
that good enough for the wild Irish *giocah?*'[2]

The bitter smile, and sharp tone with which this was uttered, went
to the soul of Murrogh.

'And has this been your lot, my poor friend?' he asked, with a sigh;
'you, whose mother's plenteous board – my dear foster-mother – is
it possible that they, who are honest enough not to betray you, would
refuse to relieve your wants?' He paused, and then added, 'I remember
when the scullogs of Connemara were noted for their hospitality, and
their door was never closed against the stranger.'

'The scullogs?' said Shane, sighing, and coming gradually to
himself; 'but it's not now as in th' ould time, and when the poor, wild
shular comes to the bawn, the curs bark, and the garlaghs cry: and
then, a vic, the pride of the Briens 'bove all – '

His voice faltered, and he dashed the big tear from his eye, with
that deeply ejaculated 'Ochone!' of Irish grief, which none but an

[1] Wanderer.
[2] Vagabond, or outlaw.

Irish bosom can heave. He wept not, however, alone. O'Brien covered his face with his hands, and wept too, but not fairly and frankly; for youth, in its mistaken pride, blushes for the feelings by which humanity is most honoured. Still the emotions he struggled to conceal, were not unobserved by one to whose lone and unreciprocated feelings such tenderness was balm, – by one, whose temperament, made up of all the warmer and more vehement affections, was counteracted, but not wholly hardened by habits, which necessity alone had rendered savage and ferocious.

'Come, come, Shane,' said O'Brien, rising, and taking his huge hands kindly in his own, 'your trials, your sufferings are now, I trust, nearly over. Had my father known your situation – but till within this last year, he has not, I understand, visited Connemara since my mother's death – now, however, come what may, while I live, and have hands and strength to labour, you cannot want. With respect to your past afflictions, I am sure, a life so miraculously saved, will not again be taken (even if you were recognized) upon the old accusation. But then, the adventure of last night was one of no small peril. That it was on my behalf too – and yet, even with all this, I am so rejoiced to see you, so delighted to see you alive, my dear old friend, that, for the moment, I can admit no other feelings.'

'Why then, are you, machree,' said Shane, with a burst of sobbing joy, 'are you glad to see your poor ould Shane, your foster-brother? And you too, a lovely fine *uasal*,[1] and a great scholar and captain!' Then dropping on his knees, and taking from his breast a bog-wood rosary, he repeated, with wild and fanatical vehemence, and in hedge Latin, '*Ave Maria, gratiæ plena: dominus tecum. Benedicta tu in mulieribus, et benedictus fructus ventris tui Jesus. Sancta Maria, mater Dei, ora pro nobis peccatoribus, nunc, et in horâ mortis nostræ – Amen.*'

'And now,' he said, putting up his rosary, and starting on his feet, 'that's all I wish or want; and won't trouble you more, machree, but just go back to th' ould place, light of foot and heart. Ay, troth! and that this blessed night, or early the morrow, any how.'

'Indeed, I think it would be wisest to do so: and the sooner the better. But, Shane, there is some one else here as interested, at least almost as interested for you as I am:' and he was about to open the annals, and inquire who was the delightful artist who had given them

---

[1] A gentleman.

so high a value, when he was struck by the sinking of Shane's head on his bosom, and the dimness of his eyes, still fixed on himself.

'You are not well,' said Murrogh, anxiously; 'what is the matter? You seem faint and weak.'

'The heart of me is wake,' said Shane, smilingly, 'that is all, shure.'

'Weak, Shane, your heart?'

'*Och, wurristroo!* it's only in regard of the place, and the thick air, not all as one on the hills of Connemara. And there's no cot nor cabin here, only great houses and castles, and the door shut, neider hob, nor hearth, nor bit, nor sup.'

'You are faint from hunger, then?' said Murrogh, with a suffocating sensation of intense sympathy.

'*Thah,*'[1] said Shane, whose English seemed exhausted with his spirits. O'Brien flew to the buffet. The cake and the usquebaugh were to him, at that moment, as the spring in the desert. He held them forth, and Shane snatched at them eagerly, and devoured them voraciously. Cheering up gradually, under their nourishing excitement, he exclaimed, at intervals, as he ate and sipped, '*Agus ne barneen bræc. Agus ne uishge buy.*'[2]

'It is all I can find,' said O'Brien, delighted to observe the effects of the small portion of nourishment produced; and now wholly engrossed by the object of his affections, his cares, and anxiety, to the total exclusion of every other idea. 'Sit down,' he continued, 'sit down, dear Shane, and do not hurry yourself; (for he was fearful that the ravenous manner in which he ate, would be injurious to him). He threw the last fragment of the old wainscot on the fire, and drawing his chair closer towards it, he contemplated with satisfaction the gradual kindling of Shane's eye, and the deepening colour of his wan cheek. Shane, having now drained the flask to its last drop, seated himself at the hearth, after the old Irish fashion, his legs drawn up (till his knees were almost on a level with his chin), and clasped by his gaunt arms; exhibiting the attitude of those, who in castle or cabin 'sat waking and watching over a coal' till the dawn should lead them to prey or poll some 'enemy's country', or till the tale-teller should lull them to sleep after the wolf chase, by such 'rambling stuff' as his wild fancy suggested.

[1] It is; yes.

[2] 'Barneen bræc,' spotted cake, a cake with currants in it. 'Uishge buy,' yellow water. Buy is the box tree, whose wood is yellow.

This last specimen of the Rapparees of the earlier part of the last century had the true Irish spirits, formed for every excitement, to madden into riotous gaiety, to sink into gloomy despondency. Intoxicated alike with jog and usquebaugh, basking in the red blaze of the fire, he now sat, the image of savage felicity; his eyes glistening, his accent chuckling, and his haggard features distorted by a play of gaiety, which rendered their expression still more wild and fierce.

'As you now sit and look on me, Shane,' said O'Brien, gazing intensely upon him, 'you recal at once the days of my happy childhood. . . .'

'*Thah,*' said Shane, rubbing his hands and smiling.

'. . . . My foster-mother, and every corner of the cabin near Dun Ængus.'

'*Musha, thah,*' said Shane, with a chuckling laugh, and smoothing back his long, lank coolun.

'She was a strange creature,' continued O'Brien; 'her mysterious disappearance from the Isles of Arran was never accounted for.'

Shane nodded his head in token of assent, and compressed his lips.

'She never settled after,' said O'Brien; 'there were some wild tales circulated of her being met in the mountains of Moycullen by wayfaring people; you, Shane, have doubtless heard the story about the ruins of the abbey?'

'She died a great saint,' said Shane, evasively, 'pace to her soul, and glory to her memory. Amen.'

O'Brien observing that the subject agitated him, changed it; and added – 'Mor ny Brien was greatly gifted; her memory was miraculous, and her voice most melodious.'

'*Thah!*' (exclaimed Shane, his stern features relaxing from their temporary compression) '*clarsagh na vallagh,* she was called far and near – ay, troth – '

'Which means the *harp of the village,* if I remember right?'

'*Musha, thah!*' said Shane, much pleased; 'and hears her voice in the mountains to this day, when the wind is asleep, keening th' ould moan!'[1]

---

[1] The Lamentations of Connaught. – See Walker's *History of Irish Music.*

The tears suddenly started to his eyes, and rolled down his haggard cheeks in big drops.

'With what delight,' said O'Brien, 'I used to listen to her stories of the tribe of Dalgais, and the feats of the heroes of our family – of Cas, son of Conal of the swift horses, and of Fionne Mac Cumhal – '

'Agus Ossin,' said Shane, suddenly brightening up, and shaking back his coolun, and wiping his eyes in his hair.

'Yes,' said O'Brien, 'I remember the effect of her Irish Cronan, that began "Corloch, haughty, bold, and brave," and Cucullin's challenge to him. You remember that, Shane?'

'*Thah!*' said Shane, swinging backwards and forwards his gigantic frame, and cheering gradually up. '*Agus an Moira Borb.*'

'Yes,' said O'Brien, rather in soliloquy than in dialogue, and wholly borne away by the subject, which now called up, not only past, but present associations; – 'that tale of Moira Borb, the Irish enchantress, the Irish Armida, is a strange coincidence with Tasso. There is something in it even more than coincidence –

> All' apparir della beltà novella
> Nasce un bisbiglio!'

'Anan!' said Shane, staring.

'And there was a spirited controversial dialogue, too, between St Patrick and Ossian,' continued O'Brien, 'which she used to sing to a wild strain.'

'*Ossin agus St Phaedrig,*' repeated Shane, making the sign of the cross.

'And that sweet old air, of which the burden was, "I am asleep, do not awaken me." '

'*Ta mi mo hoolah, na dushame,*' interrupted Shane, now not touched, but rapt.

'And Carolan's receipt, sung by old Donogh!'

'Ay, Musha,' chuckled Shane, 'a great *abra*[1] *Donogh an abhac,*[2] a great *gramog.*'[3]

'There are no impressions like those of early childhood,' said O'Brien, 'particularly when received in such scenes, and with such people.'

---

[1] A song.
[2] Donogh, the dwarf.
[3] Buffoon.

'Nil,' echoed Shane, who was now thinking in Irish, and so spoke it.

'How well I remember,' said O'Brien, 'going round St Ængus's Cross on my knees.'

'*Ængus a Naoimhe*,'[1] said Shane, blessing himself instinctively at the name of his patron saint.

'Does Conlas's rath still stand?' said O'Brien.

'Och, Musha, to the fore,' replied Shane.

'And still blazes, I suppose on the first of May, with many a merry bonfire?'

'The *Bel tean*,[2] Musha, ay.'

'What has become of that curious, long, twisted wand, which used to stand in the corner of your mother's hearth?'

'The *slahan Draotheath?*'[3] asked Shane – 'Abbess Beavoin's crosier?'

O'Brien started at the mention of a name that had so recently and so powerfully interested him.

'Och, thim has it as has a right to have it,' said Shane, mysteriously.

'I suppose you have not one story-teller, one *Sceadluidhe*, left in Arran?'

'*Virgo Maria!* Ay, plinty,' replied Shane. '*Agus* ould Fergus, the *clashmanaigh*.'[4]

'Indeed! those Arranites never die; one is tempted almost to believe their fables of longevity.'

'Shure the bed of Coemhan,'[5] said Shane, emphatically.

'How well I remember,' said O'Brien, stretching out his legs, and folding his arms, while his countenance exhibited the imaginative influences of his memory, and all its thick-coming fancies – 'How well I remember your mother placing me on that rocky bed, to recover me from my lameness, and the severe manner in which she was

---

[1] Ængus of the saints.

[2] Bel's fire.

[3] The druids' staff. The use of the crosier is said to be derived from the augur's baton, and this probably (being of Tuscan origin) came from the East. The druids likewise used the crosier; deriving it, in all likelihood, from the Phœnicians. Hence it has been thought, by some antiquarians, that the introduction of this article of furniture into the Christian church, came directly from the druids.

[4] The jester.

[5] The bed of St Coemhan, much famed for its miraculous cures, through the mediation of the saint, of infirm persons, particularly the lame and blind. – Transactions of Royal Irish Acad. vol. xiv.

rebuked by the Abbé O'Flaherty, for her attachment to such super-stitious ceremonies.'

'Ay, in troth,' said Shane, stirring up the embers with a brand.

'You remember, too, I dare say, Shane, how I got that lameness?'

'*Agus* the puffins,' said Shane, laughing, 'and the clifters! and great sport that night! And you a *donny* cratur, not that high – no, indeed – *avic Machree!*'

'Good God! what a scene! what magnificent desolation! what a subject for a Salvator! I see it all now. We stood on the summit of the cliffs, looking down the almost fathomless precipice, suddenly illumined by a beautiful *aurora borealis*.'

'Ay,' said Shane, rubbing his huge chapped hands.

'You let me down by a rope, tied round my middle. I remember its pressure, and my swinging in mid-air, till I reached the strand below; I now hear the flutter of the puffins.' – (Shane made a noise, imitating the flight of the birds.) – 'You followed; I see you now, half way down. If the rope had broken – it makes my head reel to think of it! There is a reckless hardihood in children, the result of ignorance, that – certain it is, I would not now do what I then did so carelessly – nothing could tempt me.'

'*Naen, naen!*' said Shane, shaking his head, and evidently rather guessing than understanding, the abrupt apostrophes of his quondam pupil.

'But you were then my guardian angel,' added O'Brien, smiling kindly, as, borne away by that vehemence of feeling (the virtue and the weakness of an ardent and impetuous temperament), he stretched forth his hand to the rapparee – 'And you are still' (he continued,) 'at least you would be, a barrier between me and harm.'

'Ay and troth,' said Shane, with a growling fondness, 'and the heart's blood would flow for you every dhrop and *mille*[1] welcomes.'

'Of that I have no doubt; I can have no doubt of your devotion, Shane; but, I fear it. Your desperate efforts on my behalf last night, your being now in the very neighbourhood of the military whom you attacked.'

'The *boddah Sassoni!*[2] exclaimed Shane, fiercely, his whole counten-ance assuming a ferocious expression, darkling, glowering, and

[1] A thousand.
[2] The Saxon churls.

distorted. '*Croisha na Chrishla*,[1] and they wid tiche an hair of your *vourneen urlacaen*, or blink an eye agen ye;' and he seized a carbine, which, on entering, he had deposited against the wall; and which O'Brien now, for the first time, observed.

Heart-struck at once by his devotedness, and by the insane vehemence with which it was manifested, he threw his arm over Shane's shoulder, and said, in a soothing tone, 'But I trust, my dear Shane, there will be no further occasion for your gallant and affectionate interference. My only fears now are for you. Are you aware of the risk you ran in entering the Castle last night? I am sure I saw you there.'

'Are you, *a-vic!*' said Shane, now affectedly preoccupied in piling up the embers.

'You were followed by a chair so closely that – Have you any knowledge of the person who was in it?'

'Soldier, that is your prisoner,' interrupted a voice from the further end of the room. O'Brien, with the rapidity of lightning, threw himself before Shane, who, starting on his legs, levelled his piece over O'Brien's shoulder, with the look of a wild beast, hunted to his den, and eager to protect its young. A file of soldiers now entered, halted by command, and drew up in line; while a civil officer, who accompanied them, stepped forward, accompanied by three gentlemen; and O'Brien beheld with consternation, Captain O'Mealy, Lord Walter, and Lord Charles.

There was a pause, a silence. Amazement, and a still deeper interest sat on every countenance. But, on the face of O'Brien, as it paled and reddened, as his eyes dimmed and flashed, as his compressed lips quivered and refused all utterance, was exhibited an emotion, in which every passion, save fear alone, had its share; while the deepest and direst mortification of wounded pride, at the exposure thus made of his forlorn and ruinous home, and at the strange position in which he was discovered, was almost the least easy of endurance.

He was about to address the intruders, with all the temper he could affect, but observing that when the civil officer was advancing towards him, Shane cocked his piece, he snatched the murderous weapon from his hands; and speaking to him as well as he could in Irish, he invoked his discretion, and observed to him, that resistance could then only aggravate his danger. Shane threw around him a terrible glance;

[1] Cross of Christ.

then letting fall his eyes, and shaking down his long locks, he drew his tattered mantle around him, and stood the image of sullen, silent, and ferocious despair.

O'Brien, drawing up, and assuming a look and tone of haughtiness, but ill-suited to his wretched situation, addressed the civil officer –

'Who is it, Sir, you look for here?'

'This person,' said the officer, 'whom we find with the very carbine he violently took from a soldier of the Royal Irish brigade, last night, and with which he fired at this gentleman who commanded the party.'

'You are certain of his identity?' said O'Brien. 'You can swear to his person?'

'Yes, I think I can,' replied the officer, smiling; 'It is not easy to mistake him. I saw enough of him last night in the fray of the Strugglers, and at the rescue of yourself, Mr O'Brien, out of the hands of the police. He has been traced this evening to this house, and seen entering it over an old wall in the rear, not an hour back.'

O'Brien then turned coldly and haughtily to the gentlemen, and asked, 'And to what circumstance, my lords, am I indebted for your presence, at an hour somewhat unseasonable, to say the least of it?'

'Oh!' said O'Mealy, winking at his companions, 'we were sure of finding you at home: as Lockit says, "the Captain's always at home," and so . . .'

Lord Walter here pushed back his vulgar associate, and taking off his hat, said, 'Mr O'Brien, our intrusion is indeed unseasonable, but it was as utterly unexpected both on my part, and that of Lord Charles. It requires explanation and apology. We had not the slightest idea of your being in this house, when an idle curiosity tempted us to enter it. Happening to dine to-day at the mess of the Prince's Own, with Lord Charles, where Captain O'Mealy came after dinner (on a message from Lady Knocklofty, to join her at the ball at the Rotunda), an account arrived that the unfortunate man now before us had been dogged to an old house in this neighbourhood. The strange description given of a genuine wild Irishman, and of the almost super-human feats he performed yesterday (of which Lord Charles was a witness, and, but for you, would have been a victim), induced us to accompany O'Mealy and his party, on our way into town. I have no doubt,' he added significantly, and taking O'Brien's reluctant hand, which he cordially shook, 'that a similar curiosity has likewise led you here. But since we can none of us be of service, and since we have fully satisfied our curiosity respecting this Irish champion, I think, Lord Charles, we had better proceed, and not keep Lady Knocklofty's horses waiting this tremendous night.'

'I think so too,' said Lord Charles, hesitating, and rather sideling toward O'Brien, to whom he had taken off his hat, and recognized him by a surly bend, which O'Brien had as sullenly returned. 'We are destined,' he continued, 'Mr O'Brien, to meet under singular circumstances.'

'I can have no objection,' said O'Brien, significantly, 'to meet Lord Charles Fitzcharles under any circumstances.'

'Come,' said Lord Walter, taking his friend's arm, 'let us be off; we can be of no use here, and – '

'Stay, for the love of the Lord,' interrupted O'Mealy, catching Lord Walter's sleeve; 'wait a minute, and 'pon my honour I'll be with you, before you can say Jack Robinson. Sure, you would not have me to walk to the Rotunda in my silks, pumps, and white kerseymeres: and I to lade off the first set to the tune of Money Musk with Lady Mary O'Blarney? – Pace officer, where are you? Soldiers, surround your prisoner. We'll deposit him, for the night, in the barrack depôt. Serjeant, take charge of this carbine; it is hanging evidence. Mr O'Brien, my dear, upon my honour and conscience, as a gentleman and a soldier, it grieves me greetly to sae you in such a situation, it does, 'pon my honour; and shut up at this "witching time of night," as th' immortal says, coshering and colloguing with that murdering ruffianly Irish giant there, to whom Magrah's skeleton in the natomy room of your college is but a fairy. I believe, pace officer, that is, I am afraid, we cannot well be off arresting Mr O'Brien too, till he can give an account how and why he was found here, a party concerned in this den of thieves and robbers: for that's what it is, beyond all doubt, or I am greatly mistaken. And you'll mind, Mr O'Brien, that no later than this evening, as the castle clock struck a quarter to six, just as we parted at the gate, you told me you were going to O'Brien House, to my lord your father's: and it was my fullest intention to tip you the paste-board, and give you the provoke to a mess-dinner before night. Instead of which, I find you here, to my intire surprise, in a murdering, ugly, ould, ruin, sated, quite at home, with your book and your bottle beside you, and cheek-by-jowl with your pot companion there. And you, Mr O'Brien, that pledged me your solemn word of honour, that you knew neither act nor part of . . .'

'Hold!' exclaimed O'Brien, in a tone that made O'Mealy step back some paces. For thus exposed in all his penury, – pride, rage, and indignation, gave an almost super-human expression to his countenance. There was in his look and voice something stunning, which startled even the animal courage of O'Mealy.

'Hold!' he said. 'Stop there. Whatever may be your idle suspicions, founded in ignorance, and expressed in all the insolence of your temporary authority, give them no further utterance. You *must* believe, you *dare not* doubt an assertion, to which I have pledged my honour.'

'Be aisy; be aisy, now, my dear fellow,' said O'Mealy, with a cajoling and humorous tone. 'Now, I just ask you, fair and quiet, did you not give me your word, or what came to the same thing, assured me that you knew nothing of that rebelly thief?'

'Nor did I then, Captain O'Mealy: I was utterly ignorant of his existence. Not an hour since, I most unexpectedly found in this poor and unfortunate man, an old friend, and faithful follower of my family. My long absence from Ireland, and my belief of his death, prevented me from recognizing him, in the frequent and strange rencontres we had yesterday. For the rest, let me suggest to you, and to the civil officer, under whose authority you doubtless act, that your prisoner is not quite sane; that he acts under the influence of strong mental derangement; and that his hallucination will, I trust, not fail to acquit him of the matter with which he may be charged. And now, Sir,' he continued, with an evident effort and struggle of the mind, 'with respect to this old house, which you have been pleased to name a den of thieves, it is, and has been for nearly two centuries, a family mansion; and though, since I last saw it, it has been dismantled and dilapidated, it was once the residence of my ancestor the great Earl of Inchiquin, and is now his lineal descendant's, my father's house.'

'Well, my dear fellow,' said O'Mealy, good humouredly, 'laste said is soonest minded; and as to the ould house, if I have hurt your fine feelings, upon my honour I am heartily sorry for it; and I can say no more. I suppose, the pace officer here will expect you to find some surety for your appearance for all that, in regard of your being found cheek-by-jowl with this Fin Macool here.'

'Certainly I shall, Captain O'Mealy,' said the officer. 'And Mr O'Brien, you had better accompany me at once; as it may be difficult to procure two sureties at this hour, and the night so bad.'

'There can be no difficulty whatever on the subject,' said Lord Walter; 'I offer myself for one bail.'

'And I,' said Lord Charles, 'for the other; if Mr O'Brien will do me the honour to accept of me.'

'I am much flattered,' said O'Brien, frankly, and with much feeling, 'and will gratefully accept of both, if it be really necessary.'

'A friend in need's a friend indeed,' said O'Mealy. 'Did not I tell you, my dear fellow, you were born under a lucky star? 'Pon my honour I did. It's worth while gitting into a scrape, to have lords' and dukes' sons going bail for one, – it will cut such a dash in the papers. But we must keep moving; for Lady Mary is watching for me, I'll ingage, – so, sarjeant, do your duty.'

The gentlemen drew back, and gathered round O'Brien at the fire-place, intreating him not to interfere. The soldiers moved forward upon their prisoner; who, firm, erect, and drawn up to his full gigantic height, stood like a fixture of the old building. He had imperceptibly, and step by step, drawn back (followed by his guard), till he now stood in front of the panel-door which led to the back stairs, and which was then half closed. When, however, two soldiers, perceiving his immoveable firmness, seized him by the shoulders to drag him forcibly away, his countenance darkened, his eyes flashed, and by a sudden spring he dashed them on one side, sending them reeling for several paces; and with the rapidity of thought he darted back and closed the door upon his retreat. Others of the military now rushed forward to force an entrance and pursue the fugitive; and thus, precipitating themselves on one spot of the rotten floor, the fatal and natural consequence ensued – the floor gave way. The awful, terrible, and dinning crash which followed was rendered more horrid and astounding by the shrieks of the unfortunate men, who sunk with the mass of rubbish into the yawning chasm, mingling with the report of their fire-arms, with the din of the still falling building, and the roar of the storm without. The shock given by the fall, caused a universal vibration to the whole building: rafter after rafter gave way, and beam after beam. A chimney, which fell through the tiled roof, spread increasing destruction. Gushes of thick, suffocating dust filled, for a time, the horrible abyss, and almost stifled those who still remained on a fragment of the floor, which extended a few feet beyond the great chimney-piece. These were the two lords, Captain O'Mealy, O'Brien, and the peace officer. Amidst the horror and consternation of an event so fearful, bricks and tiles still falling – doors, windows, and shutters rattling in the storm, both within and without, they still preserved sufficient presence of mind to recognize their danger, and the possibility of escape; while the cry of '*Faer ghim, faer ghim, Agus*, keep to the fire-place,' issuing from beneath the window near which they stood, convinced O'Brien that Shane was safe – a conviction, that cheered him into hope for the safety of himself and those around him.

When he could make himself heard (for, the light being extinguished, he could not be seen), he begged of all to stand quiet, and remain where they were. The hearth which they occupied, he said, was supported by holdfasts, lately erected, and the beams of that end of the floor were fresh and uninjured. He then made to the window next the chimney-piece, threw up the sash, and shouted for assistance. The building was already surrounded; men with lanterns and flambeaux were visible at a little distance; and the glittering of arms also showed that some of the soldiers had escaped, and that others had joined them from the royal barracks on the other side of the river. A lofty figure, much above the stature of those around him, forced forward through the falling bricks and tiles, and fixed a ladder against the window.

The gentlemen descended in safety, O'Brien last; but scarcely had he reached the earth, when he saw himself in Shane's arms. 'Away! away!' he said, extricating himself from the embrace. At that moment, the part of the building they had just left, fell in, with a horrible crash, and the chimney-piece, the fine monument of antiquity, was precipitated with it into the ruins. Still the outward walls held together; and by the light of the flambeaux, the back stairs were seen hanging as it were in the air, like the geometrical staircase of modern times, without visible support.

When the cloud of dust, formed by the last fall, had somewhat subsided, and the house could be approached without imminent peril, O'Brien (satisfied that Shane had escaped), busied himself in giving relief to the sufferers by this fatal event. He thought of poor Robin, buried, doubtless, with the corpse of his grandmother, beneath the ruins. He rushed on through dust and lime, followed by the humane and the courageous; and was soon joined by a party of pioneers, whose pick-axes and spades were of infinite use. Many of the soldiers, who had fallen through the floor into the hall beneath, were wounded; but all, though nearly suffocated, escaped with life, and were carried off by their comrades. Two dead bodies alone were discovered, on which the coping stone of a wall had fallen. By the glare of a flambeau, were discovered the mangled remains of the unfortunate Robin, beside those of the deceased Alice.

While O'Brien was thus penetrating into the interior of the building,

Lord Charles, Lord Walter, O'Mealy, and the constable, were fully occupied without, in preserving order and keeping out the crowd, which, in spite of rain and wind, had assembled from the neighbouring purlieus of the barracks and of Watling-street.

Every blast of wind still continued to shake the wreck of the ruined fabric; and O'Brien, believing that the walls would soon follow, was himself retiring; rejoicing that amidst the sad events of the night, his father had escaped; when, as he stumbled over heaps of rafters and lime, the faint shriek of a female voice caught his ear. Astounded, he paused, turned round, looked up, and doubting the evidence of his senses, beheld a female form standing on the still suspended stairs, between which and destruction there seemed to be but a moment of time.

The nodding ruin now received a terrible shock, from a burst of the increasing hurricane. The crowd fell hurrying back; – O'Brien plunged deeper and deeper within the walls, till he stood beneath the perilous staircase, which rocked like one of rope.

'Spring down at once,' he said, opening his arms to receive the trembling person, above whose head, fragments of the roof were falling, tile by tile. As he opened his arms, she half bent forward, as if to leap; when, from the other side, the cry of '*Faer ghim! faer ghim!*' arrested her attention; and springing down, with the light dart and hardihood of a bird, she was received in the arms of Shane. At that moment the whole pile fell in, with a tremendous roar; and O'Brien, with his arms folded over his head, sometimes beaten down, and again plunging forward, scarcely credited his senses, when he again found himself beyond the reach of danger, surrounded by the Lords Walter and Charles, O'Mealy, and a multitude of people.

The gentlemen endeavoured to carry him from the spot, and to persuade him to accompany them into town, as nothing further now remained to be done; but he was under powerful excitement, and fearful that Shane, and the object of his humane and perilous exertions, were buried in the ruins. As soon as he had recovered breath and strength, he made known his fears to the bystanders. His mind, however, was set at rest by one of the crowd, who assured him that a tall man, carrying a woman in his arms, had passed him at the Ferry slip, and by this time was on the other side. Fortunately, this information was given out of the hearing of O'Mealy and the peace officer; and O'Brien's heart, though still thrilling and palpitating, was, as far as Shane was concerned, for the present at rest. He now accompanied the gentlemen, walking arm in arm with Lord Walter, towards Lady Knocklofty's carriage, which had drawn up at a short distance, under the shelter of the *porte cochère* of Moira House, while curiosity had detained the footmen at the scene of recent action.

As neither the dress of the party, nor the state of their spirits, permitted them to join the ball at the Rotunda, Lord Walter proposed to O'Brien to set him down at the College; but he declined the offer, on the plea that the condition of his clothes (covered with the dust and rubbish of the ruin, and drenched with rain) would render a walk safer to himself, as well as spare the delicate silken hangings of Lady Knocklofty's vehicle. All that he would be prevailed on to accept, was Lord Walter's great-coat. While he was drawing it on, Lord Charles, putting his head out of the carriage window, observed, in his languid way,

'Mr O'Brien, you have said, that you could have no objection to meet me under *any* circumstances: will you allow me, then, to cut ceremony short, and make you a proposition for a meeting to-morrow?'

'Undoubtedly,' said O'Brien, coming closer to the carriage window, 'when and where you please.'

'Well, then,' said Lord Charles, 'the when, six o'clock, and the where, at our mess dinner; with Lord Walter for your second, and our friend O'Mealy for mine: and then, with glasses charged to the brim,

> Lay on, Macduff;
> And damned be he who first cries, Hold, enough.

I know this is not your Irish way of settling differences. But, hang it, – whatever an Hibernian may think, I have no great gusto for taking away the life of a man who has saved mine.'

'And who,' said O'Brien, returning the cordial shake of his hand, 'must ever value his own the more for the success of the effort. I accept your challenge, my lord, as frankly at it is given.'

'Upon my honour, this is a mighty pretty quarrel as it stands,' said O'Mealy, 'as my friend, Sir Lucius, has it. So I shall not say a word on the subject, only that I'm glad to be a party concerned.'

Lord Walter now shaking the hands of both the young men, expressed his satisfaction at the termination of an affair, in which both, or neither, had been in the wrong. The carriage then drove on, to set down the gentlemen at their respective homes; and

O'Brien, as the College clock struck eleven, entered the gates of *Alma Mater*.

END OF VOL. II

# The O'Briens and the O'Flahertys

## VOLUME THREE

# CHAPTER I

●

## *Trinity College*

Quel est donc l'objet de vos colléges, de vos académies, de tant de fondations savantes? Est-ce de donner le change au peuple, d'altérer d'avance an raison, de l'empêcher d'aller au vrai!

ROUSSEAU, *Lettre à Mons. de Beaumont.*

AMONG the penal clauses, which filled the Irish statute book from the period of the revolution, the most effective in degrading the people of all ranks, were the laws against education. Reading and writing were the peculiar privilege of protestantism: and he who had not given up transubstantiation and the infallibility of the Pope, had but little chance of enjoying the delectable adventures of Renard the Fox, or of imitating the heroism of Don Bellianis of Greece and the Seven Champions of Christendom. While the first elements of learning were thus jealously withheld from the catholic people, it is not surprising that the higher branches of science, the pathways to professional eminence, were still more rigorously guarded; and that the Gates of the Irish University were hermetically sealed against all, save the sons of ascendancy.

The young members of the great emporium of church and state prerogative, high in the conscious privileges of their caste, were, by their very position, little likely to submit to the restraints of a rigorous discipline; and the advanced age at which they were then accustomed to matriculate, did not tend to increase their subordination. At that period the road to reason was long and circuitous; there were no short cuts and by-ways to the learned languages; and the venerable college of the capital received no 'boyish troops in unhaired sauciness,' under her owlet wings. No pert precocity then started from her halls and classes, well stocked with poetry and pastry, with genius and ginger-bread. No minor poets wrote Odes to Phœbus or to Dolly, which afterwards could come forth to shame the prosaic wisdom, that had removed their authors from the grottos of Helicon, to the stalls of a cathedral. On the contrary, the students of the Irish University, some fifty years ago, came fresh from the rack-rent castles of their bashaw fathers, in the first burst of manhood. Full of restless energy, with passions awakened, and habits of turbulence formed, they were from their entrance better

> Versed in the rudiments
> Of many a desperate study,

than in those sedentary pursuits which cool the blood, 'and preach the pulse to temper.' Leaders in every civil broil which disturbed the badly policed capital; dictators in the street, and umpires in the theatre, they were popular with the populace whom they resembled, and feared by the citizens whom they annoyed. But, like the young scions of modern jesuitism on the Continent, they formed a *'jeunesse bien pensant.'* Though violating the laws, they upheld the Constitution; though breaking the King's peace, they fought staunchly for his crown and dignity; and though public disturbers of social order, and private violators of domestic happiness, they acted under the especial protection of the church, as by law established.

Still the University of Dublin, the *'Collegium Sanctæ et individuæ Trinitatis,'* was then, as now, a good old monkish and venerable institution. Founded in those semi-papistical times, when the reformation (which, as a great divine has lately declared, is only now beginning to take effect), was but a word; and erected upon the model of other institutions which sprang up under the full influence of popery, it still performed all those forms, laws, canons, and customs, which were as purely monastic, as those of any Jesuit or Dominican seminary in France or Spain. The students, for whatever profession designed, were supposed to lead the lives of the *'fratri'* of a foreign convent; and whoever beheld them in their white sacerdotal surplices, with their strongly marked Irish faces, well set off with demurely smoothed bands, celebrating their matins, vespers, or high mass done into English, in their old popish-looking chapel, might have mistaken these scions of protestant ascendancy, for the officiating *'clerici'* of an Italian Duomo, or the robust brotherhood of the Irish friary at the *'Pace'* of

Rome; where the '*lingua Toscana*,' and the brogue of Tipperary are still cultivated with equal assiduity and equal success.

Towards the latter end of the last century, the opening of the university to catholics and dissenters, and still more, the diffusion of political knowledge and public spirit through the bloodless revolution of eighty-two, produced their ennobling effects, even within the walls of the strong-hold of all ancient institutes. The spirit of the 'Trinity boys,' as they were fondly and familiarly called by the people, was then not less buoyant and vigorous, than that of their restive and restless predecessors: but it took a higher and a better direction, consonant to that greatest and best epoch of Irish story. The sparkling effervescence of the Irish temperament no longer evaporated in unprofitable ardors and ignoble contentions: and to how great an extent patriotism and science profited by the kindling of energies so fresh, and the concentration of powers so unworn, the lives and works, the eloquence and the actions of the Avonmores and the Youngs,[1] the Grattans and the Currans, afford abundant testimony and proof. Never did any country give to the world a more splendid, or more intellectual generation, than that which now burst forth to illustrate the benefits of political independence; and to prove the superiority of the age, that was dawning in the light of truth and liberality, over that which was setting in the darkness of bigotry and intolerance. A spirit was abroad, which gave to senility the vital energies of youth; and to youth the high aspiration and pertinacity of purpose of vigorous manhood. Learning raised her head from the study of useless abstraction, to catch the rising light. The historical society was established: and if national and youthful vanity found their account in the opportunities it afforded for ambitious display, if taste and judgment sometimes shrank from the ebullitions of over-excited genius, still that splendid association of youthful, fervid, and honest hearts, which nurtured the national talent of eloquence, and fostered the national spirit, was a benefaction to the country. In the dreary interval that has succeeded its dissolution, the genius, which was the sole distinction of the country – the solitary attribute which tyranny had not quenched – has sickened in the cells of 'the silent sister;' and subserviency and hypocrisy have been made the profitable substitutes for patriotism and talent.

The canons of Elizabeth were now of little avail against the spirit

---

[1] Dr Young, Bishop of Glonfert.

of the age. Swift and Molyneux were again read with avidity. Locke was not yet banished from the course of collegiate instruction. Curran, Yelverton, Grattan, Flood, Burgh, and Ponsonby, had but recently come from the meditation of their philosophical, hardy, and convincing pages; and were already shedding a glory, which effaced the memory of that dulness, that had expelled the creator of Gulliver, and had rejected the poet of Auburn. The 'Monks of the Screw,' who in the midst of their classic festivities, mingled mirth with wisdom, and gave to political philosophy the charm of eloquence, and the lustre of wit, – the Monks of the Screw had long left to other monks the gravity which is the talent of mediocrity, and the cant which is the eloquence of hypocrisy. Though some embryo Boulters and Stones were then crawling in the lowest walks of collegiate service, to attain the church's diadem, which they have since worn with such un-christian despotism; the youth of the Irish University, for the most part, followed emulously in the luminous track of their unrivalled predecessors: and men not less highly endowed, though less fortunate in their epoch, trod closely in the steps of those destined to fill a brighter, but not a more honourable page in the history of their country.

Among these juvenile aspirants for honest fame, these enthusiasts for national regeneration, the Honourable Murrogh O'Brien stood pre-eminent, as one whose unguarded frankness, buoyant spirit, and popular endowments had rendered him a subject of notoriety, from the first record of his name upon the College books. He was, indeed, the very *beau idéal* of the French and the Irish youth, who, in many important particulars, so closely resemble each other. There was, too, a brilliant, but unlucky, adaptation of his qualities, principles, and acquirements to the then reigning opinions in Ireland, which constituted him at once a leader of that portion of the students who had enlisted themselves in the popular cause: and an accidental, or an affected, resemblance to the style of Mirabeau, in his rhetorical orations at the Historical Society, had obtained him much vogue amongst his fellow students; while his military skill in the volunteer corps, which he had materially assisted in raising, had equally distinguished him among the members of the great national army.

He had thus become the subject of especial suspicion and vigilant observation to the chiefs of the university; and he had been more than once *cautioned* as to his mode of treating the subjects discussed at that society, which, like himself, had already begun to '*devancer son siècle.*'

The Historical Society of the Irish University, in its origin, and before it had attained to its high eminence, was but a mere ordinary debating club. No exception had been taken to it as long as its members confined themselves to mooting the Irish rebellion, the gun-powder plot, the restoration of his sacred majesty King Charles the Second, and such other themes as had been handed down traditionally from some archetypal exercises of church and state eloquence. Thus conducted, the institution was rather cherished than feared; as being (under the cover of a desirable exercise of the intellect) a hot-bed of servility, and a school for time-servingness. But when, awakening from the lethargy of a stultifying despotism, the youth of Ireland, and of her university, began to think, to feel, to speak, and even to write – when they took for their discussions the real subjects of national interest, a reform of the representation, and the emancipation of the catholics, then a sort of inquisition, or Star Chamber, was erected within the College walls, and the free course of debate was checked by cautions, threats, rustication, and the loss of all collegiate caste, expulsion.[1]

While such a spirit was called forth in the councils of the university, and was strengthened and authorised by its Vice-Chancellor, many of its younger members furnished but too many favourable pretexts for the exercise of its power: for they were imprudent (as the uncompro-mising and honest always are), and impetuous (as the ardent and the young cannot fail to be). Visitations, followed by censures and punishments, were frequent. Even a fellow of the College, one of the most enlightened and learned of its members, was threatened with a suspension (which was afterwards put in force), for opinions purely theoretical; while the disgrace of expulsion was held *in terrorem*, though upon what devoted head it was to fall was still a mystery.

Such was the moral condition of the Irish University, when Murrogh O'Brien was about to incur its censures, for a conduct, that, whatever might be its errors, would, twenty years before, have been passed over in silence; as one of those juvenile 'frolics, done at the heat of blood,' which then nightly disturbed the streets of the Irish capital.

O'Brien, on his return to College, after two days' absence, crossed

---

[1] 'Armed,' says a writer of the day, 'with the doctrine of libel, the great engine of oppression in all despotisms, you have invaded the student in his cell; and the subtlety of a Spanish inquisition has been employed to ensnare the artlessness of youth, and to draw generous simplicity into self-crimination.'

its threshold with a heavy and foreboding heart. Lighted by one of the porters, who accompanied him from the lodge to his own chambers in the library square (which looked from their rear into the park), he found them chill and comfortless – almost as desolate as that he had lately occupied in his paternal home. The porter, too, who only staid to light his candle, was churlish and surly; and treated him as one who was already under the ban of that empire, which was to its underlings – the world. In answer to O'Brien's question for letters or notes (for he was anxious and full of expectation as to his father), the man replied sullenly, that he believed there were both messages and letters, but that it was then too late to send them up from the lodge, and that the fire-lighter would bring them in the morning. He then retired; and O'Brien, worn out in mind and body, stiff with protracted fatigue, and the bruises he had received among the falling ruins, and chilled with the drenching rain, under which he had so long been exposed, retired to his little dormitory in utter despondency, and wholly deficient in those physical energies, from which spring the pleased alacrity of spirits and cheering aspirations of hope.

It was late when he rose on the following morning; so late, that he missed the chapel service, as he necessarily had done on the preceding day – another item in the long account which college discipline had to settle with him. As he entered his sitting-room, he found his breakfast table covered with cards, notes, and letters. There is in such mementos of friendly recollection something peculiarly cheering to spirits depressed with the consciousness of isolation. The certainty of being thought of, in the moment when some especial stroke of life's vicissitudes leads to the apprehension of a general abandonment, was gracious and gratifying. It was a solace he needed; for he was still steeped in thought from visions of the night – from adventures, at least, which might pass for visions. Intense solicitude concerning the mysterious absence of his father, at a moment so critical to his only child – anxiety for the fate of Shane – the utter ruin of his father's fortunes – and last, though scarcely least, the agitating and doubtful impression left on his mind, by the sudden apparition of that female phantom, standing on the brink of destruction, amidst the ruins of the falling house – all combined to sink his susceptible spirits to the lowest pitch of depression. He gladly, therefore, took refuge from himself in externals, and was disposed to see, in the common forms of good-will, more of courtesy and of kindness, than might even have been intended.

The visiting cards included the names of the most distinguished members of the Historical Society, some of whom had called on him, the day before, at the castle guard. There was also a letter written on coarse paper, coarsely folded, and sealed with a thimble. A slight flush coloured his pale cheek, as he threw the letter carelessly and unopened on one side: he was not wholly unused to receive letters sealed with thimbles. In the present instance, however, he could not tax himself even with a guess at the probable writer; and he threw aside the letter, and took up another of larger dimensions, and more courtly form, which was sealed with a coronet. His faint blush deepened to crimson; and he tore open the aristocratic missive with a trembling hand. It was a blank cover, containing a card for a masked ball at Knocklofty House, on the following evening – a mandate evidently issued from the office of the countess's groom of the chambers; and his name had probably been set down with the sweepings of the porter's book.

O'Brien was disappointed, he knew not why. He looked at the inclosure. The address was in a large hand; but the seal was the Knocklofty arms. There was the pearl in a field, and the motto of '*Qui me cherche, me trouve*.' The recollection of the interview in St Patrick's Hall, the exchange of the precious and elegant ring for the awful signet he still wore on his finger, recurred to his recollection, and wholly absorbed him, as he swallowed his coffee.

Gradually kindling under the cheering influence, he took up another note; having first, however, cut off the Knocklofty seal, and deposited it in his writing box. This note had lain concealed under the envelope of the Knocklofty invitation. It looked like a billet from the queen of the fairies. It was written on rose-coloured paper, and bore the fragrance of the flower whose tints it imitated. Its tiny seal was impressed with the head of a veiled Isis; and the spirit of the billet appeared, to his heated fancy, as pretty as its *matériel*. It was headed 'L'Invito,' and ran as follows:-

> If there be truth in eyes, I've read in thine
>   More than by words or breath could e'er transpire,
> A soul in sacred sympathy with mine,
>   And I'm a spirit of no common fire.
> To-morrow's eve – remember, ten's the hour –
>   Come, if hope, feeling, passion, warm thy breast;
> A mask, *en rose*, a ring, a wreath, a flower –
>   These are the signs – so leave to fate the rest.

O'Brien read over the billet a hundred times. Its contents, like its odours, were intoxicating; and its odour was so peculiar, as to breathe even upon his mental associations. It was an odour peculiar to the musky atmosphere of the Arno. A small phial, which lay in his writing box, was filled with the same distillation, the secret of which was only known to the monks of the *Santa Maria Novella*, of Florence; from whose *'fonderia'* of pious perfumery, it was sent forth, – for the emolument of the convent, and the delicious inebriation of all who partook of their hallowed essence of *'Mille fiori.'*

But whence came this pretty note and its perfume? Its fantastic contents, its seducing invitation, were assigned, with a rapid heart-beat, to Lady Knocklofty. O'Brien was perhaps vain and impassioned, with just enough of the coxcomb to misdirect a susceptibility, always on service: but it was scarcely necessary to be either, to suspect that the prepossesion of the beautiful countess, in favour of her champion, had taken a colour, of a deeper dye than that which gratitude sheds even on the most grateful feelings. O'Brien had all the sense of moral propriety which belongs to superior minds, and all that high feeling of honour, which a chivalrous profession and character combine to form and to nurture. But there are frailties incidental to the young and the ardent, which (however they may tend to violate the best interests of society), come in such an illusory guise, as to conceal their real turpitude from their victim; and which society itself appears, by a sort of tacit agreement, to view, not with approbation, but with pity and indulgence.

To have conceived, to have cherished a passion for a married woman, would never have entered into the moral abstractions of one, who, even with all his foreign habits of viewing certain *liaisons* (treated in Germany, above all other countries, as matters of course), shrunk with disgust from that corruption in private life, which is only found to flourish where public virtue is unknown. He was aware that the Irish 'high life' of the day was, in certain particulars, mounted upon springs similar to those which governed the aristocratic society of the Continent. But, however he might succumb under certain temptations, which the young and impassioned rarely resist, his principles would still have stood opposed to his conduct; and no cold-blooded sophistry in favour of what was wrong, would have advocated and excused his dereliction from what was right. O'Brien did not, for a moment, suppose himself in love with the wife of the Earl of Knocklofty, of whom he had seen and known so little. He had, indeed, thought not on the subject; but had suffered himself to be led on, flattered, seduced, and intoxicated by those gracious and gratifying sensations peculiar to his time of life, and to the impression of which, that epoch alone is susceptible. For a moment, therefore, the pleasure he received from what he believed Lady Knocklofty's poetical challenge, wholly and deliciously pre-occupied him; and he resolved, come what might in the interim, that nothing short of physical inability should prevent his giving the rendezvous to the mask, in rose, whose wreath, ring, and flower, he doubted not, would be exhibited as his signal and guide.

While he locked up the precious billet in the most secret drawer of his writing-box, the letter with the thimble impression again caught his eye. In a listless and almost unconscious curiosity, he opened it, and found a volume written in a long, narrow, old-fashioned, Italian hand, which was not quite unknown to him. He looked for the signature at the end of the fifth page, and saw, with something like pleasure, the name of Mable Mac Taaf, while, to a postscript scrawled on the envelope, appeared, 'Your affectionate aunt, Monica.' These names brought back to his heart a tide of kindly feelings, and gracious, though homely, recollections. The tenderest remembrance of his gentle and affectionate mother had rendered even the foibles and peculiarities of her elder sisters endurable, to one who was not himself of a very enduring temper; and who, in boyhood, had sometimes ill-brooked the dictatorial manner of his aunts, and their vituperation of his father. Between Terence O'Brien and the Miss Mac Taafs, a temporary reconciliation had but laid the foundation for deeper animosities; and ten years' absence from St Grellan had cancelled all bonds of kindred and propinquity between Lord Arranmore and his sisters-in-law. Although he had not forbidden his son to write to his only surviving female relations, yet when he did so, and even proposed to visit them in the summer vacation, his father had, with his characteristic manner, observed, as he read the letter addressed to them in a style at once playful and tender – 'You don't know them aunts of yours, or you forget them, Murrogh; which comes to the same thing. You might as well attempt to smooth down the back of a pet hedge-hog, as tame down the Miss Mac Taafs; who are for all the world like the cat *couchant* in the arms of the Blakes, always ready for a pounce; so take my advice, child, and lave the Miss Mac Taafs alone, and they'll lave you alone; and that's the best can happen to you.'

O'Brien did not take his father's advice. The Miss Mac Taafs were his mother's sisters; they were women; and they were now old, perhaps helpless: and however dictatorial and despotic they might be to others, they had always been kind to him. He remembered the snipes he had killed on their bogs with the brigadier's fowling-piece; he remembered, with something like pleasure, the cream and honey of Bog Moy, by the never spared abundance of which, his aunts had often sent him home sick and surfeited. He remembered the little Connemara pony, the first horse he had ever ridden, and which they had presented to him, on his first return from the Isles of Arran.

It was now five months since he had written to the ladies Bog Moy, under the influence of these reminiscences; and the letter he now endeavoured to decipher, was their tardy and not very legible answer. The Miss Mac Taafs spelled as they spoke; and they spoke as the old Irish gentry spoke in the reign of Queen Anne. The Miss Mac Taafs wrote with all the dignified verbosity with which they conversed, in that little circle, to which they were both the law and the gospel, and their digressive style was both characteristic and national. Their letters ran as follows:

'DEAR NEPHEW,
   'Your missive of the 30th of November came safely to hand; and no thanks to Paddy the post, but every blame in life – who let it drop upon the road near James Daly's dike, having got a sup in his eye, where it was found, by old Moll-of-the-rock, the *mona-shul*[1] of St Grellan, or never should have set eyes on it. It has been in the contimplation of your aunt Monica and myself to acknowledge the receipt thereof, any day, for these last three months: and the marvel is that we get lave to sit down at all in pace and quiet, and reply to the contints therein contained; seeing that we are not lift time to bless ourselves, as the papists say (to whom no disparagement; laving that to the new comers and upstarts), what with one matter, and what with another, and the place never empty noon or night, but coming and going, and coshering and gostering, and the bog saison coming down upon us all of a sudden, like an hail shower in June, in regard of the dry weather: and James Kelly (though surely a faithful servant and a trust-worthy, save in respect of the drop, poor cratur), not being as young, as he was when he mounted you on the little raghery; and them furreign undertakers

[1] *Mona shul,* a wandering woman.

at Moycullen, opening a new vein of red bog, and underselling the world; also green marble, of which more in due time. So that, what with one thing, and what with another, it is no aisy matter to get time to inform you, Murrogh O'Brien, of our good will to you, now and always: though, as your aunt Monica truly sayeth, it's little your father's son has a right to expect of us. For it's ourselves, Mable and Monica Mac Taaf, that never yet was the better of you, Terry O'Brien Lord Arranmore to the value of a brass thimble; though when you was a poor garloch of a cratur, it's us, and ours, was at your wicked will, as the saying is, and the house never free from you, for like the crickets, oncet you got in, ould Nick would not get you out on't, till you falsely abducted that poor innocent, who, – but it is no matter now, nor shall you, Murrogh O'Brien, be a screed the worse for the great injury done us by your father; of which your mother's abduction (a child in the eye of the law, and our ward as well as sister and co-heiress), was not the first nor last. But of that hereafter; this being shortly and simply to tell you, that we shall be heartily glad to see you at Bog Moy, where board and bed is at your disposal; and would be plaising to know your *raal* intintions and views in life, which, by all accounts, are like the prospects of Mam Turk on a winter's day – high and cloudy. Hearing tell of all them that comes from Dublin, that your father's a ruined man, though now a great lord, in his mansion-house in the capital: but far less well to do now, than when he was Terry O'Brien, attorney at law, in his snug red brick house, in the High-street of St Grellan, and every thing dacent, and highly respectable about him. And hears from young counsellor Costello, nephew of the ould counsellor, and of the widow and Miss Costello (great cronies at Bog Moy, though regular Ave Marias and great voteens, Father Festus Daly, P. P., director), that you carry your head above the world in Dublin college, and are the '*che shin*'[1] of the place; though nobody knows how your father keeps you there, nor for why, nor for what; since, being a lord's son, I don't see how you could, or ought to earn your own bread, either as a counsellor, or in any other way, except as chancellor of Ireland; which is a thing to be compared to Achille Head, high to look at, and far to get at; nor aisy either, to my mind. And the whole Ballyboe marvels much at your unexpected return to the country, at all, at all; the rumour

---

[1] 'Who is that?'

going that you were hand and glove with the emperor, in respect of the honour done to the memory of your great great grand-uncle, the aulic counsellor Count Mac Taaf, also my cousin Rodolphus Mac Taaf, Chancellor of the Empire; and that you would be a gineral in no time; and many young chaps here was thinking of going over to you, thinking you would make their fortunes, and get them commissions in the imparial army, which, to be sure, you might.

'But we guess it was your father's doing, who has more tricks in him than a Leprachan, always devising, and colloguing, and policizing; and has his own raisons for getting you back, I'll ingage. But Murrogh O'Brien, I would warn you well against such idle drames; and if you will be led by us, our intire and sincare advice to you is, that it is not on your father and his wild schemes, and ould Shanaos, you will depind. And as for your earning your crust and crum, by carying a bag on your arm, and a lord's coronet on your head, I hope, for the honour of the family, it's what you won't attimpt; but be, in due course of time, a raal and undoubted estated nobleman. For though your aunt, Monica, and I, might make ducks and drakes of the lands of Bog Moy, if we plased, there being no male tail; and though by marrying to-morrow (and one is never too ould to do a foolish thing, but the oulder the foolisher; not as you will see, that either myself or my sister, Monica, is a hair the worse since you left us, and will ride, walk, or dance an Irish jigg with the youngest she in the Ballyboe, be she who she may); and, as I said before, by marrying to-morrow, we could bring the title of Ballyslattery, now in abeyance, into any family, and the green knighthood; yet having, at prisint, no such intintions, we are inclined to consider you as our natural heir, if not by law, always by affection (for favour goes by liking); and I need not mind you, Murrogh, that yourself was the pet of Bog Moy, when you was a donny cratur, though it's little signs on you, never writing a line to say how it was with you – but pass for that. And would be plased that you would finish your college studies, in which I see neither rhyme nor right, seeing that when you left this ye were the greatest scholar of your age in the barony, in regard of the Latin which you spouted out like your mother's tongue, no thanks to the diocesan, but to poor Abbé O'Flaherty, – who, though a great papist, was a gentleman every bit of him, to the back bone; which is more than can be said of the Archdeacon Hunks, nor any of his breed, seed, or generation;

and governs the town and Ballyboe under thim Proudforts (now Knockloftys), who seldom see the place but in election time, of which more when we meet, in which you are much concerned. And would wish you to lose no time, but come home, as I may say – for what other home have you but Bog Moy? and think you would find the same plasing to you in every way, and especially in making head against them mushrooms and Williamites, the Knockloftys, and the new comers and undertakers at Moycullen, and their hedging, and draining, and planting, and arogating,[1] as it is called, disputing the ould millstrame, that has been allowed to go over the country, without let or hindrance, with ould Mr Martin, of Dangan, and giving the bog for nothing to them as wilt cut and dry it, and long leases, and building chimnies; and says it's a barbarous custom, ploughing, harrowing, and drawing horses, garans, and colts by the tail, after th' ould Connaught fashion "whereby," says their Scotch overseer to James Kelly, "the breed of horses is impoverished in the country," and such like talk; as if none ever ploughed, till the new undertakers of Moycullen came among us. And who are they at all? and what brings them here, building and bolstering up th' ould Abbey, and the ould dwelling-house of the O'Flahertys? But all doing from the Galway side, and Lough Corrib; and th' ould pass to the mountains, Glen Murrogh (so called after your ancestors), not opened. But of this more when we meet, only wishing you were here on the spot. Remain,

'Truely your affectionate Aunt,

'MABLE MAC TAAF.

'P.S. Plase to mintion when you mane to come – say this day fortnight; having it in contemplation to give a Jug-day to the country round, in regard of the pipe of claret from cousin Hyacinth French and Co., Bordeaux; also six beds in the barrack-room, and shakes down in plinty; also wishes you would borrow your father's coroneted coach for the journey, and not come in like a boccah![2] on a market day, sly and shabby; and if means were, would send you the Brigadier's Kevenhuller hat; but supposes you have a military three-cocked of your own – for once a colonel, always a colonel. And would heartily desire you should drive through the town in

---

[1] Irrigating.
[2] A lame beggar.

your full shute of furreign regimentals; and I'll ingage it's widow and Miss Costello will be on the *shoughraun* looking out for you at the bay window. And mind, when you come, that you don't tread on Paddy Whack's tail, for he's the darling now with your aunt Monica; and a dirty darling he is, neither wormed nor clipped, and the most troublesome cur in the barony this day – but every one to their taste. And am your affectionate,

'M. MAC T.'

'DEAR NEPHEW MURROGH,

'I slip in a line in the cover of the inclosed, just to say I join my sister, Mable, in all good wishes, and hopes to see you; "and the sight will be good for sore eyes," says Father Festus, who takes an hand at "five-and-forty" with us by times, and was coadjutor when you were in it. Plase to say, is grogram worn now? also colberteen? Would deem it a favour to inquire if a Kerry stone solitaire, of *great* value (once Lady Betty Mac Taaf's), would be trucked with advantage against a pair of silver shoe buckles and salt-cellars. – N. B. Try Skinner's Row, No. 6. Peter Blake, silversmith, of Galway, undervalues the same, though twice brought to him. Also, would like to have, if not too troublesome, a double-quilted camlet petti-coat, like Miss Costello's, eked out with grey serge behind. To be had No. 77, Corn Market, opposite the sign of the Golden Flace. – N. B. Make use of Miss Prudence Costello's name (got her by the young counsellor, a great *buckeen*). Will be surprised to hear that the ladies of Mary, John, and Joseph, much respected, are dissolved by order of the Provincial, and are transported to a new order or confraternity in Moycullen, as yet nobody knows where. Some say th' ould Abbey of Moycullen, some say Cong; having never thriven, as Father Festus says, P. P. of St Grellan, since your great grand-aunt's time of Ballyslattery, Supariour thereoff, long after the Bogmoys came over to the protestant church; and will be happy on your arrival to pay for same.

'Your loving Aunt,

'MONICA MAC TAFF.

'P.S. Wish just to mention, in a *sly way*, that if you don't mane to strew green rushes under James Kelly's feet, you may as well quit at once – governs the place intirely, and is the sense-keeper of the family. As to his not being wormed, it is not true; but give a dog an ill-name, and hang him, which is the case with Paddy Whack. See, and judge for yourself! – so called after Paddy Whack, ould Mr Robin Martin, of Dangan's Dog, young Dick's father, of whose breed he is, dam, Miss Joyce, of Joyce's county,[1] her dog Stella, first cousin once removed. So self and sister expects to see all the family on the Jug-day, long in contimplation, and hope to see you of the party. Till then, and ever, yours, etc. again with raal regard. Your affectionate aunt,

'MONICA.'

The perusal of this strange, but characteristic farago, which, under other circumstances, might have amused him to whom it was addressed, served only, in his present tone of depression, to sink his spirits still lower. His 'making head against the Knockloftys,' broadened his smile to a laugh; and the chances of going 'into the neighbourhood of Lady Knocklofty's summer residence,' increased the palpitation which even her name upon paper had excited. On the subject of titles and inheritances, however, he was completely disabused; and if his romantic imagination still gave him an interest in the historical names of his country, if a feeling of family pride still lay lingering in his mind, the mortifying position between rank and indigence, in which his father's recovered honours had placed him, combining with opinions formed under the social philosophy of the day, left his aunt's views and promises of hereditary honours without a single attraction. 'The Green Knight of the Fassagh! the Baron of Ballyslattery!! How ridiculous!' he said; 'who would go labelled into the world with such absurd titles?'

The estate of Bog Moy, indeed, might, he thought, be a substantial benefit. Although he had no great confidence in Connemara estates, he remembered the great importance he had attached to Bog Moy, and to the ladies of Bog Moy, in his childhood. They were to him like the queens or ogresses of a fairy tale – tall, gaunt, majestic, and awful. Here, then, was a hope against abject poverty, and a home against utter destitution: but on what terms! – dependence, evidently – absolute, subservient, and humiliating dependence upon two dictatorial, ignorant, old-fashioned, and eccentric women; with all the idle gossipping of a remote country neighbourhood, such as might be expected from the widow Costello; and the parish priest, James Kelly,

---

[1] A large tract of land, so called in Connaught.

Miss Costello, and Paddy Whack. 'No,' he said, as he sat clasping his hands despondingly, 'not for all the green knighthoods, the honours of Ballyslattery, and the wealth of the turf mines of Bog Moy! With robust health, the consciousness of some talent, and exhaustless energy, with Ireland in my heart, and a spirit to meet the worst and dare the worst in her cause, what have I to fear?'

There was, however, a tone of good will, of family feeling, quaintly expressed, indeed, in this letter, that was not ungracious to O'Brien's feelings. There was a home to give him temporary shelter; and in the Brigadier's tower-chamber, he might, by hard study and application, make up for the time he should lose, by a rigorous but, he frankly owned, not altogether an unmerited sentence, such as he anticipated. And now, with the hope that Shane had escaped, and was on the way back to his native mountains; and in the confidence that his father, if in town, would not fail to give him some sign of life in the course of the day, and that Lady Knocklofty would receive the homage of a visit he was about to offer her, – a visit of thanks, *pour le moins* for the protection and influence she had exerted in his favour – he arose to dress: but he found that his whole wardrobe, with Lord Walter's great-coat, had been taken away.

He threw up the window, and called to 'the boy' who attended at his chambers. But the queer old cripple, who answered to that juvenile appellation, and who in a scratch wig and ragged surtout, usually occupied the stone bench in front of the building, inhabited by such of the students as had appointed him their valet, was not, as usual, at his post. While still waiting for him, and looking listlessly out of the window, O'Brien saw the same porter, as had lighted him to his room, the night before, cross the court, followed by 'the boy', who was carrying the clothes, cap and gown, which were missing. The porter was an old familiar of the institution, jealous of its dignity, and a stern and rigorous upholder of the points of discipline which concerned his high and important calling, as the provost himself.

O'Brien perceived that his page had only taken away his clothes to brush them; and that the gruff old porter accompanied him for the purpose of delivering a college mandate. On opening, he found it to contain a summons to attend a board on the following day. While reading it, he felt the pressure of the cripple's foot upon his own, who took the opportunity of passing with the clothes into the inner room, thus to arrest his attention. He looked round abruptly, and perceived that the porter lingered at the outward door, as if to watch the underling out; who on again passing Murrogh, muttered, 'mind, Domine, you know nothing of the papers in the great-coat.' The two servants then departed together. O'Brien's first impulse was to call after the porter, and order a messenger to take home Lord Walter's coat to F. House. But instantly taking the hint that its pockets might have contained something that affected, or could injure its owner, he checked the impulse, and resolved to write to him; and to leave the note himself, in case he should not find him at home.

He had already begun his letter, when the same gruff Cerberus, who seemed to have him in especial *surveillance*, brought him the following note.

'MY DEAR O'BRIEN,

'For you must allow me to use a form of familiar intimacy, where I am desirous to become both intimate and familiar, – I write to say that I am obliged to leave town with my brother, the duke, and cannot possibly return till to-morrow afternoon, when I will call upon you in college about four o'clock. I regret that I cannot meet you at the mess of the Prince's Own – will you try, if there are any papers in my great-coat pocket, and burn them; keep the coat till my servant calls for it.

'Your's faithfully, and in haste,

'WALTER F.'

The coincidence between the warning of 'the boy,' and the direction of Lord Walter, struck O'Brien with some surprise. What papers could the brother of the Duke of F. have about his person, which it was important should be destroyed? and what, if they were not unknown to the underlings of the university, and had been examined? Without indulging further in surmise, he proceeded to fulfil his friend's injunction; but on examination, found the pockets of the great-coat empty. Either Lord Walter had been mistaken, or the papers had been removed. In so doubtful a case, he deemed it most prudent to make no inquiry, and to show no solicitude; and to this he was the more induced, because, the secret of the owner of the coat was in his keeping, and whatever might be the nature of the papers, Lord Walter's name would remain unconnected with them.

O'Brien, therefore, finished his toilette; and, though pale and haggard, from fatigue, anxiety, and emotion, there was a reflexion in his glass which might have soothed his vanity, and have told him that a cheek so pale, and a look so pensive, did not assort ill with eyes so dark, and features formed in the very mould of sentiment. Thus armed, though unconsciously, for conquest, and ignorant that ladies who profess platonism, and '*poussent les grands sentimens,*' prefer pale young men with dark eyes, to ruddy young men with light ones, he was issuing forth from the stone porch of the building, when he was met by an orderly, who inquired for the rooms of the Hon. Murrogh O'Brien. O'Brien acknowledged himself, and received the following note from the orderly, who immediately rode off:-

'Lord Charles Fitzcharles regrets, that circumstances of a particular nature will prevent him from having the pleasure of receiving Mr O'Brien at the mess dinner of the Prince's Own, on this day.'

'*Barracks, Wednesday Morning.*'

This note struck O'Brien with deep mortification, he scarcely knew why. He felt its contents almost as an insult; and had he obeyed the very Irish, and very petulant feelings of the moment, he would have answered it by a challenge to the Fifteen Acres. But to fight a man for not being able, or even willing to receive him at dinner, was rather a desperate and Bobadil measure; so tearing the paper into a thousand pieces, he hummed away his irritable and nervous feelings; and again walked forth, directing his steps to Knocklofty House, with spirits depressed, even beyond the power of the delightful visit he anticipated to raise them.

He soon reached the gates of that noble mansion, and was passed on from the porter's lodge to the vestibule, where a crowd of liveried footmen received his card, and forwarded it to a groom of the chambers, who leaned in gossiping idleness with one of his fraternity, over the balustrade of the first corridor. After an interval of a few minutes the card was returned, to be entered into the porter's book, and an answer given that her ladyship was not at home: this was possible, – was probable, – was perhaps, the fact; and yet it confounded O'Brien, and amazed him. As he took back his card, at the porter's request, to write his address on it, that it might be entered in the great record of ceremony, over which that functionary presided, Lord Kilcolman came down the great stair-case, looked at O'Brien, without recognizing him, mounted his horse, which a groom was leading about the court, and rode off.

O'Brien went forth. The summons to the board, the sudden departure of Lord Walter, the mysterious papers, the excuse of Lord Fitzcharles, the denial of Lady Knocklofty, and the insolent cut conclusive of Lord Kilcolman, combined to work powerfully upon a proud, touchy, and susceptible imagination; and before he had got a hundred yards from Knocklofty House, he not only considered himself as a very ill-used gentleman, but gradually worked up his morbid fancy to see in himself one who had lost caste, and who was cut and branded as the very pariah of society.

In this cup of mingled bitternesses, the sole palatable infusion was derived from the confiding and friendly tone of Lord Walter's letter; and the consciousness of maintaining and deserving the friendship of such a person, enabled him to treat with comparative indifference the slights of the Kilcolmans and Fitzcharles's, and assisted in restoring his spirits to something like equanimity.

His next visit was to his father's attorney in York-street: but Mr Fitton, a noted limb of the law, and conductor of the litigations of half the gentry of Connemara, whose bills of costs were the only bills they permitted themselves to pay, was on circuit; and the young men in the office had not seen Lord Arranmore for more than three weeks. All the information O'Brien could obtain, was from the head clerk, who whispered him that the execution had been for the non-payment of a bill; and that till some settlement was effected with his very refractory creditors, his lordship found it prudent to keep out of the way.

'And what settlement – what compromise can be made,' asked O'Brien, 'when no assets,' he was about to say, but he paused, and the clerk added, 'Oh, I believe matters will be settled in a day or two; a friend has come forward, and money has been advanced.'

'A friend! what friend?'

'Of that we know nothing,' said the clerk: 'he acts by an agent, with whom Mr Fitton has had several interviews; but I believe he is some foreign relation.'

O'Brien started; he knew but of one foreign relation, but of one living, who could have the means, if indeed he still had them; and this person was the secretary of the Propaganda at Rome, the Ex-superior of the Jesuit's college in the eternal city; but he was in Rome, and advanced in life beyond the given years of man. Neither had Lord Arranmore mentioned his uncle since O'Brien's return, except once or twice in a cursory way.

'Have you any idea,' he asked, 'that this kind relation is an ecclesiastic?'

'I suspect he is,' said the clerk, 'and that there is a lady in the case; at least Counsellor Blosset, the agent of the party, seemed to say as much; and a note sent us yesterday by the counsellor is in a female hand.'

'Can I see it?' asked O'Brien; and the clerk seeking among some papers, presented a note, and observed,

'You may be sure it is from a lady by the fine scent.'

The note breathed of the perfume of the *mille fiori;* and he thought was in the same hand-writing as that which he had received in the morning – a new light broke upon him. Was there – could there be some secret tye between his family and Lady Knocklofty? The interest she took in him might thus be accounted for: and if his vanity suffered some abatement by this suspicion, his feelings were not the less gratified, nor his prepossession for the fair Urganda (who thus waved her magic wand over the fortunes of his family) diminished.

Still all was mere surmise; but O'Brien without spirits or opportunity for proceeding further with his inquiries, returned to college, ordered his commons to his own room, and in the evening determined to go, perhaps for the last time, to the Historical Society.

The rumour of his inevitable expulsion had been widely spread, and was known to all but himself. Strange reports had gone abroad, which his friends, in disbelief of their veracity, and in delicacy to his feelings, had concealed from him. The accusation that would chiefly affect him, was the supposition that he belonged to some secret society of which government had intimation; but his liberal principles, some theological opinions, on points purely speculative, and an open, frank and manly advocacy of catholic emancipation, were also items in his accusation, which covered him with glory in the eyes of his young co-partners in the Historical Society. On his appearance in the society, he was received with loud cheering. Many of its ardent members, and some who have since worn the ermine, took his martyrdom as the theme of their impassioned eloquence on that night; and a declaratory resolution was proposed, that under all circumstances, Murrogh O'Brien would ever be considered as a most distinguished ornament of that society, as he had uniformly been amongst its most energetic and useful members.

This ardent rally round the victim of impending persecution, was balm to the wounded spirit of O'Brien. Among the bitterest sensations to which humanity is exposed, is the consciousness of having made great personal efforts for an ungrateful or an unworthy public. The discovery that we have over estimated the public spirit of our age, – that we have acted from a confidence in high aspirations and intense feelings, which had no existence; the sudden conviction of a wide-spreading and grovelling selfishness among the lofty pretenders to patriotism and zeal, convey not only disappointment and disgust to the mind on which they burst, but also a sense of dupery, the most irritating and intolerable. The melancholy doubt of Brutus, that the virtue to which his life had been one long sacrifice, was but a name, is the most desolating shipwreck of human hopes, which history has recorded; the tortures of Regulus, the fanaticism of Scævola, make no such call upon our sympathy.

From this pang, O'Brien was spared: the sordid calculations of egotism had not yet infected the youth of the country; nor were prudent considerations of remote and contingent dangers, ranged among the first elements of collegiate morality. Those, even, who had been but slightly acquainted with the object of the meditated attack, now officiously crowded around him, to mark their participation in his sentiments, and their contempt for his persecutors. It is melancholy to reflect that among this youthful and ardent band, were some who, incapable of that passive resistance which is so essential to a public cause, yielded in after life to the temptations of avarice and of ambition; men who sat in judgment on their former companions, and passed the sentence of an ignominious death, upon heads unstained by any crime, save that in which they had themselves so largely participated – a love, an unregulated, but an ardent love for Ireland.

# CHAPTER II

## *The Expulsion*

Rien n'est impossible; il y a des voies qui conduisent à toutes choses, et, si nous avions assez de volonté, nous aurions toujours assez de moyens.

DR LA ROCHEFOUCAULT.

IT IS an awful thing to hear some great public bell at an unwonted hour solemnly toll the tocsin of alarm, the announce of some public calamity or private misfortune, of death, of fire, of insurrection. In the gloom of a chill and truly Irish spring evening, the bell of the university, thus unseasonably clamorous, aroused the curiosity and alarm of the neighbouring citizens, as it tolled for the purpose of collecting the members of the university in procession, to accompany the provost and fellows to the great hall, for the purpose of pronouncing sentence of expulsion, and of erasing from the university books the name of him who had encountered its ban.

From the star-chamber of the learned and secret tribunal (where the delinquent is tried, heard, but not confronted with his accusers), to the examination hall, where sentence is pronounced, the distance is but short. Yet the bell had rung for some time, and the chiefs of the college had waited for some minutes in their robes for their usual attendants on public ceremonies: none swelled their train, save a few sizers, a still fewer number of the scholars of the house, and the domestic officials. At the head of these followers, the authorities proceeded to the hall; and in their presence only the name of the distinguished fellow-commoner, the Hon. Murrogh O'Brien, was erased from the books, and the fiat of his expulsion solemnly made known. At the instant of denunciation, a groan was heard from the remoter part of the hall under the gallery; a sound that seemed to burst from the oppression of a broken heart. But it passed away. None perceived who had uttered it; and the procession returned to the provost's house, with the same ceremonial with which it had set out.

Upon all such awful occasions, delicacy prevents the greater number of the students from being present at the last ceremony. The previous investigations being conducted with great privacy, and in secret committee, the students, with the usual generosity of youth, refrain from sanctioning by their presence a sentence, of whose merits they are not permitted to judge. But never had the college courts exhibited such a scene of gloomy desolation and utter desertion, as on that evening, when, after an examination of several hours before the visitors of the university, Murrogh O'Brien was found guilty of those high crimes and misdemeanors, which were, in the apprehension of the autocrats of the moment, beyond the pale of all mercy. It is melancholy to reflect that collegiate expulsion, a censure inflicted in the very outset of life, and influencing all its ulterior prospects, is necessarily not governed by any fixed and written law, but by the will of the supreme authorities. Though in all the universities of the sister kingdoms a great practical forbearance usually accompanies the exercise of this discretion, yet, in all, a capricious or vindictive sentence is possible. Nor is it to be wondered if, in the bad times of Ireland, political considerations powerfully influenced the decisions of the visitors of Trinity College, on the fate of its suspected, and perhaps calumniated students.

Even the college park, then the evening resort of the younger members of the university, was on this evening completely deserted; or if some few wandered in its deep shaded and gloomy avenues of trees, almost coeval with the foundation of the institution, they were confounded with the shadows of its old elms and oaks, and were as invisible as if they were not.

It was while the sentence of expulsion was yet pronouncing, that he on whose devoted head it was launched, rushed from the dark stone passage which leads to the Provost's house, and passed into the park. Heated, flushed, fevered, exhausted, after having been baited, worried, and cross-examined, worked into vehement and unguarded petulance, and tortured into self-crimination, or to what was deemed such, by the cold-blooded scrutiny and provoking insolence of forensic ability (for the most formidable of his judges was the most active of his examiners), O'Brien sought the refreshment of shade, silence, and solitude, with the same eagerness with which the wounded hart 'panteth after the waters.'

He felt the delicacy of his fellow-students, in the desertion which left him thus unobtruded upon; and he availed himself of it to conceal the immediate sting of mortification and to recover from the first shock of a sentence, severe beyond his worst anticipations, and preceded by an examination of the most unexpected and embarrassing nature.

It was evident that, not his conduct, but his opinions had been the chief mark of inquiry. He had been accused of popery, and at the same time of infidelity; and the whole drift of his scrutineers was less to bring home to him the riot at the Strugglers, than to involve him in the great Socratic accusation which has served in turn for striking at all opinions, and putting down the victims of every sect, – the accusation of 'believing in other gods than those by law established, and corrupting the youth of the country.'

Besides this sweeping and general charge, he was arraigned as the open leader of political faction in the college; of acting as the secret agent for the French jacobins and of being a member of a new seditious society, which the government was then watching with such suspicion and alarm, but which was, as yet, too constitutional to give a handle for legal prosecution.

Of this charge he stood accused on the evidence of some papers which had dropped from the pocket of his great-coat, while under the process of brushing, in the porter's lodge. The contents of these papers amazed him; he might have cleared himself of the imputation by revealing to whom the coat belonged. But, in denying all knowledge of the papers, he truly and rigorously kept the secret of Lord Walter; and though he felt, with bitterness and indignation, that his word, under these circumstances of partial concealment, was not believed, he had persisted in withholding the only exculpation which could vindicate his veracity.

In a temper of mind, such as these events might naturally be supposed to produce in such a character, O'Brien sought the deepest shades of the umbrageous and straight-lined avenues of trees, which then overhung the Anatomy-house, the nocturnal resort of resurrection-men, and the site of many a superstitious tale. He was pacing with steps rapid and hurried as his thoughts, when he suddenly came against some person, whose march was as precipitate as his own. It was Lord Walter Fitzwalter; their recognition was instantaneous. Lord

Walter passed his arm through O'Brien's, and turning up the avenue, said, abruptly, 'You are expelled, I hear.'

'The news has had a quick circulation,' said O'Brien, with a forced laugh; 'the bell has scarcely yet done tolling out my knell.'

'On what charges have you been expelled?' said Lord Walter, eagerly.

'Charges the most frivolous; but quite enough to establish my delinquency, under statutes which have long rested in abeyance, and have only been revived in my especial case. The true cause of my expulsion is, however, not my being "*membrum pestilens, et cœteris valdé perniciosum*," but my opinions.'

'Your opinions! – But who has denounced them?'

'Our board, like the tribunal of the Inquisition, does not permit the accused to be confronted with his accusers; but the principal evidence against me was – myself. Attacked on the score of my principles, I scorned subterfuge, and rebutted the charge by a defence still more obnoxious than the particulars of my accusation. I confessed myself the author of a pamphlet on the necessity of a reform in parliament, and catholic emancipation, for the "better quieting the country" (to use a phrase of Elizabeth's times). This was "*the very head and front of my offending – no more.*" '

Lord Walter paused for a moment, and then abruptly asked, 'What did you do with the papers you found in my great-coat pocket?'

O'Brien, after an instant's hesitation, replied, 'I found none.'

'Did you look in the breast-pocket, as I requested of you?'

'In every part of the coat. There were no papers – '

'My dear O'Brien,' said Lord Walter, pressing his hand, 'you have relieved my mind from a terrible load of anxiety. The other night, coming out of a particular society, a person, one known to me, thrust a paper into my hand, and desired me to read it attentively. I put it into the breast-pocket of my great-coat, forgot it, and was reminded of it at an early hour yesterday, when I wrote instantly to you to burn it. Being obliged to hasten without delay to my brother the Duke, who had been seized with an eminently dangerous attack of gout, I have been haunted ever since with the idea of the danger which might accrue to you, should the paper be found in your possession. I have, therefore, taken the first possible moment of return to see you, and on my arrival in town, half an hour ago, hastened to your rooms. At the gates of the college I learned the event which has occurred.'

'Are you aware of what this paper contained?' demanded O'Brien, carelessly.

'Nothing less than a plan for the separation of Ireland from England.'

'A plan,' said O'Brien, 'as physically impracticable, at the present moment, as it would always be politically unwise.'

'Exactly,' said Lord Walter; 'but all great causes have two enemies to guard against amongst their advocates, – those who, by hurrying on events before they are ripe for development, insure defeat; – and those who, by a bigoted attachment to inapplicable abstractions, and by bringing the principles of past combinations to bear upon present occurrences, miss the occasion for effecting that practical good, which can never be obtained but by consulting the genius of the times, and acting under its influence.'

'And who was the author of this notable proposition?'

'His name is – but no, hang it, he has, though perhaps unwittingly, trusted me with his secret (for I am not quite sure the paper he gave me was the one he intended), and I will not risk his name, even to you.'

'You are quite right,' said O'Brien, warmly; 'it would be a breach of trust, of – '

'Oh!' interrupted Lord Walter, smiling, 'the danger would not, I believe, be great; for I have a strange suspicion that he is an emissary of government; one of the paid fomenters of sedition, who first lay the train, and afterwards apply the spark, which makes the explosion. But a truce with the subject; and let us speak of what, just now, interests me infinitely more, your expulsion.'

'Expulsion, I believe, is not disgrace?' said O'Brien, in an anxious and inquiring tone. 'It does not necessarily lower its victim in public opinion? If it blast his prospects, it may still leave honour untainted, and character undefiled.'

'Expulsion,' said Lord Walter, 'is undoubtedly intended to be taken as a mark of disgrace; but the moral value of such authoritative decrees is not at the disposal of the tribunal which launches them. Honest and honourable men, in all times, have been expelled, excommunicated, banished, inflicted with infamous corporeal punishments, and some have died the death of the felon; yet their fair fame has come out the brighter from the fiery persecution through which it passed. The banishment of Aristides was the immortal infamy of his enemies; and the glorious patriotism of Sydney and of Russel, was not to be sullied by the tyrants who maligned and – murdered them.'

'But *I* am not Aristides!' said O'Brien, with a pettish laugh, 'nor Sydney, nor Russel. Humanity has no interests to defend in my person; and the instincts of mankind will not force opinion to do me justice.'

'True,' said Lord Walter. 'But neither is the board of pedantic muftis, headed by their superior the vice-chancellor (though one of Ireland's most implacable enemies), among those great tribunals, which impose upon mankind. The sphere of their influence extends not beyond that of their activity.'

'Such a consideration,' said O'Brien, 'is the only escape the wounded spirit finds from local littlenesses, and temporary oppressions. It is a relief to send forth one's thoughts, and to lose in the contemplation of great and general causes, the bitter sense of petty and personal inflictions. The world is indeed still before me, where to chuse; but, Lord Walter, Ireland is my vocation! If foreign rank had been my calling, I might have fought my way to ambitious distinctions, like others of my countrymen; like all men of strong volitions, who, worried and oppressed at home, find the intentions of nature in their favour justified, by the acknowledgment of their merit abroad, where no local disqualifications impede their progress. But here, in this unhappy land, stands the altar of my first and warmest vows: and in returning home, and breaking the brilliant thraldom of my past profession, I had hoped, by honest exertion, by devoted patriotism, and by some success in that liberal profession, which gives to the bar the dignity of the forum, – I had hoped, as the defender of persecuted individuals, as a champion of the great cause of political and religious freedom, to have served Ireland, and to have arrived at an honourable independence; without which man can never act as his conscience dictates, nor place himself beyond the influence of grovelling and debasing necessity. Andrew Marvel, my dear Lord Walter, did much upon his cold shoulder of mutton; but still he possessed the means of its purchase: for after all, man is not like the lily of the valley; and where the rewards of profitable labour are denied, he is shorn alike of his political and of his personal morality.

'On arriving in this country, that I might give to my new profession all the *éclat* of which it is susceptible, and that I might wholly efface the mark of my foreign education, I entered at rather a late period of life, the national university. A classical scholar, almost from my cradle (like those Irish urchins who, as Stanihurst says, in his days spouted Latin more fluently than their mother tongue), I came not unprepared for collegiate success; and I should have obtained it: but vaulting ambition hath o'erleaped itself; and the step taken in the highest consideration for the honourable profession I was about to enter, has become the stumbling-block of my destiny. Marked and branded, I go forth labelled with the disgrace of expulsion. Can such a person bring credit to any – '

'My dear O'Brien,' interrupted Lord Walter, 'you are viewing your present position under the depressing influence of a very diseased state of mind. You have but anticipated events. Expulsion from college has merely saved you from the mortification of a more mature defeat. With your feelings and your opinions, with your frank and impetuous temperament, all hope of success in any of the professions was, in this country, mere delirium. Look at Curran, Grattan, Ponsonby; under the present system, the dignities of the law are not for them. In the law, one merit alone is acknowledged, alone rewarded; and that is political subserviency. Are you for the scarlet robe of physic? "throw physic to the dogs!" A patriot physician, a physician who thinks, or feels, or reasons beyond the limits of the pharmacopœia, is no physician for the public. He may dissipate his time and his faculties in idle gossip, in intrigue, in dependance, and if he do but wear black stockings and a grave countenance, if he only attends the church or the meeting, he will undoubtedly succeed; but if he raise his regard to the greater interests of humanity, nay, if he diverges into the philosophy even of his own craft, and sees more in his profession than the phials he fills, he is an unprofitable branch, fit only to be lopped off and cast into the fire. Then as for the church – '

'*Halte-là,*' said O'Brien, smiling, 'there is no danger of my taking that broad road to intellectual and moral nothingness.'

'Well then, on summing up the evidence, it seems to me the verdict is in your favour. You are free, free to make the honest application of your talents in the way most congenial to your own nature.'

'*De l'esprit pour s'avancer! Monseigneur se moque de moi.* No, no, my Lord, in professions or out of them, here I fear the case is still the same, "*médiocre et rampant, et l'on arrive à tout,*" and so much for my expectations on *this* side the Irish channel.'

'Your entering at the present epoch,' said Lord Walter, 'into the Irish University, was certainly a false calculation; and all things considered, I do not see that the board could have acted otherwise than as they have done. For until premiums are given for patriotism, and church preferment waits upon public spirit, it is to little purpose that the language of liberty is taught in our classes, and that Demosthenes and Æschylus are illustrated from our professor's chairs.'

'Yes,' said O'Brien, kindling at the fire of Lord Walter's manner, 'we are taught the Greek, to become acquainted with its metres, not to catch the glorious spirit which breathes in the pages of its poets and its orators. We may scan lines, and string centos of poetical fragments, but woe to those students who presume to scan men or combine realities. The only classic maxim popular in college is the *populus me sibilat, at mihi plaudo;* all, however, will not do: while such studies are taught, while such authors are perused, even the Irish youth will not be slow to interpret them in their proper way.'

'Yes,' said Lord Walter; 'and eventually imitating what they must admire, they will one day unite to redress wrongs, such as Greece or Rome never suffered under. For which of the varied oppressors of those countries have rivalled the despotism of the Stones and the Boulters, the Kings and the Knockloftys!'

O'Brien's arm, as it leaned on Lord Walter's, seemed to vibrate with an electric shock, at the mention of the last name. He hemm'd away a sigh, and Lord Walter continued, 'Our youths, so deeply versed in ancient patriotism, so called upon by modern example (all Irish and humbled as they are), will one day associate for the purposes of national redemption, by its sole means, – *a national union!* – that brotherhood of affection, that community of interest, which operating from its centre, to the remotest verge of society, will effect a regeneration by means as constitutional as they are effectual.'

'And those means?' demanded O'Brien, breathlessly and impatient.

'Are reform in the representation, and the abolition of the penal code.'

'And with such means,' exclaimed O'Brien, 'and with the greatest happiness of the greatest number for its dogma, what ages of suffering might not be spared to this long-suffering land? How long have men congregated, combined, conspired for the purposes of oppression and injustice? What has not been effected by the unholy alliance of despots, by kings, by Popes, by the Jesuits of all ages, catholic and protestant, christian and infidel (for the sins of churchmen belong to their craft, and not to the religion they accidentally profess). What has not in all climes been done against the liberties of mankind by the co-operation of knaves! What might not be effected for their service by the union of the virtuous?'

'Suppose,' said Lord Walter, lowering his voice, 'such an association *did* exist, with your own maxim for its object, *the greatest happiness of the greatest number*, and with the appropriate motto of '*idem sentire, dicere, et agere*,' if such an union of strong minds and true hearts did exist, would you make the voluntary offering of your time, your talents, and your energies, of your – '

'Of my life!' interrupted O'Brien, enthusiastically; 'alas! 'tis all I have to offer.'

'Say you so,' continued Lord Walter, in a still more subdued tone; 'but suppose such a society *did* exist in embryo; as yet but feeling its way to the talent and liberality of the Irish heart; and therefore assuming for the present the secrecy and caution which is unhappily sometimes more necessary for the promotion of good, than of evil. Suppose such a society found it necessary to observe a discretion bordering on mystery, a secrecy which renders the bond of union more cohesive, its spirit more ardent; for in all human associations, the weakness of humanity must be taken into account, and the imagination enlisted on the side of reason.'

'It was in no secret association,' said O'Brien, thoughtfully, 'that the great principle of American Independence originated. It was the free and bold explosion of public opinion, which, in giving birth to the French revolution, worked openly, and in the face of day. I distrust, I dislike secrecy.'

'But Ireland, wretched Ireland has no public opinion, no public to express an opinion,' replied Lord Walter, eagerly. 'Ireland is not America, still less is it France. The knowledge, the philosophy of the one, the energy, the freshness of the other, are wanting to this land of helots. The lever, by which this inert mass is to be moved, is one of infinite delicacy. Its springs must be secret, for they are of no vulgar mechanism. Besides had you not in France your clubs, your affiliations, and something of the mystery as well as the ceremony of freemasonry?'

'Yes,' said O'Brien, 'but that is not the best aspect of the French revolution. It was the personal ambition, and petty reckless intrigues of these clubs, that palsied the national impulse; and will, eventually, I fear, check its progress, and turn aside its course. The revolution which is not based on public opinion, is at best but insurrection. Still, I will concede something to human weakness, and to the peculiar phasis of Irish society. I will allow as much mystery as will excite, with as much ceremonial as may strike on the senses without impeding real business, – and will animate philosophy without awakening the passions.'

'Exactly, exactly,' interrupted Lord Walter, eagerly. 'You have described the utmost verge of mystery intended in the present association of devoted patriots; who, to the total immolation of all personal interests and private views, have constituted themselves a body, by the name of the 'SOCIETY OF UNITED IRISHMEN OF DUBLIN.' It is to this society I would direct your views, your thoughts, your genius, and your actions.'

O'Brien replied with some astonishment: 'It is as an imputed member of this society that I have already been accused of sedition, and incipient rebellion; though I heard its name pronounced this day for the first time. This is the society which I have just heard accused of exciting the people to rebellion, of overturning the king's government, and separating Ireland from England, and of employing the sacred name of the Irish Volunteers, to cover the formation of an armed banditti, who, in due time, were, with the appellation of national guard, to overthrow the constitution, and to govern Ireland in its stead.'

'In the present state of things,' said Lord Walter, 'this is the basest of calumnies. So constitutional, indeed, has been the conduct of the society, that though some of the paid spies of government have, it is suspected, enrolled themselves among our members to betray us, they have been unable to afford even the slightest pretext for interference or prosecution. To what we may yet be driven, by the machinations of the faction who govern the country, 'twere vain to anticipate: but that men, some of them of the most illustrious families, the most independent fortunes, of the highest character, of the most brilliant talents, members of the bar, and of the church – that such men have been the founders of the society, and are among its members, is some warrant for the purity of its motives, and even for the wisdom of its object.'

'The man who addresses me,' said O'Brien, 'is, in my mind, sufficient security for its honour, its propriety, and its purity. The descendant of the princely Geraldines, the brother of a peer of the realm, one who has every thing to lose, and so little to gain, by a change – I want no other surety.'

Then suddenly stopping short in his rapid pace; and taking both the hands of the young nobleman in his with the strong compression of vehement feeling, he added, 'Lord Walter, I also am a united Irishman, united with the advocates of the cause of Ireland by all the ties of sympathy and conviction; and in all sincerity, I am ready at this moment to become a member of your society by any outward form its discretion may dictate. But I must not – I will not intrude upon your confidence, or upon that of your associates, without the fullest, the frankest exposition of who and what I am.

'You and the world, the little world which takes any note of *my* existence, know but this, that I am a member of the illustrious family of O'Brien; which founded its glory, not in the royal dignity of its sons, but in the devotion of that illustrious chieftain who defended his native land against foreign invasion, and died in the cause of national independence. They know me as the son of an eccentric nobleman, as a fellow commoner of the Irish university, and as one to whom the narrow circle of his acquaintance has given the full meed for those trifling abilities, which a vehement temperament has perhaps pushed too obviously upon public notice. But you have yet to know that the Hon. Murrogh O'Brien is the son of an ex-attorney, a pauper, bankrupt peer; that, ever at odds between his poverty and his gentility, he has for the last few months earned a penurious support by the exertion of mental labour, borrowed from the hours of his natural repose and his daily studies. You see, then, Lord Walter, before you one, who, to live, must have recourse to his head or his arm, to his pen or his musket. The story of my short life may be briefly summed up. It forms a page in the history of a country, to which it is an infliction to belong. From my birth, the victim of false impressions, – reared as the wildest of my sept, and in the wildest regions of the land, – born and educated in the Isles of Arran, amidst the temples of traditional superstition, and the ruins of barbarous grandeur, – fed upon the dream of ancient Irish glory, and in the faith of early Irish sanctity, – my first preceptor was the poor, half-civilized creature, with whom you last night found me associated; – my next instructor, the most learned, the most elegant minded of men, an Irish foreign ecclesiastic, one who, like the Culdees of old, lived an example of the pure morality he taught. Again dragged by intolerance from my sea-girt isles, and forced by that protestant Jesuitism, so similar in its means and ends to the system of Loyola, into a seminary of the established church, – kidnapped into protestantism, as my father had been before me, – witnessing the persecution of my excellent and learned friend, and the ignominious death (as I then thought) of the ruder, but not less loved guide of my childhood, I escaped from the horrors which bewildered my young imagination, by playing the truant, and embarking on board a French vessel. With an Herculean strength for my age, I worked my passage to Bordeaux; where my mother's friends heard my story, pitied, and received me. Her death ensued before the news of my safety arrived; and I was followed to France by my father, and placed in a seminary of a singular description, – one of those colleges which, under various names, have still perpetuated Jesuitism. Thence I was moved to a confraternity of a similar nature at Florence, under the inspection of the ex-superior of the Jesuits at Rome, my uncle, the celebrated Abbate O'Brien. This is no time to dwell upon my ideas, my sensations, during my residence under the tuition of the secret sons of Loyola. Indignation, disgust, an early discovery of the purposes for which I was so carefully educated, for which every acquirement, every accomplishment was pushed on me, drove me from the Italian Jesuits as I had been driven from those of the diocesan school of St Grellan. Again I fled; entered a volunteer in an Austrian regiment at Milan; and by a success which has hitherto attended all my personal efforts, recommended myself to the notice of Maréchal Lacy. In recognizing a countryman, he discovered a relation. A commission followed; the most unmerited advancement procured me the friendship of the young, the gallant Charles de Ligne, and the paternal notice and protection of his father, the Prince. I served in various campaigns until the siege of Belgrade; when a communication which my father made, of the recovery of his title, and, as I supposed, of the means of supporting his rank, determined me to gratify the longing of my heart by returning to Ireland. His letters, like the character forced on him by circumstance, were a mixture of hyperbole and mystery. Deceiving himself, he deceived me; and an accident occurred at this epoch which wound up all my purposes to the sticking place.

'In that service where the discipline of the cane still marks the degradation of the soldier, the superior officers exercise an authority, the natural result of privilege. Insulted by one who formed but a link in this chain of slavery, I resented it, and challenged the offender: and on the point of sending in my resignation, I was broken for a breach of discipline. This was unlucky, but it was inevitable; my conduct was justified by the testimony of the Prince de Ligne; who wrote a letter on the subject to my father, which I shall beg leave to put into your lordship's possession.

'In passing through France, I paused upon that great scene of human regeneration; and found my dear, my illustrious preceptor, the parish priest of St Grellan, the venerable Abbé O'Flaherty, a constitutional Bishop of France. Received into his palace, as the child of his adoption, I was presented by him to La Fayette, La Rochefoucauld, the Abbé Grégoire, Mirabeau, Ségur, and all that then and now constitute the glory of the nation. Three months' residence at such an epoch, and with such persons, did not, perhaps, exactly fit me for the country of my views and my aspirations; but I will not digress. Arrived in Ireland, and deceived by my unfortunate father, whose pride and tenderness alike concurred to conceal our mutual ruin, I mistook his habits of life, the very appearance of his antiquated dwelling, for mere eccentricity; and by much persuasion, induced him to enter me at the Irish University, and permitted him to do so under all "the pomp and circumstance" of a *filius nobilis*. Soon, however, I discovered that he was utterly insolvent, deeply in debt; and that, to gratify my wishes, he had made the sacrifice of an old Irish crown and target of gold, supposed to have been worn at the battle of Clontarf, by Brian Borrû; which he had purchased in the days of his opulence, when a thriving solicitor at St Grellan. From this moment I have never received a shilling at his hands; and, Lord Walter, to you alone I will confess it, "I have coined my brain, not, alas! to drachmas, but into the merest means of subsistence." Ireland has no literary existence. Still, *"The Anthologia,"* and the rising demand for political discussion in the pamphlet form, have opened a market for native talent. But with a false pride I cannot conquer, I have pursued my honourable vocation, as though it were a crime: how long I may be permitted to continue it with impunity, the law of libel, which is superseding all other law, must decide.

'I have only to add, that my father's ruin seems complete. What may be his intentions I know not, nor even, at this moment, where he is. It is through him that I so deeply feel this penalty of expulsion, which deprives me of the means of contributing to his future comforts.

'And now, Lord Walter, started into admiration of your character, by the exposition of principles so unexpected in one of your caste and class – anticipating the intimacy of years on the sudden prepossession of hours – won by the testimony of your interest and good-will – I have, for the first time in my life, pleaded guilty of that crime so abhorrent to proud gentility – poverty; and I would have you to understand, that I accompany the avowal by a solemn and sacred assertion, that there exists not the human being (those connected by ties of blood alone excepted) from whom I would accept of pecuniary assistance. I should consider the offer an insult; and I would forfeit, for ever, the friendship of the man I most esteem – allow me to say of yourself – rather than avail myself of its ill-directed generosity.'

'My dear O'Brien,' said Lord Walter, laughing, and pressing the arm on which he leaned, 'spare your Rousseau-ish feelings, and diatribe against presuming friendship. We younger brothers of great families are, ourselves, but noble paupers, or stipendiaries of the state, which is obliged to provide for the exigencies of our enforced mendicity. If you will accept of nothing, *I* have nothing to offer: I have hitherto lived by my good sword; for the duke, my brother, is not on the right side, and cannot quarter his cadets on the people. Every thing you have said, from the confesion of your "truant disposition," down to your romantic self-dependence, but deepens the interest I have long felt for you.'

'Long felt!' re-echoed O'Brien, with surprise.

'Yes, long. I have read a pamphlet, of which you were the suspected author; I have watched your examinations in college; I have heard you in the Historical Society; I have seen you at the head of your corps; I was witness of the spirited manner in which you conducted yourself at the castle; and all this has tended to confirm certain views with which I have been entrusted, and which have you for their object.'

'Views on me, Lord Walter!' said O'Brien, with emotion.

'Ay, views: do not suppose that the papist and protestant Jesuits exclusively possess the secret of turning the talents of highly-gifted youth to their own purposes. There are other societies who have benefited by the hint, though not exactly with the same intentions. Why should not truth and freedom adopt an agency, which slavery and superstition have found so available? In a word, we Jesuits of the Union have, for some time, marked out you, and such as you, as our destined agents; and the ex-superior of Florence and Rome had not more direct designs on your brilliant endowments, than our brotherhood of United Irishmen. The attention of our society has, from its commencement, been directed to attaching to the great cause, young men of high promise, and vigour of body and mind; whose activity and talents may assist in disseminating throughout all Ireland that spirit of unity, which can alone work the redemption of the country.

As an orator, I know you can, and as a writer, I am inclined to believe you may be of infinite service. There is, too, an extensive correspondence to be conducted with certain societies, organized upon similar principles with our own. Other agencies also are necessary; provincial and even baronial committees must be formed, and delegates must be appointed to carry on communications between the different branch associations and the great central point of union in the capital. For such missions, the time, the talents, the health, the energies, the pleasures of the volunteer must be sacrificed; and the hired officer of the despot of Austria need not blush to receive the honest remuneration earned in the service of his country. – Nay, hear me out! You have not concealed from me that the descendant from the supreme kings of Ireland, has not now, in the land of his fathers, one rood of earth he can call his own. Your frankness has left me nothing to guess; and you must live – '

'Well,' interrupted O'Brien, with a deep sigh, 'of that, my lord, more hereafter; at present, what is the preliminary step in point of form to my true and only vocation?'

'To propose you to the society, as an ordinary member, which I will do this evening; for we meet for business at half-past eight. Every candidate must be proposed by one, and seconded by another member.'

'And who is to be that other,' asked O'Brien, 'for I conclude your Lordship will do me the honour to propose me?'

'There are already some of your college acquaintance among us; a scholar of the house, for instance, one who does the honours by your talents, and boasts of his intimacy with you, Cornelius Costello.'

'He is a countryman of mine,' said O'Brien, 'and was my class-fellow in the diocesan school of St Grellan; but I have no intimacy with him. He is vulgar, trades too much on his principles, too obtrusive, pushing, pretending.'

'Humph!' said Lord Walter. 'Vulgar, perhaps, he is, but he is honest, – has been deemed eligible to become *des nôtres*. We must not refuse men, because they are vulgar, my dear O'Brien; *cela sent les côteries de Vienne*. I fear, after all, your continental liberalists look too much to revolutions *à l'eau rose*. Your young *preux*, Charles de Ligne, his princely and very aristocratic father, and others of the "high transparencies" of the Austrian court, have spoiled you for the coarse efforts of Irishmen. But men, struggling to be free, must not wait for the co-operation of the graces.'

'They are, however, no bad allies in any cause,' said O'Brien. 'Democracy *en petite maitresse* is much more formidable than jacobinism *à la pois, sarde;* and Mad. Roland, the most influential female politician in Paris, is *la femme la mieux chaussèe de son quartier.*'

'Well,' said Lord Walter, laughing, 'bring as many Mad. Rolands to our cause as you can; you are the very person to recruit for us in that line. Apropos, what do you mean to do with Albina, Countess of Knocklofty?'

O'Brien started, so as to make Lord Walter start likewise.

'Do with her! – do with Lady Knocklofty? I do not understand you, my lord.'

'Pooh! pooh! I do not want your secret, man, which, by the bye, is no secret at all; the town is full of it. Only be on your guard. Lady Knocklofty is a fine woman still, and to very young men, a very seducing woman; but then a man must be *young indeed;* and *I* was once *very, very, very,* young. Though, with all her faults and frailties, she has some good points; and while her fancy lasts, she is capable of the most romantic enterprize, and the most generous sacrifice – as charming woman ever is, under the influence of particular excitements. I know her – I know

> Il suo mobile ingegno.
> Usato amare, ed a disamare a un punto.

Trust her no further than as it leads to no consequence to yourself, or to others; and observe, keep clear of politics.'

'Good God!' said O'Brien, 'do not suppose – I am not aware – upon my honour and soul, I have not seen Lady Knocklofty since that foolish frolic of the Castle, and – '

'That is not the point,' said Lord Walter, interrupting him; 'only remember, she is the wife of the man by whose instigation the persecution of your principles, if not of your person, is carrying on.'

'But she is herself adverse to the principles of her party, opposite as day and night.'

'Oh! she has come to *that* with you already, has she?' said Lord Walter, laughing. 'You have yet to learn that all the wives of these oligarchs have a tendency to liberal principles, wherever liberal principles are professed by the most gifted, and (generally speaking) the best looking young men in Ireland. Lady Knocklofty visited young Macartney in Kilmainham, while under sentence of transportation for a libel on her husband's friend, the Chancellor; and the three Ladies

O'Blarney clubbed their pocketmoney to treat the Captain of the White Boys in his dungeon, after sentence of death had been passed on him. Women, who are in their habits and feelings aristocrats, *jusqu'au bout du doigt*, may *talk* sentimental whiggism and poetical democracy; but power and supremacy are their idols; and they will cling to those who possess both, even though they should be – their own husbands.'

O'Brien laughed, and said, '*Vous parlez en homme qui connaît son monde.*'

'Exactly,' said Lord Walter. 'Apropos, you are of course going to the fancy ball at Knocklofty House to-night?'

'I have been invited, and have accepted the invitation; but in my present position, with my present feelings – '

'What has your position to do with a mask and domino? Remember "Democracy *en petite maitresse.*" The conspiracy of Fiesco was forwarded amidst the gaities of a masked ball. So I propose that when we step out of the den in Back-lane, where our "union" meet, we turn into the first masquerade shop we find on our way, and – but first where do you dine? You are too late for commons: let us go to Daly's, it is so close.'

O'Brien agreed, and the illustrious united Irishman and his neophyte proceeded forthwith arm in arm to the 'Brook's' of the Irish capital. As they passed the library square, a few of the students were gathered in little groups at various points. At sight of O'Brien and his noble friend, they took off their caps, and (though Dr Barrett, the college Bursar, was looking from his window upon the scene) cheered them as they passed, singing in chorus:

> Wooden sons of the board, let us join hand in hand,
> 'Tis ours to discourage the youth of the land,
> Nor ever permit them, like us, to entwine
> The myrtle of Venus with Bacchus's vine.[1]

O'Brien returned the salute; his spirits rose with this courageous testimony of good will and admiration; and the *petit couvert* and Burgundy of his friendly Amphitryon, contributed to the gradual dispersion of that weight and gloom, which so readily dissipate from the elastic spirits of the youthful and the sanguine.

After an hour given to the necessary refreshment of the table, the

---

[1] Part of a song, about this time, popular in college.

two friends parted till their appointed *rendezvous* at the Tailor's Hall in Back Lane, where the United Irishmen held their meetings. Lord Walter returned home to dress; and O'Brien went back, for the last time, to college, to put up his papers, books, and clothes, that they might be in readiness when he could send for them, to the Galway Coffee-house in James's-street, – a customary haunt of his father, kept by one of Lord Arranmore's Connaught cousins, a gentleman bred and born, and of *half tribe*. Here O'Brien was certain that he could have shelter, till something definite could be decided for his future existence; and here alone there was a likelihood of meeting with his father.

When he returned to college, it was perfectly dark; and the few lamps which are destined to light the squares, were not yet lighted. As he entered the gloomy stone passage of his chambers, two figures wrapped in long mantles passed him down the stairs; the one, though doubly concealed by a cloak and darkness, was evidently a woman. Such visitants, at such hours, though strictly forbidden, were not wholly unusual in the university; and O'Brien drew up, to let the strangers pass; and then hurried on to his rooms.

He had locked the door in going forth; but when he now opened it, he was surprised to see the fire burning brightly, and the green wax taper on the writing desk still half extinguished, and sending forth a tiny stream of smoke. He relighted it; and his amazement increased to find his papers and books collected, tied up, and directed to the Galway Coffee-house, his clothes smoothed into his valise, and a sealed letter directed to him on the table. He opened it, in great trepidation, and read as follows:

'Since there exists not on earth that human being from whom you would accept pecuniary assistance, save those connected *with you by ties of blood*, one who claims the privilege you have admitted begs to administer to your present wants, by desiring your acceptance of the inclosed.'

The letter fell to the ground; the inclosure remained in O'Brien's hand, – it was a bank bill for fifty pounds. He remained for many minutes lost in the confusion of utter astonishment. He had locked his chamber door, – the key was in his pocket – his father only had a duplicate key. The mysterious visitant had evidently but just departed, for the seal of the letter was still warm. The words, too, which he had repeated in whispering confidence but an hour before to Lord Walter, were in this very letter repeated, and the most generous advantage taken of them. Yet all around him in the park had been silent and solitary. In the adjoining alley to that in which he had conversed with Lord Walter, he had for a moment fancied that he had perceived a shadowy figure walking to and fro, but it seemed to have passed away into a close walk, which opened by a private door in Nassau-street; and he had taken it for granted that it was some of the junior fellows who had the privilege of a key. There was a well-timed dexterity in this agency, an alertness, a sort of dramatic or fairy trickery, which struck on his imagination by its subtlety, ingenuity, and prompt execution. This was surely a woman's act; for the hand, though disguised, was a woman's: and what woman in Ireland was interested for him, if not her, who, however, '*mobile il suo ingegno*,' was yet 'capable of the most romantic enterprize, the most generous sacrifice!' But then, there was a claim of propinquity and blood. There was, however, almost a certainty that his father was of the party: he alone had the means of ingress. The muffled persons he had met on the stairs were the probable parties; but then Lady Knocklofty in alliance with his father! and prowling about the college park, on the night of her own fancy ball, – on the night of that day, on which her friend, the Vice-Chancellor, had condemned him to expulsion! This was too fanciful, too romantic, too wild, to admit of a moment's credence: the mystery was unfathomable! Still, however, in the whole embroglio, in the fantastic agency, the mysterious, invisible, and flattering superintendence of himself and his fortunes, there was something so gracious to his feelings, so consonant to his strongly imaginative disposition, that it operated like a philtre on his mind and spirits. There was yet another influence connected with the complicated intrigue. It reminded him of carnival adventures in Italy. His impetuous and eager passions had, more than once, plunged him into difficulties, during those saturnalia, from which he had been extricated by means as fantastic, as those under the influence of which he was now acting. Much leisure, however, was not left him for these reflections; time was hurrying on, his hours were counted. The college clock had struck eight, ere he had quite finished his toilette; and when he had made the arrangements for giving up his rooms, given his orders for the removal of his luggage, and surrendered his key to the porter who acted as *maréchal de logis*, he bid a last adieu to Alma Mater, and turned his steps towards the Tailor's Hall in Back-lane.

# CHAPTER III

●

## *The United Irishman*

Whenever the legislators endeavour to take away, or destroy the property of the people, or to reduce them to slavery, under arbitrary power, they put themselves into a state of war with the people; who are thereupon absolved from any further obedience, and are left to the common refuge which God hath provided against force and violence.

LOCKE *on Government.*

Sin va Rinaldo, dove l'amor l'invita.

ARIOSTO.

BACK-LANE, the site where liberty had for the first time raised her fane in Ireland, after ages had passed over her ruined altars, is one of those narrow, dirty, and close defiles of the old quarter of Dublin, which still represent the great streets of great capitals in those good old times, which genius in the pay of despotism has endeavoured to revive. In such thickly populated and ill ventilated '*vicoli,*' the plague was propagated, and fires were kindled, to be extinguished only after an extensive loss of the lives and properties of the inhabitants. The wisdom of our ancestors, who saw no inconvenience in what their fathers had borne, and admitted no remedy that came in the form of innovation, continued to reject, with equal tenacity, wide streets and inoculation: as equally subversive of social order, and opposed to God's providence in the government of the world.[1]

---

[1] The narrowness of streets derives from two sources. In the south of Europe, the object sought was shade. In the more northern regions, the necessity for inclosing walls to protect the towns, led to a similar mode of architecture. The taste for fresh air is,

Back-lane, inhabited only by coarse mechanics, and petty shop-keepers, had, in the early part of the century, been chosen, as an appropriate spot for erecting a catholic college for the education of catholic youth. But the intolerant spirit of the times forbad the accomplishment of this purpose; and the melancholy and monastic building, shut up in a narrow court, remained unappropriated, till it was purchased by the Corporation of Tailors; when the master's name was ostentatiously traced in the ironwork of the gateway, to the dark and narrow passage that leads to it.

O'Brien, wrapped up in a Roman *ferrajuolo* (the remains of his foreign toilet), had picked his way as he might, through the then always dirty avenue of Skinner-row, High-street, and Nicholas-street; to the utter detriment of slight pumps and silk stockings. More than once, as he applied his musked handkerchief to his nose, to cover the noxious exhalations of this region of new-born freedom, he recalled the assemblies at which he had been present, for the promotion of a similar cause, amidst the orange groves of Versailles, and the scented atmosphere of the *Jeu de Paume;* and he thought that the men who struggled for liberty in Back-lane had much greater merit, than those who congregated round her banner in the *Champs-Elysèes*, and the *Jardin du Luxembourg.*

The graphic and jocular description given of the *rendezvous* of United Irishmen, by Lord Walter, during their dinner, left O'Brien in no difficulty in making his way to it. The ill-scented passage which led to the place of meeting, was no further lighted than by the feeble rays of a dim lamp, suspended in the inner court; and it was so narrow and so dark, that he pushed against some person, who appeared to stand against its wall, at the entrance. O'Brien muttered a hasty apology; and was answered by the invocation of 'Charity, for Christ's

---

notwithstanding, an acquirement of civilization; and, like all other such acquirements, has been opposed by the organic tendency to imitation of the species, and by the stupid servile dread of innovation, artificially engendered by its teachers and misleaders. Not that any direct effort has been made to prohibit ventilation; because no corrupt interest has stood in its way; but timidity and self-distrust, once begotten by a bad system of religious and political education, sheds its baleful influence over the whole range of human thought. It is curious to remark, that England, the most fanatical and bigotted country in Europe, has likewise opposed itself, with the greatest obstinacy, to the practice of vaccination. The native land of Jenner lies open as much to the ridicule of Europe, for its imbecility respecting its ultra attachment to small-pox, as it does respecting its ultra apprehension of catholic emancipation.

sake.' There was something in the tone of voice in which this was uttered, which struck him to the heart. It was wholly unlike the drawling, whining, turgid supplications of the Dublin beggars. It had even an inflexion to which his ear was familiar; and it induced him to step back and search for his purse, light as it was. He had, however, left it in his writing-desk; but he found some silver, or what he took for silver, at the bottom of his waistcoat pocket; and he silently dropped a piece into the extended hand of the supplicant, and passed on. A simple, but most emphatic 'God bless you' still rung in his ear, and on his heart, as he crossed the little court, and ascended the steps of the Tailor's-hall; when it again struck him that the voice was familiar to him; and, at the same moment, as if by some sudden association, he was awakened to the conviction that the offering he had made to the mendicant, was a small gold coin of very ancient date, which he had purchased a week before, with some silver medals, to present to his father; but which he had left in the waistcoat he now wore. He was the more certain of this, on reflecting that the piece he had given was much too heavy for a shilling. He immediately turned back to overtake the mendicant, but he was gone; and being already beyond the time of his own appointment, he again entered the dreary building, whose dusky hall, and broad, low stairs were only lighted by a tallow candle, held in the hand of an old woman, whom the noise of his footsteps had brought out of a desolate, unfurnished room, on the right of the entrance. He inquired if Lord Walter was arrived.

'Ooh! yes, indeed,' she replied, turning her red eyes up to his face, 'this quarter of an hour or more; and bid ye be shown up to the committee room, when ye came (if you are the young gentleman he expected), and to let him know. This a-way, if you be plazed.'

O'Brien followed her up the creaking stairs, into a room on the landing place, where, laying down her candle on a long fixture table, she said 'Wait a taste, and as soon as his lordship is done spaking – for the society is sitting on business – I'll let him know.' She then disappeared.

There was something particularly dreary in this 'committee-room.' Its fireless grate was concealed by a large, ill-painted picture, representing a shivering and naked wretch, standing near a person seated on a tailor's shop-board, and cutting out a piece of cloth. O'Brien held the light down to it, and read an inscription, intimating that it was the portrait of 'J. Homodon, of Cremona, a tailerer, who gave all his gaine and labour to the poore. Canonized in his time for his miracles by Pope Innocent the Third.' It was one of those atrocious representations of humanity, given by the inferior painters of the early Italian schools, which sink the spirits to look at; and Murrogh soon turned away, and seating himself at the table, took up a torn magazine which lay before him. Chilled, spiritless, and impatient for Lord Walter's appearance, he was glad of any resource to while away the time.

The first thing he hit upon, as (beating a tattoo with his feet), he turned over the leaves, was 'Thoughts on Prudence.'

'Prudence is a quality of the human mind'. . . . 'What stupid nonsense,' he said, turning over several leaves at once, till he lighted on 'Reflections by Moonlight,' – 'Poetry of the Masque of *Ma Chère Amie*,' – 'Fashionable Pattern for working a Flounce,' – 'Private Theatricals at Knocklofty House.' This fixed his attention; and he read with almost audible utterance, 'The drama has ever been a part of elegant literature; and indeed, all the world's a stage, and all the men and women merely actors, as the immortal Shakspeare has it, etc. etc. etc. which leads to the brilliant exhibition of dramatic talent displayed at the private theatricals of Knocklofty House, on Monday the 4th instant. The play was the Beggar's Opera, followed by the Sultan. The principal characters were, the Countess Knocklofty, as Roxalana, and Captain O'Mealy as Macheath, which was allowedly given in the most capital style. It would be idle to comment on the Captain's theatrical excellence, for Madam Fame has taken that pleasing task upon herself. But we must say, his attitudes were imposing, his voice mighty melodious, and his manner of giving – "the charge is prepared," was. . . .'

Here a murmur of voices, which seemed to come from some adjoining room, interrupted the perusal of this evidently autographic criticism on the merit of Captain O'Mealy. O'Brien distinctly heard the voice of Lord Walter, speaking in a sustained tone. He arose and perceived that the sound proceeded from a door, just sufficiently opened, to discover that it gave entrance to a balcony, which dominated a somewhat spacious apartment, whence the murmur of voices issued.

As he looked down, there was something in the little senate he saw assembled, so picturesque, that its members seemed ready grouped for the purpose of a well-sketched conspiracy; and a single lamp (falling from the centre, and only dispersing the gloom of that part of the apartment over which it immediately hung) concentrated its yellow light upon heads and busts that recalled the '*grande quadro*' of Salvator's pride and glory.

At the head of the table, which occupied the centre of the apartment, and in an armchair raised by a few steps from the floor, sat the President of the society of United Irishmen. He alone was covered, and though plainly dressed, there was an air of high breeding and distinction about him; while in his bland smile were exhibited, the open physiognomy of pleasantness, and love-winning mildness, which still mark the descendants of the great Anglo-Norman Lords of the Pale, the Lords of Ormond, Orrery, and Arran, the Mount Garrets, and Kilkennys, – in former times the great oligarchs of Ireland, and in times more recent, the grace and ornament of the British Court.

The president was the Honourable Simon Butler: beside him, on a lower seat, sat the secretary. His uncovered head, and unshaded temples received the full light of the suspended lamp. It was one of those finely chiselled heads, which arrest the imagination, and seem to bear incontrovertible evidence of the certainty of physiognomical science. A dress particularly studied, was singularly contrasted with the athletic figure and antique bearing of this interesting looking person. For though unpowdered locks, and the partial uncovering of a muscular neck, by the loose tie of the silk handkerchief, had something of the simplicity of republicanism, yet the fine diamond that sparkled at the shirt breast, and the glittering of two watch-chains (the foppery of the day), exhibited an aristocracy of toilet, which did not exactly assort with the Back-lane graces. The secretary of the United Irishmen, was Archibald Hamilton Rowan.

On the opposite side sat a small, well-formed, and animated person, who was talking with singular vivacity of look and gesture, to one of extremely placid and even formal appearance. The first was the gay, gallant, and patriotic founder of the society, Theobald Wolfe Tone; the other was the celebrated and clever Doctor Drennan, a skilful physician, and an elegant writer, who might have passed, in appearance, for the demure minister of some remote village-congregation of the Scotch kirk.

A tall, elegant, and sentimental looking person sat near to them, in an attitude of interested attention, listening to the speaker, to whom, it seemed, he was about to reply. It was Thomas Addas Emmet, the son of the state physician of Ireland, – then a young lawyer of great promise, and now the Attorney-General of New York. The handsome and animated Dr Mackenna, one of the most popular writers of the day, and Oliver Bond, the representative of the most reputable class of merchants, had grouped forward their intelligent heads; while one who brought no personal beauty to the cause[1] (that letter of recommendation to all causes), James Napper Tandy, stood waiting with a packet of letters, which he had received in his former quality of secretary to the meeting.

While other leaders of the union, distinguished for their birth, talents, or principles (and it is remarkable that they were all protestants),[2] filled up the seats near the head of the table; more mixed groups less distinguished by the *beau sang*, which then came forth, in the fine forms of the genuine Irish gentry of both sects, were congregated in the obscurity of the bottom of the room. Here might be seen the square set forms, the strongly marked, but less noble features of the Scotch colonists of Ulster, the stern brow of uncompromising prosbyterianism, contrasting to the mobile, varying muscle, of trodden down catholicism; the latter drawling forth its plaintive discontents, the former announcing its immoveable resolutions.

At the moment when O'Brien was taking a rapid glance at this singular and picturesque association, Lord Walter, who stood near Hamilton Rowan, was speaking, and in the act of pronouncing the following sentence: 'Since this society is constituted for the purpose of forming a brotherhood and a community of rights among Irishmen of every religious persuasion, thereby to obtain a complete constitutional reform in the legislature, founded on the principles of civil, political, and religious liberty, I beg to propose one whose – '

Here O'Brien instantly closed the door of the balcony, and reseated himself by the flaring tallow candle, that was now fast burning down into its socket, resumed his perusal of the transcendent dramatic merits of Captain O'Mealy, and got through the whole 'Thoughts on Prudence,' without one thought on the subject, – when a sudden burst of applause reached his ear from the hall; and the next moment Lord Walter entered the room, and shaking him heartily by the hand, said, 'You have been proposed and received with acclamation. Our friend,

---

[1] When Napper Tandy was mentioned in the House of Commons as participating in the proceedings of the United Irishmen, a flippant young lawyer, then unknown to fame, got up, and in allusion to his ugliness, observed, 'that he was sorry the society could not put a better face on it.' Such were the jokes which then had their value in the Senate, and smoothed the path of the facetious utterer to nearly the highest judicial eminence.

[2] Of the twenty United Irishmen confined at Fort St George, four only were catholics.

Costello, was not here to second you as he promised; but Emmet is my fellow sponsor, for all the good things promised and vowed in your name. You have been elected without a single black ball, and nothing now remains but the form of taking the test.'

The two young friends, arm-in-arm, then descended the stairs, and entered the hall together: and never did two finer representatives of the Anglo-Norman and Milesian races of Ireland present themselves at the shrine of national independence. All made way for them, as they passed on towards the president's chair; and there was a murmur of approbation and applause, so little consonant to the wonted sobriety and awful purpose of the meeting, that the president rose from his seat, and took off his hat. At this signal, silence and order were instantly restored; and the next moment all were seated, save the neophyte and his sponsors, who stood between the secretary and chairman, when the test was presented for O'Brien's perusal. On his assenting to its purport, the whole society arose and stood uncovered, while the candidate, stepping forward, read aloud as follows:

'I, Murrogh O'Brien, in the presence of God, do pledge myself to my country that I will use all my abilities and influence in the attainment of an impartial and adequate represenattion of the Irish nation in Parliament; and as a means of absolute and immediate necessity in the establishment of this chief good of Ireland, I will endeavour, as much as lies in my ability, to forward a brotherhood of affection, an identity of interests, and a communion of rights, and a union of power among Irishmen of all religious persuasions; without which every reform in Parliament must be partial, not national, inadequate to the wants, delusive to the wishes, and insufficient for the freedom and happiness of this country.

'I do further declare, that neither hopes, fears, rewards, nor punishments shall ever induce me, directly or indirectly, to inform on, or give evidence against any member or members of this or similar societies, for any act or expression of theirs done or made, collectively or individually, in or out of this society, in pursuance of the spirit of this obligation.'

O'Brien was then introduced to the principal members present, and having accepted the situation of secretary to a baronial committee for St Grellan, in the province of Connaught, he took his leave of the society for the night, with his friend Lord Walter. Leaving the elder members to pursue the dry details of business, which have nothing to do with the *poetry* of freedom, he jumped into Lord Walter's carriage, which was drawn up at the end of the lane; and heard, with something like the heart-beat of pleasure, his order to the servant to drive to Tweedie and Lindsay's, in Parliament-street.[1]

'My servant,' said his Lordship, drawing up the glasses, to exclude the noisome smells that came 'between the wind and his nobility;' 'my servant is already there chusing us pilgrim's dresses; for a pilgrim's robe, like that of charity, covers a multitude of sins – that is, the sins of dullness and inaptitude to the noisy pleasures we are about to plunge into.'

'A propos to your man,' said O'Brien; 'he did not come for your great-coat, and you mentioned that he would.'

'I quite forgot it,' said Lord Walter, 'when once my mind was at rest about those cursed papers, which I feared might affect you.'

'And which,' said O'Brien, 'to a certain point, did affect me. It is now all over; but the fact is, those papers were taken out of my supposed pocket by the familiars of our inquisition, and were read at the board. Wild, incoherent, and ruinous to the happiness of Ireland, they were so ill-written, that I believe I stood exonerated from their composition by my judges; but they affected not to credit the assertion of my ignorance of their existence. At all events you are not even suspected; and I fancy you must be content to make a sacrifice of the coat in order to continue so; for it would be folly in you, Lord Walter, to draw upon yourself suspicions, which would injure the cause in which you are embarked, without producing any good whatever.'

'Good God!' said Lord Walter, in great trepidation, 'can you suppose that I will suffer you – is it possible that – '

'You cannot force me to reveal what I have just sworn to conceal,' said O'Brien, emphatically. 'The oath is still warm in the records of liberty, and I have promised, in the awful presence of God, that neither hope nor fear – '

'You are a noble fellow, O'Brien; but this must not be.'

'At least,' said O'Brien, 'this is not the time to argue on the needlessness and folly of betraying a friend to no purpose. That you were made the confidant of such foolish and treasonable designs, as the having such papers committed to your care would intimate, could not serve the great cause in which you have embarked; though it might serve the purposes of your enemies, and the enemies of Ireland, to ascertain the fact of your so having them, on the credit of your own testimony.'

---

[1] The Howell and James of Dublin in those days.

'I am now convinced,' said Lord Walter, musing, 'that my suspicions respecting the person who forced those papers on me are well founded. He is the intimate friend of another member of the union, whose name, if I am not deceived, is yet destined to reach posterity under the execration which follows treachery in all ages.'

Lord Walter then sunk back in the carriage, and remained silent and thoughtful, as one ill at ease with himself; while O'Brien, affecting, or feeling an elation of spirits, which scarcely belonged to his position, talked at random, and dropping the window-glass, amused himself with the questions and observations of the thickly gathering crowds, who had already begun their usual inquiry on masquerade nights in Dublin, of 'What's your charackther?' The carriage drew up before what would now be called a mart, magazine, temple of fashion, or physitechnicon; but which, then, simply indicated itself as the shop of Tweedie and Lindsay, haberdashers. All the resignation that time can bestow from its experience; or philosophy boast as the result of its maxims and tenets, youth, in its brilliant petulance of temperament, gives in a superior degree. O'Brien's spirits had already flung off their load, 'his bosom's lord sat lightly on its throne;' and, more than reconciled to his fate, he had forgotten it. Springing into the gay temple of fantastic folly, and reflected on by the brilliant lights that illuminated its altars, and not a little, perhaps, by the pretty priestesses who served them, he walked about in pleased and idle curiosity; almost fancying himself at Venice or at Rome, in the height of the carnival. Taking up and flinging down crooks and crosiers, cowls for monks, and crowns for kings, party-coloured jackets for harlequins, and ermine gowns for judges, he collected the materials for dressing his own character; and robing himself in pilgrim's weeds, 'fixed the scollop in his hat before,' and left his address as the Galway Coffee-house, that his trappings and their hire might be sent for in the morning.

Miss Lindsay, who had in the meantime dressed Lord Walter, reminded him that, though masks were not admitted at Knocklofty House, every other species of disguise was allowed, which was necessary to top the character, by colouring faces up to the disguise. Rouge, ochre, burned cork, beards, brows, mustachoes and noses, and all the artful *et cætera* of the masquerading toilet were then furnished and O'Brien undertook to officiate as the artist. When he had made up his own face, as a sample of his skill, he exhibited a perfect and beautiful model of the pilgrim of the Abruzzi, on his way to the shrines of Loretto, – to-night, a stern bandit of the Pontine marshes; to-morrow, the penitant wiping off by prayers and vigils, the crimes he had committed without pity, and without remorse; his fierceness still beating on his bent brow, and flashing from his dark eye.

'No,' said Lord Walter, looking admiringly upon him, 'I cannot compete with that; for though

> From Toscane came our worthy race,

and

> Fair Florence was some time our ancient seat,[1]

my Anglo Norman blood, has so weakened my Italian, that my appearance can never assimilate with your Milesian colouring and countenance. The utmost I can aspire to is Goldsmith's "Gentle Hermit of the Dale, the love-lorn Edwin." So, my dear Miss Lindsay, a pale, amber-coloured beard, if you please; and pray give me a robe of more tender tint, that the contrast with my friend's brown and scarlet may be more striking.'

The two young men, completely, though differently equipped for the same character, and equally dramatic in their appearance, again entered their carriage, and drove on to Knocklofty House, laughing and light-hearted, as if the one had not been that day expelled, and cast friendless and fortuneless upon the world; or the other had not just issued from that misprision of treasonable cabal, the society of United Irishmen, – where he was about to risk all that made life pleasurable, in search of the uncertain good, his generous sacrifice might bring to his unhappy country. In this rapid transition of feeling, this sudden change of objects, this versatility of thought, passion, and pursuit, there was much of youth, in all its heyday of the blood and fancy; and not a little of what is Irish, in the full development of the national temperament, – of that morbid sensibility to external impressions, which kindles at a sun-beam and sinks beneath the shadow of a cloud.

In driving down Capel-street, the carriage was surrounded and cheered at every step, by that most licentious, but most cheerful and humorous of all congregations – a Dublin mob. The answer to the reiterated question of 'What's your charackter?' 'pilgrims from *Crogh–Patrick*,' was received with loud acclamation. Pilgrims in real life, were

---

[1] Lord Surrey's Sonnet to 'the Celestial Geraldine.'

then common in Ireland; and the staff and cross were plausible and approved badges of beggary, by which many made a livelihood, extracting from credulous bigotry what charity might have denied.

In Ireland even the public pleasures and amusements smack of that disorder and coercion, which in all bad governments act and re-act on each other; giving to licensed festivity the character of suspicion and terror. Groups of military, mounted and dismounted, filled every street, and mingled with the fearless and vociferous mob. At once harmless and incontrollable, the people were permitted to annoy the passenger, by opening the carriage doors, and in some instances obliging the masks to come out, show themselves, and explain and describe their 'charackters.' The license thus granted, or rather assumed, as a prescriptive right by the populace, is rarely exceeded, except when the persons questioned resist with insolence and hauteur, and refuse to gratify the curiosity they have awakened. Then occasionally scuffles ensue, and riots, leading to dangerous consequences, occur.

The vehicle which immediately preceded Lord Walter's carriage was filled by the officers of the Prince's Own; and being stopped by the mob, they replied to the accustomed vociferations, by a command to 'Shut the door, you rascals,' and 'drive on, coachman, at your peril.'

'Droive an!' reiterated a leader of the fun, with an imitation of the English accent. 'Och then, sorrow step you'll stir, nor droive an neither, till you show yourselves, honies, and tell us your charackters:' and he forcibly opened the door, and let down the steps of the carriage.

The rage of the military occupants of the vehicle, which now knew no bounds, was expressed in a manner so violent and insulting, that the mob, under the influence of their *saturnalia*, were about to commence an assault; when suddenly catching a glimpse of the uniforms, they shut up the steps and closed the door, exclaiming in a humorous tone of utter contempt, 'Och, the poor craturs, let 'em alone. Shure, it's only th' officers, that have no charackters at all. Drive on, coachy.'

Another carriage now drew up a-breast of Lord Walter's, in which some fantastic figure was amusing the persons without, by replica in consonance with their own peculiar humour. Shouts of laughter and 'Musha, long life,' followed every reply.

'You see,' said Lord Walter, 'they are in excellent temper now. This is some person *au fait* to the national humour.'

'Long life to you, Mar'ram. Success to your ladyship! All happiness!' exclaimed a variety of broguing voices. 'Aisy, now, aisy; don't you hear the lady is spaking? And it's all what we ax to know now, Madam, is, what's your charackter?'

'Gran-uaile,' replied a sweet voice, in that rich, mellifluous brogue which is only heard on the right side of the Shannon; 'being returned from a long voyage, and finding no hospitality at the gates of Howth Castle, I'm come to ask the "*caed mille faltha*" from you.'

'Och! then, and you shall have it a thousand times over,' was the general exclamation; for all understood this allusion to a popular tradition; 'and it's on the necks of our hearts we'll draw you every step, and we'll give you a stave of your own song, any how.'

The carriage then passed on, accompanied by the mob, joining in the chorus of the then popular air of Granuaile; which, like the *lillebulero*, had not long before been applied to political purposes, with great popular effect.

'That's a clever creature, whoever she is,' said Lord Walter, as they were now permitted to drive on. 'She knows how to play with the Irish temper; I should suspect that Granuaile and Lady Honoria were one and the same person, but that the accent is purely Irish.'

'And the voice much too melodious,' said O'Brien. 'Lady Honoria's is particularly harsh and wiry. There was something peculiarly sweet in the tone of that voice, and it struck me that it had a foreign accent.'

The flaring flambeaux fixed over the gates of Knocklofty House, announced the scene of festivity; but there were so many carriages set down before that of Lord Walter and O'Brien, that they alighted; and hustled and bustled as they might, through a multitude of footmen, policemen, coachmen, chairmen, and a mob, which not even a party of the Royal Irish, with swords drawn, and with denunciations as formidable, could keep back. In the general scuffle, O'Brien got separated from Lord Walter; but still pushing on, with a flutter of the heart, in which anxiety for his friend had no part, he soon cleared the court, and entered the illuminated and garlanded hall; where a military band completed the enchantment of the fairy scene. A servant stationed at a door to the left of the entrance, informed him that it was a dressing-room, appropriated to such gentlemen as chose to change their dress, in the course of the evening; the room on the opposite side being devoted for the same purpose to the ladies.

'This is indeed in the true carnival spirit,' observed O'Brien; and he thought of Italy, and of the pro-consular government of the dull

Austrians, over that region of the imagination; whose natives, like those of Ireland, thus twine their chains with flowers, and in the amusements of an hour, forget the wrongs of an age.

He now looked around him, but looked in vain for Lord Walter. Groups of common-place characters were rushing in, on all sides; but he was struck by the singular appearance of two figures, which issued from the ladies' 'tiring-room on the left of the hall. That they were female, was only apparent by a certain graceful fulness of the bust, and by the fairy feet that twinkled in silken sandals, beneath a robe, which fell in full straight folds, from neck to ankle, circled only at the waist by a rope, supporting a cross and rosary. The head and neck were enveloped in the frightful *cappa* of the *confraternità de' penitenti*, which (with its horned termination, and two apertures seamed with black for the eyes) was the habit *à la rigueur* of the males and females of the confraternities of Italy. Such personages were familiar to O'Brien, attending the '*predica in piazza*,' of every Italian town; and devoting themselves, from penitence or piety, to certain acts of grace and humiliation, performed in this deepest of all disguises, – disguises invented by the church to carry on its great scheme of human prostration, without shocking too deeply the *amour propre* of its dupes.

The whole of this singular and truly Italian costume, from the cappa to the sandals, was of a deep rose red; like that worn by the '*assistants*' of Ischia, whose procession forms so conspicuous a part in the celebration of the jubilee at Naples.

The *Penitente* brushed lightly by O'Brien, and ascended the staircase immediately before him; but they were stopped on the corridor which led to the apartments, by a group of gentlemen, who seemed to have stationed themselves there, for the exclusive purpose of annoying the company, and interrupting the course of the evening's pleasures. Evidently inebriated, they were not otherwise *disguised*, than according to the Irish acceptation of the phrase; though the uniform they wore, gave them a singularity of appearance, which, any where but in Dublin, would have served the purposes of a masquerade. Their whole dress, including their stockings, was of a bright flame colour, save only their coat, which, lined with flame coloured silk, was of black cloth. They were the leading members of the Cherokee Club, the last successors to the 'Hell Fires,' the 'Devil's Owns,' and 'Pinking Dindies,' of more barbarous and more fierce times. Flushed and flashy as they appeared, there were among them, some of the most fashionable members of the Irish *beau monde;* Lords Kilcolman, Kilmainham, and Kilshandra, were prominent personages in the group; while Sir Phelim O'Flynn, with a long white wand, staggered about, crying 'Order, order,' in the most disorderly manner; and Captain O'Mealy, dressed as Father Paul, affected to be the chaplain of the society, and intonated at intervals, over a goblet he held in his hand,

> This bottle's the sun of our table;
>   Its beams are rosy wine;
> We, planets that are not able,
>   Without its light, to shine.

Many groups, as they ascended, and passed this formidable out-post, played them off in their own way, with all that ready but local humour, which, like other indigenous productions of Ireland, thrives best on its own soil. The appearance of the two Italian penitents, characters out of the common muster-roll of Irish masquerading, excited a considerable sensation among the Cherokees; who advanced to meet, and to surround them with a boisterous curiosity, and a characteristic war-whoop, that intimidated the penitents, till they shrank back, so as almost to oblige O'Brien to back also.

One of them, either in fear or in character, exclaimed, '*Hei mihi, quia incolatus meus prolongatus est.*'

'*Non amplius quam placebit,*' replied O'Brien to this singular apos-trophe, which both struck and amused him; and, offering an arm to either lady, he added, in English, 'Holy sisters, allow a brother of your community, and a participator in your vocation, to offer you his aid against those obstacles, which the enemy of mankind opposes to your progress, to the shrine of our common devotion.'

The fair penitents still held back, though one of them uttered a '*grazie tante, Signor Pellegrino,*' while O'Mealy, without recognizing O'Brien (for, though seeing double, he saw none the clearer), sung out –

> It was a friar, of orders grey,
>   Went forth to tell his beads;
> And he met with a lady fair,
>   Clad in a pilgrim's weeds.

'A lady fair!' cried Sir Phelim O'Flynn, who, with the rest of the party, had drawn up so as to prevent all ingress to the ante-room. 'How the devil have you found out that, Father Paul? Leave a monk alone for finding out a pretty girl: I'll be hanged if I did not take these outlandish figures for Egyptian mummies, or a new reading of blind man's buff. Pray, ladies, what's your character?'

'*Siamo penitenti rosse, della confraternità d'Ischia, in grande penitenza, alla santa casa,*' replied one of the ladies, the most elegantly formed of the two.

'We'll throuble you for change for that, Signora,' said O'Mealy, in his broadest tone of vulgarity, whispering Lord Kilshandra; 'give you my honour it's the *Bona fillola* of the Opera in Capel-street, I know her by her pretty little pasterns – smoke the foot.'

O'Brien, infinitely disgusted with the coarse, mistaken humour of the party, translated the Pilgrim's answer to ears not so familiar with their dialect as his own. 'They are saintly women, of the order of the red penitents of f'schia, pilgrims to the shrine of Loretto. So pray, good christians, impede not their pious progress, as you hope for remission of your own sins and peccadillos by prayer and penitence.'

'Then, if that's the case,' hiccuped Lord Kilcolman, looking earnestly at O'Brien, as if endeavouring to make out who he was, 'they don't pass here. We have papists enough already; and so, Signor Friar, I advise you to be off, and join your popish banditti in the south.'

'Oh! for the friar,' interrupted Lord Kilshandra, 'he has leave to quit; but we must not part with the sisterhood. Such pretty papist feet as these would find footing any where; for prettier never trod the boards, abroad or at home;' and, whispering Lord Kilcolman, he added, 'so make way for the sisters –

> If to their faith some popish errors fall,
> Look at their feet, and you'll forget them all.'

'Oh! that alters the case,' stammered Lord Kilcolman; 'for though I suspect this pilgrim is the most dangerous papist that ever came amongst us, since St Patrick; and though I am the protestant St Peter – (hiccup) – and keep the keys of – (hiccup) – '

'The cellar,' interrupted the dangerous papist; and a general laugh followed the observation.

Lord Kilcolman, easily irritated, by wit or opposition, as the dull and the drunken always are, exclaimed, inarticulately, 'Cellar or no cellar, I am, at all events, so far like the papist St Peter, and his representative the Pope, that I must be bribed well, and sell my place in Paradise to the highest bidder – '

'As you did your place in Parliament,' replied the penitent. 'What is your price, now?'

The allusion to Lord Kilcolman's recent disposal of his venal voice in one house, and of his borough in the other, excited a general titter, which respect did not permit to rise to a laugh; while annoyed and irritated by the sarcasm, he vociferated 'Come here, my dear, whatever my price may be, let me know yours, and if your face is as pretty as your foot – ' and he reeled forward to seize her hand, and mutter some insolent gallantry, when O'Brien threw himself between the masks and the Cherokees. Indignant at the unmanly spirit, which forgot alike the courtesy of gentlemen and the respect of men, he said, 'These ladies are under my protection; pray make way for them:' and backing in before the masks, with shoulders and elbows that were not to be resisted, he made a passage, through which the ladies glided unmolested, while the Cherokees raised their accustomed war-whoop, and O'Mealy sang,

> A lovely lass to a friar came,
> All on a morning early.

Lord Kilcolman at this moment endeavouring to spy under the pilgrim's cowl (which O'Brien had drawn half over his face, on first perceiving the party at the head of the stairs), exclaimed, 'I'll be d——d if that isn't Lady Knocklofty's pet rebel, Captain Right.'

O'Brien had just caught the conclusion of this allusion to himself; and irritated at the wanton insolence of these autocrats of Irish fashion, he was half inclined to take as a personal insult what was probably meant only as a general annoyance, or considered as good fun; and to throw himself again in the way of the assailants, – when a gentle and plaintive '*Ohimè*', from one of the pilgrims, who was suffering much from the pressure of the crowd, induced him to struggle with his own petulance. Abandoning his intention, therefore, he turned back to the helpless and imprudent females, who had ventured so unprotected into a scene, where protection, he now perceived, was so necessary.

Struck, as he was, with the prompt humour of her, whose Latin, Italian, and English were almost equally well pronounced, O'Mealy's suggestion, which he had overheard, recurred to him. It accounted for her singular gift of tongues, for the Italian costume, and for the hardihood with which she and her companion had ventured alone into an assembly, in which the rank of the host did not always secure the good breeding of the guests; and where the license of a masquerade permitted the expression of many an irascible feeling, which the forms of society keep in check.

O'Brien, therefore, offered an arm to either lady, which both silently accepted; and he enabled them to pierce the motley crowd of characters, which, with a terrible rush, were precipitating themselves into the ball-room, through a beautiful arch, hung with coloured lamps and flowery garlands. Immediately to the left of the entrance, he perceived a vacant sofa, and having conducted his unknown *protégées* to this desirable retreat, he was retiring with a pilgrim's salutation and saintly at his heart, and the signs of a *'masque en rose*, a wreath, a ring, a flower, *benedicite* (the flutter of a vague hope full in his imagination), when the speaking mask solicited his attention by a timidly uttered, *'Scuse, Signor Pellegrino – ma – di grazia.'*

He instantly returned; the stranger paused. O'Brien begged to know if he could be of any further use; but the penitent drooped her head, and played with her rosary, with a graceful awkwardness, that intimated one who had a request to make, but not the courage to prefer it. O'Brien, doubtful whether this was nature or art, and impatient to be off, again asked if he could seek any person, any friend.

*'Ohimè! Signor Paladino gagliardo,'* replied the penitent. 'I have no friend here, and therefore – ' she paused again.

O'Brien thought that there was something ironical in the tone, in which the flattering epithet of Ariosto was applied to him; and fearful of getting entangled with this clever and singular mask, who was 'topping her part' to the uttermost, he coldly expressed his regrets that he could be of no further use; and he was again retiring, when the mask, in an abrupt and pouting tone, exclaimed as she touched his arm, *'Ah! il est toujours plus facile de secourir son prochain, que de le supporter.'*

'I can assure you,' said O'Brien, amused by the *naïveté* of the reproach, and by its *tournure*, 'I am quite disposed to do either, in the present instance; and if you will honour me with your commands, I will fly to execute them.'

'Fly!' said the mask, 'suppose you *stay*, to execute them.'

'I should be too happy, fair saint,' said O'Brien impatiently; 'but I have engagements which will prevent my having that pleasure. However, if you have got separated from your party, and will permit me to – '

'No,' interrupted the mask, with a sigh, 'I belong to no party; not even to that of the United Irishmen.'

O'Brien started; was this coincidence, or 'a palpable hit?' Was he guessed at, or known, and betrayed? He involuntarily seated himself on the arm of the sofa; and leaning on his pilgrim's staff, he gazed with fixed attention on the figure beside him, as if he would have penetrated the muslin cappa which fell before her face: but though it betrayed the outline of a fine profile, he could not recognize a single feature; and he had the caution to reply with affected carelessness,

'If there be such a party as the United Irishmen, your vocation, fair saint, being not of this world, would, doubtlessly, exempt you, as much as your sex, from being a member of it.'

'Women have been members of societies, quite as secret, and much more discreet.'

'Indeed!' said O'Brien: 'and yet they are accused of not being able to keep a secret.'

'That is a vulgar fallacy. The fidelity of woman is the most inviolable of all human trusts. Woman can keep every secret, but – her own.'

'Trust me then with yours,' said O'Brien, insensibly interested and amused; 'and if you will not raise the envious cappa, at least tell me the name of her whom it conceals.'

'How may I trust you?' asked the mask, with a low earnestness of voice and manner.

'I will swear,' said O'Brien, 'by any oath.'

'Hush!' whispered the mask, 'you have sworn one oath too many already, to-night.'

O'Brien remained silent from consternation. He was then known by the person who addressed him. Was she friend or foe? one who came to warn, or to scan him? If a friend, who could it be? Lady Knocklofty? The idea was too romantic. If a foe, what foe? A spy perhaps of the government – one of those hinted at by Lord Walter. What an agency! It recalled the reports circulated abroad of the sisterhood of the '*Sacré Cœur*,' the newly affiliated agents of the Jesuits.

Resolved to give the conversation a light turn, and to cut it short, as soon as he could, he continued:

'Without pretending to understand your allusion, nor to take it either as a provocation or warning, I will take any vow of secrecy you please to dictate; provided it procures my personal acquaintance with the charming person I have the honour to address.'

'You were not always so ready to take vows,' said the mask drily.

O'Brien was startled by an observation, which, if not accidental, referred to a particular event in his life. 'I never,' he said, 'was half so tempted.'

'You are easily tempted,' was the half-laughing, but contemptuously uttered reply.

'Indeed!' said O'Brien, 'as, for instance, how, where, or when?'

'Everywhere, anywhere,' was the careless reply -'at a review in the Phœnix; in the presence chamber at the castle; in the park of the university; in the council-room of the Tailor's-hall. With two words you may be tempted to any enterprise, however wild; or led into any adventure, however perilous.'

'Two words!' reiterated O'Brien, eagerly – 'name them.'

'Love and liberty,' whispered the mask. O'Brien remained silent. It was now evident that he was but too well known to the extraordinary person, who thus so faithfully described him. Puzzled, beyond all power of even guessing at the Sphinx which bewildered him (whom, for a moment, he took for Lady Knocklofty, and then again suspected to be Lady Honoria); provoked, but still pleased, he scanned his companion with eyes of intense curiosity, and at last said, 'I would give all I possess, to know who you are?'

'Humph! How much may that be?' asked the pilgrim, significantly.

'Faith,' said O'Brien, piqued, but laughing, 'so little (as you seem to intimate), that I believe it is confined to mere personal property.'

'The sum of which, *par exemple*, is – '

'A heart that never resisted woman, nor flinched from man,' said O'Brien.

'A most concise inventory,' interrupted the mask; 'and to be taken for its value on the word of the appraiser. But do you count for nothing the principality of Arran, the green knighthood of the Fassagh, and the barony of Ballyslattery? Trust me, there is one here to-night, who would not be pleased to hear you say so.'

With annoyance and amazement now at their utmost, O'Brien replied, 'Indeed! and who may that be?'

'Your aunt, Mac Taaf from Bog Moy.'

'My aunt, Mac Taaf!' exclaimed O'Brien, completely the victim of an intrigue, carried on with such puzzling ingenuity; 'that is impossible – I have just had a letter from her.'

'Of what date?'

O'Brien remembered that it was dated a month back. The mask continued,

'Your aunt was at your rooms this evening, and found you absent. So she has come here to give you rendezvous.'

'So,' said O'Brien, with a laugh expressive of extreme provocation; yet struck by the coincidence between this intimation, and the note and bank bill he had received in the evening.

'Business,' said the mask, 'with Lord Knocklofty's agent brought her to town; and as an electioneering bribe, she has received a ticket for the ball, at which she has just arrived, in the well supported character of *Gran-uaile*. Shall we go in search of her?'

'Not for the world,' cried O'Brien, with vehemence.

'What an ungracious nephew,' said the mask, laughing.

O'Brien remained silent. He wished to go, but could not. An insatiable curiosity to know who his accomplished tormentor could be – a vague suspicion, scarcely amounting to a hope, that one so well, so flatteringly acquainted with him, and with all that concerned him, was, indeed, Lady Knocklofty, was still crossed by the improbability of the fact, and by a display of accomplishments, which, he believed, were not within the possession of his noble protectress. The accent, too, was either really or affectedly foreign; though the English was spoken with infinite fluency, and with a slight inflexion of the Connaught *patois*, so soft and singular in its rhythm. Could it be one of his aunts? The idea was too absurd.

While thus he mused, group after group passed; and some addressed the mask, who replied with more wit than mercy, while the other pilgrim remained mute. Lord Walter, in earnest conversation with a beautiful woman, in the character of Night, smiled and nodded to O'Brien, as much as to say, 'I see you are engaged, as well as myself.'

'There goes one,' said the mask, 'who, to guess by his words and looks, is *taillè á l'antique;* devoted as an Aristides to his country, as a Pylades to his friend, and as a Leander to his mistress; but all will not do. *On ne joue pas aux échecs avec un bon cœur.*'

'You know Lord Walter, then?'

'About as long as you do: which, it seems, is long enough for a friendship *à l'Allemande*. Still there is something honest in these uncalculated friendships. The world's friendships are so *hérissées de si, et de mais, et de sous-entendus.*'

At this moment, Lady Honoria, in the character of Psyche, winged and winning, passed on, followed by a crowd: she looked full at O'Brien, but either did not recognize, or refused to acknowledge him.

'Psyche seems *désorientée* to-night,' said the mask. 'That fatal lamp! the moment you throw a light upon love it vanishes. The allegory is obvious.'

'That is according to the nature of the love,' said O'Brien.

'There is but one love,' replied the mask, 'though there are many counterfeits.'

'The ancients had several.'

'And so too has Lady Honoria,' said the mask, laughing.

'With such wit and such beauty, how could she fail?' said O'Brien.

'For her beauty, *passe;* and pass it will of itself before long: and for her wit, it is *l'esprit d'anti-chambre, – très-gai, et un peu polisson.* But people of the world are not nice. *Tromper leur ennui en le divertissant* is their aim and object; and whoever makes them laugh by a sally, gets credit due only to a discovery. There is nothing original, nothing that comes of strong feeling and strong thinking, in the wit of Lady Honoria; *c'est une flamme sans feu.*'

Exclusively preoccupied by his mysterious and brilliant companion, whose manner had so completely changed since he had first addressed her, O'Brien had now almost forgotten the object which had brought him to a scene so ill-assorted with his position; and he was wholly given up to the spell that enthralled him, and the conjectures it gave rise to. Once before, he had been thus attacked, and thus had succumbed. The adventure, by interfering with a *rendezvous*, had saved him from a crime, and eventually from the summary penalty of such crimes, in Italy – assassination; but what was this to lead to? it was followed up with too much pertinacity, not to have some object. While thus deeply musing, his eyes accidentally bent down, and, for the first time, met those of the penitent. She was earnestly gazing on his thoughtful and almost wrapped countenance, of which the depth of expression was increased by his additional colouring, and the dress he had assumed. He thought that he recalled, in the fixed and intense expression of those eyes, the same glance which had confused him at the review in the Phœnix Park, and he ventured to observe –

'I have surely met those eyes before?'

'Yes;' said the penitent, casting them down, with a sigh; 'and yet they are not the eyes you came to meet.'

'If I were sure of that,' said O'Brien, passionately and emphatically – ' 'Tis the doubt, the hope, the fear connected with that uncertainty, that disheartens and stultifies me. If I dared ask – '

'Fairy favours,' said the penitent, 'should be accepted without inquiry. Ask no questions, obey and be patient.'

'For my patience I cannot answer, though I am disposed to an obedience the most implicit, the most devoted; but obedience implies a reciprocal tie, and I would at least know to whom I am to swear allegiance.'

'To the Queen of the Fairies,' was the reply.

'I guessed as much,' said O'Brien, full of the signature of the *invito;* 'and I here solemnly offer myself her liege man, in life and limb, and in all earthly worship of faith and truth, so help me Heaven and Allhallows!'

'Vows are but breath,' said the penitent, in a low and agitated voice; 'have you no better pledge?'

'What other do you demand?' whispered O'Brien.

'The ring that was given you in St Patrick's Hall.'

'If I had it,' said O'Brien, much agitated, 'I would not part with it for a thousand worlds; but it was taken from me while I slept, and I suspect – I hope, by the beautiful donor herself: perhaps, in repentance either of her condescension or her confidence.'

'What is that ring you wear?' asked the mask, fixing her eye upon the ungloved hand that grasped the pilgrim's staff.

'That ring – it is a bauble, of little value – '

'But of most melancholy import,' said the mask, looking more closely at it. 'If it is valueless and sad, why do you wear it?'

'It would be a history to relate,' said O'Brien impatiently; 'and this is not a moment to enter upon any tale, save one.'

'Let that be short, then,' replied the penitent, quickly, and in a low voice; 'for we are watched, and shall soon be interrupted. Leave out the tag and the moral, and come at once to the theme.'

'Gratitude,' said O'Brien, hesitating and sighing deeply.

'Gratitude! – a cold theme, and a fabulous, at least a doubtful one.'

'Fabulous?'

'Yes; little minds never feel, though they profess it; and great minds blush to own, though they should feel it. 'Tis a humiliating sentiment at the best. *Il y a peu de bienfaiteurs qui ne disent comme Satan, si cadens adoraveris me.* Have you, then, no fitter tale for a lady's ear, good Signor Pellegrino?'

'None so worthy for such a lady's ear – none that I dare venture upon now; and yet one there is, the truest and least feigned the heart of man ever dictated.'

'By its prologue, I guess 'tis an old tale with a new title-page; like the sonnets got up by the pauper poets of Italian towns; who greet every stranger with the same compliment, and change nothing in their compositions, but the name and the date.'

'Hear, at least, before your judge,' said O'Brien, petulantly, and mortified by the flippant observation.

'I hear! *guardi il cielo!*' said the mask, laughing contemptuously; 'no, Signor Pellegrino, such *rifacciamenti* are not for ears like mine; keep it for hers, whose interest it is to believe.'

'For *hers?* If you be not "the inexpressive she," then is there no truth in sympathy.'

'Vanity, like hope,' said the mask, with an emphatic movement of the head, '*dà facile credenza a quel che vuole;* and sympathy thus applied, is but another name for vanity. I, however, am not the Armida of the night.'

'Nor I the Rinaldo,' said O'Brien. 'I am not again to be misled; nor am I like other fairy victims, to be for ever flattered and tantalized, scorned and protected. Still, I would give expression to feelings as far, at least, as words can express them, and I beseech you – '

'Hush!' said the mask; '*je ne veux pas vous escamoter votre secret.* Here comes one who may have claims upon it; I have none.'

At that moment, a general movement in the company, a rush from all the other apartments, the performance of the royal anthem of God save the King, and the appearance of the officers of the vice-regal household, announced the arrival of the Lord-Lieutenant. He entered the room, leading in Lady Knocklofty, and was followed by the Duchess, attended by the Earl, who, as well as his Grace, was in the full costume of the order of St Patrick. Like the rest of his caste, his lordship affected all the forms of nationality; and never failed to parade the Irish order, to put a shamrock in his hat on Patrick's day, and to drown it in his Patrick's pot at night, with due maintenance of a custom 'more honoured in its breach than the observance.' He, indeed, boasted, on all occasions, of being a good Irishman; and, as far as ostentation and intemperance went, he had, according to the acceptation of the times, a claim to being a genuine one.

All who were seated, now arose; all who stood in groups or crowds, made way for the vice-regal procession; and the brilliant party, as they passed up the room, were saluted and hailed with an homage, to which the genial spirit of the moment contributed, at least as much as the political unanimity of the company. O'Brien alone remained motionless and transfixed, till Lady Knocklofty had so closely approached him that her drapery touched him in her passage. Her eyes met his, but with a glance of such contemptuous indignation (their only recognition), as at once confounded him, beyond all power of joining in the general act of courtesy, which the gracious smile and ready bow of the Duke exacted from all. The court master of the ceremonies now made the necessary arrangements for the opening of the lists; and the country dances began, with the exhilarating air of Patrick's Day. The ball was opened by two long sets; the one led off by the Lord-Lieutenant and his noble hostess, – the other by the Duchess and Lord Knocklofty. Groups, the most grotesque, followed: monks figured in with oyster-wenches; the devil seesawed with St Patrick, and set to the Lord Chancellor; a jack-boot turned a windmill; and a village apothecary went three hands round with Death and the Lady; while hands across, right and left, change sides, and turn your partner, were executed with a rapidity, which would have pozed the prosing performers of modern quadrilles, and would have put out of breath and patience, the sauntering figurantes of '*chaîne de dames*,' and '*demi-queue de chat*.'

In the midst of this general scene of gaity and amusing variety, O'Brien, pre-occupied and confused, saw only the terrible glance of Lady Knocklofty. More than ever perplexed and annoyed, he, for the first time, doubted that the invitation had come from her; and suspected that he was but the victim of a mystification, which, whatever was its object, had been but too successfully played off against him. Anxious to escape, and yet unwilling to leave without further explanation, his extraordinary companion, whose subtlety and adroitness had given him an almost painful impression of her character and agency, he had unconsciously reseated himself on the arm of the sofa by her side, with a countenance expressive of his agitation and his feelings.

The mask, meanwhile, was evidently amusing herself with the gay groups which flitted before her, beating time with her foot to the music, and humming a very elaborate base to the melody of Patrick's Day, with a science which showed her a perfect mistress of counterpoint.

'*Bravo!*' said her silent companion, for the first time giving signs of life, '*non va male*.'

'*Cosi, cosi*,' replied her friend; 'Irish music, like all simple melody (the effusion of feeling and of ignorance), is too irregular to admit of scientific harmony.'

'*Musica barbara!*' said the virtuosa.

'Yet Geminiani concerted some airs of Carolan; you have heard me play one,' replied the other.

'*Perrucca*,' exclaimed the fastidious *cognoscente*, in the harshest guttural tone of the true Italian organ.

'*Scuse*,' replied her companion, 'it was any thing but that. A rich melody running through a dry and learned harmony, like a fresh spring flowing into the briny deep, will preserve its sweetness still; and there is nothing of what you call *perrucca*, except where science exclusively holds the place of melody. But musical taste is a mere affair of organs and associations; to either of which there is no prescribing. Every age has its music. That which charms the ear to-day, displeases it to-morrow. *Figuratevi, cara*, the votarists of Piccini, listening to the *madriali*, which were the rage in the seventeenth century; or the devotees of our Paesiello, lending their ears to the cramped harshness of Leo and Durante.'

'*Il divino Paesiello! L'insigne maestro!*' exclaimed the Signora, with enthusiasm, as she sounded the depths of a massive snuff-box, drawn from the pilgrim's scrip, with fingers which were certainly not those of Aurora.

'*Divino*, yes, for us; but quære as to our successors. Even the strains of Paesiello may yet be put out of fashion by the more brilliant and exciting creations of some future genius; and the *Il mio ben* of the sweet Cimarosa may be pronounced by future *virtuosi*, – an *ario di sorbetto*.'

'*Non credo niente*,' said the *cognoscente*, '*è cosa impossibile*.'

'Every thing is possible,' was the reply.

'*A lei, sì*,' rejoined the Italian, significantly; while in raising her *cappa* to take her snuff, she exhibited one of those marked, withered, and furrowed visages, which are only to be found in the regions where the youth of woman is loveliest.

'*Che ne pensate?*' said the original mask, turning to O'Brien, who had almost involuntarily listened to these musical observations, by which he became insensibly as much amused as he was amazed; while his suspicions again reverted to O'Mealy's hint of the *prima donna* of the opera. 'I know,' she continued, 'you are an amateur. At least, I remember once seeing you ecstatized at the litany of the Virgin, sung on a particular festival in the Chiesa di Loretto at Rome.'

'Good heavens,' cried O'Brien, 'is that possible?'

'Yes, you stood near the *altare maggiore*, under Arpino's great picture, when one of the congregation of the *Corpo Sacro*, a sister of the convent of the *Bambin Gesù*, sung the solo.'

'Then,' said O'Brien, 'it was in Italy you have known me.'

'In Italy, in France, in Ireland, in the Isles of Arran, in Ischia, in the Campagna, and in Connemara, any where, every where,' was the careless and incoherent reply.

'*Oh! pour le coup*,' said O'Brien, now more than ever perplexed by fresh conjectures and surmises, connected with passed adventures in Italy; 'this is carrying the imbroglio of masquerading to the very head and front of its offence. That you know me but too well, is beyond all doubt. Of this you have given me a somewhat too painful assurance. For to be frank with you, you have embittered moments destined to far other sensations than those you have aroused; and have turned an expected pleasure into a positive annoyance.'

'*Ohimè!*' said the pilgrim, putting her fingers to her eyes, like a pettish child, 'you consider me then a *seccatore*, what you call in English a bore?'

'No,' said O'Brien, half laughing in spite of himself, 'not that exactly; that were an annoyance easily gotten rid of. You are the reverse of a bore. If you prosed, I should fly; but like the *lucciole* of your Italian woods, you attract attention only to evade it. You wind me up to painful excitement, only to let me down to mortifying depression.'

'I have but followed the course of your own feelings. I came not here to hurt, but to save you,' said the mask, in a deep and much affected voice.

'Indeed,' said O'Brien, 'I thank you at least for the intention. May I beg to know from what danger?'

'From the commission of a perilous fault, and of a deadly sin.'

'And they are – '

'Unavailing conspiracy and criminal love.'

'Good God!' exclaimed O'Brien; then suddenly recollecting himself, he added, 'here at least your wit fails in its divination. I presume you have taken me for another?'

'No,' said the masque, with emphatic seriousness, 'I have known you too long and too well. Your story was the dream of my earliest youth; your fate the subject of my constant occupation.'

'Indeed!' said O'Brien, affected beyond all power of concealing his emotion. 'If you are really serious, – if this is not mere *jeu d'esprit*, – if we have met before, – if you are one, who,.... ; but I must not again commit myself, till you give me more positive proof of your identity. If you indeed know me, you must know me for one at this moment, out of sorts with fortune.'

'I know you,' said the mask, 'for what you are, and for what you know not yourself to be, – one of high aspirations, but mistaken means. You are, perhaps, that foolish Roman boy who put his hand into the furnace, and only burned his fingers for his pains. Or, if not he, you are Cola di Rianza, or the simple patriot Capponi of Florence, who lost his life, and saved not his country a bit the more; or you are the gallant Fiesco, who spoiled the cause he adopted by an ill-timed explosion; or you may be Meo Patacca, or any other *capo popola* – a people's wonder and a party's dupe: one of those whom government permit to go certain lengths, that they may afterwards convert them into agents, or immolate them as victims. For such spirits have been so impersonated, as often to mar as to make the reformation they seek to effect.'

This sudden change of tone, from the deepest feeling to the coldest irony, wound up the annoyance of O'Brien to its acme; and he answered with all the coolness he could command, 'So much for what I am, – a subject of which, whether you have judged it right or wrong, I have become a little weary: and now, Madam, for yourself.'

'Oh! I? do you not then guess at me? I am Nuccia, the *trasteverina*, who prevented Meo Patacca from going to beat the infidels out of Vienna, or from some other enterprize not less safe and wise. Do you, then, forget the carnival ball at the Borghese palace, the vows you breathed, and I believed?

> Dimmi che l'ho fall'io. Ma troppo errato,
> Perché amare é grande colpa, a un cor ingrato.'

This citation, given in the *linguaggio Romanesco*, from the popular poem of Meo Patacca, confirmed O'Brien in his conjecture, that the Mask of Knocklofty House, and the '*bella Nuccia*' of the Borghese palace were one; but who this gifted and tantalizing person could be, was still the enigma. The adventure of that carnival evening had left a deeper impression on his mind, than carnival adventures are wont to make. He had gone under the influence of the spell of pleasure, which at that season, in Italy, so often tempts the young and the unwary into folly and danger; he had consented to a rendezvous with one more experienced in such adventures than himself; he had assumed the character of Meo Patacca, by an understanding with the party, who was to have appeared as Nuccia: but another Nuccia had crossed their intentions; and with a wit and spirit, a grace and intelligence, and, above every thing, with an interest and a knowledge of all that concerned him, had so worked on his volition, as to have led him from the original purpose of the night; and by thus rescuing him from a folly, had eventually protected him from a crime. This, his one sole adventure in the pleasurable but perilous scenes of Italian gallantry, had frequently visited his imagination, to cheer and warm it; and the remembrance had often recurred with a flush of pleasurable sensation, that came like sun-shine, and left the impression of its light and warmth behind it.

'If,' he said, after a long pause, 'you are indeed the Nuccia of a certain eventful evening, passed in the Palazzo Borghese, you will tell me where we first met?'

'In the ninth room of the *suite à pian-tereno*. You were standing with your eyes fixed on the picture of Love and Psyche, of Dossa da Ferrara, when I drew your attention to the "*amore divino e profano*" of Titian.'

'That is enough,' said O'Brien.

'The evening was warm, the moon was bright, you followed me to the garden, whose fountain refreshed the air, and spread around a delicious coolness. My *donna d'accompagno*

> Suzia se chiama, e non vo mai senza,

was no restraint upon vows as ardent as carnival passion ever inspired –

> Io so che solo idolo tuo me chiami
> Per farmi scherno dagli inganni tuoi.

'No, by heavens,' said O'Brien, 'I felt then all I professed; but who can for ever worship a phantom, nameless and unknown, or love with human feelings the vision of a dream? You told me then, as now, you came to save me.'

'And did I not? She whom you went to meet, the faithful, "inexpressive she," of that night, consoled herself with another Patacca, and, detected by her husband, saw her lover fall by his hand.'

O'Brien shuddered.

'Had you been but four days in Rome, instead of two, you would have better known the Duchess's character.'

'I almost fear to ask further,' said O'Brien.

'Her husband died in the dungeons of St Angelo; – for her lover was a Doria.'

'And the duchess?' said O'Brien.

'You will be shocked to hear.'

'Pray go on.'

'Married her coachman,' said the mask drily.

The blood which rushed from the heart of O'Brien, crimsoned his face.

'Oh! these duchesses,' cried the mask, with a gurgling laugh, which fell upon the ear like trickling water – 'these idol mios, with souls as warm as their suns, these bel tirannos, who alone know how to love, and lead the youth of colder climes a dance from Florence to Rome, on an absence without leave; getting them cited before courts-martial, and sent to lay siege, not to the hearts of duchesses, but to the heights of Oczakow. *O Dio buono*, how often does man mistake his vanity for his susceptibility, and the gallantry of a woman of gallantry, for any thing but what it is!'

'If you mean to say, that man is every where the dupe of woman,' said O'Brien, in a tone of evident depression and pique, '*vous prêchez un converti;* I am not the one, heaven knows, to dispute the axiom, – as you, I suspect, are the person to establish the fact; that is, if you are not some gay creature of the element, who laughs at all human ties.'

'This is not the language you held in the garden of the Borghese,' said the mask reproachfully.

'No; but then you were all woman, soft, gracious, fanciful, and – '

'Credulous,' interrupted the mask.

'Not so credulous; since, either in doubt or in timidity, you failed in your appointment in the Santa Maria Maggiore on the following day.'

'I failed neither in doubt, nor in timidity, but in obedience.'

'Obedience! to whom could such a soul as yours submit?'

'To my master and to yours.'

'Mine! that is pleasant. I acknowledge no master.'

'Yes, yours, *il est, le fut, et le doit être.*'

'Love of course?'

'No, a more potent power (though, like love, blind) – necessity, the law of gods and men.'

'A bold doctrine,' said O'Brien, 'if meant philosophically; or do you mean it literally, that you are married.'

'Wedded,' she replied, with great energy, and raising her clasped hands with a graceful movement. 'Wedded by vows, which, if vows are to be regarded, no human power can break; and this, I swear by the altar on which those vows were pledged.'

'You have a doubt then on the subject?' said O'Brien significantly, and fascinated beyond all power to move his eyes from those which now met and replied to his.

'I have a doubt upon all things, and all subjects. I am a secret member of that much persecuted sect, whose creed is more hated than catholicism in Ireland, heresy in Rome, or truth everywhere.'

'And its name?'

'The I-don't-knows – for, observe, that to acknowledge ignorance has ever been deemed a crime. Believe what is absurd, – impossible; but believe, and assert, and dogmatize (*n'importe quoi*), and you will have partisans and protectors everywhere.'

'What an extraordinary creature!' said O'Brien. 'But when is this carnival imbroglio, begun nearly two years back, to come to its *éclaircissement?*'

'To-night, I fear,' said the mask, sighing.

'When and where?' cried O'Brien, breathless, from emotion.

'This will inform you,' replied the mask, drawing a sealed paper from her bosom.

O'Brien snatched it eagerly, and was about to break the seal.

'Not here, not now,' interrupted the mask, putting her hand eagerly upon his, and as suddenly retiring it. 'See, who approaches?'

O'Brien looked up. The Duke and Lady Knocklofty, who had danced down the interminable couples of the long set, were now approaching the sofa, to which O'Brien had been chained since his entrance. Every one rose as they advanced, and the masks rose also; and made way for them, where they had been seated. Lady Knocklofty and the duke took their places without ceremony: and O'Brien, in great confusion, not knowing whether to seek the notice of Lady Knocklofty, or to avoid it, – to move away, or to remain, – stood for a moment beside the sofa, where the masks had left him.

His characteristic and distinguished person, set off by a dress calculated to give it every advantage, probably, struck the duke; for he looked at him earnestly, and then whispered Lady Knocklofty. She replied almost aloud, 'I don't know at all. We are never very fastidious upon these occasions, where number, and not selection, is the object; and persons are sometimes invited under false impressions, who, perhaps, ought not to be here. Shall we join the duchess? I see her in the next room.' Taking the duke's arm, she arose, and moved through the opening crowd into an adjoining apartment.

With the deepest mortification, with pride wounded, with every sense of delicacy, of taste, of feeling, violated, O'Brien heard himself marked out as an unbidden and an unwelcome guest, as a person asked under false impressions; and he stood writhing under the agony of his humiliating obtrusion. What did all this mean? Whence this change in Lady Knocklofty's conduct, looks, and manner? was it the result of his expulsion? was it the terrible consequence of his blasted reputation? To her, at least (his hitherto supposed 'fancy's queen'), he stood guiltless. Was this, the explication of her *'qui me cherche me trouve?'* was this the protection she had promised him in all exigencies? He trembled with stifled vexation and annoyance. Now too, for the first time, he felt the isolation of his position in this gay, fantastic multitude. The penitent mask had so surrounded him with her spells, that he had hitherto seen nothing beyond the range of her magic circle. Now the charm was broken, and he was alone, in the most fearful sense of the word, – alone in a crowd. His first impulse was again to seek the sybil, whose mysterious leaf still trembled in his hand; the next was, to consult its oracular contents. He looked on the seal as he was about to break it: its motto struck him. It was his own *'Vigueur de dessus.'* He hurried with the paper to an empty room on his left, and read, as follows:-

'If the most unfortunate of parents has yet a place in the heart of a wayward child, Murrogh O'Brien will hasten to the burying ground of the Hospital-fields, near the ruins of O'Brien House; where, by a newmade grave, at the foot of the square tower, he will meet the houseless mendicant, his charity this night sought to relieve by the donation of the inclosed.

'ARRANMORE'

The inclosed was the gold coin, bestowed on the beggar in the court of the Tailor's Hall; and that begger was – a deadly sickness came over O'Brien, at the bare suspicion – that beggar was his father! The revulsion of thought and feeling this horrible fact occasioned, was accompanied by an intolerable sensation of pain in his head and eyes, with a dizziness that obliged him for a minute to support himself on the chimney, near which he stood; and again, as his dazzled sight reverted to the terrible letter, written in his father's well known hand, the big drops gathered on his forehead, and fell upon the paper. While he still read, the *pendule* on the marble chimney piece struck twelve. There was not a moment to lose, not one to seek for the strange mysterious bearer of this letter; if indeed she might yet be found. But of her, not a second thought occurred. Pity, the most overwhelming of human sentiments, while it endures, pity for a father, who, if not more than miserable, was scarcely less than mad, took possession of every thought; not unmixed with a remorse, which, if exaggerated, was not wholly unfounded.

Hurrying from the Circe bowers (so opposed to the scene he was about to seek), with a precipitancy wild as his thoughts, he sprang into a hackney coach, and drove to the masquerade shop, where he took off his dress. Resuming his hat and coat, and discharging the carriage, he proceeded on foot to the Hospital-fields.

# CHAPTER IV

●

## *The Hospital Fields*

What is he, whose grief
Bears such an emphasis! Whose phrase of sorrow
conjures the wandering stars?

IT was already 'the dead watch and middle of the night,' when
O'Brien, having passed through the streets and lanes on the south
side of the Liffey, found himself in one of the most dreary and ruinous
suburbs of the Irish capital. Swamps and wilds to the left, were edged
with dilapidated buildings, the more melancholy in their aspect, when
a glimmer of light, issuing from a broken pane, gave indication that
there some victim of wretchedness had retired to die. To the right
appeared the then neglected banks of the river, with the high walls of
the various hospitals (the refuge for every infirmity, from the mental
aberration, for which Swift had here provided, in a dreadfully
prophetic spirit, to the most loathsome of bodily inflictions). One dark
mass, frowning and terrible above all, for a moment fixed his eye, and
arrested his steps, – the state prison of Kilmainham: and never under
the iron sceptre of the direst despotism, had power, trembling in its
strongest holds, erected a more fearful image of coercion, to supply
the influence of a wholesome and pacifying legislation. O'Brien shuddered, and passed on. A narrow, rutty lane to the right, led to the
open cemetery of the Hospital-fields. A hurry of thought, a flutter of
feeling, a feverish velocity in all the vital and moral functions of his
being, left him incapable of thought or reflection, of inference or
conjecture. In the course of his gloomy and devious route, all that
had occurred in this most eventful day, his trial, expulsion, initiation
at the club of United Irishmen, the scenes at Knocklofty House, the

sybil mask, came and went, like confused and fearful phantoms, over the surface of his imagination. But all these spectral reminiscences vanished as he entered the churchyard, the sad receptacle of posthumous wretchedness, where the earth is permitted gratuitously to receive those in death, whom it could not support in life. He plunged on through its long, rank grass, and plashy soil, over those garlanded monuments and intermingled tombs of departed indigence, which the pauper pride of surviving misery had decorated with paper crosses, and faded flowers. One 'bright particular star' shone steadily above the ruinous tower described by Lord Arranmore, and one dark unfilled grave yawned beneath it. This, then, was the appointed rendezvous.

O'Brien was already near it, and he paused for breath and force to proceed. Perceiving a human figure under the broken archway of the tower, he advanced a few steps; when a sudden thought of danger flashed on him like lightning. He was unarmed, and utterly defence-less; but he called in a firm tone, 'Who stands there?'

'Murrogh,' replied a broken, plaintive, and well known voice.

'My father!' he exclaimed; and the next moment he would have been in his father's arms, but that Lord Arranmore held him off with trembling hands, and looked on him fixedly, fondly, yet with a fearful and haggard wildness.

'Do you not recognize me, my dear father?' said O'Brien, almost suffocated with emotion: 'Do you not know me?'

'Know you!' said Lord Arranmore, still holding him off, '*heu mihi, Jesu!* know you!'

'Am I not your son, your own and only son?' exclaimed O'Brien, inarticulate from the agony of his feelings, as he grasped his father's hands, and pressed them to his eyes and forehead. Lord Arranmore's countenance, faint as was the light by which it was seen, was so changed, so haggard, and so sad, as to render him scarcely recogniz-able; and even the garments he wore might have passed on a heated imagination for the shreds and patches of mendicity. O'Brien could not proceed. His hot tears fell fast on his father's hands. After a pause, in which the old man seemed to gather force of mind and clearness of apprehension, he at length spoke.

'Murrogh, shed no tears for me, my son; but weep for yourself. My course is run, my sacrifice is accomplished, is accepted, through the merits of Him, who has suffered for the sins of all; and who has not rejected the offering of a broken and contrite heart.' He paused and threw up his eyes with an awful expression, as one occupied in mental prayer, and then continued: – 'The cup of bitterness has passed from me; but it rests in your hands. You have yet to drain it to the dregs; for the unredeemed curse of the church you have abandoned, and would persecute, – the curse, drawn down on your race, by him who betrayed his king, and slew the Lord's anointed, is still upon your young head, like the cloud that muffles the thunderbolt.'

'My dearest father!' said O'Brien, terrified at this denunciation, and at the aberration of mind which evidently produced it, 'What is it you mean? what curse do you – '

'What do I mean!' reiterated Lord Arranmore, releasing his hands from the grasp of his son. 'Rebel! Atheist! false to your king and God, worthy descendant of O'Brien the "Incendiary," – I disown you – I cast you off. You have blasted my hopes, and broken my heart; you have linked yourself with the enemies of me and mine, and are unworthy of the name you bear, and the blood that flows in your veins.'

O'Brien had long observed a change in the manners as well as person of his father; whose mode of speaking, whose very tone and accent were within the last few months much altered. He had, however, never been so much struck with the total transmutation of his parent's personal appearance, as now: and he could only answer to this wild and incoherent accusation, in a confusion of feeling, that rendered him almost as unconnected as the unfortunate parent he addressed.

'My dear, dear father,' he said, 'by whatever impressions or prejudices you are now judging me, I beseech you reserve them for another time. Consider me now, as I am, the most devoted, the most attached of sons; ready for any sacrifice, for any effort you dictate; ready to labour, to suffer, to live, to die for you; only be calm, be confident: all may yet be well. Let me, I beseech, lead you from this horrible place; its awful dreariness affects you; the very air is pestilential. We tread on human dust, we breathe an infected atmosphere. Accept of the support which nature has provided for you; drive me not from you, let me lead you home.'

'Home,' said Lord Arranmore, in a deep despairing tone, 'I have no home, I am this night homeless, houseless.'

'Gracious God!' exclaimed O'Brien, in a voice of agony, expressive of his harrowed feelings; and throwing his arms round his father, while he supported him in their fold, and sobbed upon his bosom.

With a convulsive pressure, that seemed the victory of some natural emotion over a concerted and bidden restraint, and with a vigour more borrowed from a strength of feeling than from physical force, Lord Arranmore drew his son to his heart. 'You love your poor old father, then,' he said at last in a tone of heart-breaking pathos.

'Love him! Oh God!'

'You will not, then, abandon him?'

'Did I ever? Was it not you, my dearest father, who, wrapped up in mystery, have so long left me a prey to the most melancholy conjectures.'

'Oh, Murrogh, Murrogh!' interrupted Lord Arranmore, more collectedly than he had yet spoken, 'there is, I fear, between you and me, a gulf, which neither of us can pass in this world; and in the next, my son, I fear we are parted eternally.'

'I would not believe it for a thousand worlds,' said O'Brien, now firmly convinced that his father was worked upon by some unknown influence, some mystery, as yet impenetrable. 'So far from that, again restored to you, even here, in this desolate and mortal Golgotha, I feel a joy that is inexpressible; differing, as we have ever done, upon particular opinions' (Lord Arranmore sighed almost to a groan), 'with views as opposed as our age and breeding – but of this at a more apposite time – still the ties of filial respect and tenderness have never loosed from my heart. No change of place or circumstance, neither distance nor time, has absolved or weakened them. Confide then in your child, your only son; let us leave this dreadful place; and,' he added, in a soft soothing voice, and scriptural language, 'thy home shall be my home, and thy God my God.'

Lord Arranmore started. 'Do you say this, Murrogh, from your heart? Will you now, seduced as you have been, bewitched as you are at this moment, will you leave, and for me? There is – there has been a shelter offered to your desolate and houseless father, to save his grey hairs from descending with sorrow to the grave, – to such a grave as this, which else must soon receive him.'

O'Brien shuddered, and endeavoured gently to lead him away; but in vain.

'Would you,' said Lord Arranmore, 'save from the shame of a pauper's grave the descendant of the princes of Arran, and the representative of those whose ashes sleep beneath the Druid's cromlech and the saint's altars, whose bones moulder in the consecrated earth of Dun Ængus? Would you now fly with me, where a refuge, safe and calm, honourable and holy, is prepared for me, while I yet live; and when the hour comes, now so near, when the last of the chiefs of Arran, worthy of the glorious heritage, shall descend to the tombs of his ancestors, in the isles strewed with their bones, he will go, borne on the necks of his people. The dust, blessed by St Ængus, shall still be spread over him; and his body shall sink to the narrow house, amidst the *chree* of his clan; while his soul shall ascend, through faith, to his Redeemer.'

'Good God,' interrupted O'Brien, worked upon by images, to which his spirits lent themselves but too aptly, 'I cannot bear this – hear me, I beseech you.'

'No,' said Lord Arranmore, with vehemence, 'I will hear only your assent or refusal. For you I will forfeit all – again looking on you, my son, my soul returns to you – again united, we part no more; and if you come not with me, where, for the little time I have yet to breathe and suffer, ere I go where the wicked man ceases from troubling, and the weary may be at rest, I shall remain here, to share your fate and to meet my own.'

'Let me but lead you away,' said O'Brien, in the fullest excitement of extreme wretchedness, and momentarily more struck by his father's attenuated and changed appearance. 'Let me but lead you from the inclemency of this night and the horrors of this place, and I will agree to any proposition that can ease your mind or calm your spirits, and give you confidence in the devotion of your son.'

'Then,' said Lord Arranmore, after a moment's pause, and an effort to collect himself, while he permitted his son to assist him over the graves and mounds, 'know that the ruin of your father's fortunes is imaged in the fall of the last roof he could call his own. All honour, hope, and maintenance are laid in the dust. He has done with the world, but for the tie that keeps him there, through you. Houseless, homeless, pennyless, there is yet a congregation of good and holy men, ready to receive and place him beyond the reach of the prison, that now awaits him: and there are revenues, which, for religion's sake, and inapplicable to all other purposes, will suffice to redeem him from the fangs of his creditors, – from the worldly evils that beset him on every side. While.... but this is not the time or place for further explanation. Murrogh, it is you, that have been opposed to my worldly and eternal safety. I cannot quit the world for ever, where you stand still exposed, the last branch of the tree of Maghadoire,[1] severed from its ancient stem, and left to the blast and whirlwind, its bloom withered, and its young buds scattered: I ought not to remain in it. Oh! Murrogh, Murrogh, the heart of the father, wilful and sinful, forgets its God, for the sake of the child, which he has given in his goodness or in his wrath. On the road to salvation, I pause; and drawn back to the world you inhabit, my heart still pants for you, to see you, to commune with you, to warn, to bless you, to part from you no more.'

He fell, overpowered, into the arms extended to receive him.

'Nor shall we part, my dear father,' said O'Brien. 'Had we the means of departure, even now I would fly with you, succour, protect you; and having consigned you in safety to those friends who offer you their shelter, return only to this working-day world, to earn the means of an honest and honourable existence, for us both.'

'The opportunity of departure,' said Lord Arranmore, in a hesitating voice, 'is not wanting. I cannot now enter upon a long and sorrowful story. Time presses. For three months, I have been baited, hunted, persecuted. I have also, by God's grace and his blessed Mother's, voluntarily endured much. But I am escaping from the toils; and this night, – even here, within a few paces, means of escape are provided.'

'Indeed!' said O'Brien, struck by this information, which so ill agreed with his father's destitute condition. But he in vain endeavoured to collect his thoughts: they every moment were becoming less coherent and less within his control; as a numbing and stupefying pain in his head, increased to agony. 'This is strange, is fortunate. Yesterday I learned at your lawyer's, that some relative, some foreign ecclesiastic, had come forward to arrange with your creditors; and this night I found a letter in my room with a bill, a bank bill. You have some powerful agent too; and with such an agent, I do not understand, at least I would willingly believe that a misery so unsupportable was – but my thoughts are so confused, I know not what I say.'

He paused: and Lord Arranmore replied quickly, 'I have no agent but Shane-na-Brien, himself a hunted out-law.'

'Gracious heavens! is that possible! and where is he now?'

'Safe now, I trust,' said Lord Arranmore; 'but my hour is come.'

He put up his finger, as one in the act of listening; and O'Brien at

[1] An old oak, under which the chiefs of the O'Brien family were inaugurated.

that moment heard a carriage drawing up to the entrance of the cemetery.

'Murrogh,' said his father, trembling violently under some agitating contest of feeling, 'Murrogh, judge for me; judge for your unfortunate father. Save me in this world and the next. I will not, I cannot again part from you.'

'I will attend you, Sir, whatever may be the consequence, whatever the nature of this mystery. My mind is just now terribly confused, I have gone through so much within the last four-and-twenty hours; but I feel that in following your fortunes, and my own sentiments, I am acting well.'

He articulated with difficulty, as he endeavoured to collect and arrange his scattered ideas. They had now reached the gate of the burying-ground, the carriage had drawn close to it, and the door was opened by one, who appeared to be the driver, and who alighted for the purpose.

'I will attend you, Sir,' said O'Brien, mechanically; seeing that his father still hesitated, and putting his hand to his head, he added, 'I will at least convey you safely to your friends.'

Lord Arranmore motioned him to enter. He sprang into the carriage; and his father, having given an order, in a low voice, to the driver, followed. The door was shut, the blinds were drawn up, and the carriage drove off, – at first, slowly, over the rutted road: then stopping for a few moments, it proceeded with a velocity, scarcely noticed by its younger occupant.

With folded arms, and a drooping head, – vanquished by agony of mind and body, by inordinate fatigue and exhaustion of all the faculties, physical and moral, – he lapsed into that disturbed, but absorbing slumber, which vibrates between insensibility and delirium. He had felt that something more than a moral *mal-aise* hung over him. He felt it in the pulsations of his aching head, in flushes of perturbation, and in sinkings of the heart. He had felt this, in fainter symptoms, since the night of the fall of Arranmore House; but he had, as it were, put it off. He had not 'leisure to be ill;' and, for an interval, moral energy had kept physical infirmity in abeyance. But on entering the carriage, his oppression had amounted almost to suffocation; and he had been compelled to let down the glass of the window beside him. The fresh air of the country came like balm on his senses: and the regular breathing of his father giving indication that sleep had closed on his sufferings, and forbad further conversation, he permitted the refreshing, but dangerous coolness of the night breeze, gradually to overcome the feverish agitation of his thoughts; and he sunk into forgetfulness, if not into repose.

Starting from many a broken vision, disjointed and made up of wild and incoherent images, he frequently put forth his hand, to ascertain that his father was still beside him; and this conviction being obtained, he endeavoured to connect his ideas, and to turn his thoughts to all that had recently occurred. But Lord Walter, the extraordinary, the tantalizing mask, the office he had accepted in the Society of the Union, his expulsion, his present strange situation, his father's ruin, the fall of the old house, the unlooked for re-appearance of Shane-na-Brien on the scene of life, and in the particular business of his own especial interests, mingled together, and confused imagination to delirium. Horses were changed, and daylight had broken, and the ancient and venerable town of Athenry was reached; and still, life was to him almost as if it were not.

# CHAPTER V

———————•———————

## *The Abbey of Cong*

A lowly roof, a shed
With hairy moss and winding ivy spread,
Honest enough to hide an humble hermit's head.

DRYDEN – *Hind and Panther.*

WHEN the learned orientalist and enterprizing traveller, Richard Pocoke, had overrun the east, 'to Aleppo gone,' and visited Palestine and Syria, and Jerusalem and Mesopotamia, and Candia, and Cyprus, and Giuret on the Nile, – regions belonging then only to antique fable (for space and time had not, according to the lover's wish, as yet been annihilated, by steam-boats and grasshopper-springs), he completed the measure of his life's vicissitudes by terminating his wanderings in the obscure solitudes of an Irish province; and he reposed from his labours in the purple indolence of the Irish prelacy. In reviewing the different scenes he had visited, and comparing Mount Calvary with the Scottish Dingwall, the Bishop of Elphin was wont to add – 'And yet there is a spot in Ireland, that comprizes within its verge more of the loftier features of picturesque beauty, than any once scenic combination I saw in the course of my oriental travels.' The spot alluded to was an accidental elevation, in the neighbourhood of Cong, a decayed village on the borders of Mayo and Galway; and the 'scenic combinations' were the ruins of its ancient abbey, that bathes its delicate reflections of gable and tower in the beautiful river, which runs in liquid silver beneath its walls. Its druidical monument, once revered as 'the great Cællagh'[1] of anti-christian times, – its antique

---

[1] Cællagh, – a stone, – the *caillou* of the French.

bridge, – the green rich soil, speckled by clumps of white rock, looking like Turkish tombs, – and the gushing springs bursting forth from their subterraneous caverns (to which they return by other cavities), formed the foreground of the picture; while the blue waters of Loughs Corrib and Mask, with their wooded islands and winding shores, and the stupendous mountains of Connemara, Morisk, and Mayo, broken into tumultuous disorder, and admitting through the intervals of their 'cloud-capped' heads, views of the great Atlantic, filled up the distance, and completed a scene, well worthy of the eulogium of the travelled Bishop.

This site had early attracted the attention of both church and state, by its loveliness and fertility. Here the kings of Connaught fixed their residence so early as the sixth century; and here St Fechan, the director of the conscience of Donald, supreme King of Ireland, erected, in the succeeding age, his magnificent monastery for regular canons, under the invocation of the Virgin Mary; which the rich donations of his royal penitent rendered one of the wealthiest and most beautiful of the ecclesiastical establishments in the island of Saints.

The regular canons of Cong, like those of the neighbouring monastery of Headfort, became wealthy by the commerce they carried on between the interior country and the coast; – as they were powerful from the rank of many of their royal members: and their abbots, princes palatine, held their place in those rude parliaments, where all came armed, from the heel to the neck, and prepared for other contests than those 'keen encounters of the wits,' which bring the members of modern senates into the lists of fierce, but bloodless discussion.

Thus richly endowed and influential, the Abbot of Cong became a proverbial type of all honour, wealth, and prosperity; and 'not for the Abbey of Cong,' or 'not to be made abbot,' was an appeal to probity, which testified that the asserter of his own powers of resistance was beyond the reach of all human temptation.[1] Forms persecuted did not extinguish the spirit which originated them; and though the Abbey of

[1] Saint Colgan, speaking of the Irish saints and monasteries, says, 'All that is reported of their numbers, will scarcely in after times be credited;' and though they had much diminished in the time of Henry the Eighth, so that only four hundred regular monasteries were found in Ireland, at the period of the supposed suppression of such establishments, yet there was scarcely a secular benefice, or even the poorest parish, that had not, in its origin, maintained a community of monks or nuns.

Cong (a model of the finest ecclesiastical architecture in Ireland), was left to moulder in premature ruin, and the tithes and lands, which supported its altars and its monks, went to support other monks, as useless to the community as those thus summarily dispossessed, – still from century to century the order was kept up, within some nook of its ruined walls, by one or two successive members; the elder of whom continued to be venerated by the catholic peasantry of the surrounding district, as the Abbot of Cong.

As, however, the monastery mouldered into untenantable ruin, beautifying as it fell, the Abbot and his one or two brethren (poor and lowly, patient and suffering as they were), were obliged to yield their ancient tenement to the owl that sheltered beneath its Saxon arches, and the bat that flitted through its beautiful cloisters.

But when, thus banished, the Abbot and his solitary brethren betook themselves to a little fabric, aided by the piety of the poor, out of the rubbish of the Abbey ruins, they excited no attention, and provoked no persecution; at a time even when the law of the land was most rigorous against regulars of all denominations. By degrees the Abbot's house, as it was called, assumed a better appearance. A chimney to emit smoke, and a glazed window to admit light with other tokens of mundanity, announced a better state of financial affairs, and an increase of oblations and voluntary offerings, – to the diminution of the revenue of the parish priest. Still the protestant rector of Cong (who was building his own comfortable house, by carrying off and appropriating some of the finest druidical monuments, the remains of which are still to be seen near the Abbey) did not think the 'church was in danger.'

It happened, however, about the same epoch, at which General Count O'Flaherty had re-edified the Abbey of Moycullen, in a manner the least edifying, by a conjunction of the cells and cloisters of St Bridget, with pavilions worthy of Epicurus, the Abbot's house underwent a transmutation, scarcely less striking than that, which covered the rude walls of the Santa Casa of Loretto, with gold and gems. The miserable house rose into a commodious and spacious dwelling. Although rapidly, and therefore slightly raised, and destined to be long survived by the ruins out of which it had sprung, it assumed a Gothic form and outline, which gave it an antiquated and massive air; and its little chapel had borrowed so largely from the cloisters and pointed windows of the abbey, that it looked like a prolongation, or rather well proportioned parcel of the original building. Even the altar-piece, which had been hung upside down by the rustic artificers employed to place it, would have revealed to the amazed eyes of a *cognoscente*, had any such then visited the village of Cong, a *replico* of the beautiful holy family of Annibal Caracci, of the Florence Gallery. This humble attempt to raise the once puissant establishment of regulars was ascribed to some foreign ecclesiastic, who, visiting Cong on a journey into Connemara, had been struck by the beauty of the place, and shocked at the sacrilegious neglect of one of the finest ecclesiastical ruins in Ireland; and the donation he had made to the community, was followed up by others. The plan of the Abbot's new house was attributed to one of the most distinguished members of the Royal Irish Academy, Baron O'Brien, afterwards Lord Arranmore. Notwithstanding the notoriety of these proceedings, and the visible improvement in the condition of the establishment, no show of molestation was offered by the church by law established, until one of its rural Boulters and Stones took exception at the Abbot's availing himself of a neglected salmon weir, which had belonged to his predecessors in the reign of Henry the Seventh, and which conveyed the fish alive into the cistern of the abbey kitchen from the stream. The whole artillery of the penals was then brought to bear against the community, and the order was once more dispersed, as in the time of Henry the Eighth.

The house and its pretty garden, however, remained; and it was kept in preservation, and inhabited by an old man and his wife, – the reputed proprietor living abroad. After a time, it was again occupied, by two or three respectable, middle-aged gentlemen, whose number gradually increased; but whose quiet, unobtrusive congregation excited neither suspicion nor alarm. They were known as constituting one of those confraternities, then and now so numerous in Ireland, whose members, in disgust with the world, or in love of solitude, live in community for the performance of religious practices.

At first, nameless and unconspicuous, these associates were called, 'the religious gentlemen of Cong;' and living in strict retreat, they were known only by the good they did; for they were charitable and alms-giving, and being of all professions, they applied their skill and acquirements to relieve the various ills to which the unaccommodated wretchedness of the Irish peasant stands every where exposed. Their medicine chest supplied the place of those excellent dispensaries, which, of late years, have become so general and so beneficial in Ireland. Their kitchen distributed soups, such as the Abbey refectory, in former times, dispensed to the crowding applicants. The garden teemed with simples, sovereign in every malady; and one of the members, a surgeon, superseded all the bone-setters and wise women in the country. Their paddock, which at first only fed the mule that drew their market-cart, gradually became a field; and the field grew into a farm, which in time became the source of new-light agriculture to the scollogs and middle-men of the neighbourhood: and their chapel, in consequence of the admirable preaching of a young Franciscan, who had left the convent of his order, to unite himself with the confraternity, became so much too small for the congregation, that they were obliged to raise the roof, and add a gallery round the choir.

Their affluence, from whatever sources it sprang, gained them consideration among the 'estated gentlemen' of the province; and the *suaviter in modo* of some few of the members, and the *bonhomie* of all, procured them a certain respect and good-will from the inhabitants of the neighbourhood; which was not a little increased by their occasional, though always accidental, hospitality. Though they paid no visits, they were always pleased to receive them; and though they accepted no invitations (never sleeping or eating from under their own roof), they gave them constantly and kindly to such gentlemen as came from Tuam or Ballinrobe, from their castles in Lough Corrib, or their mansions in the mountains of Galway.

Their fare, though served upon coarse, but snowy linen, and on plain yellow delf, constituted a *menu* that often startled the palates of the Connaught gourmands, *Matelottes d'anguille*, which changed the mud eels of Cong to the savour of those of St Cloud: *truites à la maître d'hôtel*, which confounded the peculiarities of the red trout of Corrib, and the white of Mask; with *soupes maigres*, which might fatten the ribs of abstinence itself, gave a new species of reputation to the community. The report even went, that their cook was a Frenchman; and that toleration, at first refused to their dogmas, was now implicitly yielded to their dinners. The bluest protestants in Galway, the most kiln-dried high churchman of Mayo, were but little inclined to persecute men 'whose port they liked.' The creed of these Reverend Amphitryons stuck not in the throats of those who swilled their claret; and the protestant Bishop of the diocese even expressed a wish to examine the tenets and the table of a confraternity, whose pastry almost excused their popery: for they had sent him a Perigord pie, which might have driven him (had the book then been in existence) to parody the remark in the *Almanach des Gourmands*, and to have said, '*Ainsi cuit, on auraît mangè le Pape.*'

It soon became the fashion of the most orthodox tables to toast the Abbot of Cong; an appellation, however, which, when applied to the superior of the confraternity, he constantly refused; – with the observation, that it would have been well for the christian world, had there never been any more powerful abbots, or more wealthy orders, than himself, and the little community over which he was but as an elder brother: a community, whose members, like the first congregated ascetics of the church, were neither separated from the world by vows, nor led into it by ambition; but who retired to live in purity, to love God above all things, and their neighbours as themselves.

When he had first mentioned the name of his confraternity, he replied to the inquiries made concerning it, that it was a peculiar *culte* of the catholic church, newly established in Italy, in honour of that sacred heart, which had beaten in human sympathy with human suffering.

Profound as was the retreat of the religious gentlemen of Cong, and inofficious as were their habits, they still appeared to have 'views on this side heaven;' or at least ties and interests, which were not all centred in the remote and romantic site to which they had retired. The community, or some one individual among them, had obtained the superintendence of a large tract of bog and mountain in Jar Connaught, including the ample ruins and fertile valley of Moycullen; which, scarce a day's journey, by land or lake, from their own retreat, was looked to with all the care, and worked with all the skill of a favourite domestic farm. There were also within the last two years certain '*allées et venues*,' of the brethren, which passed not without remark; and the little post-house of the village was put into almost daily requisition, for letters of foreign mark, and heavy postage, directed to the reverend gentleman at the head of the society. The arrival also of a very aged, but most singular and distinguished looking ecclesiastic, whose dress and air bespoke his rank, excited considerable sensation in the neighbourhood; from the circumstance of his being accompanied by two females, who were lodged at the old inn at the foot of the bridge, kept from the remotest times by the Betaghs or hereditary innkeepers of Ireland; though now so rarely frequented, as to make the event a marvel.

The ecclesiastic himself was lodged in the best room of the retreat, and served with a respect and reverence by all the brotherhood, in his occasional visits, which the titular archbishop of the province never exacted or received. The females were understood to be foreign nuns; for they were habited like Miss Joyce of Balintogher, and Miss O'Kelly of Ballinrobe, who, on the dissolution of the French monasteries, had returned to their people, for the purpose of being installed in some of the Galway or Tuam nunneries. They had remained but two days at Pat Betagh's, and had passed their time in sketching among the ruins and caves of Cong, and in stringing an old Irish harp, which had lain in a corner of Pat Betagh's best parlour for ten years. It had been deposited there as a pledge for whiskey drunk, beyond the means of the Irish muse to pay for: and as Rory Cormack, the blind harper, had been drowned on the very night of the deposit, in Lough Corrib, he had consequently never redeemed it. The religious but musical ladies found no difficulty in purchasing this harp; and when they took their departure with their venerable companion, they embarked on Lough Corrib with the instrument, a portfolio of drawings, and one of the religious gentlemen of the confraternity.

Something more than a year had elapsed, since this notable event, which had supplied the tea table, as by law established, in the parlour of the Rev. Mrs Ginkle (the rector's wife), with exhaustless sources of surmise and suspicion, when another arrival at the porch of the retreat, announced by the braying of every cur in the village, gave renewed vigour to the gossiping curiosity of the neighbourhood. A report was spread that the chaise and four, whose rattle over the Irish pavement of the main street had no less disturbed the equanimity of the cater-wauling, than it had of the canine population, had contained a maniac and his keeper, and that the former had been instantly consigned with much mystery to the hospital room of the retreat: it was moreover added, that the second personage never left that room, till carried from it in a state as dangerous, as that of the patient he had watched.

The physician from Tuam, who had been called in to assist the medical brother of the congregation, told another story; of which Mrs Ginkle believed as much as it pleased her prejudices to credit. He stated that a young gentleman, travelling into Connaught with his father, had been seized with a delirious fever on the road, in a wretched village between Athenry and Cong; and that, in utter hope-lessness of all medical aid, or necessary assistance, the anxious parent had pushed on with his charge, to profit by the skill, benevolence, and known hospitality of the confraternity, in the hope of shelter, and

of that aid which had already worked marvels in the country, not
always referred to the science of Podalirius and Machaon.

The elder gentleman was Lord Arranmore, and the unfortunate
invalid his son, the Honourable Murrogh O'Brien. The malady had
raged with a fierceness, which by no means turned out to be 'prophetic
of its end.' For three weeks, the fever had continued unabated; and
the alienation of mind was complete: on the beginning of the fourth
week, when some amendment was visible, the unhappy father (fevered
and delirious almost as the object of a solicitude, that seemed tinged
by the agony of remorse), himself sickened, and was unable to continue
his office. Stretched on his mortal couch, his physician discovered
that the noble patient was a member of some rigid order of penitents;
for he bore upon his person all the testimonials of the extremest
austerity, a shirt of hair-cloth, a girdle of rope, a discipline of sharp
infliction, and an iron cross, whose impression had sunk into his
bosom.

\* \* \* \* \*

It was towards the close of the glowing evening of one of those warm
summer's days, in Ireland so fine, so few, and far between, that the
sun, as it sunk in clouds of gold, lighted every casement in the front
of the Retreat of Cong. A long level ray of crimson brilliancy streamed
on the half-drawn curtain of the hospital room, which had been
thrown back to admit the air, and fell with peculiar effect upon the
head of one, who slept upon the raised pillows of the bed. Colourless
as Parian marble, with an expression of that pain, which had left its
impress on every feature, it was the head of Prometheus, by Salvator
Rosa. A painter's or a sculptor's eye would have dwelt with insatiate
delight on a subject which presented to either art so noble a study.
No eye save that of a simple sister of charity (one of those beneficent
beings, who, in Ireland, as elsewhere, are to be met, wherever suffering
humanity may need their assistance), now gazed on it. Dressed in the
sombre habit of her vocation, and holding back the curtain of the bed
with one hand, her figure and attitude placed in deep shadow, and
opposed to the glare of bright light which fell upon the head of the
sufferer, completed a picture, belonging to other climes and other
combinations than those, under which this singular group now
appeared.

A movement, scarcely perceptible, that passed over the face of the
sleeping invalid, displaced the principal figure in this living picture.

The curtain fell gently from the hand of the *sœur grise*, and she glided with a noiseless step out of the room, as another female entered it. This was a coarse and homely person, of middle age, dressed in the costume of the Galway peasant. The importance of a nurse was marked in her strong Irish features. Her hands were laden with the drink, which she was about to place on a little table in the corner of the room, when a low and mournful sound, that seemed to swell and die upon the air, caught her ear; and suddenly, but softly, dropping on her knees, she crossed herself and prayed. She then approached the open casement, and, after a moment, again drew in her head, and hurried away, as if urged by curiosity to inquire into the cause of some interesting and striking effect.

Meantime, as the sounds were repeated, they rose in deeper sadness, at measured intervals, and died away in sobs of more audible grief; till, in their nearer approach, they evidently awakened consciousness in the sleeping sufferer. At first, mingling with the gracious dream, which accompanies the first calm sleep of convalescence, they harmonized with its placid and soothing sensations. He thought them the blessed sounds which issued from the lips of ministering angels; but as consciousness grew stronger, and sense and reason, for the first time during a long period, awoke together, the wild and unearthly tones struck strange and unwonted upon his ear; and they caused a powerful effort at inference and combination, to enable him to ascertain the circumstances of his actual position. The effort, however, was too arduous and painful; and scarcely moving his raised head, he turned his eye towards the casement, through which the sounds were admitted, upon the sweet, soft air, that fanned his feverish temples. His feeble gaze grew stronger, as the light faded into a more sober tone; and the scene on which it rested spoke a doctrine to the sick or dying, beyond all the holy brotherhood of the *Ben Morire* ever impressed by smoke of torch and sound of bell. A brilliant rainbow hung its arch in the heavens, and spanned a scene beneath of as much beauty and sublimity as ever displayed the magnificence of the Creator. Lakes, and hills, and mountains, brightening into gay confusion, or fading into aërial tints, in the remoter distance – the full glory of the setting sun falling upon all – all looked as on the evening of the seventh day, when God, resting from his labour, saw that it was good.

The invalid stretched forth his languid glance on the scene, which the position of his couch enabled him to command; and he looked upon its loveliness, as the long suffering look upon nature in her freshness and beauty, with sensations not dearly purchased by their privations and pain.

But again that mournful cry chilled his susceptible spirits, which responded but faintly and vaguely to impressions so new and unaccustomed. The brightest external objects fail to produce their exhilarating effects, ere returning health strengthens the organs for their reception. As he gazed and listened, he perceived a train of persons moving slowly and processionally round an old stone cross, that stood at some distance, directly opposite the casement of the chamber. The sad cry, which was again half uttered, was suddenly suspended and broke into a faint murmur, as if by some abrupt and imperative command, that checked the lamentation for the dead, lest it should affect the living.

The slowly returning memory of the invalid recalled in this hullaloo the choral burden of the *caoine*, or Irish death cry, as raised in the province of Connaught; and in the movement round the cross he recognized a superstitious ceremony, practised every where, in Ireland, in conveying a body to the grave. The sound and sight did not serve to promote that exhilaration, which a slow convalescence was already bringing with it. In the course of a long and vicissitous disease, some suspensions of suffering had been accompanied with lucid intervals, and the clearing of his consciousness of all around him; and he now looked for forms that had then flitted about him, and cheered, or soothed, his frail existence, by care and kindness, or had agitated it by that restless anxiety which, while it more than shares the pain it cannot relieve, too frequently increases it. But the pale and haggard countenance of almost maniacal solicitude of him, who so often had drawn aside his curtain, and looked its anguish upon him, was now no longer near; neither was that stern brow of unsympathizing fortitude there, that was once seen to beetle over his pillow, in all the resignation, of aged insensibility; nor yet that phantom of charity, which flitted before his eyes, and confused his wandering fancy. All were now gone, and were replaced by the appearance of the homely person, who soon returned, as she had departed, muttering and praying in the low and mimic whine of the *Chree*, which had called her from her hired office, to inquire its subject.

'For whom is that death cry raised?' asked the invalid, almost startled at the unwonted coherence of his own ideas, and the perfect utterance of his own voice.

'Och, musha!' said the woman (a stranger but recently brought in, to relieve the attendant brother of the hospital, which, till the present occasion, had

> Ne'er by woman's foot been trod).

'Och, musha! sure the Keeners say 'tis the chief of the Clan Tiegs of Arranmore, who is gone to glory. But young father Francis has stopped the Chree and the Keeners, the greatest in the prowence; and there they are now going their last round, and the shular man, 'bove all, bearing the cross afore the corpse, and come in from the mountains, with the Connemara boys, to help the berrin down to the lake; and a fine berrin it is, and – '

She had now approached the bed, with the drink, which she had been busily preparing for her patient, against he should awaken; but he again lay as one in a deep slumber, his eyes closed, his lips compressed, and his colour deadly pale. When his medical attendants entered the room, they found him with a pulse that scarcely beat, and a breath that scarcely sullied the mirror presented to his lips. Nature had undergone some great revulsion, some terrible shock had been given to the nerves, through the feelings. That shock was the sudden announcement of a father's death, when the mind, all unstrung, was deprived of every energy, and unsupported by any principle of resistance to the overwhelming impression.

# CHAPTER VI

———•———

## *The Confraternity*

C'est pousser la politesse bien loin, que de se faire aimer de ceux qu'on outrage, et de savoir si bien porter les coups dont on les perce, qu'ils ne s'en aperçoivent point.

*Lettres Juives*, t.5, p. 386.

HAIL to the bright brief spring of human existence, in which care sits lightly, like clouds on a summer sky; from which sorrow flies fleetly, like mists on the morning breeze; and to which health returns with rapid revulsion, as the steel rebounds by its own elasticity, on the removal of a temporary pressure.

About three weeks from the death of the unfortunate Lord Arranmore, and on the morning of a fine July day, there sat, and thought, and wrote, in the deep embrasure of a bay window of the library of the confraternity, one who was the very personification of mental energy, rapt in the boldest dreams of speculative philosophy. An eye clear, full, and upturned, – high, intellectual, and unshaded temples, catching the ray of yellow light that struggled through the half drawn curtain, – the rich hectic hue of the blood propelled by thought over a cheek of marble paleness, – and a soul-illumined look, playing over a somewhat melancholy countenance, that 'o'er informed its tenement of clay,' combined to render the writer, as he sat in the happiest disposition of light and shade, habited in solemn black, and leaning on his elbow, one of those studies, which *virtu* has somewhat conventionally assigned to the exclusive execution of Rembrandt's inspired pencil. Who, in this fine form of intellectual life and physical energy, would have recognized the frail and feeble frame, which, three weeks before, lay struck in helpless alienation of mind on the couch of sickness? Yet such is youth, the all we know of the privileges of immortality. Such lately had been, and such now was Murrogh O'Brien. For the last four days of his convalescence, breathing the purest air, basking in the soft sunshine, gazing on the finest views, enjoying the most delightful of all sensations, a calm sequestration, with agreeable but not exciting society, surrounded by books, whose very external form rouses the mind of genius to meditation, O'Brien felt as one regenerated by probationary suffering; and with spirits the most genial, and ideas clear, distinct, and current, he employed the first days of his restoration to health on the subject, which in sickness and in health had lain nearest to his heart.

He had, while in college, begun a pamphlet 'On the State of Ireland;' and he was now occupied in finishing, revising, and clearing it off for the press. It was written with eloquence and enthusiasm, evincing that its author had felt more than he had thought on his subject. It was full of truths that were libels, and of general observations, personally applicable to certain obnoxious individuals in the council and the senate, whom popular indignation had already marked out for popular reprobation. It was honest and injudicious, and eminently perilous to the fearless writer; who, in the uncompromising probity of youth, saw only the end, and was careless of the means (as they affected himself) by which that end was to be attained.

O'Brien had already from his bed, and as soon as his hand could grasp a pen, written to Lord Walter, to account for his sudden departure, and his long silence as to its cause; and to renew his pledge to the band of well intentioned patriots, into whose service he promised to enter, as soon as his renovated health should render him capable of the mission they had honoured him with. He had been cheered by a kind, cordial, and immediate answer, full of expressions of confidence in his integrity, his honour, and devotion to the great cause, which, said Lord Walter, 'not even your Hegira or marvellous flight, under the protecting wing of Ignatius Loyola, could weaken or destroy. For I do believe that you are, at this moment, in the keeping of that warrior saint; and that your "amiable confraternity," of which you speak, is but a resuscitation of those once sovereign lords of the will and intellect of the human race, who did but follow the vocation that man has ever acknowledged, to rule and dupe his brother man.' O'Brien had more cogent reasons for believing what Lord Walter did but jocosely suggest. Yet for the moment, more amused than affected by the conviction, he willingly profited by his strange position.

From the epoch of his most singular *enlèvement* by his father, when under the influence of the strangest feelings, and excited by the feverish malady that was circulating in his veins, – from that moment when a delirious sleep and unconscious vigils had exposed him to the unwholesome airs and mists of night, his mind had been so feeble and confused, that he found an infinite difficulty in connecting his thoughts, or even in giving utterance to the solicitous curiosity, which perpetually prompted him to inquire from his father the mysterious circumstances of his recent unhappy life. One phantom, however, still floated perpetually before him, – the suspected agent of his father's wishes, the singular mask! But what he had asked concerning her, what his father had answered during the terrible night of their journey, or whether he had indeed made any inquiries, or received any satisfactory information, he could not now, even on his perfect recovery, recollect. The form of this person, who had pre-occupied his last conscious moments, had incessantly haunted him during his illness; and her voice, in a variety of languages, of tones, and inflexions, had sounded in his ears. Sometimes her image had taken the form of Lady Knocklofty, sometimes of a Sister of Charity, praying by his pillow. Sometimes, he thought he detected her in the garb of the nurse, of a priest, and of the superior of the Jesuits; for her ide best assorted with the wild incoherent images of a powerful fancy, relieved from all restraints of judgment and ratiocination.

The little information he had been enabled to acquire, or retain, of Lord Arranmore's fortunes, having been asked under feelings of more determined interest and upon more positive data, with which the passions and the imagination had nothing to do, had so well assorted with his previous knowledge of the order to which his father had bound himself body and soul (a fact he soon learned), that by inference and reflection on the concatenation of events, and by some information secretly given him by the physician who had attended his father in his last moments, he was enabled to draw a perfect conclusion, which led to the clearing up of the last act of Lord Arranmore's fitful life.

The early victim of a persecuting proselytism had abjured his enforced faith, connected as it was with the deepest wrongs and bitterest humiliations. Terence O'Brien, in his tenth year, the little sacristan of the mass cave, – in the vigour of his manhood, the protestant solicitor and high church partisan, – in his later life, had become a relapsed papist, and died in all the probationary martyrdom of a noviciate of the Jesuits. To the services of this order he had unconsciously been bound for the last twenty years, under the prevailing influence of his zealous and pertinacious uncle, the Abbate O'Brien, of Rome. To the services of this order he had been induced to devote his only son, from that period of his life, when dawning into adolescence, he exhibited such qualities as might render him an efficient and brilliant member of any society, and a support of any cause to which he should bring the full force of his natural endowments.

The first object of Lord Arranmore, under his relapsed principles, had been to separate his son from his protestant mother and aunts; and to have him secretly, but, as it were, accidentally, educated by the accomplished parish priest of Moycullen, the Abbé O'Flaherty. The retired habits of the Abbé, so displaced in the sphere to which obedience to the church had called him, had promoted the well concealed designs of his father, by removing the boy from the observation of the protestant authorities of St Grellan, until, to evade persecution in his own person, Terence O'Brien was obliged to enter his son a pupil of the diocesan school. Devoted by early oppression to perpetual evasion, Terence was himself a party to his son's flight to France, after the execution of his foster-brother, Shane-na-Brien. The supposed loss of her son broke his tender mother's heart; and this event drew, to its utmost tension, the remorseful bigotry of the proselyted, but still conforming father; and he resolved on expiating the self-attributed crime of his wife's death, by the offering of his child on the altar of religion, where, like Isaac, he lay bound and ready for immolation.

The keen perceptions of O'Brien's highly organized mind, in accordance with the strongest prejudices against Jesuitism instilled by his Jansenist preceptor, and with a deep sentiment in favour of religious reformation, implanted by his protestant mother, enabled him to break through the bonds, in which the zeal and intrigue of his father had involved him: and once convinced that he was completing his often interrupted education in a Jesuit institution, for Jesuit purposes, – with the boldness of a strong volition, he fled. Fortune, or his own high qualities, led him on through a changeful, but not undistinguished career. His strange destiny had given him the start of the home-bred youth, who ripens into maturity unpractised and undeveloped; subject to the influences of time, without the enjoyments and experience, which is alone purchaseable by bustling activity and arduous enterprise.

Saddened by the recollection of his father's evident prostration of mind, he was still soothed by the reflection that Lord Arranmore had derived gratification from the hope of extricating him from what he believed a perilous conspiracy with heretics and infidels (for such he had esteemed the protestant and presbyterian bands of reformists, which constituted the society of the United Irishmen). There was likewise another tie, which Lord Arranmore and the Abbate O'Brien had evidently wished to break, – a tie so vague, so undeveloped, so delicate, and (as O'Brien had thought) so unknown to all but his own thoughts, that he could not but wonder at the quick perception, secret information, and fastidious jealousy, with which it had been watched and thwarted. Nor could he comprehend, how that which was almost a secret to himself, should have been thus divined by two old men: in one of whom the sources of passion had been dried up from infancy, by a vocation, which had broken through all social ties; while the other, simple and credulous, and involved in temporal embarrassments and spiritual conflicts, must have had but little thought or time to start at a *liaison*, which had as yet led to nothing, and had perhaps already ended in bitter mortification and disappointment. Yet his confederacy with the United Irishmen, and his incipient predilection for the Countess Knocklofty, had been hinted at by the mysterious mask, who, he was almost convinced, acted in the service of his Jesuit relations. Who was she? a foreigner evidently, or one who had long lived in foreign lands; one who knew him personally, and who had twice sought him out, in Italy and in Ireland, and who had parted from him as lightly on each occasion, as she had met him, in fanciful mystery and careless pleasantry. If his father had known her, the secret had died with him; if she was known to his grand uncle, the secret was equally buried as if in the oblivion of the tomb. For though the Abbate O'Brien was then occupying the same dwelling with him, and was apparently the superior of the confraternity, to which his looks were laws, yet he held but little personal communication with any, nor suffered anything to transpire, but what he chose to impart; and that was so little, that O'Brien since his convalescence, had seen the awful old man but once, – when their intercourse was limited to a few cold inquiries after his health, and condolences on his father's death, spoken in Italian, and in the presence of a person who acted as a sort of Camerlingo, a foreigner and member of some religious order.

While the active fancy of O'Brien was thus fed by vague conjectures on one point, on every other he saw his way clearly. Considered intimately, and in all its bearings, the prospect was not brilliant; but as long as it lay distinctly before him, there was that within, which rendered him confident in his powers to grapple with difficulties, and to vanquish obstacles. His father had left him heir only to his misfortunes, and his ancient name; his debts, as he had told his son, had been paid out of funds, destined by that singular order the Jesuits, to liberate from worldly embarrassments, such as they might require to abandon the world for their service. Lord Arranmore's peculiar endowments were knowledge of the Irish language and customs, and his popularity with the lower orders: both powerfully available in a system, which in its first resuscitation was contented to grasp at what it *could*, until it should become capable of attaining the all it desired.

With respect to the absolute mendicity to which O'Brien had found his father reduced (a state so much at variance with the imagined donation of fifty pounds to his son, and with the protection afforded him by the order of which, by his own confession, he had taken the first vows), O'Brien had heard with a mingled sensation of pleasure and indignation, that this alms asking was one of his six spiritual exercises, or probationary experiments; and that he had availed himself of the circumstance to attack the feelings of his son, and to give more influence to the offers he was commissioned to make him. These offers were, that he should become a member of a society to which his energy and endowments might prove serviceable, which would give him the boundless command of wealth, without its responsibility and anxieties, and which might eventually place him in a sphere for centuries occupied by the direct successors of Ignatius himself, the counsellor of kings, the director of popes, the sovereign of sovereigns, the umpire of nations, and in the profane but expressive language of the institution, the '*Jesus locum Dei tenens in terra.*'

The price of a destiny thus splendid, so fabulous in sound, yet once enjoyed in fact, was no sacrifice of the passions or pleasures of life. It was but the firm internal resolution, the tacit, but solemn and irrevocable vow to live and die exclusively devoted to the interests, views, and principles of the society, by a blind and perfect obedience to its decrees, and '*prostration*[1] *of all will, virtue, and science,*' to ever order of the superior, 'such as Abraham evinced in the sacrifice of his son.' But this great mental vow, this 'internal desire,' and 'voluntary engagement under a tacit condition,' required no enforcement from monastic professions, no conventual privation and retreat. It imposed no habit, to mark by external forms, an internal separation from that world, to which its mission was wholly devoted. The Jesuit was not less a Jesuit in courts and camps, than in colleges and congregations; in the saloon of the mundane than in the cell of the ascetic; in the cabinet or the academy, than in the cloister of the *Ignorantins;* in the bowers of beauty, and in the halls of wealth and pleasure, than in the impervious forests of Valombrosa, or the trackless snows of St Bernard.

This brilliant and flattering proposition had no attraction for one, whose principles and prejudices were alike armed against it. In another age, and another aspect of society, it might have tempted his ambition, seduced his passions, and given him up unreservedly to an order, which then governed the most powerful states of Europe, and influenced the happiness, and checked the progressive illumination of millions.

In answering the paragraph in Lord Walter's letter on this subject, O'Brien observed,

'Your suspicions of the attempted revival of Jesuitism are better founded, than your apprehension of my subjection to their system. I have a charmed life, and none of Jesuit-breed can hurt Macbeth. I was brought up by my Jansenist preceptor, under the especial invocation and protection of that saint of all heretics, St Augustin; and long before reason meddled with inquiry, I had drawn my tenets against the doctrines of Loyola from the '*verites académiques*' of that arch infidel D'Alembert,[2] which were placed in my hands by my dear Abbé O'Flaherty. For, hating the tribe of encyclopedists, as Le Tellier himself would have done, had he lived in their reign, the disciple of Jansen could set aside his prejudices in favour of his doctrine; and he permitted his young pupil to look into the pages of the chief of a

---

[1] Query – Was it from the Jesuits that the Bishop of London borrowed this oft-quoted phrase? or, did it arise in his mind as a necessary result of that universal spirit of domination, common to the high churchmen of all religions?

[2] D'Alembert wrote to show that the public would sustain no loss by the suppression of Jesuitical instruction, and to point out the defects in their system of education, both in the higher and lower classes.

party, for which he believed there was no salvation. So malleable are men's principles, when brought into contest with their opinions. My Abbé, by the bye, was the very Pascal of modern times: and as I was occasionally employed as his secretary, and twice copied his admirable answers to '*Le Jansénisme confondu*' (a *brochure de circonstance*, from the secret press of the suppressed Jesuits), I sucked in my antidote, before the delicious poison of Loyola was distilled into my ears, – as it afterwards was by the zeal of my grand-uncle, and the subtle eloquence of his coadjutors; some of whom are at this moment my agreeable companions and hospitable hosts at Cong. Not to terrify you by the astounding fact, you are to know that I have some reason to believe, that I am indeed, as you jocosely suggested, in the hands of the Jesuits; and literally an inmate of one of their new probationary houses. But all will not do. I am a very type of the generation, against whose freedom the old *sbirri* of religion are secretly arming, under the encouragement of that double-minded Pope, Pius the Sixth. How much the old tact of the order is blunted, is apparent in their application of means to ends, which are totally inadequate to the exigencies of the age: if they continue in this old tack, they are lost. Some royal penitent, like Louis the XIV, may cherish them; some narrow-minded monk, elevated to the papal throne, may revive them, and princes and governments may deem it useful to protect them; but the force of circumstances, that force to which princes and nations must alike submit, that force of which Wickliff, and Luther, and Calvin, were merely instruments, – which produced the dispersion of the Jesuits, and of which Ganganelli was but the agent, will effectually prevent the successful employment of arts, adapted to another age, and to another constitution of human society. When learning and opinion were in a few hands, and the mass of mankind were sunk in ignorance and mental inactivity, the current of thought might be checked, or directed, by a well combined conspiracy of the few. But now, that the whole world is in movement, that nations are alive to their own interests, and reflect on their own affairs, the education which the public gives to itself absorbs and neutralizes the instruction prepared for it by governments and hierarchies, whenever the results of both do not coincide. Open or secret, the confederacy to govern by misleading must fail, where the many have an interest in detecting its fallacies, and a ready agent for giving utterance to their thoughts. To govern the age in which we live, ambitious spirits must place themselves at its head; and to control opinion, they must advance it. The people and the press are irresistible; and should the Jesuits again be revived, and their obsolete education again be forced upon nations by royal authority, the force put upon thought will only serve to make it expand with additional resilience.

'Still, great efforts are making in Italy to revive this long influential order. In fact, they have never really been suppressed; and though their superb palaces, called colleges, have been closed, and their classes dispersed, yet they have always maintained their congregations, their confraternities and their secret affiliations, religious and laical; which have kept up a partial influence on the feeble, the ignorant, and the voluptuous (no small portion of society in all ages). While some monastic orders leaned to the stoics, and others to the platonists, the Jesuits were ever partisans of the philosophy of Epicurus. One of their elegant and sumptuous congregations at Paris, '*La Congrégation des Messieurs*,' was still to be traced by its *débris*, when my father brought me from Bordeaux, to place me a scholar in a new-named seminary of the suppressed order, in the Rue St Jacques. The house '*des Messieurs*' was a temple of pleasure; holy altars had been removed, that theatres might be erected, and dramas were gotten up and acted by the noble catechumens, which rivalled the pious private theatricals of St Cyr.

'By means of one of these congregations (secretly favoured by the present pope and the sovereigns of Italy), assisted by that sex which brings such powerful aid to any cause it adopts, they are again endeavouring to revive their order. The name of this new association is '*La devozione del sagro cuore di Gesù*.' The foundress of this order is a young and beautiful *religieuse*, an *élève* of the Jesuits, and an uncloistered nun, of the *Bambin Gesù* monastery, and afterwards of the Florentine convent, suppressed by Leopold. Rich, or reported to be rich, greatly gifted, and highly organized, with talents for all the arts, cultivated with all the success which industry and ambition ever bring with them, this modern St Theresa, when I was in Italy, not only made her fine voice heard above all less melodious sounds in the choir of her convent, but, it is said, in the oratories of princes and the cabinets of cardinals. Acting under the direction of her masters the Jesuits, it was she who obtained from the pope, through the influence of her friend the Cardinal Rezzonico, leave to found a perpetual mass '*in honorem sacrosancti cordis Jesu*,' and she obtained indulgences for the congregation, showered upon her a *larga mano*.

'I heard her once sing in her choir at Rome, when it was the fashion to do so; and the impression left by her tone and style has never since gone from my mind. I saw her also veiled and draped as a priestess of antiquity, carrying the *sagro cuore* in a procession in honour of the new worship; and there was a life and a grace in her movement and air, which recalled all that is most admired in the antique relievos of the capitol. Imagine the aid such a creature must bring to a cause, which especially addresses itself to human passions and human weakness. You will laugh when I tell you, that I am not quite sure, that these offsets of Jesuitism are not even here employing a similar agency in their little way; and that some sister Bridget is not doubling the part of '*la Sorella Irene*,' of the convent '*del Gesù*' of Rome. I certainly saw a female figure, of a most mysterious appearance, among the falling ruins of O'Brien House. She escaped miraculously, by means, which may yet discover to me her name and vocation. Should I tell your lordship of other phantoms which have crossed my path in the female 'form divine,' you would deem the relation a wreck of my feverish delirium, and laugh at the poetic visions of typhus. Still let me caution you, should you again trust yourself to a Dublin masquerade, and be accosted by a creature, light and evanescent as the

> Gay motes that people the sunbeam;

should you find in her the humour of Sevigné, the philosophy of Tencin, with the form of a sylph and the foot of a fairy, should you find that she knows you *au fond*, and plays you off in an epigram, then fear and fly her, for she certainly is a concealed – Jesuitess. Meantime I confess that some of the spell of Loyola is upon me, and that if I had a vocation to wear out my youth 'in shapeless idleness,' I should hang up my arms in the library of the religious gentlemen of Cong.

'Their society at present includes a few French and Italian emigrants, who have fled from the obnoxious lights of the revolution, and from what they call the persecutions of the Grand Duke Leopold in Tuscany; who has suppressed many convents in his charming dominions, as being under the influence of the Jesuits, and as engaged in the furtherance of their system. Here are also some English and Irishmen, laymen and seculars, evidently retired soldiers of the disbanded army of Loyola; who have weathered out the storms, which, as they say, the mighty spirit of infidelity has conjured up against them. My great uncle, the Abbate, stands apart from all, living rather among them than with them. His dark despotic and overbearing character retains nothing of its former energy, except what wastes itself in impotent efforts at the reinstatement of his order, in which his own prolonged life is bound up. His residence here is, it seems, but temporary; and with habits isolated as his manner is imperious, he passes his time shut up in solitary supremacy; and permits the society to indulge in the '*sainte oisivete*' of the canons of Boileau.

'As yet, they have made no attempts at proselyting, nor opened any classes; though they now speak frankly of their calling, as a branch of the accomplished society of Stonihurst; which has lately pledged its allegiance to the King and government,[1] and is much respected as a loyal and religious community, and as much opposed to the revolutionary epidemia of the day, as the most furious partizans of protestant ascendancy. All Jesuits as they are, they are evidently protected by the very government that makes a vital point of withholding catholic emancipation.

'The contrast of this society, with that in which I have for years been mingling, is extremely pleasant; and suits alike to my present state of mind and of health. Their habits suit my present tastes, and leave me free from all "restraint of hospitable zeal." Shut up in their cells all day, or occupied abroad in farming, or in lounging through the romantic scenery of the neighbourhood, they hold at night a circle in their library, which might rival the *mercuriales* of Menage. It is amusing to observe with what vigour they go over the old ground of the *démêlé* of Père Bonhours, and the Trissotins of the Sévignés and the Deshoulières; with what fervid controversy they argue for and against the decision of Daubignac, '*sur combien d'heures a duré l'action de l'Heautontimorumenos*' of Terence. Here are still preserved the feuds of Perrault and Dacier. The names, bandied from mouth to mouth, are not D'Alembert, Diderot, Condorcet, Voltaire or Volney; but Heinsius, Scaliger, Balzac, Vaugelas and Voiture; whose works enrich the shelves of their library, and, with some good editions of the classics, lives of Loyola, tracts against Jansen, Spectators and Guardians, "*discours sur les agrémens de l'esprit*," essays, "*sur la délicatesse du goût*," treatises "*de honesta voluptate*," make up the catalogue of its contents.

'As yet, not one word has been addressed to me, from which I can deduce a perseverance in those views which my unfortunate father entertained for me. But so premeditated has been my residence here,

---

[1] Anno 1791.

that in the chamber in which I have been installed since my recovery, I have not only found all my clothes, books, and escrutoire which I left in my college-rooms, – but its white-washed walls are covered with the pictures of those of my ancestors, who were founders and protectors of churches and monasteries. Some of these I recently missed from my father's old mansion, of which you must have retained a fearful recollection.

'There are two pictures also, which, from the freshness of their tints, have been repaired or recently painted. One is a very characteristic portrait of General Lord Inchiquin, a celebrated apostate of our family, who joined the republican party under Cromwell. He is painted in his youth, and in the fanciful dress of Charles the First's court, which he visited with his father, when a boy. What is singularly ridiculous in this (to such little arts do these ingenious men descend) is, that it is a striking, though flattering likeness of myself. The young Lord Inchiquin is represented leaning his hand on a table, on which stands a golden crucifix, with a label beneath, inscribed "*Sub hoc signo vinces.*" The other picture is a representation of the siege of the cathedral and rock of Cashel, by the same pervert O'Brien.[1] He is here represented, mounted on a spirited charger, his sword bathed in the blood of a prostrate bishop, trampled upon by his steed. His countenance scarcely preserving a trace of the youthful calmness of his portrait, is disfigured by the fiercest passions. The beautiful Gothic windows of the cathedral are lighted by flames bursting from the body of the church, which were said to have been kindled by Inchiquin himself, and to have consumed twenty ecclesiastics. Rising above the flame and smoke that issue from its dome, appears the Archbishop of Cashel in all the pomp of his holy vestments, and all the sublimity of martyrdom. He is in the act of pronouncing that dreadful prophecy, which predicted that every curse should fall upon the family of "the

---

[1] Le peuple consterné aux approches de ce tyran, chercha en vain un asile dans l'église cathédrale. Les lieux saints ne furent pas des remparts assurés contre des cœurs barbares. Inchiquin fit donner l'assaut, et ordonna aux soldats de ne faire quartier à personne. Le massacre fut grand dans l'église, et au dehors: personne n'èchappa. On compta environ vingt ecclésiastiques, tant séculiers que réguliers, égorgés dans cette occasion, sans parler d'une multitude de peuple. Il se faisait un plaisir barbare de brûler partout les villages, les maisons, et les blends des habitans; c'est ce que lui fit donner le nom de *Murrough an toithaine*, c'est-à-dire Murrough l'incendiaire, – nom sous lequel il est encore connu dans cette province, où sa mémoire est en horreur. – *Hist, d'Irlande*, tom. iii, p. 682.

incendiary," to be redeemed only, through the expiating zeal of some distant descendant. Underneath is written "The Siege of Cashel by O'Brien the incendiary, who denied his God, betrayed his King, and died the victim of his crimes in 1650."

'The picture is painted by some artist in the service of the confraternity; for I saw a fac-simile in miniature, among the illuminations of an old family chronicle, in my father's possession, called the Green Book of St Grellan; which by the bye, was recovered from the ruins of the old house, and now lies on my table.

'And now, my dear lord, having thus "prated to you of my whereabouts," for the present, I have nothing to communicate of the future; which lies before me, vague and indistinct as the prospect that my window commands. The surface appears full of inequalities: there are swamps to sink in, and acclivities to be mastered; but there are also bright points, which may be attained, ere the night of age closes upon the hopes of life; and there are vallies and glens to fly to ere peril overtake the wanderer, or persecution strike its fangs into its victim.

'I shall leave this charming retreat early in the ensuing week. Since I began this letter, a circumstance has occurred to hasten my departure. The constituted authorities here, have found out that the invalid of the religious community is a member of the United Irishmen, and the student of Trinity College, lately expelled for atheism and sedition. They have had an interview with my uncle, who coldly and haughtily commanded me to rebut the charge, by denying it. I have of course declined to deny a fact, in which I glory, that I am an United Irishman; or refute an absurd calumny, of whose falsehood they who circulate it are best aware. I mean therefore to visit the neighbourhood of my native town of St Grellan, on an invitation long given me by my mother's sisters, two maiden ladies, who have declared me the heir to the bogs and rabbit burroughs on their estate, in the borders of Jar Connaught. I shall not through "Eden take my solitary way," but through Connemara; passing over the magnificent masses of water of Corrib. Direct your next to the Post office, St Grellan; and let the society issue their orders to theirs and your devoted servant.'

# CHAPTER VII

—————•—————

## *The Caves of Cong*

Profonda era, e nebulosa,
Tauto che per ficca: lo viso al fondo,
lo non vi discerneva alcuna cosa.

DANTE.

Questa é l'antica e memorabil grotta
. . . . . . . . .
. . . Donde una donna uscio.

ARIOSTO.

O'BRIEN'S political authorship had occupied him for two days incessantly; and on the evening of the third, having sealed up his pamphlet
with his letter to Lord Walter, he walked into the town of Cong to
deliver it to the host of the old inn, who was going, on the following
morning, 'up to Dublin, to state case, and take counsel, in regard of
a bit of an estate in Joyce's country, to which he had every right in
life, called Betagh's land to this day.' The packet was directed to Mr
Fitzpatrick, bookseller, Capel-street, Dublin; and Pat Betagh having
reiterated his assurances of its safe delivery, invited O'Brien 'just to
step in and take a tumbler with a few gentlemen, his particular friends,
who had got their feet under his mahogany, and were drinking to his
speed, success, and safe return.'

The hospitable invitation was declined, with as much courtesy and
earnestness as it was given; and O'Brien, almost suffocated with the
fumes of punch and tobacco, which issued from the parlour, where
Mr Betagh's friends were taking the stirrup-cup, hasted from the
close atmosphere of the ruined street of Cong, to the shores of its
lovely river. His head ached intensely, from the arduous occupation

of the entire day; his limbs were cramped and stiff from sedentary confinement; and as he issued from the smoky cabins, and noise of pigs, children, and dogs, he felt the fresh air as it came down in cooling breezes from the mountains, flow with a voluptuous influence on his brows, and gradually relax their painful tension.

In taking the course of the river, which, rising in the mountains, flows into Lough Corrib, and bathes, as it passes, the abbey ruins, O'Brien paused to observe the deep etching of the tower and cloistered walls upon the placid stream, relieved by the setting sun; and his train of thought involuntarily led him to penetrate the ruins, and examine their details, with more interest than he had hitherto done. In quoting largely in his pamphlet from the very Irish history of the Abbé Mac Geogheghan, written in such very pure French, he had pitched upon the story of Roderick O'Connor, the last supreme King of Ireland, and his final retreat into the Abbey of Cong. It was here (thought O'Brien, as he passed the refectory), here, perhaps, on this very spot, that O'Connor, while yet supreme King of Ireland, gave secret rendezvous to his dear friend and ally, Donald O'Brien, King of Munster: and it was under the benediction of the Abbot that both had marched against that impious son, who had always sought the ruin and death of his father, in whose life-time he had usurped his throne. It was here that, in affliction for his domestic and national misfortunes, the royal Roderick retired, resigning his barren sceptre to his son, Canchovar, '*où il employa*,' says his historian, '*le reste de sa vie, qui fut de treize ans, à se préparer pour l'éternité.*'

The sun was pouring down from the summits of Ben Leven, a flood of light upon the tomb of the unfortunate Roderick,[1] as O'Brien approached it. The monument was fast sinking to the earth, and was covered with rank weeds and briars. As he threw himself upon the long grass beside it, resting his right arm on the carved fragment of a mullioned window, while with his left hand he plucked away the dark night-shade which covered the ashes of royalty, he gave himself up to reverie, such as the place, the hour, and his own dark fortunes inspired; for the sunshine of the morning had faded from his spirits. The close of the natural day has something in it of the dreariness which belongs to the close of life, a dreariness to which the literary

---

[1] Mac Geogheghan, who wrote in a foreign country, was not aware of this tomb's existence; for he says, 'Son corps fut transporté de Cong à Clanmacanoise, et enterré avec pompe dans cette église.'

labourer is especially susceptible. The fatigue by which man earns his daily bread, forces on the strongest the 'penalty of Adam;' but the exhaustion of mental occupation, the terrible wearing of intellectual exertion (for the deep despondency of which, physical suffering has no parallel), pay back the fatal pre-eminence of genius, at a price the dullest would not envy.

O'Brien, weary from the toil of creative composition, sighed as he sat by the grave of O'Connor, and again smiled in humorous sadness, at the services performed by his ancestor Donald O'Brien, to the heroic Roderick, as contrasted with those which he himself was now discharging, in weeding his grassy and neglected tomb. While thus employed in thoughts that led to a conviction of the nothingness of all things, of the brevity of life's fitful malady (at best a paroxysm), and of the wisdom of those, who, like Roderick O'Connor, withdraw themselves from its unavailing struggles, he was suddenly roused from his sombre reflections, by a gentle rustle among the shrubs which grew upon a buttress of the venerable pile, near which he sat. A startled raven fled from his nest in the adjoining gable; and O'Brien, as he looked and listened, thought he heard the heavy footsteps of some ponderous visitant, dying along the cloisters. They faded on the air, and he again sunk upon his elbow, and fixed his eyes on the distant heights of Connemara, for which he was soon about to leave the comforts of his present retreat.

Again the sound of footsteps, with a crushing fall, seemed to approach him. He raised himself erect from the grass, but saw nothing: and all became again silent and solitary. Meantime, the surrounding scenery tinted into more perfect and picturesque beauty. The fore-ground, chequered by the massive shadows of the cloistered pile, gradually fell into deeper gloom; while a flood of yellow light poured through a Gothic door-way which was richly chiselled in its cornices with grotesque devices, and the grim heads of saints and monsters. One of these, seen imperfectly through the masses of trailing plants, seemed almost human; and O'Brien drew forth his tablets and pencil, and applied himself in the last glimmer of sunlight to sketch the gate. While thus occupied, he thought the head almost moved, and that the eye glistened with life and light. He sprang forward, to view it nearer, but it had disappeared; and, convinced that something living had introduced itself among the nondescripts of Gothic structure, he was resolved to hunt down the original he had been drawing. The fleetness of the object of his pursuit, evaded even his rapid bounds; and just

as he saw the figure skim along the walls of the refectory, and glide
into what is still called the Abbey kitchen, he fell over a fragment of
the building. The next moment, however, he was on his feet, and
then he again saw the figure standing beyond the convent wall, on
the bank of the river. Wrapped as it was in a closely veiling mantle,
he distinctly recognized that the person before him was short and
square. There was something so suspicious in this evasion, that it
reanimated his pursuit; when the low and melancholy winding of a
rural cornet or horn, arrested his steps, and he again saw the object
of his curiosity (as if startled from its covert by the sound), spring
forward and escape beyond the ruins. When again he perceived it, it
was standing on a dreary heath; but it was no longer of the same
dimensions; the short, square form, now stood lofty, gaunt, and erect.

Though half doubtful of the identity of the individual, O'Brien still
followed, till, almost breathless with fatigue, he was within a few yards
of his object; and then the vision, or phantom, suddenly sank in the
earth and disappeared. O'Brien stood thunder-struck and aghast. The
spot to which his chase had led him, was a dreary heath, speckled
with a few isolated white rocks, and fragments of a druidical Cromlech.
No shrub, or tree, or patch of vegetation cheered the scene; save that
where the figure had vanished, a clump of old scathed oaks stood,
woven and draped with ivy and creeping plants. O'Brien, as he slowly
and breathlessly approached them, recalled the tales of fairies and
lepraghauns, with which the Irish nurse had amused him during his
convalescence.

He had now reached the spot where this vision which 'seemed not
of the inhabitants of the earth, and yet was on it,' had made its
escape; and he discovered a circular cavity, which, as he looked down,
appeared to afford a ready descent by rude steps, cut in the rocky
sides of a perpendicular depth of more than an hundred feet. The
gurgling of water was heard, and some brilliant points of light were
visible beneath. He descended with eager haste, and found himself
alone in a dark and vaulted chamber of the rock. The twilight whose
rays fell from the aperture above, on the spot immediately beneath it,
reflected in rich tints from the dripping verdure, which trailed in
festoons and garlands over the interior of the cavern, and glittered
with the brilliant hues of the emerald. Further on, in the opening
cavity, stalactites and sparry incrustations caught the fading light, and
reflected it in silvery points. Beneath rolled a broad and limpid river,
whose source and exit were alike lost in the distant gloom.

O'Brien, as he proceeded with imprudent fearlessness, now first suspected that he was in the Caves of Cong, which his kind hosts had induced him to defer visiting, until the more perfect restoration of his health. But neither health nor danger were now thought of. As he groped his way along, shadowy glimpses of the mysterious figure were caught, and lost in the windings of the cave, still urging him forward; when his steps were suddenly arrested by a female form, which for a moment appeared to his dazzled eyes, weird and wild as the sybil, that led Æncas, in grottos scarcely more poetical. The apparition had darted from behind a projecting rock, with a dimly-burning brand, which her breath seemed to kindle into flame. Then setting fire to a bundle of straw, which she took from a basket on her arm, she flung it on the water, to float down the stream. Casting the glowing brand upon the rocks as she retreated, its red glare was reflected on the sparry roof, and fell upon the walls of the far retiring cavity. O'Brien had heard that a person answering to this fantastic appearance, was the oracle of those Cumean mysteries; and, divided between the thick coming fancies of his excited imagination, and his disposition to laugh at them, he was about to follow, and to reward her, for the effect she had so ingeniously produced, when another object for the moment drew off his attention. It was the person, whose evident desire to escape had led him into the cave; and who now rushing on him, seized him in his arms, and held him in an embrace of gigantic force, while he muttered in Irish what might be a blessing, or an incantation. He then as suddenly disappeared.

In the deep guttural accents, and in that iron clasp of strength and tenderness, O'Brien recognized his foster brother; but he called upon him in vain. Whatever was the cause of this reluctance to appear, he found it impossible, either by soothing solicitations to recall him, or by his own efforts to pursue him through the Cimmerian darkness, in which the extinction of the brands had left the cavern. He turned, therefore, to ask assistance from the priestess of the temple, but she too was gone. The event was singular; for she had asked no gratuity, and the fleetness of her steps belonged not to the feeble limbs of age. Yet if he had hunted Shane to these melancholy caves, who was the secret spy upon his solitary meditations in the ruins of the Abbey?

He now had only to grope his way back to the opening of the grotto. When he emerged, the mists of night were already fast settling on the dreary landscape; and the gloomy ray of many a rushlight, streaming through the casements of the cabins of Cong, directed his steps homeward. At the entrance of the village he stopped to inquire of some children, for the dwelling of the guide to the caves; and one of the urchins led the way to her cabin, which stood lone and mouldering on the edge of the Abbey grounds. He found her at her wheel in the chimney corner, spinning by a rushlight fixed in a cleft stick, fastened in the smoky beam, which traversed the chimney. He was struck by the contrast of her aged and haggard appearance, with the lightness of foot, and celerity of movement which had evaded his pursuit. 'I am come,' he said, taking a piece of silver from his pocket, 'to thank and remunerate you for the pleasure you have afforded me, by lighting up the caves, and to beg that you will accompany me there to-morrow.'

'Och, yez are welcome, and thousands,' replied the old woman, snatching at the money, and dropping it eagerly into a pouch at her side, 'and its when was it, that I did that same, a jewel machree? for I never seed your sweet comely face afore, that I mind.'

'When?' said O'Brien, in amazement: 'this evening, now, when you just left me in the caves, not half an hour back.'

'Is it me?' said the old woman, raising her voice to the shrill pitch of terror. 'Oh! mille murther! A wurrustrew the day, and Jasus keep me, amen. It was my fetch you saw, surely; if you saw the likes of me at all, at all, Mavourneen dhû; for haven't cross'd threshol, barring once't to mass, since Easter, in regard of the rheumatrix. Och! Jasus, queen of glory, look down upon me this night, and take me to comfort; for the death watch is out for me,' – and she wiped the stream from her eyes. 'And how is it I came upon yez, dear?' she continued; 'was it in my fine white winding sheet which lies there in the box convanient? Or was it in my ould cloak, and binogue, and crutch, and basket, and flint, and rushlights?'

'No,' said O'Brien, 'I saw nothing of all this; you were wrapped in a mantle.'

He paused as the old woman had impulsively risen, her eyes and mouth extended on the stretch of superstitious curiosity and personal solicitude; and then added, 'No, now I perceive it could not be you; the figure was taller and slighter.'

The old woman reseated herself at her wheel, delighted to be restored to a life which, though in the midst of pain, poverty, and age, had still charms for her. 'God is good, and his blessed Mother, amen,' she said: 'Glory be to the saints, I am to the fore still. No, honey, dear, it wasn't me, nor the likes of me, nor my arrach neither, but a great lady, glory to her name and memory, amen.'

'Indeed,' said O'Brien, 'and who was it?'

'Och, there's no harm done,' said the old woman, turning round her wheel briskly, and casting a fearful eye round her desolate hovel, 'there's no harm done, for she brings luck wherever she appears; sure it's only the *abmhasther*, the Abbess's ghost.'

'The Abbess! what Abbess?'

'Why, the Abbess Beavoin O'Flaherty.'

O'Brien started.

'Och, in truth,' continued the old woman, 'she comes over from the castle in Lough Corrib, Caisthla na Kirka, and is seen in Cong Abbey, and betimes in the caves too. But sorrow harm she'll do you, but great luck always follows the track of her traheens. There's them as would rather catch a sight of the Abbess Beavoin, than find the mark of a lepraghaun, aye, indeed faith.'

O'Brien took leave of the old woman, but the vision of Shane, the lurking person in the Abbey ruins, the strange guide in the caves, and the Abbess Beavoin, occupied his thoughts, and gave a vein of wild and fantastic imagery to his sleeping dreams, which he could not wholly shake off when awake.

In a week from this adventure, O'Brien parted from the amiable confraternity, with a regret natural to the sensible, in parting even from inanimate objects, to which they have been habituated; but most natural in one alive, even to the very quick, to kindness and to unkindness. He forgot their possible speculations on his moral independence, in their attention and hospitality. Whatever might have been their secret opinion of his waywardness, or their dislike of his principles, both religious and political, they had neither irritated him by dictation, disgusted him by interference, nor worried him by remonstrance; and they had expressed their admiration of his talents, and their friendly regret at not being destined to benefit still further by his society, in such mild and insinuating reproaches, that they left him in higher favour with himself, and consequently more pleased with them, than he had sometimes been with persons of more importance, and with associations of more beneficial tendency to the great interests of mankind.

His uncle, to whom he had announced his intention of proceeding to his aunts, in the county of Galway, had received the intelligence with the indifference of one, whose feelings were alike under the benumbing influence of age, and of systematic dissimulation. For his grand nephew he had no personal regard; for his present vocation he had more contempt than indignation; and of his future adherence to a system of which he was himself the support, or the dupe, he had no doubt whatever. He looked on the hot-headed young man as a bird, who flutters and flies to a limited distance, at the end of a string. It is the peculiar quality of zeal, united with mediocrity, to cling with a desperate pertinacity to a favourite idea, or a darling hope; and this modern St Dominick was as ready for a crusade, and as certain of its success, as he who pursued conversion even to the verge of extermination. He refused to receive his nephew's personal adieus on the night before his departure; but O'Brien had not then to learn that blood is no necessary tie, or that propinquity and kin are no bonds, where bigotry has once sown her prolific seeds of deep and bitter dissension.

The wanderer's travelling arrangements had been easily made. His wardrobe and books had been dispatched by a Galway carrier to St Grellan; and a Connemara pony (the camel of the Connaught deserts), presented to him by one of the brothers of the confraternity, afforded him the surest and pleasantest mode of passing through the mountainous wilds, to the coast scenery of Jar Connaught, and its little capital, St Grellan. The donor of this sure footed animal was one in whom O'Brien had taken much interest, and with whom he had much conversed. He was the young Franciscan preacher of Tuam, whose eloquence had brought such crowded congregations to the private chapel of the confraternity. He was far gone in a consumption, a circumstance that deepened the interest his character and manners had begotten. Though a true Irish friar, zealous and vehement, with a broad brogue and a lounging gait, there was yet about him a certain indication of one, who felt deeply, and might have been loved – of one who had made evident sacrifices of natural passions, to some sense of duty; which, whether right or wrong in its principle, called forth the pity and admiration that such sacrifices ever exact.

O'Brien, in return for his pony, had given him a miniature, on copper, of his favourite saint, St Francis of Ancisa, which he found in his writing-box, and which he had bought for a very trifle in the Piazza Navona at Rome.

'We shall meet again,' said O'Brien, in some emotion, and shaking him heartily by the hand.

'Yes!' said the young Franciscan, emphatically, and throwing up his eyes to the starry heavens, under whose canopy they were standing, 'We shall meet again; if not in this world, in the next.'

O'Brien had engaged his passage across Lough Corrib in a sail-boat, which was to start from a spot near the ruins of Cross Abbey, an old religious house, known also by the name of the Holy-rood, between Cong and the now improved, but then miserable village of Headford. The stars were still twinkling in the firmament, and the dawn was but faintly struggling through the mists of a grey and loaded atmosphere, as he turned the head of his 'hobler' from the court of 'the Retreat,' and took the road to Cross. The day came heavily on, drizzling and dreary; but as he proceeded, the weather, with all the uncertainty of the most uncertain climate in the world, suddenly changed – new objects cheered and charmed the loneliness of his way. It was the fair day of Galway, and the road soon became thronged, even at that early hour. From the mountains of Mayo, and the shores of Lough Corrib, and even from the rugged heights of Ben Leven and Mam Turk, in the wilds of Connemara, came groups of cadgers, with their panniered asses, bog-trotters, with their turf kishes, and old women, in their binogues and mantles, laden with Connemara stockings; while forms, which nature seemed to have intended for other associates and other regions, were occasionally visible among the rustic population.

In whatever direction O'Brien looked, he met bright black eyes darting their arch, yet timid glances, which alternately sought and bent beneath his own: well-developed forms, thrown into such attitudes as the rural duties in which they were involved prescribed, were set off to advantage by a dress which (though of the rudest, coarsest texture) traditionally preserved the modes of better times, when the commercial wealth, which poured into the ports of Galway and Mayo, created an artificial prosperity, in the midst of turbulence and factious warfare. Petticoats of bright scarlet and crimson,[1] set in full thick plaits round the waist, as in the time of Granuail (who probably improved the fashions of her subjects by her trip to the court of Elizabeth), were contrasted by the blue cloak, or mantle, thrown back from the shoulders, to display the brown boddice or jacket beneath. Glossy black, or golden hair, such as Ossian sang, and Carolan delighted to celebrate, was drawn becomingly off the open forehead, and fastened behind, by that modern representative of the old Irish bodkin, a

---

[1] The dress of the women, who are handsome, and have a good expression in their countenances, is peculiar; scarlet, crimson, and purple, are their favourite colours. – *Walks through Ireland*, 1817.

stout, long, black pin; while dark brows and rich colouring frequently presented such heads as the traveller sees on the banks of the Tiber. Gazing on faces from which the bloom of youth and the blush of virgin modesty were not yet banished by rude labours and matronly indifference, O'Brien saw such traces of Spanish origin, as justified the supposition, that the western coast of Ireland was colonized, if not by the sons of Milesius, at least by his Iberian descendants.

The sun had risen in cloudless splendour, and threw a long line of quivering light upon the waters of Lough Corrib, the purple mists of the distant mountains rolled up from their bases, and jocund day stood tip-toe on their summits. As the noble scene came forth to view, and expanded into beauty, the susceptible spirits of O'Brien sprang up with the breeze, which carried off upon its wing the vapours of the dawn, to that great receptacle of the elements, 'the steep Atlantic.' He drew up at the appointed place of embarkation, and was soon on board. The boat had already cleared the little creek, when a long, loud whistle, arrested the attention of the helmsman and crew, and a man running in full speed, with a kish or basket, pending from a long stick, that rested on his shoulder, appeared, hailing the crew, with many signs, both of hat and hand. The rowers rested on their oars, and the helmsman exclaimed,

'Och, its Corny the cadger, come for a cast over to the mountains, if your honor plazes; and troth, Sir, I'll engage, it's himself will pay yez, with a good song; for he is the finest poet on the lake, any how.'

'A poet,' repeated O'Brien, laughing; 'pray then put back and take him in, for the honour of the calling.'

'Long life to your honor,' said the helmsman, 'sorrow a one but knows Cornelius O'Clummaghan from Shannon river to Innis Bofin.'

'And some to their cost,' muttered a poor, pale, half naked creature, scarcely able to wield the oar he held.

'He is fine company, and has great wit,' said another; 'though some take him for an innocent; and he was welcome from Menlo Castle, to the poorest cabin in Connemara, until he got into trouble, poor lad, some years ago; but now he has come back, and has taken up a taste, and is willing to put his hand to any thing in an honest way, betimes selling a basket of scollops, or a hank of Connemara stockings, betimes a few story books, ould ballads, holy pictures, and the like, and goes on errands through the country.'

While this biographical eulogy was pronouncing, a corricle or canoe, constructed of twigs and hides, was sent ashore for the poet. The rowers meantime lay on their oars; and O'Brien, in throwing his eyes over the miscellaneous jumble of dead and live cargo, stowed into the little bark, was struck by the appearance of a scarcely human form, gathered up like a hedgehog, on the floor of the hold. A ragged mantle was drawn over the whole figure to the very head, which was bent upon the upraised knees. The deep inspirations of one who slept soundly, alone intimated that this shapeless mass was human.

'It is a poor wild cratur,' said one of the rowers, following the direction of O'Brien's eyes, and poking at the 'delicate monster' with his oar, as Trinculo does at Caliban. 'He is getting a cast over, for the love of our lady of the holy rood.'

O'Brien's attention was now drawn off by the arrival of the lake poet: he however had nothing poetical in his appearance, and resembled less in his person, than his calling, his lackadaisical fraternity of modern times. He was a low, squat, square, but athletic figure, with a countenance undecided in its expression, between cunning and idiotism; with a penthouse brow, leering mouth, and small twinkling eyes that almost met (one of nature's sure indications of a rogue). It was observed by old Barnaby Rich (a traveller in Ireland, in the days of James 1st), that 'the people of that country were most bountiful to rhymers and fools' – and in either, or in both, of these capacities, Corny the cadger was most heartily received, by the helmsman and crew; for he who amuses is the welcome guest of all classes.

As soon as he had stowed himself and his ambulating library in the boat, he made a low obeisance to O'Brien, and then addressed him in a doggerel rhyme, to a sort of whining chaunt:

'Glory be to your honor, both now and evermore;
Of health, wit, and wisdom, may God increase your store,
For myself being here, which makes my drame come true,
Poor Cornalius is bound in duty to pray for you.'

'And pray, friend,' said O'Brien, 'what was your dream?'

'I dramed your honor rowed me over, without fee or pay,
Then added a tester, to carry myself on my way.'

The rowers laughed and winked.

'You seem to cap rhymes at will,' said O'Brien: 'have you any good old Irish poetry?'

'Plinty, your honour,' was the reply.

'Have you Neilan the bard's famous invocation to Lord Thomas Fitzgerald, called the Silken Thomas?'

'No, plaze your honour, but I have Carolan's reysate for drinking.' Another laugh from the rowers, and sly wink from the improvisatore.

'Have you never heard,' continued O'Brien, 'of Ossian's chase, and dialogue with Saint Patrick?'

'Is it Oisin? Och, I know him well, Sir: Oisin – Mac Fionne – Mac Cumhal – Mac Cormac – Mac – , och sure I could repate it all, when I was a child, upon my fingers' inds.'

'What have you got in your basket, friend?' asked O'Brien.

Corny drew forth some dirty little books, and wetting his thumb, as he turned over one of the title-pages, detailed the contents and merits of each, with a genius for puffing that might have served the purpose of the first-rate London publishers. 'Here's the surprising History of the Life and Actions of Redmond O'Hanton, or Emunh Eenuch, protector of the rights and properties of his benefactors, and Captain General of the Irish tories, a most notorious, though a gentlemanlike robber. Here are, "the Feats and Actions of Phaidrig Mac Tighe," "The Miracles of St Patrick," and "The last Dying Speech of *Cahier na Gapul*, the renowned horse-stealer;" but may be, your honour would rather have the history of my books in poetry,' and clearing his voice, he fell into a sort of piperly drone, and ran over his little catalogue in a rambling rhyming measure, – a faculty by no means rare in the poor scholar, or bog poet and pedagogue of Ireland.

'Here's larning and wisdom for all ranks and all ages,
For gassoons and scollogs, and genteels and sages.
Here's the seven wise maisters, Bellianis, of Greece,
Which myself prizes more than great Jason's gold fleece.
Here's holy Saint Bridget, more fair than Briomartes,
And pretty Mrs Flanders, *opus naturæ non artis;*
And here's our patron, Saint Patrick, whose glory was grate,
Who left us the whiskey, and forbid us the mate.
So long life to his honour; here's the finest of stories,
'Tis of Redmond O'Hanlon, the chief of all Tories.
Here's the feast of O'Rourke, and the fight of O'Maras,
And the battle of Augbrim, and the fall of O'Haras.
Here's *Cahier na Gapul*, and Manus M'Connell,
With his merry man Andrew, and Randal O'Donnel,
With other great tories, Irish rogues, rapparees,

Once plenty in Ireland, as laves on the trees;
And here's miracles worked by ould father Casey,
Songs, cronans, and ballads, which cannot but plaze ye.
Here's the miners of Wicklow, the Calleen Dhas Dhu;
Here's Drimin Dub Derlish, and Bumper Squire Drew;
Here's the isles of Lough Corrib, like emeralds so green,
Forenent Tory Island, in the rear Isle Potsheen.
Here's sweet Gracy Nugent, and fair Bridget Cruise,
The Hunt of Kilruddery, and Petticoat loose;
The Hair in the corn, and Molly Astore;
With Planxties and cronans, and ballads guillore.
And what need I more, or with rigmarole laze yez,
For, if this doesn't plaze ye, the divil won't plaze yez.'

'One must be indeed difficult,' said O'Brien, laughing; 'but which is Tory Island?'

'There it is, your honour, with its fine old ruin and weather-beaten trees, bending from the sea blast. Och hone! many a brave gentleman made a bould retrait there, in the troubles, and will again, plaze God;' and he turned his disagreeable eyes leeringly on O'Brien. 'Och! there's life in a muscle, dead as he looks; and many a strange story runs the country in regard of that island: and is well known that neither baste nor bird, though many bes in it, can bellow nor warble there, in regard of Abbot Giol's prayer. For this being an island of saints, and the noise of the birds and bastes and other four-footed quadrupeds disturbing the monks at their devotions, the Abbot prayed that the gift of tongues, voice, or whistle might never flourish in the island; and it's pity but part of his prayer was put up for the faymales, and then it's to Inish Goil the boys would be looking for wives.'

'Inish Goil!' said O'Brien; 'is Tory Island Inish Goil, of which I have heard so much?'

''Tis, plaze your honour, in good Irish, and Abbot Goil's tomb lies there to this day.'

The lake poet now deviated from the topography, to the biography of the country; and having by his wandering life, *les nouvelles à la main*, he dealt out his eulogies, or vituperations, on the neighbouring gentry, according as they had administered to his wants or vanities, – as he had been feasted in the hall of an O'Connor, or banished from the kitchen of an O'Kelly. Corny appeared to be, in fact, in this respect, no unfair specimen of the *genus irritabile* of a higher class; the *amour*

*propre* of his calling apparently determining his inspirations, vindictiveness was his muse, and a cruishkeen of whiskey his butt of sack.

In listening with disgust to his scandalous chronicler, O'Brien
mentally acknowledged the justice of those severe decrees of Elizabeth's sanguinary code, which were directed against 'certen idle men
of lewd demeanour, called rhymers or poets, from whose intercourse
with the great, no small enormities did grow.' If his poetical patriotism,
imbibed with his mother's milk, induced him to credit the influence
ascribed to the bards of ancient times, as he read the poetry of Ossian,
or listened to the music of Carolan, he could detect nothing in the
poet of Lough Corrib, that savoured of 'the sweet and good intention'
attributed to the bards of the O'Neils and the Fitzgeralds. He saw in
him, indeed, a coarse, but not inadequate representation of 'the old
Irish tale-teller,' who amused his patrons, 'when they were melancholy
and could not sleep; and for a little reward or share of a stolen
cow,' praised or vituperated, with indiscriminate baseness. He soon,
therefore, turned away with a feeling of antipathy excited by the
rhymer's sinister and disagreeable countenance, and gave up his
undivided attention to the wild and splendid scenery of Lough Corrib.

As he advanced, the lake appeared almost rounded by an amphi-
theatre of hills, broken into every abrupt disunion, which could give
variety to form, and effect to light. The primitive mountains, with
their high conical peaks, formed an aerial back-ground to the
secondary range of hills; whose rugged declivities melted gradually
into the rich tones of the lowlands, which swept along the shore of
the waters. He was already well acquainted with the aspect of the
more elevated features of the Connemara mountains; and in paddling
his corricle among the rocks and breakers of their rugged shores, he
had often taken the mighty Ben Leven for his landmark; and had
listened to the tales of the Clana Earla, as the fishermen pointed to
the twelve pins of Benbola, or the fortress rock of Granuaile. But he
had seen them as distant visions, fleeting and airy as the clouds
through which they gleamed. He was now penetrating their mysterious
bosoms; and was about to tread their tangled depths, in whose fastnesses his ancestors had pursued the O'Flahertys, and had been in
their turn pursued by them, to their sea-girt realms of Arran. He
remembered when these hills were to him as Alps and Appenines:
for 'nothing is, but thinking makes it so;' and accurate ideas are the
result only of slow, sure, but often too painful experience.

The bright, broad expanse of water, over which they had glided, was now gradually narrowing into a small creek, formed by a mountain stream; against whose winding current they had some difficulty to contend, till the shallowness of the water, and the inclosure of the rocks prevented further navigation. They landed in a shady little cove, at the base of the Glan mountain, which formed the mouth of a precipitous glen. O'Brien drew from a purse, which still contained the greater part of the mysterious donation, enough to pay the crew, and more than realize the dream of Corny the cadger; and the parties separated.

The boatmen of Lough Corrib and their plebeian passengers, were occupied for a few minutes in drawing their vessel to its harbour; and then moved onwards to a stream of blue smoke, which was curling gracefully in the sunshine. Though no human habitation was visible, the smoke, in a place so wild and solitary, was a beacon never to be mistaken. It was there the 'fire burnt and cauldron bubbled,' whose secret distillation, pure and bright as it dropped, contained in its essence the elements of rapine, perjury, and murder, – that bane of the morals as of the prosperity of the people; encouraged directly by the government; and indirectly by a religion, which forbids the wholesome nourishment the wretched Irish peasant is unable to obtain, and permits the use of a poison, the source of his crimes, and the cause of much of his poverty.

# CHAPTER VIII

———————•———————

## *The Mountains*

Jam undique sylvæ et solitudo

PLINII *Epist.*

MEANTIME O'Brien, under the guidance of a lad, who was lounging
near the creek, ascended through the acclivities of Glan to a Shebean
house, which, niched in a rock like an eagle's nest, exhibited in the
turf and broom suspended over its door, an intimation that entertainment was to be had 'for man and baste.' The mountain traveller
availed himself of the notice, fed his pony, and took such refreshment
as the primitive inn of Connemara afforded. Broiled trout from the
Lough, with oaten bread, 'laughing potatoes,' milk hot from the cow,
with spirits warm from the still, and 'faithful to its fires,' and water,
that looked in hue and brilliancy like dissolved diamonds, furnished
forth no contemptible feast. To this excellent fare, was added much
information concerning the journey the traveller was about to make.
From one of the shelving acclivities of the Glan, which rose high and
sharp behind the house, the host pointed out to him, with as much
importance as if he had shown the stranger 'all the kingdoms of the
earth,' those unerring finger-posts of Nature's own elevation, the
headlands and mountain peaks. The view was sublime; it spread
before the eye, far as human vision could reach, marked and vivid, as
on a richly coloured map. The mountains of Connemara were then
savage and wild, as the absence of all cultivation could make them;
unexplored and almost unknown, save to their own inhabitants, and
to the smuggling carriers who traversed their lower range, from the
coast to the island countries. Vast tracts had been made over to new
proprietors in the beginning of the century, who had as yet made but

few efforts to examine or reclaim them; and they were inhabited only by scullogs or petty farmers, whose best crops were derived from their intercourse with the smugglers of the coast; or by herds and cottiers, hovelled in ravines, which gave a scanty herbage in winter to the lean flocks, that in summer were fed upon the dried-up loughs. The castles of residence or defence, raised in their sheltered valleys, or on the summits of the sea-beat headlands, by the factious Burkes, by the fierce O'Flahertys, and invading O'Briens of Arran, now lay in ruins; or if at all inhabited, it was only by the meadhain, or middlemen of some remote proprietor or distant absentee, unconscious of the resources of the soil he thus carelessly abandoned to his mercenary and ignorant representatives. The comparative civilization derived from the presence of chiefs, even so wild and warlike as those, who in earlier times claimed the mountains as their territories, had long yielded to the abandonment and neglect, which, from the epoch of the revolution, had fallen upon the most romantic districts, of the once most important and most interesting provinces in Ireland. All therefore was the stillness and solitude of the desert, but not its dreariness; for there was a bold breaking up of surface, an alternation of high shooting cliffs, and deep seated dells; of streams that issued in silver threads from their elevated sources, and congregated into foaming torrents as they fell into their channeled beds; of vast stools of old forest trees sending forth their scathed scraggy arms through the young green underwoods, that sprung from their roots; and of tracts of dreary moors and morasses, enlivened by those innumerable little lakes, so peculiar to Irish mountains, gleaming in the sunshine or curling in the blast; while troops of red deer looked down from the surrounding heights; and flocks of birds, startled from their aeries, ascended into the clouds!

Such were the natural accidents which gave life and movement to a scene, destitute of all human industry. While the mountain regions, viewed from the elevated spot where O'Brien stood, seemed to swell and fade into distant acclivities, forming endless chains towards the north and west, the lowland plains, and narrow strip of rocky coast, to which this rude region formed so bold a back-ground, were spread beneath to the south. Misty and soft as they lay in the sunny mid-day lights, it was difficult to descry those landmarks which were pointed out and named by the experienced host; but the more remote head-lands of Achille and Bencooler stood out, distinct and lofty above all, the watch-towers of the mightiest ocean of the universe, the land ramparts of the old world, and yet the nearest spot of earth to the new.

'And now,' said the host, pointing out the bird's-eye view of O'Brien's journey, 'you must cross the mountains, by the mam or glen between Glan mountain and the mountains of Lough Ambro; and then coming down on the Lakes of Ardcrow and Hindella, where you will go down the rapids with Emunh-na-Lung,[1] the ferryman; and still keeping the Leam mountain to the left or east, and the twelve pins to the west, you must go straight forward, down the bridle track, by the bed of the Sueeb river, and you will arrive at once upon Jar Connaught; and afore night you will find yourself with Lough Glenmurrough to the left, the Bay of Rosemuck to the right, and the town of St Grellan, down convanient forenent you.'

O'Brien took down the wild names of this verbal itinerary in his tablets; and assured by his *cicerone* that he would never want a clean shakedown and a '*caed mille faltha*,' while there was a thatched roof in Connemara, he mounted his pony, and began to take his solitary way.

He gazed on all around with enthusiastic emotion. National vanity and early associations influenced his picturesque perceptions, which in themselves were strong and clear. Excited by the scene, by the rapid circulation of his blood, and by the rarefied air he breathed, full of those spirits which engender hope and kindle fancy, his temperament responded to his position; and impressions were received, and ideas combined, such as he had never before experienced. But while new and astounding views of nature, gave new and imposing images to a mind the most creative and imaginative, still they excited sensations rather than sentiments. Confused, exalted, almost inebriated, he felt equal to any enterprize, and capable of any sacrifice, which had for its object that country, so strongly illustrated by the beautiful (but desolate and neglected) scenery around him. With his mind, like his steps, wandering, from point to point, and from thought to thought, he wondered that in regions so sublime, the Irish heart ever quailed, the Irish spirit ever drooped; and that men, who were masters of such natural ramparts, had not rather died in their defiles, than have submitted to the oppressor. 'But, alas!' he added in soliloquy, 'minds, not mountains, are the true ramparts of liberty.'

Thus pre-occupied, he passed unwittingly from one steep to another

---

[1] '*Emunh na Lung*,' Ned of the oar.

(his mountain pony almost directing his march), like one who dreams and walks, where waking consciousness would shudder to tread; till reaching an elevated cliff, which, by stopping the pony, awakened him to self-possession, he smiled at the recklessness of his own enthusiasm. The defile, unmarked by any track, appeared to lead only to a precipitous fall of rocks; and the sure-footed animal with instinctive caution, stood still.

O'Brien, in utter forgetfulness of the instructions of his host, and perplexed as he was, was yet free from the slightest suspicion of personal danger. He knew that in Ireland, the more remote the track of civilization, the safer is the way. There, crime, arising out of political misrule, is only directed against political oppression: and though at that period, numerous bands of peasantry had in the south armed themselves, and were in open rebellion against the greatest of all Irish grievances, the tithes, yet in Connaught, where the wretched natives, in the early part of the century, had been 'brayed as in a mortar,' all was the peace of spiritless resignation, – the calm which broods upon the ruin of the tempest that has passed.

O'Brien, thus puzzled as to the course he should pursue, sat patting the back of his pony, when he thought he heard a rustling in the mimic forest of brushwood, quickbeam, and witch-hazle, which richly covered the sides of the rocks, to the left of the defile, from the summit to the base. Throwing up his eyes, he fancied he saw a figure moving through the masses of brambles and verdure; but at that moment his attention was drawn off. A horseman suddenly bounded across his narrow pathway, endeavouring to rein in his steed, and 'humbly axing pardon of the gentleman for startling his animal.' It was Corny the cadger; he appeared to have issued, with a sort of pantomimic effect, from a fissure in a high, black, dripping rock, which rose perpendicularly to the left of the pass; but the furze and underwood he had cleared away, by springing his horse boldly through them, had concealed the mouth of the defile, which appeared to open in a bridle-way, or short cut from the shore of the lake below. He was mounted on a stout garron, between two paniers; and accounted for his appearance, by saying, that he had been dispatched in great haste by a dealer in fish below, on the lake, across the mountains to Killery Bay, where a great glut of turbot had been caught. His employer, he said, served the religious gentlemen of Cong and Tuam; and the two next days were black fasts. He then offered his services to the traveller as far as their way lay in the same direction, with a simple earnestness, that almost obliterated the disagreeable impression made by his sinister countenance. He remarked that, instead of proceeding forward, 'his honour must turn back a taste, and take the little *luib*[1] to the left, which would bring him to a bridle track to the head of Lough Ardcrow.'

O'Brien gladly availed himself of this information, though somewhat startled by the cadger's appearance; and Corny continued:

'Och, sorrow step of ground from the foot of Mam Turk to the top of Ben Leven, but I know better nor my pater or credo. Jasus pardon me' (crossing himself devoutly), 'and dioul would be in me, if I did not: for many a sore step I have made in 'em, as scholar, cadger, and cosherer.'

'Are you a Connemara man?' asked O'Brien, with a scrutinizing look; for, though glad to be guided, he still did not like his guide.

'I am not, plaze your honour, but am all as one; having served 'Squire Joyce, of Joyce's country, for two years and more, and carried the post, and had my bit, and my sup, and my rag, in regard of a trifle of a good turn I did the 'Squire, when he was high sheriff.'

'What was that?' demanded Murrogh carelessly.

'Why I was walking the world, in them times, as a poor scholar, with my satchel and copies (for larning was then in fashion, not all as one as since them schools were set up); and hearing that the Galway bailiffs were on the hunt for the high sheriff, in respect of a trifle of debt to a Galway marchant for limins and sugar (all the daling, troth, ever he had with any of them; his estate finding everything, barring the claret, which comes from his cousin-germain in Bourdeaux), what does myself do, but helps them to a boat to cross the lake in, taking care to let out the bottom, when they were little more than half way; and being then a light bit of a gassoon, and swiming like a barnacle, it was not long till I got safe to 'Squire Joyce's in good time to put the high sheriff on his diffince; and when all the constables in the country came down upon him in a posse, myself carried his honour over to the Hy Tartagh or O'Flaherty's Mountains, and lodged him safe in the ould ruins of the Abbey, till the hue and cry was over; and then brought him back in great state to his own place, and had the run of the house ever after; and might to this day, only for a little trouble I fell into (and was a wronged man, and an innocent, if ever there was one), in respect to a taste of smuggling.' Here Corny sighed

---

[1] A glen

out an 'Och hone!' 'So, after that, when I came back from foreign parts, I took to cadgering, and crosses these mountains with a bit of fish, or a kish of kelp, or whatever is going, ten times a year, and more; and sells a print of a priest, or a story-book or ballad to the fishermen; – any thing to get honest bread. But minds ever to keep the bridle ways and high roads, and goes straight from Balinrobe to Cong, and from Cong across the Lough, down upon St Grellan town, or the Killeries; in respect of my accident, Jasus be good to us. Amen.'

'And what was your accident?' asked O'Brien, more in courtesy than in curiosity.

'Och! plaze your honour, I don't like to be discoursing about it. This a-way, if you plaze, Sir, dear, to the left. But it's what I was never rightly myself after that, any how, though it's now fourteen years agone; and it's far I have been, and much I have seen since then; and the like of that, at home or abroad, never came across me afore or since.'

'And pray what was it, friend?' asked O'Brien, whose curiosity now was worked upon by this 'swelling prologue of a mighty theme,' which the cadger was evidently more anxious to relate, than he was to hear.

'What was it, Sir, dear? Och, then to your left again, if you plaze. This Mam has the divil's own twists in it; but once we track the neck of the mountain above, we'll see the whole bog and Turlogh of Ardcrow, like a sheet of paper before us. What was it, your honour? Och, then it's a long story, and to this day sorrow night's lodging need I want, nor bit nor sup neither, as long as I'd be willing to tell the cottiers, aye troth, and the best scollogs in Connemara, and was called into Miss Joyce's parlour to tell that same. And ould Mr Martin, of Dangan, God bless him, when I'd bring a kish of fish to the gates, it's what he'd have me into Madam Martin's iligant room, and, Corny, he'd say, it's a long time since we'd have your story of the Abbey of Moycullen and the ghost of Abbess Beavoin O'Flaherty.'

At the mention of these names, O'Brien listened with an awakened interest, and increased curiosity; and Corny went on in his rambling manner.

'And so, then, I'd scrape my best bow, and stand with my caubeen in my hand, forenent the buffet, and every servant in the house with his head in at the door, and the quality sated on the settee; I'd clear my voice, and – you may throw your reins on the baste's neck, your honour, and let her take her own way up the hill, for she'll never decaive you – I'd clear my voice, and just humouring it awhile, till I'd get into a proper tune, I'd begin this way. In the name of God, and the blessed Virgin, and the whole court of heaven, amen. It came to pass on the eve of the pattern of the feast of Saint Grellan, glory be to his honour, that I, Cornelius O'Clummaghan, scholar, cadger, and cosherer, commonly called the poet of Loch Corrib, having loaded my garron and kishes down below, among the caves of Killery Bay, and being bound to Balinrobe on a trifle of business for a frind, as often I was, and will again, plaze God, began my journey through the mountains of Connemara, fresh and fasting, with the wind full in my teeth, and a say fog full in my back, my bit of a dudeen[1] stuck in the cord of my caubeen,[2] with a slip of sally in one hand, and my padreens in the other. Now every one knows, that the short cut from Killery harbour to Balinrobe, is by the pass of Barnaderig, and through Joyce's country to the ferry of Cuffeen, at Loch Mask, which brings you down to Balinrobe town, in no time; but having a raison of my own, for not going th'ould bridle track, which is well known to man and baste, I took my way by the skirts of Lough Feo, striking into the heart's core of the Kylemore hills, and keeping my eye on the twelve pins of Benbola, by way of a mile-post, never losing sight of the track of Benknock, until I cleared the hills of Shannonayola, and found myself late and lone, in the great pass of Mamclogheleer, as myself thought; for now yez will mind, I lost sight of the twelve pins, and took the sun as my guide, it going due-west, and I going due-east; and thought I couldn't miss my way, barring the night came on, nor then itself, in regard of the stars, and so walking on aisy and quiet beside the garron, she being heavily laden, and I beguiling the way as I could, betimes lighting my pipe from a smothered sod, that I stuck in one of the kishes, betimes taking a thimbleful out of my cruishkeen, which was belted with a suggan at my side – betimes dropping a bead, and saying an ave or decade, – and betimes lilting up an ould planxty, or repating a taste of Don Belianis, or the seven wise maisters, or any skreed of larning, that turned up in my mynd; when what should I hear, as I thought, but voices talking English among the rocks, on the top of me, which was remarkable; little English being then talked in Connemara, any how; but couldn't see a christian, barring a great goss hawk, that came screaming down the

[1] Short pipe.
[2] Hat.

cliffs, and then cutting along the *rasach*,[1] was soon out of sight. A bad sign it was! and it wasn't for nothing the bird quit her nest; and the next minute, what should I hear, Sir, honey, but the shot of a musket, and then another, and then a shout faint and far, like the howl of a hound at midnight, and then a great rustling and floustering among the atharwood[2] above, and then a floundering and a flapping down the cliffs, from rock to raith,[3] and then comes tumbling the carcase of a man, just like a wounded curlew, till all battered and bloody, he lies staked on the point of a crag, as close to myself, as yez are now, gintleman dear, at this present moment. Diab-hal! I thought the sowl would have left the body of me; the more so, as the head of the corpse being turned to me, and the eyes of it staring out of the socket, in my face, what should I see, but th'ugly countenance of a great crony and cosherer of my own, one Darby Lynch of the Cladagh, who had been hunted in the mountains two days before, by them boddaghs of Revenues, who had been sent down to bring ruin upon the place, all in respect of a taste of tay, and a trifle of tobacco, that Darby, poor boy, forgot to inter in the port, and to save trouble, had landed them down among the rocks in the caves of Killery Bay. Och troth, then I saw it was time for myself to be on the *scuirlang*;[4] and without waiting, to raise the *keenthecaun*[5] over the dead man, I cuts the cable of my kishes, and jumping the garron, dashes down a bit of rasagh or shrubbery glen, and on I went over stone and stream, thinking of nothing at all, but how to get rid of them boddaghs of Revenues, who brought me into trouble afore; and seeing at last that I had missed my mark, and was on th'ould channel of a torrent, that had taken it into its head to go another way, just for variety (which often it does), I turns the garron up the first bit of a *luib* that I met, and short and sweet it was like the road to sin; for all of a sudden it opened into a sort of a *bainseoch* of a place, without track or trace, mark or mearn,

[1] A wild place.

[2] 'Atharwood,' an old Irish term for hawthorn, quickbeam, birch, witch-hazle; such as usually grow in mountains, ravines, and wild places.

[3] Brake.

[4] On the move.

[5] A corruption from the word *caoinan*, or Irish dirge, still howled at funerals in most parts of Ireland. Although there is not in the Irish language, the professional Caoinans are called Keeners. Each province had formerly its own *ullaloo*, called the Munster cry, or Ulster cry, etc. etc. etc. and may still have.

but overgrown with *loso wood*,[1] so that the garron couldn't make a step, without tearing through bosheens of fern and furze, ivy and thorn bush, the soul! and looking up at the sun, it was then myself first seed that we were taking the same road, cheek by jowl, and that instead of getting on, it was backward I was going, as the devil tells his padrheens, god bless us! but what had I for it? sorrow thing! so I takes the first turn, which led to a glin or pass properly so called, and the way was broad below, and the rocks were meeting and hugging above the head of me, like gossips at a fair, so that what light was in it, came in at the far ind, at which myself wint out, as soon as I convainently could; and if I did, where should I find myself, but in a four ways place, at the top of Glan Murrogh, and within sight of th'ould haunted ruins of the Abbey of Moycullen; and then troth you would not give an Englishman's button, or what's less, an Irishman's skewer, for my life; for now mind me well, Sir, dear, what should I see, standing bolt upright against a rock afore me, lone and lofty, grand and grey, but a fine ancient ould stone crass, and the crass in a circle; and down the main trunk, the figure of a nun with her hands on her breast, cut out of the hard stone; and above her head, cut in the same, these words in the finest of Latin (yez understand Latin, Sir, dear), '*Orate pro me, Beavoin O'Flaherty,*' and a little green rath, as green as ever grew on fairy ground, rising near; and a torrent which, in regard of the rath, is called Pool na Fouika,[2] dashing down from a tall comely cliff behind all; and it was then to my moan, I well guessed the place, it was my sore luck to stand in!' Here Corny paused, and taking off his hat, wiped his moist forehead with the sleeve of his coat.

'And what place was it?' asked O'Brien anxiously.

'Why what place could it be? Wasn't there the four ways! and the Abbess Beavoin's crass, and the Pool na Fouika, and the rath; and put that and that together, and what place could it be, but *Croisneer ny Croise,*[3] that often I heard tell of, and never wished to see.'

'Well?' ejaculated Murrogh interrogatively.

'Well, no, but ill, your honour, and the worst of luck that ever befell me, for if there is a *bainseoch*[4] on the face of the creation, it's that

[1] Creeping plants.
[2] The fairy's waterfall.
[3] The barrier of the cross.
[4] A desert place.

same, Go Dein Deudh – That it was in the stocks of Creag Grellan, I was standing that minute, or up to my neck in Lough Feo, in place of where I was. So putting myself under the purtection of God, and the whole court of Heaven, for what else had I for it, I dropt on my knees before the crass, to pray for the sowl of Beavoin O'Flaherty, as it was my duty and devotion to do, taking a drop of the cruiskeen just to raise the heart of me, which was sick and faint; but what would you have of it, sorrow prayer, I could pray no more than if I was a Turk, or a heathen, or heretick – I that served mass, and could do it again with any boy within the verge of Mitre land. Och hone! it was then I gave myself up for a lost man, a desolate christian, a raal *Baintrebbah;*[1] and flopping down upon my two bare knees, and thinking of nothing at that present time, better to do, I begins to thump my breast, as if I was saying my "culpa mea," and fixed my eyes on the crass, and rehearsed aloud "Orate pro me Evelyn O'Flaherty," which was all I could do, for the sowl of me; and if I did, what should make response close at my ear, crying "Amen," but a voice, if voice I may call it, that was like the moan of the Banshee in a stormy night, faint and fearful. And I, starting on the feet of me, not maning to do that neither, only couldn't help myself; and saw as plain as this twig in my fist, standing in the woody pass forenent me, the figure of a faymale nun, the very moral of the stone image on the crass. Och! then I pledge you my conscience, it's little I saw or heard after that, any way; for the sight lift my eyes intirely, and there came a roaring in my head you might have heard from this to Mam Turk; and what happened then, or what as wonge with me, body and sowl, or where I was, or what I was, it's what I never could tell, to this blessed minute; but believes it's many a mile I travelled between that and day. And when I opened my eyes, one fine morning, I found myself lying as flat as a bannock on the bare soil, at the foot of the rock, with the sun shining over me, and a tall, swarthy woman standing beside me, in her smock and mantle; her long grey coolun hanging down, after the fashion of the Isles of Arran, and a leather girdle round her middle, and looking, as I thought, very like a seal.[2] This was more of the yarn; for I knew *her* any how to be neither worse nor better than a *Binied.*

[1] An excommunicated person.

[2] There is a popular superstition along the coast of Connemara, that the islands of Clare and Arran were at one period peopled by a race half seal, half human, or as they called them, mermen.

' "What call have ye here, ye *Arab hallagh?*" says she; which, in hard Irish, manes, "ye divil's bit."

' "Sorrow call, at all at all, Maram," says I, "and it wasn't with my own good will I came in it."

' "Up, and away then, you *gramog,*" says she, "and the divil your master be your speed, for this is holy ground, not made for his imps to sport in."

'Sport, thinks I to myself; but I said nothing, only scrambled upon my feet, and made her a genteel bow.

' "There," says the Binied, pointing to the garron, that was taking her morning male of a whisp of grass, "there's the garron; use her, while you have her, which won't be long; for Feadhree's curse is upon him and his rider!"

'And so, troth, I wanted no more bidding, but mounting my garron, turned her head to the spine of the mountain; but the Binied making a snatch at the suggan that bridled him, twists him round another way.

' "That's your road," says she, "for it leads to the gallows of St Grellan, to which you are bound, and that's my prophecy," says she, "and mind the words of the Banfhaoh;" and then giving the garron a skelp of a long *cipin* she held in her fist, off it went, as if the divil was her speed, sure enough, over stick and stone, hill and turlogh, till she landed me safe at the foot of gibbet hill.

'And now, young gintleman, jewel, yez will little marvel, if the people would rather be after taking a round of fifty cantreds of bog land than make a short cut by the pass of Croisneer ny Croise, for it's a marked place; and luck or grace never fell on him yet, that left the track of his foot in it; as I know to my great moan and grief, in regard of my kishes, which was the ruination of me intirely, God help me! to say nothing of my lovely fine garron, which died of the crupple, two days after I got back, as the Binied foretold!'

'But how had you roused the wrath of the Binied?' asked his auditor insensibly interested in a detail so improbable, yet so much in keeping with the superstitious reminiscences of his early childhood.

'Och! then, an ould grudge to me and mine. For, do you see, my father had a hand in bringing Mor-ny-Brien's husband (for that was her name) to the gallows, a great rapparee and a wood hunter.

'Mor-ny-Brien!' repeated her foster-son, endeavouring to suppress his emotion, as he observed the eye of Corny glancing at him under its penthouse lid. 'Was she the person you met in the mountains of the Hy Tartagh?'

'Ay, in troth, Sir; a great follower of the O'Briens of Arran, and mother of that imp of the divil and fairy-begotten garlagh, Shane-na-Brien, who was hanged for murdering a pace officer at Michael's Cross, twelve years ago.'

At that moment a loud shrill blast from a rude mountain horn, repeated in endless echoes, came so close on the ears of the narrator, that it seemed to issue from the rocks, near which they were riding. O'Brien's pony stood still as if spell-bound, but the cadger's horse became so unruly, that he was unable to rein it. He was, indeed, as much incapacitated for the effort, by the sudden change which came over himself, as by the fear of the animal he rode. His hands trembled, a ghastly paleness over-spread his countenance; his eyes, strained from their sockets, were fixed upon some object on the rocks above, which fastened them with a basilisk's gaze; and his quivering lips vainly endeavoured to mutter some incoherent prayer, when a second blast released his horse from all restraint. Dashing forward with ungovernable violence, the animal soon carried him through the windings of the ravine, till he was lost to O'Brien's view. The mountain pony, on the contrary, remained quietly on the spot, as if the fearful blast, which scared away 'the horse and his rider,' was recognized as a familiar sound. She neighed and pricked up her ears, and pawed the earth, as in reply to a signal not unknown to her. Meantime O'Brien's eyes were intently fixed upon the spot, where the apparition stood, which had frightened the astounded cadger, and in which O'Brien distinctly recognized the figure of Shane-na-Brien. His gigantic form cutting darkly against the yellow sky, he stood leaning on his *galb* or staff, and looked like the very genius of the wild and solitary place, with the picturesque savagery of which his form so well assorted.

But while O'Brien gazed and hailed him, Shane drew back into the thicket, and the cry of *'faere ghim! faere ghim!'* notified that caution was necessary and protection at hand. The wild and warlike cry was followed by the low and modulated tones of the Irish bugle or cornet, which softened down to a plaintive melancholy, as they descended the mountain. To his amazement O'Brien perceived that his intelligent pony followed the music till it ceased; when he found himself at the foot of the mountain, and within view of the smoke of a human habitation.

He was now convinced that Shane was accompanying him on his journey; and that he was the unaccommodated individual who had lain mantled in the bottom of the boat. In the horn, whose tones were so skilfully modulated, he recognized an instrument on which Shane had taught him to perform in his childhood. It was the cornet, or as it is called in Irish, the 'musical stick;'[1] and the soft, wild music which was produced from it, was an air still known to the peasantry of Connaught, by the name of the 'gathering of the kine,' whose rich, flowing, and somewhat melancholy melody, chaunted at eve by some female voice from a distant style, draws the obedient cattle home by the spell of its magic sounds. The docile instincts of the acute little animal, whose properties were so well adapted to the region in which it was bred, struck him with admiration; and justified all he had heard of the once celebrated race of Connemara 'hobblers.' While caressing the pony with his hand and voice, as it stood to take breath after its arduous descent, he smiled as the notion crossed him, that the animal was a true Jesuit, and worthy, by its docility and intelligence, of the *manège* from which he had taken it.

While permitting his horse to drink from a spring which gushed from a rock, the lowest of the mass, O'Brien was struck with the wildness of the scene around him. It was a *turlogh*, or dried-up moss, encompassed by the steep hills that lie at the base of the Shannonfala mountains, and stretched between them to the very verge of the Loughs Hindilla and Ardcrow. Between these masses of water darted down one of those rapids, described by the host of the Shebean; but O'Brien looked in vain for Emunh na Lung, the ferryman; and found no mode of crossing, save in a corricle laid up under a witch-hazle that dipped into the water.

While standing in some perplexity, his ear was suddenly struck by a deep, low, and sobbing moan, that seemed to issue from a ravine that lay to the left of the rocks through which he had descended; and on approaching the spot, he perceived an infant laid out upon a plank, just within the fracture of the mountains, leading to a little dell, which some wretched beings had apparently chosen for their last asylum, wherein to starve and die. Some loose stones and sods, heaped rudely together, against the side of a rough, but sheltering rock, intimated a human dwelling; and a little stream of turbid smoke issuing from an

[1] The cornac, or musical stick, is the horn of some animal, with a brass mouth-piece; and is still used.

aperture in the green roof, spoke it to be then actually inhabited. The appalling image awed, but by no means checked, the warm, prompt, and sympathising feelings of the solitary spectator, He dropt a piece of silver into the broken trencher, which was placed at the feet of the infant corpse, for the purpose of receiving the contribution of the wanderer, who might pass by a place so lonely and isolated. Familiar as O'Brien had been with such objects in his early youth, and well acquainted with the barbarous Irish custom of exposing the dead, for the purpose of obtaining means of interment; still influenced perhaps by feelings predisposed to sadness, he shuddered at the spectacle, and was again backing his pony into the main path, when it struck him that this might be the hut of Emunh na Lung. At this moment the thick fall of many feet arrested his attention; a group of squalid, naked children, crowded to the door of the hut, followed by a tall, gaunt, spectral figure, who paused upon its threshold, and looked the very genius of famine. It was evident, that this Irish Ugolino was the wretched father of these wretched children; one of whom, with its shoulders drawn up to its ears, its bristled hair standing on end, with all the traces of neglect and want marked on its pinched features and squalid looks, came slyly, and yet joyfully forward, to snatch the silver shilling, which glittered in the trencher: and then holding it up to the man, screamed '*tighim, tighim*' (see, see). The father snatched the money, looked earnestly at it, then glancing his dark and sunken eye at the young and charitable stranger, he nodded his thanks, sullenly and dejectedly, but without making any further appeal to the benevolence he had awakened. O'Brien was deeply affected; he feared to advance – yet his feelings would not suffer him to retreat, without some effort to inquire into, and relieve such misery.

'Is there a fever in your house?' he demanded doubtingly, while occupied in untying the knotted strings of his purse.

'No faver,' replied the man, doggedly.

'What did that child die of?' asked O'Brien, pointing to the livid little corpse, which looked the victim of typhus.

'Hunger,' said the man, sternly.

O'Brien shuddered. 'And that moan?' he asked, with some difficulty of articulation.

''Tis the woman!'

'The woman! your wife?' Another sullen nod of the head was the distinct answer. The highest order of despair is but little demonstrative.

'What is the matter with her?' The man hesitated a reply, either from want of English or of power to express himself; at last he said —

'Have you Irish?'

'Enough to understand you,' replied O'Brien, in the same language. The man pushed back the crouching children, with the humour and petulance of famished misery, and stepping up to O'Brien, told his story in the fewest possible words, and in that language, whose concise idiom gives emphasis to whatever it conveys. He had been a petty farmer down in the low lands: he was reduced to become a cottier, a turf cutter: marshy bogs and scanty maintenance had brought down disease upon himself and his family. He became a pauper, without strength, and with too large a family to 'walk the world' (the Irish pauper's usual resource). He raised, therefore, a hut, and constructed a buirling on the edge of Lough Ardcrow; but the service of the ferry was inadequate to support his family, which was starving around him. His wife had lately lain in, the infant had died for want of its natural nourishment, and the mother was fast following it to its untimely grave: 'that was all,' he said, taking up the oar of his little boat to prepare for his office.

'All!' said O'Brien, dismounting and articulating with great difficulty. One of the children took his bridle, and he entered the cabin, scarcely conscious that he did so: for his heart was full, and his recollection not very perfect. The house was, as might be expected, destitute of all human accommodation. A bundle of furze smoked under an aperture in one corner; a dying woman, squalid and meagre, lay extended on a bed of heather in another, covered only by a torn blanket. The livid tints of dissolution already discoloured her face: she was evidently running down fast, and each moan was less audible than the last. A difficulty of breathing, a something that rose hysterically to the throat, and prevented utterance, for a moment kept O'Brien silent. At last he said, addressing the man, who stood with his hands folded, his lips compressed, as one made up to suffering,

'Have you nothing to give her?'

'Nothing!' was the emphatic reply, uttered in a tone of reckless, but almost placid despondency.

'Gracious God! what is to be done? A little nourishment might yet save her. Is there no cabin, no farm house within reach, where we could purchase her a little milk, till something better is procured?'

'There is,' was the cool reply.

'Where?' said Murrogh, eagerly, and hastening to mount his horse. 'Direct me where to find it, and I will go myself.'

'Will you?' said the man, falteringly, and following him to the threshold, 'will you?' As he spoke, his rigid muscles relaxing from their stern compression, every strong line and lineament of his haggard face yielding to the sudden impulse of long uncalled-on feelings, he 'wept Irish'. That deep, convulsive sob, which the high wrought sensibility of the most sensibly organized people in the world, sends out from their labouring breast, now burst tumultuously from the quivering lips of one, in whose chilled, but still all human heart, neither want, contumely, nor despair, had been able to dry those fine sources of emotion, so falsely attributed to the civilized and the refined alone.

In a moment O'Brien was mounted. The eldest of the children was placed before him as his guide; the little animal they rode, picking his steps along the ridge of a gullet, perilous to tread and fearful to look at. In ten minutes it brought them into the slovenly bawn of a mountain scullog's cabin, which lay sheltered in a little slip of valley, near Lough Hindilla, surrounded by all those symptoms of thriftless and negligent prosperity, which distinguished the farming smuggler of Connemara. The baying of a cur dog brought an old woman from the cabin. O'Brien told his story in three words; he wanted milk for a poor herd's wife in the mountains, who was dying for want of nourishment; and he held up a half-crown-piece as a running commentary on his brief text. The woman readily filled a bottle with milk, warm from the cow, and added to it a small wheaten cake. While taking ample payment for all, she was beginning a string of gossiping questions in Irish-English, prologued by the remark of how impossible it was to feed the poor cottiers of the mountains for ever, – when O'Brien cut her short, by giving the spur to his pony; and with a haste incredible, retracing the perilous path he came, he returned to the objects of his commiseration. The eagerness with which the poor woman bit the vessel that conveyed the nutrition, for which she was perishing, was more than a recompense for the service his charity had bestowed; while his feelings were still further taxed by the prostration of the unfortunate father at his feet.

In a few minutes, he was with his pony in the boat, and Emunh na Lung, standing erect, and governing with one oar the progress of the vessel, he made a rapid descent into the adjoining lake. O'Brien landed, and remounted; and he did not refuse his hand to the wild

Connaught ferryman, who pressed it to his eyes and lips. Under the protection of a heartfelt blessing, he proceeded on his journey.

Pausing for a moment, to look back at the wild scenery he had passed, another winding blast from Shane's bugle seemed to bid him adieu, as he now entered the lines of comparative civilization. The sun, as it reddened the vast bosom of the Atlantic, danced on some remote spire that sparkled like a meteor in midair: and the bridle track, which led to the beautiful coast, that lay in the distance, taking a turn, he soon came on the high road to St Grellan. There again he paused for a moment; all the associations of early life, all the feelings of that patriotism, which is so much made up of localities, came out in full development. He saw the dark mass of building in the midst of a dreary plain, which he identified as Bog Moy House, his future residence. He saw the young plantations and rich woods of Beauregard (the long uninhabited, but magnificent seat of the Proudforts), which lay on the road from St Grellan to Galway. He saw the glittering sashes of the Bishop's palace, at a short distance from the town, and the heavy atmosphere of turf smoke, which hung over the town itself. Agitated by many feelings of 'good and ill together,' he struck into the rutted way, which was by courtesy called the high road; and as the last gleam of sun faded from the bay, entered the suburb, which was still called O'Brien's gate.

At a period, when the largest cities of the Irish provinces presented images of the desolation and violence, which, down to the close of the last century, marked the general character of the country, the smaller towns consisted of little more than one or two good modern houses (the residences of the church and state authorities), a jail, a barrack, and a surrounding cluster of the vilest cribs, raised of dry stones, – with a few old houses, antique towers, and perhaps a battered castle, or a ruined convent.

O'Brien having passed the gate which bore his name, and which still had the old inscription upon it – 'From the ferocious O'Flahertys, deliver us, oh Lord!' and having waded through the long, dirty suburbs of mud hovels, called the Cladagh, the first object which struck his eye was the ruin of the old Nunnery of Mary, John, and Joseph, converted into a barrack; where an English regiment was mustered for evening parade, in its cloistered court. The contrast with the scenes through which he had so recently passed, was striking; nor was he more prepared for the transmutation which, in traversing the main street of the town, he thought it had undergone since last he had seen it. Either his inexperience had formerly endowed it with a beauty and importance, which in fact it did not possess, or it was now much decayed and deteriorated: for it appeared to him mean, old, filthy, and wholly without police. The trade of this second city of the country was indicated by an oaten cake, thrust out of a sashless window, on a deal board, or a pole struck in the thatch of a cabin, with a turf at the end of it; while 'good dry lodgings' was scrawled over the door of many a hovel, whose threshold was washed by the overflowings of the unchannelled street; which ran in muddy torrents, as the acquired inequalities of the pavement directed. In other places, 'entertainment for man and baste,' indicated that whiskey and straw might be had for a moderate remuneration, by the equestrian, who was not able to 'pay the damage' of the great inn.

The great inn (itself a most dilapidated building. and once the town mansion of the O'Flahertys), was distinguished by a shattered sign of the O'Flaherty Arms, which lay against the door-case of the squalid entry; the walls, from which it had swung for half a century, being too frail to support any longer with safety so cumbrous an appendage. The long main street and market-place were peopled with a bare-footed, ragged population; among whom a few officers, looking like beings of a superior creation, picked their way to the parade, at the summons of a drum, whose roll alone disturbed the silence of this nest of ruin and wretchedness.

O'Brien hesitated whether he should, or should not, put up at the O'Flaherty Arms; for both himself and his steed were weary, after a voyage and journey of eighteen hours. A house of entertainment, however, on the opposite side of the way, by its appearance determined him to pass the night at St Grellan, and to proceed to Bog Moy, a distance of five miles, on the following morning. It was a spacious and handsomely fronted fabric, newly built, and with some of its windows not yet glazed. Over the door was written, 'THE TONTINE HOTEL;' and on a flaring escutcheon appeared the splendidly emblazoned arms of the Proudforts, upon a field or the pearl of Lough Corrib, with the motto of '*Qui me cherche, me trouve.*' O'Brien read, and sighed.

On dismounting, he was received, if reception it could be called, by a ragged, tipsey waiter, who lounged at the door; and who tottered before him into a large, chill, and comfortless room, with furniture as old and battered, as the walls were fresh and new.

'I should be glad to have a supper and well-aired bed-room immediately,' said O'Brien.

'A supper and a well-aired bed-room,' replied the waiter, carelessly, as he arranged the pepper, mustard, and vinegar cruets that stood on an old sideboard.

'Yes,' said O'Brien, 'I suppose there is no difficulty?'

'Difficulty; 'pon my credit I can't say.'

'Send your master,' said O'Brien.

'My master,' said the man, surveying the traveller, who had come in on a Connemara pony, with only a light valise strapped behind him; 'my master dines with the other revenue gentlemen at the collector's, and isn't at home.'

'Well then, send your mistress.'

'The mistress! Och! the mistress never attinds customers, if she's in it; but she isn't. She and Miss Maria Theresa are gone to a dry drum, and won't be home the Lord knows whin. It's my intire opinion,' he added, putting his hands in his waistcoat-pockets, crossing his legs, and leaning back against the sideboard, 'that the O'Flaherty Arms would have answered ye better, than the Tontine; for none stops here but the highest of quality.'

'It is my opinion, too,' said O'Brien, laughing in spite of himself, at this specimen of the Irish mode of doing business, and of getting up crack inns under the patronage of the autocrats of the land; and, hurrying out, he bade the boy who had charge of his pony, to follow him to the other inn. There, in spite of its appearance, he found a hearty welcome, a good bed-room (if not a particularly neat one), and a bill of fare consisting of the usual 'boiled fowl, bacon, and greens,' which never fail at a genuine Irish inn: where the bacon lies on the hob ready to be cut, and the fowl in the roost over it ready to be killed.

Before he partook of the fare, for which his mountain journey had so well prepared him, and which, as usual, required the preparatory operations of 'first catching the fowl,' and then killing it, O'Brien went to visit his pony. It was already under the hands of the *baccah*, who acted as groom in the stable-yard of the O'Flaherty Arms; and it was surrounded by some of those loungers, who are always to be found in the inn yards of Ireland. They were all considering the pony with curiosity and admiration.

'It isn't for nothing you brought the gapul, plaze your honour?' said the baccah, as O'Brien examined one of her feet.

'Do you think her of value?' asked the owner.

'Do I, is it, Sir? – troth, I surely do,' was the baccah's reply, as he rubbed down the sides of the little animal with renewed vigour; 'she'll bring her own price any day, in fair or market, in Galway county or out of it. I'll ingage it's herself carried you well over rock and rathe, bog and mountain; for she's as cute as ever a baste in the barony.'

'You know her, then?' said O'Brien.

'Know her! It's few but knows *gapul na phouka;*[1] sure she's of the Shulah's breaking,' he added, turning to the loungers.

'Then,' said one of them, 'it's herself's the *luibin*[2] of a gapul; for it was his father before him had the notes for making a cute cratur of a Connemara pony.'

'Why, then,' said another, 'it's a pity but it's himself he would break in, instead of the gapuls; for a wilder poor cratur doesn't breathe the breath of life this day. There be some wud tell you he's a fairy man, and others wud be after saying he's the arrach of Shane-na-Brien: ay, by my conscience, or Shane himself, who was hanged for the murther at St Michael's Crass; – Christ save us, and bless the mark.'

'I never seed the Shulah but oncet,' said the baccah, 'and that was Lammas day, 'bove all the days of the year, in the mountains of Moycullen. And it was himself was taking that very pony, quiet as she stands there, down to the wood of Dim, on Lough Corrib, where the horse-dailers lays the price for the ponies; he breaks on the *Claghan-na-tomparagh,*[3] and finds his bargain there the next day: for the Shulah will not put his *comhluadar*[4] upon any man, barring it's a priest, a friar, or a nun. And I'll ingage a good bargain it is; for a garlah in the cradle might deal with the Shulah, ay, indeed. So they say none ever saw the Shulah in town, or townland, which is mighty wonderful; only in respect of the great penance and sore sin upon his poor soul; for, do you mind, meet him where you will, by night or day, by Luib or Lough, it's telling his padreens he'll be, and going over his decades, and the seven penitentials.'

O'Brien, now perceiving that his steed was in good hands, and had all that prepossession in her favour which is through life so serviceable to man or beast, left him to the baccah; convinced that Gapul-na-

[1] The fairy's pony.
[2] Cunning, crafty one.
[3] The stone of the pirates.
[4] 'Company.'

phouka was a pupil of Shane's, who, it appeared, supported his wild existence, by breaking in those mountain horses, which, like himself, were indigenous to the regions, where alone the breed of ponies and of Shulah men were still extant.

The suspicion of who Shane was, the confidence placed in his probity, the indisposition of the common people to profit by their suspicion, and receive the reward for his apprehension, afforded O'Brien food for meditation, no less than Shane's mysterious conduct towards himself. The fidelity to his pecuniary engagements, in his strange commerce with the horse dealers, was nothing new or peculiar. In the midst of the most lawless burnings and destruction of property, the genuine Irish peasant is scrupulously honest in his intercourse with his neighbours: and O'Brien's heart bore ample testimony that the virtue was not solitary in his foster-brother. He knew him to be brave, persevering in action, and enduring of privation, faithful to the death in his attachments, an affectionate son, an incorruptible follower, with a heart that beat with a rude, but impulsive sympathy for the sufferings of others, and glowed with a genuine, though ill understood love of country. Yet is this man (he thought), a murderer, an outlaw, ready for every violence, – his hand armed against civilization, as civilization is armed against him, – and the whole tenor of his life at variance with the best interests of society! The world may make its conventional virtues and vices, and civil associations may dictate forms, but the source of good is in the feelings and affections of the animal. Even when bad government, or the undue pressure of ill-arranged externals, turns them the most irresistibly aside from their natural career, and enforces a disordered reaction, their principle itself remains unchanged; and the man thus situated makes for himself a code of compensating morality, which fits him for the peculiar circumstances of his untoward and difficult position.

In the midst of such reflections, intermixed with musing on Shane's perpetual watchfulness over his foster-brother's safety, and his inexpicable unwillingness to encounter him, even in the security and remoteness of the mountain fastnesses, the supper appeared; which his landlord set before him with a flask of claret (then, for reasons unassigned by the vendors, so cheap and so genuine in the county of Galway), and a county newspaper. In glancing his eye over the stale intelligence of this provincial journal, towards the end of his repast, O'Brien was caught by the appearance of his own name in a conspicuous column. He read as follows:-

'Died, on the first of June, at the retreat of the religious gentlemen of Cong, the Right Hon. Terentius O'Brien Lord Arranmore, the lineal descendant and representative of the Clan Tieg O'Briens, Princes of the Isles of Arran. His lordship was distinguished for his patriotism and loyalty, and, above all, for his great antiquarian lore, and for the efforts he had made to revive the literature of his country, as it existed in those times, when, if a learned man was missing from Europe, it was said, *amandatus est in Hiberniam.*

'His lordship having in his early childhood been seduced to abandon the religion of his fathers, he returned to it in mature life, from a sincere conviction; and bent on ending his days in the odour of sanctity, he retired from the world, and became a member of the confraternity of religious gentlemen of Cong. His remains were conveyed to the great Isle of Arran with a pomp suitable to his rank, and were attended to the water's edge by the greatest concourse of persons ever assembled in this province upon a similar occasion since the funeral obsequies of the great Lord Clanrickard.

'His Lordship is succeeded in his titles and estates by his only son, the Hon. Murrogh O'Brien, grand nephew of the celebrated Abbé Don Ignatius O'Brien (secretary of the college of the Propaganda of Rome), great great nephew of Field Marshal Count Taaf, of the Mac Taafs of Jar Connaught, and nephew to the Misses Mac Taaf, of Bog Moy House, in the county of Galway, and Ballyslattery, in the county Mayo.

'His Lordship has served with distinction in the armies of His Imperial Majesty the Emperor of Germany; to which service it is supposed he will return, having settled his affairs in this country. His Lordship is in his twenty-fifth year and unmarried. His presumptive heir is Turlogh Giol O'Brien, Esq. of the Isles of Arran.'

O'Brien read this paragraph with a moisture in his eyes that obscured their vision, and with a smile occasionally curling his lips, that indicated his opinion of this purely Irish exhibition of pride in all its hyperbole. The pompous announce of titles and estates sounded in his ear like a mockery. The lordly appellation was, indeed, not new to him; for the polite and punctilious inmates of the Retreat had not failed to give him, in conversation, all the additions to which they attached so much consequence: neither was he wholly insensible to the possession of a title, respectable for its antiquity in the eyes of the world. He had, however, hesitated on its assumption, under the total ruin of his fortunes, and the consequent neccessity of earning his bread; nor was he wholly uninfluenced by an abstract contempt for aristocratic distinctions, which formed part of his philosophy, without entirely destroying the prejudices of early education; but, on more mature reflection, he changed his mind, and determined not to abandon his only possession – a possession which had caused his father the sacrifice of his independent fortune. The title was his right; and though unsupported by wealth, was still a barrier between him and that neglect, for which he was not yet prepared; while, by raising him above the mass, he believed it would inevitably increase the utility of those efforts, which he was more than ever determined to make for the civil and religious liberties of his countrymen.

END OF VOL. III

# The O'Briens and
# the O'Flahertys

$\bullet$

# VOLUME FOUR

# CHAPTER I

———•———

## *Bog Moy House*

Sic siti lætantar lares.
The ruin speaks that some time it was a worthy building

*Cymbeline.*

LORD ARRANMORE had just returned from the refreshing luxury of a
sea bath, on the following morning, when the opportune arrival of a
Galway carrier enabled him to appear before his aunts, with such
advantages of dress, as never fail to have their value, when brought
to the aid of great personal endowments. As soon as he had breakfasted, and given his pony in charge to the 'garloch', who was to ride
it to Bog Moy, he freighted the St Grellan chaise (the only public
vehicle in the town), with his books and wardrobe; and committing
himself fearlessly to its dislocating machinery, set off for Bog Moy.

Twelve years had so changed and improved his appearance, that if
there were any persons in the town of St Grellan, retaining a recollection of the young Clan Tieg O'Brien of Arran, who now saw him,
they no longer recognized in the elegant foreign-looking stranger, who
had 'put up at the O'Flaherty Arms,' the ungainly, but comely boy,
whose early talents and boyish adventures had left a due impression
behind them, and were still the theme of occasional gossip over the
winter's fire in the neighbourhood.

It was not till half an hour before his departure, that the address
on his luggage announced him to his host as Lord Arranmore, whose
father's funeral had recently passed through St Grellan, on its way
for embarkation to the isles.

The Connaught imagination immediately took wing. Rank, riches,
a colonelcy in the Irish Brigade, and a claim to half the estates in the

province, were soon added; and before Lord Arranmore entered his chaise, the news had fled through the High-street, reached the Cladagh, brought a crowd of idlers, beggars, and Isle of Arran boys, to the door, and filled all the windows in the town with gazers, of that sex, which, accused everywhere of the habit of window-gazing, more inveterately indulge it in the country towns of Ireland, even than in those of Spain. It was as dreary and drizzling a day as the 'great father of waters,' the Atlantic, ever sent to throw gloom over the town of St Grellan, when Lord Arranmore began his short journey to Bog Moy. The day was, besides, a great catholic holiday, the festival of St Grellan, the patron saint of the Ballyboe. The streets were all mud, the houses all smoke, and the gaiety of the town was still further eclipsed by the shops being half shut. He in vain endeavoured to recall, as the chaise jolted through the long, ill-paved, and rutted street, the 'fair city that lifted herself on high,' in the imagination of his boyhood. All its dimensions seemed contracted: the High-street and Four-ways (the *corso* and the *carrefour* of his childish admiration), whose splendour and bustle used to fill him with wonder, when he came in from the isles, or the mountains, now seemed dwindled and deserted. In the Four-ways, however, appeared groups, which identified its old destination: it was surrounded by shebean and pot-houses, and filled with females squatted in the mud, and selling Connemara stockings, eggs, fish, and other vendible commodities; while spalpeens and cottiers, leaning on their sleaghans[1] and scythes, lounged around the great stone cross in the centre, waiting to be hired after mass, and too often waiting in vain.

The High-street, too, was distinguished by many of its old features. It was still paraded by those *batteurs du pavé* in all Irish towns, the squireens; some galloping ostentatiously through the town on their new hunters, purchased by an I.O.U., more readily given, than redeemed; while the dismounted cavalry, seated on the counters of the best shops, amused their strenuous idleness with such 'bald, disjointed chat' as the news of the neighbourhood furnished them withal, repaying with a horse-laugh and a halfpenny the wit of the half-idiot, half-knave, who stood at the door, or bestowing a largess of equal value on the mendicant cripple, who, packed into a barrow, was wheeled from door to door by the 'christian' for charity (ready

---

[1] Turf spades.

'to do that, or more, for sweet Jesus's sake'), or by the buckeens, who would do that, or anything, 'just for fun, or a bit of a frolic.'

Early as it was, the belles of St Grellan were already clacking their pattens to prayers or parade, equally earnest in their double vocation of faith and flirtation; or were seen dangling their legs over the sides of a low-backed car, on their way to the '*salt watther;*' while the few not thus employed with this world or the next, sat suspended, like Mahomet's coffin, between both, in their window, too much occupied with other persons' affairs, to be very attentive to their own. From all these, the pochay of the O'Flaherty Arms elicited observation and comments; not only from the unusual circumstance of the turn out itself (a rare event), but from the handsome head put forward alternately from every window, not permanently closed by a wooden blind. All who had heard of the arrival of Lord Arranmore at once recognized the stranger (who was taking the coast road to Bog Moy, the tide being out), to be the son of the well-known, though long absent Baron O'Brien; and all who had not heard of that event, were full of queries and conjectures concerning the *che shin*,[1] whose black stock denoted his military calling, and whose unpowdered head was an innovation that portended some revolution in the Galway fashions, which had held their ground unchanged since the days of George the Second, and the great Lord Clanrickard.

Among the spectators of him whose 'youth and comeliness did pluck all gaze his way,' there were two, in whom his apparition, as he passed the bay window at which they were stationed, struck especial emotion,

> As though they saw some wond'rous monument.

These were the widow and Miss Costello, the friends and gossips of the Miss Mac Taafs, by whom the event of Lord Arranmore's arrival was devoutly wished, and long looked-for. From this watch tower of their perpetual vigilance, where, 'from morn till noon, from noon till dewy eve,' entrenched in snuff-boxes and pocket-handkerchiefs, with their knitting in their hands, with Pastorini's prophecies on one side, and Betsy Thoughtless on the other, they took cognizance of every transaction, private and public, religious and commercial, that occurred in the town. No little voteen picked her way to mass in the morning or mall in the evening; no dry-dum was given by the dowagers

---

[1] Literally, 'Who is that?' a notable person.

of one sex, nor jorum of punch by the dowagers of the other; not a pair of Connemara stockings was sold in the Four-ways, nor a basket of fish disposed of in the Cladagh, to the cadgers of Galway and Tuam, without their knowledge and commentary.

In the handsome head thrust through the left window of the St Grellan chaise, and in the dark, bright eyes, raised to the widow's bay window, which she construed into a look of recognition, the ladies at once discovered the long-expected and often talked-of guest of Bog Moy; for whose sake many an intended party, and above all the '*Jug Day*,'[1] two years in contemplation, at Bog Moy, had been deferred by their dear friends, the Miss Mac Taafs.

'I declare to Jasus, Prudence Costello,' exclaimed the widow, as the old chaise rattled by, and the fine eyes flashed upwards, 'I declare to Jasus, if that ar'n't Lord Arranmore at last, gone the coast road to Bog Moy! Why don't you return his salute, girl?'

Prudence Costello did return the salute tenfold; if a slight inclination of the head, extorted by 'the nods, and becks, and wreathed smiles' of the widow, could be so called. Throwing back a door, which literally opened into the kitchen (according to the Connaught establishment of that day, when every story had its own kitchen), the widow cried out, 'Mary Blake, slip on your Connemaras, and run down to the O'Flaherty Arms, and inquire if it's Lord Arranmore that has just set off by the coast-road in the pochay, that's my girleen.'

Mary Blake dropped her work 'right willingly;' and without waiting to slip on her Connemara stockings, slipped her feet into her pumps, and ran down to the O'Flaherty Arms. The intelligence she brought back was of a nature to induce the widow Costello to expedite an order to Jenny Lynch to have the car at the door by three o'clock: 'for we're going to take tay at Bog Moy the evening.'

The best quilt and feather-bed were put in requisition for the service of the low-backed car; and the sober wardrobe of the widow and Miss Costello (the one still affecting weeds as an inconsolable widow, and the other black, as a sentimental devotee, inconsolable for being neither widow nor wife), supplied its most becoming gravities, for welcoming home one whom they considered as hereditary prince

---

[1] The Jug Day was that, on which a pipe of claret, imported from France, was first broached in the old Connaught houses; and when the friends and neighbours were invited to give their opinions of the merit of the importation.

of the Isles of Arran, the Lord of Arranmore, and the heir of Bog Moy and Ballyslattery.

Never had Lord Arranmore, in his wanderings in far distant lands, looked upon scenes of classic association with more intense interest and curiosity, than he now sought out objects familiar to his recollection, on the road from St Grellan to Bog Moy; a road once so well known, but which seemed so strangely changed, since he had 'plucked geese, played truant, and whipped top' on it. Nothing could be more dreary or desolate than the country through which he was passing; there was nothing to meet the feelings of the most moderate philanthropist, or to satisfy the hopes of the least sanguine agriculturist; – nothing either prosperous or picturesque. There were but few symptoms of artifical cultivation, and no neat farming, no close enclosures, no secure fences, no budding hedgerows, and doubled-faced ditches, no sod or pipe drains, nor one faint dawning ray of the new light of modern husbandry. The agricultural state of the province was represented by swampy fields for pasturage, divided by stone mearings, with patches of earth, as yet unsown, but intended for a scanty provision of corn (for little grain was then raised in a land which had once supplied foreign markets).[1] Of the old woods which once fringed the bases of the Connemara hills, and of which some stunted remains were still visible in his childhood, there was now as little trace, as of any attempt at new and improving plantation; and to one more deeply read in the Irish story, than apprized of the actual state of Ireland, the name of the *woody island* would have appeared to have been given to it in irony or in reproach. The axe of the stranger had indeed been early laid to the root of the Irish forests, when they were the only fortresses of the brave hardy native, – when to cut down an army it was necessary to root up a wood, – and when heroes and oaks, Irish champions and Scotch firs, fell together. The little, however, which was then spared, fell before the wants of the people, in the beginning of the eighteenth century. The noblest forest trees were consumed as fuel, and the uncertainty of every tenure, under the penal code, at

---

[1] 'The people had not the folly to improve the property they had scarcely rescued from the gripe of forfeiture, being aware that its cultivation only invited fresh litigation. Thus Warner observes: "Whereas permanency of tenure, stable property, and even durable security in land or money, are prohibited the Irish papists by law, which obliges them to keep their lands waste, instead of improving them, in order to prevent, as much as possible, any temptation to leases in reversion, which protestants only can take." ' – *History of Ireland.*

that period, prevented that succession of coppice and planting, which might soon have supplied the place of the original produce. The mansions of the gentry were few and desolate; and the neglect and discomfort of their exterior gave no adequate idea of the quantity of claret drank at a vast expense in the interior. The population was as dreary as the country, being made up of a few squalid beggars, on their way to increase the mendicity of Galway town, or to be shipped off to the West Indies, – an occasional pedestrian, going from Bally to Bally, with his brogues and hose on his shoulders instead of his feet, – or perhaps a scollog and his wife, mounted on a barebacked garron, only shod before, according to the economy of those times. Here and there an equestrian of the higher order, the squireen, followed by his wise man, driver, or overseer, was distinguished afar off by the naked children, peopling every dunghill, as a 'brass-buttoned gentleman.'

Lord Arranmore's first glance at Bog Moy convinced him that there, at least, nothing had been changed. The morass or boggy plain, in which it stood, was as unreclaimed as when he had last shot snipes upon it, within a few paces of the house. In the midst of its brown surface appeared the only verdant spot in the demesne, a horsepond in its 'mantle of green.' There, still flourished, or decayed, a few old stunted trees, called the Orchard or '*Avalgort*,' with a mound covered with furze, called the '*Fin avain*,' or Vinery.[1] There too mouldered the ancient Dovecote; and the well of 'sweet water,' under its vaulted arch of rudely cut stone; a wall of stone or clay encompassed the bawn (a square of two hundred feet), the only pleasure-ground, which in former times 'the unquiet state of the land' permitted to the gentry of Ireland. Up to the commencement of the last century, the flocks of the most wealthy landholders were attended by armed herdsmen, who with spears for crooks, took their watch in the morning upon some high crag, to spy the neighbouring enemy, and at night drove their charge into the bawn, which afforded shelter alike for man and for beast. The bawn had been flanked by four square towers; one of which was in good preservation, and distinguished by the name of the Brigadier's Tower. Not so the mansion. Since Lord Arranmore had seen it, it had become confusion worse confounded: preserving the remains of all the various changes from its first erection of 'cage-work

---

[1] In an old Irish almanack of the fourteenth century, once in the possession of Colonel Vallancey, the time of gathering grapes and drinking the new wine is mentioned.

and couples,' through its progress of clay and stone and lime; 'a castle begun,' and a modern mansion never finished. On the outside of the bawn walls, rose a cluster of hovels, whose smoke rolled in masses from their chimneys down upon the road. These were the remains of the dwellings of tenants 'planted and estated on the land,' who had once been returned as constituting eleven families able to make twenty-five men at arms, and now the shelter of a band of Miss Mac Taaf's cottiers or under-tenants. It was dignified by the name of the town of Bog Moy.

Lord Arranmore drew up before one of these huts, which lying next the bawn gateway (without a gate), served as the lodge: and on the gassoon's inquiry, in Irish, if the Ban Tiernas were at home, the answer was given, that they were on the little bog convenient to the place. The future lord of Bog Moy alighted; and ordering the chaise and pony to proceed to the house, took a little 'thatched headed' urchin for his guide, and walked towards the bog which was so convenient, as to be separated from the pleasure-ground or garden-plot only by the dilapidated walls of the bawn. A 'mearing' of loose stones marked the separation of this favourite bit of bog from the turlogh through which its red veins ran.

Upon this meering Lord Arranmore leaned for a moment, to contemplate the singular scene and well-remembered persons before him. The Miss Mac Taafs were both on the ground, and both standing enough in profile, to give him a full and perfect view of their figure, without being seen by them. His first opinion was, that they were utterly unchanged; and that like the dried specimens of natural history, they had bidden defiance to time. Tall, stately, and erect, their weather-beaten countenance and strongly marked features were neither faded, nor fallen in. The deep red hue of a frosty and vigorous senility still coloured their unwrinkled faces. Their hair, well powdered and pomatumed, was drawn up by the roots from their high foreheads, over their lofty 'systems;' and their long, lank, necks, rose like towers, above their projecting busts; which with their straight, sticky, tight-laced waists, terminating in the artificial rotundity of a half-dress bell-hoop, gave them the proportions of an hour-glass. They wore grey camlet riding habits, with large black Birmingham buttons (to mark the slight mourning for their deceased brother-in-law); while petticoats, fastened as pins did or did not their office, shewed more of the quilted marseilles and stuff beneath, than the precision of the toilet required: both of which, from their contact with the water of the bog, merited the epithet of 'Slappersallagh,' bestowed on their wearers by Terence O'Brien. Their habit-shirts, chitterlings, and cravats, though trimmed with Trawlee lace, seemed by their colour to evince that yellow starch, put out of fashion by the ruff of the murderous Mrs Turner in England, was still to be had in Ireland. Their large, broad silver watches, pendant from their girdles by many steel chains, shewed that their owners took as little account of time, as time had taken of them. 'Worn for show, not use,' they were still without those hands, which it had been in the contemplation of the Miss Mac Taafs to have replaced by the first opportunity, for the last five years. High-crowned black-beaver hats, with two stiff upright, black feathers, that seemed to bridle like their wearers, and a large buckle and band, completed the costume of these venerable specimens of human architecture: the *tout-ensemble* recalling to the nephew the very figures and dresses, which had struck him with admiration and awe, when first brought in from the Isles of Arran, by his foster mother, to pay his duty to his aunts, and ask their blessing, eighteen years before.

The Miss Mac Taafs, in their sixty-first year (for they were twins), might have sunk with safety ten or twelve years of their age. Their minds and persons were composed of that fibre which constitutes nature's veriest huckaback. Impressions fell lightly on both; and years and feelings alike left them unworn and uninjured.

The eldest Miss Mac Taaf, – the eldest but by an hour, the representative of the Green Knights and Barons of Ballyslattery, who stood erect, with her right hand leaning on a walking-cane umbrella, was laying down the law in a loud oracular voice, sometimes in Irish, sometimes in English, to an old man, who stood bare-headed and footed before her. Her directions, though evidently 'the law and the gospel' were strengthened by an occasional reference to a person, who sat on a clump of turf, with pen and paper in hand, and an ink-horn at his button-hole; such as, 'and here James Kelly will tell you the same, Dan Hogan; and you know we consider James Kelly as the sense-keeper of Bog Moy;' to which assertion, James Kelly, by a confirmatory nod of the head, fully assented.

While Miss Mac Taaf and her premier were thus engaged in the legislative department, Miss Monica was busily employed in the executive. She stood a little in advance, her back supported against a turf-clump. Paddy Whack was seated beside her on his hinder legs, and was looking into her face, watching for the stick which she occasionally threw into the water, 'to keep the baste quiet.' She was, however, then occupied in counting the kishes of turf wheeled off, and receiving a tally from each driver as he passed, which she strung upon a cord. Sometimes chiding, sometimes praising, frequently soliciting, and always interfering, she kept up a constant fire of words, which were answered with more respect than coherency, by the rustic interlocutors. 'Thady Flaherty, it's what I hear, your bracket cow calved last week, and your woman never sent up a drop of the strippings[1] to the great house.'

'Och! then she won't be so, Marram, I'll engage, God bless you, Miss Monica.'

'Drop that chip of bog wood now, Jemmeen Joyce, is it to stale the timber, ye were let to come and help your daddy on the bog?' 'Onor ny Costello, where's the tribute hose ye were knitting for me, in lieu of the ducks?' 'What is it ye are grubbing up there, instead of clamping the sods? Show it here now: is it another copper Shamus?'[2]

'No, plaze your honour, Miss Monica, Marram; it's an ould horseshoe, the great luck!'

'Well, if it's only an old neile, I have often told you, that, as ladies of the manor, we have right to every screed found on the Fassagh. Take it up to the great house, Onor ny Costello.'

Thus occupied during some hours, they were on the point of breaking up their council, as the sun in its course announced the hour which gathered the cottiers to their mid-day meal of potatoes and milk at the great house, when a little gassoon ran up to Miss Mac Taaf, and presented her a slip of paper, on which was written, 'A stranger claims *connagh* and *meales* of the ladies of Bog Moy, after the old fashion of Irish hospitality.'

Miss Mac Taaf put on her spectacles to read this note, which Miss Monica perused, over her sister's shoulder. Both ladies raised their large Irish eyes, when the gassoon, in answer to their *che shin* (who is it?) pointed to the writer. They looked earnestly, and moved forward with stateliness, when the stranger, vaulting lightly over the mearing, took a hand of each lady, and pressed it with equal grace and cordiality to his lips: exclaiming, 'My dear aunts, has Murrogh O'Brien no longer a place in your recollection?'

'Chroist Jeesus, Murrogh O'Brien, is it you choild?' demanded both

[1] The first milk after the calf is dropped.

[2] 'A copper James;' i.e. one of James the Second's copper tokens, issued during his short reign in Ireland.

ladies, in a breath, and with a pleasurable amazement, tempered by that habitual stateliness, with which no emotion, either of pleasure or of pain, ever materially interfered.

Equally charmed at the arrival of their titled nephew, and struck by the change in his person, they stood returning with cordial interest, the shake of the hand which followed his more courtly salutation. Looking with eyes eloquent in their curiosity and surprise, they continued welcoming him to Bog Moy, and passing comments on his person and dress, in rapid alternation; while James Kelly and Paddy Whack, now both 'on their legs,' stood wondering and waiting for an explanation (the one bowing his head, the other wagging his tail): *sheagans* and shovels were suspended; barrows stood still, and ears and eyes, all opened to their fullest extent, soon conveyed to the gossiping followers of the Mac Taafs, the welcome news that the mistress's nephew, the heir of Bog Moy, and Clan Tieg O'Brien of the Isles, had arrived among them, by the style and title (soon announced) of Lord Arranmore. Caubeens and barrads were now flung in the air, the '*chree*' of the Mac Taafs was raised by the men, taken up by the women, and sent back by the boys; and was followed by the burden of an old Irish song, that always comes so readily to Irish lips:

> Welcome, heartily,
> Welcome, Grammachree;
> Welcome, heartily,
> Welcome, joy.

A half holiday was now asked for and granted, and a half cruiskeen[1] was voluntarily promised; and these modern representatives of the old Irish Clans, showering blessings on the party, which now together quitted the bog for the bawn, were left to enjoy the hope of idleness and poteen, the only enjoyments and luxuries with which they were acquainted.

Lord Arranmore, with an arm of either aunt drawn through his own, and with ears that lent themselves more readily to their questions, than his tongue did to the answers they required, proceeded with them to the house, accompanied by Paddy Whack and James Kelly; the former trotting behind, the latter somewhat in advance, on his

---

[1] Cruiskeen, – a pitcher. Thus used absolutely, the contained liquor understood is always whiskey.

way to announce in the kitchen the arrival of the young Lord and Tierna. Meantime, inquiries were intermingled with sarcasms on the recent life, conversion, and death of O'Brien's father; on the arts and seductions of the confraternity at Cong; on his own situation and appearance; together with references to his visit to the Retreat; hopes of his unaltered attachment to the church established; hints at their own intentions in his favour; and an implied conviction that he was now come home to 'settle down for life at Bog Moy, which, sooner or later, would be his own;' the whole composing a farrago, uttered by the elder, and reiterated by her *double*, the younger Miss Mac Taaf, to which it would have been impossible to have made reply or observation. None indeed was expected: the volubility of the Miss Mac Taafs was a *sostenuto*, uninterrupted by any inflexion of tone, or pause of ideas; and their habits of dictation, and their confidence in their own infallibility (the natural self-sufficiency of persons living out of the world), excluded all chance of expressing either a difference or a coincidence with their opinions.

Their nephew, however, was in a temper to be amused with every thing, and annoyed by nothing: and when Miss Mac Taaf observed, in the pompous accent, which Irish provincial ladies assume to subdue the peculiar brogue of their province, 'But choild, I am amazed to see you as peel as peeper, and as thin as a lauth. Whoy, I expected to see you with cheeks as red as roses, and shoulders the full of a door,' – he replied:

'Campaigns through half Europe, dear aunt, and a typhus in Ireland, with other recent and melancholy events, but little favourable to the roses of high health, have, indeed, sent me back to you something less florid and fleshy, than when I was wont to come to Bog Moy, to shoot snipes at Christmas, and to fatten on cream and honey with poor old Norah ny Costello.'

'Well, choild, never moind; though poor Norah is gone, the crame and honey are to the fore; and I'll ingage, you won't be long at Bog Moy, till you are as stout as big Ben Joyce, and as fresh-coloured as the Flahertys of Killery. So, I hear, you got pandy at college, for getting into a 'ruction, as young Counsellor Costello wrote down to the widow. Well, sorrow pity you, Murrogh O'Brien; what call had you there, you (that had been in great furreign colleges, and living with kings and emperors abroad, and in the high road to be a field-marshal, like your great uncle), to come back and make a schoolboy of yourself, instead of coming down at once to Bog Moy House, where pace and plinty, and the heartiest of welcomes awaited you, and every comfort in life; and heir, as it is well known you are, far and near, to the toitles and estates belonging thereto, and the country round ready to be cap in hand to you. And there it stands,' added Miss Mac Taaf, passing through a breach made in the bawn wall, by the brawny shoulders of the herd, who thus gave ingress and egress to the cattle, collected as of old, within its protecting circle – 'there it stands, just as you left it; and a troifle will make it the prettiest pile, in Connaught, as it is the oldest, except the Abbey and Castle of Moycullen. And have it in contemplation to take down the rist of the old roof, and other great improvements, plaze God; and there you see is the bee (bay) of St Grellan, forent ye, and the mountains of Connemara to your rare.'

Lord Arranmore was much pleased by the manner in which his aunts had taken the affair of his expulsion; and cheered by their affectionate reception, he beheld even the dreary and dilapidated mansion (to which they were, with such pride and pleasure, conducting him), with less disgust than he would have done, under feelings less gracious than those, for which his mountain journey, and returning health and spirits, had prepared him. Still he was struck with the slovenliness, and disorder, and strange substitutions of the bawn and house. An old cart stopped up the gateway, to keep out the stray cattle and the cottiers; an old hat was thrust through the broken pane in the hall-door fanlight; the offices were lying in ruins to the left; and to the right, the garden plot, where still many a flower grew, encumbered with weeds, marked a fatal inattention to that order and arrangement, which, wherever they exist, are the surest signs of civilization and security. The ancient seat of one of the oldest protestant families in the country, was indeed stamped with all those tokens of thriftlessness and neglect, which prejudice falsely, invidiously, and exclusively assigns to the catholic population of Ireland.

Lord Arranmore remembered the respect and admiration he had formerly felt for Bog Moy House, and was surprised to find how much it had shrunk in dimensions and grandeur, in an imagination schooled by the experience of 'other and better worlds.' Yet, minor and trivial dilapidations excepted, nothing was changed in the interval of his absence. The fallen roof, which had caused the wing it had once covered to be shut up, had been overthrown forty years before. The beam which propped a tottering gable, was nearly as frail and decayed, as the ruin it upheld; and many a glassless window was still stopped, as in times of yore, with such materials as chance, 'high arbiter,' had brought to hand in the hour of need. The parts of the building, however, which were habitable, were capable of accommodating many guests; the purpose for which, in the estimation of its truly hospitable and Irish owners, a house alone was built; and the Miss Mac Taafs, contented that this was the case, did not give an immediate or definite date to the improvements and restorations, which ever and anon floated 'in their contemplation,' as they had done in that of their uncle, the Brigadier, before them, for nearly half a century.

At the approach of the party, the whole domestic establishment turned out to welcome their future lord; and from Granie-ny-Joyce (the second in rank and command to the *dames suzeraines* themselves), down to 'the ould woman,' who for twenty years had occupied a stool near the *bocaen* or chimney corner, nobody knew why – (the *girleen baan*, the *boccah*, and the boy about the place included) – all were assembled at the hall door. The only person 'reported missing,' was James Kelly, who answered for his immediate appearance from the pantry, by replying to Miss Mac Taaf's shrill cry of 'Where are ye, James Kelly, and what are you about, man?' by exclaiming, 'Arn't I drawing on my state small-clothes, Miss Mac Taaf, in honour of his lordship?'

'Jeemes Kelly's niver in the way, when most wanted,' said Miss Monica, as they entered the parlour.

'Why, then, that's more than can be said for your pet, Monica Mac Taaf,' replied her sister, giving Paddy a kick, as he ran under her legs; 'he's always in the way, like the parish church, wanted or not. And now, choild,' she added, addressing her nephew with cordiality, 'you are welcome to Bog Moy; and long may you live to enjoy it,' and she imprinted an audible kiss on either side of his face, after the French and old Irish fashion. Miss Monica reiterated the salutation, and Granie-ny-Joyce, the *girleen baun*, and the 'old woman,' who stood foremost of the group, near the parlour-door, seemed well inclined to follow the example. They were, however, dismissed in Irish, by Miss Mac Taaf, who seating herself, on an old, rickety, upright, straw-bottomed settee; and placing her kinsman beside her, threw her eyes over his person with a scrutinizing glance.

'Well, Monica Mac Taaf,' she observed to her sister, who had taken the place on the other side, 'would ye ever have known this fine *comhlindrah*[1] of a fellow here, to be the *stalking Voragah*[2] that went off mitching twelve years ago, the Lord knows where.'

'Why, then, never would,' said Miss Monica, taking snuff, 'only for the Mac Taaf nose, and his being the very moral of Sir Columb over the chimney, and ever was from a baby up, and liker now than ever.'

O'Brien raised his eye to Sir Columb, whose grim visage and lank figure in armour was so humorously frightful, that he rose to conceal the too ready smile it was impossible to suppress. Although the picture, like the rest of the furniture, was an old acquaintance, yet, as if it were a novelty, he now read aloud the inscription printed beneath:-

'This is the true pourtrayture of the coragious Colonell Sir Columb Mac Taaf, Knight, who routed Colonell Ingoldesby in his own difference in the pass between Cong and Headfort, and was afterwards knighted for said service by his excellencie the Duke of Tyrconnell. Sold by Patrick Smith, at y'Cross and Bible, Backlane, 1652.'

'Niver moind that now, choild,' said Miss Mac Taaf, dictatorially, 'but come and sit down here. You have seen that picture a million of times: you will find nothing changed here, thank God, since ye went. There is the voyadore you used to play Jack Straws on, and the sideboard, and the ancient ould buffet. And there is your great uncle Flavius's silver tankard, and the first cheny tay-pot ever used in the county Galway; and you see th' ould Persia carpet houlding to the fore: and hopes them will come after us will do the place as much justice as we have done.'

'Ay,' said Miss Monica, 'I hope so too. It would be a great heartbreak to see an iota changed in it.'

'But Murrogh, dear,' continued Miss Mac Taaf. '(for it's Murrogh we'll call you in private, after the ould fashion, and keep my lord for company), what sort of an head is that ye have got, without a dust of powder, or a taste of toupee? Why, boy, it's just the same curly *caen dub* that ye went away with.'

'I hope you will find both heart and head as little changed as your own Bog Moy,' said O'Brien, smiling.

'Oh, I'll ingage the heart's in the right place, choild; but for the head, Murrogh O'Brien, I'd be better plased to see it more in the mode, craped, and powdered, and buckled, with a fashionable club,

---

[1] A handsome foppish fellow.
[2] *Stac na Voragah*, 'the stake in the market place,' applied to any tall, ungainly person.

like young Counsellor Costello's, and not like Jemmy Skirret's water dog.'

'But, my dear aunt, I assure you it is in the very extreme of the fashion, – of the Paris fashion, at least – where crêping and powdering are now as much out of date, as the long love-locks of my brave ancestor, Sir Columb, there.'

'Why, what sort of a *Cauthah*[1] is it at all?' said Miss Mac Taaf, running her fingers through the luxuriant tresses of his hair.

'It is called the *Brutus* head,' he replied, with some annoyance, and drawing back.

'Brutish enough!' interrupted Miss Mac Taaf, with a stately laugh, which was taken up by Miss Monica; 'and would not take the half of what I'm worth, to show you with that head in the cathedral church of St Grellan, when the eyes of the whole congregation and the bishop's pew will be on you. Monica Mac Taaf, moind me to sind in the boy about the place for Gill Duff-na-Kiruwan in the morning to dress his hair like a christian, and bring out an assortment of cues, till his own grows naturally. You remember Gill Duff-na-Kiruwan, I'll ingage, Murrogh, "system, tete, and perriwig maker," in the High-street; and has the good blood in his veins for all that, and might claim kin to the Castle-Kiruwans this day, high as they hould them-selves. And I declare to goodness, Monica Mac Taaf, the creature ha'n't a rag of weepers to his cuffs, and he in father's mourning. Well if your poor foolish mother was living, or if it was with ourselves ye had been left, it isn't in this neglected state you would have return'd to us. But never moind, choild; we'll tack you on something, and smarten ye up, agen the Jug Day: for we have it in contimplation to ask the county round, in regard of the tapping of the pipe of claret sent over to us by our cousins, French and Co., of Bourdeaux; and only waited for your coming home; and we'll get you, when you are rested a taste, to write cards of compliments for same. What's gone wiht th' ould pack, Monica, that stood in the buffet?'

'Why, shure, Jeemes Kelly carried them off to the kitchen before they were half done with, sister Mable, though I told him ye wanted them. But who dare gainsay Jeemes Kelly?'

'Why then, I'll shurely part with Jeemes Kelly when he laste thinks of it,' said Miss Mac Taaf, whose partiality to her sense-keeper could not stand the loss of a pack of cards, which had not been more

[1] The matted hair of the ancient Irish.

than three years on service; and which were destined to contain the compliments and invitations of the Jug Day.

'It's what he's getting the head of you entirely,' said Miss Monica, 'and thinks the place is his own, as much as the brigadier ever did; and small blame to him, since it's yourself will let nobody cross him, and he disguised from morning till night. I would have him up before the altar, the first day Father Festus holds a station, and book-swear him too for a year and a day, against sup or drop. I'll ingage I'd make a good servant of you yet, Jemmy Kelly, if it's to me ye were left.'

'Well, there he is,' said her sister, angrily; 'take him to yourself, Monica Mac Taaf, and do your worst with him; but as for turning out the cratur on the wide world, like a mangy hound, after twenty years' service, it's what I won't do, Monica Mac Taaf; and, indeed, has long had it in contimplation to make him own man and body servant to Murrogh, which would put him out of the way of temptation; for it's coshering and gostering with the tinants that lades him astray. And ye must have a man in livery to ride after ye, Murrogh; for you must go and make your obeisance to th' ould families; and, same time, Jeemes Kelly can drop cards for the Jug Day, and the sooner the better. For though you are a lord, we can't be sending out old Donaghni-Crone, the town-crier, to insense the people of your return, with a "uaisht! uaisht!" But you must mount your aunt Monica's filly, and ride first to the Lynches of Cloghballymore.'

'And to the Burkes of Derry-na-Cloghna,' said Miss Monica, rubbing up her recollection, as she rubbed her high forehead.

'And the Darcys of Kiltalla,' said Miss Mac Taaf.

'And the O'Flahertys of Tallikihan,' said her sister.

'And the Gno-beg O'Flaherty-more,' added Miss Mac Taaf.

'And the Skirrets of Claer-yn-dowl and Ballyduff, and the Joyces of Joyce's country,' continued Miss Monica.

'And the Drumshambos, and the Dangans, and the Marble Hills, and a *mille*[1] others,' said her sister.

'For though,' said Miss Mac Taaf, 'we don't want to send you out to make cuttings on the county, like a Cromwellian scout-master, nor to make an house haunter, nor a wanderer, nor a wagger about streets and townlands, of you, like the young squirantry of the newcomers, yet it is right ye should make yourself known to the ancient ould families, in and about county Galway, Mayo, and Clare, where you

[1] A thousand.

will meet with the greatest of respect, in regard of the Mac Taafs. And as to the O'Briens, I lave that to spake for itself; for being a lord and a nobleman, as you surely are, in right of your father, though if it was not for us, Terry O'Brien, and ours, and the Brigadier's coffer, and the great recourse ye had to us and it, and a black day it was, abducting and seducing that poor *omadaun* of a cratur, Bridget Mac Taaf, for which if ye did not rot in Galway jail, it's us ye had to thank for it; for it's laid down in the statutes, "that if any person or persons, by fraud, flattery, fear, or false promises" – But far be it from us, choild, to make you suffer for the sins of your parents; so come, now, and we'll show you the ways of the place, and you shall choose your own bed in the barrack-room, out of six, for life, as I may say; only must be contint with a shake down in the Brigadier's tower, on the Jug Day, maning to put the four young Blakes, two Bells, and three Bodkins, in Bachelor's hall, as we call the barrack: and as to the six young O'Flahertys, it's little bed they'll trouble that night.' The Misses Mac Taaf then rose, and sailing on majestically before their wearied and silent nephew, showed off the lions of Bog Moy, with as much ostentatious pride in its fusty rooms, mouldering furniture, its make-shifts and substitutions, as the rural *Conte* of Romagna exhibits his '*apartimenti nobilit*' to wondering travellers; and then retreats to his own slovenly attic, to share with his domestic the *buona mano* which forms so considerable an *item* in his revenue.

Those who have basked in the sunshine of an Irish welcome, can alone tell how intoxicating is its cordiality; and how many sins against taste, manners, and even against the independence of its object, it redeems. Lord Arranmore, with all the fear before his eyes of Gill Duff-na-Kiruwan's crêping irons, powder-puff, and scented pomatum, and his horror of the bed in the barrack-room, and the weepers to be tacked to his cuffs, with no faint forebodings of the diatribes to be dinned in his ears against his father's abduction of his mother, and the endless visitations to be made in Galway, Clare, and Mayo, was still more amused than annoyed, during the first hours after his arrival, by manners and habits, a phraseology and accent, which seemed wholly to have changed their character since he had last visited Bog Moy. His aunts, on their part, like all persons dwelling in solitude, to whom the least important event affords a sensation, were charmed to the extremest excitement by his arrival; and before the '*boy about the place*' followed the party to the Brigadier's tower, to announce that 'dinner was dishing,' Lord Arranmore, with a Jesuitism worthy of the school from which he had just issued, had subverted many of the rules, and repealed many of the laws, which threatened to intrench upon his personal independence, or habitual comforts. Point after point was gradually abandoned (for the time being, at least) to the insinuating earnestness, which in begging a respite, obtained a reprieve; and Miss Mac Taaf, unable to resist manners to which she was so wholly unaccustomed, and softened by a pleasurable excitement she so rarely experienced, yielded, without being conscious of her submission, to the suggestions of her nephew, or mistook them for her own –

E rendea ad ascoltar dolce concento.

This was indeed the sole, glorious, golden opportunity, which might ever occur for changing her high resolves: for to the newly arrived guest and restored friend, the Irish affections refuse nothing.

It was therefore agreed upon that Lord Arranmore, to assert the privileges of his 'order,' should await the visits of the neighbourhood, before he paid any; that during 'the dry saison,' he should occupy the only habitable room in the Brigadier's tower (his foreign habits and campaigning life, as he observed, rendering an airy situation preferable to a close room, even with the *agrément* of six well-tenanted beds); that the crêping irons of Gill Duff-na-Kiruwan should not be called into service, until his aunts gave the *Brutus* a trial, and had endeavoured to reconcile themselves to its simplicity: and, lastly, an assurance that weepers were no longer worn at Court being solemnly pledged, the bill to reform his toilette was 'ordered to be read that day six months.'

'And now,' said Miss Mac Taaf, as she stood in the embrasure of the loop-hole of the Brigadier's tower, 'I hope you are plased, choild, for ye see ye have your own way in every thing. Every man to his taste, as Pat Foley said, when he kissed his cow: but how any living christian can prefer this lonely, ould gazebo here, away from every sowl, to the barrack-room, where there is always a chance of somebody dropping in, it's what I can't concaive. However, we'll have the place readied up any how to-morrow for ye – and the swallow's nests swept out of the chimney, and the Brigadier's press-bed shaken well out, and a rattling turf fire kindled, to give it a sprightly look, and teebles and cheers put into the pleace. Then there's the Brigadier's fusil, and a map of the town lands, so you won't want amusement: and to be shure, a finer view none need desire than lies round ye, with the best bit of red bog in the country under your nose, and forenent you the mountains of Connemara, and the *bee* (bay) in your *rare* (rear). And look, choild, as far as you can see to the lift, that's the gleamings of Lough Corrib; and under the shelter of that mountain, which stands out bolt upright, ye may see th' ould woods, and new plantations of Beauregard, as them upstarts of Knock-loftys call it, instead of the fine ould name of Clogh-na-Corrig, which – but Chroist Jasus, choild, what is it ails ye! Why, ye are as red as a turkey cock, and now again as peel as peeper.'

'I am perfectly well, aunt, only a little subject to flush, since my last illness,' said Lord Arranmore; and he added carelessly, 'Is the Knocklofty family in the country?'

'Not that I heared tell,' replied Miss Mac Taaf. 'And now, Murrogh O'Brien, Lord Arranmore, once for all, and not to trouble you any more on the subject, there is one earnest request I have to make to you, and that is, that I lay my solemn command and injunction on you, as you value my feevour and regards, not to have any call or communication with any of the upstarts, patentees, or new comers of the pleece; among whom I reckon above all, the Hunks' family, and thim Knockloftys, who wasn't in existence two hundred years back, though they now look down upon th' ancient ould residenters, and cut their jokes upon the "neetives," as that new Lady Knocklofty, and her friend Lady Honora, call'd us all, last summer, and that turncoat, their poor cousin and follower, Miss Kitty Maguire, that sowl'd her religions for a mess of pottage, and had the impudence to draw a pourtraiture of your aunt Monica and self, as the Leedies of *Cushlanne-na-Haliah*,[1] who scolded themselves to death, as the story goes.

---

[1] The story goes, that two old ladies of the family of the O'Flahertys becoming heiresses to the castle in question, took possession of the towers which are still standing on Lough Corrib; but not being able to adjust the partition of the property, an endless casue of quarrel arose. One of these ladies was nearly blind, and the other sadly afflicted with the asthma. Day after day they scolded at each other, from the rising of the sun till the going down of the same; until the asthmatic lady, as might be expected, found herself breathless, and on the point of yielding the last word. Taking advantage, however, of her sister's infirmity of vision, she dressed up a figure in her own clothes, and placing it in her tower window, retreated to her boat, to recruit her forces in the cool air of Lough Corrib. The myopic lady meantime, perceiving the window occupied, continued her diapason of invective, and receiving no answer, was only more irritated and inflamed by the implied contempt. The conclusion was inevitable. Death alone could put an end to such an unequal combat; and the lady of Cushlanue-na-Haliah, was found, one fine morning, lifeless in her 'bower window.'

But if ould Dennis Daly dies (and he's not expected, I hear), they'll be running down to the country, and be wanting to put their *comluaider* on Bog Moy, as they did afore. But vote or voice they'll not get from us or ours; for we'll support th' ould blood of the country against all the Cromwellians and Williamites in the land, and call upon and expect you to do likewise, Lord Arranmore; and will engage that if you put yourself at the head of the Bog Moys and Ballyslatterys, and joins Martin's Connemaras and Daly's Dunsandals, yez will keep the county in your own hands, and sit, plaze God, for St Grellan in the parliament yet.'

With this prophecy, echoed by Miss Monica's 'I'll ingage, troth, will ye,' the ladies of Bog Moy descended the broken steps of the Brigadier's tower; continuing to amuse their nephew with various details of the insolent airs of the party of Beauregard, on the occasion of their last visit to the country: and ended, as they entered the dining-room, with the expressed hope that it would be long before they paid another – a prayer in which Lord Arranmore most devoutly joined.

# CHAPTER II

### *The Jug Day*

Our country's honour roofed.

SHAKESPEARE.

THE flanking turret of the bawn of Bog Moy, distinguished as the Brigadier's tower, had obtained that name in consequence of the siege which the Brigadier Flavius Mac Taaf had maintained against a host of creditors: and the Brigadier might have long retained possession of a place, within whose precincts the 'king's writ could not run,' had he not been compelled to surrender, on the summons of an apoplexy. Since his death the fortress had remained unoccupied, except by an old overseer, whose recent demise had again left it untenanted. Though abandoned to neglect, its massive walls (eight feet in thickness) had preserved it dry: and when the swallows' nests were destroyed, 'the place readied up,' and a few such articles of furniture conveyed to it, as might be spared from the not very abundant *garde-meuble* of Bog Moy House: and when a huge turf fire blazed on its spacious ungrated hearth (necessary even in July), it was, if not comfortable, habitable. Beneath its roof, its new tenant might at least hope for that silence and solitude which would stand in the place of other enjoyments, and to pursue his studies uninterrupted by the dictation of his aunts, the endless gossip of the widow, Miss Costello, and Father Festus, or by the probable descent of the Os and Macs, tribes and half-tribes, who from the boasts of the Misses Mac Taaf, he concluded would drop in, in their passage from the interior to St Grellan, with the good intent of bestowing all their tediousness upon the inmates of the mansion.

In such a tower, in such a spot, surrounded by bogs and morasses, the most elegant dramatic writer of his day produced one of the most charming and classical comedies in the English language.[1] Whatever gives concentration to genius, and excludes the distraction of external objects, is favourable to its labours. Some few writers, indeed, have thrown off their happiest productions amidst the bustle of business, or the excitement of pleasure, – as the deaf are said to hear best during the rolling of a drum. But, though Shakespeare may have written amidst the distraction of the green-room, and Farquhar composed in the confusion of a country inn, still the activity of the senses, is, generally speaking, but little compatible with energy of intellect.

Rude as was this ruinous retreat, still here he had hoped to woo and win back that mood of mind which the unmeaning common-places and illiterate garrulity of the inmates of Bog Moy had effectually put to flight. But the woods of Beauregard, seen faintly, as they were, in the remote distance, kept up a feverish recollection of scenes and persons, which assumed a brighter and more attractive aspect, from their contrast with his present isolated and coarse mode of existence. The intellectual intercourse of the Historical Society; the military festivities of the Dublin Volunteers; his adventures at the castle, and at Knocklofty House, the Sybil mask, too, all arose in rapid association; but he endeavoured to forget all,

> E'en as a flattering dream of worthless fancy:

to think, as thought might be most profitable to himself and others, and to pour the whole force of his mind upon such subjects of literary and national interest, as might serve the great cause to which he had devoted himself from sentiment, before principle had suggested its adoption as a duty.

A few days' residence at Bog Moy, however, convinced him, that there he could not long remain; that a dependence the most insupportable must be the inevitable purchase of a residence, in no instance attractive – a dependence, whose irksomeness could not long be relieved by the laughable absurdities, which at first had turned disgust into amusement. Perpetually urged to be useful, though rarely permitted to be so – condemned to listless inactivity, yet denied the repose of leisure: exciting jealousy by his interference, and resentment

---

[1] Cumberland wrote his 'West Indian' in an old turret in his father's episcopal residence in Ireland. See his *Memoirs*.

by his neglect; he lived under the perpetual infliction of the vigilance and dictation of both his aunts. Even this childish subjection, to which they sought to reduce him, was scarcely more annoying, than the penalty imposed on his patience and taste, by the dull, monotonous details of their endless *commérage*. With views as narrow as their sphere of action, and with a sharpness of temperament, concentrated in their own little interests, their eternal expression of their petty grievances and fancied injuries was humorously contrasted with the remote obscurity of their lives and position. Impressed with the highest sense of their own consequence, full of contempt for all that was not of their own castle, class, and sphere, they were yet jealous at the fancied neglect, even of those on whom they looked down; and, perpetually at variance with each other, they were only united in an endless endeavour to repel fancied aggression, and mutually to support their own very questionable personal importance. Such as they were, the *Ban Tiernas*, of fair chieftains of Bog Moy, were strong, but not rare illustrations of the fallacy of those theories, which give to the world every vice, and to solitude every virtue.

If retirement encourages those formal peculiarities which are at variance with the minor moralities of social intercourse, it is no less hostile to the development of regulated benevolence; which alone springs from an enlarged and practical philanthropy. In solitude the heart narrows, the feelings of personality acquire preponderance; and self, magnified by the remoteness of other objects of comparison or affection, becomes the exclusive principle of existence.

All these foibles of temper, temperament, and position, came out daily and momentarily in the Miss Mac Taafs, after the flush of their first pleasurable excitement, occasioned by their nephew's arrival, had subsided. Isolated by their topographical situation (for Bog Moy, when the tide was out, was only accessible by a bridle way), their only habitual visitants were the widow and Miss Costello, and their director; the two former repaying the hospitality of their comparatively wealthy friends, by feeding their peccant humours with the local scandal of St Grellan; and the latter (as far removed from the cultivation and refinement of his predecessor, the Abbé O'Flaherty, as from the bigotry and zeal of the Abbate O'Brien), was neither of an age, nor of habits to render his society more than endurable, to one who had all the fastidious intolerance of youth, which time and experience eventually breaks down to universal indulgence. With the numerous cousins, friends, and followers, 'kith, kin, and relations' of whom Miss Mac Taaf had spoken, he perceived they held but little communication. The distance of their residences was considerable; the ways impassable; and the habits of his aunts home-bred and indolent. Nothing therefore less than some great family festival, like the Jug Day, sufficed to draw together the representatives of the ancient chiefs of Connemara and Jar Connaught from their nooks in the mountains, or their courts and castles 'on the other side of Galway town.'

By the great protestant authorities, the Hunkses, the Proudforts, and their dependants, the Miss Mac Taafs were looked upon, like other very old protestant families, as half papists and whole Jacobites (a race in those remote regions, even then not quite extinct); their old fashion, manners, and habits, and above all, their having neither carriage nor horses, were likewise impediments to a social intercourse in that quarter: though it was always 'in their contemplation' to remedy the last objection, when they could 'ready up the family coach,' which mouldered under a shed in the bawn; and when James Kelly could get time to look after the two long tailed greys, 'the only bastes with which they could drive into St Grellan town, after the Mac Taaf fashion, as introduced by Lady Betty Burke.'

Lord Arranmore thus living in utter isolation, without either the enjoyments of solitude or the distractions of society, had no opportunity for sounding the political feelings of the country; and he looked forward to the Jug Day, no less as an occasion for acquiring information for the society of the Union in Dublin, than as relief from the tedious sameness of his present existence. Meantime letters from Lord Walter cheered him, by accounts of the success of his pamphlet; a success, however, which threatened to draw down on its author the vengeance of the party against which it was directed.

The *last of the* old pack of cards had now been sent out by 'Paddy the post,' and distributed through the country; and Lord Arranmore counted upon a general gathering of the clans: but where the numerous guests were to be stowed (even with the aid of the priest's house, which the Miss Mac Taafs had put into requisition), he had not the least idea.

In about three weeks after the arrival of the future lord of Bog Moy, the long expected, long contemplated Jug Day arrived. But no vulgar bustle, no flutter of hope or fear, no vague apprehension of who would, or would not accept the invitation, disturbed the habitual stateliness of the Miss Mac Taafs. Nothing of that horrible anxiety which clouds the gaieties of the demi-ton of more refined society, lest the great should stay away, and the little come, ruffled their equanimity. Each lady, sailing about with her hands dropped into the depths of her capacious pockets, gave orders for certain 'cuttings and cosherings' on the county, which were always exacted upon such occasions. Tributary poultry, and tributary fish, came teeming in from tenants on sea and land, in kreels and kishes, with guizzard-trout from Lough Corrib, butcher's meat from St Grellan, and whiskey from every still in the Barony. Linen was drawn forth from chests and coffers, which, for colour and antiquity, resembled the '*linge de Sorbonne*' quoted by Menage: and moulds were prepared by the indefatigable Grannie-ny-Joyce, which might have come within the meaning of the bye-laws of the town, directed against 'candelles which give ne light ne sight.'

Cadgers came crowding to the back way, and beggars to the bawn. Pipers and harpers assembled from all parts: and the pipe of claret, in honour of which the feast was given, and which occupied the withdrawing-room, that had long served the purposes of a cellar, was crowned with green branches, and raised on a lofty bier within view of the guests: the silver tankard of the Brigadier was placed beside it.

'As "the Jug Day" intimated an invitation of twenty-four hours, at least, no particular time was fixed upon for the dinner: and the guests, well aware that they could not come too early nor remain too late, poured in, as their own convenience, distance of residence, or previous occupations dictated. Two stately old coaches and four, with a chaise-marine and chariot, came by the coast-road, the 'tide being out;' guests from the coast, dependant on high water, sailed at an earlier hour into the creek of Bog Moy, from the seats on Killery Bay, and the headlands of Achille. The greater number, male and female, rode single or double over moor and mountain, 'the bog being dry,' – an event on which much of the hospitable intercourse of the Barony depended, and which was frequently announced in the invitation, to insure its acceptance.

It was in vain that the ladies of the feast endeavoured to press their refractory, and now most unpopular nephew, into the service of the day; that a spigot was conveyed to his keeping for tapping the pipe, and filling the 'first jug;' that he was ordered to help Father Festus in making and mixing the punch (an operation performed with a certain hocus-pocus air, peculiar to the genuine parish priest of the second or third class); it was in vain that he was requested to have 'an eye about the place;' and see that when the stables were full, the bastes should be turned into the paddock, and plenty of hay thrown down for them. With 'an eye' only to his own sense of personal dignity, he had made a sudden retreat from spigot and tankard, from pipe and punch; and having passed the early part of the day among the rocks of the sea shore, with Polybius in his hand, and a dreadful anticipation of the bore of the coming evening in his head, he returned only in time to dress for dinner. Bolted in his tower by the very bar which had excluded the Brigadier's invading creditors, he beheld from his loop-hole, the gradual *coming in* of the 'mere Irish', as they descended from brake or hill on saddle or pillion, or were jolted along the rutted road to the bawn, on low-backed cars,[1] or carriages. The women, who came on horseback, he observed were nearly all clothed in the same singular costume; viz., enormous full-plaited cloth skirts, capotes, and calashes: and neither valise nor saddle-bag gave note of preparation for a more splendid or elegant toilette.

Meantime, the boy about the place, the *girleen bawn*, and as many other boys and girls as the exigencies of the day had pressed into the *valétaille* of Bog Moy, had been sent to seek out him, in whose honour the feast was principally given. Unable therefore to defer any longer his appearance, Lord Arranmore sallied forth to encounter annoyances, in part made up of his own fastidiousness and of that over-refinement of taste, which youth so often affects, even to itself.

As the fallen roof of 'th' ould withdrawing-room' had not been restored, – as the floor of the new withdrawing-room (now the cellar), had never been laid down, – as the dining-room was strictly appropriated on the Jug day to its proper purpose, and was scaffolded round with tables somewhat precariously, but rather picturesquely placed, in what Miss Mac Taaf called 'horse-shoe fashion,' – the best bedroom, which opened into the dining-room, was constituted a *salon de reception* for the time being – an expedient often resorted to in the remote parts of Ireland, in days not very long gone by. As this room, which was literally on a ground-floor, was rarely inhabited, its damp and fusty atmosphere required a fire to render it endurable, even in

---

[1] A low-backed car is the common vehicle used for the purposes of husbandry. It has no springs, and moves on wheels made of solid pieces of wood. Upon such occasions as the present, a feather bed and counterpane were formerly spread over the car, for the double purpose of state and ease; and the author has seen as much beauty, and almost as much diamonds, thus transported to the seat of rural festivity, as she ever beheld gracing the dinners of the British metropolis.

summer: and the swallows of Bog Moy, not contented with the chimneys of the Brigadier's tower, had made so considerable a lodgment in that of the room in question, that more smoke was sent back than emitted through its channel.

When, therefore, Lord Arranmore opened the door, on making his first appearance, a sudden gush of smoke rushed down into the chamber, and scattered the ashes in such dark thick clouds, that he could see nothing distinctly, but that the room was crowded to suffocation.

'Weary on the smoke,' said Miss Mac Taaf, making a motion with one hand to waft aside its vapours, and holding out the other to her nephew to lead him forward, and present him in form to the company. While struggling with her temper, she muttered in his ear, 'This is pretty behaviour, Murrogh O'Brien; – and the party made on purpose to introduce you to the ould families. Well, never mind now, but *foghal foh*, as your father used to say.' Then stepping forward majestically, she presented 'her nephew, Lord Arranmore,' separately to each guest, male and female, to the third and fourth generation; evidently vain of the high-sounding title and splendid personal appearance of the young relation, for whom she was reserving such a lecture, as she conceived his dependence, and her own authority over him, entitled her to pronounce.

One 'dissonant consonant' name followed another, with genealogical illustrations as unpronounceable as those of the Hebrews; and cousinships, twenty times removed, were claimed and acknowledged, till Lord Arranmore (wearied and annoyed beyond all measure, at the awkwardness and formality of the ceremony, which seemed to have no end), took refuge behind one of the massive head columns of 'the best bed,' upon which several ladies were seated, chatting and laughing with the most perfect ease and frankness, neither silenced nor interrupted by the approach of the noble stranger. Every seat in the room, indeed, was occupied by the female guests, while the men stood in groups in the centre and near the door, with all the propriety of separation observed in a cathedral. All, however, talked gaily and unreservedly: no rustic bashfulness, none of the awkward reserve and vulgar timidity usually observable in provincial society, embarrassed the conversation. Sheep and justices, grand juries and road-jobbings, the usual conversational resources of country gentlemen, were indeed amply discussed; but good stories, and bon-mots, and sallies of humour, were plentifully poured forth to enliven the mere details of country and local topics.

As the smoke passed off, and the atmosphere cleared up, Lord Arranmore observed with surprise that there was present, not only more personal beauty than he had ever seen assembled in so limited a circle, but that even a considerable elegance and sumptuousness of dress distinguished the female part of the company. The slough of over-all cloth petticoats and capots having been cast off in the hall, a display of French silks, and point lace, of fashions from Bordeaux, and flowers from Oporto, was exhibited, which might have put the *petites maîtresses* of the capital to the blush; and which proved that the intercourse kept up between the Connaught gentry and their exiled kindred and commercial correspondents on the Continent was even still in considerable activity. He was struck, too, by the general animation and *éveillé* look of all: every eye beamed life; every countenance was full of intelligence: and though the brogue of many was sufficiently obvious, and the prettiest lips made *weavers* rhyme to *savours*, *meat* to *fate*, and *mean* to *gain* (as Swift did, long after he had associated with the Harleys and the Bolingbrokes), yet to voices as soft as the smiles that accompanied them, much might be forgiven on the score of mere pronunciation.

'Do you wish to sit down?' asked a lady (herself seated on the bed, in the shade of its moth-eaten damask curtain), and she made a movement which seconded the invitation.

Lord Arranmore felt no very decided inclination to accept the proffered seat. The person who made the offer did not appear particularly attractive; partaking of none of the advantages of the toilette, which enhanced the charms of many of the younger members of the society. She was dressed soberly and dowdily, in a grey camlet habit, with a head-dress then worn in Ireland, called a *bonne grâce*, a sort of deep and simple bonnet, affected alike by the religious ladies and those of the better order of peasantry. To judge by a small gold cross, pendant from her bosom, she was evidently one of those lay nuns, whom the dissolution of convents, incidental to the French revolution, had driven home from the Continent, to their friends in Ireland; or perhaps a *chanoinesse* of some of those foreign orders, to which such Irish catholic ladies as can claim admission by quarterings since the flood, are occasionally elected.

Dreading to encounter another devout Miss Costello, in the lady thus habited *en précieuse*, Lord Arranmore hesitated to accept the proffered place, and bowed coldly.

'Oh, no ceremony,' she added carelessly, 'there is room enough; and you may have some time to wait for dinner. In Connaught, as in France, *'ni les princesses"* (as Mademoiselle Montpensier tells us), *"ni les gens de la première qualité. n'ont point d'heure précise pour se mettre à table."* Time belongs to another class of persons than princes or chiefs, Irish or French: so you had better sit down.'

Struck by a manner so off-handed, a tone so pleasant, and a voice so mellifluous, in spite of its brogue and foreign accent, Lord Arranmore took the seat which was offered him on the best bed, observing:

'Irish manners resemble the French in many respects.'

'Yes,' said the lady of the *bonna grâce*, 'we have only to fancy this *la ruelle* (the object of ambition to the coteries of the Longuevilles and the Nemours of the past age, and of the Grammonts and Polignacs of the present), and the thing is as correct as possible; though in England it would *faire frémir* the least prudish. What revolutions, by the bye, in church and state, has not the *ruelle* effected – what leagues and frondes.'

'Wherever woman presides,' said Lord Arranmore, amused and surprised by a style of conversation so unexpected in such a place, 'there must be placed the focus of all power and influence. The most important events in the history of man are indeed referable to the *ruelle* and *boudoir;* which, after all, are the true counsel boards and star chambers, in which his destiny is decided.'

'Which only shows,' said the lady, 'that man is governed by his passions and his vanity; for the agency of woman is rarely directed to any higher faculties or feelings.'

'I cannot exactly agree with you, Madam,' he replied, warming in the conversation: 'I believe there are women whose intellectual superiority gives them a higher vocation in society, and a more decided influence over its events, than even those personal charms, which, however irresistible, must still have the informing soul to give them their full effect.'

'*L'esprit de la plupart des femmes,*' said the lady, smiling, '*sert plus à fortifier leur folieque leur raison;* and I suspect a cunning woman will always have more influence than a clever one. Pray, who is that very pretty person, in the dirty lace and sparkling diamonds, who, like others of the belles present, reminds one of the heroines of the old romances, "*force pierreries, et point de linge blanc.*" '

'I don't know in the least,' said Lord Arranmore, laughing. 'I am almost a stranger here myself; and though my introduction was sufficiently formal, it confused me so much that I have not retained a single name.'

'Yes,' said the *bonne grâce*, shrugging her shoulders, 'I observe it; *quelle corvée!*'

'But who would not be "*corvéable et taillable à merci et miséricorde,*' if the reward were to be the place I now occupy,' replied Lord Arranmore, with warmth and with a gallantry as sincere as it was graceful. For though he could not very well discover the age or figure of his muffled interlocutor, he was charmed with an intelligence, a frankness, an indescribable something, which lurked in certain tones and modulations of her voice, that attracted perhaps by their adaptation to the peculiar taste of the hearer.

'I do not think, however,' said the lady, evading the compliment, 'that my name was inflicted upon you: the fact is, I was not on the master roll of the Jug Day: I have only stepped in, like many others, in the tail of my sept; and have not yet been presented myself to the ladies of Bog Moy: for I got at once hitched here, out of the line of fire – and smoke too!'

'My aunts cannot fail to be delighted with the presentation of such a guest,' said Lord Arranmore; 'will you allow me the honour?' and half rose.

'No, no,' said the lady, eagerly, 'I am only worthy to be confounded with the crowd: besides I am altogether *déplacée* here: my calling is not to feasts, but to fasts,' (and she looked at her cross), 'and my name has long ceased to be popular at Bog Moy.'

'Good heavens! what is in a name?' demanded O'Brien, warmly, and still more fascinated; but vainly endeavouring to get a view of the face of the speaker.

'Every thing in Connaught,' replied the *bonne grâce;* 'it is the sign of feuds and alliances, of hatreds and of loves, of ancient inheritances and recent usurpations. What an abridgment of the history of the land, for instance, is the story of the "O'Briens and the O'Flahertys," names that to Irish ears speak volumes?'

'Yes,' said O'Brien, startled at the observation; 'their local ambition and private passions, concentrated as they were upon this petty sphere of action, were an epitome of all that has shaken the world, under the high sounding names of the Cæsars and the Alexanders.'

'Exactly,' said the *bonne grâce.* 'I remember hearing in my infancy from my foster-mother, the story of my celebrated ancestors, Murrogh O'Brien, and the Abbess of Moycullen.'

'Were they *your* ancestors?' demanded Lord Arranmore, in some emotion. 'May I beg to know the name of the person I have the honour of addressing?'

'Beavoin O'Flaherty,' was the reply.

O'Brien started on his legs: the lady rose too, glided away, and piercing into the laughing, talking group, which had gathered round the open door, as if to recognize some acquaintance, was merged in the crowd. At that moment James Kelly, in a most stentorian voice, announced that 'the dinner was dished.' Miss Mac Taaf, now sailing up to her nephew, seized his hand, and leading him to a venerable looking old lady, in a flowered sack and velvet hood, exclaimed, 'Lord Arranmore, lade out Lady O'Flaherty, of Limon field, who I believe now that the Moycullens are not to the fore, is the greatest lady in the county; for' (she added, addressing an elderly gentleman) 'though I know you Burkes and De Burgos have the true Norman blood in your veins, and an English earldom, and an Irish marquisate in your family since the invasion, yet it's a rule in Bog Moy, that the Milesians ever take the wall of the Strongbownians; and no disrespect meant neither to the English by descent, nor to the thirteen tribes, no, nor the half tribes; since all here, are gentry bred and born; and not a Cromwellian, nor a Williamite in the whole party, I'll engage.'

This exordium being pronounced, and followed by a general applause, O'Brien was permitted to lead out the Dowager Lady O'Flaherty – one of those noble representatives of Irish beauty, and of Irish gentility, who, down to the close of the last century, were to be found in the remote provinces of Ireland; and who in their courtly manners and stately habits, preserved the dignified graces of the Irish court of those days, when the Ormondes and Tyrconnels presided over its almost regal drawing-rooms. Supported by a high gold-headed cane, on one side, and on the other by the arm of Lord Arranmore, this venerable subject of many of Carolan's inspirations, moved slowly on, followed by the O'Maillies of Achille and Clare Island, the Joyces of Joyce's country, and others of the great aboriginal families of Connemara and Mayo. Then came the Darcys, the Dalys, the Skirrets, and the Frenches, with the Burkes, Blakes, Bells, and Bodkins, and all that filled up the list of tribes of Galway of those who could and those who could not claim cousinship.[1] The protestant clergyman of the parish of Bog Moy (a parish without a congregation), bowed out Father Festus, the priest of a congregation without a church, and the provost of St Grellan gave the *pas* to the Mayor of Galway.

Sixty persons to be seated, where there was not comfortable accommodation for half the number, required no little pains and ingenuity: and the horseshoe table would have been very inadequate to the wants of the guests, but for the never failing aid of the side-board, side-tables, and window-stools, which with a 'plate on the knee,' and a 'bit in the corner,' at last provided for all. After much crushing, squeezing, and laughing (all in the most perfect good humour and courtesy), the whole company were finally seated. Lord Arranmore at the head of the centre table, between his elder aunt, and the Dowager Lady O'Flaherty, presided as the representative of the late Brigadier; while Miss Mable, supported by a Joyce, and a Blake, did the honours at the further extremity.

Grace being said by the minister of the established church (while the Roman catholic guests cast down their eyes, moved their lips, and crossed themselves under the table-cloth, with a bashful and proscribed look), – Miss Mac Taaf stood up, and with a cordial welcome in her eye, said aloud, 'Much good may it do ye all;' to which all bowed their heads. A rush of attendants, of all sorts and sizes, ages and ranks, including the servants of the guests, liveried and unliveried, – and the striking up of the pipes and harp (the performers being ceremoniously seated at a table, on which wine and glasses were placed), on the outside of the door, announced that the 'hour of attack' had arrived; and never did a more hospitable board offer to appetites, sharpened by sea and mountain air, a more abundant feast. No expected *relevé* (except such as were necessary to supply the place of the vanished contents of some favourite dish), kept the appetites of the *gustateurs* in suspense. Rounds of beef were the *pièces de resistance*, which none resisted. Haunches of venison and legs of mutton were *entrées* and *entremets*, that required no substitution. Pastry and poultry formed the *hors d'oeuvres;* and a *dormant* of a creel of potatoes and a bowl of fresh butter left no wish for more brilliant or

---

[1] The feuds of the *Bianchi* and *Neri* of Florence were poor and cold types of the dissentions which long distracted the town of Galway concerning the right to 'call cousin;' a right claimed by the half tribes, and refused to them by the whole.

less substantial fare: while a vacant place was left for the soup, which was always served last. Jorums of punch were stationed round the capacious hearth; port and sherry were ranged along the tables; and the door opening into the withdrawing-room, disclosed to view the cask of claret, the idol, to which such sacrifices were to be made, on altars so well attended and so devoutly served. The Brigadier's tankard, brightened for the occasion by James Kelly, was now filled to the brim with 'the regal, purple stream,' and placed before Lord Arranmore; and before the palate was blunted by the coarser contact of port or punch, the new tap was tasted. The flavour, body, and odour, were universally approved, in terms worthy of the *convives du grand De La Reyniére;* and it required no skill in augury to divine, that the claret would be out, before the company.

All were now occupied with eating, drinking, talking, laughing, helping and being helped; while old-fashioned breeding disposed every guest to be cordially at the service of his neighbour: – 'Allow me to trouble you for a slice of your round, rather rare;'[1] was answered by, 'Sir, the trouble's a pleasure.' 'Give me lave to call on you for a cut of your haunch, when you are at leisure,' was replied to affirmatively, with 'the honour of a glass of wine;' and a cross fire of 'Miss Joyce, shall we make up that little quarrel we had?' – 'Port, if you plaze, Sir' – 'Hand me the tankard' – 'James Kelly, tell Miss Prudence Costello, I shall be happy to hob-and-nob with her, if she is not better engaged,' etc. etc., continued without intermission; and exhibited a courtesy, which not long ago prevailed in the highest circles; – a courtesy which, however quaintly expressed, was well worth the cold and formal reserve of what is now considered refinement, in the school of modern egotism.

Meantime, Lord Arranmore, prompted by his aunt, and nudged by James Kelly 'to press the bashful stranger to his food,' did the honours to a circle, in which bashfulness was certainly not a distinguishing characteristic. His situation was irksome, in proportion as his thoughts diverged from the menial duties imposed upon him, in search of the *bonne grâce*, which had hidden from his eyes a face, that he was most anxious to behold. There was something in the voice, as well as the words, of this anomalous visitant at Bog Moy (even before she had announced a name having a poetical and fanciful interest in his imagination), which pre-occupied him, and which had even struck him

[1] Anglicè 'raw.'

forcibly, as not new to his ear. What a style of conversation, too! after the tedious prosing of Widow Costella, Father Festus, and the Miss Mac Taafs; what a transient restoration to the world of intellect! He looked down either side of the horse-shoe table, in vain. On either side, indeed, bright eyes, that seemed lying in wait for his, sparkled to his inquiring glance: for many of the fair Os and Macs had '*données dans la seigneurie, à bride abattue;*' and mistaking his scrutinizing glance, they replied by a nod of assent, that engaged him in a keen encounter of 'wine and smiles' for which he was utterly unprepared.

At last, however, he discovered the object of his search at a side-table at the lower end of the room. She was seated in profile, leaning on her elbow and playing with her fork, in apparent attention to Father Festus; who, never more in his vocation than when presiding over the rites of hospitality, was keeping his 'table in a roar.' Lord Arranmore from that moment was wholly engrossed by the only person who had an interest for him, and he was about to send James Kelly to request permission to take wine with her, when Miss Monica Mac Taaf (who, by her position at the foot of the table, commanded a view of the bawn through the open windows), exclaimed, with intense amazement – 'The Lord bless us! who can this be! a coach and four, and a great party of horsemen and military officers?'

Miss Mac Taaf turned round her head, asking, 'Is it the Walscourt livery?'

'No; it looks like the Browns of the Neale, or of Castle Mac Garret,' said old Mr Joyce.

'Why, then, upon my honour and credit,' said Miss Mac Taaf, rising and approaching the window, with the leg of a duck in her hand, and a napkin pinned over the breast of her *corbeau* (as she called her raven habit, or dress of ceremony), 'if it isn't the Knocklofty coach; and didn't know they were in the country, and thinks they might have waited till they were called on, any how. Jeemes Kelly, man, run to the door.'

'To come at this hour, too!' said Lady O'Flaherty; 'though that is just like them: their last morning visit to Lemon Field was paid, as Sir John and myself had sat down to cribbage, after tea.'

'Why, then, come when they might,' said Mr Blake, 'they could never take a happier moment to see Bog Moy in all its glory. It will give them an idea of county Galway hospitality, they have as yet shown little inclination to follow themselves; so I hope you'll admit them, Miss Mac Taaf?'

A similar thought had crossed Miss Mac Taaf herself. Not

> At the royal feast for Persia won,
> By Philip's godlike son,

did Philip's 'godlike son' himself look upon 'his valiant peers around,' with more pride and triumph, than Miss Mac Taaf surveyed her horse-shoe table, occupied by the members of the oldest steps and tribes in the province: and being secretly flattered with this first visit from Lady Knocklofty, she turned to the company and observed,

'It shall never be said the door of Bog Moy was closed at maile times to friend or foe; so I'll go and receive them, and ask them to take pot-luck, if no body has any objection.'

A general consent was announced; and Miss Mac Taaf, wholly preoccupied, and unconscious of the duck's leg in her hand, or the napkin on the breast of her *corbeau*, sallied forth to the hall door, to which a *vis-à-vis* had drawn up, driven four-in-hand by Lord Charles Fitzcharles, and followed by a young lady on horse-back, and some gentlemen in military uniform.

Several of the male guests had also risen from table, and accompanied Miss Mac Taaf to the door, which was so close to the dining-room window as to give to all within the full benefit of what was passing; and all eyes and all ears were now directed to the same point.

'My dear Miss Mac Taaf,' said Lady Knocklofty, alighting, followed by Lady Honoria Stratton (while Miss Macguire, assisted from her horse by Captain O'Mealy, the general of the district, and his aide-de-camp, joined them) – 'My dear Miss Mac Taaf, I have a thousand apologies to make, in the first place, for not acknowledging your hospitable invitation, which I only received yesterday, on my return from Lord Altamont's (where I have left Lord Knocklofty in attendance on his Excellency the Duke), and, in the next, for having kept you waiting dinner till such an unconscionable hour, as I fear we have done.'

'*My* invitation! – Kept *me* waiting! – the Lord save us!' exclaimed Miss Mac Taaf, raising her eyes, and the hand with the duck's leg; while the other was shaken by the great lady, with true electioneering cordiality.

'It was all Lord Charles's fault,' said Lady Honoria; while both ladies, with much difficulty, kept their countenances.

'But, pray,' said Lady Knocklofty, 'do not let us detain you from your guests. We will follow you to the dining-room. I hope you will excuse our *demi-toilette*. You see, Miss Mac Taaf, I have taken you at your word, and brought the party at Beauregard, as you desired.'

'As *I* desired?' repeated Miss Mac Taaf, in utter confusion of ideas, and still standing in motionless surprise.

'Miss Mac Taaf,' said Lady Knocklofty, introducing her suite, 'Major O'Mealy, General Egerton; – Lord Charles, come down off the box, and give the horses to the grooms; – Lord Charles Fitzcharles, Captain Horace Montague, A. D. C. Miss Maguire and Lady Honoria you know, I believe, already.'

Miss Mac Taaf was now utterly confounded; she endeavoured, but in vain, to recover her thoughts and stateliness; and to make a curtesy, that should express her possession of both: for no French ultrá of the old regime was ever more anxious to '*représenter noblement et avec dignité*,' than the chieftainess of Bog Moy.

'You cannot have mistaken the day,' said Lady Honoria. 'Miss Mac Taaf looks as if she scarcely expected you?'

'I hope not. I am sure I have not,' said Lady Knocklofty; 'but I have the card with me;' and she shook a card from her scented handkerchief, as if its touch would have been contamination. 'There it is,' she said; 'some one pick it up.'

The only 'one' who had presence of mind to do so, was James Kelly, who, standing at his mistress's elbow with a plate in his hand, exclaimed, 'It's the ould knave of clubs, shure enough, Miss Mac Taaf: I'd know his ugly face any where, in regard to having dropped it into the dripping-pan; and there's the mark to this day.'

A general titter among the great party followed the observation; and young Counsellor Lynch, whose modesty seldom lay in the way of his advancement, joined the laugh, with an intelligent look of mutual understanding with the Knocklofty party, and read the card aloud.

'The Miss Mac Taafs (Mable and Monica) present regards, and request the pleasure of the Earl and Countess Knocklofty, and the party at Beauregard's, company to a Jug Day at Bog Moy, Tuesday, July 20. – N. B. Beds for the ladies, and a shake down for the gentlemen, if wanted.'

'Well,' said Miss Mac Taaf, recovering from her confusion, and with all the ancient hospitality of the sept, and all the natural courtesy of an old Irish gentlewoman, 'well I know neither act nor part of that card, though it shurely is a card of th'ould pack, if not my writing; and, I suppose, it's some of the St Grellan humbugging; but any how,

Lady Knocklofty, I am happy to have the honour of seeing you and your's at Bog Moy; and if you will take pot-luck, you will find a hearty welcome, and good cheer left to the fore; – to say nothing of the best blood in the country assembled to receive you.'

Without further ceremony, Lady Knocklofty and her party accepted the invitation; and she expressed her anger at the liberty taken with her with such a smile as, to an attentive observer, would have betrayed the secret of the hoax, and placed it to the account of its true authors.

Miss Mac Taaf, with her head on high, stately and stern, led the way, followed by the three dames of quality, Lord Charles, General Egerton, the Aide-de-Camp, and O'Mealy. The latter personage had been appointed to the office of Brigade Major of St Grellan by Lord Knocklofty, on the disbanding of the Royal Irish – broken (as it had been raised), to answer some private interest of the founder. Nothing under the effrontery of the dashing party, which now entered the dining-room, primed for fun and ready for frolic, could have withstood the awkward formality of the introduction; as Miss Mac Taaf presented each, 'according to the scrip,' to the heads of all the families present, who all rose. When the ceremony was over, the new party took their places; for although it might have puzzled the most accurate calculator of *âmes et demi-âmes*, where to place an additional number of guests, the board of Bog Moy seemed to afford a general accommodation to all consigned to it, and in a few minutes the new comers were seated at the upper end of the table.

With that charming courtesy, which distinguishes Connaught manners, and which springs from kindly feelings, and a deep reverence for all the rites of hospitality, those who had previously occupied the first seats had risen, and resigned their places to the Knocklofty party, shifting for themselves as they might. 'Clane plates' were called for by Miss Mac Taaf, with an order for fresh relays of dishes, re-echoed by James Kelly at the sideboard, and reiterated from servant to servant, to the remotest confines of the kitchen. Old Mr Joyce called on Lord Charles to take wine; Counsellor Lynch begged to be allowed that honour with Lady Knocklofty; and a general challenge following, the new arrivals were welcomed with such claret as Lord Charles and the General declared they had never before tasted.

Meantime the bright eyes of the three great ladies, assisted by their glasses, were turned with much curiosity and amusement on the company.

'Well,' said Miss Mac Taaf, 'I am hoighly deloighted to have an

opportunity of showing your ladyship the ra'al rank and beauty of the
country. For though this is not a pleasure I ever dramed of, and
though there has long been a trifling difference between your family
and ours, yet if ye had found the door of Bog Moy shut agen you at
dinner time, you would have done well, to serve the Mac Taafs, as
Granuaile served the Howths,'

'And how was that, my dear Miss Mac Taaf?' said Lady Knocklofty,
leaving untouched the pile of venison that smoked before her, and
taking a survey of the table, through her glass.

'Why, my lady, she carried off the heir of the family; which is what
I should be very sorry you would do with our heir; and I beg to
present to your Ladyship, my nephew Lord – Jasus, what's gone with
Murrogh?'

'Murrogh' had in the first incursion of the grandees into the dining
room, availed himself of the rising *en masse* to escape from his durance
at the head of the table; and hoping to evade observation, by
confounding himself with a group of young men, who crowded round
a side table, till he could find a moment for complete eclipse, he was
on the point of darting forth, and flying he knew not, cared not
whither, when his aunt's speech directed every eye to his person, and
arrested his flight. At that moment, a low voice close to his ear,
muttered '*fais ce que dois, arrive que pourra:*' the counsel acted like
magic: he instantly returned to his place, and his aunt presented him
to Lady Knocklofty, saying – 'This is the heir I alluded to; and you
see, your Ladyship might do worse than follow Grace O'Mailly's
example. Lord Arranmore, my dear, this is the Countess Knocklofty
– Lady Honora Stratton – Miss Macguire – and as to the gentlemen
I'll lave them till after dinner.'

Lord Arranmore, struggling against the most painful confusion, still
mastered his emotions, to his uttermost power of self-controul; and
with all the ease he could command, bowed to the parties presented
to him. A movement of something like recognition, with evident
surprise, was made in return. Lady Knocklofty inclined her head
coldly, and blushed deeply through her rouge; and Lord Charles,
with a sort of shy cordiality, acknowledged the acquaintance; while
O'Mealy, an ape in all things, went no further than the courtesy of
his principal led him.

Lady Honoria, the first to recover from the unexpectedness of his
*rencontre*, and anxious to divert the attention of the company from the
too evident confusion of her friend, now drew out Miss Mac Taaf

(who in the meantime presented her sister at the foot of 'the horse shoe,' as the co-heiress of the estate of Bog Moy, and the lordship of Ballyslattery, now in abeyance). Sending away her plate of 'boiled duck, smothered in onions,' and calling for soup, Lady Honoria put up her glass to the black, grim pictures over the chimney piece, and asked 'Are those family pictures, Miss Mac Taaf? They are very well done.'

'They are,' said Miss Mac Taaf. 'The cintre, Lady Honora, is the portraiture of the courageous Colonel Columb Mac Taaf, who defeated Colonel Ingoldesby at the pass of Cong, – Jeemes Kelly, is it on the Persia carpet ye lave them dishes? what are the cheers for, man?' – (James Kelly in vain sought a vacant chair for the dish he was replacing with a tureen of soup) – 'which Colonel Ingoldesby was an upstart of Cromwell's, of whom the story runs, that the first of the Hunkses that ever showed his face in Connaught was his foot-boy.'

'I declare,' said Miss Macguire, 'I took that for a picture of King William; the nose is so like.'

'It is the Mac Taaf nose, Miss Macguire,' said Miss Mac Taaf: 'who carried their noses, and their heads too, as high as any Williamite in the land. If you look at my nephew there, you'll see he is the very moral of Colonel Columb. The nose in particular, as the verse runs,

> Whoever the comeliest beauty would spy,
> See the nose of the Taafs, and th' O'Brien's bright eye.

Nobody would mistake him. He has thim both, we flatter ourselves: so hold up y' head, choild, there's money bid for ye.'

Every eye-glass was now alternately directed to the picture of Sir Columb, and to his descendant; and every lip was curled with a suppressed smile.

'And pray,' said Lady Honoria, puckering up her mouth, 'who is the lady with a cat under her arm, and a piece of gingerbread in her hand?'

'The cat happens to be an Italian greyhound, Lady Honora, and the piece of gingerbread is the – bible,' said Miss Mac Taaf, drawing up. 'The lady is our great great grandmother, Lady Mac Taaf; an English lady, and daughter of Sir Roger Gammon, who came over to Ireland, as Escheator of Connaught. Through his pious efforts, and the grace of God, the Mac Taafs embraced the reformed religion. It was on occasion of this alliance with the Gammons, that we first quartered the boar in the family arms.'

'And the *bore*, I suppose, has remained in the family ever since?' said Lady Honoria, gravely.

'Ever since, Lady Honora,' said Miss Mac Taaf, as gravely. 'But, Lord save us, what's gone with the goose?' an interrogation to which none could reply, until a certain gnawing noise under the table announced that Paddy Whack had availed himself of Miss Mac Taaf's preoccupation, and was doing those honours by the Solan goose, which she had neglected.

'Well, it does not signify, Jeemes Kelly,' exclaimed Miss Mac Taaf, much irritated, 'I'll have that cur hanged up to-morrow, if I live – at all events, turned out of the place.'

'If you turn him out, sister Mable,' said Miss Monica, kindling, 'you will turn me out too; for, love me, love my dog, that's my motto. And if Jeemes Kelly was minding what he was about, the goose would be still to the fore.'

A sisterly storm was now evidently brewing; which was, however, averted by the interference of General Egerton, who alone kept his countenance with perfect good breeding, during the whole scene. He requested Miss Mac Taaf to take wine, passed fresh eulogiums on the claret, inquired the name of her wine merchant, and asked if Paddy Whack was an Irish wolf-dog, – a race of which he had heard and read so much

'Is it he the hound,' said Miss Mac Taaf, with much inveteracy, 'he is a spalpeen of a cabin cur, Giniral, and as arrant a colley as ever caught a colt by the heels.'

Miss Monica reddened, and was whispered by the widow Costello, 'to keep quiet before the company.'

'But if you wish to see a raal Irish wolf-dog,' continued her sister, 'look behind you, Giniral, there is the portraiture of the famous *Sus an chios*,[1] and its celebrated lady.'

'Which is the lady?' asked Lady Honoria; 'and which the wolf-dog?'

'Which you please, young gentleman,' whispered Miss Macguire, after the manner of the show-man, while the courteous General, to cover the ridicule, put up his glass, and observed, 'a very majestic looking person indeed. Pray who is she, Miss Mac Taaf?'

'That, Giniral, is our celebrated ancestress by the mother's side, Granuaile, or Grace O'Mailly, who kept the country round in awe and terror, and built the first tower in this pile, which came into our

[1] Honeysuckle.

family by the marriage of her daughter by Richard Burke, her third husband, with Emunh Mac Taaf. She was the terror of the nation along the coasts, and moored her· large vessels in Clare Island, and her small craft in *Carrig-na-Uile*. Allow me to help you, Gineral, to some drawn butter?'

The General, in accepting an offer which deluged his plate, observed, 'I think I can perceive a very strong likeness between this eminent lady and yourself, Miss Mac Taaf.'

'So I am tould, Gineral,' said Miss Mac Taaf, much pleased; 'and there are some think I've more of the O'Mailly, than the Mac Taaf.'

'Here is an O'Mealy, I can answer for it,' said Lady Honoria, 'who would be flattered by the resemblance: I mean our friend the Major.'

Miss Mac Taaf turned her stag-like eyes on the Major, whose name she had not before caught: and the inspection was evidently in favour of its object; who pulled up his stock, and calling up one of his best looks, returned her glances with a smile of infinite insinuation.

The persons with whom O'Mealy was now engaged, produced a very different effect on his mind, from that which they had made on his party. His early impressions of the grandeur and consequence of the old families of Munster and Connaught (whose names were to him as those of the Guelfs and Ghibelines), were still fresh. He remembered the day, when to have been admitted into such a circle was beyond the reach of his hopes, as it had ever been the great object of his emulation. The plenteous board at which he was seated, and the quarters which Bog Moy might offer to the Brigade Major of St Grellan, when Beauregard should be deserted, suggested the idea of securing the good graces of its stately mistress. When, therefore, Miss Mac Taaf, pleased with his comely appearance, asked him, 'And are you an O'Mailly, Meejor?' he replied, in a soft voice, 'I have that honour and glory, Miss Mac Taaf.'

'And of which of the families?' asked the lady. This was a puzzler.

'Of which of the families is it, Miss Mac Taaf?' reiterated the Major, evasively, pulling up his stock.

'Ay,' said Miss Mac Taaf, 'are ye of the O'Maillys of Clare Island, of whom the story goes that they were the discindants of the Mermaids, whose beautiful singing is heard to this day off the island? Or are ye of the O'Maillys, Lords of *Umhaille*, or the owls' country; called to this day *Bru na Umhaille*, or the race of the owls?'

'Oh!' said Lady Honoria, 'that is not the genus in ornithology to which the Major belongs, though he may be a descendant of the

Mermaids; for he certainly inherits their musical talents; of which, I am sure, he will be happy to give you a specimen, when the cloth is removed, Miss Mac Taaf.'

'We must not wait for that, Lady Honora,' said Miss Mac Taaf, who was passionately fond of music, and thought it never could be ill-timed: and although the Major had scarcely swallowed his last morsel of venison, and washed it down with a glass of claret, she proceeded to ask him, 'Might we take the liberty of troubling you, Meejor, for a song?'

The Major, always pleased to be called out, and now resolved on pushing his relationship with the heiress of Bog Moy, replied, 'With the greatest pleasure, Madam. Have you any favourite air you would wish in preference?'

'Any thing Irish, Meejor,' replied Miss Mac Taaf. 'May be you'd feavour us with "Molly Astore." '

'I am happy to have it in my power to obleege you, Miss Mac Taaf, and will give you the new words, as sung in the new opera at Lady Ely's private theyatricals.'

'Any words plazes you, must be plazing to me, Meejor. Mr Joyce, keep silence there, at the ind of the table.'

The stillness of the tomb instantly prevailed, and every body looked as melancholy, as if about to descend into it; while the *Magnus Apollo* of the moment, canvassing the several tables with looks of conscious merit, and anticipated success, cleared his voice, took another glass of claret, pulled up his stock, fluttered out his whiskers, and running through a few modulations, at last began, – directing his looks and the words of the song to the lady of Bog Moy.

> Had I a heart for falsehood fram'd,
> 	I ne'er could injure you;
> For though your tongue no promise claim'd,
> 	Your charms would make me true, etc. etc.

Applause, loud and long, followed this beautiful air; which being sung with true Irish pathos, and the finest possible voice, produced an enthusiastic effect upon organs, the most adapted to respond to such an influence. The tears had come into Miss Mac Taaf's eyes, as she listened; and wiping away the pearly brine, she said, 'Cousin O'Mailly, I'll take a glass of wine with you, and to your health and song.'

'Cousin O'Mailly,' delighted with the acknowledged relationship, accepted the challenge, with 'the greatest of pleasure, Madam,' and Miss Mac Taaf continued: –

'And now, Meejor, you have every right and title to call upon whom you plaze, till you rest yourself, before we ask you again; and there's Miss Prudence Costello, who has a sweet little pipe of her own, as any in the county; and will give us, "Guardian Angels" without further pressing, I'll ingage.'

'Guardian Angels,' were now called for by all; and Miss Prudence Costello, who was the most impudent looking person in the world, threw round her large swimming eyes, that seemed to roll *en coulisse*, and declared 'that she could not attimpt to sing after the Meejor.' The Major, however, pressed, as majors will press; and after much pretty delay, and affected bashfulness, Miss Prudence promised to give 'Guardian Angels,' provided her sister, the widow, would join in and help her out. The widow, whose voice and looks were any thing but recusant, sighed and hemmed: and then pitching her voice to her sister's, after reiterated cries of silence, both ladies started off in perfect unison. With eyes cast down, and bosoms heaving, and looks of gentle sentimental martyrdom stamped on their broad, comely countenances, they sung with emphasis –

> Guardian angels! now direct me,
> Send to me the swain I love;
> Cupid, with your bow protect me,
> Help me, all ye powers above.

'The powers above' did not, however, help the widow and Miss Costello, but deserted them in the very beginning of the next verse, which they in vain endeavoured to recollect. After many hems, and ineffectual attempts upon their truant memory, Miss Prudence set off, on Mr Joyce's suggestion, with 'her own favourite little song of, "Hark, sweet tally-ho, ho, ho!"' and when she came to the *refrain*, of –

> All my fancy lies in Nancy,
> Hark, sweet Tally-ho!

she turned her eyes on the young heir of Bog Moy, with an expression by no means equivocal as to 'all *her* fancy;' and the soft impeachment to which he was no stranger, completed an embarrassment, that had already placed him in the purgatory reserved for the proud and the feeling. Under the most insupportable mortification, his changing colour betrayed a confusion it was now no longer in his power to conceal. The well applauded 'Hark, sweet tally-ho!' was followed by the songstress's earnest 'Ahs,' and 'Ohs,' applied to old Mr Joyce, to sing 'Bumpers, Squire Jones,' a song for which the jolly old gentleman was celebrated all over the country. This he gave with great humour and effect, first in Carolan's own Irish words, and then in the excellent translation, which had been made of it by a judge of the land,[1] commencing with –

> Ye good fellows all,
> Who love to be told where there's claret, good store,
>     Attend to the call
> Of one who's ne'er frighted,
> But greatly delighted
>     With six bottles more.
>     Be sure you don't pass,
>     The good house Moneyglass,
> Which the jolly red god so peculiarly owns;
>     'Twill well suit your humour,
>     For, pray what would you more
> Than mirth, and good claret, and bumpers, 'Squire Jones.
>     etc. etc. etc.

'Bumpers, Squire Jones,' was as usual encored and toasted, with three times three: and the cloth being in the interim removed, James Kelly announced to Miss Mac Taaf, 'that the tay was wet, and the griddle cake, and sally lun buttered and served.' She arose, gave 'the king' (the preliminary to the departure of the ladies); after which they withdrew to the best bed-room, amidst many prayers and supplications to remain, – always expected as matter of form from the gentlemen.

While some flounced on the bed, and others sprang out of the windows, and romped on the bawn, the 'great ladies' who had already ordered their carriage, gathered round the Miss Mac Taafs: and if to learn the particulars of whatever concerned the family of the Taafs, from the flood down to the present moment, was an object of interest and curiosity, they were amply gratified, through the garrulity of that self-love, which always finds its account in autobiography. In these particulars, were included the birth, parentage, and education of their nephew; his military career abroad, and the prospects that awaited him at home. 'if he behaved himself to their liking; the inheritance of

---

[1] Bumpers, Squire Jones, was translated by Baron Dawson, from Carolan's 'Planxty Jones,' written in honour of Squire Jones, of Moneyglass, in the county Leitrim.

Bog Moy, and the reversionary honours of the Barony of Ballyslattery, and the Green Knighthood of the Fassagh; together with their intention of looking out for a suitable match for him.

'The ould blood in protestant veins,' said Miss Mac Taaf; 'one of the Lady Burkes of the Clanrickards, or the Lady O Briens, of the Inchiquins, both his blood relations. And now, Lady Knocklofty,' she added, in the honesty of her heart (won over by the well-applied flattery of Lady Knocklofty and her party, but firm to her principles), 'though I shall be happy to see you and yours, at Bog Moy House, whenever ye may plase to feavor us, in the way of the ould Irish hospitality, yet I will tell ye frankly and fairly, that vote or voice of me or mine, or of the tinants on the property, shall never be given to my lord; for if th'ould blood does not stand by th'ould blood, what's to become of the country? Aud Dinnis Daly, ye are the man for my money, if the King of England was to set up for the place tomorrow against ye?'

This was said with as honest and as dignified a determination, as that with which Old Bess of Hardwick assured the reigning minister of England, 'your man sha'nt stand.'

'Well, my dear Miss Mac Taaf,' said Lady Knocklofty, 'I cannot expect you will do for us, what ye would not do for the King; but leaving you and my lord to talk county politics when you meet, allow me to say, that I shall be happy to follow up this acquaintance, originating, as it has, in some vulgar practical joke of the town's people; and I hope that you will soon give us the pleasure of your company at Beauregard, where we expect the Lord-Lieutenant in a few days from West Port.'

The ladies then sent to let the gentlemen know that they were going. None of the gentlemen, however, attended the summons. O'Mealy was perfectly at home, and had his own reasons for remaining; and the General, Lord Charles, and Captain Montague, desirous to see the frolic out, delighted with the claret and the company, and calculating on the humours of the ball, supper, and raking pot of tea, of which the pretty Mrs Burke had informed her neighbour, Lord Charles (with such a commentary of eyes and smiles as detained him to whom they were directed) – they requested to have their horses left, and consigned the four-in-hand to the groom.

The three ladies now departed, attended to their carriage, and bowed off by nearly all the gentlemen who crowded to the door. On the return of the party to the dining-room, the claret jugs were again replenished, the punch was placed by Father Festus on the table, and the company continued their joyous orgies till midnight, when the hall was cleared out for the ball. As many as had preserved their centre of gravity were now busied in looking for partners for jigs and country dances. Lord Charles and Captain Montague secured the two reigning toasts, the beautiful Mrs Burke, and the lovely Honor Blake; while Captain O'Mealy followed in the wake of Miss Mac Taaf, as she sailed about inquiring for her nephew, to lead out Miss O'Flaherty, of Lemon Field, and to open the ball, to the tune of Planxty Connor; exclaiming, vociferously, 'What's gone with Murrogh? Did any one see my nephew, Lord Arranmore? Meejor O'Mailly, would you do me the feavour to tell my nephew, that I lay my injunctions on him to lave off – he that never drinks – and open the ball with Miss O'Flaherty.'

The Major assured Miss Mac Taaf that his lordship had left the dining-room at an early hour, resigning the chair to old Mr Joyce, on the plea of headache, as he had heard him say.

Miss Mac Taaf now expedited an estafette to the tower, to the orchard, to the vineyard; but Lord Arranmore was no more to be found, than the heir of the St Lawrences', after the visitation of Granuaile to Howth Castle.

'Well, 'pon my honour and credit, now, after all,' said Major O'Mealy, 'I would not wonder, Miss Mac Taaf, if Lady Knocklofty had kidnapped my lord, your nephew, after the manner of our great ancestor, you know.'

'Nor I, neither,' whispered Lord Charles to Captain Montague.

While emissaries were sent in search of the truant hope of the family, the ball was opened by Lord Charles and Mrs Burke; Miss Mac Taaf consented to move a minuet with Mr Joyce (a custom of theirs for the last thirty years, upon similar occasions); and jigs, danced with a grace and spirit which astonished the members of English *bon ton*, gave the lovely animated performers another 'renown,' than that acquired by simple 'tiring each other down.'

A supper, plenteous as the dinner, and quite as substantial, was served up, as soon as the last lingering devotees of the claret had left the dining-room; and the morning sun, as it rose, shone upon the un-wearied votaries of pleasure, celebrating the last rites of the Jug Day over the raking pot of tea, which assembled as many of the party, as had not found it absolutely necessary to avail themselves of Miss

Mac Taaf's barrack-beds and shakes-down.[1] Horses, carriages, and cars, then filled the bawn, while sails were hoisted in the creek; and of the merits of the claret, not a doubt was left in the mind of Miss Mac Taaf, for – not a drop was left in the cask.

---

[1] The shake-down, barbarous as it may seem, had its precedent in those courts, to which we are now referred as models of manners. Down to the days of the Stuarts, the laying down at night and taking up in the morning of beds prevailed, from the king's own bedchamber, even to the steps of the canopy of state; where the esquire of the body flung his shake-down under *the dais*.

# CHAPTER III

———•———

## *Beauregard*

Starvami sempre a contemplar quel volto,
Ogni pensiero, ogni mio bel disegno
In lei finira.

ARIOSTO.

THE sovereign ladies of Bog Moy, with all the love of power, and habit of exercising it, incidental to those who have not been broken down to a reciprocation of rights and privileges in the world's great school, ill brooked the independence of their nephew; whose comings and goings, whose wanderings, late and early, and preference of a book and a ramble, to their society, had already caused much bitter reproach and wearisome dictation. His elder aunt had more than once hinted that greater deference was expected from one who was destined to owe every thing to her favour; but when she learned that he had deserted the party, and vacated his place at the head of a table, where he had been placed to represent the Brigadier, her resentment was at its height. His evasion was deemed contempt; and anger and indignation stifled every anxiety, which his protracted absence might naturally have excited.

But when the night advanced, the morning and mid-day came, and the guests were all departed, save the Costellos and Father Festus (who were invited to stay and partake of the fragments of the feast, and talk over its events), and still no tidings were received of their absent nephew, their apprehension for his safety prevailed over every other sentiment and consideration: and all the horrors of bog-holes, precipices, unlucky places, and fairy grounds, were conjured up in fantastic array to account for his disappearance.

The Miss Mac Taafs, who loved a sensation, even a painful one, would not be comforted; and they were on the point of dispatching the priest, in addition to the numerous other emissaries, in search of the object of their alarm, when a horseman in the Knocklofty livery galloped past the parlour-window; and the next moment James Kelly, not yet quite sober, brought in two letters.

'It's Murrogh's sale, thank God,' said Miss Taaf, eagerly breaking open one letter; while Miss Monica, cutting round the seal of the other, said, 'And this is the Knocklofty coronet.'

They read as follows:-

'MY DEAR AUNT,

'A thousand apologies, and a thousand regrets for the anxiety and annoyance, which, I fear or flatter myself, my absence must have occasioned. I was literally driven from the festivities of Bog Moy, by an insupportable head-ache, which rendered me incapable and unworthy of enjoying them. I sought my usual remedy, the open air; and with the intention of joining the ladies at the tea-table, on my return sauntered over the cliffs. Pursuing my walk, however, further than I had intended, I had unconsciously arrived at that fearful precipice, *Carrig-na-Phouka*, when I perceived, on the strand beneath, a carriage and four, without a driver, the tide advancing, and (as well as I could discern at that fearful distance, and by the fading light) some female figures standing on the sands. I saw, at once, the dilemma; and scrambling down, as well as I could – ('The Lord bless me!' said Miss Mac Taaf, raising her eyes and hands; "scrambling down Carrig-na-Phouka! where even the puffin-clifters scarce venture to go") – and found that Lady Knocklofty's coachman had, under James Kelly's auspices, rendered himself incapable of sitting on the coach-box, – that the groom was not more sober, – and that the tide was rapidly approaching the strand road. In short, you will imagine the rest. I mounted the box, and had the good fortune to convey the ladies in safety to Beaure-gard; which, by the by, we did not reach till long after midnight. Here I am, then, and here I must remain, till you send me the pony and a valise, with a change of dress, when you may expect me, with all possible expedition, at Bog Moy.

'Your affectionate

'ARRANMORE.

Miss Monica next read her letter,

'Beauregard.

'MY DEAR MISS MAC TAAF,

'As I find Lord Arranmore is sending for dressing things, I take the opportunity of assuring you that he has not suffered by his gallantry; and that having risked his life to save ours, in the most perilous descent from the cliffs to the strand (where we should have perished but for his timely assistance and great presence of mind), he has sustained no other injury, than getting drenched with the spray of the tide, which all but overwhelmed us. You deserve the penalty of his absence, for making my servants so drunk; but I hope to hear you have not suffered from your delightful Jug Day: and remain, with compliments to Miss Monica,

'My dear Miss Mac Taaf,

'Very truly yours,

'ALBINA KNOCKLOFTY.'

As Miss Mac Taaf felt it to be highly necessary to reply to so civil a note, and as highly politic to 'lay her injunctions and commands' on her nephew to return home immediately, – and as writing notes at Bog Moy was not an occupation of daily occurrence and practised facility, the Knocklofty groom was ordered 'to put and step in, and get entertainment in the kitchen while the answers were preparing.' It was evening before the pony was caught, the valise filled, the letters written, and the groom permitted to depart (much in the same state as his fellow servants had been sent from the hospitable threshold of Bog Moy, on the preceding evening).

The incident altogether opened a new vein of discussion to the party assembled in the best bed-room; and the civilities of Lady Knocklofty, her visit, and even the accident which marked her return home, were all considered by the Miss Mac Taafs as the results of deep calculation, and of a premeditated attack upon their own political independence, and on the heart and hand of their nephew and heir. 'But Murrogh O'Brien,' apostrophized Miss Mac Taaf, tapping violently the lid of her snuff-box, 'I'd sooner see ye in your winding-sheet, young and comely as you are, this day, than wedded to a follower of the Proudforts; and so the Honourable Miss Kitty Macguire may carry her honourability to another market: for over rood or acre of Ballyslattery or Bog Moy she'll never reign, with my good will or consint.'

'Nor with mine,' said Miss Monica.

'Why, then, long may ye reign over it yourselves,' said the priest, 'for better can't come, and worse may.'

Beauregard was one of those remote and superb seats, which in Ireland, and more particularly along the western and southern coasts of the island, rise like fairy structures, in the midst of dreariness and desolation. Wealth, taste, and luxury had given the word,

> ——The desart smiled,
> And Paradise was opened in the wild,

The castle stood upon an eminence, over the Atlantic Ocean, of which it commanded a sublime view, to the verge of the horizon; and it was sheltered by mountains piled upon mountains, – in the glens and recesses of which, the late Lord Proudfort had planted with a success which bore ample testimony of the fitness of the soil to such oranmental cultivation; and authenticated all that has been sung of the 'woody Morven.' The spacious mansion was furnished in all the cumbrous sumptuosity of the day. Massive sofas and *bergères* from Paris, carpets from Turkey, and crystal lustres from Venice, supplied the place of the nobler works of art; while mirrors, covering every wall, occupied the spaces, which, in the houses of the old Anglo-Irish families, the Butlers, and Burkes, and the Talbots, are filled with the portraits of Vandyke and Lely.

On arriving at this sumptuous palace, the ladies expressed their acknowledgments to Lord Arranmore, even to the very hyperbole of gratitude: and a supper *en partie quarée*, in Lady Knocklofty's dressing-room, enlivened by the wit of Lady Honoria, and the humour of Miss Macguire, was rendered delightful to him by the increasing softness and courtesy of his noble hostess; which formed a striking contrast to the noisy and heart-whole joviality he had left behind him at Bog Moy. The circumstances of the adventure which had again rendered Lady Knocklofty and her friend Lady Honoria his debtors to so large an amount, and the humours of the Jug Day, formed the principal topics of conversation: and though, in deference to their nephew, the Miss Mac Taafs were spared, nobody else escaped. The finery of the dresses was criticised and laughed at, and the beauty of the women, about which Lord Charles had raved, was utterly denied.

'Animal beauty, indeed, there was,' said Lady Honoria; 'but "*belle et bête*' is all that can be said of them. What do you say, Lord Arranmore?'

'There certainly was a great deal of animal beauty, Madam; a sort of beauty, however, *soit dit en passant,* that goes well with every other; and without which, I fear more intellectual charms go for very little.'

'Oh, shocking!' said Lady Honoria. 'Is this your doctrine?'

'For so sentimental a looking person, it is rather a coarse one,' said Lady Knocklofty.

'I do not say it is *my* creed,' said Lord Arranmore; 'but I find it is a very prevailing heresy among the rest of my sex.'

'He is quite right,' said Lady Honoria: 'men are wretches, so there's no more to be said about them. There was one, however, among the women in the bed-room, that was a clever, odd creature enough.'

'What, the sort of nun, or *Madame la Chanoinesse,*' asked Miss Macguire, 'that I saw talking to you at the window?'

Lord Arranmore was all ear.

'Oh, yes, by-the-by,' said Lady Knocklofty, 'the woman in the bonnet. I heard her speaking French to you, which surprised me not a little.'

'She speaks it like a *petite maitresse du fauborg St Germain,*' replied Lady Honoria.

'Lord Arranmore, you are eating nothing,' said Lady Knocklofty; 'though you must have earned an appetite by your long drive, and arduous exertions. Good heavens! how could you venture down that horrible cliff? did it not make your shudder to look down?'

'Oh!' he replied laughing, 'Like Panurge, *je ne crains que le danger;* and my early education in the Isles of Arran ... but I beg your ladyship's pardon, you were speaking of the lady in the deep bonnet.'

'What did she say to you, Lady Honoria?' asked Miss Macguire.

'Not much; but it was extremely piquant – sarcastic, indeed. I told her that our turn would come next, and she said *"pourquoi pas? moquons-nous des autres, et qu'ils se moquent de nous: c'est bien fait de toute part."* '

'Oh! she found you out, my dear,' said Lady Knocklofty. 'It was a pretty sentiment, however, for a *religieuse.*'

'Yes,' said Lady Honoria, 'but she told me she had got a plenary indulgence from the pope, for saying and doing odd things, for a century to come, in return for the sacrifice of coming to Ireland, to reform some order – I forget what – which she said amounts to nothing, but teaching the nuns to wear clean linen and wash their hands.'

'But are nuns allowed to wander about this way?' asked Lady

Knocklofty, yawning, yet looking under her eyes, and observing the interest with which Lord Arranmore listened to these details.

'Yes,' said Miss Macguire; 'one of the nuns of Galway is the toast of the county, and parades her veil and rosary every night on the Mall. To go into a nunnery here, is to take out a brevet of coquetry.'[1]

'How came she at Miss Mac Taaf's, do you know, Lord Arranmore?' asked Lady Knocklofty.

'No, Madam, I never saw her before (heard her, I should say), for I scarcely saw her, even then.'

'I suspect,' said Lady Honoria, smiling significantly, 'she came in, like other people, on the invitation of the knave of clubs; for Miss Monica knew nothing about her, and was just going to make some inquiries, when we came away.'

'How odd!' said Lady Knocklofty, yawning again, and twirling a ring on her third finger, which now divided the attention of Lord Arranmore, with this account of the *bonne grâce*. It was the pearl of Lough Corrib.

'Come,' said Lady Honoria, now yawning, or affecting to yawn, as she took a candle, 'it is time to go to bed, – I never was so weary,' – and kissing her friend on either cheek, she wished Lord Arranmore good night, gave a nod to Miss Macguire, and departed, Miss Macguire following her example.

'Lord Arranmore,' said Lady Knocklofty; 'after so much fatigue, you will be happy to retire also. Shall I ring the bell for the groom of the chambers, to show you to your room?'

'The night is so fine,' said Lord Arranmore, looking through the glass-door that opened on a balcony, near which he was standing, 'and I feel so little disposed to sleep, that I believe, now I have the pleasure of seeing your ladyship perfectly safe, I will walk down to the beach, and get into one of those fishing-boats, which will soon put out; and so relieve my aunts from their anxiety, as soon as I possibly can.'

Lady Knocklofty now rose too, and approaching the window, which she threw open, said, 'We cannot possibly part with you thus; you must not always arrogate to yourself the power of conferring obligations, and escaping even from the expression of the gratitude they excite. Come,

---

[1] This is now no longer true. Through the influence of protestant persecution, all catholic institutions are daily acquiring new force; and (bigotry engendering bigotry) the papist grows more papistical, as the protestant becomes more proselytising.

you must remain; and I will send for your dressing things, and write to *my aunts* Mac Taafs, to beg you off; and promise that they shall have their "faithless tassel back again." Besides, "I have a long arrear of – hate – to settle with Alonzo," ' and she dropped her eyes and smiled.

'And I, Madam,' said Lord Arranmore, in considerable emotion, 'I have also – ' At that moment, the groom of the chambers entered.

'Morrison,' said Lady Knocklofty, 'bring in chamber-lights, and get me a glass of lemonade: and be in the ante-room to conduct Lord Arranmore to his bed-chamber.'

Morrison bowed obedience, and retired to execute his orders.

Lady Knocklofty now passed the glass-door and advanced to the balcony, which hung immediately over a beautifully wooded inlet of the sea. A long line of silver moon-light was reflected from its glassy waters; while the morning-star was already glittering above a dark and rocky promontory to the left of the castle. 'What a lovely night! what a sublime scene!' said Lady Knocklofty, throwing her arms over the balustrade of the balcony. O'Brien folded his, as he stood beside her, more occupied by herself, than even by the sublime and magnificent scenes to which she directed his attention. 'When I am here,' she said, 'I wonder how I can exist elsewhere. These are the scenes, and these the objects for which I was intended' (and she raised her eyes to his face). 'You will scarcely believe how little I belong to the world, in which my ill (or as that world supposed, my good) fortune has thrown me. It is impossible, Lord Arranmore, to describe the emotions with which these scenes inspire me, – or the religious enthusiasm they awaken. Do you not think that such objects communicate to the mind a portion of their own grandeur, and raise it to a loftier cast?'

'I can believe their influence, Madam,' said Lord Arranmore, 'for I have felt it; but I can imagine a position, in which even such scenes lose their influence, and where there is that within the heart, which dulls "all feeling else, save what beats there." '

'Can there then be any state of feeling, which an hour so calm, a scene so sublime – I had almost said so holy – would not exclusively engross? Can there be an emotion they would not compose, a thought they would not soothe?' asked Lady Knocklofty.

'Yes, Madam, I feel at this moment that there is,' said Lord Arranmore. He paused, confused and agitated. Alone, and at such an hour, in such a place, with one who had once so deeply interested him, and who, through good and evil report, had still occupied his thoughts, he was at a loss how to proceed; but Lady Knocklofty had now turned her full and softened eyes, with a look of anxious inquiry, on his face, and he yielded to the impetuous frankness of his nature, to his usual impulse to

Parlar prima, e pensar poi,

and without any preliminary observation, he begged a moment's audience, and then entered at once upon the events of his recent life, his conduct and his feelings, as far as they were connected with the interest she had taken in his fate, with the party to which she was attached. While dwelling with an uncalled-for vehemence on his gratitude, his respect, his admiration for herself, he gave to sentiments of mere gallantry, drawn forth by the presence of their object, a warmth more consonant to the excitement of the moment, than to the nature of the feelings which prompted them.

Lady Knocklofty listened with the deepest attention, leaning her cheek upon her hand, her eyes turned full upon his, and her quick respiration almost fluttering the curls upon his brow, and heaving the muslin scarf thrown over her bosom.

'I have always believed you,' she said, when he had ceased to speak, 'more sinned against than sinning; and party runs so high in this wretched country, while the government people feel themselves so imperiously called upon to put down every symptom of a revolutionary nature, that – But this is not the point. Some of my dearest friends are among *your* party – Lord Walter, for instance. It was not, then, the political crimes alluded to, that injured you in my opinion; my feelings were more at home, more selfish. What did you mean by returning me my ring?'

'I return your ring, Lady Knocklofty? Gracious heavens!'

'And with that insulting inuendo, too; which, however well it might have become the standard of the Irish Brigade, was, when addressed to one, who, in the fulness of her gratitude (which vanity might have construed into another sentiment!) – '

'Good God! What can your ladyship allude to? The ring, the precious ring, that is now on your finger, was drawn most mysteriously from mine, as I lay asleep in St Patrick's Hall, and exchanged for that which I now wear.'

'It was sent to me,' said Lady Knocklofty, 'wrapped up in a fold of paper, on which was written, *"Fais ce que doy, arrive que pourra."* '

Lord Arranmore changed colour; the voice and counsel of the *bonne grâce* seemed to sound again in his ear, even from the lips of one, who made him feel every moment how difficult it was, in particular positions, to follow the admonition.

'Lady Knocklofty,' he said, after a pause, 'I am the victim of some mysterious agency – be it for my good, or for my ill – of whose existence I am only conscious by the influence it exerts over my actions. By whom my ring was purloined, I know not. I had, indeed, suspected that it was yourself; and that, *joué de tout part*, this trick made a part of the general frolic, in which I played so very foolish a part.'

'Then it was not you, who sent it back to its imprudent donor,' said Lady Knocklofty; 'and, covering an insult in an epigram, made her doubly feel her folly and indiscretion?'

'Me! Good heavens! what in my character, my conduct (even little as you can know of either), could lead your ladyship to indulge a suspicion so derogatory to the feelings of a gentleman – of a man? Give me back,' (said O'Brien, with eagerness), 'that precious ring: I reclaim it in right, in justice; it is the only indemnification I *can* receive for the injury you have inflicted on one, who (many as may be his faults and frailties) is yet guiltless in all where woman is concerned.'

The white hand, on which the ring gleamed, lay on the balustrade, like snow in the moonshine. Lady Knocklofty sighed and smiled, and said, 'No, I must not, ought not, cannot give it again. Remember, *fais ce que doy*.

'And I will take the advice as my wishes construe it,' said Lord Arranmore, ardently; and raising the unresisting hand, timidly and reverentially, he had nearly drawn off the ring, when a loud, shrill blast suddenly and sadly sounded from beneath. Lady Knocklofty started, and drew back her hand; and the ring fell into the deep waters below.

Both remained for a moment silent. To one, that solemn, savage sound, came with an awful effect; for the erring are always superstitious. To the other, it came as a well-known warning – it was the mountain modulation of Shane's sylvan horn. A moment afterwards the splash of an oar was heard; but the shadows of the beetling rocks concealed the boat – if boat there was – which might have skirted the indentures of the shore, and contained this strange haunter of woods and waters.

'How wild, how strange!' said Lady Knocklofty shuddering.

'I fear,' said Lord Arranmore, 'I fear the sudden sound has alarmed you. It probably came from some fishing boat cruising about the creeks.'

'It has indeed shaken me,' said Lady Knocklofty softly, 'for I am horribly nervous: but suppose we take it as a warning.'

'Perhaps I should,' said Lord Arranmore; 'for if there is danger, it can be to me alone.'

'I trust there is none to either; and for you, though chance has led you into the enemy's camp, you are at least protected by the laws of war.'

'But,' said Lord Arranmore, smiling, 'I am here without the knowledge of the commander of the forces, and being neither hostage nor prisoner, I cannot claim the protection of those laws.'

'No,' said Lady Knocklofty, 'a prisoner you certainly are not; and if *you will* go at this unseasonable hour, and after such fatigues, my carriage shall attend you; but – '

'*Will* go! Good Heavens! Lady Knocklofty, I must, I ought: restored to your good opinion, flattered, perhaps intoxicated by your condescension – But judge for me; the guest of Lord Knocklofty I can never be, and your guest, in his absence, I ought not to be.'

'So young and so discreet! and yet discretion is not the virtue I suspect you of,' replied Lady Knocklofty significantly.

'You would wrong your judgment, if you did; but there is a certain feeling of self-respect, a voice that will be heard.'

'Come, come,' said Lady Knocklofty, 'place your feelings of self-respect in abeyance for the present; and listen to a voice that is not used to solicit in vain. Instead of embarking in a fishing-boat for the port of Bog Moy, you shall commit yourself to a well-aired bed, to which Morrison, you see, is ready to pilot you. Still I enter into your feelings, and respect them; and had I such a son, thus would I wish him to act.' She sighed softly.

'And had I such a mother,' said Lord Arranmore, taking her hand, 'I would – '

'Endeavour to run away from her, as you do now from me,' interrupted Lady Knocklofty, laughing, and struggling to release her hand.

'And fail in the attempt, as *I* do now,' said Lord Arranmore.

'Then you will stay,' said Lady Knocklofty, playfully, 'under this fatal roof, for one night at least. Hark! do you not hear "the raven himself is hoarse that croaks the entrance of Duncan under our battlements." '

'I hear but one sound,' replied Lord Arranmore with great

animation, "'tis the voice of a syren! and I will not affect to resist a spell to which the wisest have yielded. I accept your ladyship's hospitality for this night, and to-morrow – '

'Oh! for to-morrow,' said Lady Knocklofty, gaily, ' "sufficient to the day is the evil thereof;" but I will sign a bond of release, if you have any fears for your personal liberty.'

'I confess I have,' he replied eagerly; 'but for the bond!'

'For the present, however;' said Lady Knocklofty, throwing down her eyes, 'you must accept my note of hand.' Lord Arranmore pressed the hand thus graciously presented to him, to his lips, with uncontrollable ardour; and Lady Knocklofty withdrawing it, in apparent confusion, re-entered the dressing-room, and called Morrison to conduct Lord Arranmore to his room. Morrison, who was dozing in the ante-chamber, entered, Lady Knocklofty rang for her maid, but suddenly turning round, and beckoning her guest back to the window, she said, in a low voice,

'It is right I should tell you (for perhaps you are not aware) how deeply you have been calumniated by our side of the house. I do not allude alone to heresy and schism, atheism and sedition; but there is a rumour that you were dismissed your regiment under circumstances which render it a delicate matter for military men to cultivate your acquaintance. This, my young friend, Lord Charles, is most desirous to do; and, in short, you must take an opportunity of talking with him to-morrow, after breakfast. Know him, and like him for my sake.'

Lord Arranmore turned pale with rage and indignation. His lips trembled with emotion. 'Can I see Lord Charles now?' he demanded eagerly.

'He is not yet returned, of course, or we should have heard of it,' replied Lady Knocklofty.

Lord Arranmore now stood biting his lips and looking at his nails; and the conflicts portrayed on his changeful features, evinced that thoughts dark and stormy as thunder clouds were passing over his mind. Lady Knocklofty gazed on him with that expression with which a virtuoso eyes some splendid production of art.

'I am sorry,' she said, 'that what I have mentioned has affected you. Pray think no more of it, till to-morrow at least. It was right you should know it before you met Lord Charles at breakfast.'

'Certainly,' said Lord Arranmore; 'and I owe your ladyship a thousand thanks for putting it into my power to enter upon my defence against the blackest and most libellous calumny that the wickedness of party ever invented, to wring the feelings, and blast the reputation of its victim. And yet, Lady Knocklofty, I cannot, will not, stoop to justify myself from this groundless, infamous charge. If Lord Charles believes it, let him. To explain would be to commit the only dignity I have left. But to you – '

He drew forth a pocket-book, and taking from it a letter, he continued, 'This letter was written to my father on my leaving the Austrian service. I had already tendered my resignation, which the Prince de Ligne did me the honour not to accept; giving me time to re-consider my purpose. Meanwhile the insolence of a superior officer, who affected to treat an Irish gentleman as he was daily treating his subaltern officers – But I will not obtrude upon your ladyship a wearisome detail of circumstances, without interest for you, and full of disgust for me. *Pour trancher le mot*, my challenge was refused, and I was permitted to retire.'

Lady Knocklofty took the letter and said, 'I find it is a service of danger to accuse you; it only increases the prepossession which it is your privilege to inspire. Well, *fiez-vous à moi*, and now, good night, and fair-boding dreams.'

'Good night, dear Lady Knocklofty,' said Lord Arranmore, soothed by her smiles, and more than soothed by her flattery. Bowing on the hand, again presented him, he followed the groom of the chambers along the carpeted corridors to the elegant sleeping-room prepared for him; a strange contrast to the bawn, and the tower, and the Brigadier's press bed at Bog Moy.

'What a creature!' said Lady Knocklofty; which in a woman's lips means everything expressive of admiration or of contempt, according to the inflexion of voice or expression of smile with which it is accompanied. A deep sigh was the comment on this text; and, throwing herself into the cushioned depths of her fauteuil, while her maid placed a *peignoir* over her shoulders and relieved her tresses from the confinement of black pins and bandeaus, she opened the letter of the Prince de Ligne, and read as follows:

'*A Milord Arranmore, etc. etc.*

'MILORD,

'Votre fils a fait une grande indiscretion; il ne fera jamais une bassesse. Il s'est cru obligé de se battre avec un officier supérieur, et la discipline autrichienne s'est crue obligée de lui donner sa démission; c'est dans l'ordre. Il a été mon aide-de-camp, je voudrais bien qu'il le fût encore. Je vous le renvoie avec regret, mais avec honneur. Il est peu docile, il ne sera jamais rampant. Depuis l'age de quinze ans, volontaire dans mon régiment, il a eu des petites aventures très-brillantes dans toutes les campagnes. Mais ce brave militaire n'est plus soldat – il m'assure qu'il ne le sera jamais. Cependant il sera toujours courtois chevalier, prêt à venger les injures des femmes, et à redresser les torts de la societé. Voilà une vocation assez dangereuse! Emoussez sa fougue par quelque profession sobre, et il deviendra bon citoyen; mais gardez-vous bien de lui ôter ce fen de l'âme, source, peut-être, de quelques imprudences, mais aussi de tontes les vertus.

Je suis, milord,

Avec la plus haute considération,

etc. etc. etc.

'LE PRINCE DE LIGNE.'

In an elegant breakfast-room, opening into a lawn, studded with flower beds, and commanding the ocean with its numerous isles and islets, Lord Arranmore found himself on the morning following his arrival at Beauregard. Although it was mid-day, no one had yet attended the breakfast-table, and he had ample leisure to reflect on the unlooked-for events of the preceding evening.

These incidents had not only occupied the sleepless vigils of Lord Arranmore, but furnished endless sources of reflection – as alone and spiritless he occupied, for far more than an hour, the sofa in the breakfast parlour. More than once he started, and asked himself if all were not a dream, – a question which the re-appearance of his masked tormentor upon the scene, in a time and place so little expected, rendered not unnatural. He was now convinced that the voice of the *bonne grâce* was not unknown to him; and connecting it with her advice conveyed in his own motto, her peculiar foreign accent, and her spirited conversation, he was almost led to believe that this reformer of Irish convents was one of the *Penitenti Rosse* of the fancy ball in Dublin; the Nuccia of the Carnival in Rome, – perhaps the harpist at the castle, the vision of O'Brien House, the guide of the grotto at Cong, and, in a word,

Le fantôme mysterieux qui troubla son repos,

by an almost supernatural agency, wherever his wayward destiny had led him. Her transmutations, various as they were, seemed to him but to realize the artifices of Annibal (as described by his favourite historian, Polybius), 'who procured artificial suits of hair, adapted to persons of every age, and habits that corresponded with them; and varying his dress continually, lay so well concealed, that not those alone who had seen him transiently, but even his intimate acquaintance could scarcely know him.'

What the object of this female Annibal might be, he could not conjecture. The sum of all his reflections, inferences, and combinations was, that she was Irish by birth, foreign by breeding; – that her name was O'Flaherty, and her residence a religious retreat in the mountains of Moycullen; – that she was interested in his destiny, for others or for himself; – that she had been known to his father, as she was to his uncle and to Shane (one whom he now believed the agent of all). But if this 'airy nothing' had indeed a local habitation and a name, what a woman! how organized! how gifted! how accomplished! She justified all that he had heard of the talents and acquirements of the sister Irene of Rome, the foundress of *Cuore Sagro*. If with such a mind her preson corresponded – if with such an intellect and such talents, she had the eyes, the smile of Lady Knocklofty, – such eyes such smiles as gleamed on him at parting the night before, – he sighed and shuddered; and folding his hands on his brows, threw back his head on the sofa, and wished he was safely away, even at Bog Moy.

'*Il existe une morale fondée sur la nature de l'homme, indépendante de toutes les opinions spéculatives, antérieure à toutes les conventions.*'[1] This moral existed, and in great intensity, in the mind of him who now applied to himself the observation of one he loved to read and cite; but what passions had not this *morale* to combat? Lord Arranmore determined, cost what it might, to return that day to Bog Moy; yet three days, three delightful days, elapsed without his putting the sage resolution into practice. The letter of the Prince de Ligne had produced all the influence it was calculated to exert upon minds, on which the rank and celebrity of the writer were more powerful than even his genius and his worth.

With Lord Charles it reinstated him as a gallant and distinguished officer. With the worldly Lady Honoria, and with Miss Macguire, the *homme comme il faut*, the aide-de-camp and friend of the Prince de

---

[1] Franklin, cité par Condorcet, dans son éloge de ce philosophe.

Ligne, was a far different personage from the son of a pauper peer and relapsed papist, 'whom nobody knew.'

Lady Honoria had now also other views, than when she had preached discretion to her fair friend and disciple, on the occasion of the review in the Phœnix Park. Mr Stratton was ill in Dublin of an incurable disease, increased by daily intemperance. The influence she had obtained over Lord Knocklofty, through his vanity and indolence, was now becoming a habit, – the tyrant of weak minds and of idle ones. Nature and fate, she believed, combined to complete the ruin of Lady Knocklofty. Nothing could save her: and as somebody must inevitably benefit by her errors (a wife being a necessary appendage to a great man), she saw no reason why she should not be the future lady of Proudfort House, and of Beauregard, as well as another. Sometimes, indeed, her wavering calculations had been directed to influencing the Duke, sometimes to winning upon Lord Charles, who was *aux écoutes:* but now they were all concentrated on the point most consonant with her wishes, by the re-appearance of that individual upon the scene, whom, in her long experience of the fancies and passions, platonic or capricious, of Lady Knocklofty, was the person who had most worked on her imagination; or on that very equivocal species of sensibility, she called her heart.

She had purposely left them a *champ libre* for that mutual explanation, which must inevitably take place. The confident of all Lady Knocklofty's secret thoughts, she guessed, that the re-action would be favourable to the restoration of the offender to her good graces. When therefore she heard Lord Arranmore retire to his chamber, she stole softly to Lady Knocklofty's dressing-room, and found her in the first raptures of the perusal of the Prince de Ligne's letter. The maid was immediately dismissed.

'There,' said Lady Knocklofty, 'you see my first impression was right; and that this "boy with the eyes," turns out a hero of romance after all.'

Lady Honoria read the letter with attention.

'Is not this a charming character?' asked Lady Knocklofty.

'*Tant pis pour vous, ma belle,*' said Lady Honoria, with an admonitory shake of the head.

'However,' said Lady Knocklofty, 'you know my way. I must be amused, and above all, in this tiresome place.'

'Amused!' said Lady Honoria, shaking her head again, and looking moral.

'Come, come,' said Lady Knocklofty, smiling, 'let me have my frolic out.'

'Your frolic, child! – your fever, you mean; an intermitting one, however, for I thought you were "dismissed cured," long since.'

'Psha! I never was on the sick list; or if I were, I am now so perfectly convalescent, that you may trust me. I mean nothing but "*a little sport withal*," as Rosalind says, to enable me to get through this eternal electioneering summer; nor no further in sport neither, than with safety of a pure blush I may in honour come off again.'

'Well, to quote from your own Rosalind, *en tout bien et tout honneur*, of course,' said Lady Honoria, laughing; 'one thing is very clear, with respect to your "gentle, strong, and valiant Orlando," viz. that it rests only with you "to cry *hem* and have him," if such an idle victory can be an object to you.'

'I am not so sure of that,' said Lady Knocklofty, shaking her head; 'and in the difficulty of the conquest lies, perhaps, its sole value. His Irish spirit is sadly at odds with his Irish gallantry; and to fall in love out of the ranks of opposition, he considers a misprision of nationality; in fact, he has as good as told me so.'

'And therefore you are *piqué au jeu*,' observed Lady Honoria. 'Oh! there is nothing like the quintessential *coquetterie* of you women of sentiment.'

'Come, now, confess,' said Lady Knocklofty, 'that to vanquish the proud resistance of this *Ame Paladin*, will be an amusing task for a dull summer at least; and that it will

> Be pastime passing excellent,
> If it be husbanded with modesty,

to witness the struggle between patriotism and prepossession in that young and ardent mind. What a principle to overcome! what prejudice to vanquish!'

'But you do not mean to let Lord K. and the Duke find him here? You will let the "foolish fluttering thing" go back to his cage at Bog Moy, after a day or two?'

'Certainly: just birdlime his feathers as a warning against presumption, and then let him go. In short, there is a pleasure in making a conquest, even though you should turn it to no account.'

'To what account can you turn it?' said Lady Honoria, yawning, 'except you could reconcile Lord K. to him, in the case of old Daly's death, and a new election; then, indeed, the influence of his popular name might be of use.'

'A good idea,' said Lady Knocklofty. 'My dear Honoria, they ought to make you Chancellor of the Exchequer; your resources are exhaustless.'

'Such as they are, my dear Albina, they are always at your service,' said Lady Honoria; and the dear friends and confidants then again kissed, and parted for the night.

On the morning following this 'colloquy sublime,' the entrance of Miss Macguire with her keys of office (that is, of the tea-store), put to flight the train of thoughts, and scattered the thick-coming visions, which gave to the attitude and countenance of Lord Arranmore, the character of one absorbed in waking dreams of deepest reverie. Smiling upon the aide-de-camp of the Prince de Ligne, as she had never smiled upon the prisoner of the castle-guard, whom she had assisted to play off, for the amusement of Lord Kilcolman, she now rallied him upon his deep abstraction, and hinted her suspicions, that some of the fair Os and Macs of the Irish Paphos, from whom they had conveyed him away, were the cause of it. There was something so obviously false and heartless in this pleasantry, that Lord Arranmore replied to it coldly; and he was relieved, though somewhat embarrassed, by the entrance of Lady Knocklofty, leaning on the arm of Lord Charles. They entered from the lawn, on which the breakfast-room opened by a French window. Lord Charles almost rushed on him, with an unmeasured cordiality, characterized by his usual awkwardness and *brusquerie*. He shook both his hands; and without alluding to the past, muttered something, that seemed intended for an apology, or a compliment; it was not easy to discover which.

The entrance of Lady Honoria gave a turn to the conversation, and the Jug Day at Bog Moy formed its principal topic.

'When did you get home, Lord Charles?' asked Lady Knocklofty; 'and where did you leave the General and Horace Montague?'

'At their quarters in St Grellan: they are going to a review at Galway; and they only arrived in time to dress and be off.'

'And the Brigade Major?' asked Miss Macguire, laughing, 'Cousin O'Mailly, of the Owl's country?'

'Oh! by Jove, I never saw a fellow so happy. Lord Arranmore, he'll cut you out, you may depend upon that. I heard your aunt invite him to shoot on the bog; and offer him the services of Paddy Whack, and a bed in the barrack-room.'

'I assure you,' said Lady Honoria, 'he asked me gravely, if there was raally a knighthood in the family like the knight of Kerry's.'

'Of course, you swore to the fact,' said Lady Knocklofty.

'Of course. But seriously, Lord Arranmore, I advise you to have a strict eye to your elder aunt; for O'Mealy is evidently enamoured *des beaux yeux de sa cassette*, and if you are not quite sure of the intail – ' Lady Honoria stopped short, observing, that on the subject of his aunts, Lord Arranmore *n'entendait pas raillerie;* and then added, in another tone, 'Joking apart, O'Mealy is such a ways-and-means fellow, that I have no doubt he will make Bog Moy his head quarters, when the Knockloftys are gone.'

'And excellent quarters they are,' said Lord Charles. 'Never tasted such claret in all my life. How it did flow, by Jove! Then the women! what lovely creatures. There is not a rout in London could show such a turn out: and amazing good manners too, I can tell you. There is nothing in your Dublin set like that Mrs Paddy Lynch, with her large eyes, and the dimple in her chin. By Jove! only think of the four Miss Roistrums, as compared with these Connaught beauties.'

'The comparison is not fair,' said Miss Macguire, piqued for the honour of Dublin society. 'The Miss Roistrums are your *tic douloureux*, Lord C.; besides, they are bad specimens. They owe their place in society, to their father's place under government; and are handed down from viceroy to viceroy, and regiment to regiment, with state-chairs and barrack-fixtures. Pray don't quote them, when you go back to your set in London, as specimens of the Dublin beauties.'

'Why, one sees them every where,' said Lord Charles; 'while quantities of pretty creatures, whom one only meets at the park, the theatre, or the rotunda, are kept back, because they don't belong to the official set. One does not come to Ireland to be rode rough-shod over by the demi-ton of London. Why, there are those nine Miss Flamboroughs, as we call them, who give themselves such airs here, and cut right and left in the *hauteur* of their "insolence of office." In London, it is quite another thing with them.'

'But, still, they are so very pleasant, and talk so much, and so well,' said Miss Macguire.

'Yes, and talk and look so like, that Falkland of our's made love t'other night to Miss Emmeline, thinking she was his old London flame, Miss Anna Maria.'

'*N'importe*,' said Lady Honoria: 'It is a joint-stock concern, a family firm, – we call it the New Consolidated London Assurance Company

– and, provided you deal with the house, it matters not with which of the partners.'

Every body laughed.

'Bravo,' said Lord Charles. 'You Irish women are so pretty and so witty, and give such good nick-names, you might carry all before you, if you were only true to yourselves. What do you say, Lord Arranmore?'

'I am of the non-importation confederacy, of course,' said Lord Arranmore, laughing. 'Beauty is the staple commodity of the country, and superior to any fabric which foreign policy would impose on us. But it is the old fashion of Ireland to neglect its native produce, and to give the preference to whatever comes marked with the stamp of a distant market.'

Lord Arranmore now rose to take his leave; but against this proposition there was a general outcry. The silken flag of a beautiful barge, which was that day to take the party to the Isles of Arran, was fluttering through the trees, in the bay below.

'A long-planned expedition,' said Lady Knocklofty, 'for which you, Lord Arranmore, are yourself accountable; and we could not possibly undertake our voyage of discovery under better auspices, than when piloted by the chief of the Isles.'

The proposal was irresistible: but yet Lord Arranmore resisted. 'He had only his evening dress, – was in shoes and stockings.' That was easily remedied; Lord Charles had made up some jackets and trowsers for the boating parties of Beauregard; and a suit of them was at his service.

But his aunts! He was desirous to relieve the anxiety which his absence must naturally awaken.

A man and horse would do that much more expeditiously.

The man and horse were accordingly dispatched; and the chief of the Isles of Arran once more visited the rocks of his nativity, and realm of his fancied inheritance, under circumstances the least probable, and least 'dreamed of in his philosophy.'

# CHAPTER IV

———— • ————

## *The Excursions*

Noi ci mettemmo per un bosco
Che da nessun sentiero era segnato.

DANTE.

Your accent is something finer, than you could purchase in so removed a
dwelling.

*As You Like It.*

BRIGHT skies and favouring gales, with eyes and spirits as sunny and
as light, gave promise of a halcyon voyage to the gay pilgrims bound
to the Isle of Saints, as the party from Beauregard, reinforced by two
young *militaires* from St Grellan, put off from the shore. Every feature
of the beautiful Bay of Galway had its effect. The mountains of
Connemara stood out from the clear and cloudless horizon; numerous
islands spotted the glossy surface of the deep; and green shores and
gliding barks gave touches of home scenery and a busy movement to
the whole, which took from the usual dreariness of sea views.

Lady Knocklofty observed to O'Brien, with whom she conversed
in a low tone, that 'it was all enchantment,' and he felt that it was so:
yet, like other spells, it operated with a mingled sensation of sadness
and pleasure; and more pleased with others than with himself, he
sighed to think, that he was revisiting the Isles of Arran, under
auspices the least appropriate to such an occasion.

Scarcely, however, had the barge approached the first and smaller
of the isles, when the wind changed, and a thick sea-fog sprung up
and veiled out every speck of land. The pilot, unable to make for the
port of Arranmore, with wind and tide against him, was glad to avail

himself of the impatience and entreaties of the ladies, to run into the first of the islands which presented itself. They had scarcely landed, when the fog discharged itself in a heavy rain; and the hovel of a kelp gatherer, situated among the rocks, was the only asylum against the 'pitiless pelting of the storm,' which the thinly inhabited and rocky spot afforded.

Here an excellent cold dinner, the object and reward of all parties of pleasure, with wines of the choicest description, and all the *fun* of those little *desagrémens*, which constitute the *agrémens* of all such expeditions, occupied and amused the time, though it did not fulfil the intentions of the party.

Towards evening, however, the deluge suddenly ceased; a brilliant rainbow threw its arch of promise across the calm sky, the winds were hushed, and without a 'breath the blue wave to curl,' even had there been a wave (which there was not) to be curled by them. The party re-embarked at sunset; the sails were furled, the oars plied, and moonlight seas, and a balmy atmosphere, with the exhilaration produced by Burgundy and Champagne, in some of the party, and with causes as exciting in others, rendered the prolonged voyage home still more delightful than the shorter transit of the outward-bound crew had proved in the morning. It was midnight when the voyagers entered the well lighted dining-room of Beauregard; where a supper was served, which did not want the zest of a keen appetite to recommend it to the palates of the guests. A note from Miss Mac Taaf was put into Lord Arranmore's hands, as he had just seated himself by Lady Knocklofty at the table, which ran as follows:-

'DEAR MURROGH,

'I must take lave to inform you that I am highly displazed with your whole behaviour and conduct in regard of the Brigadier, who never left his own table as long as he could sit at it nor after, more particularly on a Jug Day. No scrambler over rocks nor cliffs nor book-worm; and wonders much ye got to the bottom with life, being the first bird or baste ever climbed down *Carrig-na-Phouka*. And am highly delighted ye saved Lady Knocklofty's life under God's mercy to whom all praise with best regards, and would have written as intended (also my sister Monica) but not a scrap of paper left in the place, though have meditated sending for half a quire by Paddy the post from St Grellan this week back for which call on your return at Mrs Costello's. I send a change of linen with your foreign riding coat, also the pony and boy tied up in your white French cambrick pocket handkerchief. No need of saddle-bags which you can ride home the boy walking. And lay my commands and injunctions on you to return to dinner, not forgetting the lock of the Brigadier's fusil at Peter ynch's – Major O'Mailly shooting himself here tomorrow – so mind you are back to the minute, as you value the regard of your affectionate Aunt,

'MABLE MAC TAFF'

Lord Arranmore coloured as he read, twisted up the incoherent farrago, and crammed it into his pocket; indignant at the servitude to which this despotic old woman sought to reduce him, and resolved to resist it, even for the short time he intended to remain at Bog Moy.

'That note bodes no good to our gipsy party in the mountains tomorrow, I suspect,' said Lady Knocklofty, whose eyes were fixed on his countenance, on which annoyance was strongly painted. He smiled, and answered,

'My aunts desire their best compliments to your Ladyship, and congratulate you on your safe arrival at Beauregard.'

'But is Cinderella's hour come?' asked Lady Honoria, jeeringly – 'that's the point; or does the ill-natured old fairy refuse a further furlough?'

'The old fairy,' replied Lord Arranmore, 'has every claim to my respect; but none upon my time. It is at your Ladyship's service, in any way you please to dispose of it.'

'Take care what you say,' said Lady Honoria: 'you know not how much you may commit yourself. The man who makes me professions, gives me breath; but he who gives me his time . . . Ask Lady Knocklofty if that is not the *pierre de touche; elle s'y connait, bonne femme.*'

'Oh! pray don't apply to me,' said Lady Knocklofty, 'I have no maxims on any subject; I am the slave of impulse, and wholly led by my feelings, not by my experience: any one may deceive me, as long as I deceive myself, and that' (she added with a sigh) 'I generally do.'

'That is the true secret of deceiving others in time,' said Lady Honoria. *'On commence par être dupe, on finit par être fripon.* That is we begin by being *sensible*, and we end by feigning it.'

'My hour is not then come,' said Lady Knocklofty. 'I fear – I feel it is far off.'

'But it will come,' replied Lady Honoria; 'it is the natural course of things!'

'I may grow old,' observed Lady Knocklofty, passionately, 'but never insensible.'

'When you are old, my dear, you may grow what you like, but don't talk of it – to live to look through spectacles, and see nothing but wrinkles! Ouf!'

Everybody asserted, that she, beyond all her sex, never could grow old.

'So the men told Ninon,' said Lady Honoria, 'and yet while *entre les deux âges*, what was her confession – "*Tout le monde me dit, que j'ai moins à me plaindre du temps qu'une autre; mais de quel façon que ce soit, si l'on m'avait proposé une telle vie, je me serais pendue.*" '

'The most horrible of all fates,' said Lady Knocklofty, 'is not to live to grow old; it is to preserve the feelings fresh, when the person is withered – and yet there are hearts, which time cannot reach.'

'Oh! for your Lady Pentweasles, and Lady Wishforts, your green hearts and grey hairs, I give them up,' said Lady Honoria, laughing, and every body laughed with her.

The men all thought Lady Honoria very clever; but they felt that the credulous and passionate Lady Knocklofty was irresistible: the conversation was then abruptly turned by Lady Knocklofty to the intended excursion of the following day.

Among the wildest and most romantic sites of the lower range of the Connemara mountains, and at ten miles distance from Beauregard, Lord Knocklofty had recently built and furnished a beautiful sporting lodge, to which, from its situation, he had given the name of 'the Heaths.' To this lodge he was about to repair in the early part of the ensuing week, with a large party from Lord Altamont's (the Lord Lieutenant included). To inspect the necessary preparations for so distinguished a company, in so remote a place, Lady Knocklofty had planned a gipsy party into the mountains for the following day. Servants and sumpter-horses were to precede her; and as the Heaths were only approachable (after the first four miles) by bridleways, through the ravines and mams of the uncivilized region, the whole party went of necessity on horseback. Lord Arranmore had spoken of his return to Bog Moy on the next morning, yet no one was surprised to see him *de la partie*. Lady Knocklofty was a most accomplished horse-woman; she never looked so well as on horseback – the dress, the air, the exercise became her; it was her stronghold of coquetry, to which she never failed to resort in all cases of emergency: and as her two fair friends rode almost as well as herself, a *cavalcata* answered the views and purposes of all, and all took the field with grace and spirit.

The party was reinforced by the General and his Aides-de-Camp, all feathers and aiguillettes; and as it passed the gates of Beauregard, it had that gallant air which characterized the courtly cavalry of White-hall, or Newmarket, when the monarch himself acted as the *cavalierot to* to the Stuart or Jennings of the day.

Lord Arranmore rode a favourite mare of Lady Knocklofty's (which seemed as much inclined to keep close to its mistress, as its rider), having lent his sure-footed pony to Miss Macguire. He had got entangled in this second party by the provoking hit at his dependence, launched by Lady Honoria; at least he attributed the change in his intention to the circumstance, which, perhaps, might have influenced, but certainly did not exclusively occasion it. His whole existence, since he had left Bog Moy, had been a thraldom. Dissatisfied with himself, every principle at variance with his position, he had got involved in lines the most delicate, and difficult to break through. Long and dangerous *tête-à-têtes* (the more dangerous, because their soft muttering was sanctioned by being carried on in society) had put him in possession of a secret, which men of the world well know how to appreciate, but which, to one, ardent and inexperienced, whose very 'virtues had turned traitors to themselves,' was estimated by another standard than that which the world supplies.

Not even the seductions of Lady Knocklofty (and her habitually haughty, high-spirited demeanour rendered them but more seducing), had touched his heart. But at five and twenty there are other avenues to the frailties of nature than that of the heart. Lord Arranmore sighed to think that he had not even the excuse of feeling, to sanction his weakness, which, however, he placed to the account of gratitude; and he began this gipsy expedition with the firm resolution, that it should be his last. To provide against the possibility of again falling into temptation, he had dispatched 'the boy' with everything but the riding-dress he wore, to Bog Moy; and he resolved to return to the Brigadier's tower, and to all the horrors of his temporary dependence, that night.

The gipsy expedition was begun immediately after breakfast, in all the brilliancy of spirits incidental to that first, fresh season of the day. The ornamental grounds, the flourishing plantations, and old stunted woods of Beauregard were soon passed. The verdure of its pasturage, and the yellow blossom of its meadows and corn fields, were gradually exchanged for the brown plains of peat bog and heathy swamps, studded with turf stacks; while a few half-naked cottiers, walking up to their middle in the boggy soil, and bearing bushes and stones to patch the bog road lately laid down by the great lord of the district, exhibited in their famished looks and squalid rags, a painful contrast to the splendid party, who turned aside their eyes, as they passed, in pity or disgust.

The high, wild mountains of Connemara soon came upon the eye in all their real ruggedness, and divested of those aërial tints with which distance had hitherto beautified them; and their gap, or pass, dark and narrow, was entered with feelings almost of awe and apprehension. On either side, the ravine (scarcely admitting two persons to ride abreast) rose in a long line of lofty and magnificent precipices, shattered by the elements, into the boldest and most grotesque forms, ridge shelving above ridge, like artificial galleries. Hollows filled with dark vapours, or gleaming with living waters; mountains, succeeding to mountains, receding, softening, and again starting forward upon the horizon, and admitting through their breaks blue glimpses of the distant ocean, or nearer gleams of the waters of Lough Corrib, cheated the weariness of the way, by that changeful variety which mountain scenery alone possesses.

Escaping from a mam, whose rock appeared ready to split and fall upon the heads of the intruders, and suddenly descending a green and slippery track, which fell to the margin of a chain of small lakes, – and now again ascending another bridle-way, among hills covered with a stool of stunted wood, – the elegant spectators of these savage regions, while they exhausted every phrase of admiration which Thomson or Delille had supplied, began to exhibit symptoms of impatience and weariness; and to express wishes for the termination of the expedition, which were still disappointed and delayed. The General held up his repeater and touched the spring, as a warning to the party: it struck four. The guide, a gamekeeper attached to the establishment at the Heaths, was again and again interrogated as to their position. Did he see the lodge? In which direction did it lie? How far was it off? etc. etc. etc., to all which he replied as he could: 'Och, you can see it, my lady, if yez were on the top of that rock there; and saw something very like it a good bit ago, but thinks it was *Cushlanne-a-Haliah*, or the Hag's castle, where th' ould lady scoulded herself to death.'

'That must be my aunt Mac Taaf,' whispered Lady Honoria to Miss Macguire.

The guide was then called upon for the story of 'the ould lady,' and a quarter of an hour was thus beguiled. Lady Honoria, however (who hated parties of pleasure, but liked any thing better than remaining at home and alone), at length called after Lady Knocklofty, who rode in advance, in close conversation with Lord Arranmore.

'Lady K. we must certainly have a shakedown at the Heaths to-night, if indeed we reach the lodge before to-morrow morning.'

'I always intended it,' said Lady Knocklofty, laughing over her shoulder, 'and have provided for you all accordingly.'

Every body expressed their surprise, but none their satisfaction at this intelligence.

'*Quelle perfidie!*' exclaimed Lady Honoria. 'I hope then, you have provided a compass; and are not without flints and matches, and other necessaries for bivouacking, wherever we may happen to find ourselves at night-fall.'

'I have forgotten nothing,' said Lady Knocklofty: 'a cargo of night-caps and tooth-brushes accompany us; for you know our friend, Lord Charles, like the Dean of St Grellan, is mighty particular who he lends his tooth-brush to; but come, cheer up, you will soon find yourself in a palace in the desert, like the enchanted castle, in *la Belle et la Bête.*'

'*Ma belle, c'était bien bête de se fier à vous,*' said Lady Honoria, 'I, at least, ought to know you better.'

'But look at that sublime view, Honoria! Lord Charles, have you anything like that in Cumberland?'

'Never tried, by Jove; never looked beyond the covers. A grove of fine chimneys, on the sweet, shady side of Pall Mall, for me.'

'How can you be insensible to such scenes?' said Lady Knocklofty. 'Good heavens, what a prospect!'

'The prospect of a soup and a sofa,' said Lady Honoria pettishly, 'would be the only prospect that could have a charm for me at present.'

'Exactly,' said Lord Charles, 'that's my idea too, Lady Honoria, of the sublime and beautiful.'

'Well, you are earning the enjoyment of both,' said Lady Knocklofty, endeavouring to keep up the spirits of her party, to the level of her own, which were all abroad. 'Look at that mass of tremendous rock, all sunshine on one side, and deep obscurity on the other – what a curious effect!'

'I wish I was *on the other*,' said Lady Honoria, 'for I am done to a turn, *grillée aux os;* the heat is insupportable; do let us escape from this *côte rôtie*.'

'Well, *courage, mon enfant*, we must be now nearly at our journey's end; for the last time I was here, I rode with my lord, and Lord Clanrickard, in two hours and a half from gate to gate; though we went the old road: this is the new line.' She then asked the guide, what difference there was in the distance between the two roads?

'Why then I would not take on me to say, my lady,' replied the guide, taking off his hat, and wiping his forehead, with a look of some perplexity, as the party now rode up to him, 'for never came this new line afore; only, just, it was your ladyship's orders.'

'Never!' exclaimed Lady Honoria.

'Never!' repeated the whole party, in various tones of impatience and annoyance.

'No, in troth, never,' replied the guide.

'Then,' said Lady Honoria, with much ill temper, 'we may as well give up the ghost. I'm already in a fever; *je n'en peux plus*, and here, it appears, all resource is cut off.'

The gentlemen affected to laugh; but were not a little perplexed. It was clear that the guide had lost his way, or rather had never known it. There was, however, no alternative, and they continued to follow as he led. Every trace of a road, or even of a path, was now gradually disappearing; and the horses floundered on, through rough masses of rock, rising out of the quaking swamps of a peaty vegetable soil, till the ravine terminated abruptly over one of those deep and desolate hollows, which resemble the gaping crater of an extinct volcano. A dark, grey pool filled its lowest depths, overshadowed by a semicircular range of sheltering precipices, whose shaggy points were involved in the electric clouds, they had drawn from the surrounding atmosphere. A narrow stream appeared to unite this sequestered spot to some lake, on the other side of its barren rocks; but neither track, nor man, nor path, nor pass, nor living form, cheered the hopeless prospect – which, clouded by the now lurid and lowering atmosphere, was the very *lascia speranza* of the desolate region.

Every body quitted their horses.

'Here is a pretty *cul de sac*,' said Lady Honoria, throwing herself on a bank of heather. 'Even if we find our way back, we have full four hours' ride, without relief or refreshment.'

Lady Knocklofty and Miss Macguire took their places beside her:

and the grooms led the horses to a natural basin of water, dripping from the rocks; while the gentlemen took the guide a little in advance (to free themselves from the embarrassment of the ladies' questions and complaints), and entered on a consultation. But the guide had lost all presence of mind in losing his way. His intelligence all depended upon the sensible objects, with which it was associated; and of these he had lost sight, after the first hour of their journey. He had, in fact, taken a totally different road from that recently laid down by Lord Knocklofty's engineer, the precursor of one, to whose talents and industry the regions of Connemara are now so deeply indebted.[1]

While others were consulting and conjecturing, Lord Arranmore, to whom these regions were familiar, and by whom such obstacles had often been encountered, substituted experiment for inference, and separating from the party, in quest of some means of escape from the embarrassments in which they were involved, he caught the figure of a lonely fisherman who was throwing out his line from a little canoe, in the depths below. He resolved therefore to descend the precipice, and obtain such information as this probably native inhabitant of the region could best give them. The steep was not without danger; but his confidence in his own agility, address, and well practised activity, was authorized by similar feats, performed in similar difficulties. He had already begun his descent from cliff to cliff, and from point to point, when, as he paused upon a slippy and rapid descent, almost apprehensive to proceed further, a loud, wild blast, from a mountain horn, called forth a thousand echoes from the rocks. It was the warning tone, which, in such notes, had often checked the reckless temerity of his boyish enterprises, and had of late so frequently sounded in moments of exigency and peril.

He threw up his eyes, and perceived a figure perched on the pinnacle of a rock over the heads of the party he had left, who were sheltering from the sun under its beetling shadows. A form more appropriate to the region could scarcely be imagined, than this image of 'the giant Danger,' bestriding the toppling cliff, of which its rugged and boldly defined limbs seemed a part.

Lord Arranmore again ascended, in the assurance that a guide was at hand, and that his good or evil genius still followed his steps. In his ascent he perceived a pathway up the rocks, which had hitherto escaped his notice, and that of the party: and though the figure of

[1] H. Nimmo, Esq.

Shane had vanished, like a wreath of mountain vapour, still as the path led to the spot where he had disappeared, Lord Arranmore pursued it; and suddenly found himself upon the smooth summit of a table-mountain, which commanded a view, contrasting with that from which he had ascended, to an extent only to be met with in those altitudes, where nature seems relieved from her own laws, and sports in the wildest and most capricious freedom.

It was a broad and fertile glen, centered by a beautiful lake, and sheltered on all sides, save one, by hills and rocks of various forms and tints, to which the receding and ruder mountains formed a background. The clouds, which had obscured the other and steeper side of the acclivity, were here broken into fleecy vapours; and the sun poured a full flood of yellow radiance, tinging every hill and hollow, pool and torrent, and brightening the clustered walls and picturesque chimneys of a pile, which (half in ruin, half in preservation) lay along the edge of the lake. It was manifestly one of those relics of ecclesiastical architecture which, rude as they may be, are still in Ireland so superior to every other monument of antiquity. The lake confounded its waters with an inlet of the sea, which, like many others, indenting this coast, run in a long and narrow channel between the hills. On the brow of one of these hills, appeared a cluster of cottages, surrounded by symptoms of verdure and cultivation; while a mill, turned by a mountain torrent, intimated some considerable progress in industry, and civilization, very little to be expected in a region so remote. Several figures were seen moving from various directions upon one point, and that point was the fabric which commanded the whole.

A transition so immediate, from wild and houndless sterility, to a scene of such repose and loveliness, seemed more the work of magic, than of accident. Lord Arranmore gazed in emotion; and for a moment, perceived not that the mountain-sheep cropping the scented herbage from the flat on which he stood, were attended by a boy, who lay under the branches of a stunted oak. The boy had, however, been looking upon him, from his first appearance, with a bashful, pleased, and sideling look.

'What old building is that?' demanded Lord Arranmore, in as much Irish as he could command.

'The Abbey of Moycullen,' said the child.

'Is it inhabited?'

'Och, yes, by the religious ladies of the Holy Heart.'

A sudden revulsion of the whole frame, brought Lord Arranmore's blood from the heart to the head. The boy, who had now risen, fondly taking his hand, stood looking in his eyes with a glance of recognition.

'You know me?' said Lord Arranmore, endeavouring to recollect him.

'*Agus* the *Uasal*, shure.'[1]

'And your name, my child?'

'Padreen, the son of Emunh-na-Lung. That's my daddy, sure;' and the boy pointed to a man, who was sculling over the ferry-boat with some passengers, to the other side of the lake. Lord Arranmore now recognized one of the objects of his commiseration at Ardcrow; and he shook the child's hand heartily.

'Your father, then,' he said, 'is the ferryman of this lake, now?'

'Aye, indeed?' said the boy.

Lord Arranmore paused and gazed. This then was, in all probability, the habitation of one, who, to his imagination, had not appeared like 'an inhabitant of earth;' and to this deep and lonely seclusion, to this fertile, fruitful domain, the church had again found its way, after the lapse and persecution of centuries. For a moment, too deeply interested to think of any thing but the scene before him, and the object with which he believed it to be intimately connected, he forgot those whom he had left behind, as if they had never existed: a shrill whistle from the guide, followed by the repetition of his own name, re-echoed among the nether rocks, brought him back to the remembrance of an association, so little in harmony with the scene of his contemplation. His first feeling was that of a miser, who suddenly discovering a hidden treasure, trembles lest others should follow in his track, and share his prize. He felt no desire to throw his party in the way of the ladies of Moycullen. It seemed a species of sacrilege. He knew not why, – he stopped not to inquire, – yet when the guide, followed by Captain Montague, appeared within a few paces of him, he felt something like embarrassment.

He had been missed, and the party were full of anxiety for his safety. The mountain-horn had called their attention to the spot from which it had sounded; and the pony ridden by Miss Macguire, as if led by the sound, had directed its steps towards the ravine, whose mouth, concealed by brush-wood, afforded a tolerable ascent. The

[1] The Gentleman.

party were toiling up on foot; and the horses, led by the grooms, followed.

The scene, which discovered itself to the gaze of all, produced many exclamations of wonder and admiration. The descent was easy and over a mossy soil; and the guides learned from the shepherd boy, that there was a wheel-way along the edge of the lake, which led to the shore of the Bay, where there was a fishery, and boats which plied to St Grellan, and a bridle track along the strand. This was most welcome information. It raised the spirits and roused the energies of all.

'So,' said Lady Honoria, 'we have only been playing the old part of the King of France and his merry men, first "marching up the hill, and then marching down again." '

'This view,' said Lady Knocklofty, 'is worth all we have suffered. What old building is that on the edge of the lake?'

'It's what they call it, the Retrate of the Religious Ladies,' said the guide.

'Then,' said Lady Honoria, with great glee, 'this is probably the dwelling of the *religieuse* of Bog Moy, who said, if I would take convent fare, – *roba di convento*, she called it – she would be glad to see me. So pray let us row over, and beg her hospitality, for I am famished.'

'By all means,' said the General. 'It will be quite a Mont St Bernard adventure.'

'I never saw a nun in all my life, except on the stage,' said the younger aide-de-camp; 'I would give anything to see a real nun.'

'I dare say it will be fun alive,' said Lord Charles, rubbing his hands.

'We shall come in for a mouthful of vespers, too,' said Miss Macguire: 'this is just the time.'

'And a mouthful of something more substantial, too, I hope,' said Lady Honoria, 'though it be but a hot potato.'

Lady Knocklofty objected; she thought it best to get home as fast as they could. What did Lord Arranmore think?

He was quite of her ladyship's opinion. But the question being put to the vote, the no's carried it. The party therefore descended the heights and reached the lake, just as Emuhn-na-Lung and one of his sons were putting out from the opposite side. The boat was hailed, and the rower, instantly recognizing his benefactor, sprung on shore, and, unmindful of the splendid company which surrounded him, fell at Lord Arranmore's feet: with all the promptitude of Irish gratitude and its hyberbole, he burst into tears, kissed his hands, and uttered many exclamations of surprise and delight, at so unexpected a meeting.

'Here is a scene!' said Lady Honoria.

'What does it all mean, Lord Arranmore?' demanded Lady Knocklofty, in the hope she would be called on for a sensation.

He hastily explained; but the ferryman, full of his own good luck, entered more in detail upon its history, adding, 'that nothing but luck had followed him ever since the hour he had met with his honour's goodness; for that shortly after he was visited in his poor cabin, by the suparior of the confraternity, and the Reverend Mother had taken him into her service, and given the childer plinty of larning, and the ateing and the drinking *goloure*.'

'Then pray row us over to the Reverend Mother,' said Lady Honoria, stepping into the boat, 'for you could not possibly be a fitter object of her charity than we are.' The rest of the party followed, and Lord Arranmore (last, and least willingly) gave his arm to Lady Knocklofty, who was bored and out of temper. The grooms, under the guidance of the shepherd-boy, took the horses towards the shore; where, at the distance of a mile, was a *tighleana*, or house of reception, opposite to which, stood a second ferry. The boat then put off; the oars sparkled in the sun-beams; the scene they were approaching came forward, in distinct features, as they advanced, and in less than a quarter of an hour, the party landed.

With a simultaneous expression of surprise and admiration, they paused. The Abbey of Moycullen, after the lapse of ages, still preserved all its beautiful Gothic forms; and, submitting more to the aggressions of time, than of man (though grey and moss-covered, mouldering and decayed), still exhibited a most striking and picturesque exterior. The intricacies of the mountain passes, which led to it by land, had probably saved it from the spoliations of Cromwell's soldiery; though the ferocious fanatics had penetrated into the deepest gorges of the Galway mountains, wherever monastic establishments had held out the lure of plunder.[1] The curiously-ribbed oak-roof of the church, with its arched and ornamented entrance of the Saxon Gothic, its great window, perfect in its delicate tracery, and recently filled with stained glass, together with its belfry and cloisters, were in the highest preservation; while, lying partly in ruin, were still visible

---

[1] Not very far from Moycullen, at Aughnanure, twenty-seven priests were put to death by the Cromwellites.

the old refectory, chauntry, and cells of its once opulent community; and a modern building, which harmonized externally with the rest, had been built by the late Count O'Flaherty, and was now the residence (according to the ferryman, who served as cicerone to the party) of the religious ladies of the Abbey.

As the party advanced from the lake along the greensward that spread before the Abbey church, they halted to examine an escutcheon or lozenge, hanging over the arch of its principal entrance. It represented a woman in the habit of a nun, offering a heart irradiated by a glory, to a monk in the vesture of Loyola, with the motto of *In hoc signo vinces*. This singular sign (on which Lady Honoria made observations, which to the pious would have sounded like sacrilege) attracted the eyes of all, and increased the general amazement; for it was understood by none, save Lord Arranmore, who sighed as he gazed at it, – when suddenly the low sweet peal of the flute-stop of an organ, directed every sense to itself. The accidental rising of the dark curtain (dropped before the entrance, as in foreign churches), by the hand of some peasant votarist, gave a transient view of the interior of the church; and the gipsy party, with every other intention in abeyance, passed the *velum* of the temple, and entered the sanctuary.

The perspective was striking. The church, though small, was most characteristic of the remote times in which it was raised; and the lights which penetrated the fine Gothic window, at its extremity, fell with singular effect on the delicate tracery and pillars. The high altar was richly decorated with all the paraphernalia, which the catholic church has borrowed from the Jewish. The altar-piece was a well-painted illustration of 'Suffer little children to come unto me; for of such is the kingdom of God:' and little children, clean and well-dressed, to the number of thirty, were seated, with looks demure and folded hands, round the steps of the altar. A venerable ecclesiastic was celebrating the vesper service before the holy table, while the responses were chaunted by female voices, accompanied by the organ. The chancel was separated from the nave by a screen: the latter was crowded to excess by a congregation of the peasantry; and in the former, with their eyes riveted to the psalters from which they were singing, stood the sisters of the community of the Holy Heart. In the midst, upon a raised chair, sat the Superior, with a superb missal open on the desk before her, on which her folded hands, just escaping from the long and sweeping sleeves of her habit, were laid. Her ample robe and voluminous veil, her *pose* and air might have well become a

*Jeanne de Plaisance*, or other princess of the church, in the sixteenth century, to whom conscious power and the habit of command had communicated a haughty ease of demeanour, characterising alike the movements and the repose of the possessor. Once, and only once, the Reverend Mother turned her head, and raised her eyes from the missal to which they were directed. It was at the moment when the entrance of the strangers, for whom all had made way, occasioned some slight disturbance. She again, however, let them fall, and remained dignified and motionless until the symphony of the anthem, which closed the service, commenced, when one of the choral sisters replaced her missal with a music-book, bowed the knee, and retired to her stall. The music selected was a *Salve Regina*, whose simple counterpoint was well adapted to the not very educated voices of the choir. One voice, however, in the solo part, was strikingly superior to the rest. It was a *contralto* of the rarest description, rich and clouded, yet less remarkable for its quality than for the highly finished Italian manner of its execution. It was the voice of the Superior: and in its mellow and well modulated tones, was recognized by some of the strangers the voice of the Italian harpist of the castle; while to the one alone to whom it communicated emotions the most mixed and powerful, it produced the full conviction that he again listened to the accents which, even in the land of the Syrens, had taken 'the prisoned soul, and wrapt it in Elysium.'

The voice ceased. The organ in full *diapason*, commenced a voluntary. The community, preceded by their Superior, departed by a door that opened from the choir into the interior of the edifice. The officiating priest retired into the sacristy, and the sacristan extinguished the wax lights that burned on the altar, and veiled the shrine, and closed the sacred volume. The peasant congregation, each dropping a knee before the high altar, and dipping a finger into the stone vase of holy water, made their exit; and the party from Beauregard still remained leaning against the screen, where they had taken their stand on entering, wholly occupied with sensations of surprise and pleasure.

Released, however, from the silence imposed by the sacred ceremony, they soon broke forth in expressions of amazement and admiration. To the young men, the sisters (a very clumsy set of persons) appeared angels; by the women they were pronounced dowdies, who in ordinary dresses would have been coarse and vulgar. Upon the subject of the Superior, there was a more general agreement:

all felt the imposing influence of her dignified and abstracted manner. 'As she sat' (said the gallant old General), 'with only her pretty white hands to be seen, she reminded me of the charming portrait of the Abbess of Fontevrault –

> Elle avait au bout de ses manches
> Une paire de mains si blanches,
> Que je voudrais, en vérité,
> En avoir été souffleté,'

'It is very extraordinary,' said Miss Macguire; 'but I am persuaded that her voice is that of the Italian harpist at the castle, which threw old Lord Muckross into such raptures, and which Lady Honoria pronounced to be *le plus bel asthme du monde*.'

'I wish we had got a better view of her face,' said Lord Charles, 'but she shouldered us out very explicitly. Lady Honoria, where is the convent fare you promised us?'

'I saw nothing that resembled my close bonnet acquaintance,' said Lady Honoria. 'I am afraid she is not of them. But, *coûte qui coûte*, we must try our luck; so, Lady K., send in a message to request leave to view the interior, and trust to Irish hospitality for the rest.'

Lady Knocklofty, though least amused and most amazed of her party, declared she would rather suffer any inconvenience, than take so great a liberty with a person of so forbidding a deportment as the Superior.

'Forbidding?' repeated Miss Macguire; 'Oh, I assure you that it is only the *tournure* of the convent, and is put on and off with the veil and scapular.'

'To be sure it is,' said Lady Honoria; 'you may trust Kitty Macguire on these points – *elle s'y connaît*.'

At that moment the sister who had played the organ descended from the organ loft, and Lady Honoria solicited her attention as she passed, by requesting her to present the Countess of Knocklofty's compliments; when she was stopped short by the sister waving her forefinger before her face (the common movement of Italian negation), and saying, '*Non intendo l'Inglese, signora.*'

'Who speaks Italian here?' said Lady Honoria.

'Lord Arranmore, you do, of course – come forward and translate for us.'

Lord Arranmore had hitherto remained apart, with his eyes fixed on an altar-piece of a small lateral chapel, in the endeavour to conceal his pre-occupation, by a feigned admiration of a very indifferent work of art. Thus called upon, he turned round; and in spite of every attempted mastery over himself, he coloured to the eyes as he recognized in the organist, the elder of the *Penitenti Rosse* of the fancy ball. Lady Honoria repeated the message, of which he was the interpreter, and the foreign nun immediately retired to deliver it.

'Only think,' said Lady Honoria, 'of their having brought over a foreigner to teach these creatures music? What are the papists driving at?'

'What indeed!' said the General, smiling. 'That Abbess completely realizes my ideas of a dangerous papist.'

'By Jove,' said Lord Charles, 'I should like to be of this church militant. That old Father Confessor has a fine time of it.'

Other common-places followed, till one of the sisters returned, and bowing first to the altar, advanced with a slight inclination of her head, her hands folded sanctimoniously before her, and her demure and downcast looks humorously contrasted with her handsome, broad, and very mundane countenance. In a strong brogue she delivered the Reverend Mother's compliments to Lady Knocklofty, inviting the party to partake of such poor refreshment as the place afforded, since there was nothing in the Abbey that was worthy of their inspection. As she spoke, she cast a furtive look at the military, and added, as from herself, with a smile that somewhat deranged the sanctity of her countenance, 'It is seldom that the like of ye trouble this place, for few visit it; not all as one, as Mary, John, and Joseph: God be with it!'

As she spoke, she opened the door of the screen, and led the way to the interior.

Inclined as the party were to draw out the discontented sister, *ci-devant* of Mary, John, and Joseph, there was no time left for the mystification; for walking rapidly before them across a little court, she threw open a door and ushered them into the refectory. It was a plain, low-roofed apartment, lined with bog oak, and lighted by small Gothic windows, and furnished with a suitable simplicity. A long table down the middle of the room, with wooden benches on either side, a reading desk at the further extremity, with a *replico* of the picture of the Holy Heart suspended from it, and a good copy of Raphael's St Cecilia, included the whole of its *mobilier*.

The table was already served by a female domestic in a lay habit; the Italian organist and the sister of Mary, John, and Joseph, doing the honours. The service of the table was remarkable for its homeliness; but the mountain wanderers, who looked forward to potatoes and butter, as the probable fare of an Irish convent, were less surprised by coarse linen and yellow delf, than by delicacies worthy of the *calendrier nutritif:* these were a perigord pie, a *pot de confiture*, some dried fruits, and dessert wine that might have put '*le menu de la table à l'apogée de sa gloire*.'

The party were taken by surprise, and exchanged looks; for the foreign lady not only kept them in check by her presence, but with the sharp and prying glance of a *Sœur Ecoute*, evidently produced the same effect on her Irish sister. Lady Honoria endeavoured, in vain, to discover if her acquaintance of Bog Moy was of the sisterhood. In answer to her side-wind questions, Sister Bridget replied, that though the community were not yet cloistered (and she laid a strong emphasis on the word), and it was not yet the custom in Ireland to lock up those, whom natural vocation had given voluntarily to God, yet that none of the community went beyond the Abbey grounds, except the Superior, who had the church's leave to go out on its service.

'And what is the Reverend Mother's name?' asked Lady Knocklofty.

'Madame Beavoin O'Flaherty,' was the reply.

Lord Arranmore rose from the table, and again seated himself, in obvious perturbation, increased by the fixed and penetrating glances of Lady Knocklofty.

The Italian nun here rose to withdraw, beckoning the communicative Sister Bridget to follow her.

'We should like extremely,' said Lady Honoria, perceiving that the Italian understood English (whether she could, or would not speak it), 'to have the honour of being presented to the Reverend Mother, and of offering her our acknowledgments for her very hospitable entertainment.'

The Italian motioned to her sister to take the message; and Lady Honoria, hastily writing a few complimentary lines on a drawing card of Captain Montague's, Sister Bridget undertook to deliver a request, in which all present, from various motives, were interested. In a few moments the sister returned, and presented a slip of paper to Lady Honoria, who read as follows:-

'The Reverend Mother, Superior of the community of the Holy Heart, will receive the Countess Knocklofty and her party; but she wishes it to be understood, that in complying with a request, which will by no means repay the curiosity that originates it, the Reverend

Mother hopes her acquiescence may be deemed less a precedent than a concession.'

'Humph!' said Lady Honoria, in a low voice, 'there is nothing like the humility of the church. This reminds me of the haughty Abbess of the Carmelites, who shut the door of her convent in the faces of *les Tantes du Roi*, when I was in Paris.'

'Are we to await the pleasure of your superior here, or to follow you, Madam, to the presence?' demanded Lady Knocklofty, haughtily, much mortified at such want of deference to one, whose consequence she supposed could not be unknown, even in so remote and barbarous a district. The Italian answered by leading the way, and an expressive gesticulation not to be mistaken.

'*Cela passe outre!*' whispered Lady Honoria.

'Yes,' said Lady Knocklofty, 'it is all nonsense, and we had better go at once; I am bored to death with this mummery.'

'We are *in for it* now,' said Miss Macguire; 'but I dare say it will be good fun, for Sister Bridget is doubtless but a type of Mother O'Flaherty.'

In this hope the party followed their leader across a small cloistered court, filled with flowers, which the Italian told Lord Arranmore was called the Abbot's Garden. It led by a low archway into a corridor, which connected the original building with the additions made by Count O'Flaherty. It had been painted in *fresco*, with subjects but little suited to its present purpose: they were evidently taken from the heathen mythology, and represented, among other subjects, the sacrifice of Iphigenia – the altar, the priest, the victim, and her sudden 'translation to the skies;' with such an accompaniment of Zephyrs and Cupids, as indicated that something more was meant, than met the eye. A counterpart, representing Europa crossing the Hellespont, was separated from it by vases, dancing figures, and arabesques, which likewise ran beneath the frieze; and along the corners of the walls.

'The thing,' said Lady Honoria, pausing, 'is not only "rich and rare," but one wonders how the – hem! – it got there.'

'These are the representations, painted by the naughty count, which the Archdeacon complained of, I suppose,' said Lady Knocklofty; 'and curious ones they are, for the walls of the retreat of a religious community.'

'*Si chiama il torre del Conte,*' said the Italian to Lord Arranmore, pointing to an inscription over the door, which terminated this singular gallery. It was,

Amicitiæ et Libertati, S.

'Translate for the benefit of the country ladies, my dear General,' said Lady Knocklofty, now becoming insensibly interested.

'Sacred to friendship and to liberty,' said the General; 'a singular motto for the dwelling of one who has abandoned all earthly affections, and resigned her personal freedom, perhaps, for ever.'

The opening of the door cut short all further observation. The Italian introduced the visitors as *la Contessa Knocklofty, e la sua società*. For a moment the party forgot their high airs of superiority and habitual tendency to mystify all that were not of their own set. Startled by the appearance of every thing around them, and most by the occupant of the singular and elegant apartment, they stood for a moment, with that expression of constraint, which marks an involuntary subjugation to an unexpected and imposing exterior. The apartment was the *rez de chaussée* of an octagon tower; and it opened by its windows on one of the lesser lakes, which formed a chain with the greater, and escaped into the recesses of the wooded mountains, behind the Abbey.

Its walls were of one of those colourless colours, which are so well adapted to give relief to the paintings which decorated them. These were portraits of the *mothers* of the church, or saintly women of all ages, set in massive frames of finely carved oak. The furniture, though sombre in its hues, was luxuriously contrived. The fauteuil, on which the Abbess reclined, and the table that stood before her, were pictures in themselves. Whoever had seen the splendid portrait of Pope Julius II by Raphael, would at once have recognized the original of these close and picturesque imitations in the *accessoires* of that wonderful production. The lady was seated at an open casement. Her table was piled with volumes richly bound, one of which lay open before her; and from the implements scattered about, she appeared to have been painting in it. A finely carved ebony crucifix stood before her. Her dress was a religious habit, with ample sleeves to the wrist, and confined by a girdle beneath the bust. The folds of her veil and *sogolo* were so arranged, as to give a strong resemblance of the bust of the *Vestale* in the Capitol.

Her countenance was rich in expression, passionate and intellectual, even in repose; it resembled the female heads of Correggio. Her features were mobile and full of play, and her complexion was of that tint, only found in Italy, – pale, but not fair; and of that high polish, peculiar to the skins of southern regions. Her eyes were Irish eyes, large, grey, deep set, and fringed, and arched by long, dark lashes and brows; the extreme whiteness of the muslin round her face, formed a striking contrast to tints so mellow, and traits so marked. A slight flush passed across her transparent cheek, as she rose to receive her fashionable visitors; and her smile, displacing the almost awful gravity of her look, at the entrance of her guests, exhibited perhaps something too much of her white and regular teeth, and gave an almost fearful expression to her countenance. It was a beautiful smile, but too acute, and seemed to indicate a spirit that 'o'er informed its tenement of clay.' Her real, or affected dignity, put even the effrontery of Lady Knocklofty and Lady Honoria out of countenance. Though they had entered *armées de toute pièce* from that exhaustless depôt, their habitual assurance, yet conventional insolence, shrank before the natural influence of evident intellectual superiority; and when she motioned them to a sofa opposite to her, they took their places with some little embarrassment. The gentlemen sat, or stood, as they pleased: the General and his aides-de-camp at an open window, Lord Charles on the arm of the sofa, and Lord Arranmore behind Lady Knocklofty, and leaning over its back.

'I fear,' said Lady Knocklofty, recovering her *air prononcé*, 'that we intrude on you; but our natural desire to see a person so celebrated, must be our excuse.'

'Celebrated!' interrupted the lady, coldly; 'I did not suspect I was even *known;* this remote solitude is not much adapted to bestow celebrity!'

'At least,' said Lady Honoria, coming to her friend's assistance, 'our desire to see one so worthy to be celebrated, a person so distinguished.'

'Distinguished!' repeated the Reverend Mother, opening her large eyes, with a look and tone so *naïve*, that its *naïveté* might almost pass for knavery.

'Is it not a distinction?' said Lady Honoria, a little posed how to proceed, 'to have the courage – the devotion, to retire to "these dark solitudes and awful cells," with endowments every way qualified to adorn and to enjoy society! With such musical talents alone, with such a voice, you might aspire to——'

'To be a *seconda donna*,' interrupted the Superior, 'in some provincial opera in Italy, with a salary of ten *lire* a night; or to obtain the patronage of some great London lady, till I sang myself out of fashion;

and then share the fate of so many others; *fêtée* today, far beyond my merits, forgotten tomorrow, far below my deserts; or perhaps I might even make my way to the Irish capital, and be called upon for a hunting song, in the midst of a bravura, or be interrupted in a concerto on the harp to play magical music, and symphonize "Hunt the slipper," or "Puss in the corner." '

Every body started, some smiled, and looks of intelligence and surprise were mutually exchanged.

'Oh! you doubt the fact,' continued the Reverend Mother, in the same strain of irony. 'A friend of mine, however, was thus used, who brought *her* endowments to adorn the society of Dublin, and had hoped to make her fortune in that "land of song," which has taken a harp for its arms; but she saw at once the fallacy of her hopes, and resigned them.'

'But you, Madam,' said the courteous General, approaching the table, and throwing his eyes over a beautiful illumination she was painting on a leaf of a missal, 'you at least could fear no failure; such talents must command success every where, as well as deserve it;' and he added, with the air of one who announced a discovery, 'talent, like knowledge, is power.'

'Talent is only available when seconded by the *prestige* of fashion,' replied the Superior, coldly; 'knowledge may be power, in nations, but wealth is the power of individuals. Those,' she added, throwing herself back in her fauteuil, 'whose endowments are of the highest caste, and who have not their age along with them, will find their knowledge not power, but impediment; and they will be soon taught that the light thrown upon a society, which is not prepared to reflect it, serves but to consume the spirit that kindles it. 'Tis the bursting of a rocket, before it is launched; but the world is governed by common-places.'

Every body remained silent, while, as if to fill up the awkwardness of the pause, the Superior, turning to Lady Knocklofty, observed,

'I cannot imagine how your Ladyship and your party, got into that line of mountain, which led you down upon this glen. There is an old pass, recently repaired and opened, which leads down by the coast, to the town of St Grellan: likewise it is a short and beautiful sail from Beauregard to the inlet, which communicates with our lakes, and by which you might penetrate into our hills, with the aid of burlings and corricles (the native means of navigating the shallows, and passing the rapids of this romantic solitude), that is, if *toutefois* your object be to visit the wilds of Connemara, so rarely sought by such wanderers.'

'Our object,' said Lady Honoria, whose brilliant flippancy yielded to the superior influence of one, who sat like an intelligence in the midst of inferior agents; 'our object here, Madam, has been most agreeably disappointed. We set forth to take an early dinner *au bout du banc*, at a sporting lodge of Lord Knocklofty's, called the Heaths; but our guide having misguided us, we have been thrown upon your hospitality, for a refreshment, that was becoming very necessary indeed: and we have been equally delighted with all we have seen and heard, for which, in the name of the party, I beg to offer our best thanks.'

The lady bowed slightly, and coldly observed, 'There is nothing to see or hear in this lonely and rude retreat, to repay so much fatigue as you must have encountered. I once rode over these mountains; they are terrible in their little way, even after the Alps and Appennines, for they are much less accommodated; but the *Heaths* lie more towards Lough Corrib; you can see the belfry of the office, from a terrace which I have cut on one of those shelving hills on the other side of this little lake; and you can reach it still,' she said, looking at a time-piece, that lay on the table, 'before sunset. You shall have a guide to conduct you, and the bridle way is much better than any you have passed.'

'A broad hint,' whispered Lady Knocklofty to Lady Honoria; for though her imagination lent itself freely to this singular scene and person, she was still impatient, and distressed at the whole adventure, and added, 'pray let us be off.'

'However intricate the ways we have come,' said Captain Montague, who, with the rest of the gentlemen, made an attempt to move, 'I fear we shall find it more difficult to get away, than we did to arrive.'

'We must make the effort, however,' said Lady Knocklofty petu-lantly, 'for we cannot intrude longer on this lady, whose time is doubtless precious, as well as sacred,' and she rose as she spoke.

Every one now of necessity arose: the Superior rose also, and observed,

'Time here is indeed *urgent comptant*. Like other new colonists in barbarous regions, our labour is the currency by which we live.'

'There is nothing very *barbarous* here, however,' said Miss Macguire. 'This beautiful apartment reminds me of the Abbesses' *parloirs* in the great convents of France. May I beg to know of what order is this convent?'

'We are a confraternity of no particular religious order: we are at least, as yet, subject to no rules; but are one of those religious societies so common in Italy, and particularly in Florence – a sort of *demi-religieuses*,' she added, smiling.

'Macchiavel,' said Lord Arranmore, in a pointed manner, and now for the first time giving signs of life, 'Macchiavel was a member of one of those *nameless* orders, I believe.'

'So I have read,' said the Abbess, throwing down her eyes, and colouring slightly at the abruptness of the observation. 'Macchiavel was a worthy and a pious man; but acted and wrote under peculiar circumstances, and with views wholly mistaken or misinterpreted.'

'Then,' said Lady Honoria, always ready to go out of her way, to say a smart thing, though rarely saying 'a wise one,' 'we may apply to your catholic communities, what the Irish traveller said of Spain – *point de religion, et beaucoup de dévotion.*'

'Which is the reverse of what may be said of your protestant communities, Madam,' said the Abbess – '*Point de dévotion, et beaucoup de religion.*'

Every body laughed, and Lady Honoria, more accustomed to be laughed with than to be laughed at, said, petulantly, 'I assure you we Irish protestants are deficient in neither: the proof is, that we are daily making converts from your infallible church. Here, for example, is our last conquest; you will allow we have reason to be proud of it,' and she drew forward Miss Macguire, by no means pleased at being thus distinguished for her apostacy.

'Yes,' said the Superior, fixing her penetrating eyes upon the convert, 'if you are sure of it. But there is something so papistical in the expression of that young lady's face (for, trust me, religions have their physiognomies), that I suspect she is like Fra Paolo, *catholique en gros, et protestante en détail.*'

Miss Macguire blushed deeper than she had done for the last half of her life; and the General, evidently infatuated with the Reverend Mother, observed, 'You are a dangerous person, Madam, if you read faces thus, *à livre ouvert.*'

'Rosalba,' she replied, 'learned to know characters from her constant study of countenances, "*ed anch' io son pittore.*" '

'So I perceive,' said the General, 'and a very charming one, too. I presume these pictures are from your easel; they have the true character of the Italian school. Are they original, or copies?'

'Copies' (was the reply) 'from Montegna, Da Vinci, and Raphael; the last, I think, who painted pious women, because, about that time, the agency of such spirits ceased to be in demand.'

'The fashion, however, may be revived,' said Lord Arranmore, with the emphasis of one who spoke under some strong or acrimonious feeling, 'and with the effect, which the subtlety of female agency has always produced.'

'By Jove! if all pious women were as pretty as these,' said Lord Charles, looking round him, 'a charming fashion it would be: I would be a monk myself. I say, General, look at that lovely creature, with the angel touching her with an arrow tipped with flame; there is nothing in the Windsor gallery like that. Look, Lady K., is it not like the Duchess?'

'I am no judge of pictures,' said Lady Knocklofty, who had moved towards the door, in vain; for every one had gathered before the beautiful portrait, which, as a close and admirable copy, was well worth their attention.

'That is a copy of the famous St Teresa, at Genoa. The master is disputed. It is so inferior to the original, you cannot judge of the merit of the composition,' said the fair artist.

'I never saw a saint with eyes so like a sinner,' said Lord Charles.

'And yet she *was* a saint,' said the Superior, gravely: 'the church owed her much.'

'The church has owed such women every thing,' said Lord Arranmore, vehemently; 'and Dante's apostrophe of "*Ahi, Constantino*," should have been addressed to Helena, rather than to her imperial husband.'

'Faith has always been upheld by sacrifice; and who so fit to make it as woman?' demanded the Superior, turning her fine eyes, for the first time, on him who made the observation.

'Faith may also be upheld by imposition,' said Lord Arranmore, pointedly. 'It is well known that this St Teresa was an agent of the pope's, whose councils she considerably influenced.'

'She was a chosen vessel of the church,' said the Superior, dropping all that was mundane in her look and manner, and folding her hands on her bosom, 'to forward the salvation of her erring children.'

'She was a chosen instrument to forward a system, injurious alike to the liberties and happiness of mankind,' said Lord Arranmore, with more acrimony than the subject demanded.

'And well chosen, too,' said the General, 'if she was as lovely as that picture represents her, –

> From lips like those what precepts fail to move?'

'Her beauty is on record,' said Lord Arranmore, pointedly; 'it was perfect; and her versatile talents may be estimated by their effect, at a time when the monastic system was breaking up. She was sent forth armed by the church, and by her own peculiar powers, for the mission; and quitting her luxurious convent of Mount Carmel, she contrived to submit thirteen great monasteries to her reform, till her reputation was carried beyond the bounds of christian Europe. Her writings are still but too popular in Italy.'

'She was an author, too?' asked the General.

'Many extraordinary works are attributed to her,' said Lord Arranmore. 'Her *Action de grace* is full of grace; and her *Chemin de perfection* is written in a manner very little calculated to answer the end it proposes; while her hymns are worthy of Sappho.'

'There is one sentiment, at least,' said the *religieuse*, with the meek manner of one accustomed to stand the brunt of such attacks, 'which may plead her cause with souls as sensible as her own – and that is *ohimè! quanto son infelicissimi i dannati, non possono amare.*'[1] She raised her eyes as she spoke, with a supplicating softness, as if to deprecate the critical severity, which had been so unsparingly directed against her favourite saint; and then let them fall beneath the shadow of their long lashes. In this look was concentrated all the intelligence 'which soul to soul affordeth,' when words are denied.

Lord Arranmore turned away, and muttered between his teeth unconsciously, 'The Jesuitess!' then pausing before another picture, he said; 'here is a saint of another style.'

'Yes,' said the Superior, mistaking, or affecting to mistake his meaning, ''tis an attempt at the manner of old Montegna, as you, General, will perceive, by the formality of the figure and the golden ground: it is St Catherine of Siena.'

'It is a most faithful imitation of that school,' said the General, much flattered by her reference to his judgment; 'what, pray, was the vocation of this shrewd looking saint?'

---

[1] Alas! how unhappy are the damned; they cannot love.

'Her mission,' said the Superior, 'was one of great activity, and belonged more to this world than the next. It was she who made up the breach between the Florentines and Pope Gregory the Eleventh. It was she who removed the chair of St Peter from Avignon to Rome, and brought back the truant pontiff from the shores of the Rhone to the Tiber. It was she who gave the victory to the Urbanites over the Clementines: and by prayer and preaching brought over all Italy to the cause of her favourite pope.'

'By prayer and preaching!' returned Lord Arranmore, 'say rather by her perfect beauty and consummate art. She was educated for the mission she so ably filled, and her natural eloquence and energy did the rest.'

'Lord Arranmore,' said Lady Knocklofty (who, 'patience perforce,' had again resumed her seat on the sofa), 'it appears that you are wonderfully well read in the lives of the saints.'

'The study, Madam, made part of my college course abroad, and came in under the head of divinity.'

'And a very proper head to come under,' said the gallant General, 'if the dead saints were as divine as the living,' and he looked full at the Superior, who either did not make, or did not choose to acknowledge the application.

She was occupied in showing a small and beautiful portrait on ivory to the two young men and Lady Honoria. The subject was dressed much in the same habit as she herself wore; and the countenance, like hers, was more remarkable for its brilliant intelligence than its sanctity.

'Now,' said Lady Honoria, 'in spite of the veil and rosary, that was a most mundane creature, or I am much mistaken. If coquetry had ever been canonized, I should say *la voilà*.'

'It was one,' said the Abbess, 'accused of having more spirit than grace, and it was said of her, *qu'elle avait de tous les genres d'esprit*. When this miniature was painted, she was a nun in the Monastery of St Fleuri. It hangs here more for its value as a work of art, than from any estimation of the original; for the nun of St Fleuri broke the vows, forced on the helplessness of her youth; and returned to a world, to which her genius was more adapted, than to the seclusion of a monastery: it is the portrait of the famous Madame de Tencin.'

'And yet,' said Lord Arranmore, 'this arch-intrigante of the most intriguing times, this *femme d'état*, would in other times have respected her vows, and yet have fulfilled her natural vocation; and as the agent and adjunct of popes and cardinals, she would have carried on a system which, in all times, has been best carried on by the subtlety of woman. In the fourteenth century, she would have been a Catherine of Siena; in the fifteenth a Saint Teresa; and in the present age she *might* have made an abortive effort, to restore a system, which does not belong to it.'

'She had one merit at least,' said the Superior, meekly: 'she was capable of great devotedness. Her friendship knew no obstacles, acknowledged no impossibility, when to serve or to save, to rescue or redeem the object of her partiality or protection, was in question.'

'Her protection!' muttered Lord Arranmore, with bitterness.

'Say no more, my dear Madam,' said the General, 'or, all protestant as I am, I shall fall before the shrine of this mundane saint, and worship her image.'

'I never saw a more equivocal countenance,' said Lady Knocklofty; 'it has the look of a handsome imp.'

She rose as she spoke. Her patience and temper were now alike exhausted; with that quickness, which renders woman, where her most powerful passions are concerned, omniscient, she had detected the sudden pre-occupation, and total change of manners, of Lord Arranmore, from the moment they had passed the curtain at the church door. His relaxed attentions to herself, his frequent change of colour and countenance, his piqued and pointed manner, when addressing the Superior, and his intense inquiring eye, as he gazed on her, evinced that this was not their first interview; and from this inference, a thousand painful and mortifying conclusions followed. Whatever was the nature of her partiality for one, whose character and condition were at such variance with her own position, whether it was the caprice of an unregulated imagination, or of a passion still less defensible – he had long occupied her thoughts; and for the last few days his presence and society had given interest to a mode of life she detested, and rendered the solitudes of Beauregard, not only endurable, but delightful. Now, however, making an effort at self command, she tapped the General on the shoulder, and observed, 'Come General, lest we should lose the most agreeable sinner in the world, I must tear you from the saints: I perceive the Reverend Mother is bent upon your conversion, and I have no doubt that what she undertakes, she will perform.'

'*Je ne demande pas mieux*,' said the General, drawing up, and looking as alert as fifty years '*bien sonnées*' would let him.

'Saint Ignatius was a soldier,' said the Abbess, with grave simplicity.

'Yes,' said the General; 'but if I remain here much longer, I must belong to the army of martyrs; and as that is a service for which I have no vocation, I shall seek safety in flight. I am ready to attend your Ladyship,' and he turned with a sigh to Lady Knocklofty.

Every body smiled at this *malentendu*, except the person to whom it was addressed; whose compressed lips, and knitted brows, but ill assorted with any expression of amusement. She turned shortly on the Superior, and rather bowed, than spoke her acknowledgments. The party then took their leave; and the Reverend Mother, resuming her dignified air, which had evidently been laid aside, for a conventional meekness, whenever religion came in question, accompanied the visitors to the extremity of the corridor. There they were received by the Italian sister, who conducted them back through the church. A boat with four oars, that resembled a pleasure barge, now neared the shore, for their reception. The party were soon seated, under an awning which had been spread against the ardour of the evening sun, and were launched on the placid bosom of the breathless lake.

'Well, this has been an adventure,' said Miss Macguire, 'worth all we have endured to come at it. It was quite delightful.'

'I am quite of another opinion,' said Lady Knocklofty, sulkily.

The men however all agreed with Miss Macguire, and were loud in their commendations, Lord Arranmore alone excepted, who had taken an oar, and was plying it with energy, by no means called for by the occasion. Each now pronounced a eulogium upon their hostess, after their own peculiar way; but it was evident that her habit and singular manner had gone for as much as her personal attractions and intelligence.

'What do you think of her, Honoria?' asked Lady Knocklofty, abruptly.

'Why, as Madame de Sévigné says of somebody, "*c'est la plus belle vocation pour la coquetterie.*" '

'Exactly,' said Lady Knocklofty, with a petulant laugh, 'you have hit off the *Reverend Mother* to admiration. Lord Knocklofty will be a little surprised to learn, what sort of a community he has got in his neighbourhood. This is a very different thing from the poor slovenly daudles of the St Grellan convent.'

'I am convinced, Lord Arranmore,' said Lady Honoria, 'she is the very person in the close bonnet, I met at your aunts'; but as she did not seem willing to acknowledge the acquaintance, good breeding forbade my recalling it.'

'Did good breeding forbid you also from acknowledging the acquaintance, Lord Arranmore?' asked Lady Knocklofty, significantly; 'or were *you* too cut by this reverend lady? for it struck me that this visitor at Bog Moy was not so totally a stranger to you.'

Lord Arranmore, taken off his guard by the suddenness of the question, answered with some embarrassment: 'I really don't know: that is, I think, with Lady Honoria, that the Superior, and the lady with whom I chatted for a few minutes at my aunts', may be one and the same person.'

'Come,' said Lord Charles, laughing, 'you are pushing him too hard. See how he blushes, "celestial rosy red;" as Miss Roistrum said of my new uniform. I say, Arranmore, when next you go to the Abbey to confession, take me along with you: as I am no epicure, Sister Bridget will answer me, for a little pious flirtation.'

Here the boat reached the shore; and the ladies, impatient to be off, ordered their horses. One, however, was 'reported absent without leave,' as the young aide-de-camp announced it. It was Lord Arranmore's pony, which had strayed away; 'But,' said the host of the Shebeen, 'it will soon be found, and restored safe and sound to the owner, if it was gold.' What was remarkable in this event, was, that the saddle had not strayed with the animal, but was found lying in the shed, which was dignified with the name of stable. It was remarked, however, that the saddle was much too large, and that the pony might easily have gotten rid of it.

The difficulty thus created was not easily surmounted; and Lord Arranmore, who insisted on giving up the mare he rode to Miss Macguire, was compelled to await the tide, and return himself by boat.

'We shall wait supper for you,' said Lady Honoria; while Lady Knocklofty scarcely returned his bow, as she rode off.

'I shall not fail,' was the reply made with the most absent air.

'Honoria' (said Lady Knocklofty, as the two friends rode side by side), ''tis all over. There ends my dream, like so many others.'

'Why, child, if a dream can amuse you, what prevents you from dreaming on?'

'You see what I mean, I perceive,' said Lady Knocklofty, with a deep sigh.

'Oh! yes,' replied Lady Honoria, laughing: '*le sage entend à demi-*

*mot.* You suspect that this Abbess is an acquaintance, of some sort or other, of Lord Arranmore's?'

'And what do you think – you who are so observing?'

'That there was evidently some intelligence between them – that he was piqued – and that she was coquetting with her saintly eyes and sinful smile. But an old love is the safest of all loves: besides, you have amused yourself up to your bent with your Orlando; who, in spite of his patriotism, is on the high road to be desperately in love with you.'

'Yes, *on the high road*,' said Lady Knocklofty, shaking, her head; 'he was, I believe, *déterré!* but it is nothing to start such game, if one does not run it fairly down.'

'Well, and you have run it down.'

'No,' said Lady Knocklofty, 'far from it: yet it was royal sport too while it lasted.'

'Why it was a *heart* (hart) to be sure,' said Lady Honoria, 'and therefore *royal sport*, if you will; but any bush, if beaten, may turn out as good game.'

'No,' said Lady Knocklofty, 'there is nothing like him –

> Natura il fece, e poi ruppe la stampa.'

'What! has he taught you Italian already?' said Lady Honoria, laughing. 'You have been an apt scholar.'

'I made him teach me that line, which he applied to Shakspeare, but which is equally applicable to himself.'

'If you have come to books and Italian, your case is desperate; *cela sent la grande passion*, instead of an innocent flirtation, to get rid of a wet day in the country. You make me tremble, child. How can you be so *fresh?* Is this the way you "make sport withal?"' '

Here the gentlemen rode up, and the broad, strand road, permitting the party to ride abreast, the conversation became general. Without further adventure, the amused but wearied wanderers arrived at Beauregard.

# CHAPTER V

———— • ————

## *The Interview*

LORD ARRANMORE stood on the beach, as the party from which he was now so unexpectedly released rode away. He had impatiently watched the fading of their shadows from the pebbly shore, as they departed; and when a sudden turn in the cliffs concealed them from his view, he breathed with a long and deep drawn respiration, as one who was released by their absence. Eager for silence and solitude, he turned away from the little creek, where a party of fishermen had just entered, for fresh water. He was well aware that at any moment a boat might be procured; and he turned back upon his steps, and walked rapidly up a ravine along the lake.

> His noble and most sovereign reason,
> Like sweet bells, jangled out of tune,

was a chaos of perturbation. – The dream of his thoughts – the spirit of his adventures – the destiny that had linked itself to him, and, in voice and form, in passing glances and partial revelations, had pursued him, from the choir of the Gesú Bambino, to the pavilions of the Borghese palace – from the saloons of the castle, to the fallen ruins of O'Brien's house – from the caves of Cong, to the smoky chambers of Bog Moy – had now been manifested to him, in the palpable form of a young and beautiful woman! – of a woman, however, veiled and vowed to a religion, to which it was possible that her ambition and her prejudices were alike devoted.

When he thus detected in the Superior of an obscure Irish convent, the influential member of a powerful community at Rome, – when he detected in the sister Irene (the foundress of a new *culte*, and the well known agent of the Jesuits at Florence) an Irishwoman, his amazement was mingled with something of national pride. But other and remoter considerations all faded, before the conviction, that this gifted, powerful, lovely person had been long interested and occupied with himself and his wayward fortunes. To what purpose, – for what object, – or to what end, he resolved to learn from her own lips, in an immediate interview. With passions

> ——that, like the Pontic sea,
> Ne'er knew retiring ebb, –

with a vehemence of temper that had led to all the good or ill of his short but chequered life, he was still impelled on; and he paused not to reflect. To feel and to act, had been the habit of his life; and piqued by the indiscriminating indifference, with which the Superior had received him, in common with his very common-place associates, – annoyed by the insiduous meekness, with which she had appealed to him, in behalf of those women, who like herself had acted a part through life (thus treating him as a dupe, and probably considering him one), he resolved to oppose the intrepidity of frankness to the mystery of intrigue; and to demand the explanation of a conduct, into which he had a right to inquire, since it had influenced his own peace, and interfered with his actions. Firm of purpose, he was yet undecided as to the moment for putting it into execution. His petulance and ardour led him at once back to the Abbey, to the octagon tower, to the cell of the sorceress, where, surrounded by the implements of her arts, she appeared more dangerous in her dignified grace and sanctimonious reserve, than she had even been in the brilliancy of her wit at Proudfort House, or in the playfulness of her fantastic character in the garden of the Borghese. But that he should obtain admission to her presence at that moment was more than doubtful; and would necessitate a breach of his engagement at Beauregard. He sighed from his inmost soul, the deep sobbing sigh of remorse, of regret, that he had ever entered that Alcina's palace, – the first, the solitary event in his life, which had committed his principles, and impaired his self-respect. Still the feelings of a kind – (and he blushed to think how kind) – of a confiding woman, were at stake. He had but too well observed that he had already awakened those suspicions, which place the tender and susceptible on the rack of doubt. And for whom was he to wound this warm-hearted, imprudent, but generous woman? For one who was upholding a system he detested, and who, if not an impostor, was at least a dupe; – while Lady Knocklofty was simply, and only – a woman! To return instantly, and for the last time, to

Beauregard, was therefore a resolve, to which he had painfully come, at the moment when he had reached a point that gave a full view of Moycullen Abbey.

Beguiled by thoughts as hurried as his steps, he had wandered to the ferry, which the party had first crossed, under the guidance of Emunh na Lung. The sun had already sunk beneath the horizon, leaving a yellow flush upon the remote line of the distant sea; and tinging the summits of the mountains, with tints, that vanished while they were looked upon. Every line, and point, and arch, and gate of the Abbey was sketched upon the stilly bosom of the lake. The breathless air fanned no leaf, nor bent the reed which feathered the water's edge. The boat-house had been deserted and shut up; the boat (fastened by a rope to the stump of a tree) had no undulation. The solitary but agitated spectator of this scene of peace stood with folded arms, the moral contrast of its material tranquillity. He gazed wistfully, with thoughts suspended between desire and resolve, and still hesitated in all the torment of indecision. The light insensibly faded, and the shadows lengthened, forms mellowed into mists, and mists to darkness, and solitude itself looked more solitary; until the moon, rising majestically, gave a new character to the scene, of which the idealism was singularly augmented by the tones of a harp, which came floating over the silent waters, as soft and silvery as the pure light of which they seemed the harbingers. Their 'sole auditor' hesitated no longer. The tones of the harp breathed on his excited senses, like

> No sound that the earth owns;

and obeying their almost supernatural solicitings, he resolved on seeking out, at once,

> The Goddess on whom those airs attend;

and eagerly and tremblingly, he uncoiled the rope of the ferry boat, sprung into it, and pushed off for the opposite shore.

At that moment, the melancholy winding of Shane's horn came floating down from the heights, from beneath which the boat had just escaped. Lord Arranmore looked up in the direction whence the sound proceeded, and beheld the dark outline of a human figure, standing on the point of the rock above. For once, however, the warning sound had lost its influence. Whatever peril now awaited him, he scoffed at. A mind energized by passion, an imagination heated by excitement, an habitual love of adventure, an impatience of mystery, and above all, a secret infatuation, beyond what the senses can awaken (which, unknown to himself, was operating with increasing intensity, in favour of the extraordinary person, into whose presence accident had at last so strangely led him) – all conspired to impel him to his purpose.

He was already on the further shore, and had drawn up his boat. The sounds of the harp had died away; the moon was clouded, and the Abbey, in the repose and majesty of its silent ruins, looked the very sanctuary of holy and innocent sequestration. To proceed, he felt was almost sacrilege: he paused for a moment; and then crossing with a noiseless step the dewy grass, he approached, and raised the curtain of the ever open door of the chapel. All within was still and dark, save where before a pictured representation of the Holy Heart, a lamp shed its concentrated light full on the head of St Ignatius, the principal figure in the group. He dropped the curtain and shuddered; and again he hesitated; but urged irresistibly onwards, he passed before the facade of the antiquated pile; and doubling the angle formed by the transept of the church, encountered an iron railing, which separated that part of the Abbey, at all hours accessible to the public, from the building erected by Count O'Flaherty, and now the habitation of the community. By a bound he cleared the barrier, and found himself on a greensward, that dipped into the waters of the lesser lake, and fronted a most irregular building. As yet he had found no door of entrance; no light, no sound, gave guidance to his steps; till as he advanced, a long and tremulous ray, dancing on the water, led him to the spot from which it issued. With steps, slow, silent, and stealthy as those of a midnight murderer, he advanced, and paused, and advanced again. A glass-door, which opened almost on the verge of the lake, discovered, that the light which played upon the waters, proceeded from a lamp standing on a table within. The interior of the apartment lay open to his view; and he perceived the Superior of a community which was already buried in the forgetfulness of sleep, seated between the window and the table, with her head reclined on her arms, and her arms folded upon her harp. Again he paused. He heard the strong beating of his own heart; and the sound but increased its palpitations. Agitated, doubtful for a moment whether to retreat or advance, he endeavoured, upon the very threshold of his wishes, to collect his thoughts, to subdue his emotion, to arm himself with equanimity and presence of mind, for an interview, thus sought under the most unwarrantable circumstances. He stood at the vestibule of the temple, where this priestess of Jesuitism celebrated her rites, and prepared her illusions. This idea armed him; and treading heavily, to announce his approach, and to prevent the consequences of a sudden alarm, he advanced to the open door.

It was, perhaps, in the confidence of her profound retreat, and the safety of her chosen solitude, that the Superior was rather startled than alarmed at this intrusion. On hearing the approaching footsteps, she merely raised her head, and with a composure of mind, announced by the firmness of her voice, demanded who was there? adding, in a tone of inquiry, 'Shane?'

'No, Madam,' said Lord Arranmore, with a voice faltering, in spite of every effort to steady its tones, and uncovering his head, as he inclined it; 'No, Madam, it is not Shane; but it is one, as unlinked to the great chain of society – it is one as much out of sorts with fate and fortune, who, perhaps inexcusable in his intrusion, thus ventures respectfully to solicit a moment of your attention.'

While he spoke, the lady had risen, and drawn herself up to the full height of her stature; and with a command over her emotions, if any such had been awakened, she calmly said, in a low, interrogating tone, 'Lord Arranmore, I believe?'

'I blush to answer, Madam, to a title so unsupported by all which alone gives such sounds value; but the unfortunate person who now obtrudes himself upon your notice, is Lord Arranmore.'

'The inheritance of a great name,' replied the lady, coldly, 'is an awful responsibility, not always acquitted by the adscititious circumstances which accompany it. But it is generally attended by a knowledge of those forms, which good taste, in any rank, never violates. May I beg to know, my lord, the purport of this extraordinary visit, at this unusual hour, and paid in this very indecorous manner?'

She had now advanced; and folding her arms within her long, full sleeves, leaned against the side of the glass door, in an easy and commanding attitude, as one who gave audience to some suppliant rustic, whose interests led him to consult the oracular decisions of his village *suzeraine*.

'I cannot speak, Madam, while you stand,' he replied

She resumed her seat, without inviting him to enter; but he advanced, and took the place she had a moment before occupied at the door.

'I feel, Madam,' he continued, 'the full impropriety of this intrusion. It is not, however, the result of temerity, but of that necessity, which you once pronounced to be "the master of gods and men." I stand not here to plead for its fitness, but to demand of you the spring, the secret of those events, which have urged me to a violation of the common forms of society, and placed me in the awkward position in which I now appear before you.'

'You must excuse me, my Lord Arranmore,' said the lady, imperatively. 'To whatever your allusions may point, this is not a moment to explain them. I am here, the head of a religious flock: my example is of more consequence than my precepts. Your intrusion here is a flagrant impropriety; to endure it, is to sanction it. Whatever right you may suppose you have to question me (and *I* admit of none), you must choose another and a fitter time. I desire you will withdraw.'

'Madame O'Flaherty,' replied Lord Arranmore, (with a decision of manner as peremptory as her own), 'for I find that the Sister Irene of the Bambin Gesú, the Nuccia of the Borghese, the Pilgrim of Proudfort House, now chooses to assume the representation of the tender and unfortunate Abbess, who once reigned over these solitudes, and by a name consecrated in the superstitious reverence of the country – by the name of Beavoin O'Flaherty, to——'

'To what does all this verbiage lead?' interrupted the Superior, half rising, in scornful impatience, from her seat. 'The name I bear is mine, by every right that birth and inheritance can give. It was my father's name; and has descended to me, from the brave toparchs of this now neglected region, the last of whom is represented in my person: and now, my lord, this being said, I have only to reiterate my desire, that you will take your leave.'

'Then,' said Lord Arranmore, advancing a step within the room, and heedless of an order evidently less peremptorily announced than the first, – 'then you are the daughter and heiress of Count O'Flaherty, from whom this small portion of his inheritance was won by my unfortunate father; – a victory which terminated in the utter ruin, alike of his fortune and his mind.'

His voice was full of emotion. He paused for a moment, and then added with rapidity, 'You are not perhaps aware, Madam, that the return made to my father was the seduction of his sister, one as lovely and as gifted as yourself, of one sacrificed on the altar of superstition, a victim to that system which you are here to revive.'

'You would not make me answerable for my father's sins?' demanded the Superior, now not unmoved by an emotion so infectious.

'No, Madam, but I would awaken some feeling for my father's wrongs.'

'In what manner do you call on me to evince it?'

'By showing some sympathy for his son's misfortunes.'

'You jest, Lord Arranmore,' she replied, with a bitter smile. 'The boon companion of the dissipated and the great, the *protégé* of a lady, whose power is absolute, whose will is law; the associate of the despots of the soil and the enemies of Ireland – what can you want from one who belongs to the persecuted and degraded caste? What sympathy can the member of a sect, which has been thrown beyond the pale of all sympathy, grant to the guest of the Earl of Knocklofty, to the *protégé* of his – wife?'

'I am neither the guest of the one, nor the *protégé* of the other,' he replied, trembling with angry emotion. 'Chance has linked me for a moment with a party, which in prudence, perhaps, I should not have known; and which from inclination, I should never have sought. The accident, however, which formed so unnatural a combination, has dissolved it: the link is severed, and – for ever.'

'Your resolve is, doubtless, taken on mature deliberation?' said the Superior, giving peculiar signification to the question, by the tone and smile with which it was asked.

The blood rushed to Lord Arranmore's face at the implied sarcasm; yet to blame was to be interested, and the conviction encouraged him. He had now, by an insidious progress, so far advanced into the room, as even to lean over the harp, supporting his head upon his hand, with eyes fixed earnestly on the extraordinary but beautiful countenance before him. After a silent and dangerous pause, he observed, with a faint smile,

'What are the deliberations of man, when a breath, a glance, a tone is sufficient to overturn the deepest and the wisest? Your words, Madam, have effected all that reason should have done, but did not; and my resolve dates no farther back, than your reproach.'

She waved her head expressively, not approvingly.

'Such,' she said, 'was the plea, and such the temperament of Count O'Flaherty, with whose faults you have but just reproached his child. Alas! with all his sins, he *was* but what you *are*.'

'And what was that?' demanded Lord Arranmore, eagerly.

'An Irishman,' was the cool reply.

'That, I trust, is not a disgrace?'

There was a sort of ironical hesitation, a humourous play of feature, as the Superior replied, 'Why – a – perhaps not a disgrace; but it is sometimes almost a ridicule; and it is always a misfortune. With some it is a farce; with others a tragedy, according as the person, on whom so fatal a birth-right is inflicted, is an O'Mealy, or an O'Brien. To be born an Irishman is a dark destiny at the best; the last that the wise would contend with, or the proud encounter. – Here, indeed, as everywhere, mediocrity is safe; dulness is its own protection, and insensibility its own shield: but genius and feeling, the pride, the hope, the ambition of patriotism, the bitter indignation which spurns at oppression, the generous sympathy which ranges itself on the side of the oppressed, – if there are lands where such virtues thrive and flourish, and force forward the cause of human happiness, Ireland is not one of them. Here virtue is made to turn traitor to itself; and the same passions that rouse the patriot to any sacrifice, urge him into the snares of the profligate. Here the fortitude of long endurance corrupts into obsequiousness; and the spirit of the gallant maddens into lawless intemperance. Here genius is the object of suspicion to dull rulers, and of insult to petty underlings; and all that bends not – falls. Fly then, Lord Arranmore, for here none like you, have ever lived and thriven. You start at advice so abruptly given, and from one who has so little right to advise; but I lay aside every personal consideration, to avail myself of this one, this only (but far from prudent), occasion, to warn you of your danger. Trust me, by remaining here, you will but mar the cause you hope to aid. Honest, but indiscreet, gifted with every talent, but that which is necessary to direct all, you will, as others have done, and (I say it in fearful prophecy, are destined still to do) fall a victim, without effecting the good for which you suffer. Nay, Lord Arranmore, you must hear me out; you have hunted the sybil to her cell, and now you must patiently listen to her gloomy oracles. Take the future upon the word of the past. Fly, while you have yet the power: the world is all before you. Every where, talents such as yours will avail, save only at home! Whatever may be your vocation, the pathway of ambition is open to you. In France, your preceptor, the Bishop O'Flaherty, has but to receive and make you known. In Italy, in Spain, your uncle, the Abate O'Brien, is still powerful; Russia wants officers of European intellect, to discipline her Tartar legions; and in Germany, the Prince de Ligne will do for his distinguished aide-de-camp all that influence can effect for talent in that land, where influence is paramount. I do not direct your views to England; but I implore you to leave Ireland, where you cannot do good, but may cause evil. Means shall not be wanting to send you forth, as becomes your rank – means coming from a hand you have already said you would not reject, – the hand of your nearest living relation, which is now, for the first and for the last time, held out to you in the cordial amity of kindred.'

She paused; her countenance irradiated with the animated energy of her awakened spirit, her colour deepened by the obvious emotion she had excited. Lord Arranmore seized the extended hand, and fell at her feet, while, wholly involved in the most powerful feelings, fascinated, bewildered, he pressed it to temples that throbbed with delirious pulsation, to lips that burned like living fire. Madame O'Flaherty rose in confusion, in agitation, and in anger.

'My Lord,' she said, 'you must go – go this instant. This is not what I expected – what I have deserved. Your extraordinary appearance has anticipated and hurried on intentions, previously conceived: make me not to repent that it has done so. Do not turn an interview of importance to you, to the purposes of mere idle and habitual gallantry. Reserve such flattering insults for Lady Knocklofty, or any other lady of the high Irish autocratic society you frequent, whose manners belong to their system: they neither suit the time, nor place, nor person to whom you have the bad taste to address them. Let go my hand instantly, or – '

She had already taken up the silver bell that stood upon the table near her, but Lord Arranmore snatched it from her.

'Whatever may be the penalty of my disobedience to this imperative command,' he said, with passionate vehemence, 'I *will not* comply with it! I am here, by a law superior to your own – all-powerful as you are – by the law of that instinct, which urges every being to inquire into the means by which his happiness is influenced, his actions interfered with, his feelings worked upon, and his destiny taken out of his own hands. You have too long assumed a power, only belonging to Providence itself. Whoever you are, remember, that by assuming protection over me, you give me the rights of the protected. Who are you, that would lay me under obligations, which, if your offers are sincere, as they are extensive, should bind me to you for ever? You have said that the hand so freely given, so fearfully withdrawn, was the hand of my nearest relation. Who and what I am, you but too well know; and thus bending a knee which never bent before to created being, I demand who and what you are? I ask it, in earnest supplication, – I demand it, as a right. And I vow by all that is sacred not to quit this place, or this position, come what may, till you satisfy doubts, and lay suspicions, that have become the torment and occupation of my life.'

All the equanimity, the presence of mind possessed, or dignity assumed by the Superior, now gave way in a natural feminine emotion, before the vehement and peremptory expression of manly passion; her countenance changed, her voice grew tremulous.

'This,' she said, 'is not the time nor the place suited to such a revelation: I cannot here tell you all, and, perhaps, what I can reveal is of the least importance.' After a moment's pause, she added, in a hurried manner, 'I am the daughter of Count O'Flaherty, and of that unfortunate Italian nun, whom the restless energy of your uncle and of mine, brought over to this country, for purposes utterly unavailing. My mother's abduction had been communicated to her uncle, the Abate O'Brien, by your indignant father, who had vainly challenged the seducer. The bravest officer in the French service refused to risk the life of the man whose services he had repaid by such injury; and in one so petulant and fierce, this was a redeeming forbearance: let it plead for him. My mother's crime, which in Italy or Spain would have subjugated her to the living incarceration of the "*Vude in pacem*," was, in Ireland, safe from the vengeance of the ecclesiastic authorities; and the error which the church could not punish, it took measures to redeem. By the Abate's influence, dispensations were procured from Rome, and after twelve months of sinful existence, the Abbess of St Bridget became the wife of her seducer; who, under the moral influence of his kinsman, the Abbé O'Flaherty, submitted to a yoke which, with him, broke for ever the tie of passion. The ceremony which legitimized my birth, preceded it but by a day. Your foster-mother assisted at my entrance into life, when my mother, vowing me to the Virgin as an expiatory offering on the altars she had violated, impressed upon my brow this holy sign, the indelible mark of my destiny and immolation.' (As she spoke, she raised her veil, and discovered a small black cross imprinted on the centre of her white and polished forehead.[1])

Lord Arranmore looked and shuddered, almost breathless, from intense interest and deep emotion –

---

[1] This was a very ancient custom in Ireland, where it is still practised. Ludlow alludes to it in his *Memoirs*. The mark is impressed with gunpowder, in the way so commonly employed by sailors.

'In the solitudes of Moycullen,' continued the Superior, 'passed the ten first years of my romantic life, amidst such associates as gave to your ardent mind its first direction. I shared with you, in my infancy, the affectionate solicitude and the wild legends of Mor-ny-Brien, and even the instructions of her wilder son.'

'Good God!' interrupted Lord Arranmore; 'how extraordinary! I well remember her long and frequent absences from the Isles of Arran. I certainly, too, received some impressions of your name – your eyes – that have floated like half-forgotten dreams in my memory, but have never been effaced.'

'We occasionally, I believe, shared the same cradle in infancy,' continued the Superior, casting down her eyes. 'I profited too by the instructions of the Abbé O'Flaherty.'

'You were known, then,' said Lord Arranmore, 'to all that surrounded me; – my father, my fosterers, my preceptor; and to me alone your existence was a secret.'

'It was so to all, save those whom you have mentioned. For the honour of the church and the sept, my mother's abduction was covered by such little strategems, as easily appease the curiosity and lull the suspicions of ignorance and superstition. Year after year her removal to some remote country was proposed, but was rendered impracticable by her state of mind and health: and those who were of necessity admitted to the secret, were sworn upon the cross of *Onor-ny-Cruise*, not to reveal it, so long as my unfortunate mother remained in a country, where catholicism, persecuted and calumniated, needed all the support, which the virtues and discretions of its professors could give it. – But to continue: my father was recalled to France shortly after my birth, and never returned. My mother, with all the passions of an Italian, and the conscientious sensibility of a devotee, gradually fell a victim to remorse, awakened by disappointed affection: her mental malady took the fearful form of religious melancholy. I became the companion and vigilant guide of her wild wanderings. Pity and affection so early developed, ripened intellect, and sharpened it, into premature acuteness. I was also the pupil of her lucid intervals: she was a superior musician and linguist. I early benefited by her instructions, as I inherited her organization for the arts; but if I acquired her talents, I imbibed her enthusiasm and adopted her illusions.'

'Her illusions!' reiterated Lord Arranmore, in the deepest emotion. 'You are not, with all your powerful endowments, a dupe as well as a victim; and deceiving others, you are yourself undeceived.'

'Your decision, Lord Arranmore,' she replied coldly, her dark brows knitting into a singular expression of sternness – 'your decision is more prompt than liberal.'

'Forgive me, Madam,' he replied, in confusion, 'I beseech you. I am but – I am but guessing at a character, which defies all ordinary calculation of human intelligence and conduct. – Pray, proceed.'

'Strange means,' she added emphatically, 'were taken to subtilize my mind, from childhood; but they failed to deprave it. Intellect, well awakened, and blended with strong sympathies, can rarely be turned to false purposes. The utmost development of mind can lead but to truth; and the sublimest philosophy teaches but to increase the sum of human happiness. Brought up to propagate dogmas, I soon arrived at facts; and the veil dropped, – and for ever. Educated for the purpose of obtaining an influence over the minds of others, I obtained a mastery even over those for whose service and secret views I was instructed. I have become their directing spirit, not their slave; and I wield the power and influence they have given me, for purposes directly opposed to their intentions.'

'Are you not, then,' interrupted her delighted auditor, eagerly, – 'are you not here to give grace and splendour to institutions which had fallen into desuetude in Ireland, – establishments offensive to the Deity, because incompatible with the true duties and destinies of the species?'

'If I have been brought here for that end, I have wielded my influence for far other purposes. You have heard and seen; there is nothing here that recalls the unaccommodated, slovenly devotion of the old establishment of Mary, John, and Joseph: education is here going on upon a liberal plan, to fit woman for the useful, blessed duties, that belong to her sex, as wife and mother, – by the arts, which soothe and soften life. I have brought over with me, the "*Sœur Choriste*" of my convent in Rome, to whom I am indebted for the cultivation of my musical talents. Music is the natural language of an Italian, and I avail myself of its influence, as did the legislators of old. For the rest, – time is occupied; and intellect, once awakened, will soon find its level. You have heard the cheerful noise of that merry mill, turned by a torrent, which is no longer a mere feature of pictur-esque desolation: you have seen the dwelling of the peasant, no longer a part of the soil, out of which it rises. Such is my Jesuitism, the only Jesuitism the age will bear, or Ireland, I trust, submit to. But time presses, and digression now, even for self-defence is ill-placed. – The

death of both my parents threw me into the power of my bigoted
grand-uncle; who received me at the foot of Mount Cenis, from your
father's hands. What followed I will not detain you to relate; my
natural endowments answered the purposes of my employers, and
were cultivated to the uttermost: for, from the *petites maîtressess* of the
Faubourg St Germain, to the powerful superiors of Italian convents,
Jesuitism has always borrowed its agency from female arts, and female
subtlety. I became in Italy the foundress of a new worship, the
protected of popes and cardinals; and I retained the *prestiges* of my
monastic position, with the advantages of every social distinction:
bound to an order and its interests, – I was yet permitted to live in
the world.'

She paused – her mobile countenance wholly changed its character.
A look of arch gravity gave a new expression to her features; and
there was a tremulous movement round her beautiful mouth, as if she
feared to smile, and vainly tried to look serious. The interest of her
auditor, which deepened with every word she uttered, was now at its
acmé; but he could only utter – 'Well, Madam!'

She continued – 'It was at this period, that "my spiriting" was
employed to rescue from the dangers of that world, one marked out
by ancient prophecy to be the saviour of his country, and the restorer
of the rights and the creeds of his forefathers. It so happened that
this future champion, this hope of his family and his country, was a
refractory young Jesuit, who, when still in his *parvæ*, and deep in the
innocent studies of Ludovicus Vives, had chosen to think for himself,
to burst his bonds, and to break the chain of prophetic event he was
born to fulful.'

She paused again, and a significant and humorous smile passed
over her features.

'Of the person, Madam,' said Lord Arranmore, 'thus contemptuously alluded to, I am not ignorant; but the prophecy, – I beseech
you go on.'

'If your lordship were as deeply read in the history of this unfortunate country, as I from necessity have long been, you must have
known that the Irish have ever been superstitiously governed by their
dependence on these prophecies. Such a prophecy was imagined to
have you for its object. A mole on the cheek ( the antitype of that of
Brian Borru); your birth in the ruins of Dun Ængus on the festival
of St Ignatius, were conclusive in your favour, and you became the
object of the incessant vigilance and interference of our visionary

relations. The confidant of the general schemes of the order, I could not but become acquainted with this particular underplot of your grand uncle, and with his views on you. Our common ancestors and fosterage, our common destiny worked upon my rather Irish imagination, and your resistance to a thraldom which pressed so heavily on myself, your struggles, and extraordinary and adventurous life, still farther interested and engaged me. Accident led me to a nearer insight into your views and character, at the carnival in Rome; and when an opportunity occurred of doing you an important service, I availed myself of it, something perhaps beyond the boundary of that conventual propriety which governs the sex in ordinary life. Obliged by my position to avoid making myself known, the adventure necessarily assumed an air of romance, which in our subsequent intercourse it has been my – caprice perhaps to continue.'

'Your caprice?' repeated Lord Arranmore, in uncontrollable emotion.

'I must not be interrupted,' said the Superior, resuming her imperative manner; 'time presses, and I pass over all that is not essential to tell. At the time of your leaving Rome, I was employed to found an affiliation of our establishment at Florence; – but the spell was broken. A prince and a prelate for once were leagued with public opinion; and Leopold and Ricci succeeding in baffling the views of the order, and dispersing the devotees of the Holy Heart: – our house was suppressed. The French revolution, with other changes in Tuscany, made by the Grand Duke, followed up the blow; and I accompanied my aged grand uncle to the Netherlands, and thence to England; where alone his scattered order found shelter and protection. Still thrown by my sex and helplessness on my uncle's protection, I again accompanied him to Ireland, where my little property, inherited from my father, was held in trust for me. It was then that I resolved on establishing this house; to improve the female members of my persecuted sect; to take them out of the hands of vulgar bigotry, – to refine, to liberalize. This, indeed, I have not effected, by the means I should have preferred, but my agency is limited. Availing myself of the Abate O'Brien's imperturbable zeal and intentions, and of the influence of the popular religion I profess, I have established on the domains of my forefathers the institution in which you find me. I have worked with all the means afforded me. This, however, is not a moment to devote to *my* views; it belongs to your interests – to your safety.

'In a recent visit to Dublin with the Abate, for the purpose of assisting your father and my uncle in his pecuniary involvements, you again came within the sphere of my observation at the review in the Phœnix Park. You might have remarked a foreign-built carriage which had got locked into the wheel of Lady Knocklofty's phaeton, close by the spot where you were stationed?'

'Yes, Madam, and I have heard her ladyship allude to the singular persons it contained.'

'Becoming the involuntary auditor of a conversation, which gave me a glimpse of the danger to which my cousin was exposed, I resolved to attempt his rescue, and – you know, or have probably guessed the rest.'

'I know – I have guessed nothing!' replied her anxious questioner: 'it is for the Sphynx herself to expound her own enigmas.'

'And yet,' she replied, with a faint smile, 'Œdipus was no conjuror; any school-boy might have guessed the riddle that made the fortune of his sagacity: for, after all, he had only to deal – with a woman.'

'Only, indeed!' exclaimed Lord Arranmore, passionately.

'And a woman is so easily seen through; her feelings lie so obviously on the surface, her highest moral powers are so imperiously governed by her affections – '

'Her affections, Madam!' interrupted Lord Arranmore; 'did you say her affections?'

'Her sympathies, I should have said,' replied Madame O'Flaherty, colouring deeply; 'and when her pity combines with her ingenuity, and both are called forth for the same object, then she becomes omnipotent. But to proceed: it was a curious coincidence, that I should have been a witness of the fray in which you were so deeply committed (for I was lodged in the Franciscan convent in Wine Tavern-street); I availed myself of access obtained for other purposes, to the castle, where I was sure of learning what might be your fate; I was in St Patrick's Hall, waiting for the means of returning home, during your interview with Lady Knocklofty; and while you slept, I exchanged the gift of a *femme galante*, – for the awful signet of St Ignatius, a family relic presented to me by your father, which I used to arrest your passions, through the influence of your imagination.'

Lord Arranmore would have interrupted her, but she went on rapidly. 'I was engaged in making a drawing of the antique mantlepice of O'Brien House, when your arrival drove me into concealment; when I nearly met my death in that horrible accident from which you would, and Shane did, rescue me; and here (*par parenthèse*) I will add, that my influence over Shane is of old date: it began in Connemara, where I was the "delicate Ariel" of this Irish Caliban; it was continued at Rome during his pilgrimage of penance, and has been confirmed by my assumption of the office of Abbess of Moycullen: the devotion of clanship and hallucination of mind have done the rest. Still anxious to serve and to save you, I accompanied your unfortunate father to the university, on the evening of your expulsion. He ventured to the hall of examination, and I awaited your sentence in the alley, from which I could not escape without discovery. I overheard your implication in schemes, as pure in their motive, and patriotic in their ends, as they were visionary in their means, and impracticable in their conduct. It was myself and your father who left the note and money in your rooms, during your absence with Lord Walter: and it was still your *éternelle cousine*, accompanied by her *sœur choriste*, who gave you *rendez-vous* on her own invitation (for the brashy *invito* worthy of the pen of such women as your Lady Knocklofty, was a *tour de page*, played off on your credulity, by the Reverend Mother of Moycullen).'

Lord Arranmore coloured to the eyes, bit his lips, and reiterated, 'My credulity, indeed!'

Madame O'Flaherty, with a shy, sly, downcast look, continued: 'It was I, too, who worked your father, through his fanaticism and paternal solicitude, to the scene of the hospital fields, for the purpose of removing you from the seductions, which your virtues and passions alike rendered dangerous to you. It was I, who, as a *sœur de charité*, assisted at your sick bed, as I should have done at that of any other who stood in such need of my assistance. It was I who met you in the caves of Cong, which curiosity had led me to visit by torch-light, under the guidance of Shane, who upon the occasion of this nocturnal visit to Cong, first detected the *espionnage* of a person employed to watch your movements by the constituted authorities. From that moment Shane has never lost sight of you, and has occasionally "done my spiriting," not indeed gently, but ably. It was I who, with an effrontery worthy of Lady Honoria Stratton herself, came uninvited to the Jug Day; partly *pour m'égayer*, and partly – but here ends my Jesuitry. I saw you safely lodged beneath your aunts' roof, but saw you still with regret exposed to an influence you are the least calculated to resist. You are, however, your own keeper. It neither is my office, nor my inclination, further to interfere.'

She paused, and cast down her eyes, and then added, 'Since the

Sphynx is destined to remain in her desert, to reign in lonely solitude, and at best to excite the curiosity of some chance wanderer, whom accident brings to her remote region, you will not, I trust, misconstrue the interest she has taken in your behalf; though somewhat, perhaps, too fantastically manifested. But,' (and she hesitated and looked significantly) 'men (and above all, such men), are always more readily convinced through their sensations, than their reason – for arguments are words, but images are facts; and a scene got up, is always well worth a case stated. I could not argue with you; I would not lecture, – and – a –'

'In a word, Madam,' interrupted Lord Arranmore, piqued, through all his raptures and admiration, 'the Ariel appointed to watch over the "shallow monster," by the pious Prospero of the Jesuit society, has acted much as her prototype did; and amused her own superior intelligence, while she played with the weakness and folly of the subject committed to her power.'

'At least,' she replied, smiling, 'give me credit for the purity of my motives, however capriciously evinced.'

'I will give you credit for any amount of obligation you please to claim,' replied her infatuated auditor; 'but I beseech you, wrench not from me the belief, that, all lonely as I am in this wide world, there *is* one who feels for me that interest, which angels are said to feel for man! and that an agency so poetically wielded in my behalf, is not all the result of a caprice, or part of a system.'

He looked full at her, as if he would have read her soul in her eyes, but they were downcast, and fastened on the earth.

'I cannot now,' she said, after a long pause, 'tell all that my be told; and to tell less, may be dangerous alike to both. Your impetuosity and most unexpected intrusion have hurried on an event, which I wanted only a favourable opportunity to bring about. For the rest, trust to me, when I tell you, that there is not a moment to lose: for your sake, for both our sakes, you must leave this country. It is also for your safety (and I speak not of your moral safety), that you return no more to Beauregard. Lord Knocklofty is already there. He was seen with his suite, this evening, while his wife was here, passing the new line from the Heaths to St Grellan. The Lord-Lieutenant has been suddenly recalled to Dublin, for the purpose of issuing a proclamation, for the suppression of the Volunteers. Your last political *brochure* has attracted the attention of government; and the first steps of a prosecution are taken against the publisher. Your gallant and imprudent friend, Lord Walter, has found it expedient to leave Ireland.

'This intelligence I have this night received; and I was on the point of conveying it to you, by Shane, whom I awaited here, when your unexpected intrusion rendered it unnecessary.'

'I swear solemnly by all that man holds dearest, to obey you to the letter, as a superior intelligence,' said Lord Arranmore, rising, and approaching her, 'if you promise that this interview shall not be the last; that you will yet communicate with me?'

'I promise,' interrupted the Superior, rising, and taking his hand to lead him forth, while pointing to the starry firmament, which illuminated and canopied a scene of infinite sublimity – 'I promise,' she added, with solemnity, 'by these great mysteries of nature, by which we are surrounded – mysteries of which we ourselves make a part, I promise, provided you leave the time and place to me.'

'Provided I leave it?' said Lord Arranmore, waving his head, and pressing the hand he held to his lips (which was no longer withdrawn). 'Alas! What am I? What avails my intentions? There is a destiny, which has long governed the events of my life, preoccupied my thoughts, and left me without will or power to act, but by its sovereign inspirations. The sport, or perhaps, after all, the dupe of this assumed supremacy, my position is indeed far from dignified: but such as it is, I would not now exchange it, even for the independence I worship, and for which I have already made such unavailing sacrifices. So long as you honour me by an interest so flattering, – so long as you condescend to guide, it shall be my glory to be guided; but speak no more of me: one word, my lovely cousin, of yourself – of your strange and most uncongenial destiny. It is your advice that I should fly this unhappy country; it is my amazement, that you should remain here.'

'I cannot, like you' (she said with energy), 'act for Ireland, – write for her – die for her! but I will do more, *I will live in Ireland;* and trust me, to do so, is the purest proof of patriotism, that those, unprotected by power and faction, can give. 'Tis a perpetuated struggle to the liberal; to the feeling, to those prone to sympathise, and unable to relieve, it is a perpetuated martyrdom – but this is no time for such discussion. Hark! 'tis Shane's horn.'

Lord Arranmore, startled by the information, listened, and the sound of Shane's melancholy horn was distinctly, though distantly heard.

'That,' said Madame O'Flaherty, in great perturbation, and withdrawing her hand, 'announces the arrival of one who must not find you here; and now farewell.'

'Of one!' said Lord Arranmore, with anxiety; 'whom do you expect?'

'Our uncle, the Abate O'Brien.'

'Ours!' he repeated, as they proceeded to the edge of the lake, where his boat now undulated in the mountain breeze. 'Ah, *ma belle cousine*, to have any tie in common with such a being, even one so dark and formidable! – '

'*Ah! mon beau cousin*,' interrupted Madame O'Flaherty, in an animated accent, 'this is no time for sentiment; I have promised, let that suffice – farewell:' and disengaging her hand, which he had again taken, she suddenly retreated to the glass-door, closed it, and taking her lamp, disappeared into the interior of the building.

The splash of oars was now distinctly heard through the profound silence of the night; and the next moment, the shooting of a boat down one of the rapids which connect the series of lesser lakes, was visible. Lord Arranmore sprang into his own canoe, and vigorously plying his oar, gained the opposite side unobserved.

Exhausted by emotion, the most powerful he had ever experienced, fascinated to the spot, unable to tear himself from its vicinity, he threw himself on the bank under the shadow of an old fantastic beech, and within full view of that Abbey, the dwelling of her, who for the moment occupied every thought and faculty of his existence. If eloquence be but 'the putting together of passionate words, and applying them to the passions of the hearers,'[1] the musical, fluent, and graceful details of the Superior, her deep philosophy, and deeper feeling, even her imperfect accent, and foreign rhythm, had all the charms of eloquence with one, whose passions had lent themselves to every word she uttered. But the inference was still more intoxicating than the facts. Neither the pride nor the prudery of the Superior had enabled her to conceal a deeper interest, than her guarded words revealed; and that was a conviction which absorbed or banished every other idea. All the ambition of self-love was realized in this belief. Not for a moment did a sense of his own perilous situation darken, by its gloom, the bright, warm visions that fevered and convulsed him (for he had already determined to resign himself to justice, and stand between his publisher and the law). The moonbeams which played through the branches under which he lay, were not brighter than the waking

---

[1] Hobbes.

dreams, that cheered his visionary reveries. To him, the small space that moonlight shone upon, was the world, or well worth all the world beside. In solitudes so lovely and remote, with a female so far above the level of her sex, almost of his own, what a life might be enjoyed! All that love and liberty could lavish on one, whose devotion to both was the crowning sentiment of his existence, might be here possessed to their fullest extent. In such sites his ancestors had lived, and loved, and wandered, and preserved their wild, and not always joyous independence; and he imagined circumstances which might render even the life of an Irish outlaw more than endurable. Thus wrapped in visions of the highest mental excitement, he dreamed and slept.

# CHAPTER VI

---•---

## *The Festival of St Beavoin*

Report me and my cause aright to the unsatisfied.

SHAKSPEARE.

Id commune malum: semel insanivimus omnes.

IT is a splendid enjoyment to awaken to light and life with nature herself, and surrounded by her greatest works to participate in her brilliant renovation: but there is a more precious sensation still; 'tis when the eyes, long closed in deep and obvious sleep, open upon some devoted being, whose fostering care has watched over the helplessness of our slumbers. The representative of the Clan Teig O'Briens, had slept, as his ancestors had so often done before him, with earth for his couch, and heaven for his canopy; and with a faithful follower watching beside him. He arose with the sun from his bed of heather, refreshed indeed, but confused by his strange position. The mountains, the lakes, the Abbey, all the sublime objects, on which his senses had dwelt in the dim, mysterious light of a waning moon, and under the influence of a dreaming fancy, were now spread before him, in the full reality of form and colour. The branches of the beech, under which he had lain, had been woven into an impervious canopy above his head; while, at the entrance of this fantastic bower, sat one who hummed the Lullaby of other times, which brought repose to the wearied. It was Shane-na-Brien. The object of his vigils gazed on him for a moment unobserved; and then springing upon and embracing him in a grasp, firm and nervous as the giant's own, he said, 'Now, then, my dear Shane, you are mine: for once you cannot, and shall not escape me.'

Shane made no resistance, but looked on him with an expression of wild delight, and then cowering at his feet, and caressing his hands, he said, with a suffocated accent of pleasure –

'Och! musha, the great joy to be near ye, cushleen-ma-cree; and the pinance – and the vow – and too much joy for poor Shane, the murderer, *croishna Chrishna!*'

'You avoided me, then, as a penance?' said Lord Arranmore, smiling, and raising him from the earth.

'Musha, ay! only a vow upon the cross for two months and a day, and a bit of a promise to the blessed and holy lady, the Reverend Mother; and now ye have met, and shure I'll ingage she tould you all herself, and the Broah Tanah;[1] and never lost sight of ye day or night, but ever on the track of your traheens; ay, troth, like the brach on the slot of the deer; and saw ye often on the edge of the pit, and the Breagaslagh[2] on the steps of ye.'

Through these wild and incoherent phrases, Lord Arranmore could just discover that a vow of penance and of obedience to the Superior had prevented Shane from indulging in his society, even in the moments when he might have done so with safety; and that there was some danger hanging over himself, which had been averted by the vigilance, with which his foster-brother had haunted his steps.

While these thoughts were passing through his mind, and he was preparing to follow Shane to the cabin of Emunh-na-Lung, where he was assured that a good breakfast, and *mille* welcomes awaited him, he was suddenly struck by a change of countenance in his companion, and by a crouching movement and a firing up of his eye. The next moment, Shane, with a tiger's spring, darted down the declivity near which they stood, and disappeared in a copse of furze. Immediately a discharge of fire-arms was heard, and Lord Arranmore, in horror and consternation, bounded forward to follow; when Shane returning, met him, coolly wiping the pan of a pistol, which he replaced in his bosom. 'Is any body hurt?' demanded Lord Arranmore, in great perturbation. 'Whom have you fired at?'

'The dioul takes care of his own,' said Shane, sullenly; 'he has escaped now; but he's a sold man, the Breagaslagh – the informer – the blood-seller.'

[1] The ancient prophecy.
[2] A deceitful person, or traitor.

'Of whom do you speak?' said Lord Arranmore, shocked by the frenzy of Shane's rolling eye, and the distortion of every savage feature.

'Of him, whose bought word hung me at St Michael's Cross,' replied Shane, in Irish; 'of him who follows you in the mountains to betray you; the blood-hound of the Sassoni that hunts the hart to its covert; the informer of the Hunks creatures of St Grellan, and the *Braither-na-Earla*,[1] Corny the cadger, who has the *brianna*,[2] to dog and take you, *ma Cushleen;* but,' he added in a low mutter, while raising his clenched hands and bloodshot eyes to the heavens, 'but that moon, waning as it is, shall yet shine upon his corpse:' and he continued to move his lips in inarticulate and frenzied sounds, and preserving the same strongly marked attitude of religious invocation.

'Miserable man!' exclaimed Lord Arranmore, shuddering in horror at the state of a country, where such things could be, and yet pass unheeded; and shocked at the sanguinary frenzy of the wild and unfortunate being, with whom his own wayward destiny had thus linked him, – 'miserable man, would you, while still in penance for one involuntary murder, plan the destruction of a fellow-creature in cold blood?'

'Musha! shure God is good,' said Shane, sternly, and blessing himself; 'and there's mercy for the pinitent, *laudate Dominum de cælis*, amen. And shure I would not vex you, dear, only the ould Brehon law, a thumb, and have sworn it by the hand of my father, and my mother's grave – and it must be done, *judica me, Deus!*'

Lord Arranmore saw that this was not a moment to argue with one whose reason was in temporary abeyance; and whose faith and feelings, alike at variance with all judgment, nourished hallucinations, which under other circumstances they might have corrected or subdued. He stood therefore, a moment, in deep and dark meditation, awakened by his observation of the unhappy, fevered creature before him, who continued to mutter incoherent prayers in Irish and in Latin; till gradually and slowly coming to himself, his countenance fell into an expression of extreme exhaustion. Burying his rugged head in his huge hands, he wept; then wiping away the tears with his long malted locks, he turned his haggard and melancholy eyes on his foster brother,

---

[1] The Earl's overseer, or driver. Such persons were often used as informers during the rebellion of 1798.
[2] The warrant.

and in a voice of shame and contrition, said, 'Ma Cushleen, shure, dear, you'll bear with poor Shane.'

Lord Arranmore took his extended hand and pressed it kindly; endeavouring to calm his agitation by a change of objects, he expressed a wish to go to the cabin of Emuh-na-Lung. Shane cheered up, seized his long twisted cipen, which lay on the ground, and led the way. Lord Arranmore followed in spiritless silence to the cabin, where the grateful Emunh and his children, prepared by Shane for his arrival, waited on the threshold to receive him, and where a frugal but wholesome breakfast was in readiness against his arrival.

Thus humbly, but, he believed, safely, lodged in regions every way correspondent to his feelings and his views; unrestrained by society, unfettered in his movements, by its duties and its forms, the late dweller in courts, and camps, and colleges, found that a mountain and woodland life,

> More sweet
> Than that of painted pomp,

was infinitely preferable to a cell in Galway gaol or a dungeon in Kilmainham. There was here none to distract his thoughts from the object which now ruled them with sovereign influence; none 'to cope him in his sullen fits,' or thwart him in the indulgence of those wild, but delicious reveries, which had preluded his sweet refreshing slumbers of the preceding evening. Here he determined to avoid the annoyance of his threatened caption, and to await the trial to which he was resolved to surrender himself.

He determined, therefore, to write to his publisher to inform him of the fact. He had also to acquaint his father's lawyer of his situation, and to direct him to make all necessary inquiries concerning his precise position, and prepare his defence. With his plans thus arranged, it became necessary that he should collect as much of his papers and wardrobe, as was necessary for his immediate use, to take leave of his aunts, with whatever excuse might present itself at the moment, and to return to Emuh-na-Lung's cabin, which he had fixed upon for his headquarters.

With his mind lightened by these resolutions, his heart far otherwise pre-occupied than by his own personal safety, with spirits revived, and a volition roused to firm resolve, wholly engaged with the exciting present, and leaving fate to futurity, he mounted his pony (which he was not surprised to find in Shane's possession), and took the road to St Grellan. His inquiries at the post-office were answered by a letter from Lord Walter, dated from Dover, explaining the motives of his temporary absence, and one from his publisher, announcing that the government had issued a warrant for Lord Arranmore's apprehension; and, in consequence of his disappearance, had likewise commenced proceedings against himself.

He immediately adjourned to an obscure public-house, between St Grellan and Bog Moy, where in a long letter to Lord Walter he detailed the state of that part of the country, to which his mission had been directed; and explained the total absence of all immediate discontent in the catholic gentry, who (remote from official persecution, and living in habits of kindly intercourse with the old protestant families, their rents well paid, their cellars well stocked), slept over the degradation of their caste, and were ignorant or unmoved by the events which were passing in the distant capital. Six hundred years of oppression were now producing their moral effects. The conscientious notions of passive obedience of the catholic, were then fortified by the seared and callous feelings of the man; while the pride and ambition (which under happier circumstances have since so honourably, and in spite of some errors, so usefully directed their views and their energies to the future), were exchanged for a silly, but too national vanity, which centred itself in the oft cited past –

> When Malachi wore his collar of gold,
> Which he won from the proud invader.

Upon a population so dispersed, no political impression was feasible. The few who had sense and education sufficent to appreciate their disqualifications at their proper value, could not convene their less awakened countrymen, to arouse them by the infectious eloquence so peculiar to the Irish temperament. Orators could not fire, where there were no auditors to listen: and even, if all felt aggrieved, a constitutional resistance would have been a physical impossibility. In the corporate towns, as in those of other parts of the kingdom, fuel for disaffection was not wanting: trading loyalty and borough patriotism, showed themselves in all the petty oppression of subaltern authority, and in all the gratuitous insult of triumphant faction; but in the great towns, the catholics were decidedly inferior in influence and wealth, and the possibility of resistance was not even suspected. The United Irishmen had, therefore, nothing to expect from a population so unawakened, and so dispersed.

Of his own personal views, Lord Arranmore could say little, for as yet they were floating and undecided; and on the subject which most nearly touched him, the discovery of a near relation in the person of 'the Jesuitess' of a former communication, he was silent.

By the same post, letters were dispatched to Mr Fitzpatrick, the publisher, and to Mr Fitton, the attorney; and the sun had set before Lord Arranmore took the road to Bog Moy. The darkness of a gloomy, drizzling night was already falling on the desolate domain of his now rather uncertain inheritance. Bog and waste, sea and mountain, swift-drifting clouds, and pattering showers, formed a combination of dreariness and gloom which gave to the red blaze of the turf fire, which shone through the parlour window of Bog Moy House, a splendour not its own, and seemed to render the hospitable hearth on which it burned the very focus of comfort. As Lord Arranmore approached the ever-open door, the full-raised chaunt of Major O'Mealy's well-known sonorous voice caught his ear. He alighted, and glancing his eye through the window, perceived a party at supper in all the enjoyment of true Irish conviviality. The Major was seated, *en maitre*, at the foot of the table, Miss Mac Taaf at the head, and Mrs and Miss Costello, Father Festus, and Miss Monica on either side. James Kelly, stifling with laughter, was stationed at the sideboard; while the rest of the household, from 'the ould woman' to the 'boy about the place,' were gathered round the door, purposely left open for such an auditory in all genuine Irish houses.

To appear in such a circle, for the purposes which had brought Lord Arranmore to Bog Moy House, was impossible. Taking, therefore, the priest's lantern, which burned on the table in the hall, he proceeded to his tower. There, packing up in a valise the things necessary to his immediate wants, with all his papers, and a few of his books, he remained, only to pen a hasty note to his aunt, promising to explain his sudden departure at an early opportunity, and expressing the gratitude and affection he felt for his quaint, old fashioned, but kind-hearted and affectionate relations. This note he sealed, and left on the table; then taking his portmanteau, and extinguishing the light, he mounted his pony, and took his road towards the cabin of his refuge in the mountains.

Within a mile of his destined home, Lord Arranmore was met by Shane-na-Brien, whose warning cornet he had more than once heard on his approach. Weary and dispirited, he exchanged but few words with his foster-brother, who trotted beside him, humming an ancient cronan, the melancholy and monotonous drone of which, served but to deepen the depression it was meant to cheer. The welcome which awaited him was as warm as an Irish heart ever gave: and the bed prepared for him had the best property than can distinguish the couch of the weary, cleanliness. Every thing in this humble shed was of suitable simplicity; but the descendant of the supreme kings of Ireland thought of the wanderings of O'Donnel amidst the snows of the Dublin mountains, of O'Neil's bed of fern and rocky table, and acknowledged that his own position gained by the comparison.

Lord Arranmore's first act, on the morning following his arrival, was to dispatch a note by Shane to the Superior of the ladies of the *cuore sacro*. He thought he was fulfilling a duty, in informing one, so actively interested and so nearly related to him, of his intentions, and of the steps he had taken to retain his liberty, until it became necessary to resign himself to the law. He saw not that he was obeying an impulse stronger than his reason or will to direct it.

He concluded his note by observing, 'Come what may, I will stand the trial that awaits me; for though falsehood, leagued with corruption and protected by power, may accuse, there is still an impregnable barrier for innocence in the trial by jury.'

With a hurry of perturbation which defeated its own purpose, he tore open the answer received to this note, and read as follows: –

'To admire the principle on which you act, is not to approve its application. You are about to make an unavailing sacrifice. Trial by jury is of no value, where influence strikes the panel, and prejudice and faction govern the conscience of the juryman. Like the other institutes of a free people, it is inapplicable to the circumstances of our proconsular despotism. Stay, and you are lost; fly, and you may yet serve that cause in other countries, which in your own you will now but mar.

'BEAVOIN O'FLAHERTY.'

He instantly replied, and dispatched his answer by Shane.

'MADAM,

'I have nothing left but honour. It is a possession I will not forfeit, even though you command me. I will not fly. But I will wait here for a time, in the hope of the accomplishment of your promise; and then I shall give myself up to those laws, which it is my doctrine to uphold, and must not be my practice to despise or evade.

'I have the honour to be,

'Etc., etc., etc.,

'ARRANMORE.'

To this second note no answer was returned. From the incoherent replies of Shane to his numerous questions, he could gather nothing, except that the Superior had met him in the old chauntry of the Abbey, an unfrequented spot, the burial-vault of the O'Flaherty, accessible only to Shane himself, by a subterranean entrance, and to the Abbess, by a door, of which she kept the key. To this meagre intelligence was added, the knowledge that the Abbate O'Brien was still at the Abbey; and that great preparations were making for celebrating the festival of the Foundress, at which many of the catholic clergy of the country were to attend.

This was ungracious and provoking intelligence. Was Ireland then urged by its persecutions, to preserve those superstitious rites, which even the most catholic countries were now yielding to the progress of illumination? Connected with this reflection, was one of a more personal nature. The continued presence of his uncle must be a restriction upon his cousin's movements, and it added to the necessity of his own concealment. He adopted therefore a disguise, which confounded him with the simple inhabitants of the region: a coarse jacket, and trowsers of rateen, with a slouched hat of rye-straw, left him distinguishable from the peasantry of the country only by those personal endowments, which dress cannot conceal. He now almost lived upon the lake, in the little *buirling*, which was just large enough to permit him to ply his oars; sometimes gliding under the shadows of its dismal rocks, and sometimes lying beneath the shadow of the alders, whose branches fringed the sedgy banks. Occasionally the tones of a harp, stealing over the waters from the octagon tower, repaid him for these hours of listless, but impatient concealment. Once only he ventured to land, when penetrating the ruins of the Abbey, he was nearly discovered by the officiating priest, who attended to celebrate mass and vespers. Pursued to the lake, he plunged into it, and swam across. The incident excited suspicion, and was talked of at the Abbey, where it awakened considerable alarm. For it was known that a party at St Grellan, who had recently assumed a particular colour, had a few days before burned a catholic chapel (a rare occurrence in those times), unpunished by the magistrates, and unnoticed by the government. A strong re-action to the supposed operations of the United Irishmen was developing itself; and every thing catholic was threatened with the vengeance of the protestant agitators. One of the authorities of St Grellan had visited Moycullen, to inquire into the nature of the establishment, and some of the familiars of the Proudforts had been prowling in the neighbourhood.

At the instigation of Shane, who was evidently but the organ of his sovereign mistress, Lord Arranmore absented himself for a few days, visiting, with his fosterer for a guide, some of the romantic sites in the upper regions of Bembola and Mam Turk. It was in such scenes, that the peculiar qualities of Shane came forth in singular adaptation. Light, rapid, and measured in his movements, this representative of the ancient *Turbicolæ*, pursued his way with unshod feet, and unsheltered head, in a quick, even dog-trot, throwing out from his broad, brawny, and naked chest, a deep, short-heaved respiration. Sometimes, as he skirted a precipice (while his *protégé* wound beneath in a narrow gorge), he balanced his long pole, with a skill admirably adapted to his perilous, but self-chosen position; sometimes bounding down with fearless alacrity, he plunged the pointed end of his staff in the boggy earth, and then making it a *point d'appui*, sprung over the treacherous rut, which a causeway of tangled brushwood hid out from all ken but his. Of this excursion, Lord Arranmore took advantage to work upon the unsettled reason of Shane, and to wean him from his murderous designs against Corny the cadger. But the hallucination was too fixed to be permanently removed, and though he had momentary power over the ideas and the tears of his foster brother, yet on the slightest allusion to the treachery of the informer, Shane relapsed into his wildness and insanity. Lord Arranmore therefore determined to place him under the surveillance of Emunh, and to employ the well-known influence of Madame O'Flaherty and the clergy to bind him by a vow.

In spite, however, of Lord Arranmore's prudent resolves, and the solicitations of Shane to extend their wanderings, the morning of the third day found them returned to Emunh's cottage. Emunh had brought from St Grellan a letter from Mr Fitton, directed by Lord Arranmore's order, under the name of O'Flaherty, so general in the district. It informed him of the near approach of his trial, and of the necessity of his immediate surrender. There was not a moment to lose. Of the sum of money left by his father and cousin, twenty guineas

still remained; and this sufficed for the present. He determined therefore to ride to Galway that night, accompanied by Emunh, to bring
back the pony, and to proceed by the coach to Dublin, on the following
morning. To get rid of Shane was a preliminary step, which was
happily rendered unnecessary by his own sudden disappearance. He
was seen running down the declivity, with his canoe on his shoulder,
flinging it on the lake, and sculling to the opposite side. The lake
indeed, on this day, was all alive: boats gliding down the rapids,
passing up from the port, or crossing from the opposite mountains,
centred before the porch of the Abbey church: for it was the long-
expected festival of St Beavoin.

To this shrine Lord Arranmore resolved to direct a last pilgrimage.
The silence of his powerful cousin, the protracted accomplishment of
her promise, her deep seclusion, contrasted with the active life she
led before his arrival, were mortifying circumstances, which, during
the few last agitated days of his life, gradually undermined his vague,
but anxious hopes. Was it indifference? was it caprice? or was it
submission to that imperious relation, who seemed to have taken up
his fixed abode at the Abbey? There was now no time for conjecture
or delay. Pausing only to write a few lines, to inform her of the cause
of his immediate departure, and to intreat a moment's interview, the
object of which he scarcely knew himself (if it were not once again to
see her, and bid her adieu for ever), he made a succinct toilet, assumed
his disguise, threw himself into Emunh's boat, and mingled with the
devotees, who were crowding the nave of the church to suffocation.

The preparations for the service were rendered unusually solemn,
by the coincidence of a mass for the dead. The remains of a member
of the confraternity of Cong had that day been conveyed to the tomb
of his ancestors, in the chauntry in the Abbey. Lord Arranmore
shuddered to learn that it was his young and interesting friend, the
Franciscan monk, whose melancholy prophecy was thus fulfilled.

On entering the body of the church, and taking his place in an
obscure corner, he raised his hat before his face, for other purposes
than those of mental devotion. He looked around him, and observed
that the altar was hung in that mournful attire, which the church has
been accustomed to use in the last obsequies of her departed children,
since the days of St Ambrose. The sanctuary was occupied by the
high priest and his ministers, who were chaunting the solemn service
for the dead, alternately with the choir. The full and heavy notes of
the catholic ritual, the moving appeals for mercy, were strikingly

imposing. One object, however, alone fascinated the eyes of the concealed spectator, and engrossed every feeling. It was the Superior of the community! – She was much changed: there was nothing in her appearance of that spirited dignity, which had characterized her air and demeanour, when he had last seen her in the choir. The deadly paleness of her cheek, the strong expression of anxiety, which knitted her dark brows, and the melancholy of her fixed and abstracted gaze, convinced him, that she had not brought a disengaged spirit to the awful ceremony, at which she so pompously presided: for she sat in a stall, apart, richly robed, and with the well preserved crosier of the ancient Abbesses of Moycullen, beside her.

One person alone divided for a moment Lord Arranmore's attention, with this all engrossing object, and that was the high priest himself. He resembled, as he stood at the altar, none of his order by whom he was assisted, whose submissive and obsequious countenances, were strongly contrasted with the stern physiognomy of the haughty Hierarch of a once almost omnipotent church. Lofty above the rest in stature, although loaded by years almost beyond the age of man, his singular and severe visage evidently excited in the beholders a reverence bordering on fear. The majesty of his air was increased by the magnificence of his vestments (relieved by the shabby, faded costume of the attendant priests); and as he stood in front of the altar, he threw round his still flashing eyes, in triumph: as if, in the revived splendour of these long neglected ceremonies, he beheld the accomplishment of hopes long cherished, the reward of a pertinacious ambition, the crowning object and end of his labours and his life.

Lord Arranmore shuddered, as he gazed upon this awful personage. It was the Superior of the Jesuit college at Rome, the Secretary of the Propaganda, the ever ruling and mastering spirit of his unfortunate father – the Abbate O'Brien; for whom high-sounding dignities abroad were but as feathers in the balance, when weighed against the hope of restoring his church and order to their ancient supremacy, in his native land. Here he now stood; and though but presiding at the altars of a poor and remote Irish convent, he imaged, in his person, the pertinacity of ecclesiastical ambition, and the spirit of an order, not to be laid by the authority of princes, and vanquishable only by public opinion.

Lord Arranmore, wholly pre-occupied by the scene before him, alternately directed his anxious eyes, from the presiding priest, to the lovely, but absorbing Superior; and forgetful of his own perilous position, of the circumstances in which he was involved, and the purposes for which he had assumed his disguise, – he had impetuously advanced, and placed himself directly opposite to the stall of the Abbess, unconsciously maintaining his upright position, when all around him was prostrate. In that awful moment, when the elevation of the Host images the hallowed presence of 'God on earth,' – when the altar bell tingled, and a low voice uttered the '*Sanctus, sanctus, sanctus,*' – at that awful moment a murmur was heard, a band of armed men rushed to the spot, where Lord Arranmore stood; he was suddenly seized – resisted – escaped his assailant, and again was surrounded. The next moment a pistol was fired, and an uproar, a conflict ensued, whose horror was increased by the sense of sacrilegious violation entertained by the catholic congregation. Aloft above all, and in front of the object of attack, stood Shane-na-Brien; wild, infuriate, he held in his grasp, with maniacal force, the wretched victim of his long cherished vengeance, and was dragging him to the steps of the altar, as if to immolate him at the shrine of that Deity, whose rites he had impiously profaned; – it was Corny the cadger!

But even the maniac paused in his frenzy at the spectacle which at this moment presented itself. The inferior clergy had rushed among the people, as if to exert their powerful influence to preserve peace, and to prevent murder. But the high priest, the Caiaphas of the temple, stood motionless and erect, as if awaiting the martyrdom he was ready to undergo. Here ended his short-lived triumph; an age was summed up in an instant. The ghastly colour of his visage suddenly altered to a blood-red suffusion. His eye shot forth one flash of unearthly fire – a rattling sound died on his convulsed lips; and raising the crucifix on high, which he held with the last gasp of vital force, he fell dead upon the altar steps, which were covered with his blood. In the eyes of the congregation it was the blood of a martyr. The signal was given – the scene which followed was indescribable.

To execute a warrant from the Secretary of State was the pretence for the indecent violation of the temple of God; to scare catholicism from its altars, to insult, to outrage, and to provoke, were the motives which determined this choice of time and place. From the first moment when Lord Arranmore, foreseeing what must ensue, had shaken off his assailant Corny, he had endeavoured to reach the stall of the Superior, and to protect her from danger and insult. In the effort he had caught his uncle's eye, observed the sudden change in his countenance, and was hastening to his assistance, when he was himself knocked down, upon the altar steps, beside his dying relation. To all that followed he was insensible: and when he recovered his reason, he found himself lying on the earth, his head supported on a monument, and a small pitcher of water by his side. He drank freely and was much refreshed. He had been stunned by a blow on the back of his head, but not much hurt; and he looked round him and gradually recovered his powers of perception.

The dreary place he occupied was of Gothic architecture, and filled with very old and rude monuments. One grated window, in the further end, looked upon a lake, whose water dashed against its massive buttresses. He guessed, rather than knew, that he was in the old chauntry, mentioned by Shane, to whom, he took it for granted, he owed his safety. On approaching the window, the reviving influence of the air quickly dispelled the faintness left by the blow. The opening at which he stood looked diagonally upon the Abbey church; and from the great window above the altar, a dense body of smoke rose in wreathed and voluminous folds. Shouts of savage triumph were mingled with the crash of broken wood-work: while, in the intervals, the low crackling of combustion was distinctly audible. As he remained for a moment fixed to the spot, a tremendous crash announced the fall of the Abbey roof, which was followed by a burst of light, reflected in livid redness on the lake, above the lustre of a meridian but clouded atmosphere. Groups of the peasantry were seen contending with the rioters beneath the walls; and at remote distances, women and children flying from the contest, and horsemen and pedestrians hurrying to the rescue of their friends, or to extinguish the fire.

Lord Arranmore flew to the low arched door, but it was fastened on the outside, and he sought in vain for any other egress. With the fury of an enraged tiger, he hurried through the gloomy house of death; he examined every tomb and penetrated every recess, but no traces of the subterraneous entrance of which Shane had spoken met his eye. He mounted to the stone embrasure of the window, and strove with the whole force of desperation, to wrench the iron grating from the stone, – but in vain. In the full conviction of the inutility of his efforts, he threw himself on the earth in an agony of mind, in which every form of insult and danger that unprotected female helplessness could encounter, rose in rapid and terrible succession to torture and to madden him. One object, however, predominated in his fancy over every other; and the dreadful apprehension for his cousin's safety, the talented, the sensitive, the lovely Abbess, his benefactress, his guardian angel, banished every recollection even of his own horrible lot: for if Shane had fallen in the affray, or had been made a prisoner by the police, what was the destiny which awaited him in this living tomb?

By degrees, however, the sounds of tumult died away. The fire in the church had either subsided, or had been extinguished. Hour passed after hour, and each with the tediousness of an age. The lake upon which the chauntry stood, was rarely navigated; and no sounds from the interior gave indication that a human being still lingered round the ruin. At last the splash of an oar was heard, and coasting beneath the shadow of the craggy rocks, a boat was seen winning its devious and stealthy way to the window of the chauntry. Lord Arranmore's heart beat quick; he put his hand out through the bars; a note, fastened to the point of a boat-hook, was thrust through the window; and the boat again glided silently within the protecting shadows of the rocks.

Lord Arranmore tore open the paper, and recognized with transport his cousin's writing. It ran as follows:

'Those for whom probably you are most interested, are safe. Think only of yourself. Means for your evasion are prepared. You will be conducted to Emunh's cottage after sun-set; flight will be still in your power: act as prudence and principle may direct; and for the promise so solemnly given, believe that it shall be fulfilled at a more convenient season. For the present it must be deferred. 'B. O.'

Soothed and pacified, and furnished with the materials for gracious meditation, Lord Arranmore was enabled to pass the interval which preceded his enlargement with patience. Released from his apprehensions for his cousin's safety, he sought and found gratification in this new instance of the interest she manifested on his behalf; and the brief missive, cool and concise as it was, still came from her, and had his safety for its object. At the time appointed Emunh appeared, and leading the way through a vaulted passage, terminated by a flight of steps, conducted the prisoner to an opening upon the rocks, where a boat was moored, beneath the shelter of projecting underwood.

On the way over, Emunh, in reply to Lord Arranmore's anxious questions, detailed in a low voice the events of the day. The death of the aged Abate had roused the peasantry to ungovernable madness. The Fencibles, who had been stationed at a small distance from the Abbey, were called to the assistance of the police; and in the conflict which ensued, having obtained possession of the church, they demolished the seats, altars, and stall-work. Piling the wreck of their fury into a heap, they had kindled a fire, which soon reached to the dry oak rafters; and having destroyed the roof, burned itself out. In the meantime, the catholic gentry who had attended the funeral, having conducted the ladies of the community to a remote and secure part of the building, had aided in appeasing the riot. Many of the peasantry had been made prisoners; but Shane, who had fought with a desperate fury, had escaped to the mountains, hotly pursued by Corny the cadger, and a detachment of the military.

On arriving at an unfrequented spot, on the opposite side of the lake, Lord Arranmore and his guide entered a lonely and untrodden glen, which after a quarter of an hour's brisk walking, brought them to Emunh's cottage. There, refreshments were already provided, of which the former stood in much need. The welcome meal being hastily dispatched, Emunh led Lord Arranmore's pony to the door, ready saddled, with the valise strapped in its place; and urging the necessity of immediate departure, presented a letter which he said came from the Superior. It was an inclosure containing two fifty pound notes, and the address of Mad. O'Flaherty at the Franciscan convent, in Dublin.

Lord Arranmore sighed as he unwillingly put up the inclosure (of which he resolved to make no use), until he should have an opportunity of restoring it to the generous donor. The offering wounded him; – one line from the hand that made it, would have been worth millions. But there was no time left for the indulgence of feelings, natural in one whose warm passions brooked no disappointment, and whose pride was sharpened by adversity to a morbid excess. Forcing a small remuneration upon his humble but grateful host, he bade him a hurried farewell, and struck into the bridle-way, which led to the high road to Galway.

It was lonely and deserted. The setting sun was struggling through masses of dark and stormy clouds, and shot its long yellow rays over the distant ocean, casting a lurid light upon the highest tops of the mountains. The solitary sojourner in wilds so dreary had advanced for a considerable time at a brisk pace; but, by degrees, he had dropped his bridle on his horse's neck, insensible to his 'whereabouts,' unconscious of external objects, with one deep-seated and master-thought overruling every other, he was lost in reverie, when the clanking sound of a horse's feet caught his ear and roused his attention. He seized his bridle, and gave spur to his little steed; but his progress was arrested by the approach of a person of muffled and mysterious appearance, preceded by a ragged boy, who seemed to act as guide. Lord Arranmore's first impulse was to plunge into the copse to his left, to avoid one, who was perhaps in pursuit of him; but he soon perceived that the intruder was a female, in the coarse dress of the country, a blue mantel and deep hood.

He drew aside to let the traveller pass, but glancing his eye beneath her close-drawn hood, he discovered the agitated countenance of Lady Knocklofty. He halted in the shock of utter amazement; and in deep and uncontrollable emotion, exclaimed, as he alighted and approached her,

'Gracious heavens! is it possible? Lady Knocklofty here?'

'It is possible!' she replied, in a voice tremulous with agitation; 'it is pitiable – it is true.' A silence of a moment ensued; when she added, with a deep-drawn sigh, 'Yes, Lord Arranmore; you see before you the unfortunate, the imprudent, but not the ungrateful Lady Knocklofty.' Lord Arranmore gave his horse to the boy, and taking the reins of Lady Knocklofty's, walked beside her. Another pause ensued, and he then said,

'To meet you in so wild a place, in so unsuitable a dress, and unseasonable an hour, unaccompanied by friends, unattended by servants, what can this mean? – what has led you here?'

She abruptly replied, 'You!' and the answer but deepened his consternation. He was unable, or unwilling to reply; and she continued, 'You see before you one whose pride is humbled in the dust, whose strength is her weakness, and whose sense is overpowered by her sensibility. My duty to my husband, to my children, my self-respect, my regard for reputation, are not merely surmounted, they are unfelt. Your liberty, your life, are in danger. To rescue, to save you, to warn you of your danger, and to offer you the means of escape, have led me into these solitary regions, unattended, unprotected.'

'Think not of me, dearest and most generous Lady Knocklofty – think but of yourself – your precious self,' he exclaimed in most passionate emotion. 'The evening is already falling – you are alone – you are far distant from Beauregard. Be the consequence what it may, I will accompany you back. If my hours of liberty, or even of life are counted, could my last moments be better employed than in the service of the noblest, the most generous of created beings?'

'Never,' said Lady Knocklofty, with passionate vehemence, while her tears dropped on the hand that now pressed upon hers; 'and I swear by that sinking sun, never to return to my home, my children, till I have placed you beyond the reach of that persecution, which they with whom I am fatally linked, have raised against you. For me, I am wrecked beyond the reach of all redemption.'

Gratitude, admiration, pity, every sentiment (save perhaps respect) agitated the object of this most generous infatuation. Confounded, alarmed, he knew not what step to take. 'Let me, at least,' he said, mounting his horse and holding the bridle of hers, 'let me conduct you homeward, while I reveal to you my means of escape. This ravine enters into the new line of road to St Grellan, and – '

Lady Knocklofty snatched the reins from his hand – 'Ungrateful and insensible!' she said, 'I know your infatuation for one as cold as she is false renders you insensible to the feelings of humanity.' She turned her horse's head, and motioned Lord Arranmore, as if to dismiss him.

'Be the consequence what it may,' he said, 'I will not leave you thus. For myself, I am reckless, and I am now hastening to Dublin to stand my trial.'

'Then you are lost!' interrupted Lady Knocklofty, impetuously. 'This day I have heard your doom pronounced. The libel is not all that is laid against you; charges of a most treasonable nature, on evidence as apparently convincing as I know it to be false, which involves you in the proceedings of men, who are the dupes and the victims of hired instigators and spies. I have seen the Chancellor's letters to my husband; and it is determined to make an example of the first well born and marking personage they can catch in their toils: you are that person. I have not lost a moment in seeking you. Think not that I am deceived by this appearance of generosity. Nothing that concerns you is unknown to me. I, too, have my spies; and I heard from my informers that you were in these mountains, that you were lurking about the Abbey, and that you had been seen at midnight conducted to your boat by your . . . Abbess.'

'Gracious God!' said Lord Arranmore, striking his forehead, in an agony beyond his power of concealment, at having thus imprudently committed one for whom he felt so much, and to whom he stood so deeply indebted.

'Lord Arranmore,' continued Lady Knocklofty, drawing from the breast of her habit her handkerchief, which she bathed in her tears, 'your conduct was not grateful, it was not humane . . .' Her sobs interrupted her words.

'If the sacrifice of my life could dry those precious tears,' he said, tenderly and softly, 'it should be offered at your feet. But, dear Lady Knocklofty – '

'I want no sacrifice. I ask but to be permitted to save you; and to leave to others the recompense of a wayward heart, which gives itself capriciously; not gratefully.'

'To owe my liberty, my life to you, would render both more valuable. But again I urge you, think not of me, consider only yourself, consider where you now are!'

'Where alone I can be useful to you,' she interrupted him. 'Nobody knows the imprudent step I have taken, but my friend Lady Honoria. Let me not err in vain; we are now within a mile of the Heaths: that bright point of light is its vane. I mean to pass the night there. This gate leads to its young plantations.' She advanced and pushed open an iron gate with the end of her whip, as she spoke. Lord Arranmore followed her along the margin of a lake, and she continued: 'I will not take you to the house. Neither the innocence of my conduct, nor the purity of my motives, would save me from censure, were it known that you accompany me. But alight; and if that fishing-house is open, I will communicate there what else I have to say.'

Wild and agitated as herself, Lord Arranmore obeyed her, whom it was now so difficult to resist. A manly pity, a deep but honest commiseration, gratitude the most profound, and fears for her safety and reputation, the most acute, were the feelings by which he was governed; unmixed with one thought which virtue itself might disapprove. To leave her in such a moment, was to be more, or less than man: he advanced and perceived that the boat-house was open. The interior was dimly illumined by the fading twilight; but it appeared to be an elegant pavilion, decorated by the hand of luxury and taste. In assisting Lady Knocklofty from her horse, he was shocked by her pale and altered appearance, and by the feebleness of her movements, as he supported her on his arm. He led her to a sofa, and leaned over a chair beside her. She wept freely; and relieved by this indulgence, she recovered her self-possession, and drew from her bosom a packet of papers: – 'There,' she said, 'are copies of the informations which have been lodged against you. The facts they contain may serve you in – your hour of trial.'

Lord Arranmore pressed the generous hand that offered them to his lips. 'My hour of trial!' he exclaimed, with emotion. 'Oh, Lady Knocklofty!'

*    *    *    *    *

The storms of a night, in which all the elements had been thrown into fearful contest, were gradually subsiding into the low broken sobs of the gushing wind, the distant roll of retreating thunder, and the faint gleam of innocuous lightning. The grey, faint dawn was struggling through the vapours, which canopied the summits of Bembola and Mam Turk; when upon the brink of one of the precipices of the Glan Mountain, a human figure appeared, which well belonged to a scene so wild, so awful, and so desolate. The fugitive (for such he must have been, unhoused, and wandering in such an hour and place) had just emerged from a narrow ravine of furze and brambles; and was tearing, with wondrous strength, the tangled branches of a scathed beech tree, to obtain a passage into the glen beneath. He had cleared a way, and was plunging headlong down, when (all reckless as he seemed) he was withheld by that instinct that survives even the love of life itself.

The increasing light (for though the moon had not yet set, the dawn was faintly breaking) rendered the peril of his position fearfully obvious: yet not more fearful than his own appearance. There was blood upon his hands, his eye was wild and sunk, his colour ghastly, his features distorted. His uncovered head had caught, in its thick and matted locks, fragments of burrs and thistles, which he had encountered in his flight; his clothes were torn, his neck was bare, and his whole exterior bespoke one hunted to the death. It was an awful, an affecting spectacle: and the more affecting, because on that forlorn figure and distorted countenance, were still visible traces of the finest impression of God's own mark, when 'after his own image he made man.' The fugitive was Murrogh O'Brien, Lord Arranmore.

He had eluded the pursuit of justice. He had escaped from the officers, who had traced him to the Circean bower, whose threshold he had crossed, in the consciousness of an unsullied life; and from which he had escaped, with life indeed, but not unsullied. On the first alarm, he had sprung from an open window into the lake, urged only by the hope of saving her from shame, who had plunged him into crime. Weighed down by the dripping waters, which he had endeavoured to wring from his saturated clothes, he had flung off his coat and cravat; and exposed to the thunderstorm, which shook even the mighty regions in which he wandered, he continued to ascend the acclivities of the Glan Mountain, in the hope of crossing to Lough Corrib.

The first glimmering of the dawn disclosing to him the dangers of his horrible position, he let go the branches he had torn aside with his lacerated hands; and ascending a craggy rock, perceived a bridle track; while a column of smoke staining the pure morning sky, announced the proximity of some human habitation.

As he advanced, his steps were arrested by a low, faint moan. He paused. It might be the complaint of some dying animal; but his own wretchedness was in sympathy with all that suffered; and he proceeded to the spot whence the sound had issued. A groan of human agony came from the glen beneath the shelving rock on which he stood. Thrown, as he himself was, beyond the pale of humanity, he still was tremulously alive to its sympathies; and descending the rocks with as rapid a step as their steepness would admit, he found himself in a deep, dark, narrow glen, whose shaggy rocks almost closed over his head; while the moon, shining faintly above, concentrated its rays on the body of a man, who lay upon his face weltering in his blood. A gory track was visible on the salient points of the rocky declivity, intimating that the wretched being had been hurled from the summit, on which he had received his death-wound. The victim still breathed; but a torrent of blood was gushing from his breast.

Lord Arranmore raised the dying man in his arms; and as his eyes fell upon the face, he recognized the distorted features of Corny the cadger. With an impulse of horror, he was on the point of letting him drop, when the victim grasped him in the strong gripe of death, and raised his dim eyes with a look of such agony, that, turning aside his own, he could only articulate, 'Wretched man, what has brought you to this?'

The cadger, with an effort at articulation, which convulsed every hideous lineament, endeavoured to pronounce the name of his murderer; when a shrill, loud blast from a horn echoed through the rocks above the glen. At that sound the dying man gave one fearful spring from the arms of his supporter, and fell a corpse upon the earth; while the appalling figure of Shane, half way down the rocks, with one hand pointing to the vapoury and waning moon, and the other clenched, as in triumph over the dead body, added to the horror of the scene.

The wretched and solitary spectator of this awful tragedy, himself unobserved by Shane, now stood motionless, with every faculty frozen and palsied, unable, and perhaps unwilling to communicate with the perpetrator of a deed so bloody. Time, however, was not allowed him, either for reflection or for action; a sudden burst of sound roused him from his contemplation, and the next moment he beheld the mouth of the glen filled with armed men. He was instantly surrounded, seized, and bound. The horror of his fate overwhelmed him; he had neither the wish nor the power to resist. Manacled and chained, he was placed on horseback before a dragoon. The dead body, laid upon a bier of woven branches, was raised upon the shoulders of two smugglers, who had conducted the soldiers through the mountains; one of whom had seen Lord Arranmore's escape from the lake into the ravines of the pass. The party proceeded; and the exhausted and almost senseless prisoner was lodged in the gaol of Galway. The next morning he was conveyed in a chaise and four, escorted by a troop of horse, to Dublin; and on his reaching that capital (where, as the leader of the most brilliant of the Irish Volunteers, as the orator of the Historical Society, and the most gifted member of the University, he had but a few months before 'won golden opinions from all sorts of men'), he was lodged in the state prison of Kilmainham, in whose dungeons some of Ireland's most distinguished sons were then incarcerated.

His prison chamber rose above that high and terrible wall, then deemed so lofty, as to need no sentinel to add to its security. On the opposite bank, at a small distance, there stood an old and formless pile of ruined walls.

The arrest of a young nobleman, so gifted, so accused, and in public supposition so guilty, excited a strong sensation in the metropolis, where the reign of terror, which preceded the horrible epoch of the Rebellion, had already begun to spread dismay, and to agitate the public mind. The public papers were full of reports concerning the murder perpetrated in the Glan Mountain. The manner in which Lord Arranmore had been taken, – alone, – at day-break, – by the side of the corpse, from which life had scarce departed, all corroborated the probability of his guilt. He was likewise smeared with blood, and so overpowered by his own emotions, as to offer no defence, and to make no resistance: but above all, a warrant for his arrest was found in the pocket of the dead man, who, it was supposed, had fallen in a contest with the object of his pursuit. These just grounds of suspicion were almost confirmed by the obstinate and desponding silence of the prisoner, from the moment of his captivity.

From the time, however, when he was visited by his counsel (for none others were admitted to him), considerable exertions were made for his defence. On the second week of his detention, which resembled the *carcere duro* of an Austrian prison, his day of trial was appointed. Curran, Fletcher, and others of the most distinguished members of the bar were engaged for his defence. The court and all its avenues were crowded to suffocation. Multitudes of the people, with anxious countenances, were gathered in close array, muttering their feelings and opinions, as they drew back, to admit the carriages of the judges and the lawyers, employed on either side. Within the halls, men of the highest rank, members of the government, and of both houses, were pressing and rushing on, to seek for places, already pre-occupied by others, as anxious, as curious, and as influential as themselves. The leading members of the society of United Irishmen, with a sympathy and courage, which distinguished them in all the legal prosecutions of their brethren, were congregated near the dock. Convinced of the innocence of the prisoner, and suspicious of the foul purpose to which appearances might be turned against him, they saw the necessity for their countenance and support; and no personal considerations of danger could prevail with them to absent themselves. Many females also of the highest distinction, and most noted fashion (the particular friend of Albina Countess Knocklofty, whose protection of the accused was not forgotten), were seated on the bench. The three Ladies O'Blarney were conspicuous, with their three white pocket handker-chiefs, the insignia of their well-prepared sensibility. The good Lady Mary was accommodated with a seat next the judge. Her ladyship had, from the first committal of the accused, exhibited as much zeal in behalf of his soul, as her husband had shown perseverance in urging forward the prosecution of his person. She had sent him tracts, and had written him frequent letters on faith and justification; and though he had taken no notice of her pious endeavours, she counted upon, and announced his conversion, as among the triumphs which graced her mission. In his personal sufferings, she had no sympathy; but in his salvation, as it was to be worked through her instrumentality, she had a deep interest. And now –

> The charge was prepared, the lawyers were met,
> The judges arrayed – a terrible show,

and a silence the most awful followed. The panel being sworn, and the clerk of the crown standing in readiness to read the indictment, a short pause ensued; which was succeeded by a low buzzing whisper, while all eyes were directed to the still empty dock. As the delay was protracted, anxiety increased. The judge whispered an officer of the court below him, and then desired the sheriff aloud to produce his prisoner. The sheriff disappeared, and in a few moments returned, pale and breathless, to announce that his prisoner had – escaped!

A loud murmur, amounting almost to approbation, arose among the crowd, at the extreme verge of the court; while something like disappointment was visible on the countenances of the female auditory. The three Ladies O'Blarney put up their three white pocket handkerchiefs, and ordered their carriage to a morning concert at the Rotunda. Lady Mary desired her coachman to take Kilmainham (in his way to an auxiliary supplementary branch society for converting Tippoo Saib and his subjects), to make inquiries concerning the flight of her proselyte. Inquiries were made; but the only details she could learn, were, that certain mysterious characters had been found chalked on the ruins opposite his prison window, that a knotted rope had been found hanging over the lofty wall of Kilmainham, and that the impression of a gigantic foot was traced beneath.[1]

A letter was found on the prisoner's table, addressed to the judges. It was a simple and solemn denial of the political crimes charged against him; and more especially of the murder of the informer. On the former point, opinions varied, with the prejudices and the interests of those who expressed them. But there was so evident an embarrassment in the short explanation he gave of the circumstances which brought him to the spot where he was taken, that the murder was almost unanimously laid to his account, until his reputation was cleared by the voluntary confession of – the murderer himself. It was Shane-na-Brien; who, whatever might have been his motive – whether a desire to clear his foster-brother from the horrible imputation, a weariness of life – or the hope of expiating in this world, a crime for which he believed eternal punishment awaited him in the next – surrendered himself to justice, and was, on his own declarations, convicted and executed.

Of the Abbey of Moycullen, nothing but its ruins remain. Its fair

---

[1] Such are the literal details of the escape of an United Irishman, who has since been made known to fame, as one of the most gallant officers in the French service.

members, again restored to the bosoms of their families (woman's best sanctuary), still cherish a feeling of admiration almost religious, for the gifted and extraordinary Superior, under whose auspices they had been for a time congregated; and whose immediate departure from Ireland was believed to be connected with the flight of Lord Arranmore. To her agency, indeed, was attributed all the ingenuity with which the escape of the prisoner was conducted; and the gossiping of the town of St Grellan had exaggerated circumstances, till, to the heated imaginations of its visionary inhabitants, they appeared a fulfilment of the old prophecies, predicted in the old times, of the inseparable connexion between the destinies of THE O'BRIENS AND THE O'FLAHERTYS.

# CHAPTER VII

————•————

## *Conclusion*

Time is like a fashionable host,
That slightly shakes his parting guest by th' hand,
And then with arms outstretched, as he would fly,
Welcomes the comer.

SHAKSPEARE.

La révolution ne vient pas de tel ou tel homme, de tel ou tel livre; elle vient des choses.

CHATEAUBRIAND.

THE French Revolution was the result of causes deep-seated in the institutions it destroyed. Its frequent re-organization gave to it a succession of characters, each differing from the other. The reign of terror was the shortest, but its impression was the most permanent. The consular *régime* was the most perfect, but seems to have been the soonest forgotten. It, however, in its first epoch, met the hopes, and reconciled the opinions of all. The liberals looked with confidence to the re-establishment of rational liberty; the royalists looked to the return of the Bourbons; and France in 1802, typified by England in 1660, beheld in Napoleon Bonaparte another Monk. The church, after her complete prostration, elevated to her ancient alliance with the state, dignified the conqueror of Italy, and of the Pope, with the name of her 'restorer.' The people called for *panem et circenses*, and obtained both; and he in whom '*la puissance de la révolution*' now centered – the destiny of kings, and the pacificator of Europe, – as yet avoided all occasion of shocking public opinion, and refrained from assuming all external forms of power, beyond what might become the Chief Magistrate of a republic.

It happened one evening, that as the First Consul was writing in his cabinet after dinner, and the ladies of his family, with the Generals Rapp, Bessières, Lannes, and Lebrun were taking coffee in the saloon, a proposal, made by Madame Murat, to go to the Opera to hear the grand oratorio of Haydn, which was the rage of the day, was acceded to *à l'unanimité*. The General Lannes was deputed to invite the Chief Consul, who instantly adopted the proposition. The *'piquet d'escorte'* was ordered, the carriages drew up, and Mad. Bonaparte, lingering behind while *'le brusque et brave Rapp'* arranged her shawl 'after the manner of the Egyptian ladies,' was called upon by her lovely sister-in-law with *'dépêchez-vous donc, ma sœur, voilà Bonaparte qui s'en va.'*

The visit to the opera, thus uncalculated, was yet, in consequence of some strange reports, expected: and either this expectation, or the attraction of Haydn's Creation, had filled the house almost to suffocation, at an unusually early hour. Long before *le premier coup d'archet* was heard in the orchestra, the arrival of some high foreign *donna d'importanza* had called forth all the interested civilities of the members of the box-keeping department. The *contrôleur* from his little office, cried aloud to the *ouvreuse de loges*, *'Citoyenne ouvreuse, la loge, s'il vous plait, de Son Excellence la princesse de Fustiburg.'* As this was the first night that *Son Excellence*, the wife of the Austrian Plenipotentiary, had visited the opera, her titles rang sweetly in the ears of the attendants on the *bureau de l'Opéra*. Theatrical personages are all aristocrats; and *'la loge de Son Excellence la Princesse de Fustiburg,'* seemed to find a deathless echo through the corridors and the saloons; while *la citoyenne ouvreuse*, scudding respectfully before the Princess, threw open the box door, drew forth the *fauteuil*, arranged the cushions, let down the *grille*, and presented *l'imprimé*, or the book of the oratorio.

The Princess was a true German princess in appearance. Full, fair, and fresh, for one who had evidently passed her *première jeunesse*, she was not without pretensions; and she had given to her somewhat redundant *embonpoint* all the advantages of a splendid toilet. In passing to her box, she had fixed the attention of a group of military, who stood laughing and chatting, in expectation of the commencement of the music; when one among them (but not of them, for he had a decidedly British *tournure*, and was in the dress of a *pekin*) suddenly started off, brushed by the box-keeper, and abruptly entering the box, exclaimed –

'Heavenly powers! can I believe my eyes? Kitty, my sweetest, is it possible? Can it really be you? Well, this is too much happiness!' and, shutting the door, he pressed the fair hand he had seized to his lips, exclaiming, 'Surely you have not forgotten me, Miss Macguire?'

'Lord Kilcolman, I believe,' replied the lady, drawing up. After the first evident shock of her surprise had subsided, she fixed her eyes steadily, but somewhat humorously, upon him, and added, 'I really did not at first recollect you; how much you are altered. You have grown so very thin and yellow, that you are quite *méconnaissable*.'

'And you too, my lovely friend, are altered, but it is not for the worse, by Jupiter. I give you my honour, you are a thousand times handsomer than ever – may I perish, if I flatter.'

'I heard you were dead, Lord K.,' said the lady, coolly pinning her *imprimé* to the front of the box.

'There never was the least foundation for the report, I give you my honour. It originated solely in my voyage to the Dead Sea: but never mind me, talk only of your lovely self. By all that's precious, I have not felt so much pleasure since I parted from you in the little study at Knocklofty House, an age back. But tell me, dear, what has brought you to this place? Who is the Prince Fusty, something, this elegant set out belongs to?'

'He is the Austrian minister.'

'The Austrian minister! to be sure he is, I remember now all about him. Then I suppose you are here, with your aunt the Countess Macguire, with whom, I understand, you went to live at Vienna; and who is, by all accounts, the minister's minister.'

'No,' said the lady, drily, 'I am here with the minister himself.'

'With the minister himself! you take away my breath; and in what capacity, my sweetest?'

'In the capacity of his wife.'

'Heavenly powers! do you tell me that? Ah! Kitty, you who – ' and his lordship actually brought those tears to his eyes, which the nervousness of dissipation so easily calls forth.

'Why, what would you have me do?' said the lady, screwing up her pretty mouth, and looking down pensively. 'You would not have me pass my life in weeping for your infidelity and breach of promise?'

'Infidelity! and breach of promise! By all the powers, you wrong me, Miss Macguire! that is, Princess, I mane. You knew my unfortunate situation: cleaned out of the last shilling at Daly's, and eased of my last acre in Tipperary; threatened by my creditors, and tormented by my mother, to make that odious match which was to set all to rights; urged, too, by my political friends, with respect to the union which was then brewing; in short, paint to yourself for a moment, the minister's niece with twenty thousand pounds fortune, a foreign embassy, and a pension for life. Could you blame me, Kitty, dearest?'

'Oh, no, my love, no!' hummed the Princess, after the manner of Miss Macguire; 'but could *you* blame *me*, my lord, if in my despair, I – I – consented to become – '

'Ah, you creature!' sighed his lordship, languishingly.

'A Princess of the empire,' continued Miss Macguire, humorously.

'Upon your honour! and are you a real Princess?'

'Real and undoubted, as you are a real Irish peer. But come, Lord K., we have each of us fulfilled our destinies; so a truce with sentiment and reminiscences. I hate thinking of the past; it's worth nothing: so pray, let's talk of the present. In the first place, what could have possibly brought *you* here? *Je n'en reviens pas.*'

'Why, dearest, having joined the allied army as a volunteer, on my return from Jerusalem, I——.'

'From Jerusalem! ha! ha! ha! *cela passe outre*. What in the world could have taken you to Jerusalem?'

'Faith, I don't know; that is, it's a long story. When I returned to England from my embassy, and our party was out, and poor Lady K. dead, I found there was no getting on, especially for us Irish Union lords, and the whigs coming in, and that sort of thing. So I got tired of the clubs and *ennuyé de ma personne*, as we say in France, and I thought I'd just take a trip to Jerusalem.'

'But, why to Jerusalem?' asked the Princess still tittering, 'what an odd place to go to, *pour se désennuyer*, and a distant one. How came you to fix upon it?'

''Pon my soul and honour, I don't know, if it wasn't to eat Jerusalem artichokes on their own soil: one must have an object, you know.'

'To be sure: and was that the only object which determined your pilgrimage?'

'Not entirely. The fact is, do you see, there is no getting on in that tiresome dull London, if one isn't labelled and ticketed, somehow or other, for something. Rank there is a mere drug; and Irish rank goes for less than nothing. But a man, you know, who has been at Jerusalem! I defy you, by Jupiter, to throw a man in a corner, who has been at Jerusalem! You see how Lord Kilshandra got on, and Lord Stillorgan, after they had published their books, and got all those d——d hard names and jaw-breakers into them.'

'You don't really mean to turn author,' said the Princess, with one of her Miss Macguire comical looks.

'Faith, I don't know; but I give you my honour, my Journal is the most amusing thing you ever read. O'Mealy too has collected some scraps of Jerusalem songs, which he learned from the little black-eyed daughters of Sion there, which I might introduce: there is one that begins – 'pon my honour, I forget it now; but it is all about *pooshum*, and *nooshum*, and is the sweetest little thing you ever heard, as O'Mealy sings it. He swears too, it's all Irish.'

'O'Mealy!' almost screamed her Excellency, in a convulsion of laughter. 'You are not really serious? You don't mean that O'Mealy went with you to Jerusalem?'

'Indeed he did, poor fellow, every foot of the way; and I was very near laving him behind me, in the valley of Jehosaphat, as we say in Jerusalem. For at a pic-nic dinner, that I gave at the pool of Bethesda, he drank more Greek wine than agreed with his head; and so he fell asleep under the cedars of Lebanon, within view of the temple of Solomon (the finest thing, upon my honour, you ever saw in your life, and every way superior to our parliament-house), where he caught a quinsey, which has left him no more voice than a frog: so, '*Othello's occupation's gone*,' as he says himself, from the celebrated Shakspeare, and I, of course, am bound to provide for him.'

'Provide for him!' said the Princess, still laughing, 'why, he was handsomely provided for, when I left Ireland, as Sir Barnaby O'Mealy, lord of Bog Moy: for he took the Green Knighthood, on his marriage with old Miss Mac Taaf, in spite of the Red Book.'

'Oh! but that turned out a bad spec. The old girl was such a lawyer, that she kept what she could in her own hands; and he run out all *he* could, sold the personals, brought the old house about her ears, shut her up in the Brigadier's tower, and then fled for the same. He got into trouble too, poor fellow; was shortly after shut up for a time in gaol, then came to London, applied to me in his distress, and became my tiger; and there he is, as large as life, 'pon my honour.'

'Where, where, for heaven's sake?' said the Princess, taking up her glass.

'There,' said Lord Kilcolman, 'in the *parterre*, leaning over the back of the *parquet*, ogling that pretty little *citoyenne* in the *baignoire* to the left.'

The Princess had no difficulty in detecting, in the flashy, dashing *ci-devant jeune homme*, whose bloated red face was set off by a pair of black moustaches, in addition to his original bushy well-powdered whiskers, the former led captain of Knocklofty House, and the *Primo Tenore* of the private theatricals of Dublin.

'Well, all this is much too droll,' she exclaimed, more amused than she had been since she left Ireland. 'I take it for granted, then, that if you and your tiger joined the allied army, on your return from Jerusalem, you are now prisoners of war, on parole.'

'Exactly, upon my honour: and never was so happy in all my life. What between the Boulevards and the Champs Élysées, the cafés, and the claret, and the theatres, and the estaminets, I will say, there is nothing in the world like the society of Paris – *Kyrie Eleison!* as we say in Jerusalem; what a difference, between Paris and London! But tell me, when did you hear any thing of the Knockloftys? I have lost sight of all that set for years.'

'I had a letter to-day from the present Lady.'

'The present lady! what do you mean? Is poor Albina dead?'

'Oh no! she is only Duchess of Ludlow; and her friend, Lady Honoria, is the present Lady Knocklofty.'

'You amaze me, Kitty – Princess, I should say. What the devil does that all mane?'

'Why it means, that Lord Knocklofty got a divorce three years ago.'

'A divorce! I thought it would come to that; who pays the damage?'

'Poor, good-natured, indolent Lord Charles, now Duke of Ludlow, whom you may remember in the Prince's Own in Dublin, some years back.'

'Mashallah! as we say in Jerusalem, *est-il possible?* Why, when I left Ireland, she was talked of about that young, insolent, rebelly O'Brien, that she wanted to cram down the throats of every one, – he, who was hanged afterwards in the rebellion, or something of the sort, as O'Mealy tells me.'

'He would have been hanged, or *something of that sort*,' said the Princess, laughing, 'if he had not escaped from Kilmainham, where he was put up for a suspicion of murder, or libel, or both; but that affair of her Ladyship's blew over. Lord K. did not want to be bored, and would believe nothing – at least would *hear* nothing; though there was a strange story about a boat-house and a pony. When, however, the Knockloftys gave up Ireland, preparatory to the getting up of the Union (which Lord Knocklofty was the principal person in bringing about), and settled in London, they renewed their intimacy with Lord Charles, who, you know, was always a dowager fancier; and so, like all young men *qui se laissent aimer*, he made no resistance. The thing, however, might have gone on for ever; but Lady Knocklofty was vain of her conquest, and would have a *scene:* some say she was urged to it by Lady Honoria, who had lived with the Knockloftys ever since the death of Mr Stratton.

'But be that as it may, Lady K., one fine day, rubbed off her rouge, let down her hair, called her 'friends, lovers, countrymen,' about her, made a speech from Lady Townly, acknowledged herself unworthy to be Countess Knocklofty any longer, stepped into a hackney coach, threw herself upon poor Lord Charles's honour, and is now, 'Pamela, or Virtue Rewarded,' alias Duchess of Ludlow. Lady Honoria, however, who has taken her place, finds that London *bon ton*, though headed by her beautiful friend, the Ex-Lady Lieutenant, will not admit Irish ladies into its particular set, who have been blown on in their own country. Besides, I believe Lady Honoria is altogether *trop prononcée* for the high societies of London; and I perceive by the tone of her letter, that, in the hope of a speedy peace, and the return of the emigrants to France, she is doing the honours by them all in London, *pour se ménager une retraite à Paris*, one of these days. This is all I know of the old set, most of whom I believe are dead: so no more reminiscences, for Heaven's sake. The Prince will be here immediately; and remember that we high transparencies are all *dans les hautes étiquettes:* so pray let go my hand, Lord K.'

'Ah! Kitty, ye creature!' sighed Lord K., imploringly – but Kitty had resumed her *air de princesse;* and Lord Kilcolman, with a maudlin look, and an Irish sigh, sunk back in his *fauteuil*.

The orchestra now gave note of preparation for the commencement of the oratorio; and the throwing open of the box door announced the arrival of his Excellency the Hochfurstlich Durchlaucht, the Prince Von Fustiburg, a sovereign prince of a thousand acres, and lord of the lives, properties, and liberties of as many subjects. He was a tall, meagre, formal, elderly gentleman, dressed in a court suit, covered with orders, and glittering with stars. This *enfant gâté* of the Aulic Council of Vienna, and worthy disciple of its *déraison politique*, fancied that he had come to Paris, to assist in settling the fate of nations; and he brought to the task, a mind made up of precedents, authorities.

etiquettes, and all the rubbish of by-gone diplomacy, wholly inapplicable to the new order of things. Wrapt in the consciousness of his own importance, he was received and treated by the man, who then represented the spirit of the age, and was its type and sign, as his imperial master had been before him – *en grande ganache!*

The Princess presented the Earl of Kilcolman as an English Peer, a prisoner of war, an old friend, and a distinguished compatriot; and the Prince received him with all the ceremony due to his rank; offering him, as a preliminary courtesy, a pinch of snuff, from a box, the lid of which was illustrated by the most foolish face in Europe, set round with the most brilliant diamonds.

The ceremonial of presentation over, the Princess gave up her attention, not to the music, which had begun, but to the audience; and particularly to a side-box, within two of her own, to which every eye was now turned. The *grille* had been just lowered; and two officers, in general's uniforms, entered. The younger of the two came forward, and raising his glass, seemed to reconnoitre the audience, whom his presence had thrown into movement, with great *sang-froid*.

'Who is that young General?' asked the Princess; 'I mean the pale, sallow, thoughtful-looking one, with his hair divided on his forehead, and hanging *en oreilles de chien?*'

'*Mein Gott,*' said the Prince, '*er ist der Consul,* 'tis the General Bonaparte.'

The Princess and Lord Kilcolman both rose in eager curiosity, and fixed their eyes intently on one who was then fixing the gaze of worlds: they were so near the box of the First Consul, as to hear him say in his clear, sharp voice, to an officer, who entered, '*Et Josephine?*'

The arrival of Madame Bonaparte was the reply to this inquiry, which was made in some emotion; and the First Consul coolly added, '*Ces coquins-là ont voulu me faire sauter. Rapp, faites-moi apporter l'imprimé de l'oratorio.*'

There was at this moment a simultaneous rising: a general murmur of applause expressed that the Consul at that moment excited some very lively and powerful interest. The fine music of Haydn went for nothing; and the plaudits of the audience were loud and long.

'*Qu'est-ce que cela veut dire, Monsieur de Vaudrémont?*' demanded the Prince, of a gentleman who had just entered the box, pale, fluttered, and in evident emotion.

'*Cela veut dire,*' said Monsieur de Vaudrémont, 'that the audience have just heard, that the First Consul, on his way to the opera, was near being blown up by the explosion of an infernal machine, and that the police, for once, have been taken *au dépourvu*.'

'*Mein Gott! mein Gott!*' said the Prince, 'is it possible, *der mann des Schictsals?*'[1]

'*Eh, mon Dieu, oui*,' said the ex-noble, '*on ne peut s'empêcher de reconnaitre dans ses destinées une providence, qui l'a marqué de loin pour l'accomplissement de ses vues.*'

'Count,' said the Princess, 'what an admirer you are of Bonaparte, you, who were such a devoted adherent of the Bourbons!'

'*Eh, ... eh, ... eh, que voulez-vous?*' replied the page of Marie Antoinette, afterwards *chambellan* of the Empress Marie Louise, and *gentilhomme de la chambre* to Charles the Tenth; – one, who represented in his person that particular class of the French nobility, who had been the first to fly their country in its exigency, and to avail themselves (in its prosperity) of the amnesty in favour of the *prévenus d'émigration*. The idol of the aristocratic coteries of London, where he had been received as *l'homme immobile de la monarchie*, the Count de Vaudrémont, had accepted a little mission of courtesy from Louis XVIII at the court of Vienna; but instead of returning to play whist in the modest parlours of Hartwell, he was the first to get his name '*raye*,' and to *faire anti-chambre* to the Bonapartes, under the magnificent towers of the Bourbons. Admirably fitted by his old courtly habits of gossip and *médisance*, to administer to the master weakness of Napoleon, he became the founder of *la police de caquetage*, which afterwards so deeply embittered the life of his employer; and he was as rarely missed from the saloons of St-Cloud, where he played *saute-mouton* for the amusement of the consular family, as from the state apartments of the Tuileries, where he taught the *parvenus* of the day the etiquettes, in which they soon learned to excel their teacher: for the forms that impose most, are those most easily acquired.

The first act of the Creation was now finished, when a box which had hitherto remained closed, near to that of the prince, was thrown open, and a general officer, attended by his two aides-de-camp, came forward. He was rendered conspicuous by being the only General present who did not wear the new decoration of the Legion of Honour; for though many of the military accepted it with reluctance, few had the courage to refuse what all considered as a return to old institutions. This was probably remarked by a little party of Liberals in the pit,

---

[1] The man of destiny; the name then given by the Germans to Bonaparte.

who rose, and cheered the person more distinguished by the absence of that mark of note than he could have been by its adoption. The General, however, had possibly some other claims to popularity; for the manner in which he was received by the audience, seemed no less marked and emphatic than that of the Chief Consul; though the applause was much less universally bestowed.

The person, thus noticed, was in the very prime of life, of lofty stature, and commanding air; and so distinguished by personal advantages, that the Princess, fixing her lorgnette steadily at him, asked, 'Who is that magnificent looking person, Monsieur de Vaudrémont? I think I have seen him before.'

'*Ha! par exemple!*' said the Ex-Count, who had the *Memoires du genre humain* at his fingers' ends, 'that is, or would be a personage, a modern Alcibiades: like the Athenian General, he has figured as a statesman, a soldier, and a philosopher; *d'ailleurs fort joli garçon.*'

'But, who is he?' asked the Princess, still fixing her glass.

'He is one of our Generals *mal vus, "un Général suspect"*. He belongs to a faction equally violent against royalists and jacobins; although the First Consul, in his wisdom, has set the example of a necessary fusion of parties, by admitting the Ex-Grand-Seigneur, Talleyrand, and the Ex-Montaguard Fouché, to his councils and confidence – '

'But who is he?' again interrupted the Princess, with increasing curiosity and earnestness.

'He is one of the heroes of the Italian campaign, though you see he is not decorated with the new order of the Legion of Honour. In fact, he is at the head of those officers who have shown the most decided repugnance to its establishment; and he even had the insolence to tell the First Consul the other day, that such distinctions "*n'etaient que les hochets du despotisme:*" to which Bonaparte replied, "*Eh bien, c'est avec des hochets qu'on a toujours mené les hommes.*" '

'But his name?' said the Princess, 'his name first, and memoirs after! – his name?'

'It is General O'Brien, an Irishman by birth. Those Irishmen! *nous en avons comme s'il en pleuvait.*'

The Princess almost started, and exchanged a significant look with Lord Kilcolman, whose opera-glass followed the direction of her own, while she muttered in English, 'I thought so; Lady Knocklofty's *hero*, something changed, but not disimproved.'

'By Jupiter, I believe so,' said Lord Kilcolman.

'But it's impossible – a fellow like that, that no one would speak to in Ireland! – he a General in the French service! and little Boney, so clever and clear-sighted. Poh! 'tis impossible.'

''Tis true, however,' said the Princess, still speaking English; 'it is not easy to mistake him.'

'Nor to forget him either,' said Lord Kilcolman, with the air of a man who had a right to be piqued.

'These Irishmen,' continued Mons. de Vaudrémont, '*se fourrent partout*. There are the Generals Clarke, Lawless, Harty, Kilmaine, *et tant d'autres*.'

'All of whom,' muttered Lord Kilcolman, 'would have run the risk of being hanged, had they staid at home.'

'*Plait-il?*' demanded the Ex-Count.

'Oh! nothing,' replied the Princess, smiling; 'only my Lord observes that had these Generals remained at home, they would, no doubt, have been *elevated* as they deserve.'

'*Eh! sans doute! ce sont de braves gens.* There's General Clarke, for instance, who, from a simple lieutenant, has become – '

'Never mind General Clarke, tell us more of General O'Brien,' said the Princess, impatiently.

'*Et! voilà les femmes!*' shrugged the Prince; '*qu'un homme soit beau!*'

'*Eh bien*,' interrupted the Princess, and addressing the Count.

'Well, this Irish General is a perfect hero of romance. He narrowly escaped being hanged in Ireland, as some of his countrymen here relate; for the Irish have always a *coup de patte* to bestow upon each other. But, *c'est égal*. Thrown on the coast of France, where he was driven by stress of weather, having escaped from his own country in an open boat, he was taken up for a spy – sent to Paris – did not give what was deemed a satisfactory account of himself, – and had a letter found on his person signed by the noted aristocrat, the Prince de Ligne. That was enough. *Pardi!* he was condemned – ordered for execution – thrown into a dungeon, in order to be sent with the next batch to the guillotine, on the following morning; and *that* morning – it was the 9th Thermidor. Then arrived the insurrection, which ended in the death of Robespierre; and nothing more was thought for months of the prisoners, till a *sœur de charité* (an order tolerated when religion itself was proscribed), took up the mission of seeking out the victims which the atrocious Robespierre had left to pine in their dungeons; *et voilà mon général*, not only restored to liberty, but actually discovering in the present *ancien évéque de C——* (the celebrated Abbé O'Flaherty, so influential in the Convention), an old friend and near relation. Well, this O'Brien *a de l'esprit*, and a great talent for popular writing. He was immediately employed, became the Magnus Apollo of Cambacérès, Boissy d'Anglas, Carnot, and others, who have since styled themselves Constitutional Liberals. But this did not last long. The royalist reaction broke out, and took the *dessus: et voilà mon drôle qui s'insurge!* and narrowly escaped deportation, or worse; and now, seeing clearly enough that existing arrangements were but provisional, and that nothing permanent was possible, except *war*, forthwith our modern Alcibiades quitted the senate and took the field, and, for once in his life, he was right. The army was his true vocation. He was bred, *sous tente*, and distinguished himself in every campaign, till, from a simple volunteer, he has become *comme vous le voyez*, a Lieutenant-General of the Republic. In the campaigns of Italy he performed prodigies of valour, was soon found out and distinguished by Bonaparte; but is now risking all, by opposing the First Consul in every effort to bring back social order. "General," said the First Consul to him, immediately after the inauguration of the *Concordat* in Notre Dame, "*Général, comment avez-vous trouvé la cérémonie?*" '

' "*Il n'y manquait*" (replied the hot-headed Irishman) "*qu'un million d'hommes, qui ont été tués, pour détruire ce que vous rétablissez.*"[1] And yet this man is cried up for his talent, and lives with Cabanis, and all the philosophers! – *Ah! que les gens d'esprit sont bêtes.*'

The Princess and the Peer had only withdrawn their eyes from the subject of these details, to exchange looks with each other. They had, from the first mention of his name, recognized in the French General, the unfortunate Lord Arranmore; and though much changed, – though the gloss and glow of youth were all dimmed and faded, – yet in his fine melancholy and marked countenance, they still detected that peculiar beauty of a passionate and energetic expression, which had first attracted the attention of Albina Countess of Knocklofty, at the review in the Phœnix Park. But the melancholy which clouded his brow, and seemed its habitual character, dispersed like mid-day vapours from before a summer's sun, as he turned round to give his

[1] 'General, what do you think of the ceremony?'
'It wanted nothing but the million of men who have been slain, to destroy all that you are now restoring.'

hand to a lady, who entered the box, leaning on the arm of a gentleman *en habit bourgeois*.

'By Jupiter! what a beautiful woman,' exclaimed Lord Kilcolman. 'What a dress! she looks like the priestess of the sun, in the new ballet.'

'*Ah! voilà la fin du roman!*' said the Count, taking snuff. 'Madame Bonaparte has been called *la bonne étoile* of her husband; that beautiful woman, your priestess of the sun, my lord, is *la mauvaise étoile de notre Général;* she it is that governs him and misleads him in his present opposition.'

'Ah! for heaven's sake, *contez-nous cela,*' said the Princess, with renewed earnestness and interest in the subject.

'Some pretend that this priestess of the sun, who is an *ex-religieuse*, is neither more nor less than the very sister of charity, who restored the General to liberty; and it is well known that she is "the Lady of Lodi" (as she is called in a little vaudeville written on the subject) who defended herself in her château on the banks of the Adda, where she lived in great retreat, at the head of a sort of semi-religious society. She is very rich, and inherits the wealth of a certain Jesuit uncle, whose name I forget. The château was attacked by a skirmishing party of French soldiers, whom she kept at bay till the arrival of the main army; when, throwing herself at the feet of the General of division, he recognized in the heroine of Lodi, *la sœur de charité;* and permitted her to march out of her fortress *tambour battant*, and with all the honours of war – *Vous devinez, Madame la Princesse, le dénouement?* The General and his captive were married shortly after the battle of Lodi, at Milan, in the presence of Bonaparte. The bridegroom was ordered from the altar of the Duomo, to the siege of Mantua; and before he rejoined his bride in Paris, the army of Italy, accomplishing the great work of the revolution, sent back its heroes to be crowned in the Capitol.

'In the interval which has occurred since the treaty of Campo Formio, the constitutional party has begun an energetic but unavailing opposition to the measures of the First Consul; and this faction has no more active members than the General and Madame O'Brien. Of her, one may say, as my friend Talleyrand said, the other night, of another pretty woman, "*C'est la tête de Cromwell sur le corps d'une jolie femme.*" Graceful, eloquent, adroit, and veiling all under an air of simplicity and *bonhomie*, she is, in fact, a perfect Aspasia, and is exercising *sur notre belle jeunesse de France*, the same influence which her prototype obtained over the Athenian youth; *enfin, c'est une femme très-dangereuse*, and it is thought will soon receive an order to quit Paris. *En attendant*, her saloons are nightly crowded with malcontents: you are sure of meeting there Lanjuinais, Grégoire, Garat, Le Noir, La Roche, Constant, Chenier, and the celebrated Cabanis (with whom she now entered the box, all of whom are occupied *en faisant des empiétemens*, on the new system, which can only end in their own ruin – *comme de raison.*'

Here the dropping of the curtain and the rising of the consular family were signals for the Austrian Prince and the *ci-devant homme immobile de la monarchie*, to hurry to pay their respects to the First Consul, on his escape from assassination. Madame la Princesse, giving her arm to the Earl of Kilcolman, asked, 'And now, Lord K., who do you think the *héroine de Lodi* turns out to be?'

'Upon my honour,' said the Earl, 'I have not the laste idaye; but she is one of the finest looking creatures I ever saw, though not in her teens. What luck that O'Brien has always had.'

'Why, is it possible you do not remember her? She is very little changed, except that she has more *embonpoint*, and is differently dressed.'

'Give you my honour and soul I have no recollection who she is – not the laste in life.'

'She is, as the Count would say, *ni plus ni moins* than Madame O'Flaherty, the Superior of that Irish convent, where –'

'What Irish convent?'

'Oh! I thought you had been of our gipsy party among the mountains of Connemara, where this Aspasia – but the crowd is intolerable; will you come and sup at the embassy?'

'I will, with all my heart and soul,' replied Lord Kilcolman, backing his way through the multitude (all hurrying to see the First Consul pass), with shoulders only manufactured in Tipperary.

'I'll tell you all then;' said the Princess. 'There is, I assure you, *de quoi faire un roman*, if it were well treated.'

'And why not write it yourself?' said Lord Kilcolman, pressing the fair arm that leaned upon his: 'you are such a *talented* creature!'

'If I did, every body would say I put them into my book,' said the Princess, 'for all the blockheads and blockheadesses think themselves printable; and draw what you may, "each cries, that was levelled at him." '

'Upon my honour that's the raison I prefer writing my journey to

Jerusalem. I defy any one to take offence at a book written just about nothing at all.'

'Don't be too sure of that,' said her Excellency.

**THE END**

**Pandora Press**
FICTION

Already published:

*The Wild Irish Girl*
Lady Morgan
*Introduced by Brigid Brophy*

The young and hot-blooded Horatio travels incognito to his wealthy father's estates in Ireland – an Ireland abandoned to the whim of indifferent and oppressive absentee landlords. There he falls hopelessly in love with Glorvina, the enigmatic, beautiful and impoverished 'heiress' to estates now belonging to Horatio's father. But, as the plot progresses, Horatio finds that his beloved and her strange and wild homeland are more complex than they had at first apeared.

*The Wild Irish Girl* is at once a romance and a political fable, and a tragically unprophetic one at that; Lady Morgan could not have been more mistaken in her vision of a politically and religiously united Ireland. Ironically, this 'simple love story' with its portrayal of the culpability and arrogance of the English occupiers only serves to emphasise how impossible were Lady Morgan's hopes for a country she obviously so dearly loved.
0-86358-097-1

*The Female Quixote*
*The Adventures of Arabella*
Charlotte Lennox
*Introduced by Sandra Shulman*

"I will despatch you tomorrow morning, with my orders to him, to live, or at least, to proceed no further in his design of dying, till he has further cause"

So speak Arabella, the delightful heroine of this eighteenth-century novel, who (like the famous Don) lives her life under the illusion that nothing has changed since the days of chivalry and romance and that aspiring suitors will cheerfully die for her at the drop of a handkerchief.

Written in 1752, this light-hearted, sparkling comedy of misunderstandings is really a tongue-in-cheek look at the difference between romance and reality, but all ends happily and Arabella is let down into the real world with a gentle bump.
0-86358-080-7   Price £4.95 net

*Patronage*
Maria Edgeworth
*Introduced by Eva Figes*

An ambitious work, and Maria Edgeworth's most commercially successful novel, *Patronage* is an astute and humorous portrayal of the
British class system and the different ways in which men and women
make their way in the world.

Written in 1814, this magnificent novel is not only a comedy of manners
but also a meditation on the concept of 'patronage', both financial and
sexual. The plot revolves around two families – the Percys and the
Falconers – whose fortunes mirror and contrast each other. The Falconers accept patronage from Lord Oldborough but by the end of the
book it is the Percys who are perceived as possessing the great mortal
worth and wealth by dint of their own efforts.
0–86358–106–4   Price £6.95 net


*Belinda*
Maria Edgeworth
*Introduced by Eva Figes*

Like her contemporary, Jane Austen, Maria Edgeworth concealed
beneath a seemingly effortless lightness of touch and humour, an
awareness of the poignancy and sadness of everyday domestic existence.

Written in 1811, this is the story of Belinda and the two men who court
her.

Around this conventional literary cliché, Maria Edgeworth has woven
an extraordinarily complex and powerful narrative, so that a romantic
comedy of manners becomes, in her hands, a rich and subtle counterpoint of themes – love, fidelity, passion, cynicism and the position of
women in society – with characters all equally memorable, whether
virtuous like Belinda, 'wicked' like Lady Delacour or feckless like
Vincent.
0–86358–074–2

*Helen*
Maria Edgeworth
*Introduced by Maggie Gee*

In which the heroine, Helen, finds her honesty and integrity pitted against the well-meaning but morally ambiguous behaviour of her friend, Cecelia. The conflicting loyalties of the two young women, caught between patriarchal authority, with its moral absolutes, and their affection for one another, are played out against the broader political ideals of the wise and tolerant Lady Davenant.

First published in 1834, Maria Edgeworth's comedy of social and sexual manners was greatly admired by many later writers, including Elizabeth Gaskell, who used it as a model for her own *Wives and Daughters*.
0-86358-104-8   Price £5.95 net


*The History of Miss Betsy Thoughtless*
Eliza Haywood
*Introduced by Dale Spender*

In which the lovable heroine, Betsy, is shown the error of her thoughtless ways and after many adventures marries Trueworth.

First published in 1751, this long and extraordinary novel gathers into its net a multitude of sexual and social concerns; abortion, divorce, marriage laws and the double standards governing men's and women's behaviour in the eighteenth century.

Betsy's growth to maturity is played out against the realisation that the institution of marriage is a personal as well as a social commitment for women, who must try to take control of their own lives – overcoming chauvinistic social conventions. But despite its more tragic episodes, this is a happy book: witty, adventurous and touching.
0-86358-090-4   Price £5.95 net

*Memoirs of Emma Courtney*
Mary Hays
*Introduced by Sally Cline*

'While men pursue interest, honour, pleasure . . . women, who have too much delicacy, sense and spirit to degrade themselves by the vilest of all interchanges, remain insulated beings. Hence, the eccentricities of conduct of which women of superior minds have been accused – the struggles, the despairing though generous struggles, of an ardent spirit, denied scope for its exertions! The strong feelings, and strong energies, which properly directed, in a field sufficiently wide, might – ah! what might they not have aided? But forced back, and pent up, they ravage and destroy the mind which gave them birth.'

Written in 1796, *Memoirs of Emma Courtney*, shows what happens when Emma falls hopelessly in love and all her carefully thought out, and fought out, independence is threatened by the intensity of her feelings. Based on Mary Hays' own relationship with William Frend, her first novel shocked the public by its frank exploration of sexual politics and the passionate nature of the heroine, who does not follow convention by waiting for a man's declaration of love.

A remarkable work in its unusual plea for women's emotional and sexual emancipation and in its impassioned desire to break through the barriers of restriction and prejudice which governed women's behaviour in the eighteenth century.
0-86358-132-3   Price £4.95 net

*Helen*
Maria Edgeworth
*Introduced by Maggie Gee*

In which the heroine, Helen, finds her honesty and integrity pitted against the well-meaning but morally ambiguous behaviour of her friend, Cecelia. The conflicting loyalties of the two young women, caught between patriarchal authority, with its moral absolutes, and their affection for one another, are played out against the broader political ideals of the wise and tolerant Lady Davenant.

First published in 1834, Maria Edgeworth's comedy of social and sexual manners was greatly admired by many later writers, including Elizabeth Gaskell, who used it as a model for her own *Wives and Daughters*.
0-86358-104-8   Price £5.95 net


*The History of Miss Betsy Thoughtless*
Eliza Haywood
*Introduced by Dale Spender*

In which the lovable heroine, Betsy, is shown the error of her thoughtless ways and after many adventures marries Trueworth.

First published in 1751, this long and extraordinary novel gathers into its net a multitude of sexual and social concerns; abortion, divorce, marriage laws and the double standards governing men's and women's behaviour in the eighteenth century.

Betsy's growth to maturity is played out against the realisation that the institution of marriage is a personal as well as a social commitment for women, who must try to take control of their own lives – overcoming chauvinistic social conventions. But despite its more tragic episodes, this is a happy book: witty, adventurous and touching.
0-86358-090-4   Price £5.95 net

*Memoirs of Emma Courtney*
Mary Hays
*Introduced by Sally Cline*

'While men pursue interest, honour, pleasure . . . women, who have too much delicacy, sense and spirit to degrade themselves by the vilest of all interchanges, remain insulated beings. Hence, the eccentricities of conduct of which women of superior minds have been accused – the struggles, the despairing though generous struggles, of an ardent spirit, denied scope for its exertions! The strong feelings, and strong energies, which properly directed, in a field sufficiently wide, might – ah! what might they not have aided? But forced back, and pent up, they ravage and destroy the mind which gave them birth.'

Written in 1796, *Memoirs of Emma Courtney*, shows what happens when Emma falls hopelessly in love and all her carefully thought out, and fought out, independence is threatened by the intensity of her feelings. Based on Mary Hays' own relationship with William Frend, her first novel shocked the public by its frank exploration of sexual politics and the passionate nature of the heroine, who does not follow convention by waiting for a man's declaration of love.

A remarkable work in its unusual plea for women's emotional and sexual emancipation and in its impassioned desire to break through the barriers of restriction and prejudice which governed women's behaviour in the eighteenth century.

0-86358-132-3   Price £4.95 net